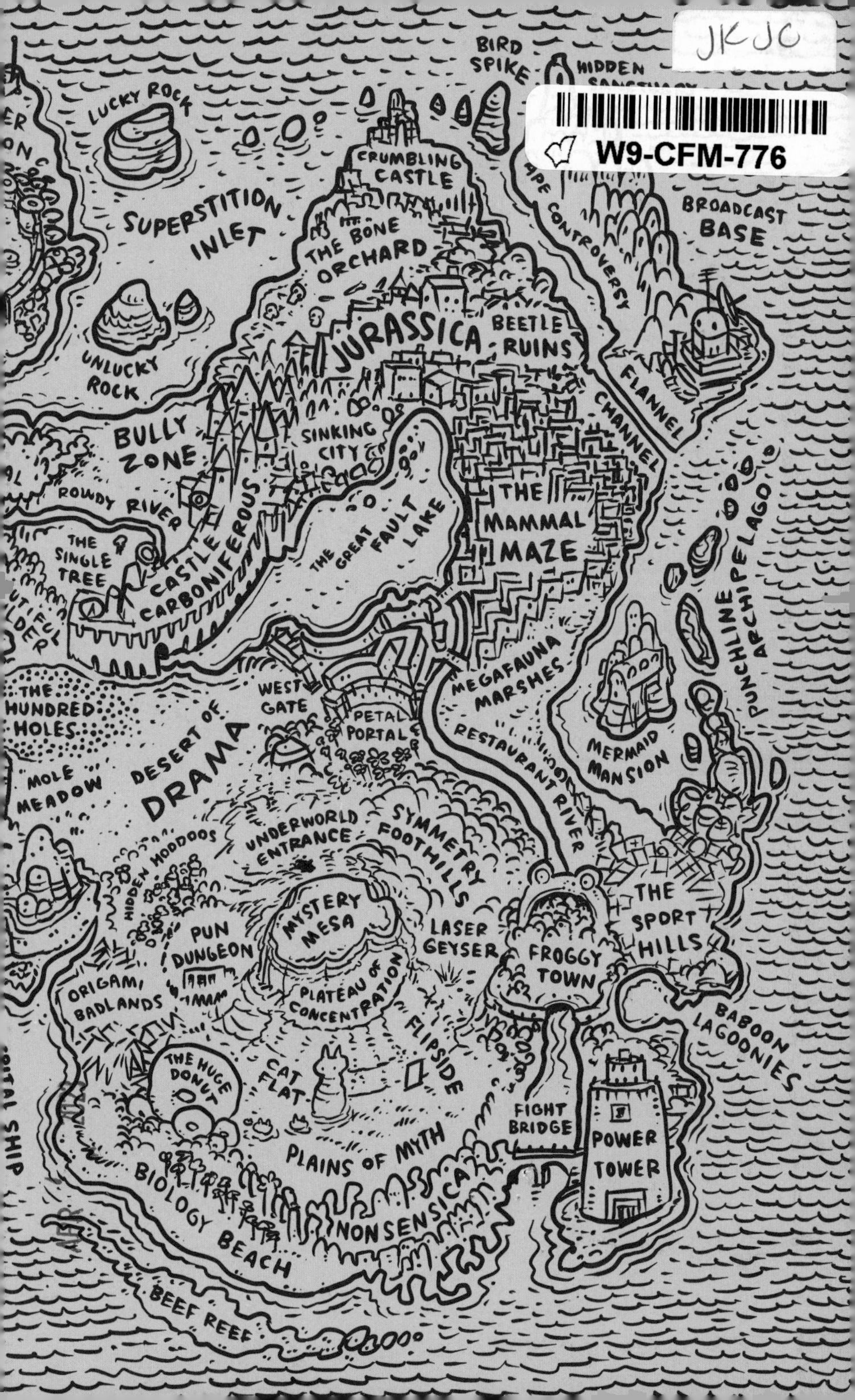
BIRD SPIKE
HIDDEN
LUCKY ROCK
CRUMBLING CASTLE
SUPERSTITION INLET
THE BONE ORCHARD
CONTROVERSY
BROADCAST BASE
UNLUCKY ROCK
JURASSICA
BEETLE RUINS
FLANNEL CHANNEL
BULLY ZONE
SINKING CITY
ROWDY RIVER
CASTLE CARBONIFEROUS
THE GREAT FAULT LAKE
THE MAMMAL MAZE
THE SINGLE TREE
PUNCHLINE ARCHIPELAGO
THE HUNDRED HOLES
WEST GATE
PETAL PORTAL
MEGAFAUNA MARSHES
DESERT OF DRAMA
RESTAURANT RIVER
MERMAID MANSION
MOLE MEADOW
UNDERWORLD ENTRANCE
SYMMETRY FOOTHILLS
HIDDEN HOODOOS
MYSTERY MESA
PUN DUNGEON
LASER GEYSER
FROGGY TOWN
THE SPORT HILLS
ORIGAMI BADLANDS
PLATEAU of CONCENTRATION
BABOON LAGOONIES
FLIPSIDE
THE HUGE DONUT
CAT FLAT
FIGHT BRIDGE
POWER TOWER
PLAINS OF MYTH
BIOLOGY BEACH
NONSENSICA
BEEF REEF

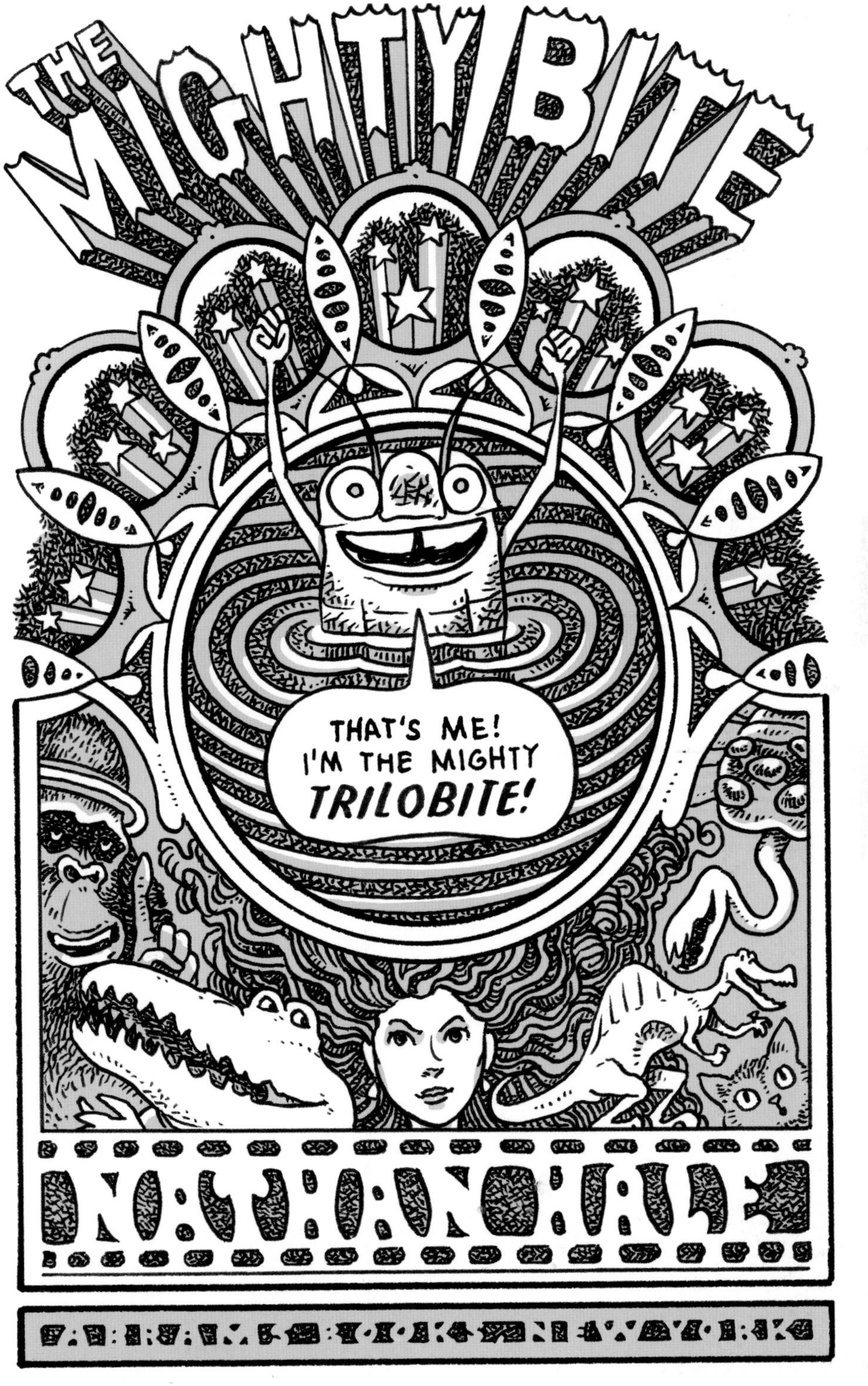
THE MIGHTY BITE
THAT'S ME! I'M THE MIGHTY TRILOBITE!

Library of Congress Control Number 2022942221

ISBN 978-1-4197-6553-7

Text and illustrations © 2023 Nathan Hale
Book design by Nathan Hale, design assistance by Charice Silverman
Color by Lucy Hale

All of the text in this book was hand lettered. The drawing and lettering
were created using Sakura Pigma pens on Strathmore Bristol paper.
Color was added in Clip Studio Paint.

Printed and bound in China
10 9 8 7 6 5 4 3 2 1

Amulet Books are available at special discounts when purchased in
quantity for premiums and promotions as well as fundraising or
educational use. Special editions can also be created to specification. For
details, contact specialsales@abramsbooks.com or the address below.

Amulet Books® is a registered trademark of Harry N. Abrams, Inc.

ABRAMS The Art of Books
195 Broadway, New York, NY 10007
abramsbooks.com

Hey hey!
This one's for Lindsey K!

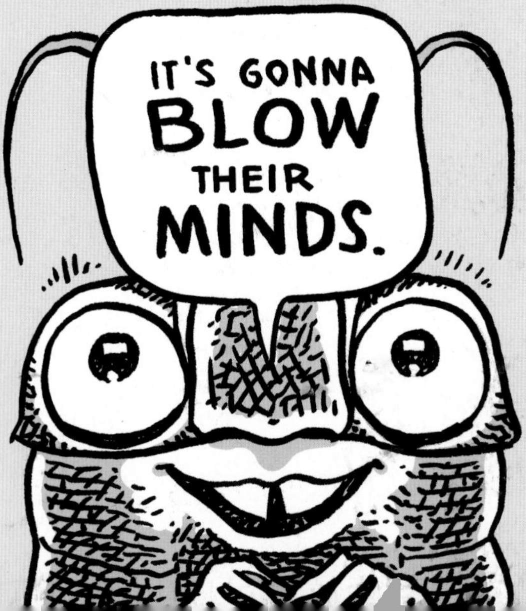
IT'S GONNA BLOW THEIR MINDS.

CHAPTER 1

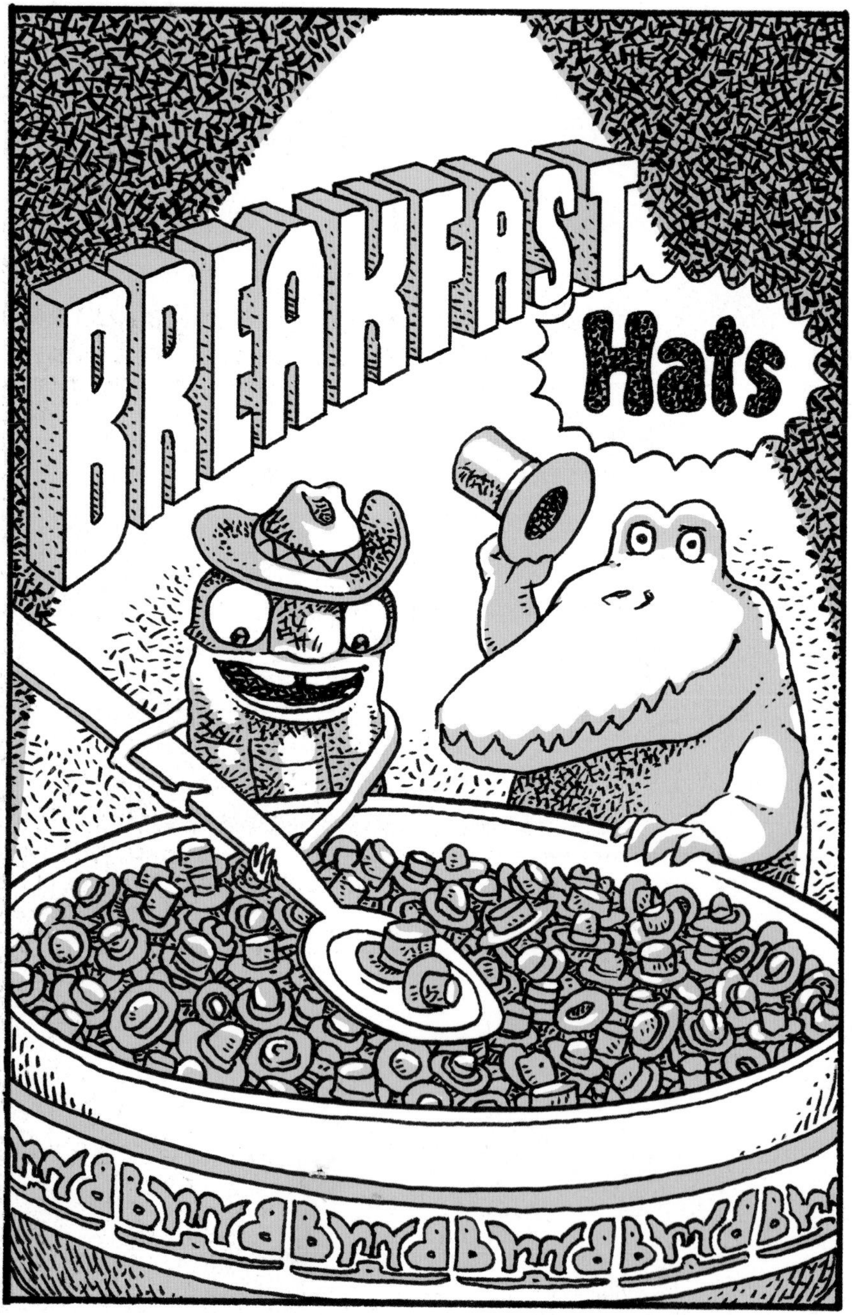
BREAKFAST
Hats

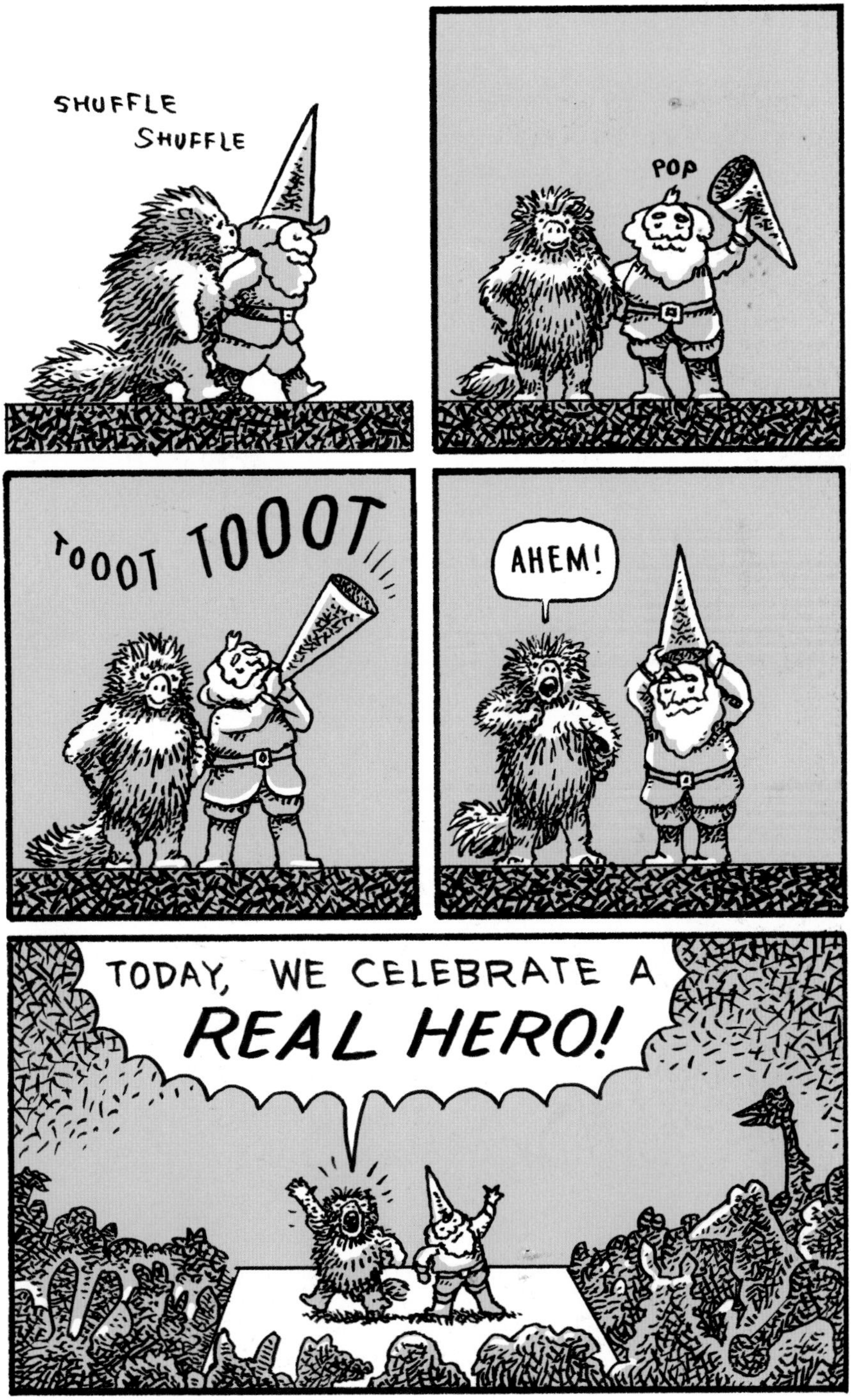
SHUFFLE
SHUFFLE
POP
TOOOT TOOOT
AHEM!
TODAY, WE CELEBRATE A *REAL HERO!*

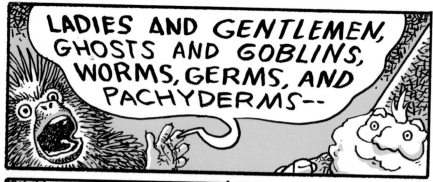

LADIES AND *GENTLEMEN*, GHOSTS AND GOBLINS, WORMS, GERMS, AND PACHYDERMS--

CLAP YOUR HANDS!

STOMP YOUR FEET!

CLOP YOUR HOOVES!

FLUFF YOUR FEATHERS!

RATTLE *YOUR* CLAWS!

AND POP YOUR SUCTION CUPS TOGETHER!

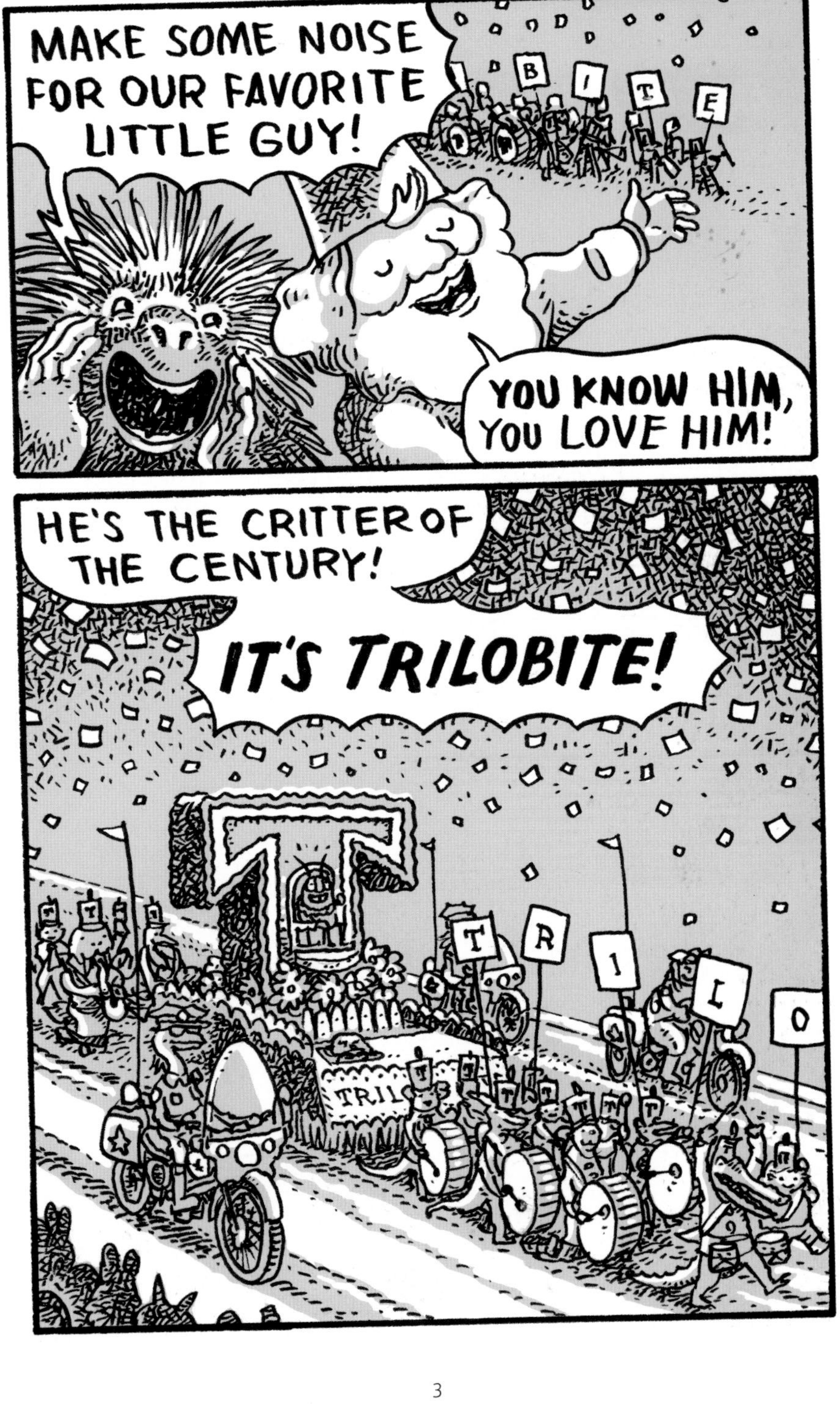
MAKE SOME NOISE FOR OUR FAVORITE LITTLE GUY!
YOU KNOW HIM, YOU LOVE HIM!
HE'S THE CRITTER OF THE CENTURY!
IT'S TRILOBITE!

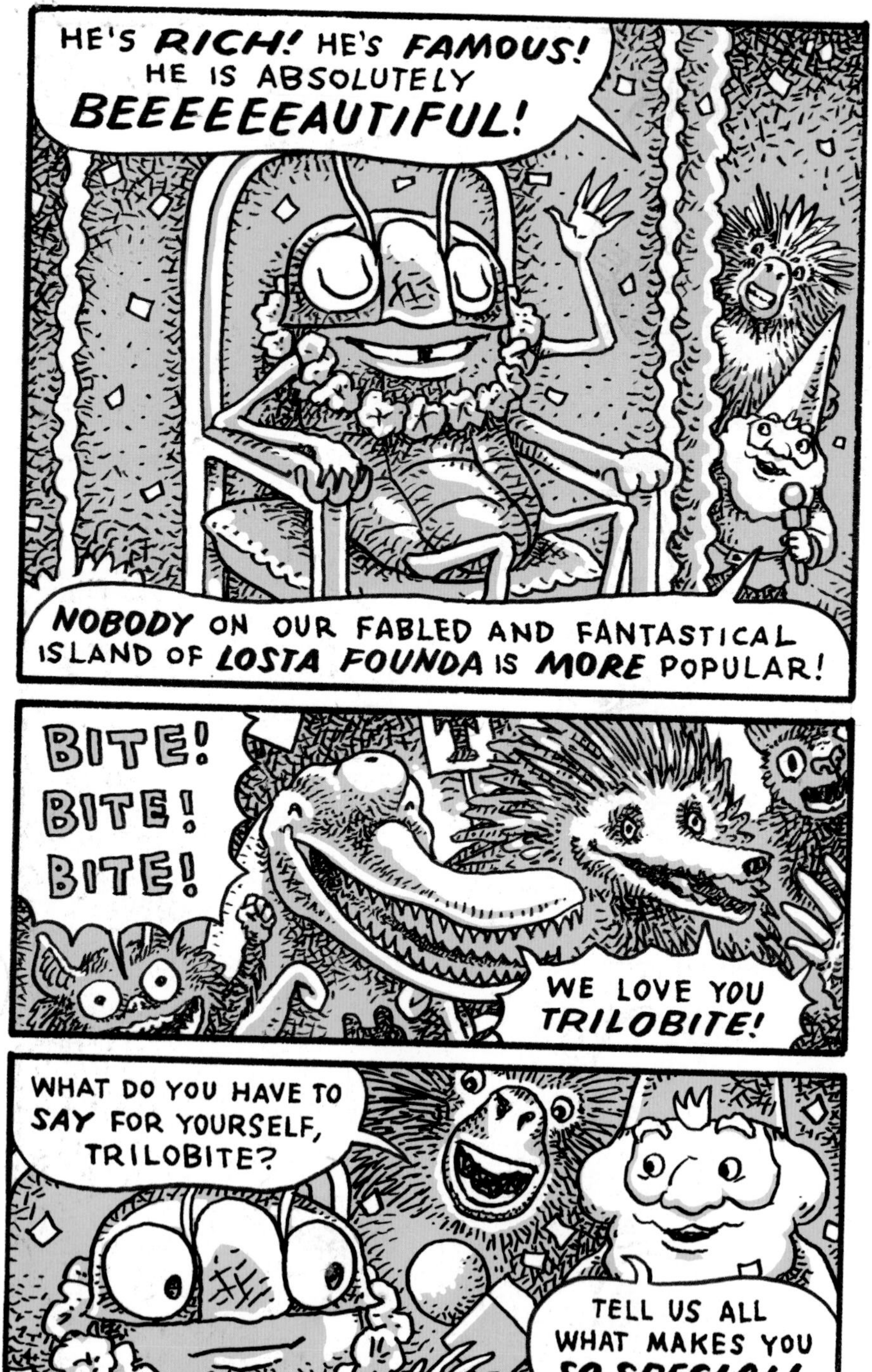
HE'S RICH! HE'S FAMOUS! HE IS ABSOLUTELY BEEEEEEEAUTIFUL!
NOBODY ON OUR FABLED AND FANTASTICAL ISLAND OF LOSTA FOUNDA IS MORE POPULAR!
BITE! BITE! BITE!
WE LOVE YOU TRILOBITE!
WHAT DO YOU HAVE TO SAY FOR YOURSELF, TRILOBITE?
TELL US ALL WHAT MAKES YOU SO SPECIAL!

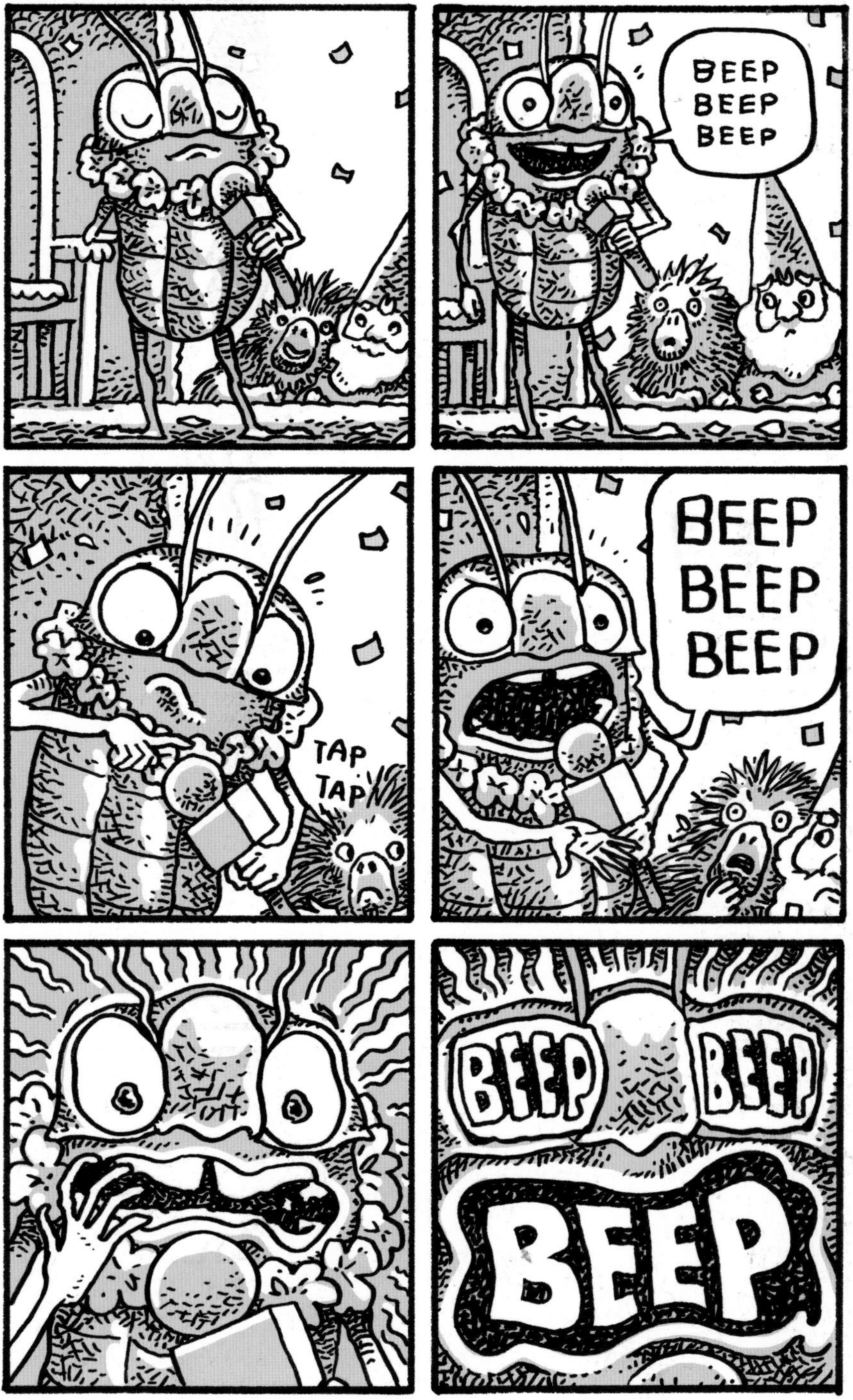
BEEP
BEEP
BEEP
TAP
TAP
BEEP
BEEP
BEEP
BEEP
BEEP
BEEP

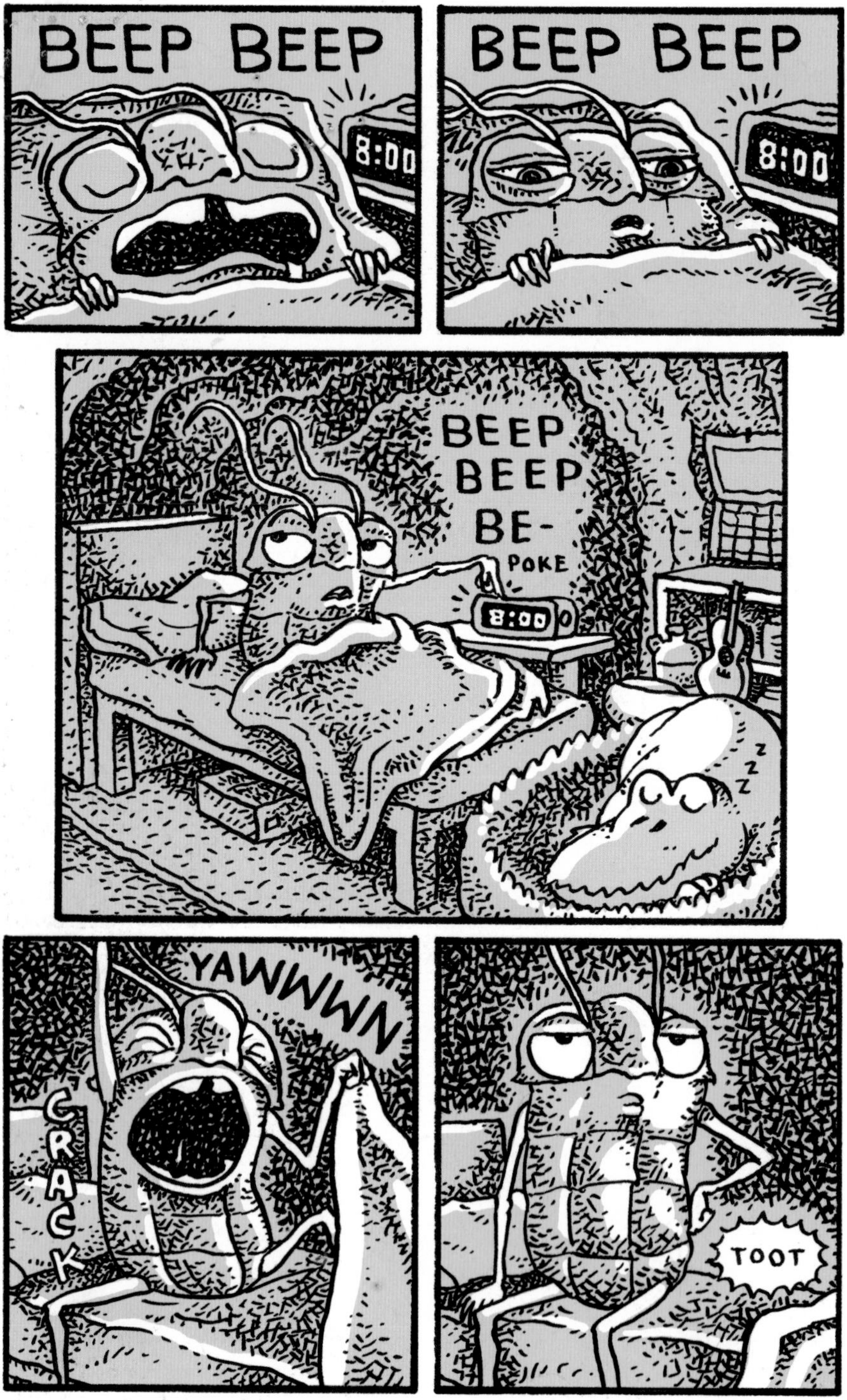
BEEP BEEP
8:00
BEEP BEEP
8:00
BEEP
BEEP
BE-
POKE
8:00
Z
Z
Z
YAWWWN
CRACK
TOOT

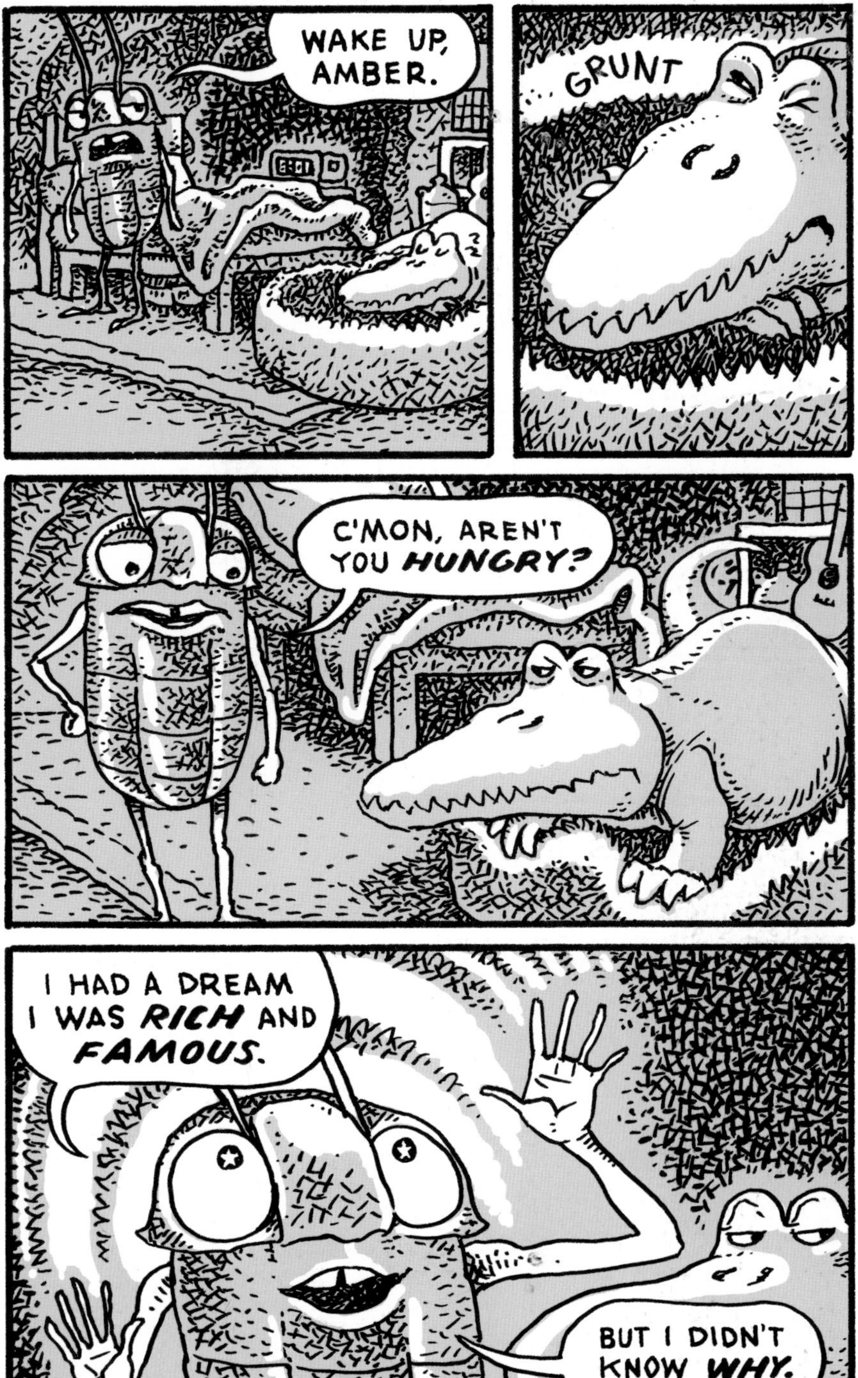
WAKE UP, AMBER.
GRUNT
C'MON, AREN'T YOU HUNGRY?
I HAD A DREAM I WAS RICH AND FAMOUS.
BUT I DIDN'T KNOW WHY.

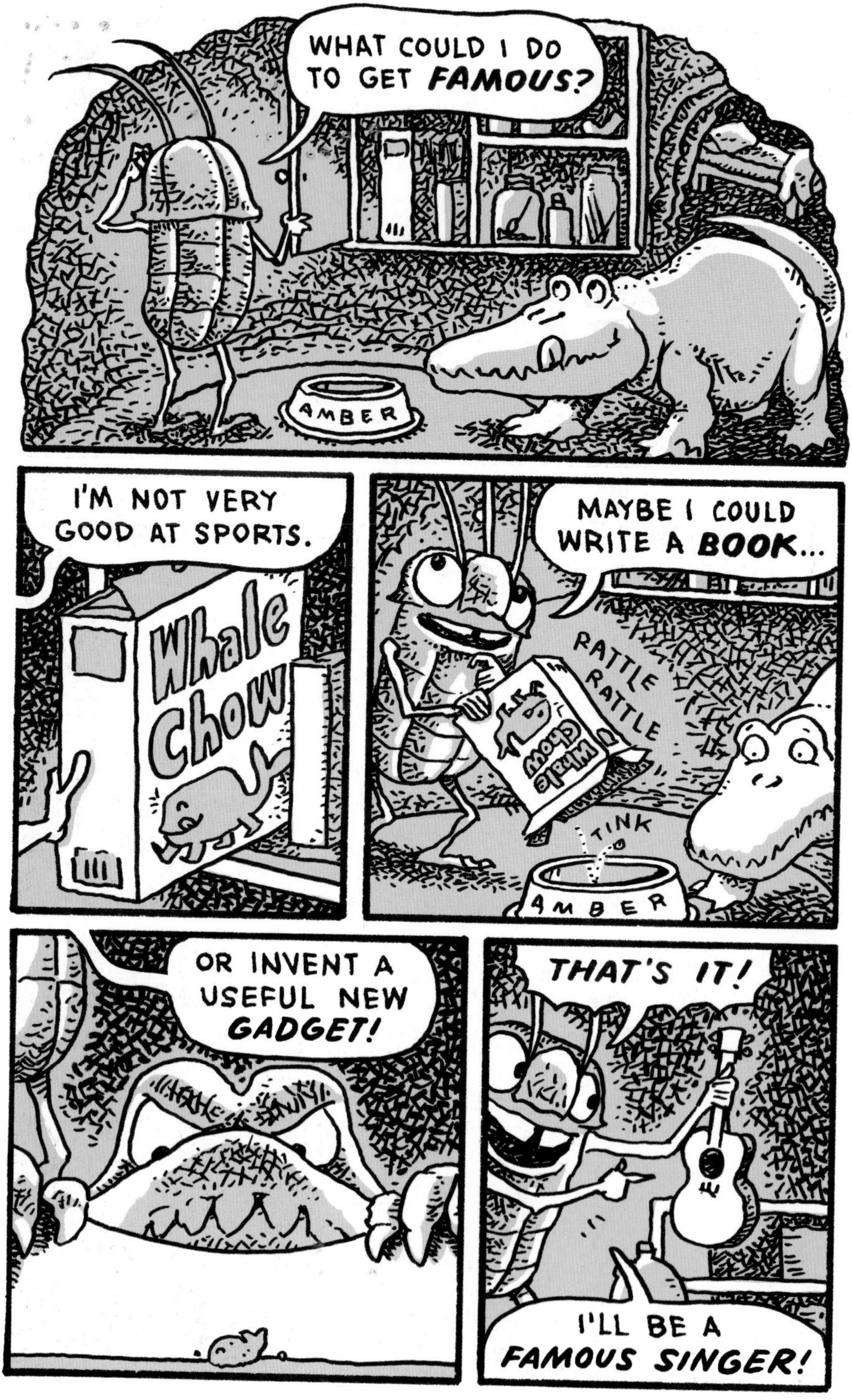
WHAT COULD I DO TO GET FAMOUS?
AMBER
I'M NOT VERY GOOD AT SPORTS.
Whale Chow
MAYBE I COULD WRITE A BOOK...
RATTLE RATTLE
Whale Chow
TINK
AMBER
OR INVENT A USEFUL NEW GADGET!
THAT'S IT!
I'LL BE A FAMOUS SINGER!

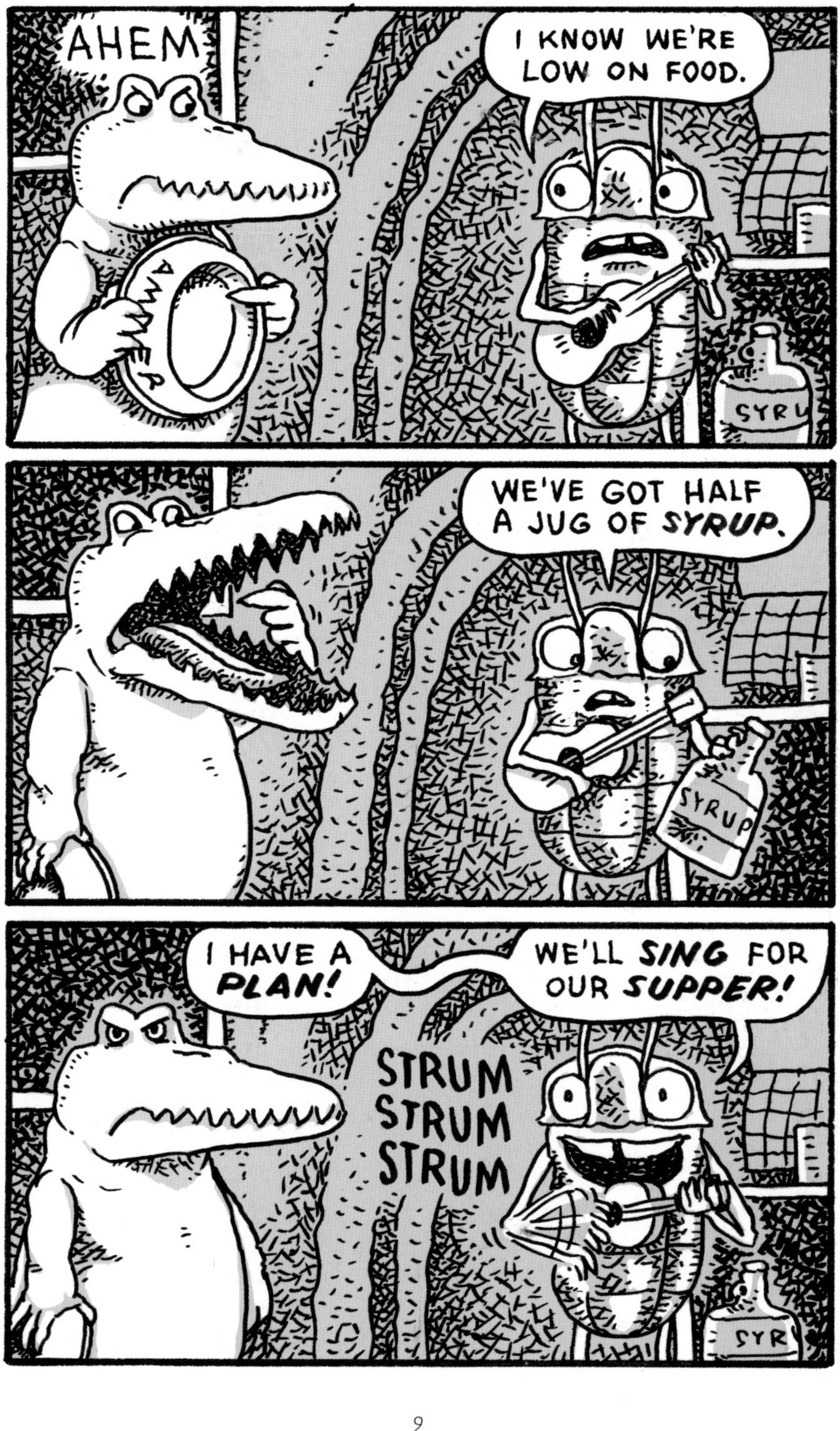
AHEM
I KNOW WE'RE LOW ON FOOD.
SYRU
WE'VE GOT HALF A JUG OF SYRUP.
SYRUP
I HAVE A PLAN!
WE'LL SING FOR OUR SUPPER!
STRUM STRUM STRUM
SYR

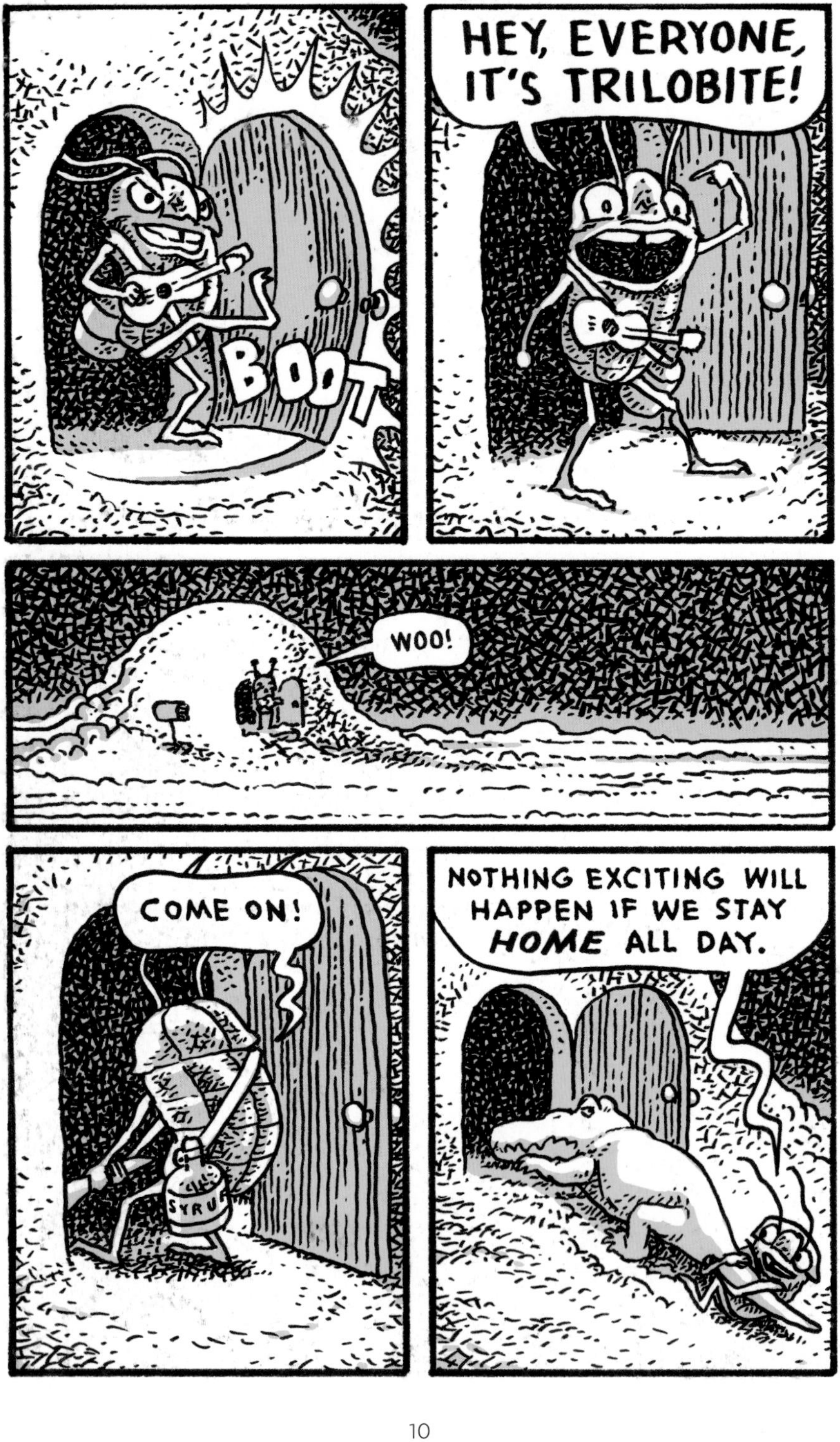
BOOT
HEY, EVERYONE, IT'S TRILOBITE!
WOO!
COME ON!
SYRUP
NOTHING EXCITING WILL HAPPEN IF WE STAY *HOME* ALL DAY.

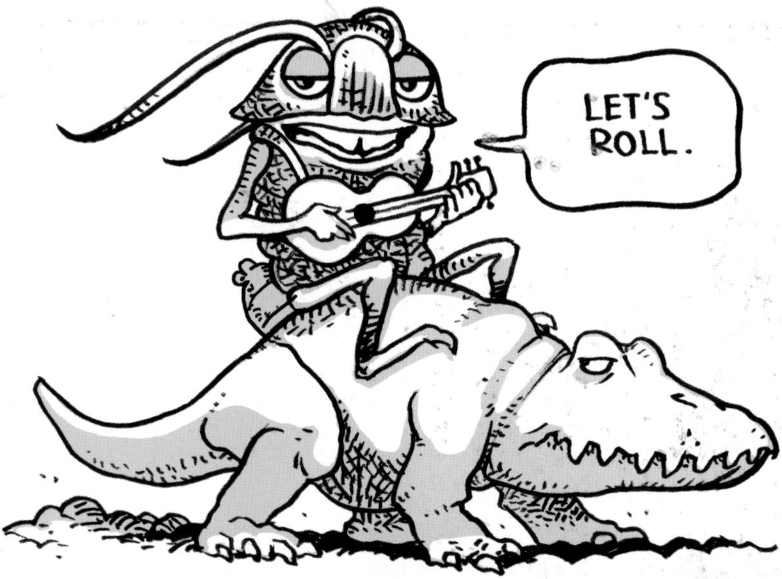
LET'S ROLL.

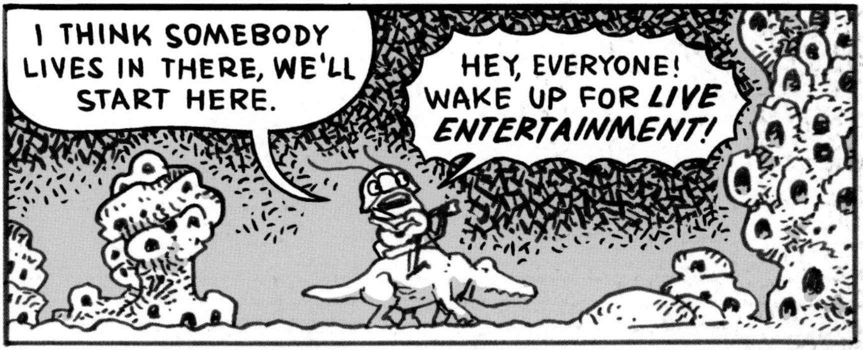
I THINK SOMEBODY LIVES IN THERE, WE'LL START HERE.
HEY, EVERYONE! WAKE UP FOR *LIVE ENTERTAINMENT!*

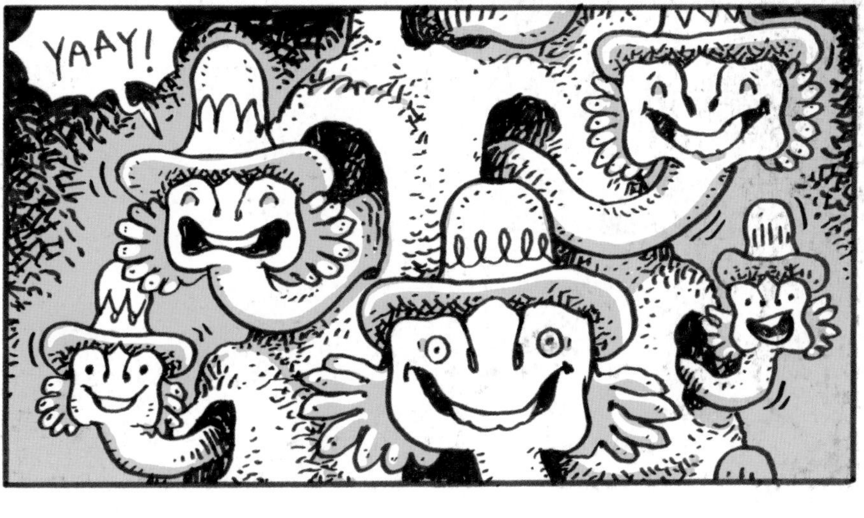
YAAY!

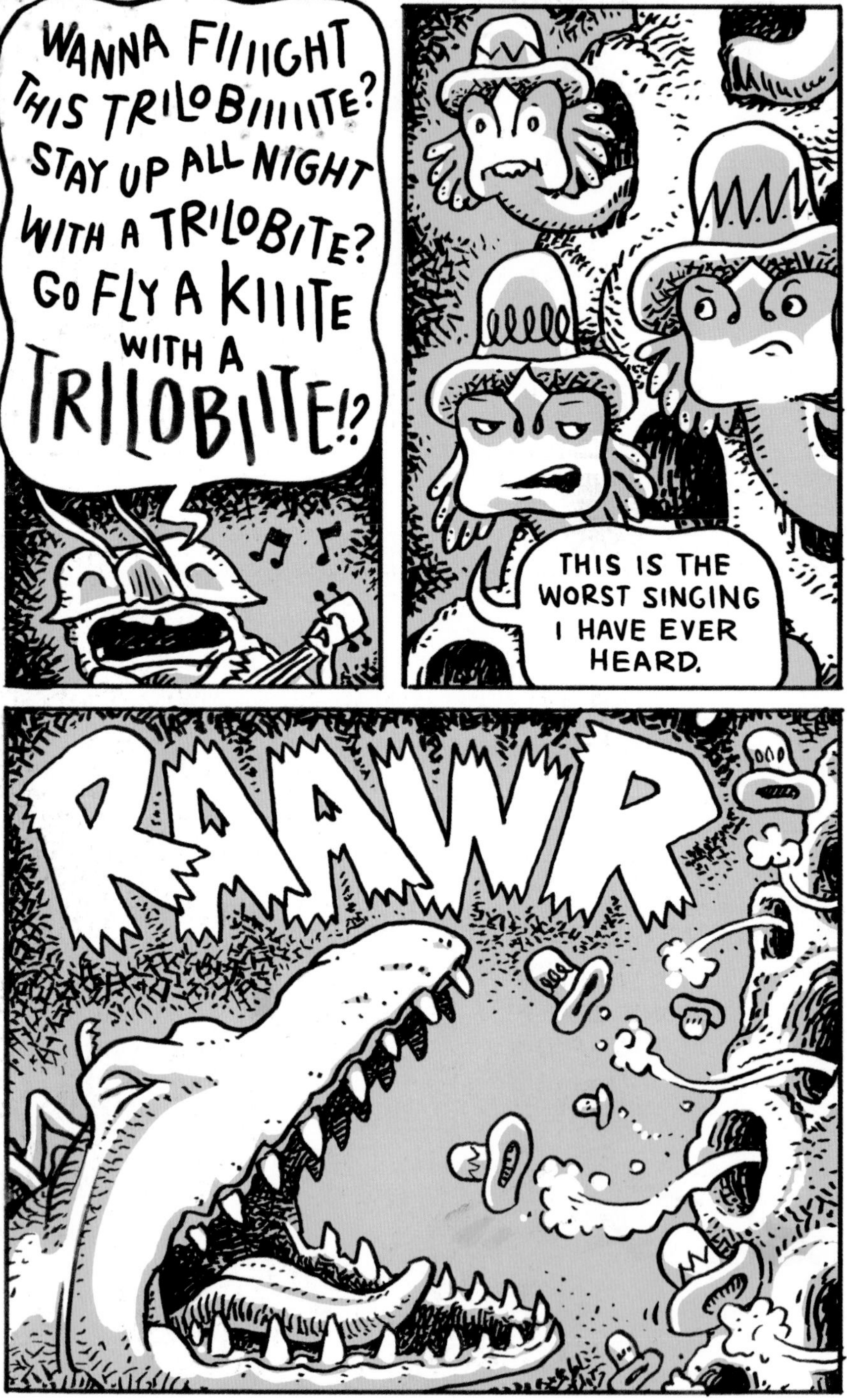
WANNA FIIIIGHT THIS TRILOBIIIIITE? STAY UP ALL NIGHT WITH A TRILOBITE? GO FLY A KIIIITE WITH A TRILOBIIITE!?
THIS IS THE WORST SINGING I HAVE EVER HEARD.
RAAWR

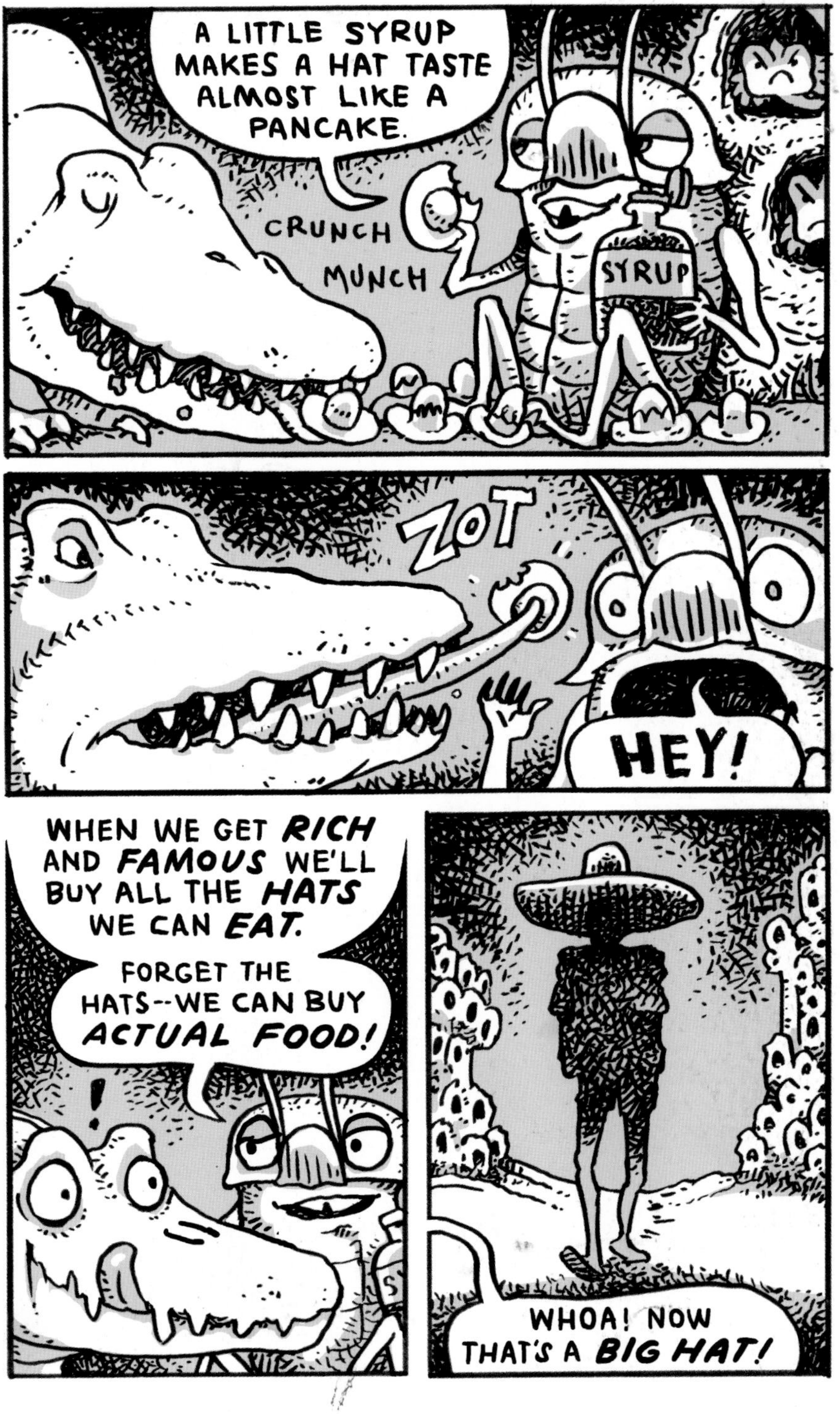
A LITTLE SYRUP MAKES A HAT TASTE ALMOST LIKE A PANCAKE.
CRUNCH
MUNCH
SYRUP
ZOT
HEY!
WHEN WE GET RICH AND FAMOUS WE'LL BUY ALL THE HATS WE CAN EAT.
FORGET THE HATS--WE CAN BUY ACTUAL FOOD!
!
WHOA! NOW THAT'S A BIG HAT!

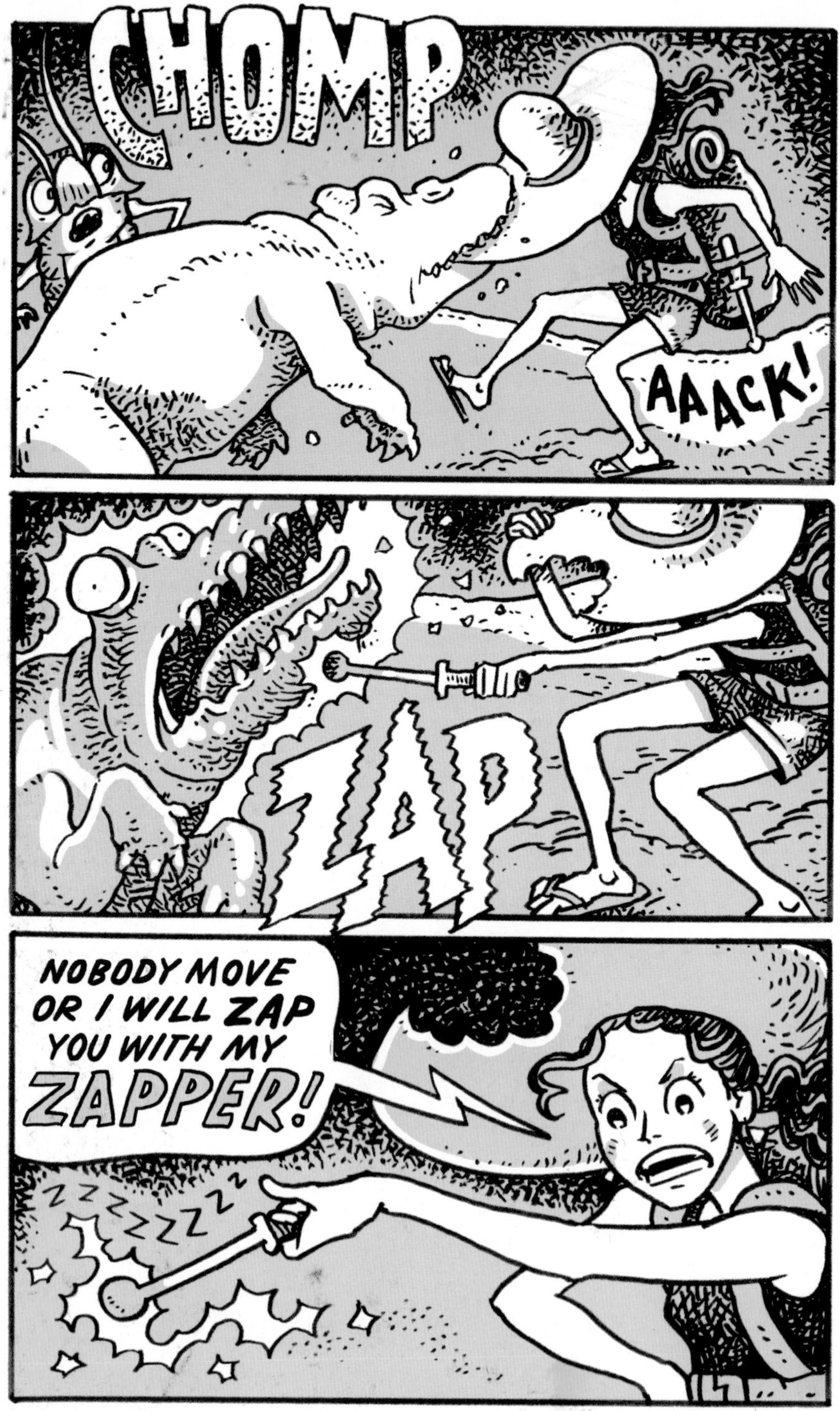
CHOMP
AAACK!
ZAP
NOBODY MOVE OR I WILL ZAP YOU WITH MY ZAPPER!
Z Z Z Z Z Z Z Z Z

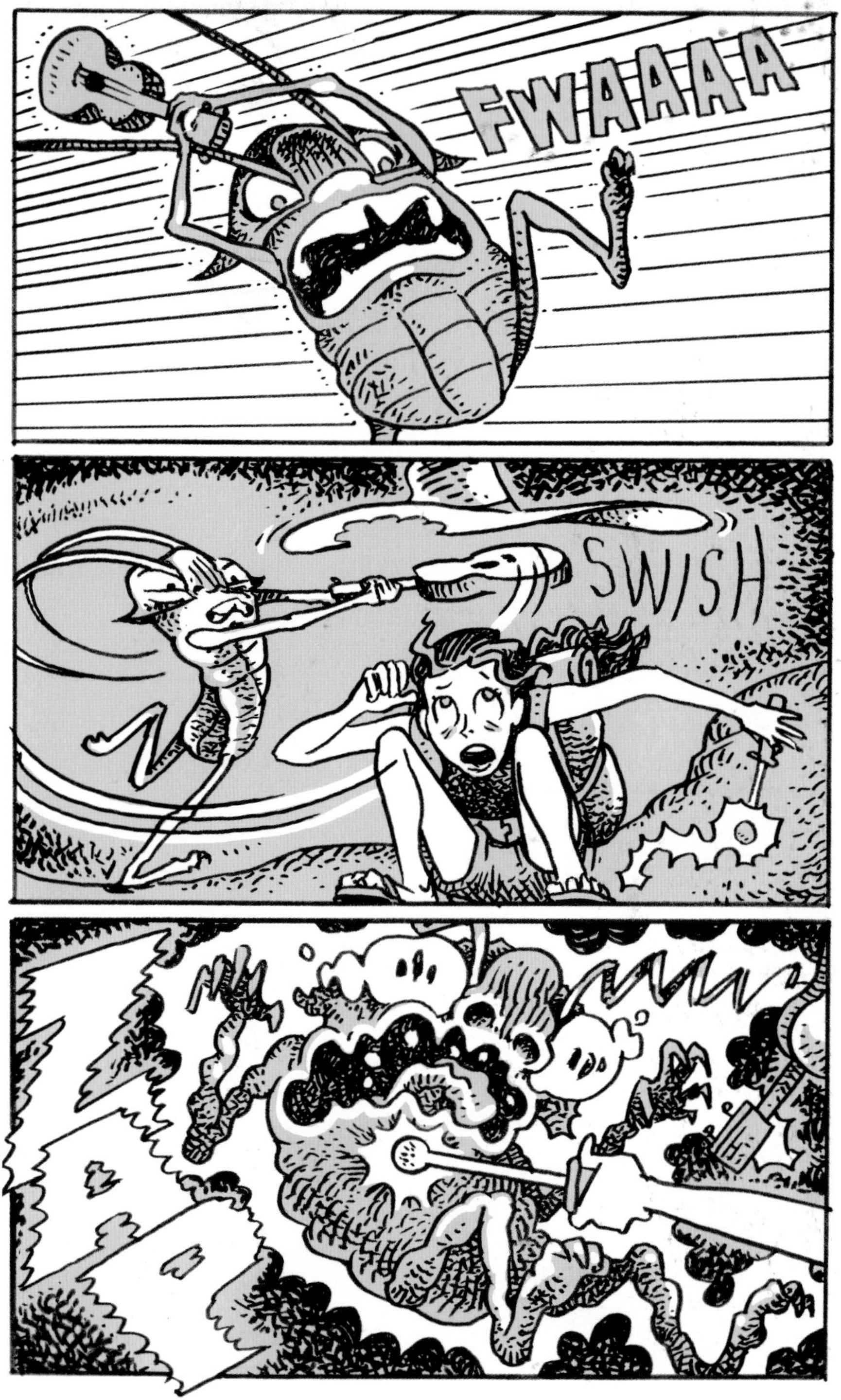
FWAAAA
SWISH

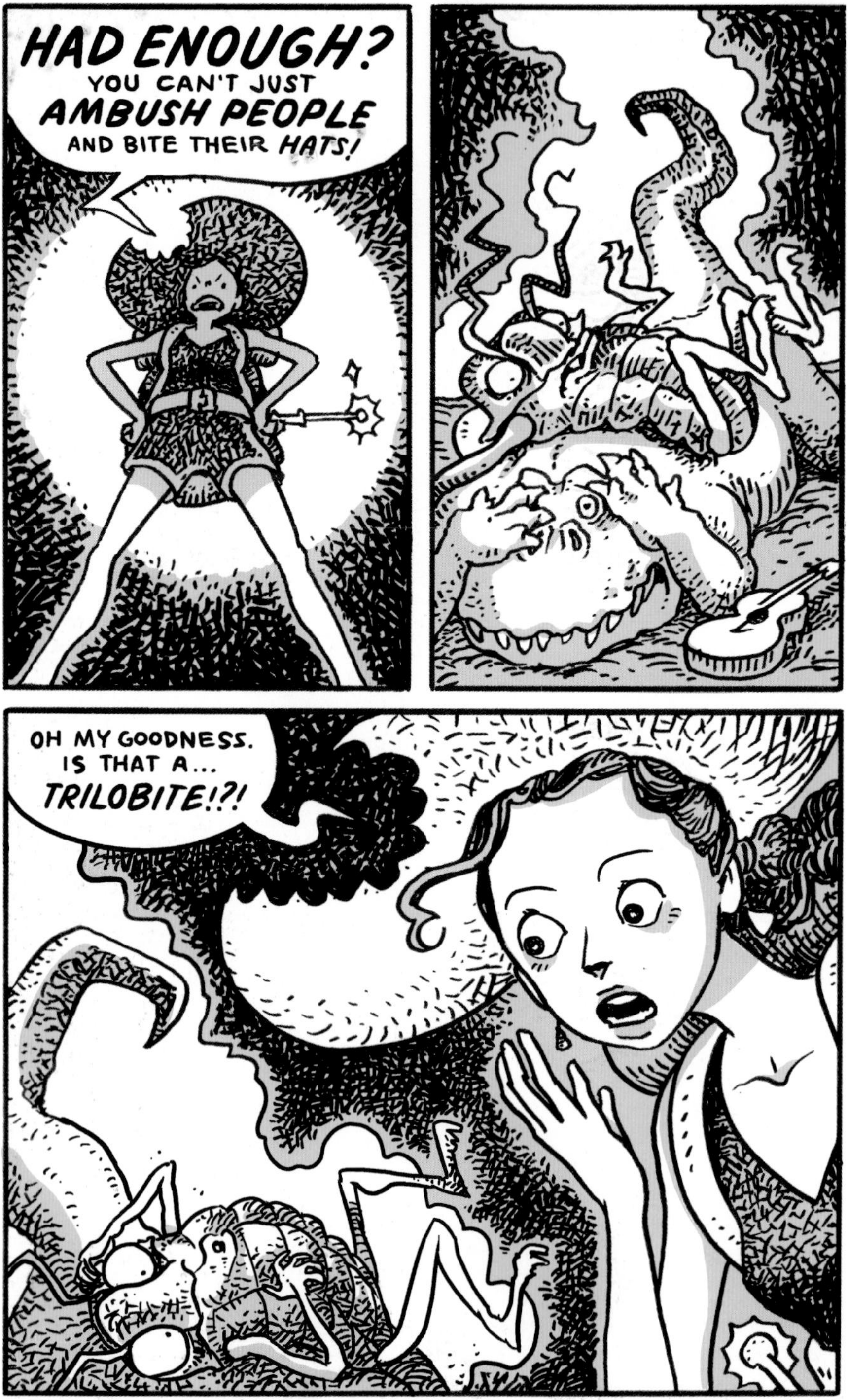
HAD ENOUGH? YOU CAN'T JUST AMBUSH PEOPLE AND BITE THEIR HATS!
OH MY GOODNESS. IS THAT A... TRILOBITE!?!

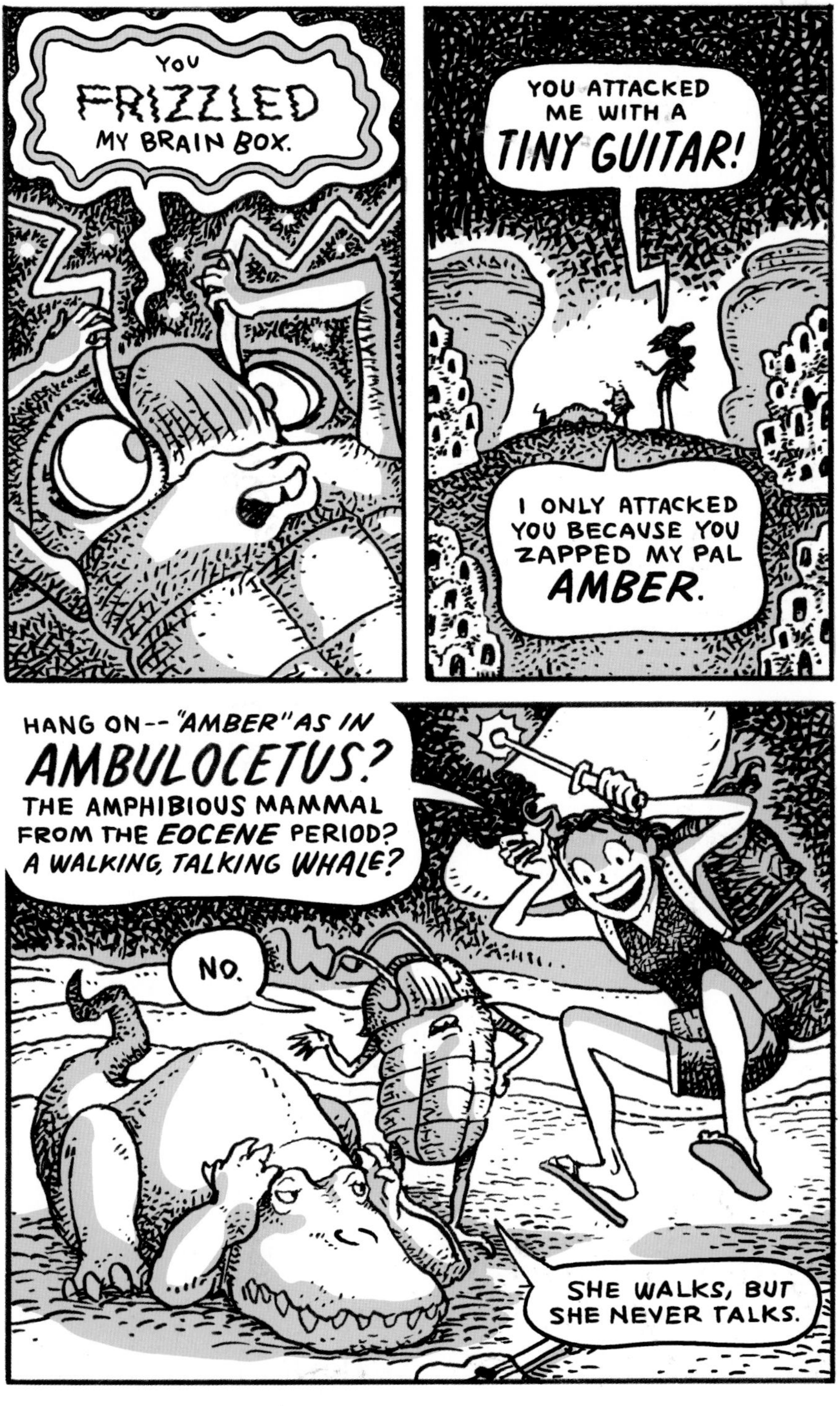
YOU FRIZZLED MY BRAIN BOX.
YOU ATTACKED ME WITH A TINY GUITAR!
I ONLY ATTACKED YOU BECAUSE YOU ZAPPED MY PAL AMBER.
HANG ON-- "AMBER" AS IN AMBULOCETUS? THE AMPHIBIOUS MAMMAL FROM THE EOCENE PERIOD? A WALKING, TALKING WHALE?
NO.
SHE WALKS, BUT SHE NEVER TALKS.

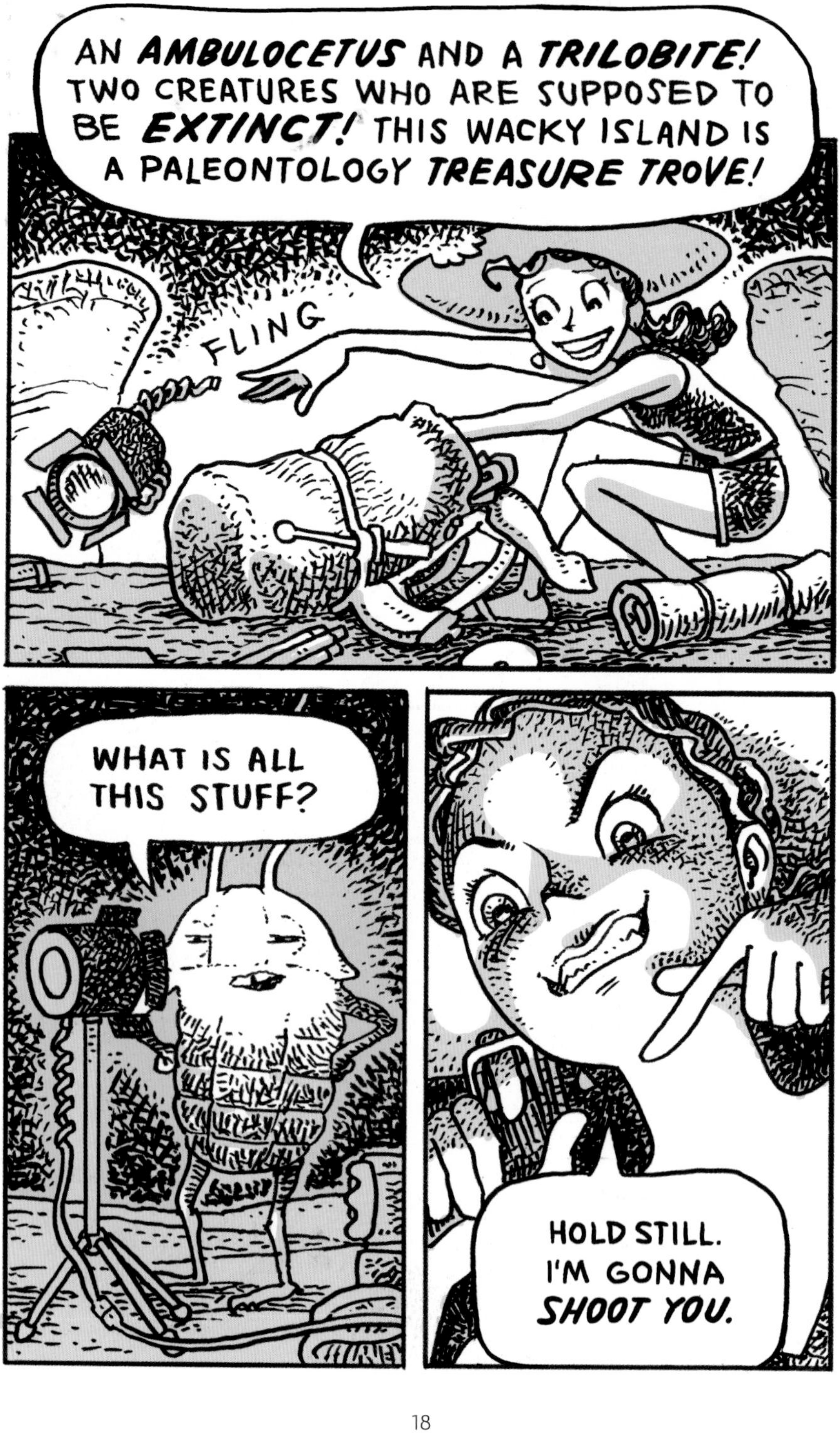
AN AMBULOCETUS AND A TRILOBITE! TWO CREATURES WHO ARE SUPPOSED TO BE EXTINCT! THIS WACKY ISLAND IS A PALEONTOLOGY TREASURE TROVE!
FLING
WHAT IS ALL THIS STUFF?
HOLD STILL. I'M GONNA SHOOT YOU.

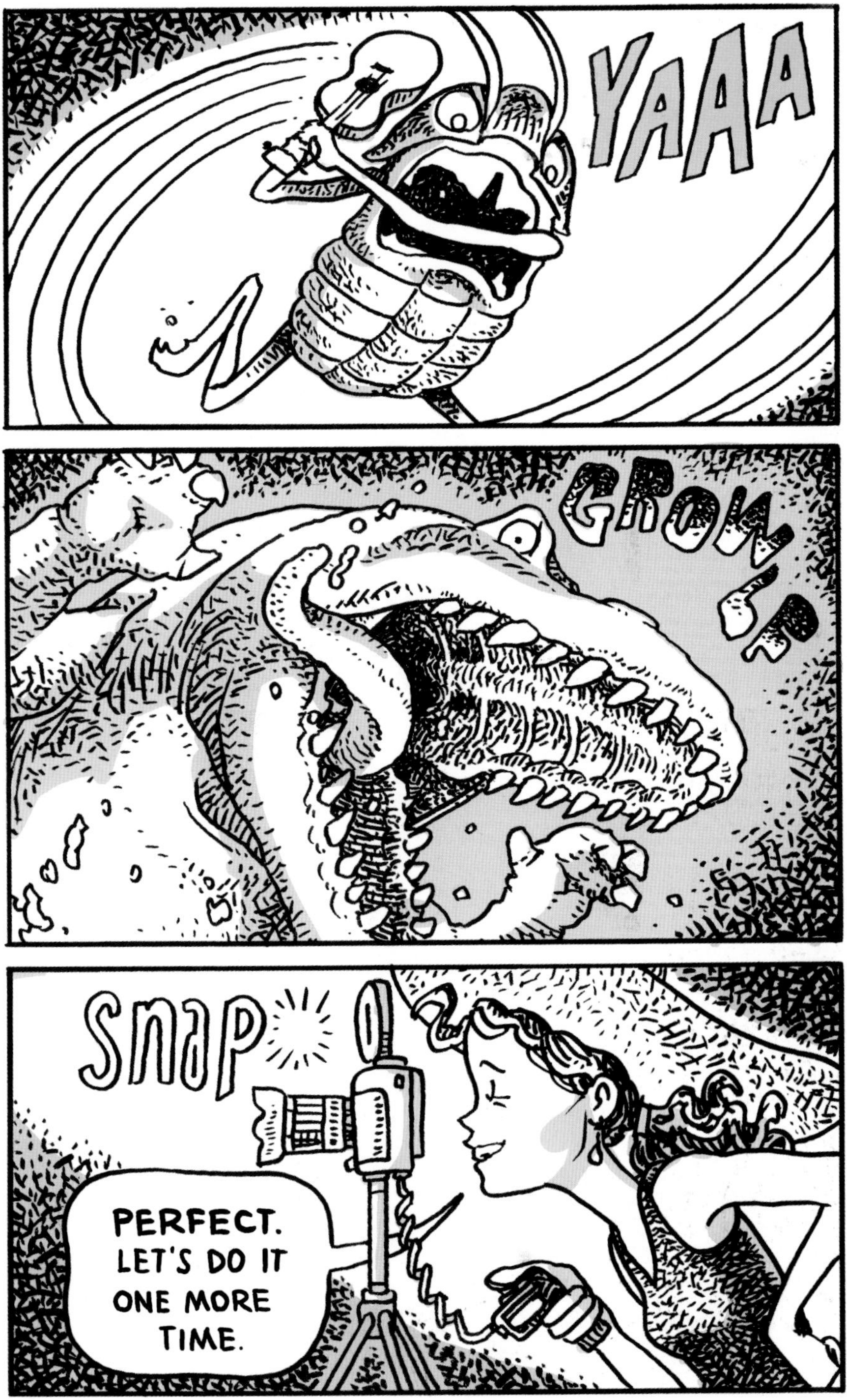
YAAA
GROWLR
SNAP
PERFECT. LET'S DO IT ONE MORE TIME.

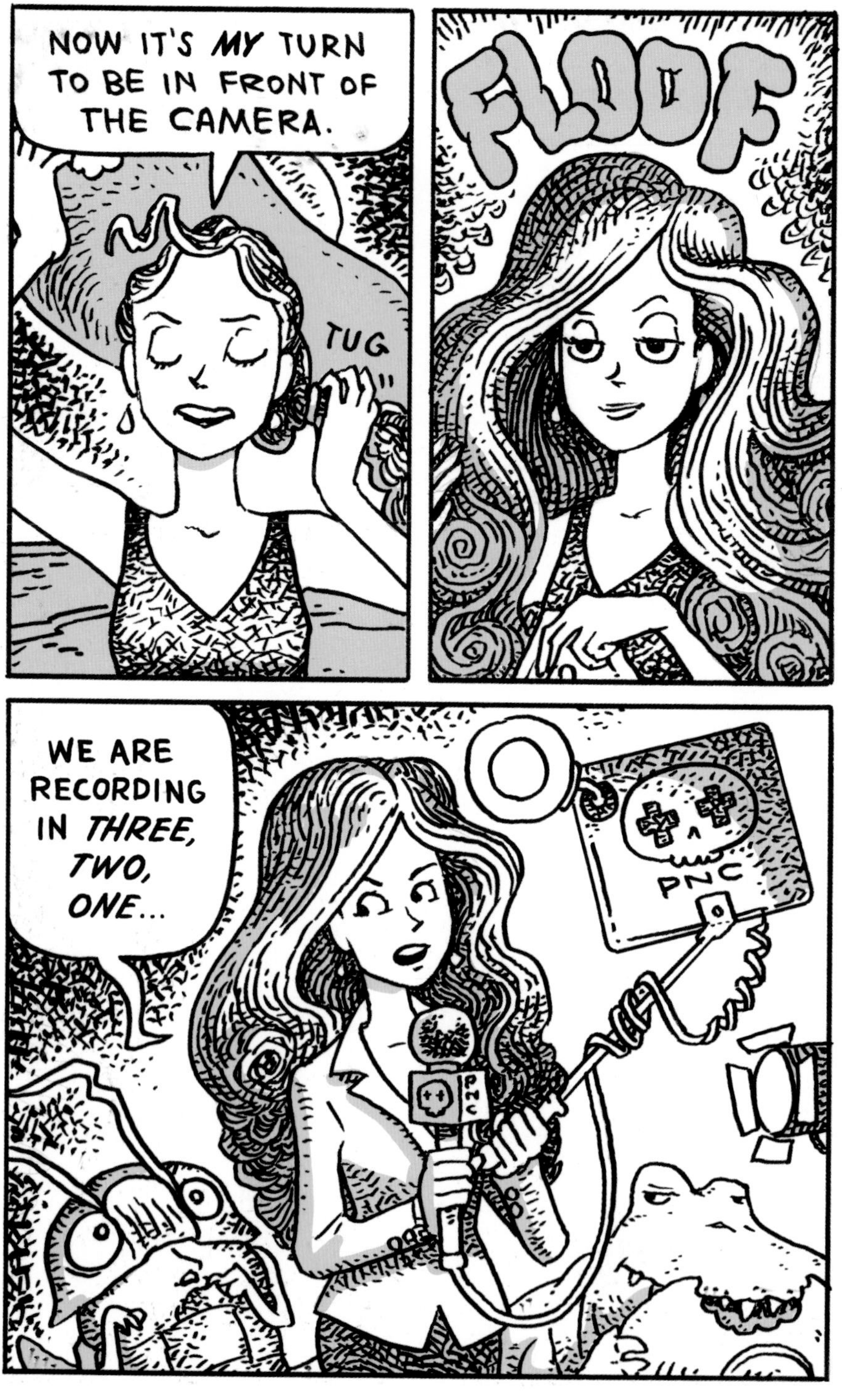
NOW IT'S MY TURN TO BE IN FRONT OF THE CAMERA.
TUG
FLOOF
PNC
WE ARE RECORDING IN THREE, TWO, ONE...

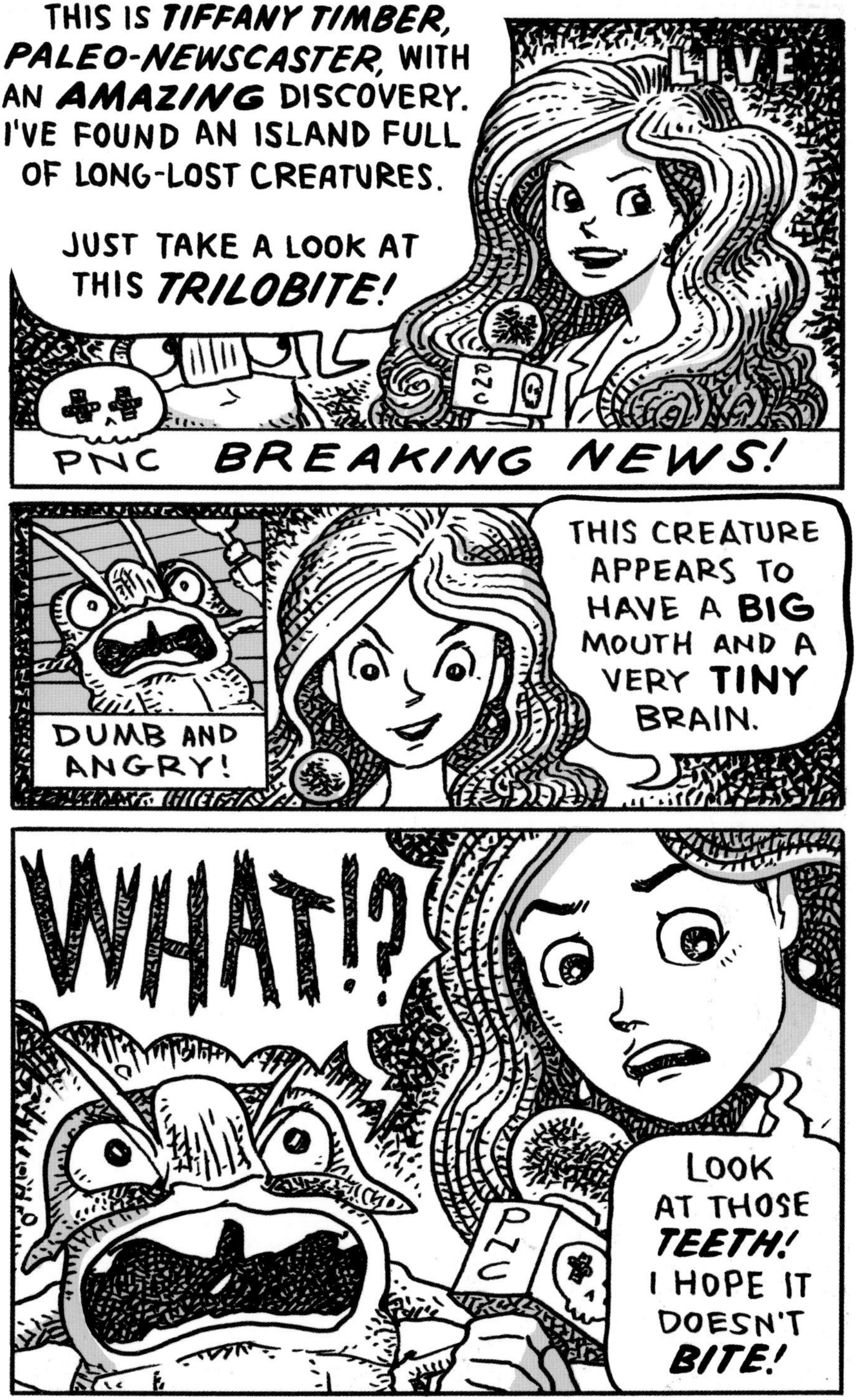
THIS IS TIFFANY TIMBER, PALEO-NEWSCASTER, WITH AN AMAZING DISCOVERY. I'VE FOUND AN ISLAND FULL OF LONG-LOST CREATURES.
JUST TAKE A LOOK AT THIS TRILOBITE!
LIVE
PNC
PNC BREAKING NEWS!
DUMB AND ANGRY!
THIS CREATURE APPEARS TO HAVE A BIG MOUTH AND A VERY TINY BRAIN.
WHAT!?
LOOK AT THOSE TEETH! I HOPE IT DOESN'T BITE!
PNC

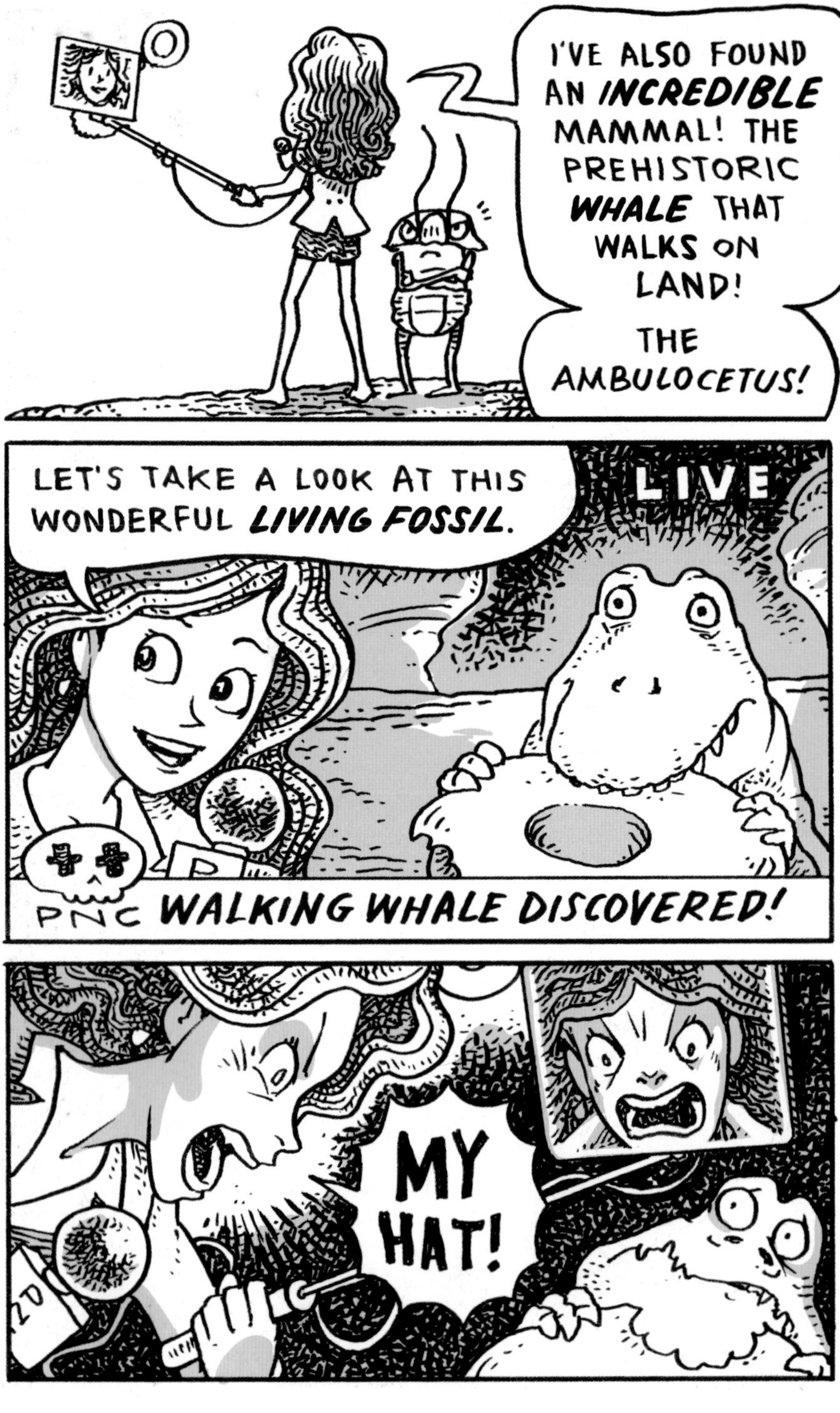
I'VE ALSO FOUND AN INCREDIBLE MAMMAL! THE PREHISTORIC WHALE THAT WALKS ON LAND!
THE AMBULOCETUS!
LET'S TAKE A LOOK AT THIS WONDERFUL LIVING FOSSIL.
LIVE
PNC WALKING WHALE DISCOVERED!
MY HAT!

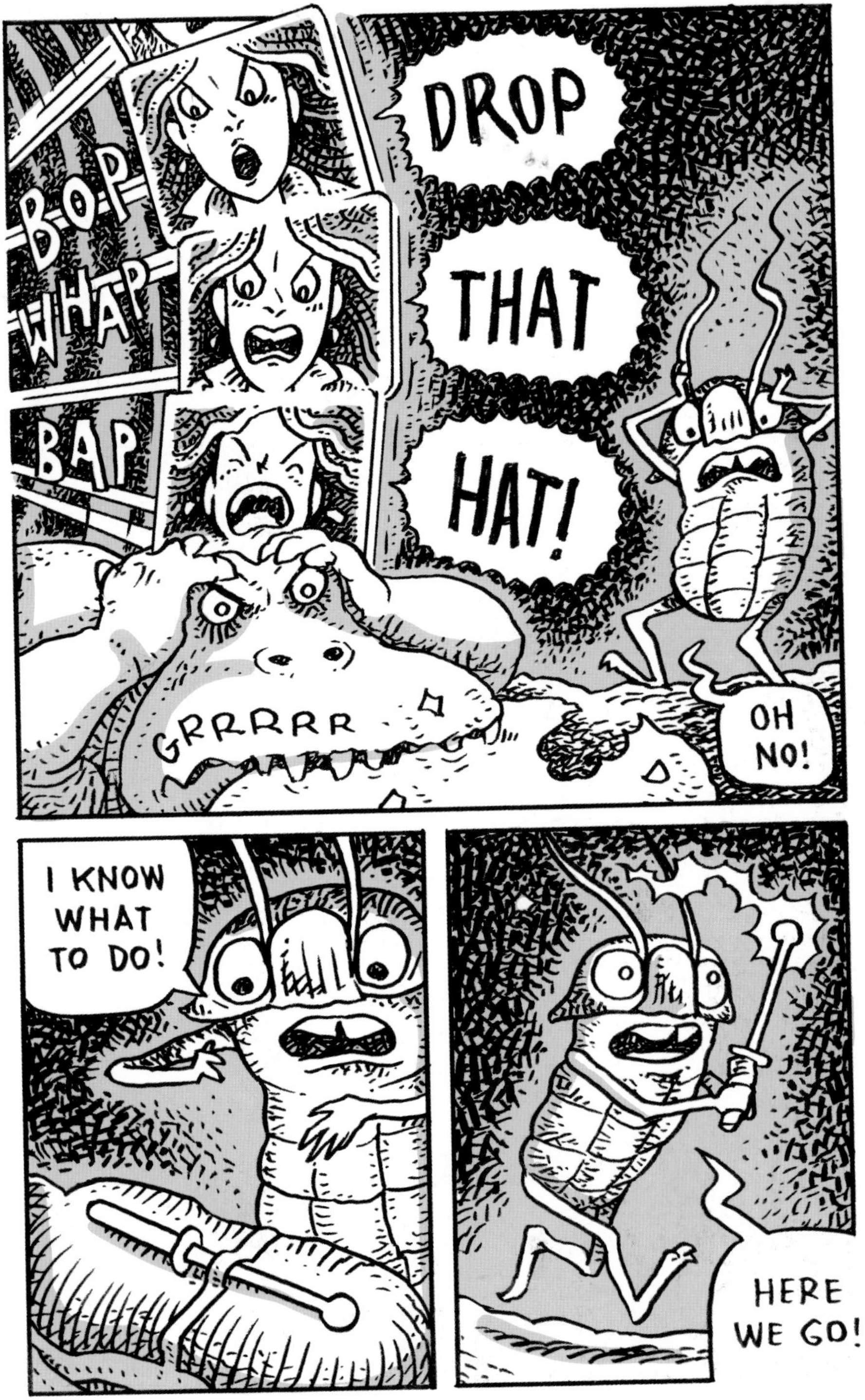
BOP
WHAP
BAP
DROP
THAT
HAT!
GRRRRRR
OH NO!
I KNOW WHAT TO DO!
HERE WE GO!

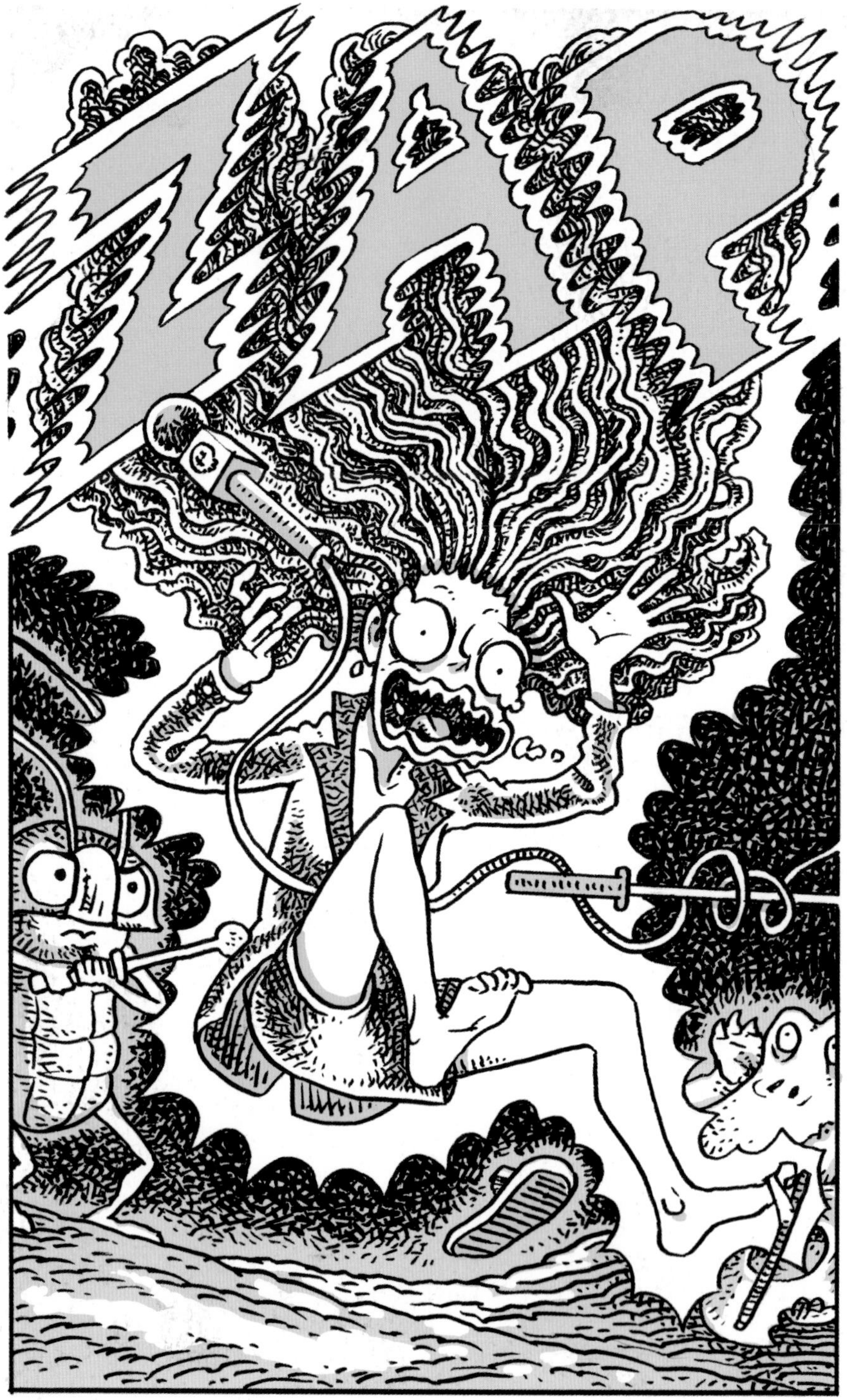
ZAP

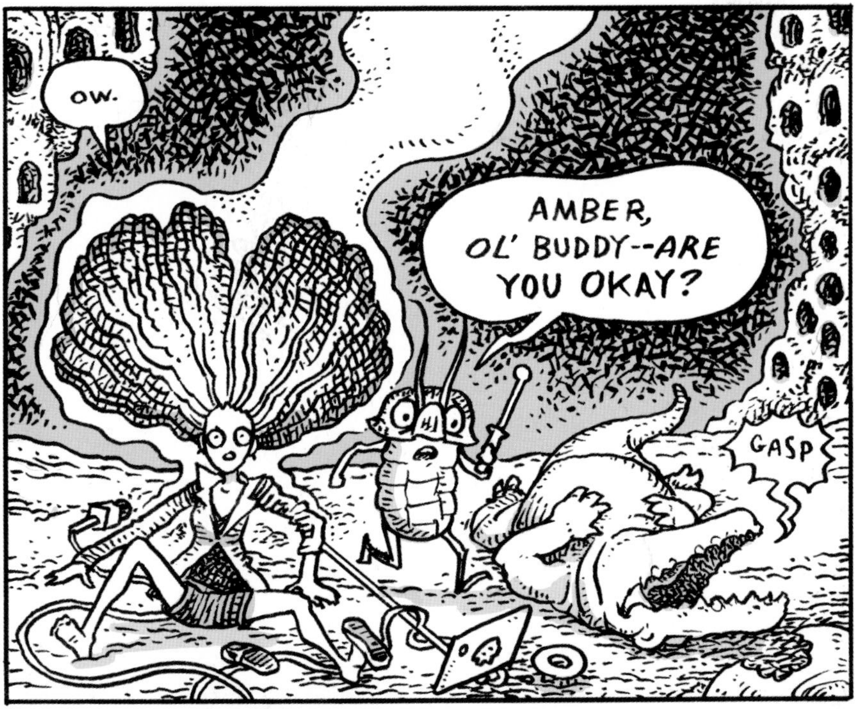
OW.
AMBER, OL' BUDDY--ARE YOU OKAY?
GASP

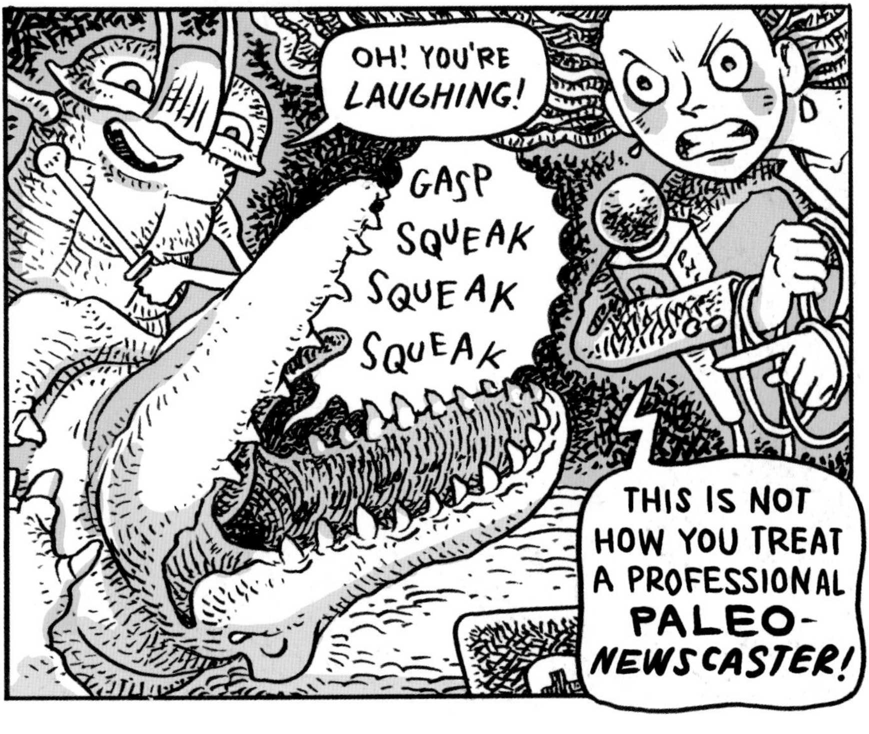
OH! YOU'RE LAUGHING!
GASP
SQUEAK
SQUEAK
SQUEAK
THIS IS NOT HOW YOU TREAT A PROFESSIONAL PALEO-NEWSCASTER!

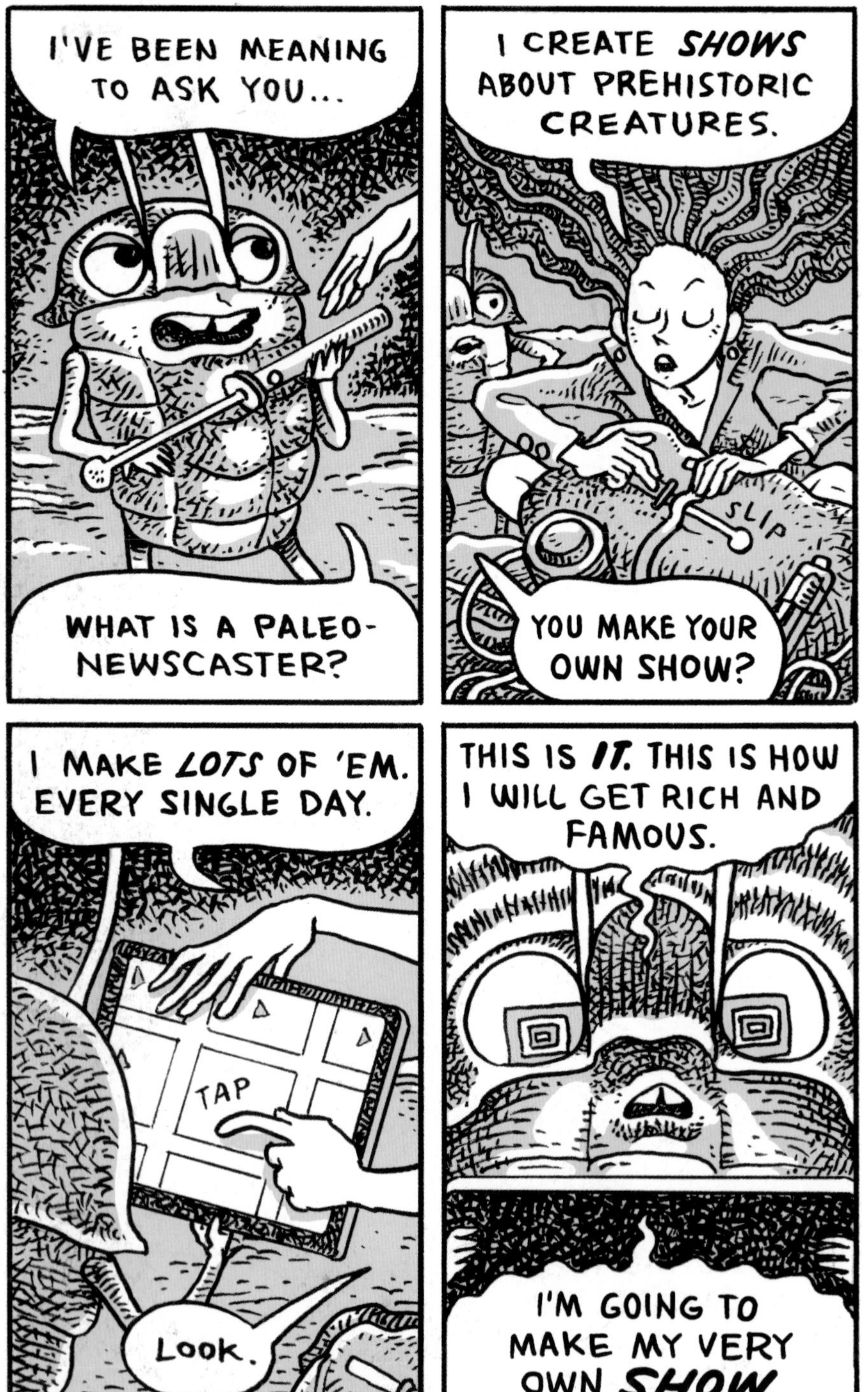
I'VE BEEN MEANING TO ASK YOU...
WHAT IS A PALEO-NEWSCASTER?
I CREATE SHOWS ABOUT PREHISTORIC CREATURES.
SLIP
YOU MAKE YOUR OWN SHOW?
I MAKE LOTS OF 'EM. EVERY SINGLE DAY.
TAP
LOOK.
THIS IS IT. THIS IS HOW I WILL GET RICH AND FAMOUS.
I'M GOING TO MAKE MY VERY OWN SHOW.

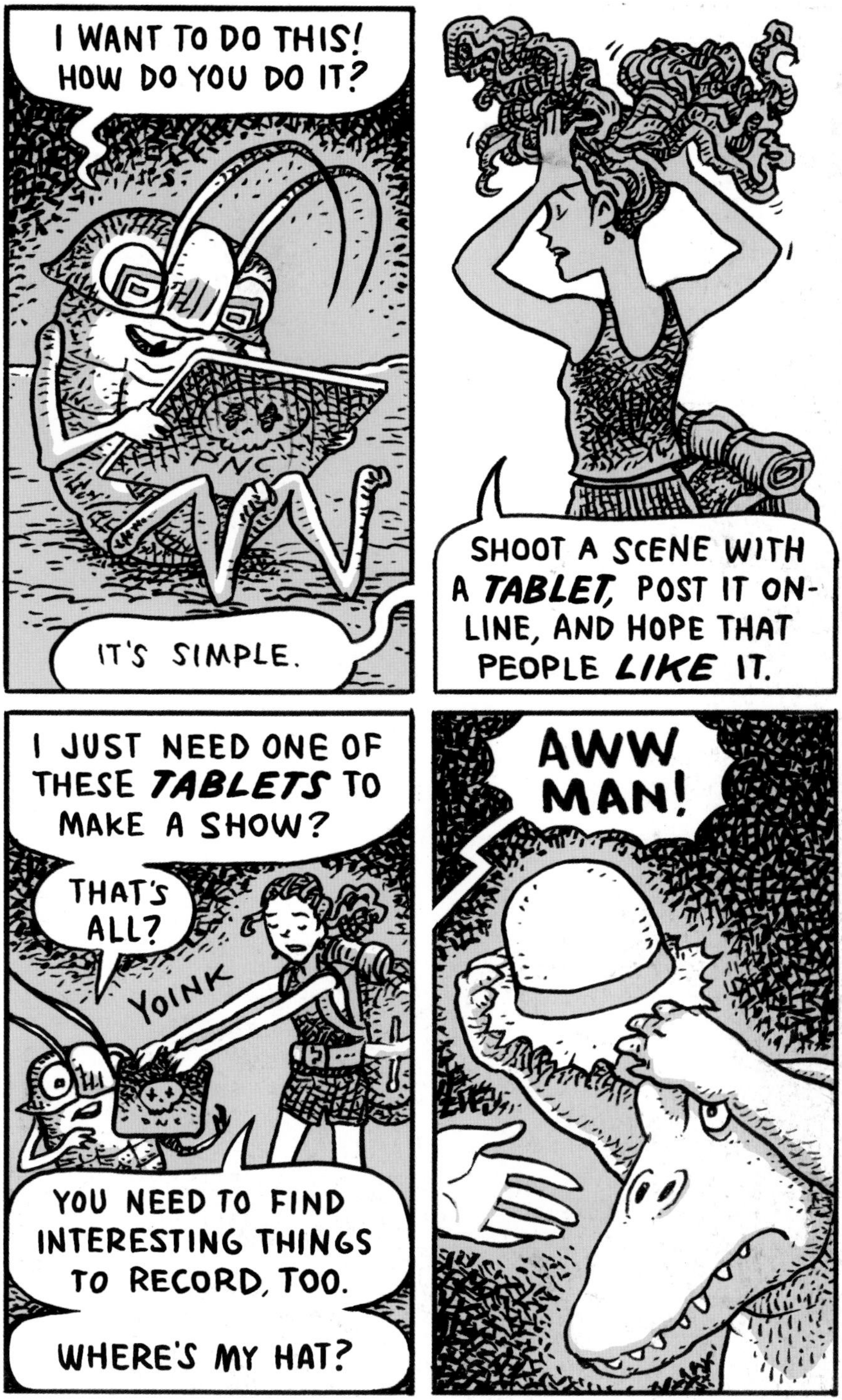
I WANT TO DO THIS! HOW DO YOU DO IT?
IT'S SIMPLE.
SHOOT A SCENE WITH A *TABLET,* POST IT ONLINE, AND HOPE THAT PEOPLE *LIKE* IT.
I JUST NEED ONE OF THESE *TABLETS* TO MAKE A SHOW?
THAT'S ALL?
YOINK
YOU NEED TO FIND INTERESTING THINGS TO RECORD, TOO.
WHERE'S MY HAT?
AWW MAN!

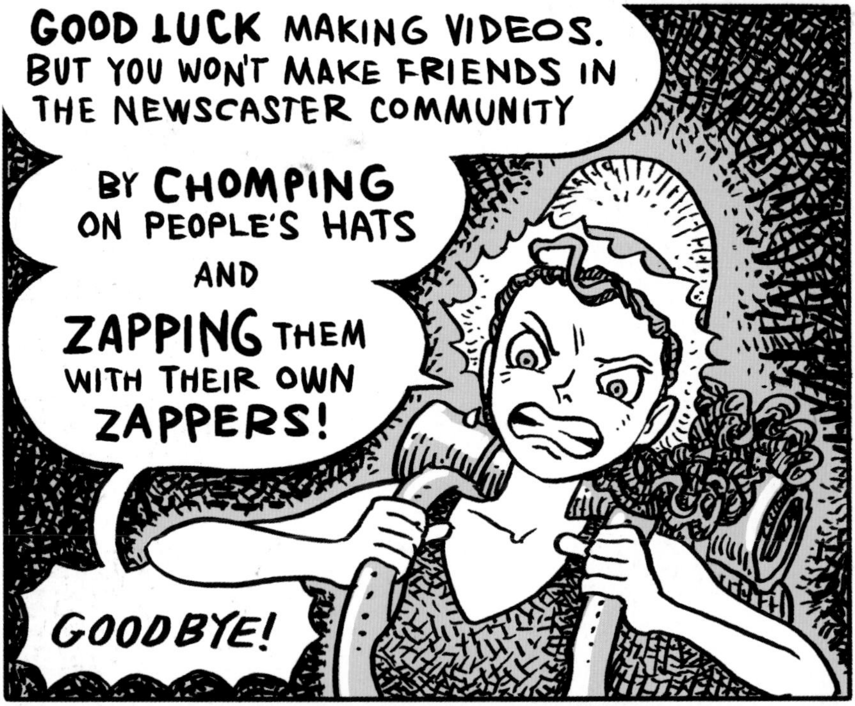
GOOD LUCK MAKING VIDEOS. BUT YOU WON'T MAKE FRIENDS IN THE NEWSCASTER COMMUNITY
BY CHOMPING ON PEOPLE'S HATS AND ZAPPING THEM WITH THEIR OWN ZAPPERS!
GOODBYE!

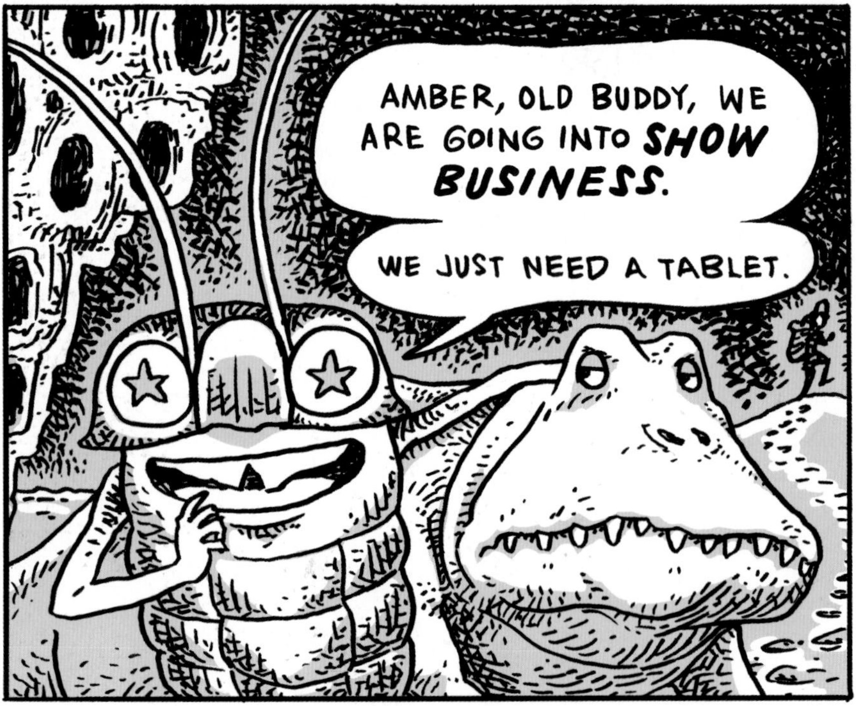
AMBER, OLD BUDDY, WE ARE GOING INTO SHOW BUSINESS.
WE JUST NEED A TABLET.

CHAPTER 2

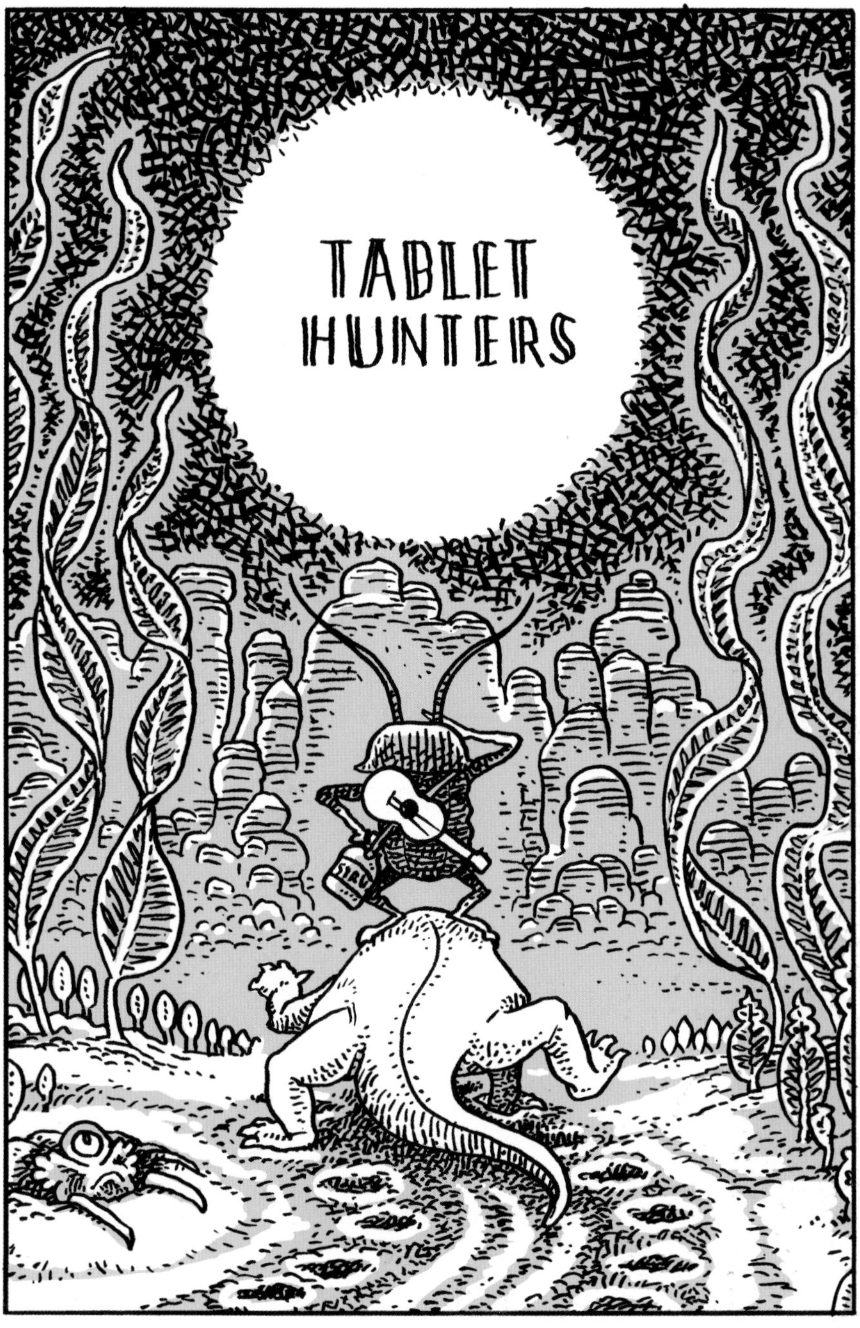
TABLET
HUNTERS

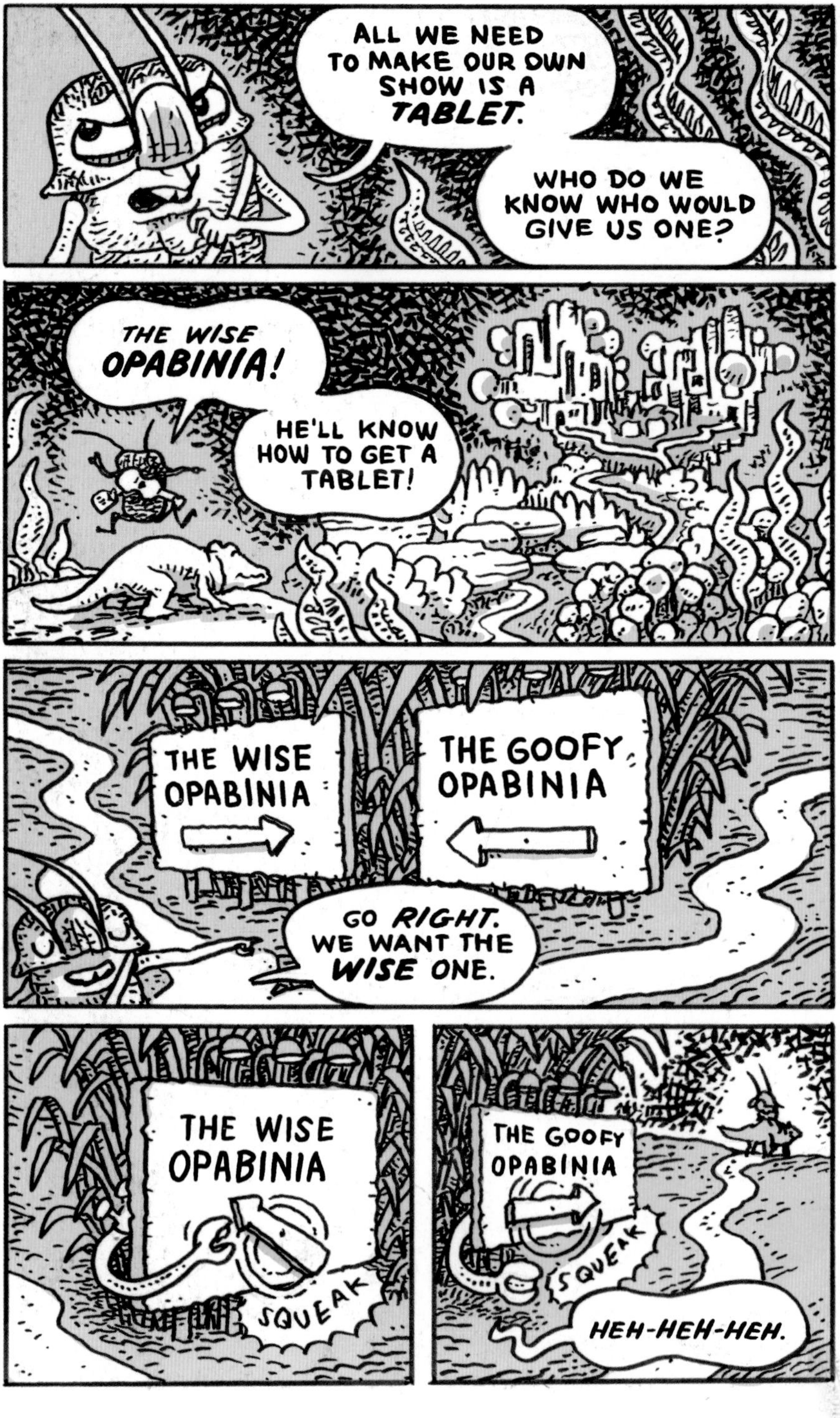
ALL WE NEED TO MAKE OUR OWN SHOW IS A *TABLET*.
WHO DO WE KNOW WHO WOULD GIVE US ONE?
THE WISE ***OPABINIA!***
HE'LL KNOW HOW TO GET A TABLET!
THE WISE OPABINIA
THE GOOFY OPABINIA
GO *RIGHT*. WE WANT THE ***WISE*** ONE.
THE WISE OPABINIA
SQUEAK
THE GOOFY OPABINIA
SQUEAK
HEH-HEH-HEH.

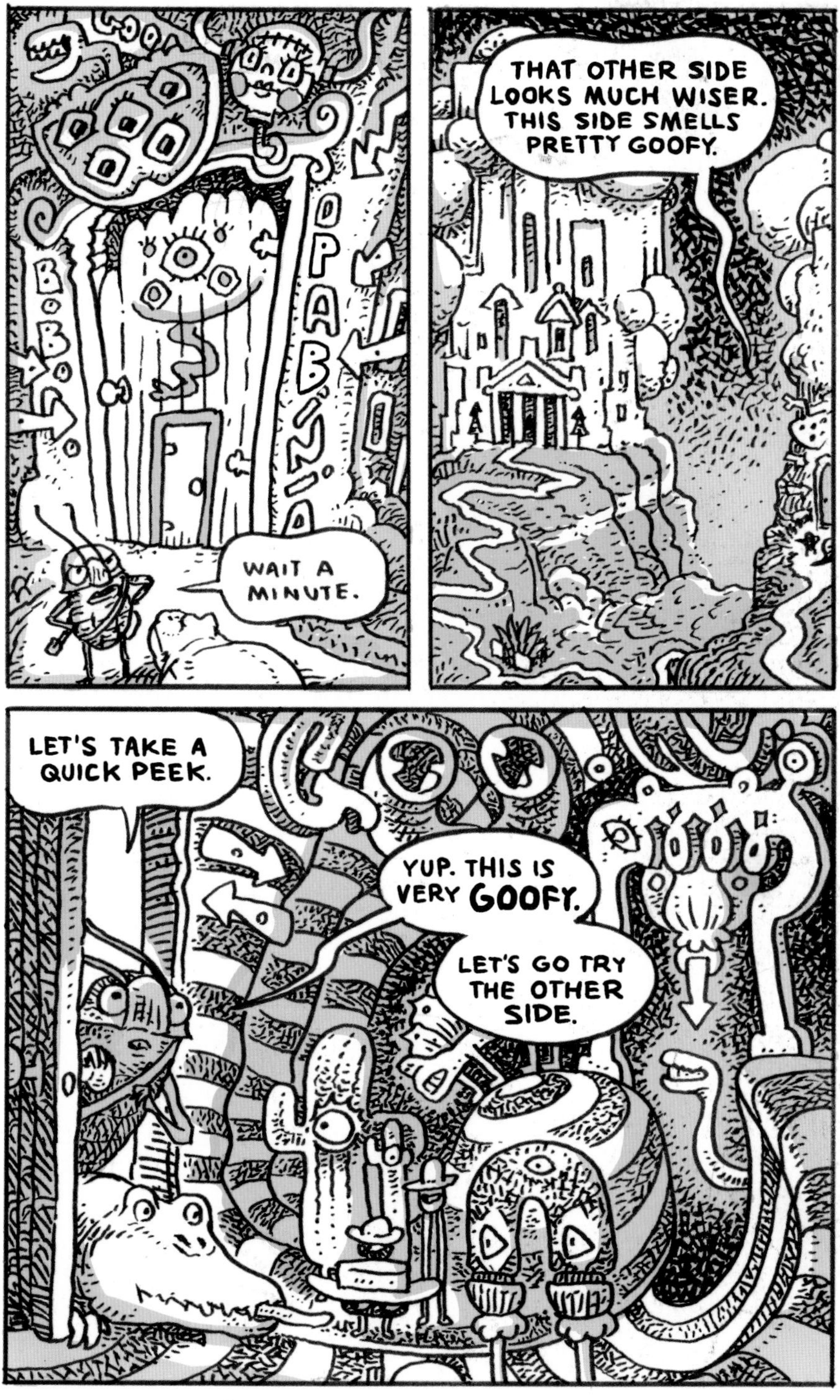
BOBO
OPABINIA
WAIT A MINUTE.
THAT OTHER SIDE LOOKS MUCH WISER. THIS SIDE SMELLS PRETTY GOOFY.
LET'S TAKE A QUICK PEEK.
YUP. THIS IS VERY GOOFY.
LET'S GO TRY THE OTHER SIDE.

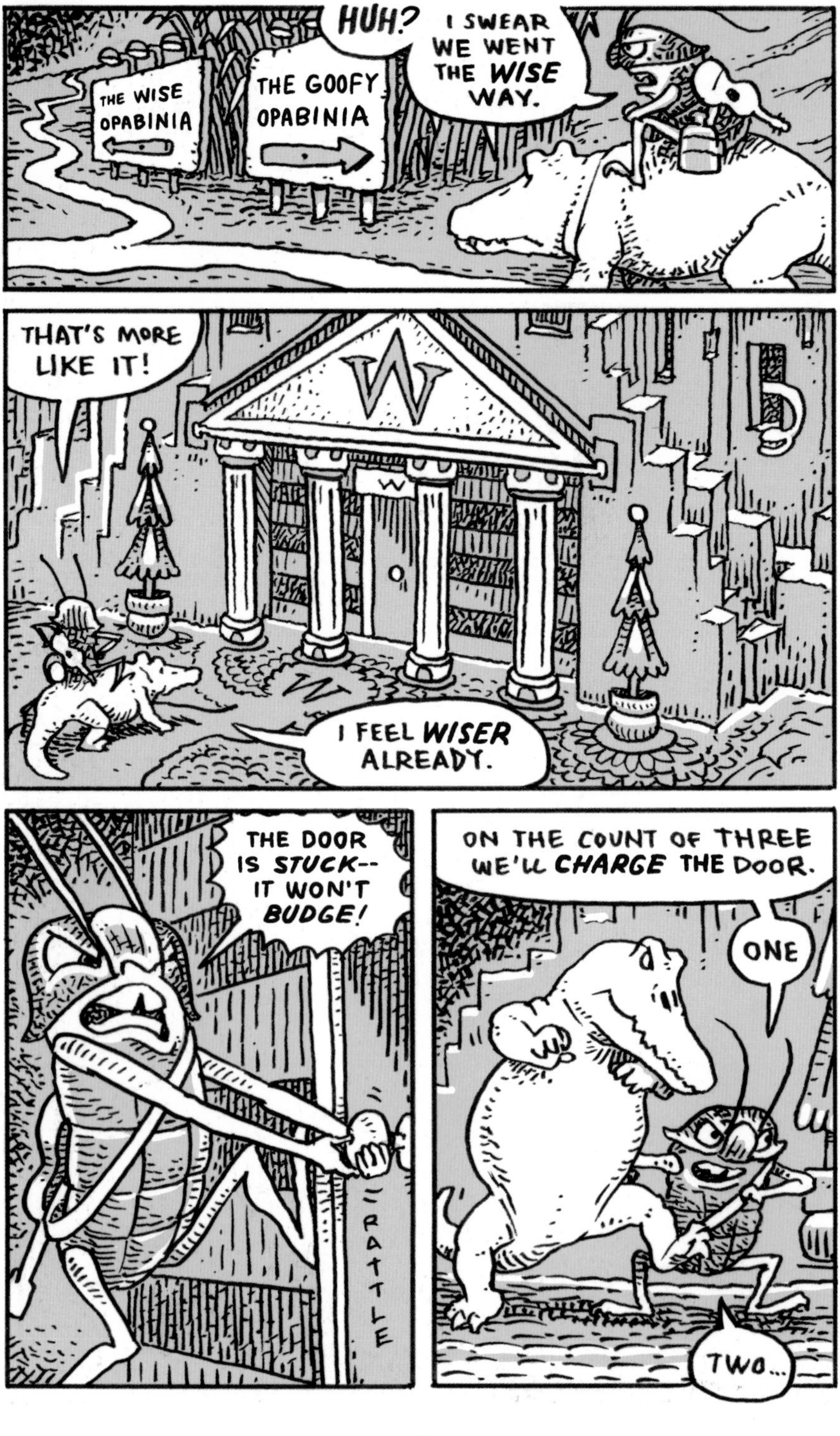
THE WISE OPABINIA
THE GOOFY OPABINIA
HUH?
I SWEAR WE WENT THE WISE WAY.
THAT'S MORE LIKE IT!
I FEEL WISER ALREADY.
THE DOOR IS STUCK-- IT WON'T BUDGE!
RATTLE
ON THE COUNT OF THREE WE'LL CHARGE THE DOOR.
ONE
TWO...

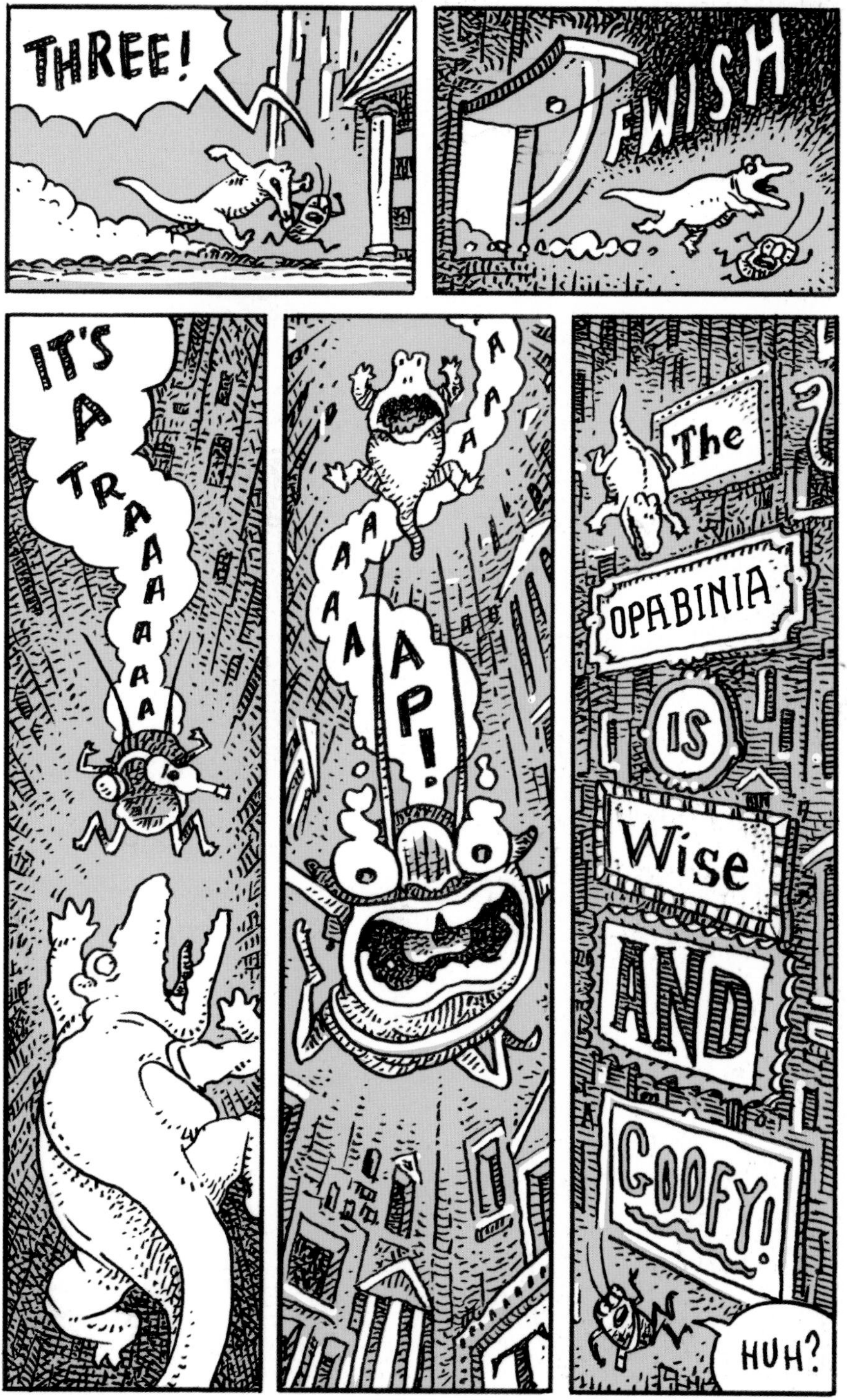
THREE!
FWISH
IT'S A TRAAAAAAAAAAAAAAAAP!
The
OPABINIA
IS
Wise
AND
GOOFY!
HUH?

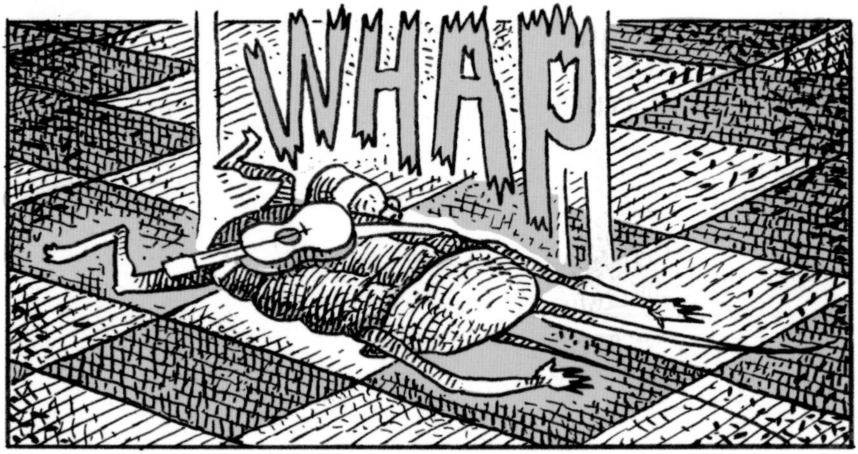
WHAP

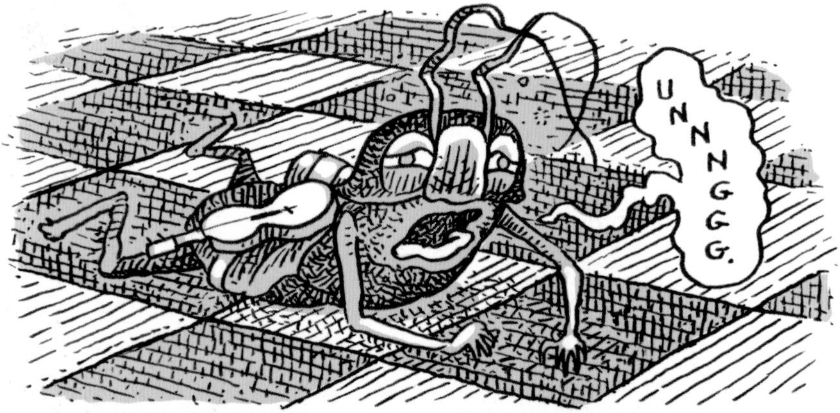
UNNNGGG.

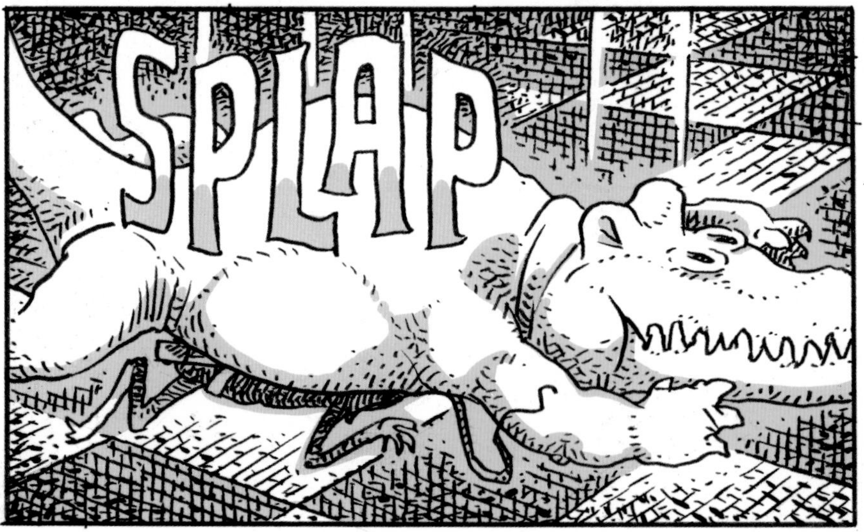
SPLAP

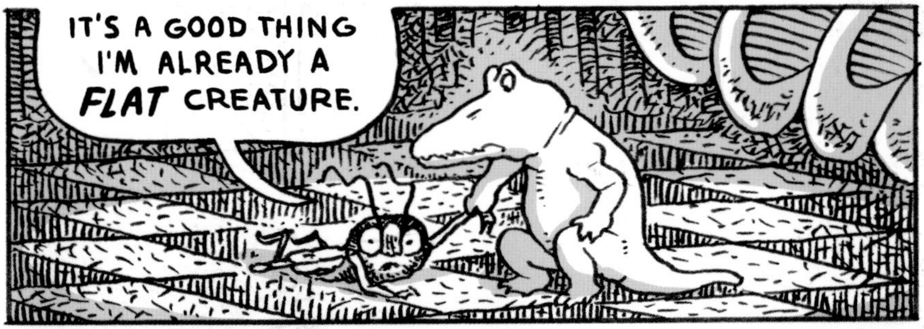
IT'S A GOOD THING I'M ALREADY A FLAT CREATURE.

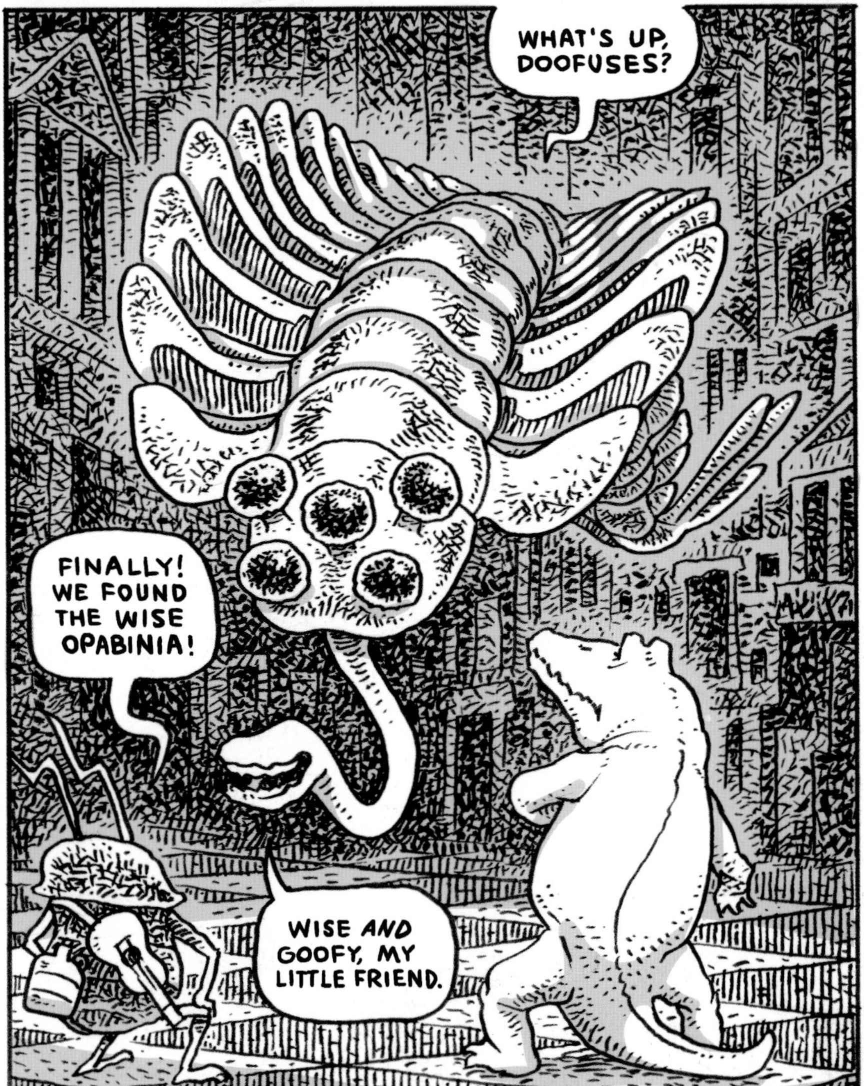
WHAT'S UP, DOOFUSES?
FINALLY! WE FOUND THE WISE OPABINIA!
WISE AND GOOFY, MY LITTLE FRIEND.

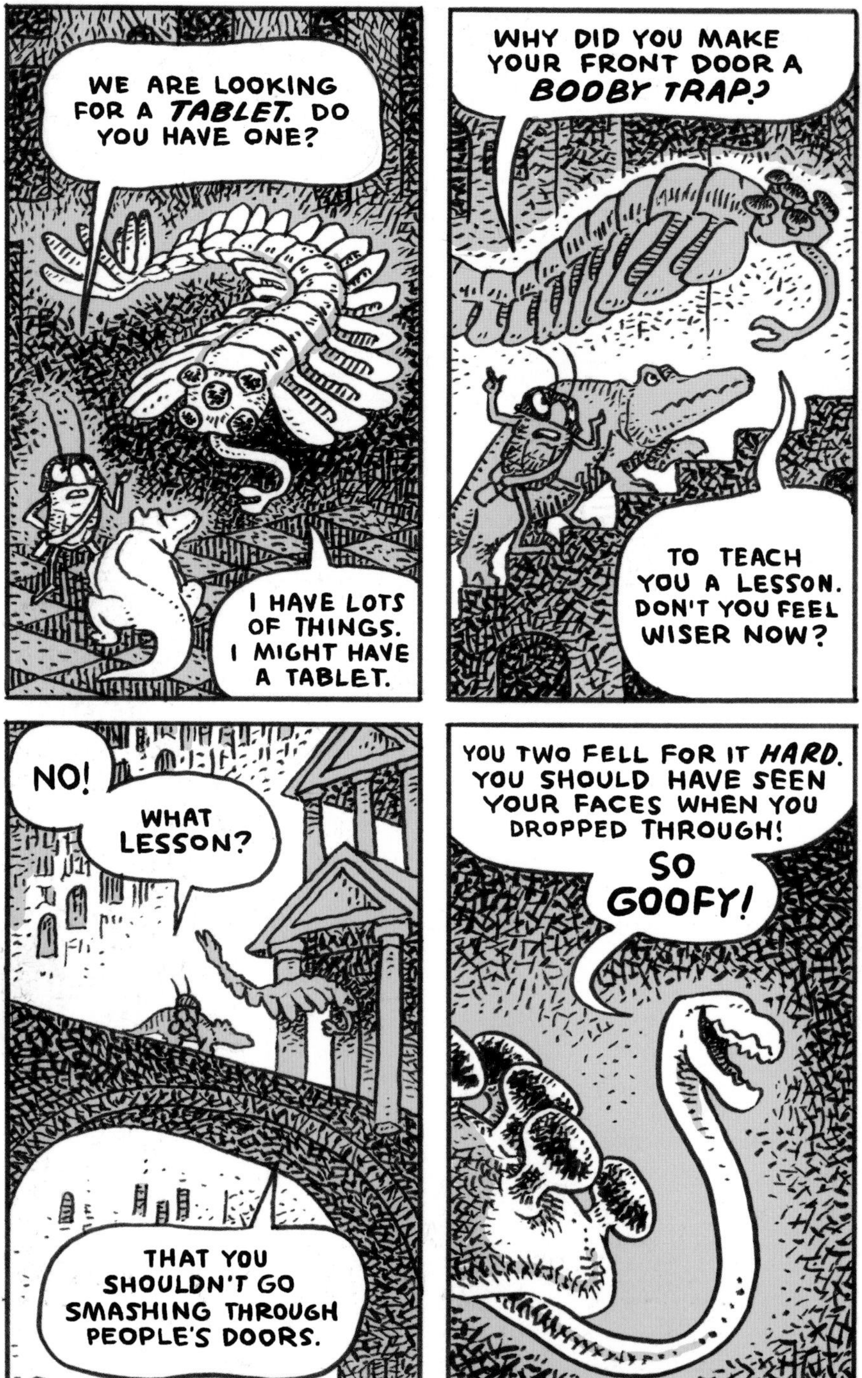
WE ARE LOOKING FOR A TABLET. DO YOU HAVE ONE?
I HAVE LOTS OF THINGS. I MIGHT HAVE A TABLET.
WHY DID YOU MAKE YOUR FRONT DOOR A BOOBY TRAP?
TO TEACH YOU A LESSON. DON'T YOU FEEL WISER NOW?
NO!
WHAT LESSON?
THAT YOU SHOULDN'T GO SMASHING THROUGH PEOPLE'S DOORS.
YOU TWO FELL FOR IT HARD. YOU SHOULD HAVE SEEN YOUR FACES WHEN YOU DROPPED THROUGH!
SO GOOFY!

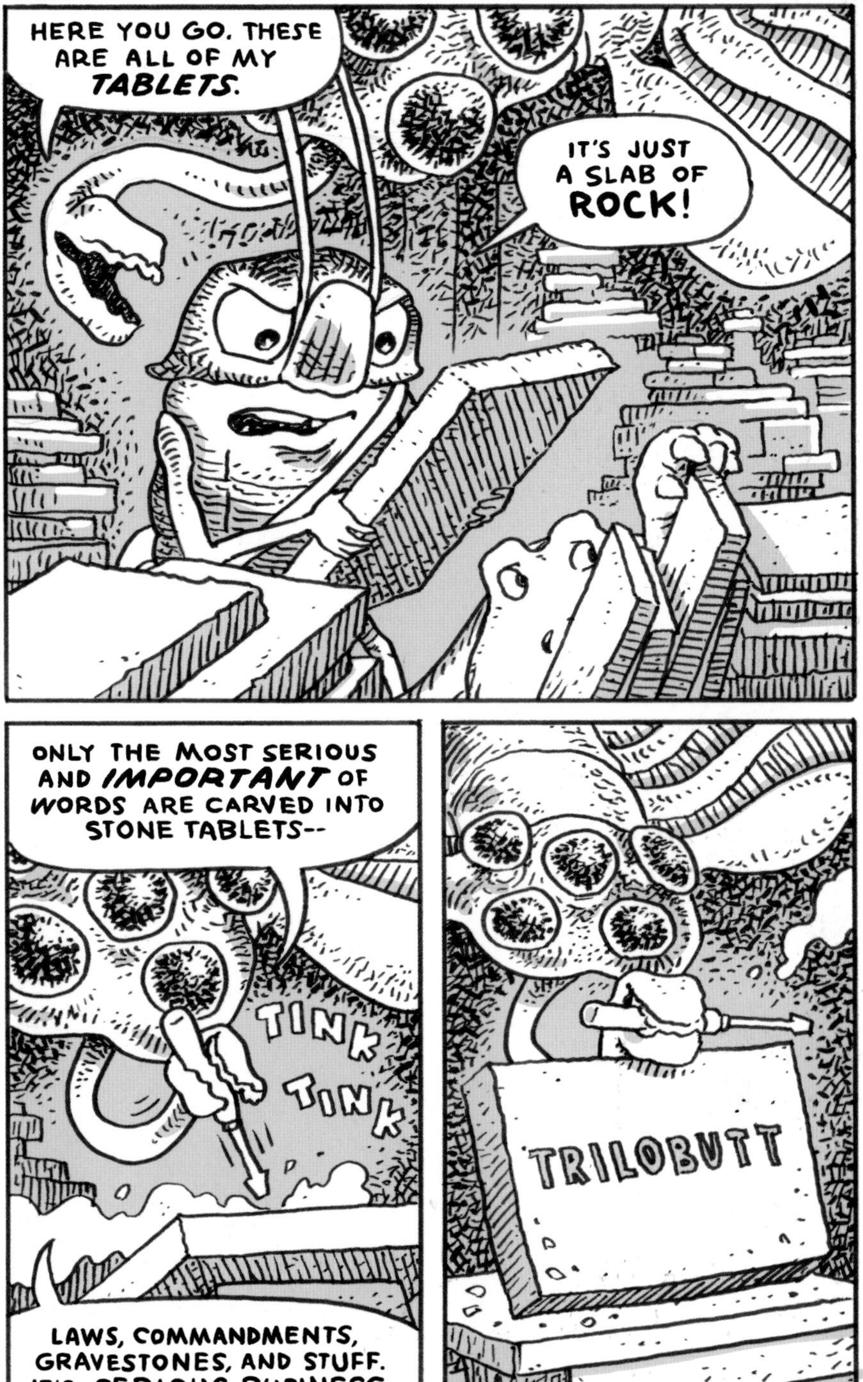
HERE YOU GO. THESE ARE ALL OF MY TABLETS.
IT'S JUST A SLAB OF ROCK!
ONLY THE MOST SERIOUS AND IMPORTANT OF WORDS ARE CARVED INTO STONE TABLETS--
TINK
TINK
LAWS, COMMANDMENTS, GRAVESTONES, AND STUFF. IT'S SERIOUS BUSINESS.
TRILOBUTT

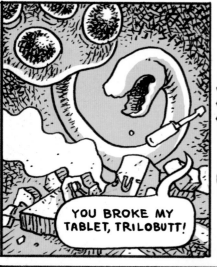

THAT'S **NOT** THE KIND OF TABLET WE WANT!

WE WANT TO MAKE A **SHOW!** WE WANT THE THING WITH A **SCREEN** THAT YOU LOOK THROUGH!

YOU BROKE MY TABLET, TRILOBUTT!

A **CAMERA!?** WHY DIDN'T YOU SAY?

I'VE GOT **LOADS** OF CAMERAS!

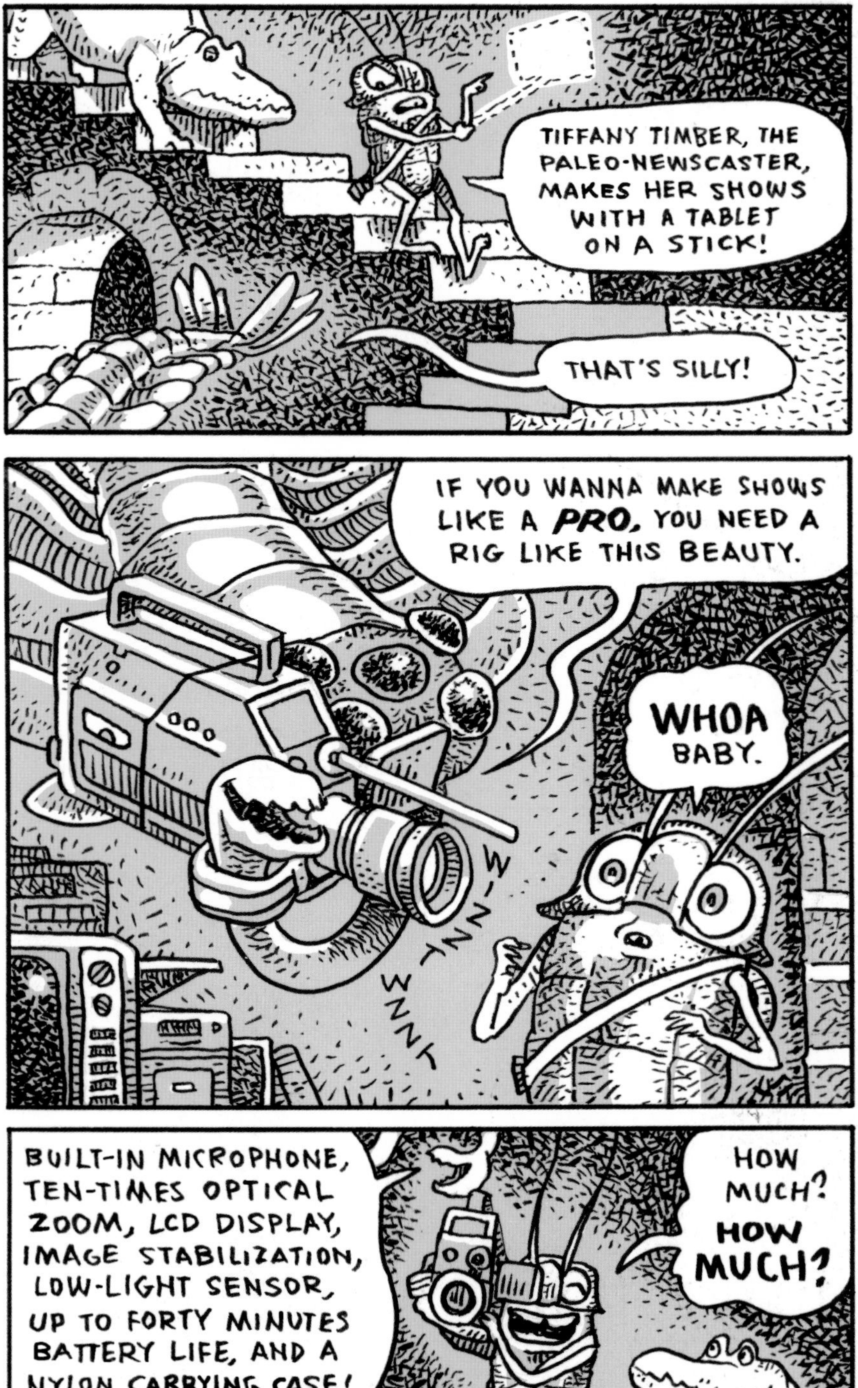
TIFFANY TIMBER, THE PALEO-NEWSCASTER, MAKES HER SHOWS WITH A TABLET ON A STICK!
THAT'S SILLY!
IF YOU WANNA MAKE SHOWS LIKE A *PRO,* YOU NEED A RIG LIKE THIS BEAUTY.
WHOA BABY.
W-ZZZT
WZZZT
BUILT-IN MICROPHONE, TEN-TIMES OPTICAL ZOOM, LCD DISPLAY, IMAGE STABILIZATION, LOW-LIGHT SENSOR, UP TO FORTY MINUTES BATTERY LIFE, AND A NYLON CARRYING CASE!
HOW MUCH? HOW MUCH?

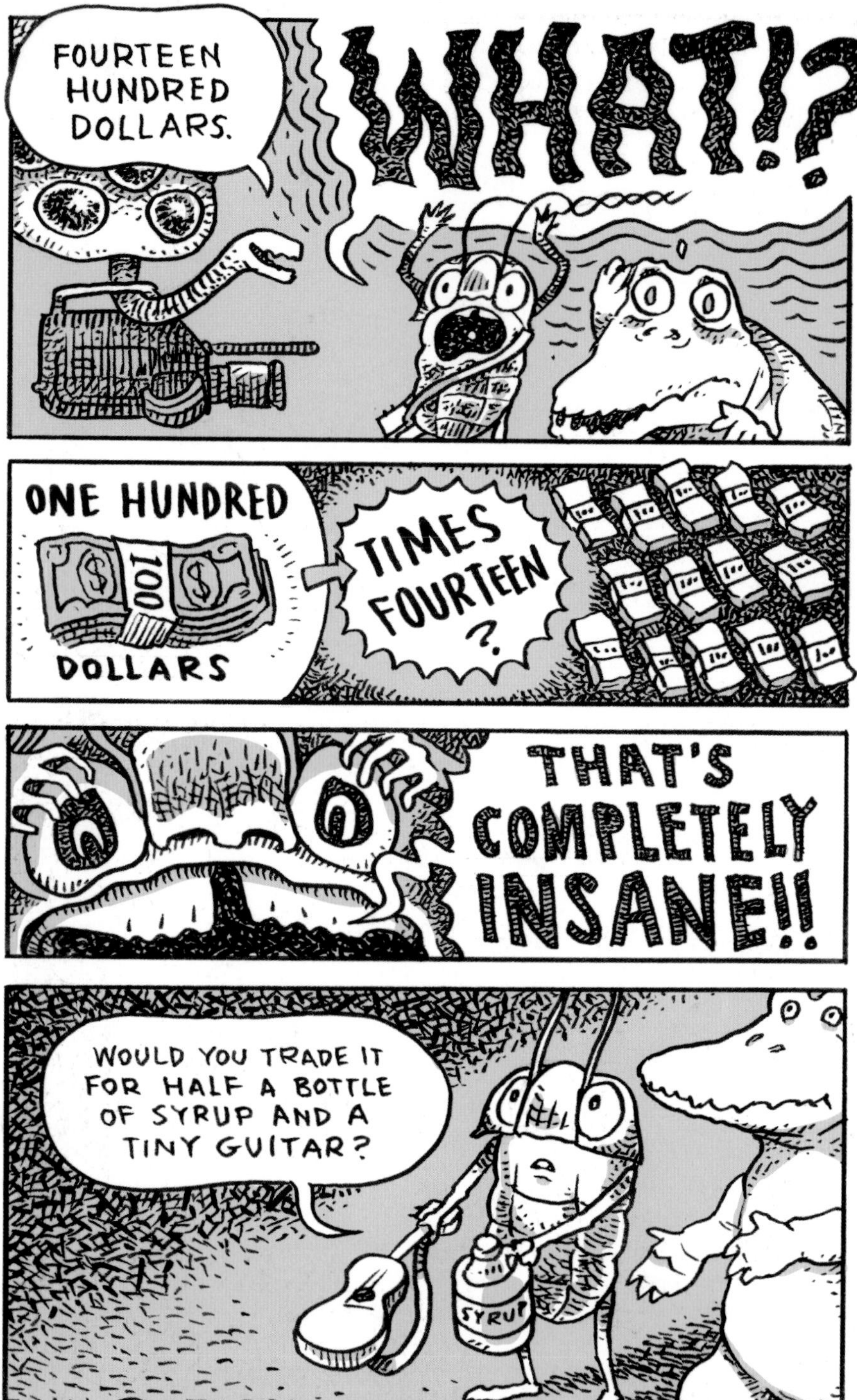
FOURTEEN HUNDRED DOLLARS.
WHAT!?
ONE HUNDRED
100
DOLLARS
TIMES FOURTEEN ?
THAT'S COMPLETELY INSANE!!
WOULD YOU TRADE IT FOR HALF A BOTTLE OF SYRUP AND A TINY GUITAR?
SYRUP

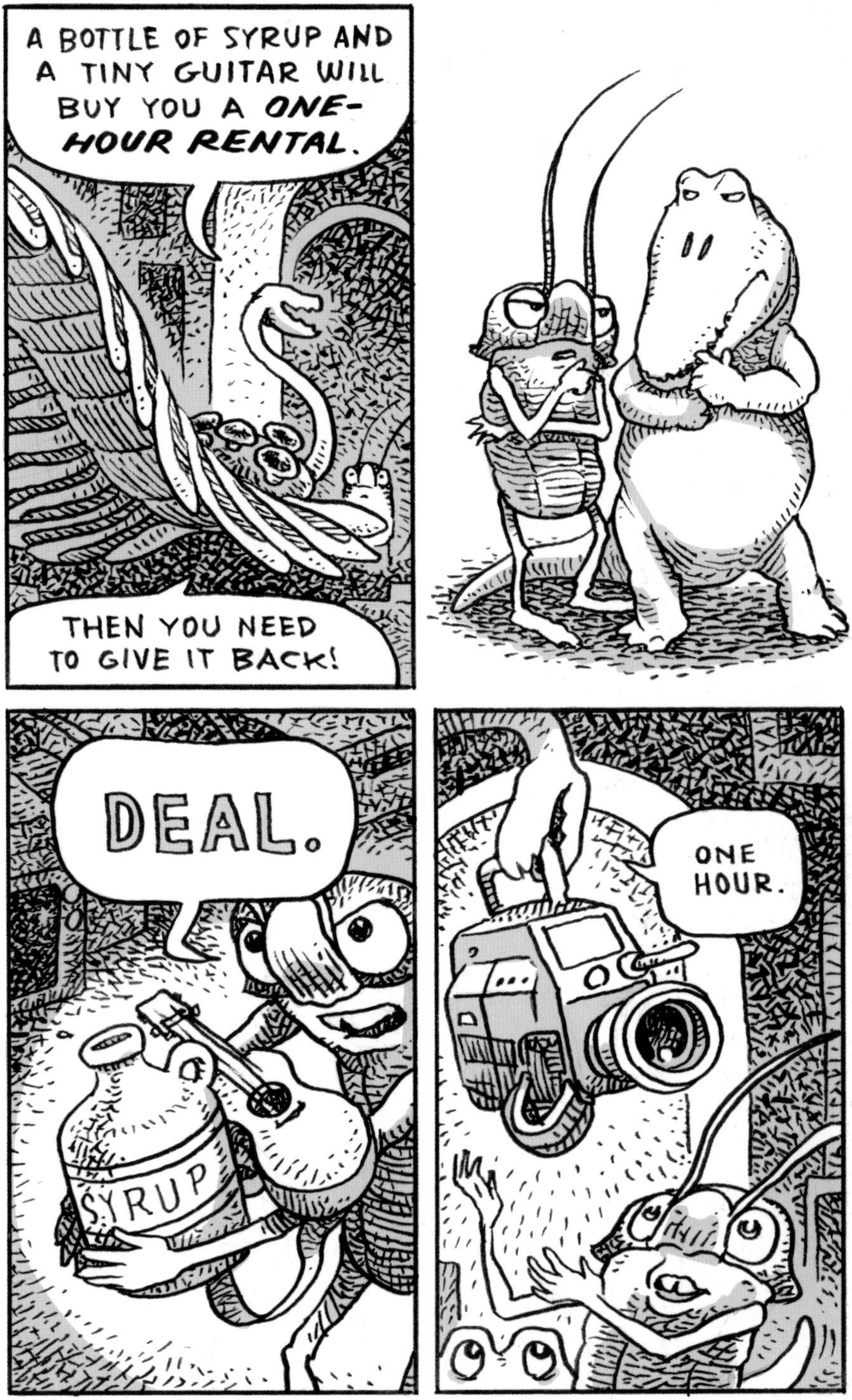
A BOTTLE OF SYRUP AND A TINY GUITAR WILL BUY YOU A ONE-HOUR RENTAL.
THEN YOU NEED TO GIVE IT BACK!
DEAL.
SYRUP
ONE HOUR.

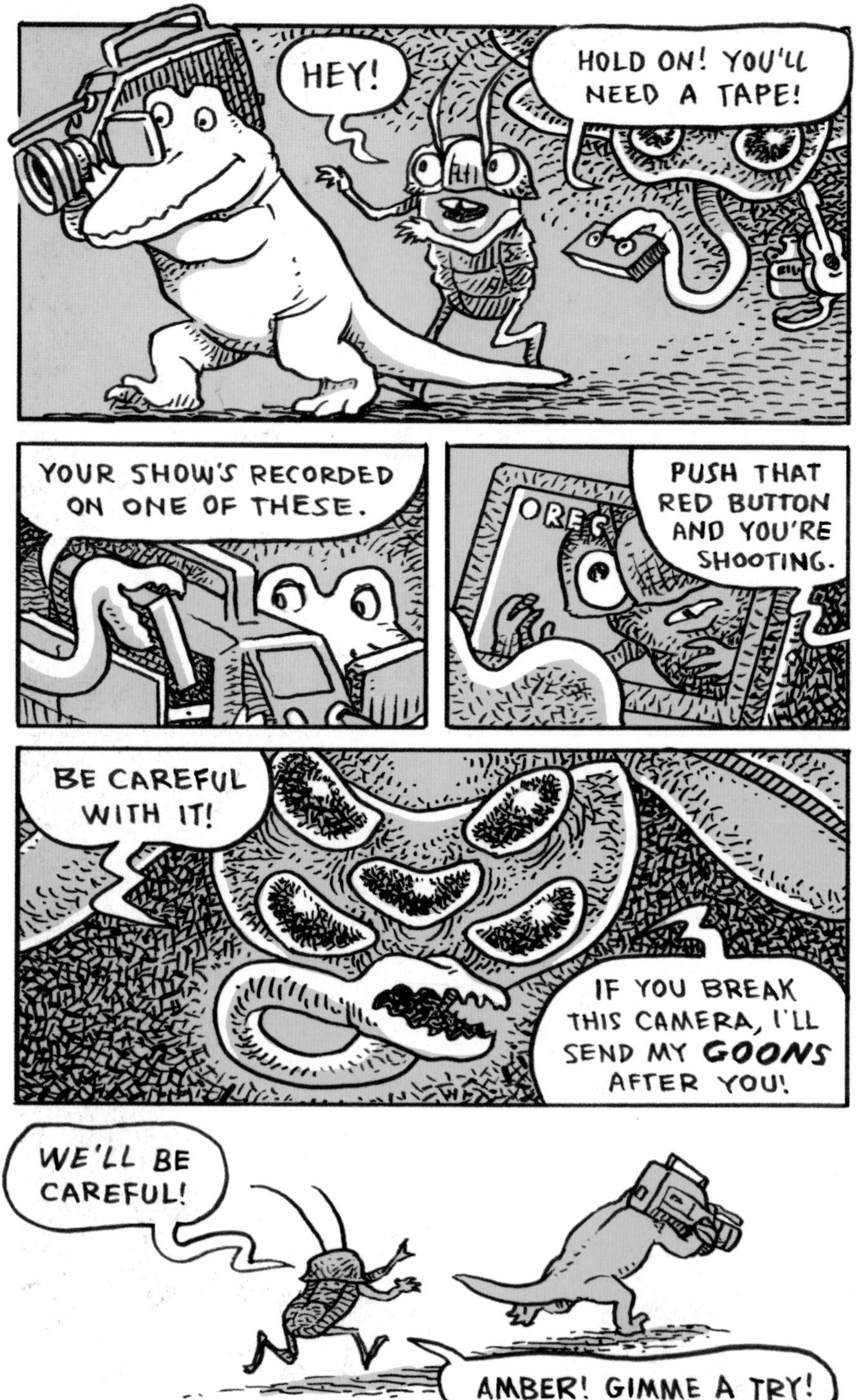
HEY!
HOLD ON! YOU'LL NEED A TAPE!
YOUR SHOW'S RECORDED ON ONE OF THESE.
REC
PUSH THAT RED BUTTON AND YOU'RE SHOOTING.
BE CAREFUL WITH IT!
IF YOU BREAK THIS CAMERA, I'LL SEND MY **GOONS** AFTER YOU!
WE'LL BE CAREFUL!
AMBER! GIMME A TRY!

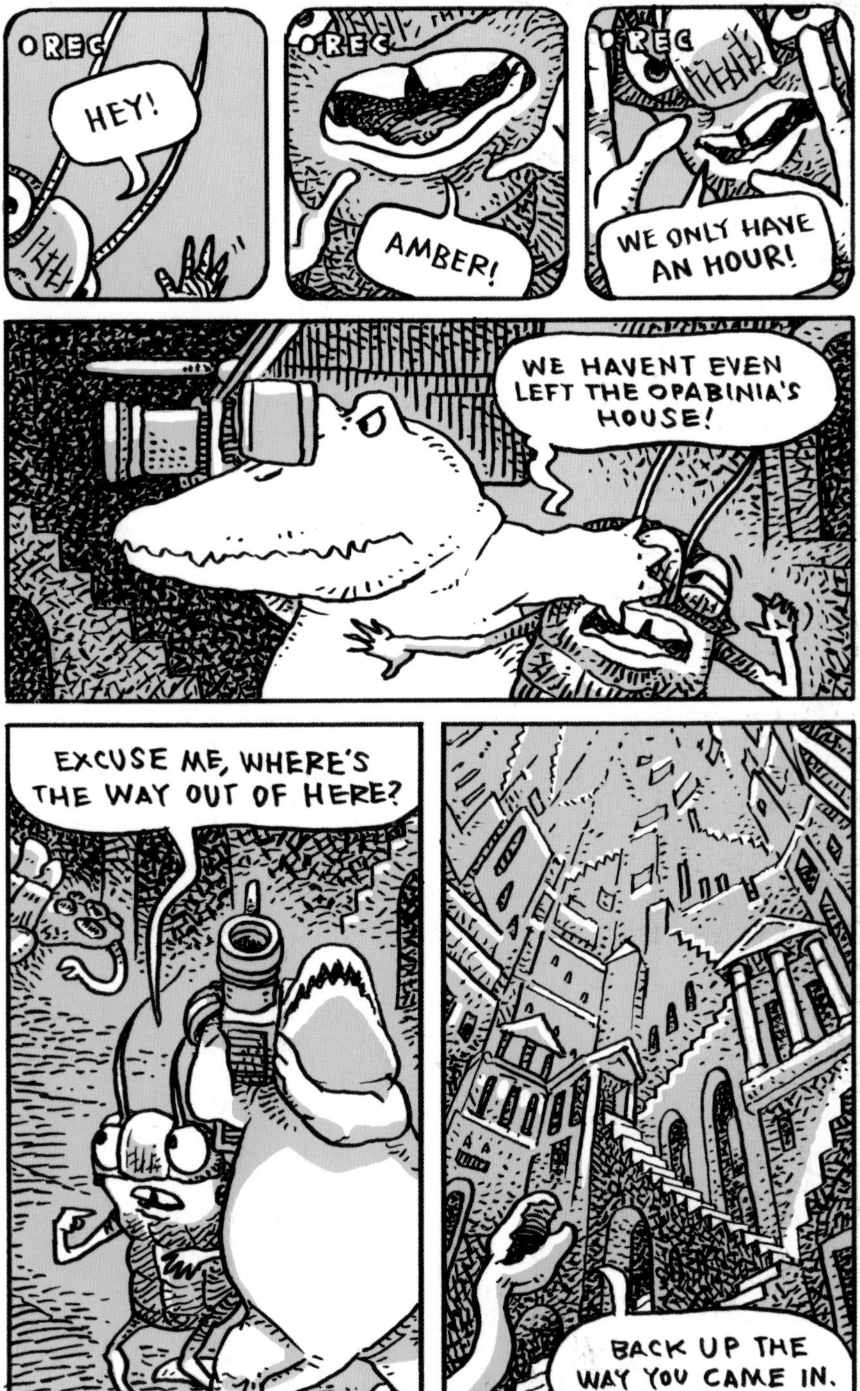
REC
HEY!
REC
AMBER!
REC
WE ONLY HAVE AN HOUR!
WE HAVENT EVEN LEFT THE OPABINIA'S HOUSE!
EXCUSE ME, WHERE'S THE WAY OUT OF HERE?
BACK UP THE WAY YOU CAME IN.

THE LADDER IS MUCH FASTER THAN THE STAIRS, YOU KNOW.
JUST GIMME THE CAMERA! YOU CAN'T CLIMB WITH IT!
HNNGGG
CHOMP
OKAY, WE'RE TAKING THE STAIRS!

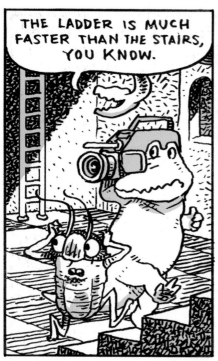

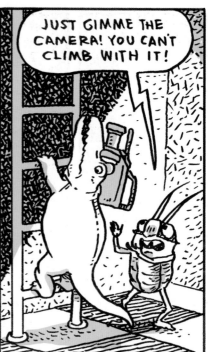

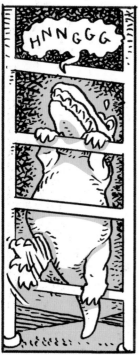

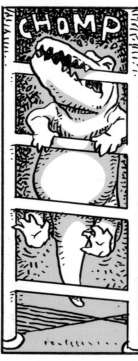

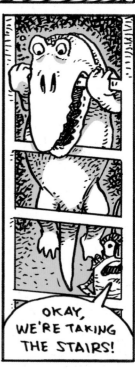

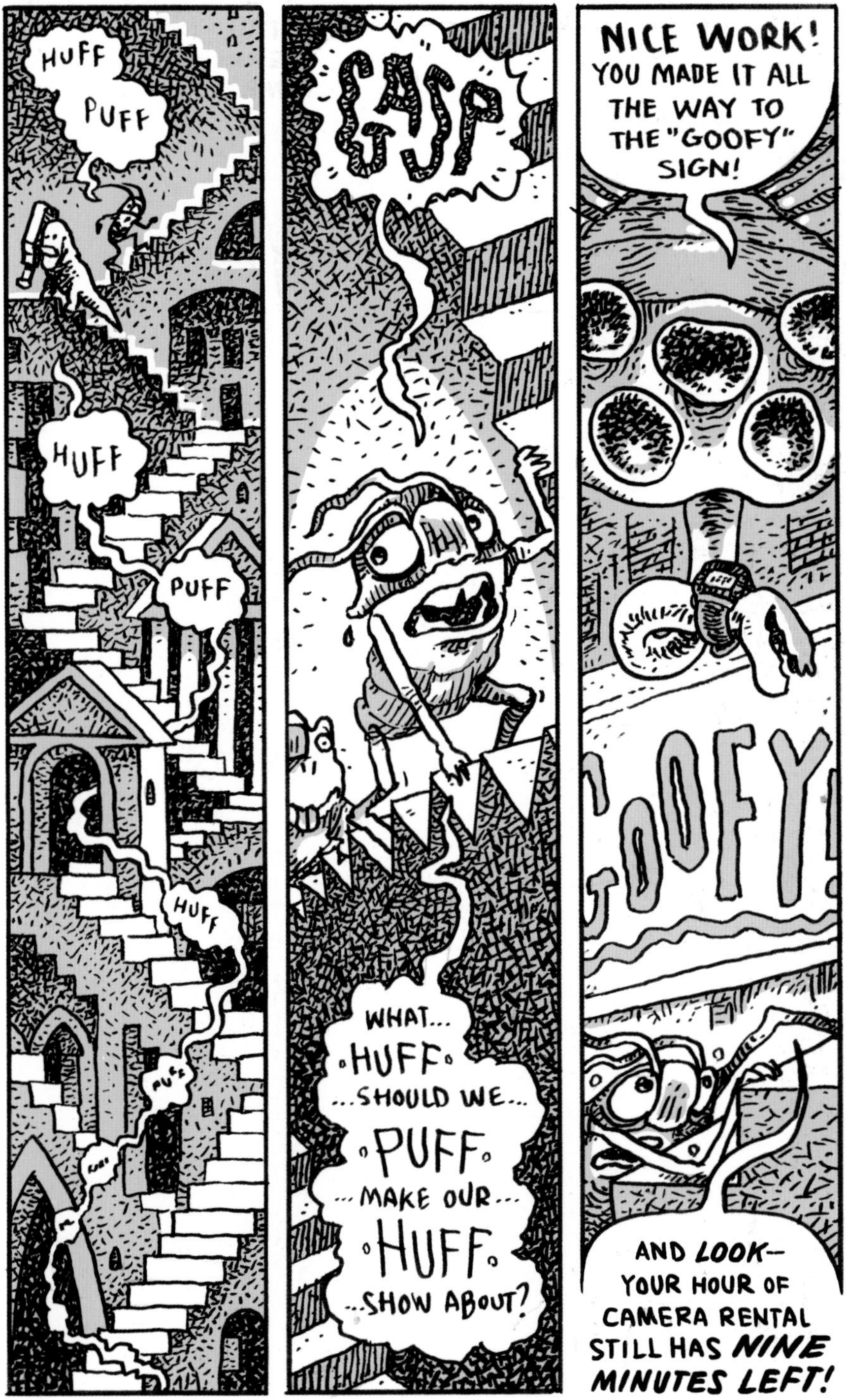

HUFF
PUFF
HUFF
PUFF
HUFF
GASP
WHAT... HUFF ...SHOULD WE... PUFF ...MAKE OUR... HUFF ...SHOW ABOUT?
NICE WORK! YOU MADE IT ALL THE WAY TO THE "GOOFY" SIGN!
GOOFY!
AND *LOOK*— YOUR HOUR OF CAMERA RENTAL STILL HAS ***NINE MINUTES LEFT!***

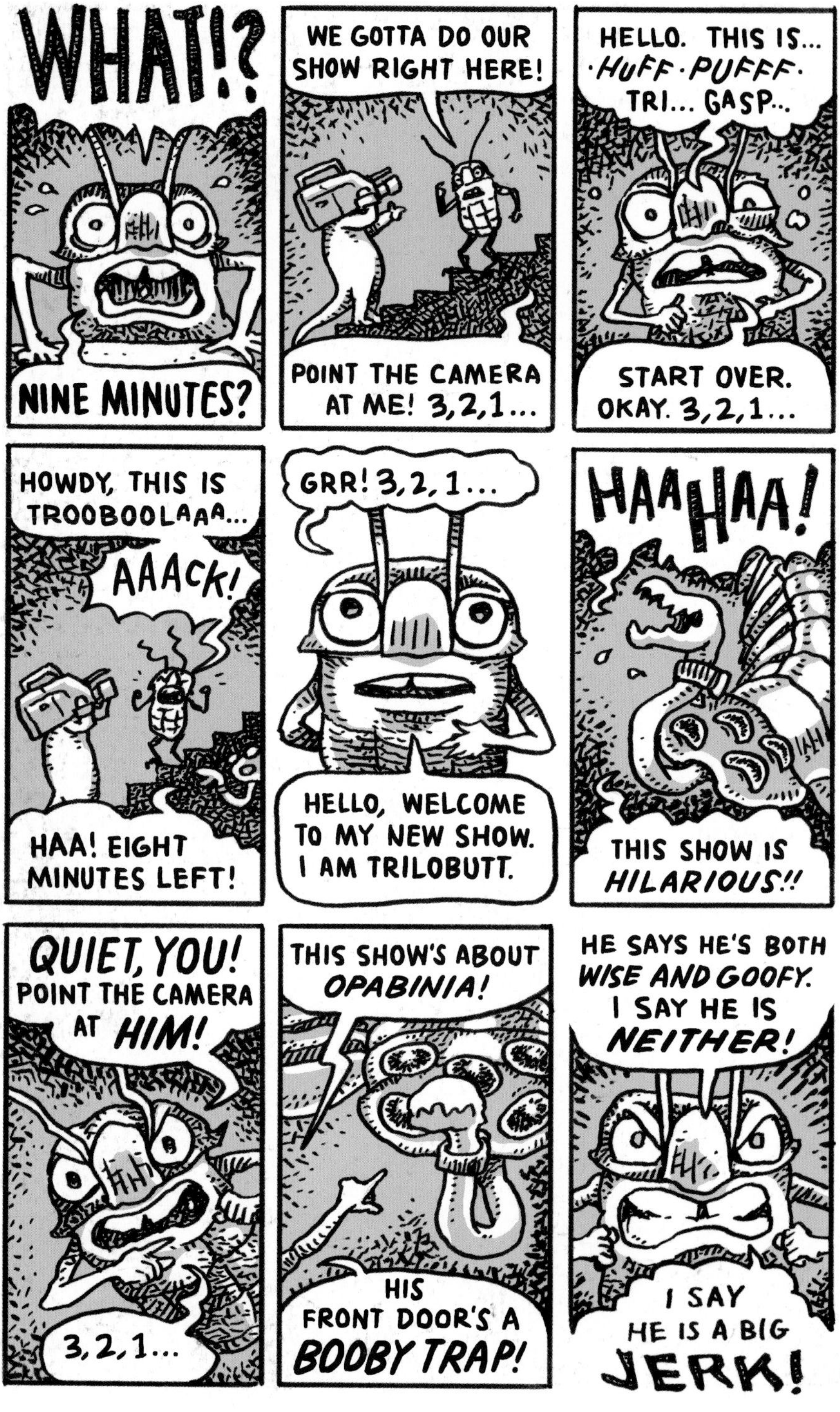
WHAT!?
NINE MINUTES?
WE GOTTA DO OUR SHOW RIGHT HERE!
POINT THE CAMERA AT ME! 3,2,1...
HELLO. THIS IS... ·HUFF·PUFFF· TRI... GASP...
START OVER. OKAY. 3,2,1...
HOWDY, THIS IS TROOBOOLAAA...
AAACK!
HAA! EIGHT MINUTES LEFT!
GRR! 3,2,1...
HELLO, WELCOME TO MY NEW SHOW. I AM TRILOBUTT.
HAAHAA!
THIS SHOW IS HILARIOUS!!
QUIET, YOU! POINT THE CAMERA AT HIM!
3,2,1...
THIS SHOW'S ABOUT OPABINIA!
HIS FRONT DOOR'S A BOOBY TRAP!
HE SAYS HE'S BOTH WISE AND GOOFY. I SAY HE IS NEITHER!
I SAY HE IS A BIG JERK!

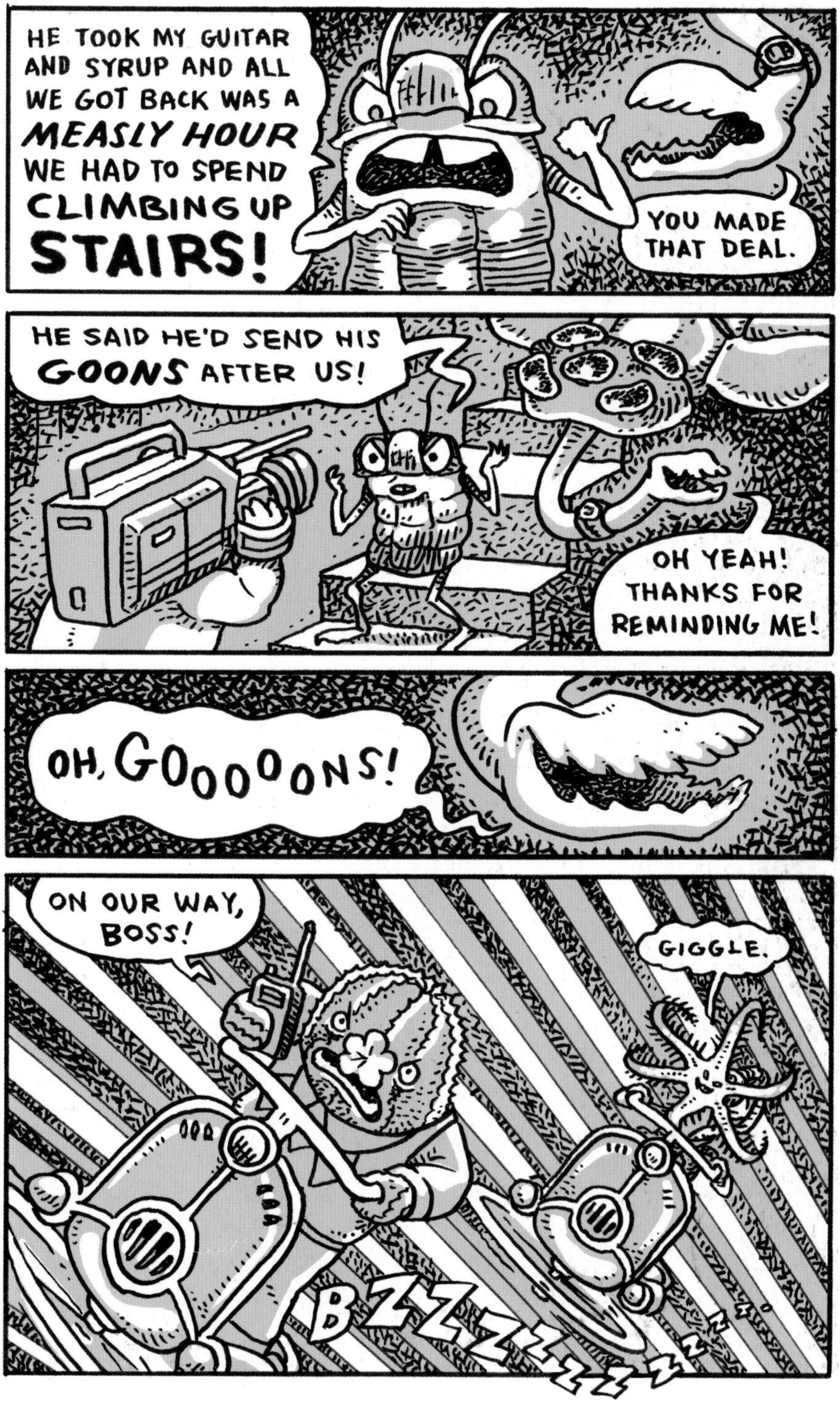
HE TOOK MY GUITAR AND SYRUP AND ALL WE GOT BACK WAS A MEASLY HOUR WE HAD TO SPEND CLIMBING UP STAIRS!
YOU MADE THAT DEAL.
HE SAID HE'D SEND HIS GOONS AFTER US!
OH YEAH! THANKS FOR REMINDING ME!
OH, GOOOOOONS!
ON OUR WAY, BOSS!
GIGGLE.
BZZZZZZZZZ

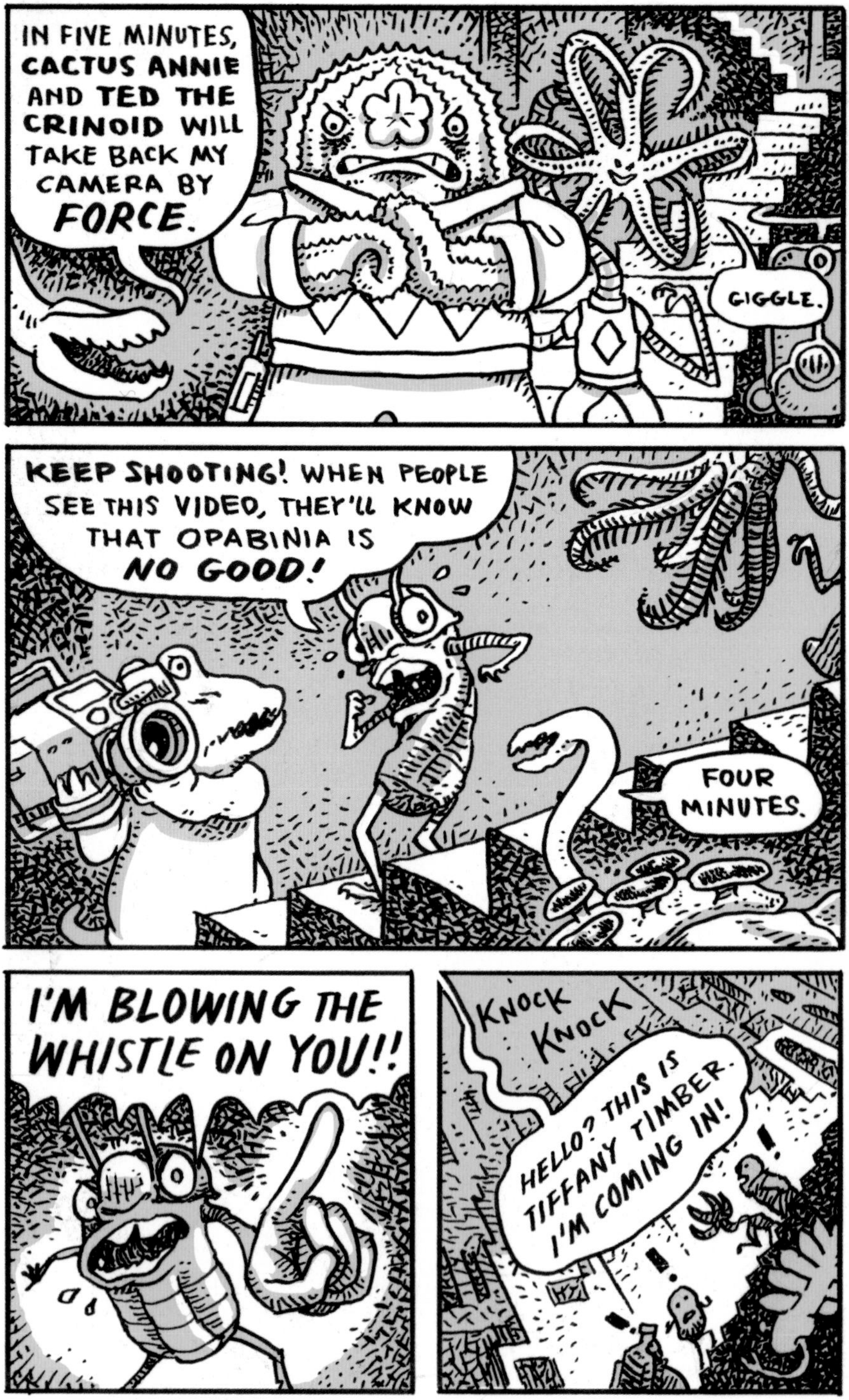
IN FIVE MINUTES, CACTUS ANNIE AND TED THE CRINOID WILL TAKE BACK MY CAMERA BY FORCE.
GIGGLE.
KEEP SHOOTING! WHEN PEOPLE SEE THIS VIDEO, THEY'LL KNOW THAT OPABINIA IS NO GOOD!
FOUR MINUTES.
I'M BLOWING THE WHISTLE ON YOU!!
KNOCK KNOCK
HELLO? THIS IS TIFFANY TIMBER. I'M COMING IN!

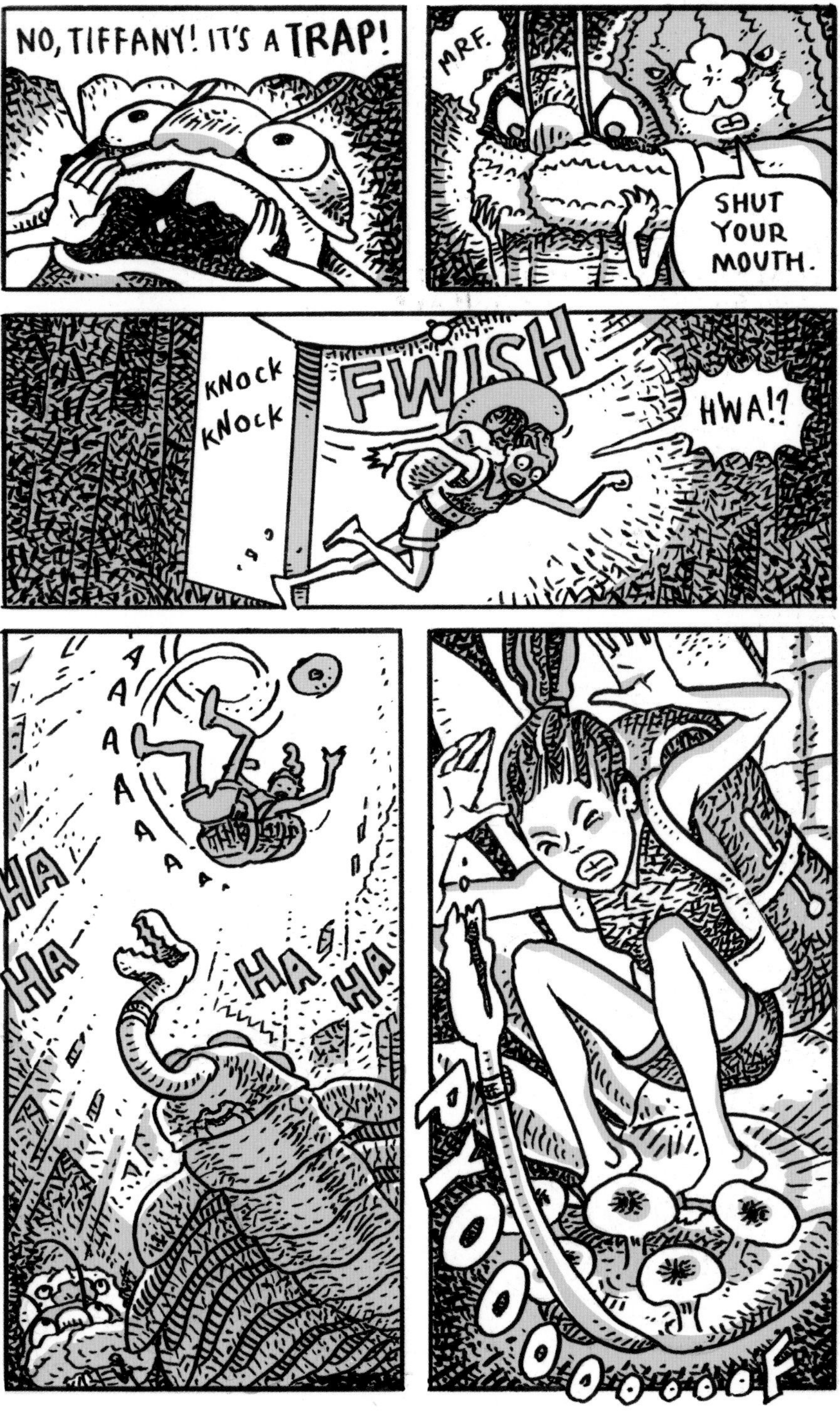
NO, TIFFANY! IT'S A TRAP!
MRF.
SHUT YOUR MOUTH.
KNOCK KNOCK
FWISH
HWA!?
AAAAAAAA...
HA HA
HA HA
RYOOOO.....F

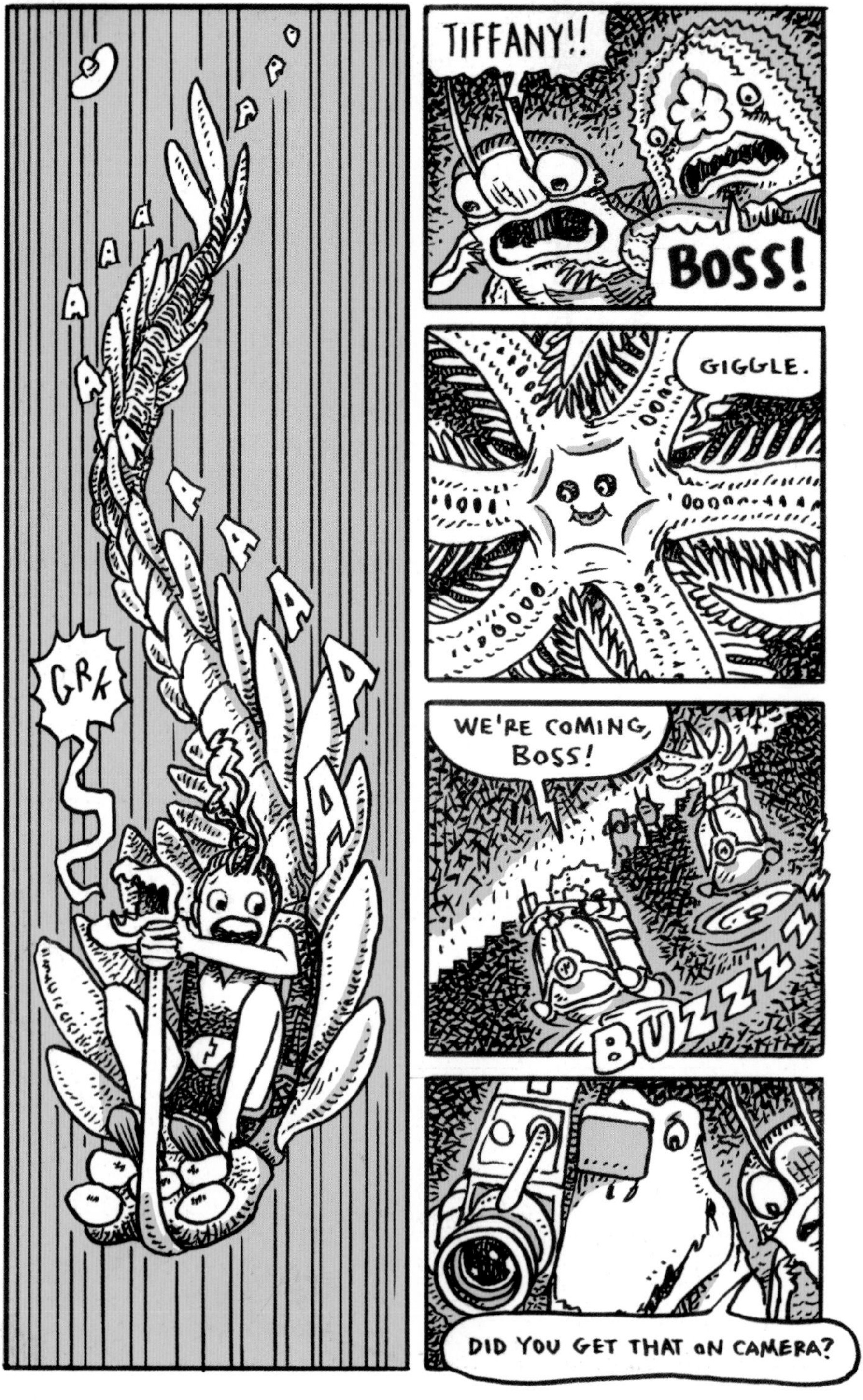
AAAAAAAAAAAAA
GRK
TIFFANY!!
BOSS!
GIGGLE.
WE'RE COMING, BOSS!
BUZZZZZ
DID YOU GET THAT ON CAMERA?

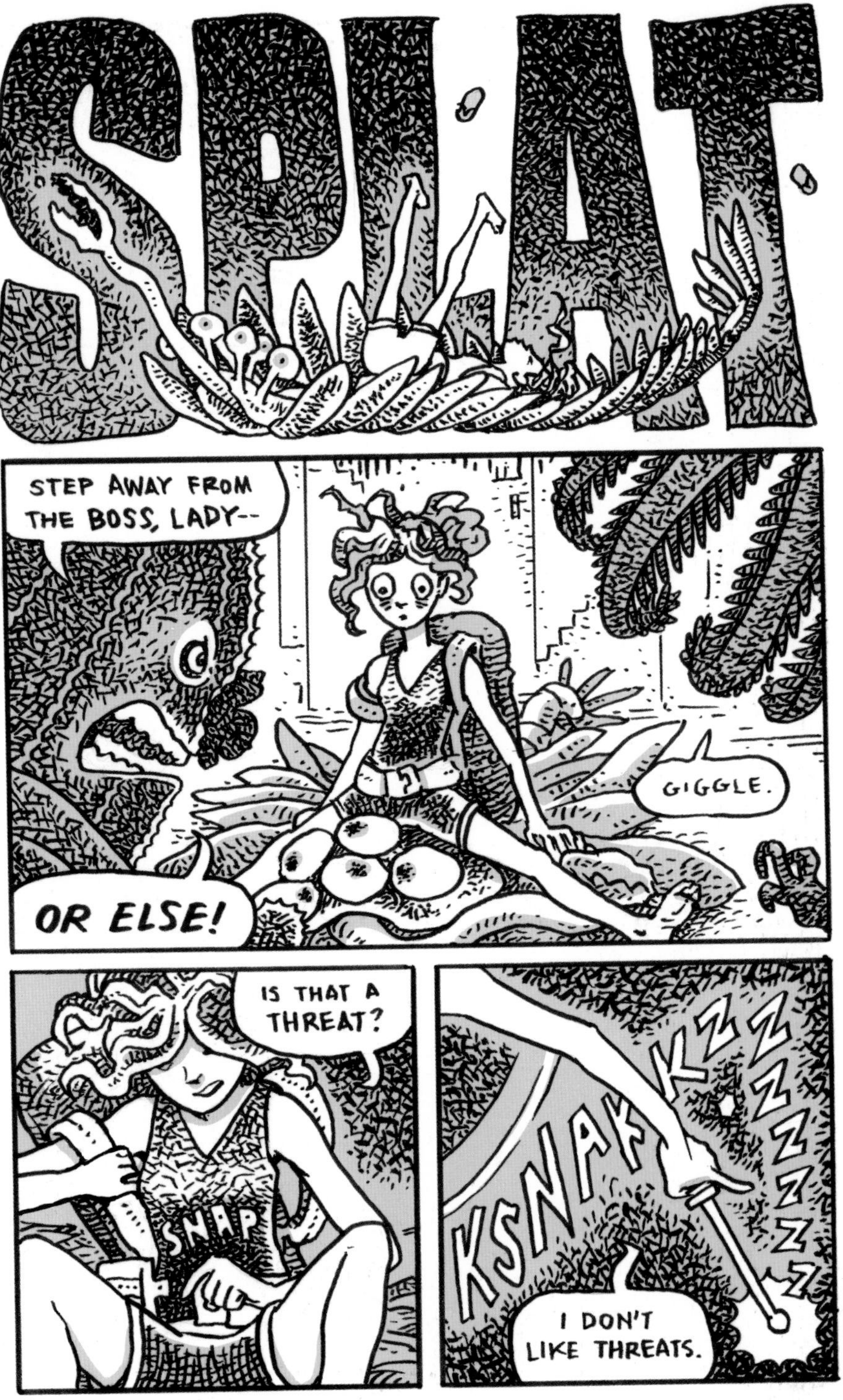
SPLAT
STEP AWAY FROM THE BOSS, LADY--
OR ELSE!
GIGGLE.
IS THAT A THREAT?
SNAP
KSNAK KZZZZZZZZ
I DON'T LIKE THREATS.

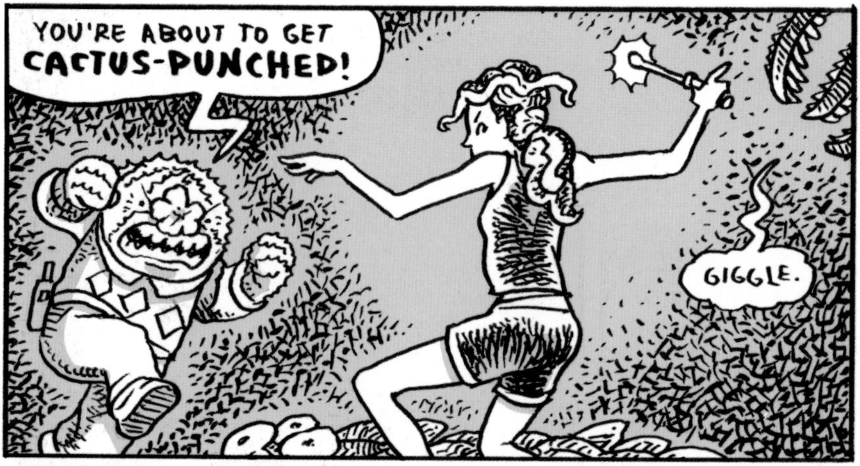
YOU'RE ABOUT TO GET CACTUS-PUNCHED!
GIGGLE.

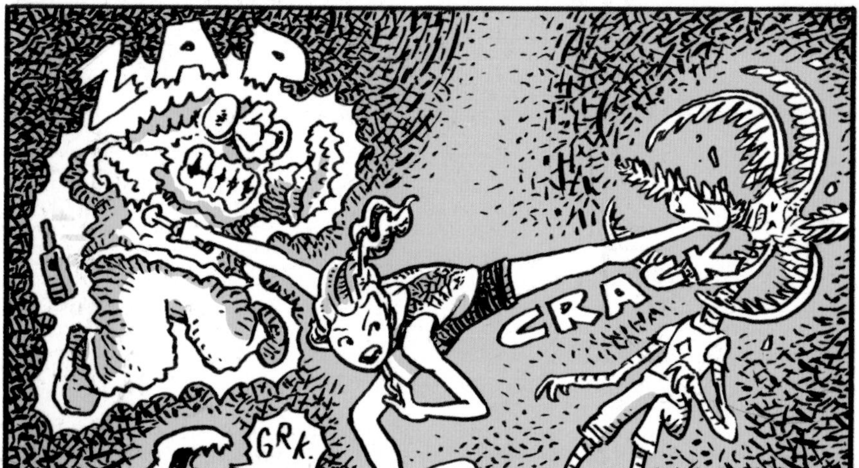
ZAP
CRACK
GRK.

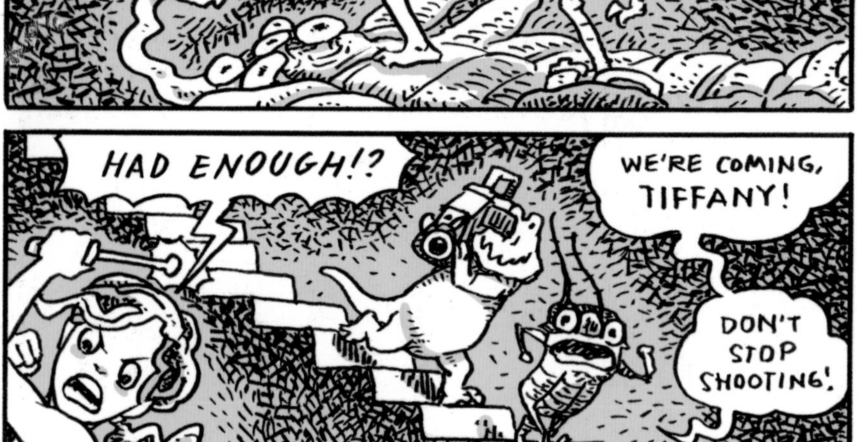
HAD ENOUGH!?
WE'RE COMING, TIFFANY!
DON'T STOP SHOOTING!

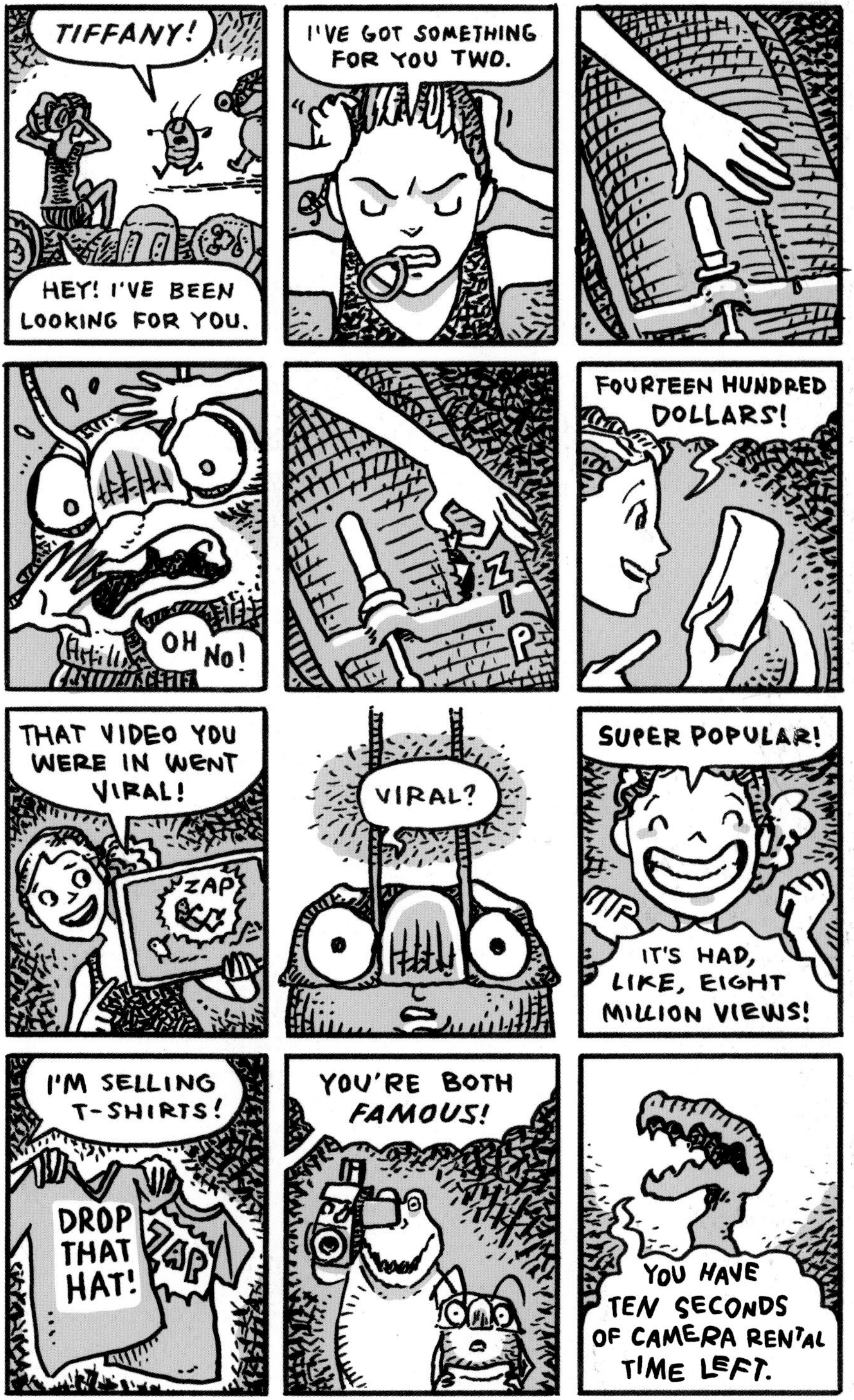
TIFFANY!
HEY! I'VE BEEN LOOKING FOR YOU.
I'VE GOT SOMETHING FOR YOU TWO.
OH No!
ZIP
FOURTEEN HUNDRED DOLLARS!
THAT VIDEO YOU WERE IN WENT VIRAL!
ZAP
VIRAL?
SUPER POPULAR!
IT'S HAD, LIKE, EIGHT MILLION VIEWS!
I'M SELLING T-SHIRTS!
DROP THAT HAT!
ZAP
YOU'RE BOTH *FAMOUS!*
YOU HAVE TEN SECONDS OF CAMERA RENTAL TIME LEFT.

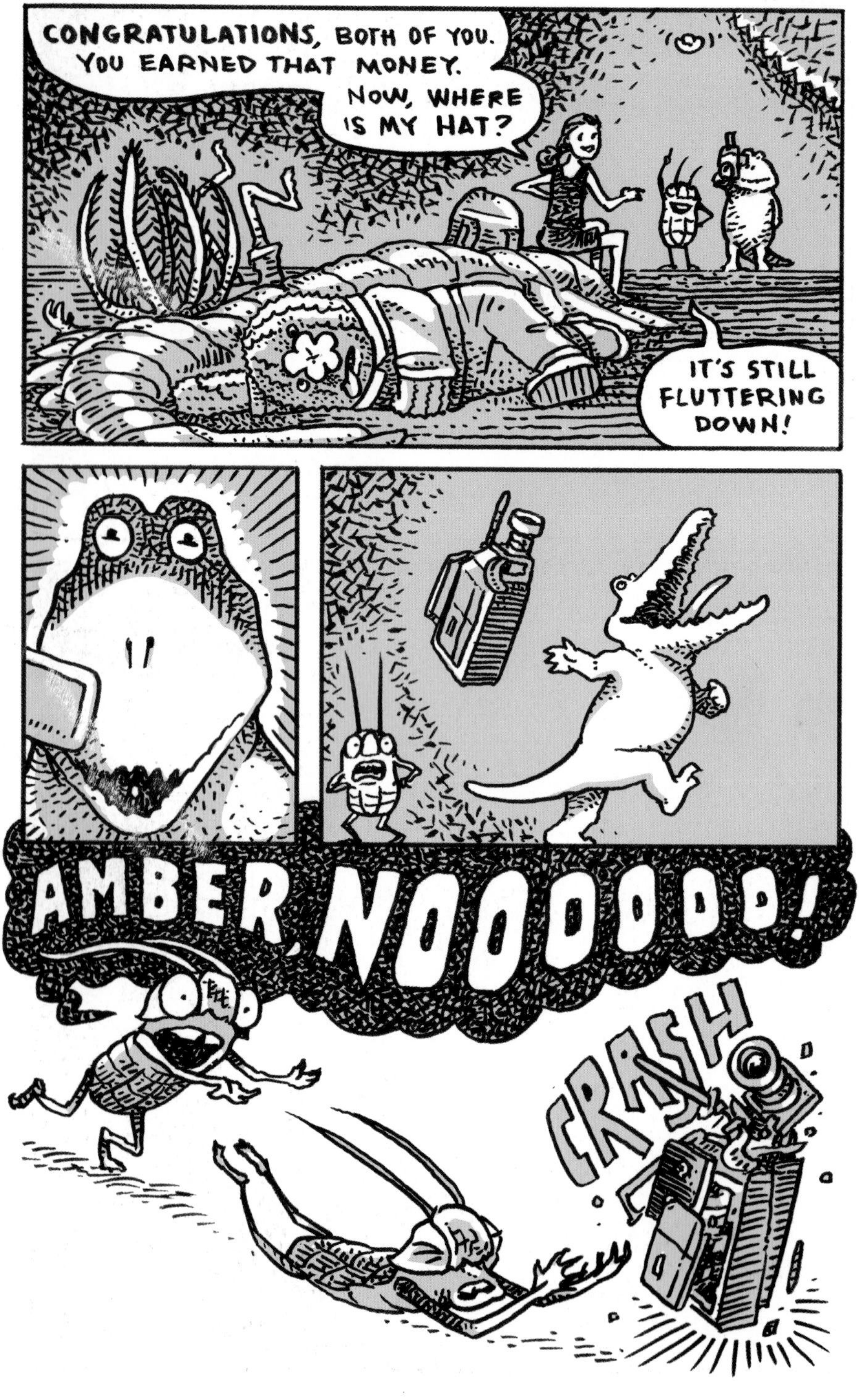
CONGRATULATIONS, BOTH OF YOU. YOU EARNED THAT MONEY.
NOW, WHERE IS MY HAT?
IT'S STILL FLUTTERING DOWN!
AMBER, NOOOOOO!
CRASH

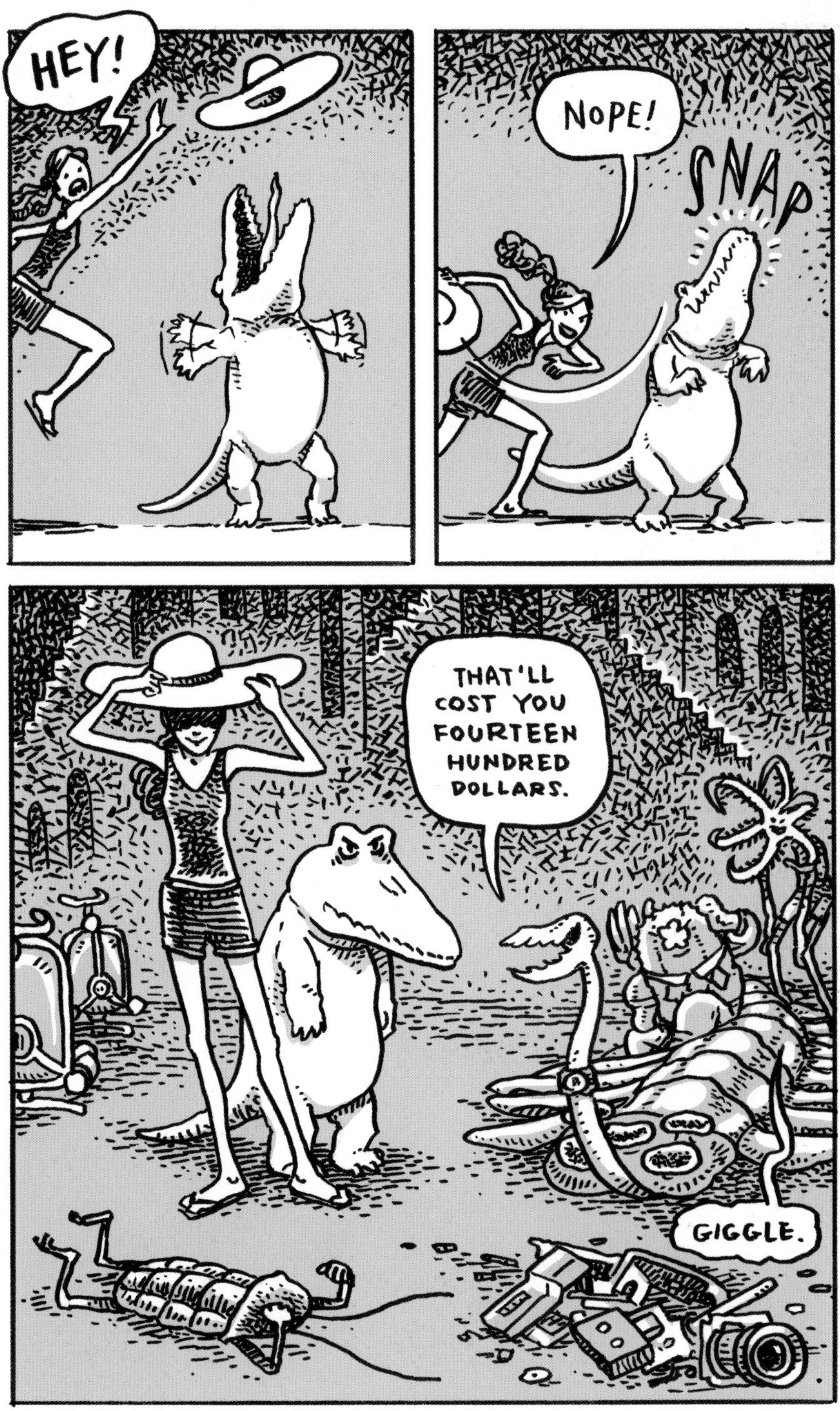
HEY!
NOPE!
SNAP
THAT'LL COST YOU FOURTEEN HUNDRED DOLLARS.
GIGGLE.

CHAPTER 3

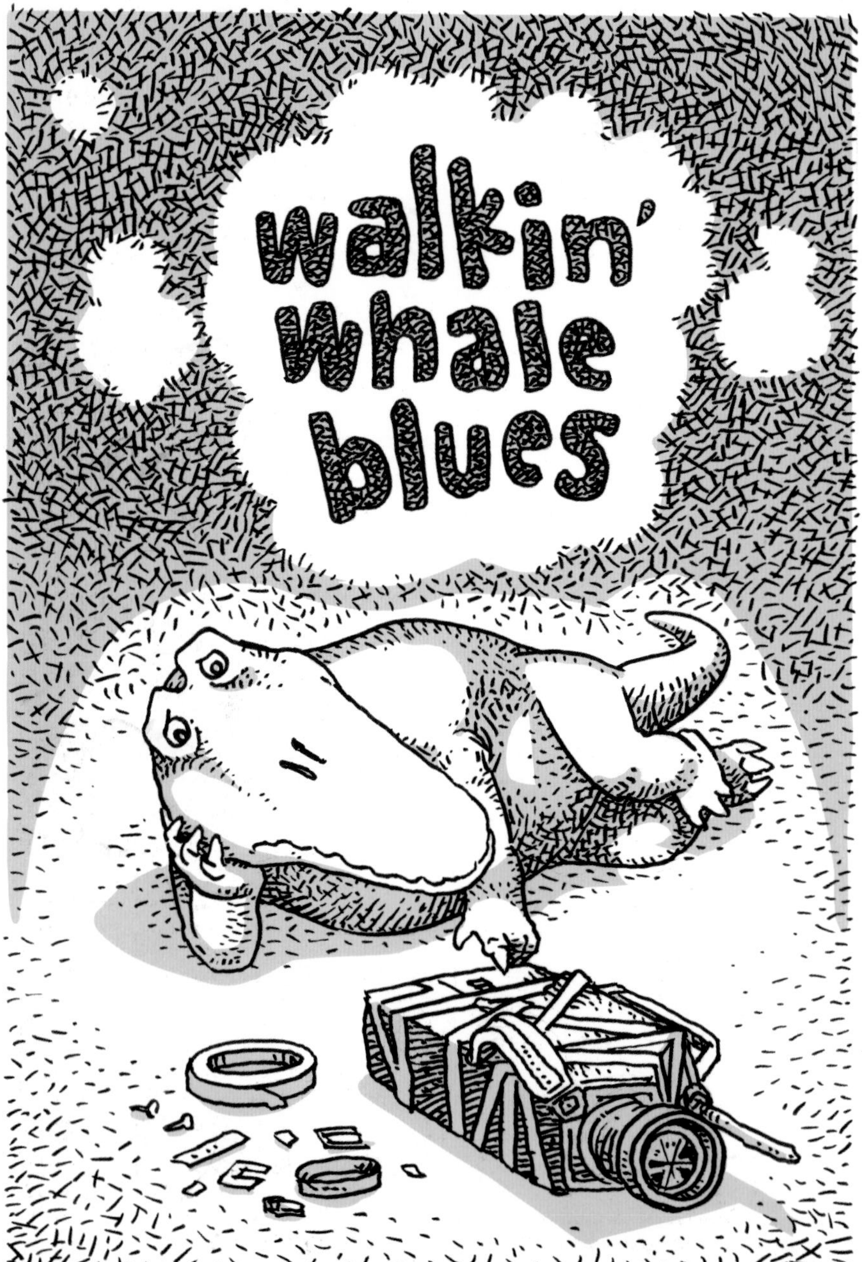
walkin' whale blues

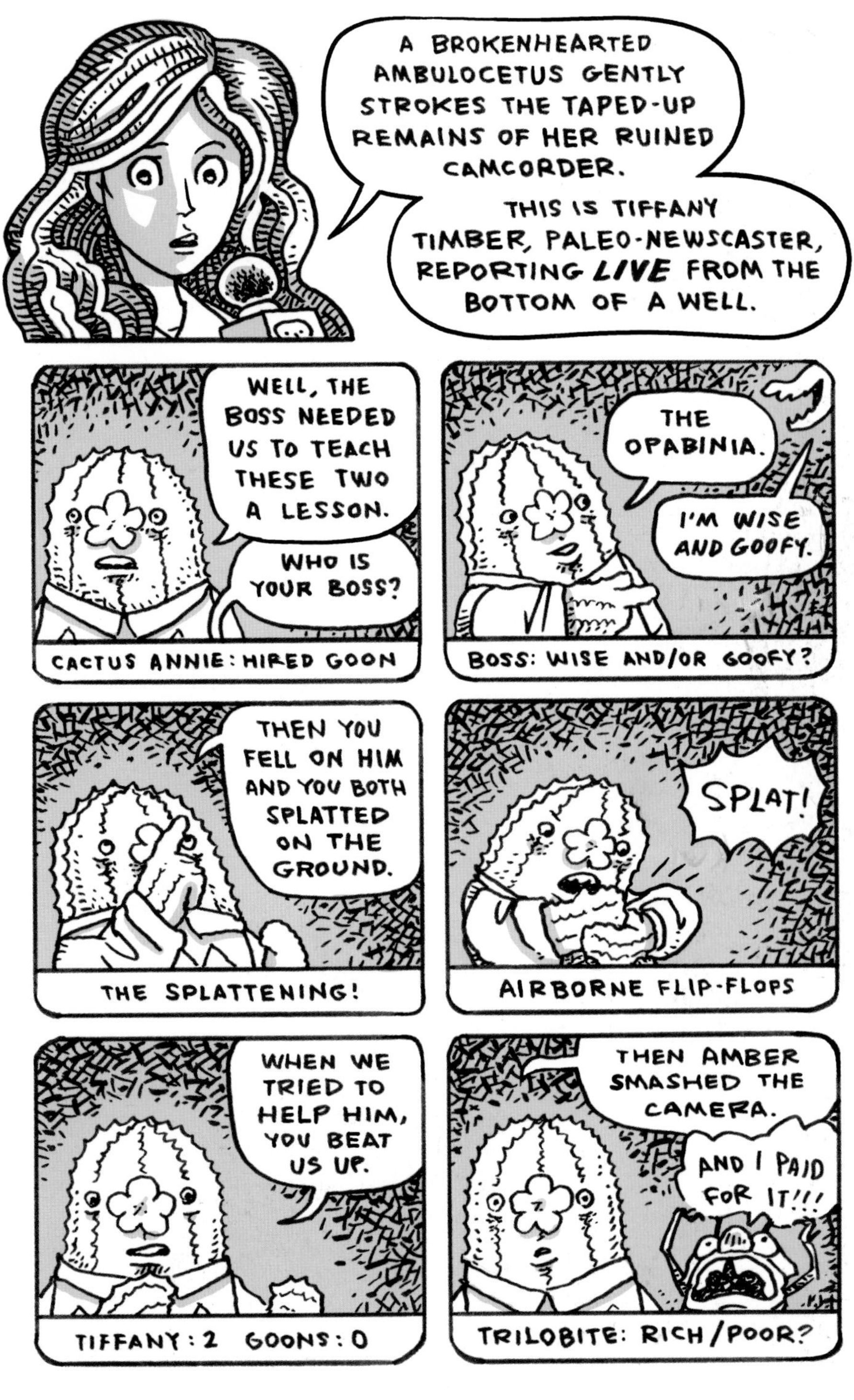
A BROKENHEARTED AMBULOCETUS GENTLY STROKES THE TAPED-UP REMAINS OF HER RUINED CAMCORDER.
THIS IS TIFFANY TIMBER, PALEO-NEWSCASTER, REPORTING *LIVE* FROM THE BOTTOM OF A WELL.
WELL, THE BOSS NEEDED US TO TEACH THESE TWO A LESSON.
WHO IS YOUR BOSS?
CACTUS ANNIE: HIRED GOON
THE OPABINIA.
I'M WISE AND GOOFY.
BOSS: WISE AND/OR GOOFY?
THEN YOU FELL ON HIM AND YOU BOTH SPLATTED ON THE GROUND.
THE SPLATTENING!
SPLAT!
AIRBORNE FLIP-FLOPS
WHEN WE TRIED TO HELP HIM, YOU BEAT US UP.
TIFFANY: 2 GOONS: 0
THEN AMBER SMASHED THE CAMERA.
AND I PAID FOR IT!!!
TRILOBITE: RICH/POOR?

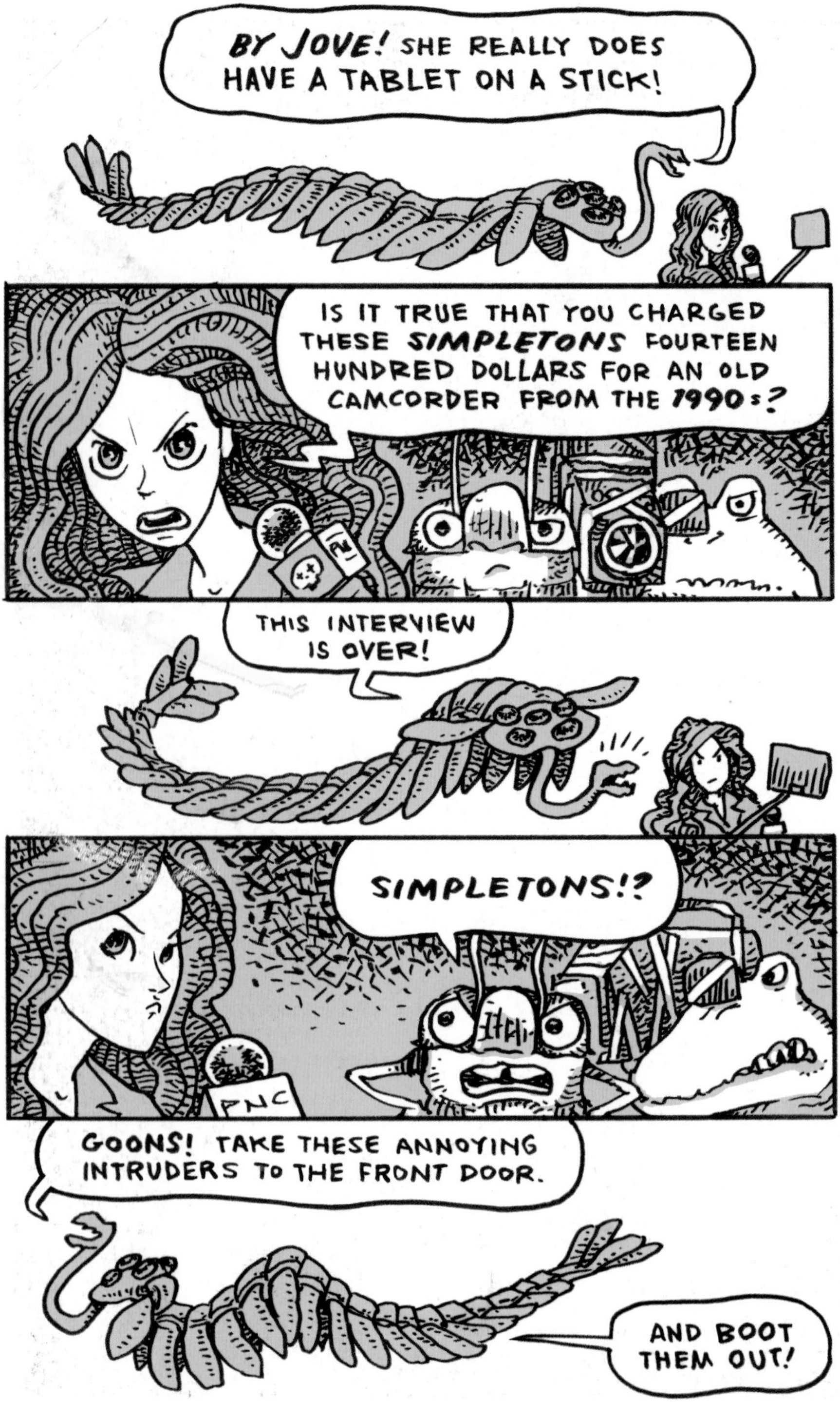

BY JOVE! SHE REALLY DOES HAVE A TABLET ON A STICK!
IS IT TRUE THAT YOU CHARGED THESE SIMPLETONS FOURTEEN HUNDRED DOLLARS FOR AN OLD CAMCORDER FROM THE 1990s?
PNC
THIS INTERVIEW IS OVER!
SIMPLETONS!?
PNC
GOONS! TAKE THESE ANNOYING INTRUDERS TO THE FRONT DOOR.
AND BOOT THEM OUT!

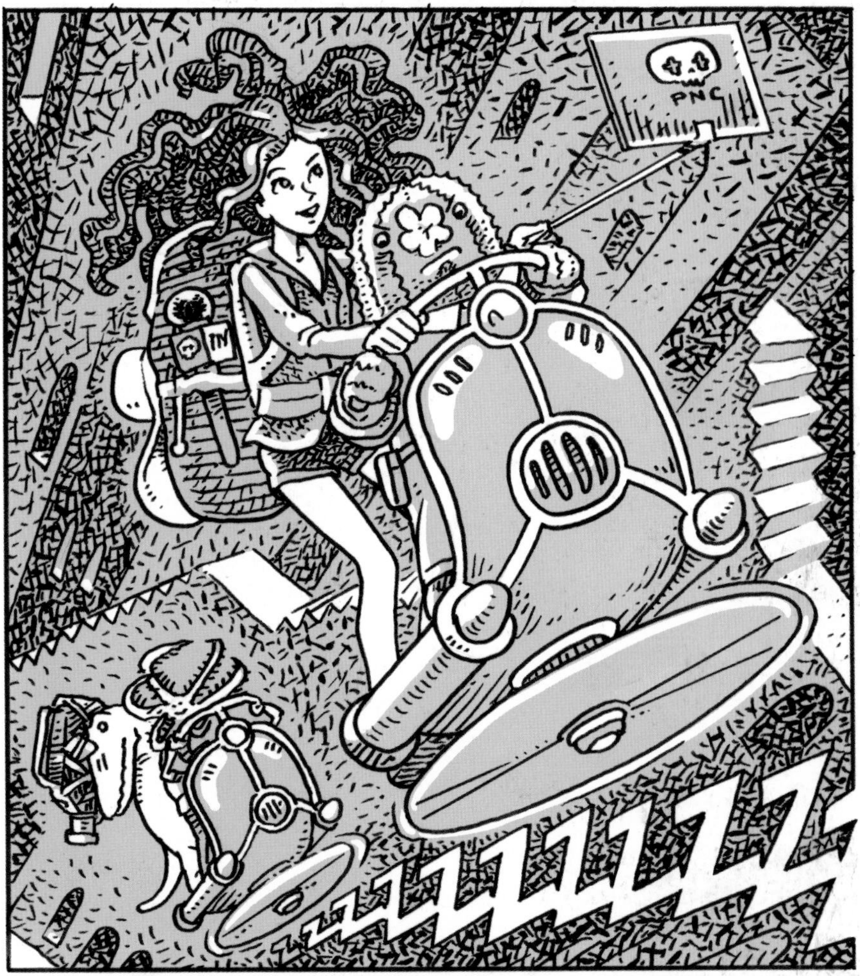
PNC
ZZZZZZZZZZ

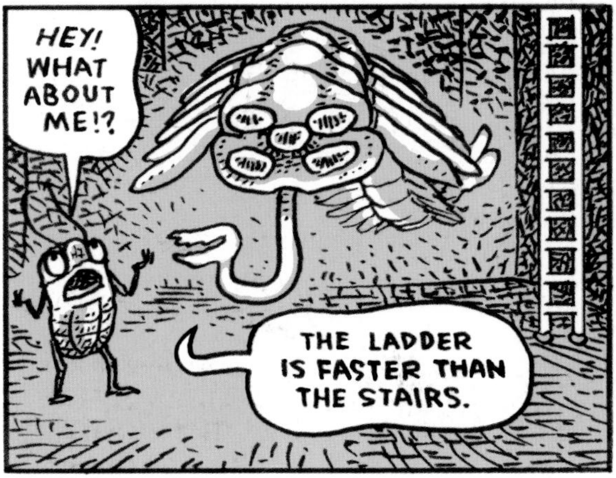
HEY! WHAT ABOUT ME!?
THE LADDER IS FASTER THAN THE STAIRS.

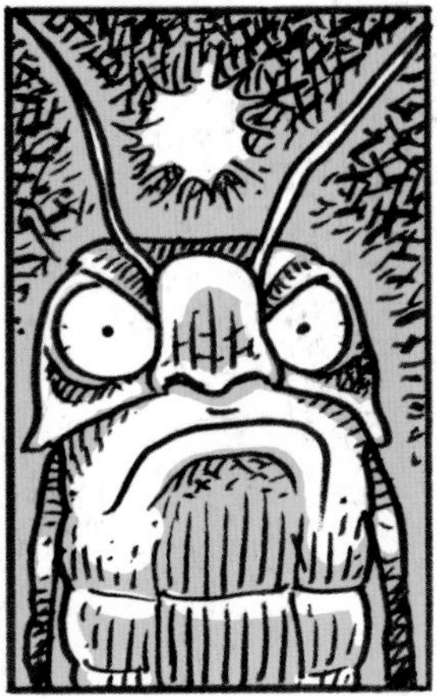

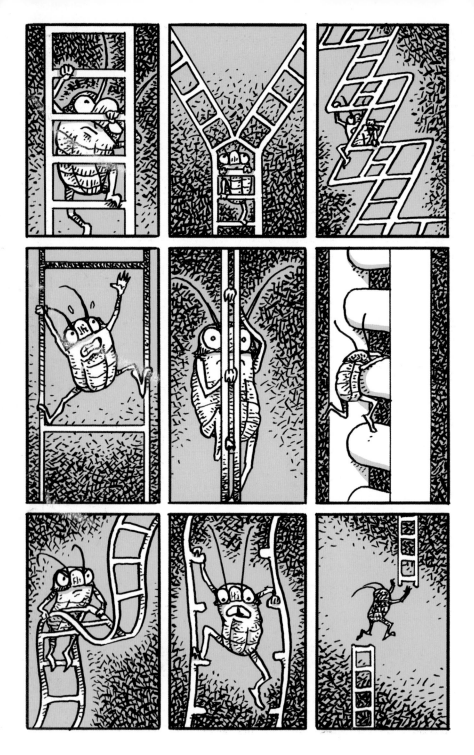

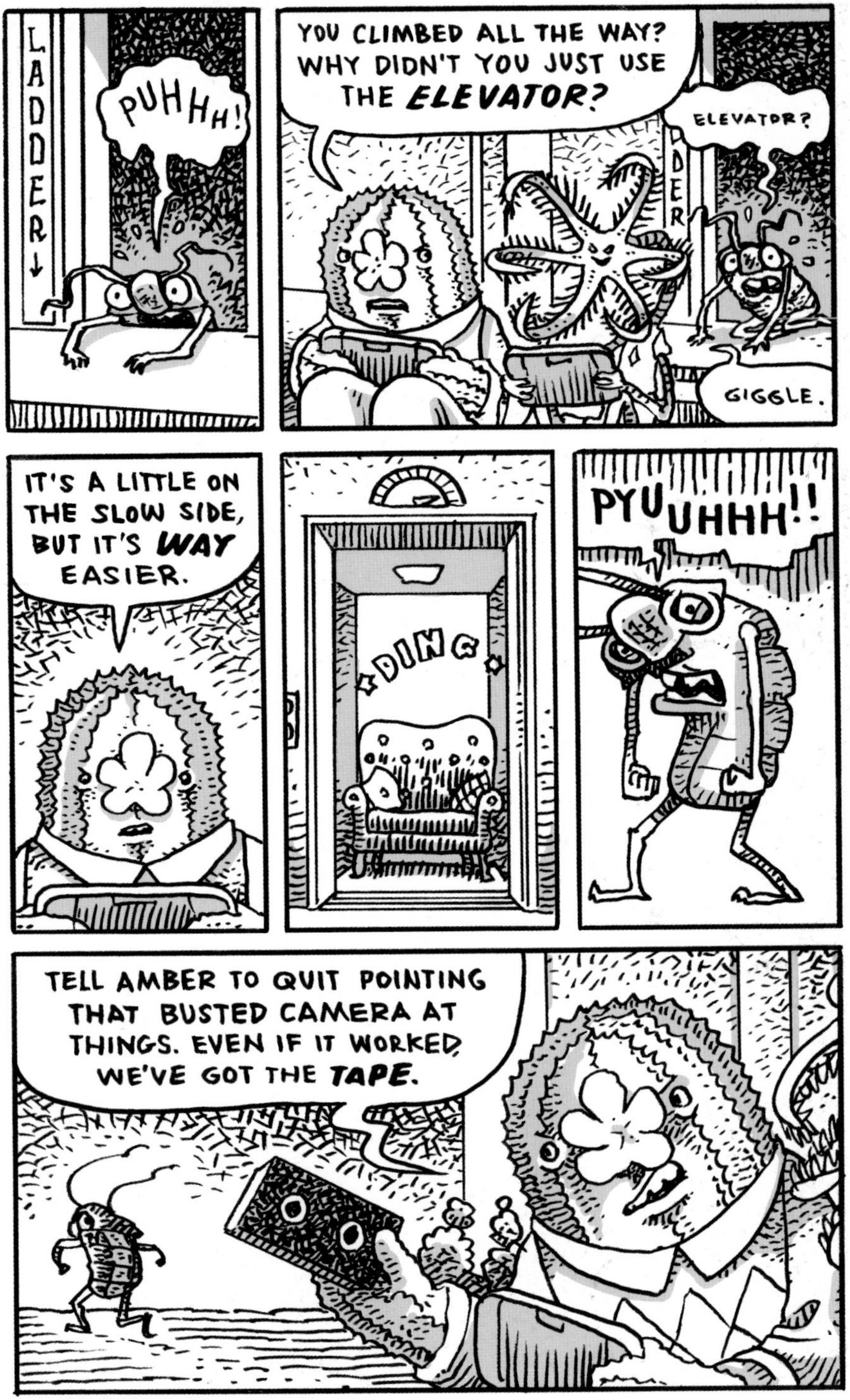
LADDER↓
PUHHH!
YOU CLIMBED ALL THE WAY? WHY DIDN'T YOU JUST USE THE ELEVATOR?
ELEVATOR?
DER
GIGGLE.
IT'S A LITTLE ON THE SLOW SIDE, BUT IT'S WAY EASIER.
DING
PYUUHHH!!
TELL AMBER TO QUIT POINTING THAT BUSTED CAMERA AT THINGS. EVEN IF IT WORKED, WE'VE GOT THE TAPE.

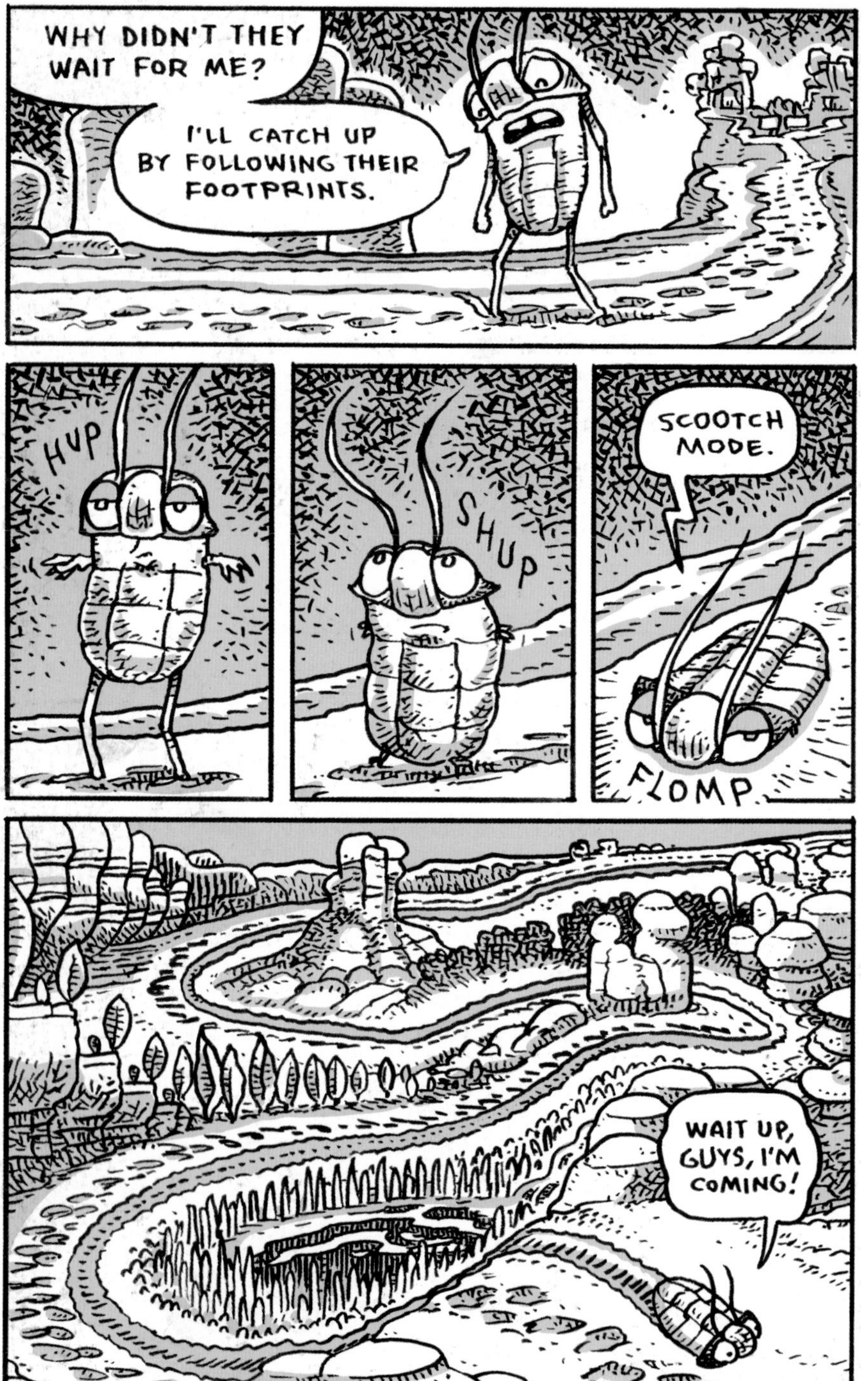
WHY DIDN'T THEY WAIT FOR ME?
I'LL CATCH UP BY FOLLOWING THEIR FOOTPRINTS.
HUP
SHUP
SCOOTCH MODE.
FLOMP
WAIT UP, GUYS, I'M COMING!

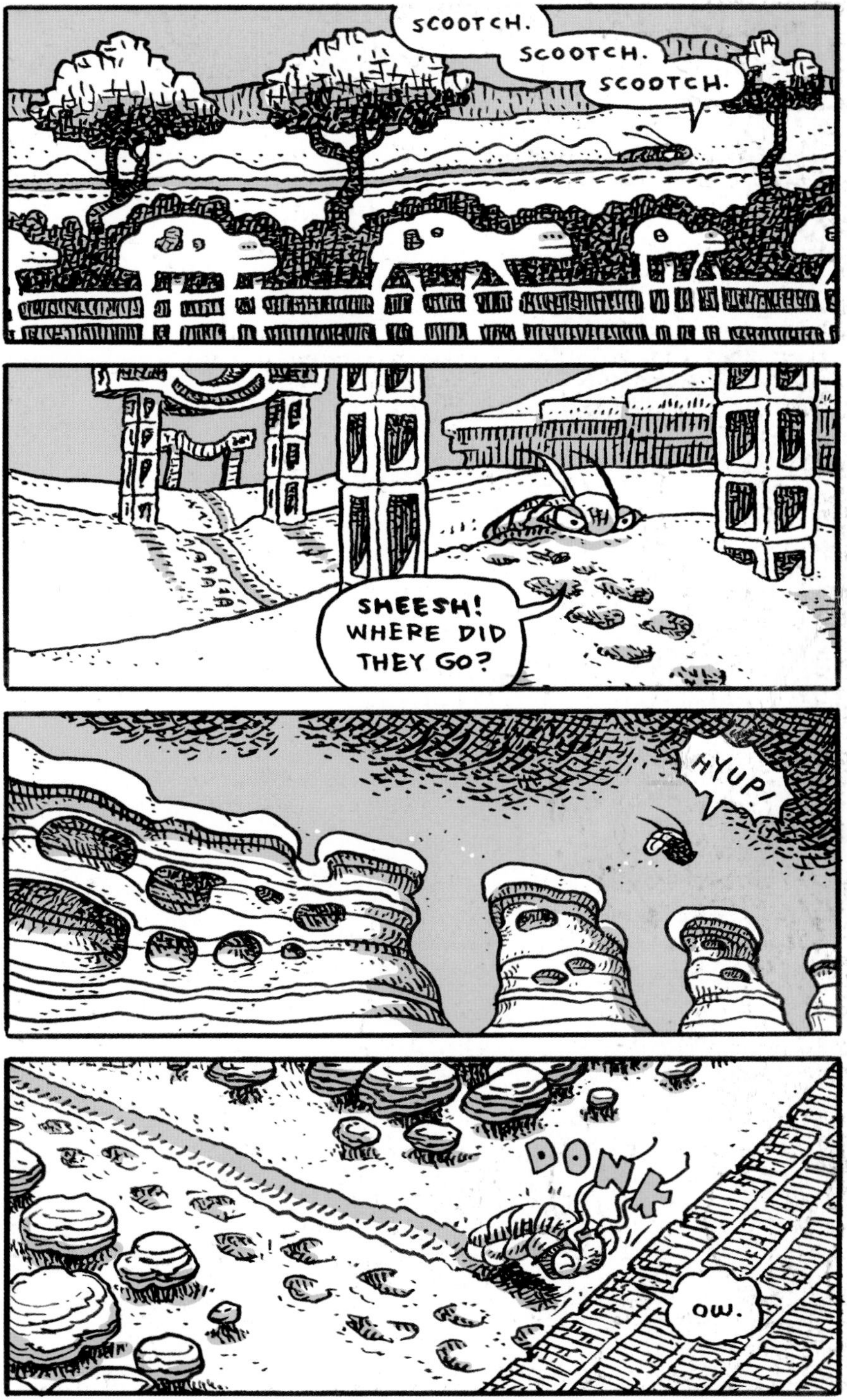
SCOOTCH.
SCOOTCH.
SCOOTCH.
SHEESH! WHERE DID THEY GO?
HYUP!
DONK
OW.

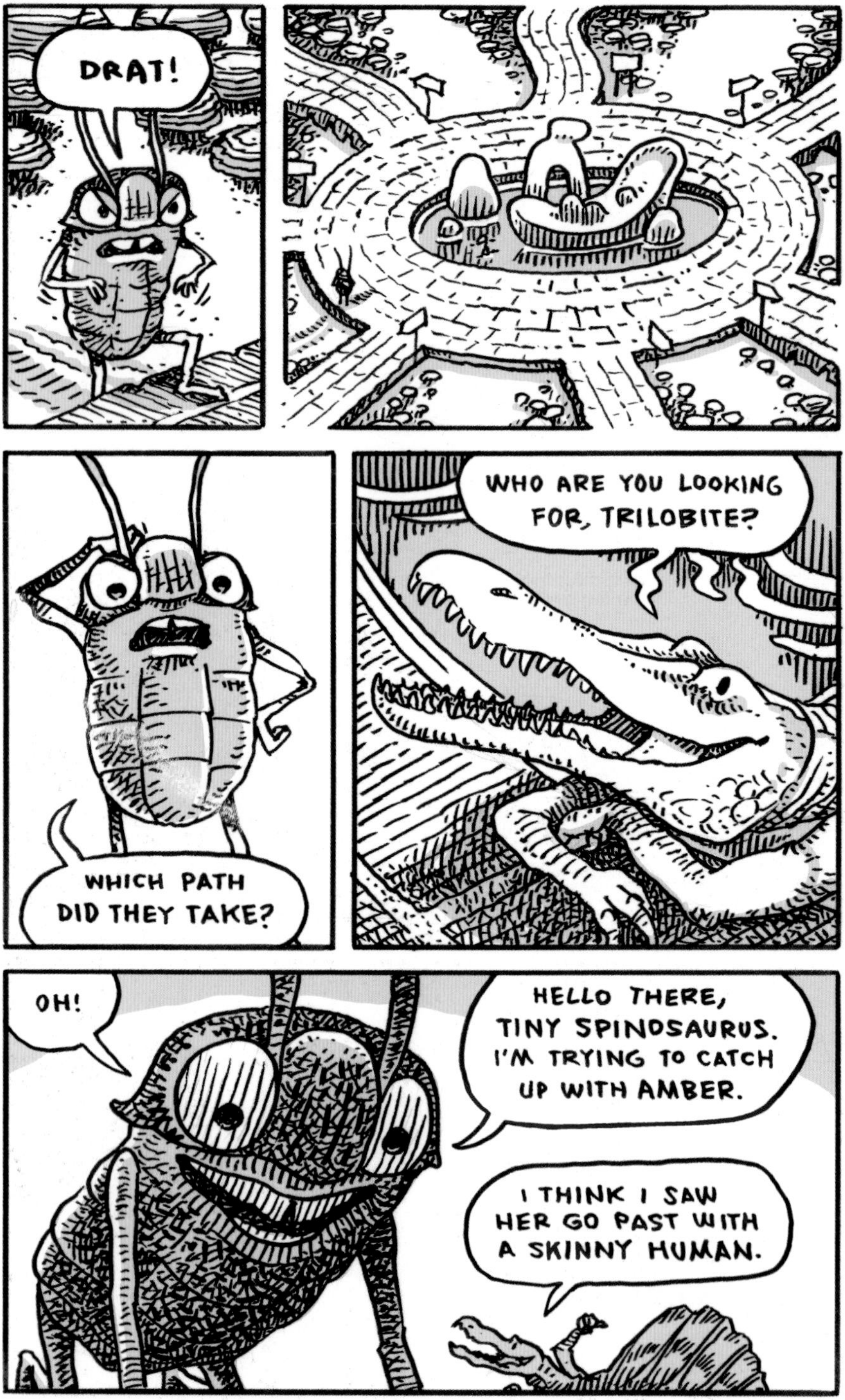
DRAT!
WHICH PATH DID THEY TAKE?
WHO ARE YOU LOOKING FOR, TRILOBITE?
OH!
HELLO THERE, TINY SPINOSAURUS. I'M TRYING TO CATCH UP WITH AMBER.
I THINK I SAW HER GO PAST WITH A SKINNY HUMAN.

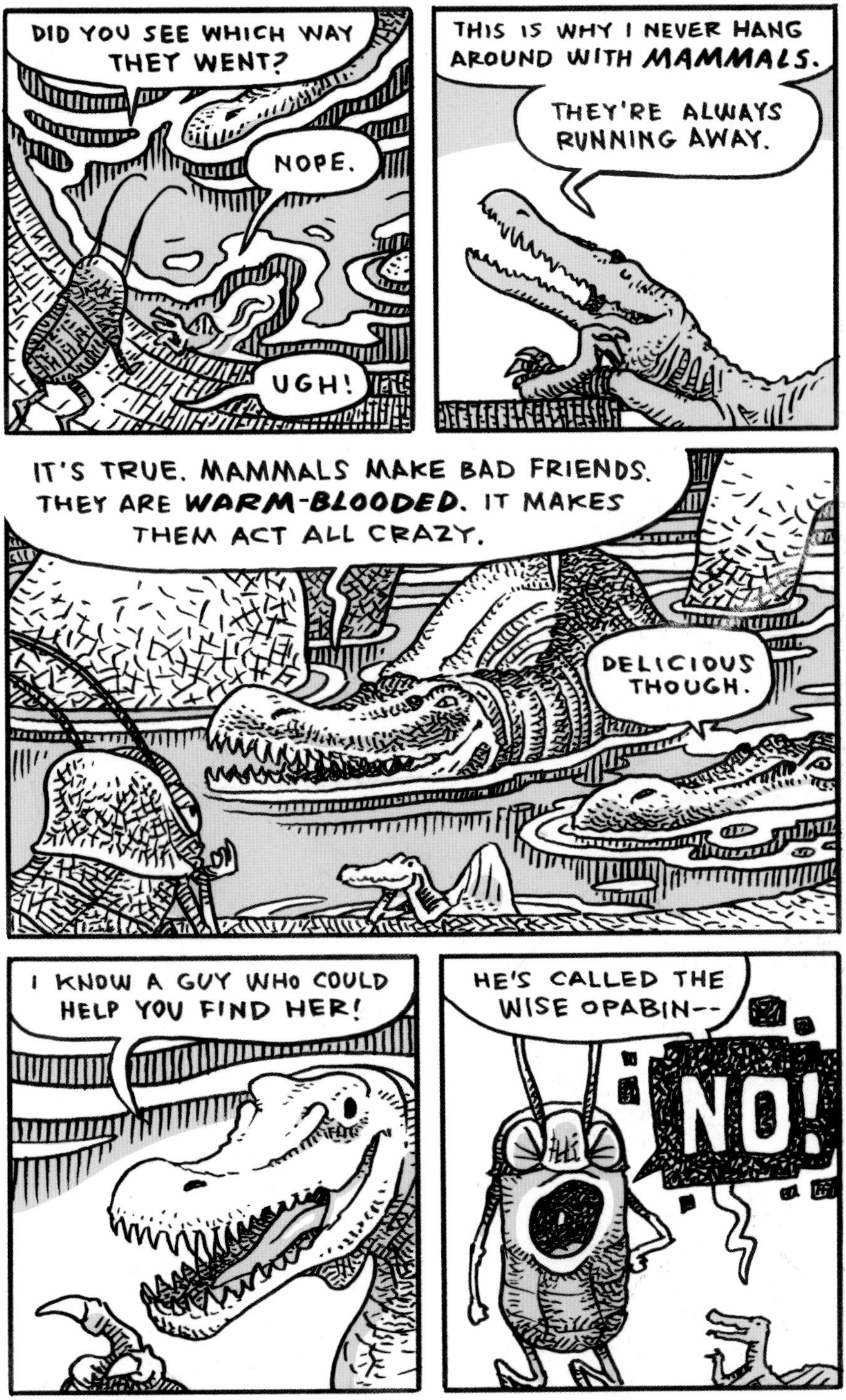
DID YOU SEE WHICH WAY THEY WENT?
NOPE.
UGH!
THIS IS WHY I NEVER HANG AROUND WITH MAMMALS.
THEY'RE ALWAYS RUNNING AWAY.
IT'S TRUE. MAMMALS MAKE BAD FRIENDS. THEY ARE WARM-BLOODED. IT MAKES THEM ACT ALL CRAZY.
DELICIOUS THOUGH.
I KNOW A GUY WHO COULD HELP YOU FIND HER!
HE'S CALLED THE WISE OPABIN--
NO!

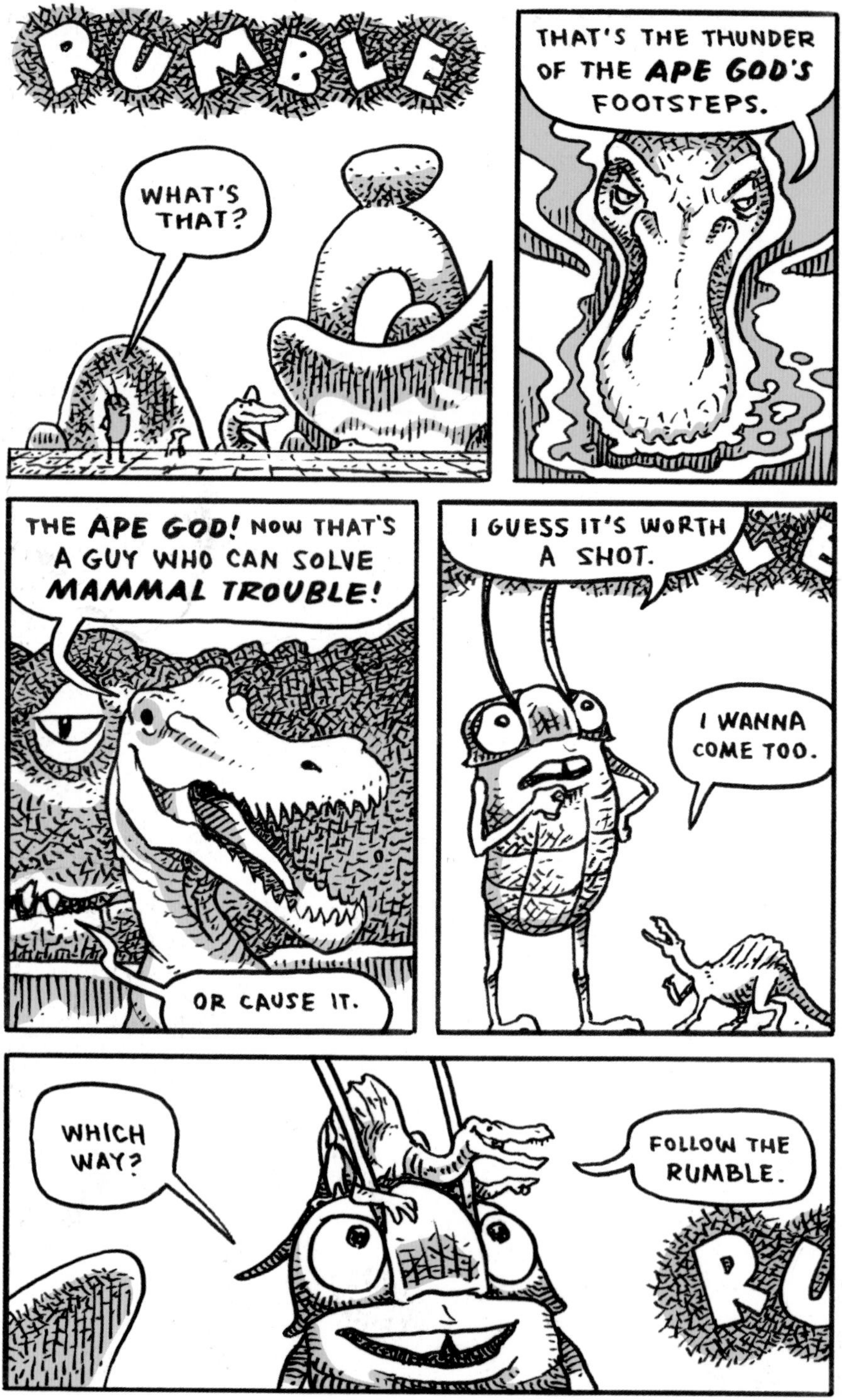
RUMBLE
WHAT'S THAT?
THAT'S THE THUNDER OF THE APE GOD'S FOOTSTEPS.
THE APE GOD! NOW THAT'S A GUY WHO CAN SOLVE MAMMAL TROUBLE!
OR CAUSE IT.
I GUESS IT'S WORTH A SHOT.
I WANNA COME TOO.
WHICH WAY?
FOLLOW THE RUMBLE.

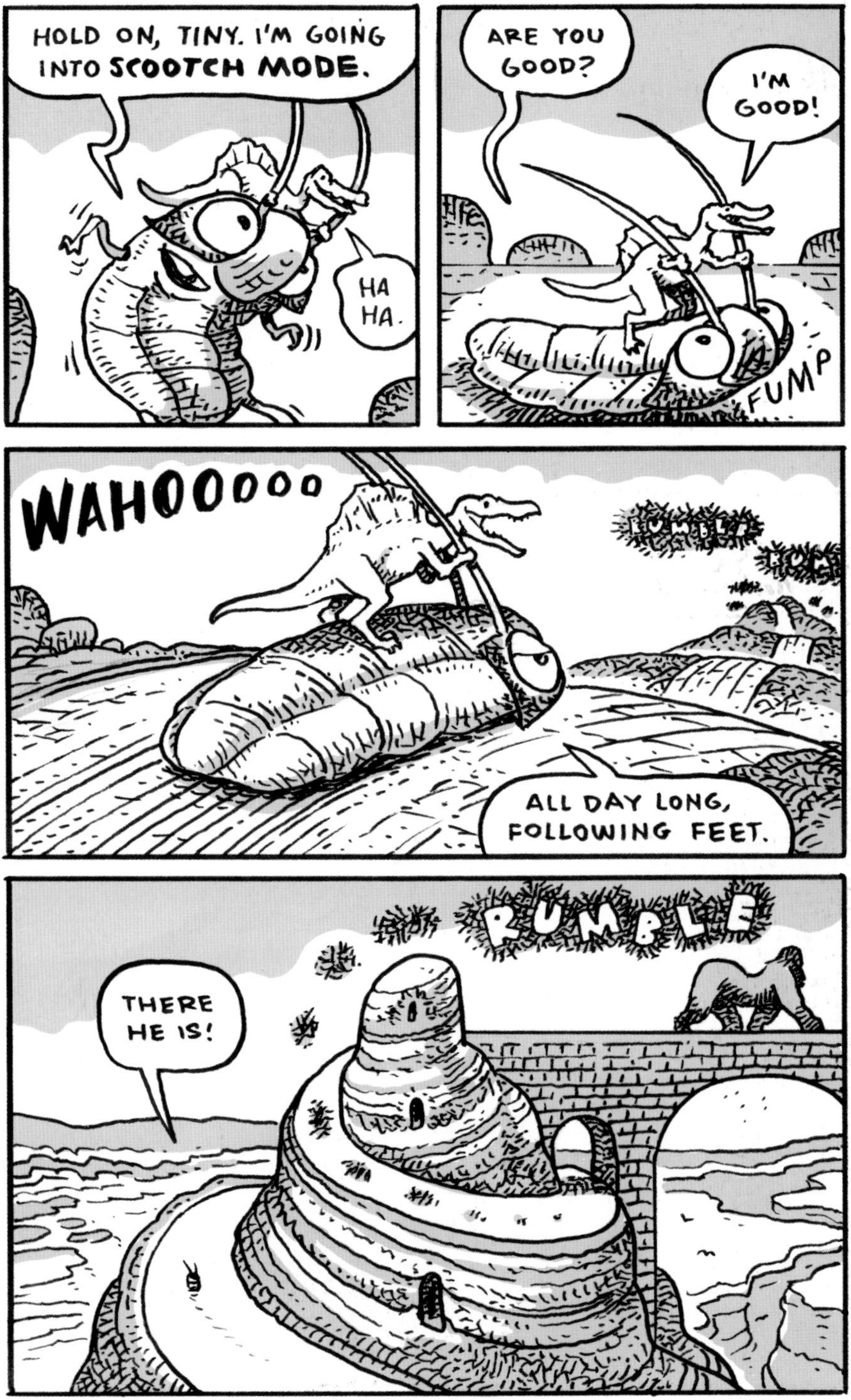
HOLD ON, TINY. I'M GOING INTO SCOOTCH MODE.
HA HA.
ARE YOU GOOD?
I'M GOOD!
FUMP
WAHOOOOO
ALL DAY LONG, FOLLOWING FEET.
RUMBLE
THERE HE IS!

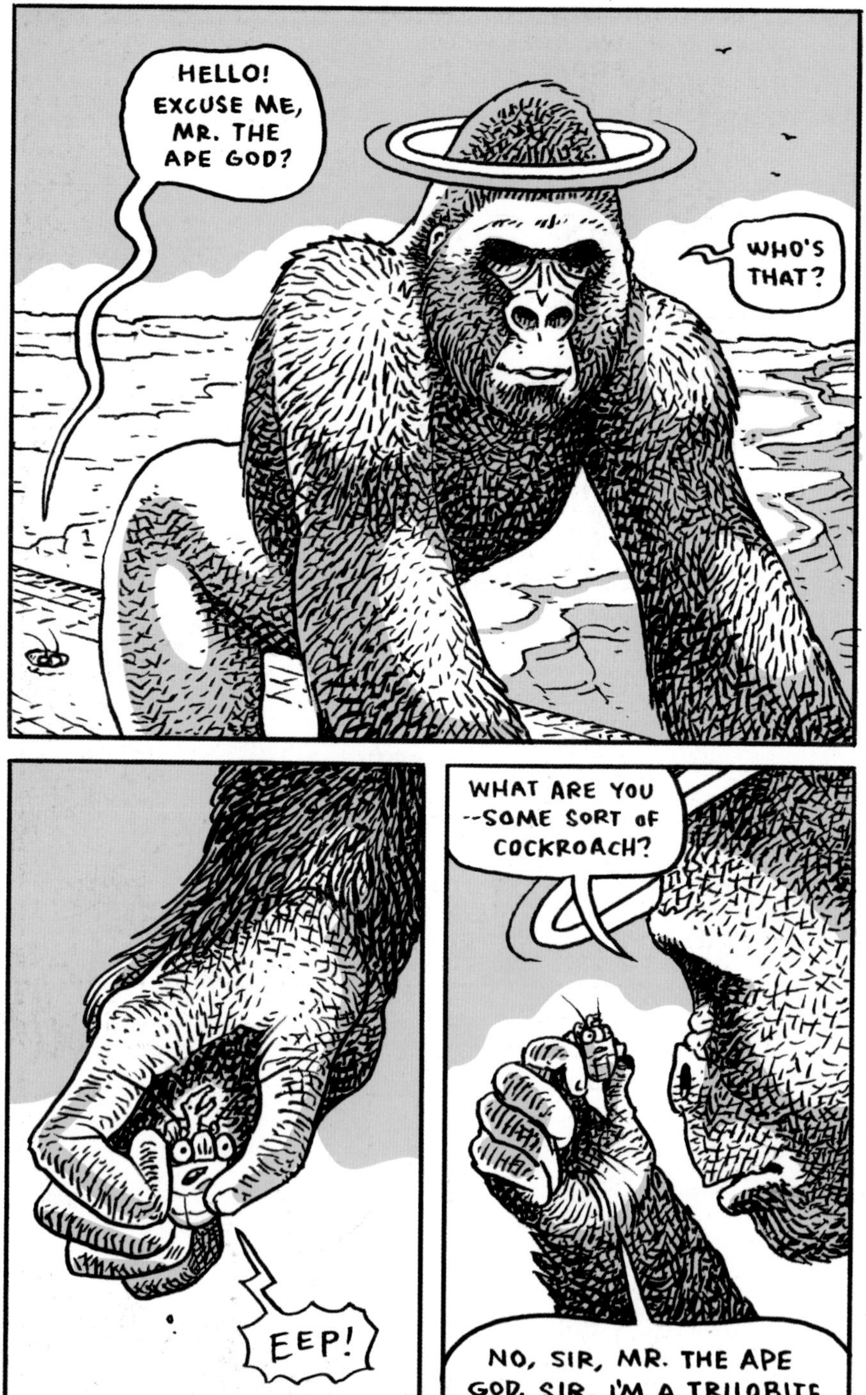
HELLO! EXCUSE ME, MR. THE APE GOD?
WHO'S THAT?
EEP!
WHAT ARE YOU --SOME SORT OF COCKROACH?
NO, SIR, MR. THE APE GOD, SIR, I'M A TRILOBITE.

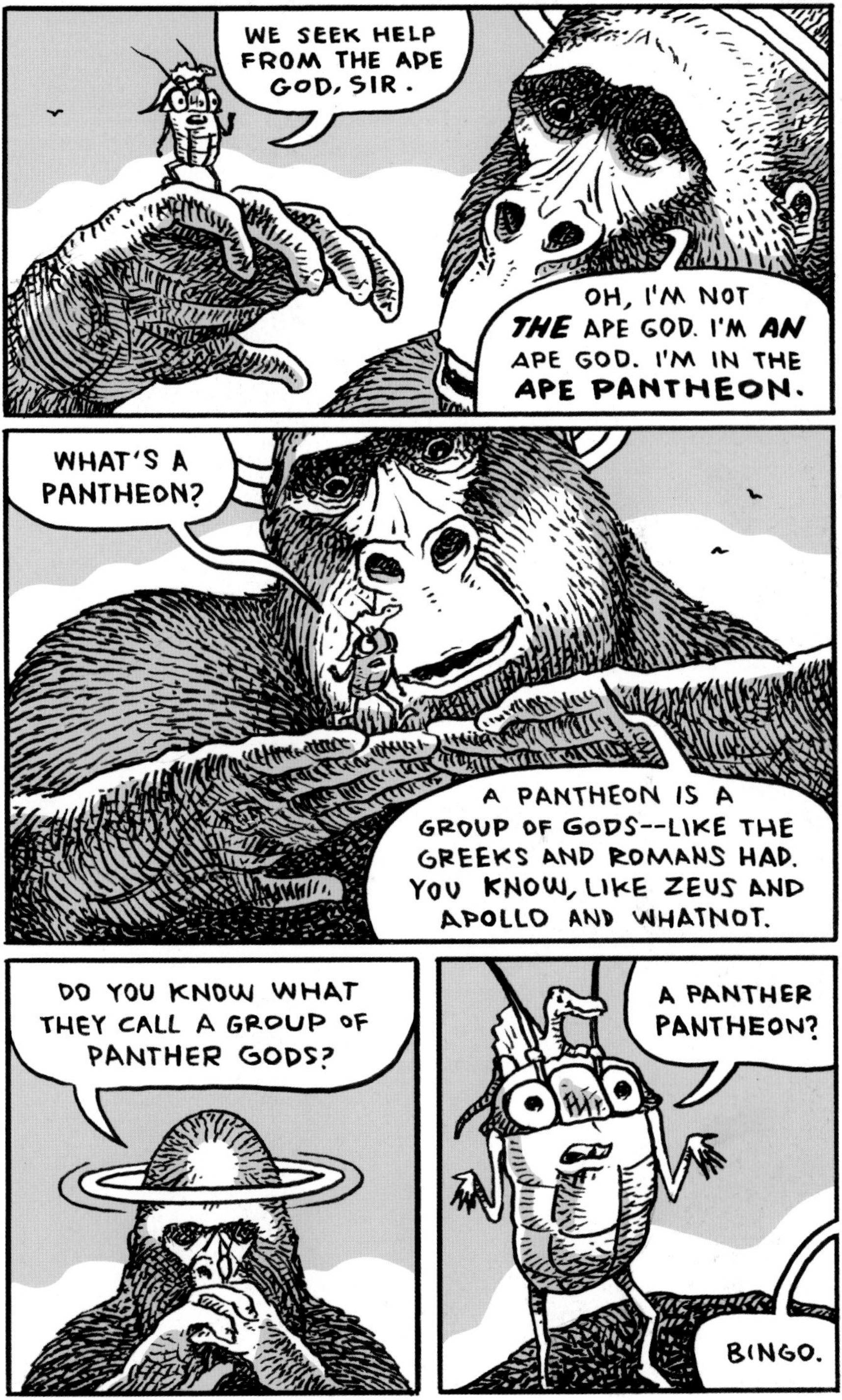
WE SEEK HELP FROM THE APE GOD, SIR.
OH, I'M NOT *THE* APE GOD. I'M *AN* APE GOD. I'M IN THE **APE PANTHEON.**
WHAT'S A PANTHEON?
A PANTHEON IS A GROUP OF GODS--LIKE THE GREEKS AND ROMANS HAD. YOU KNOW, LIKE ZEUS AND APOLLO AND WHATNOT.
DO YOU KNOW WHAT THEY CALL A GROUP OF PANTHER GODS?
A PANTHER PANTHEON?
BINGO.

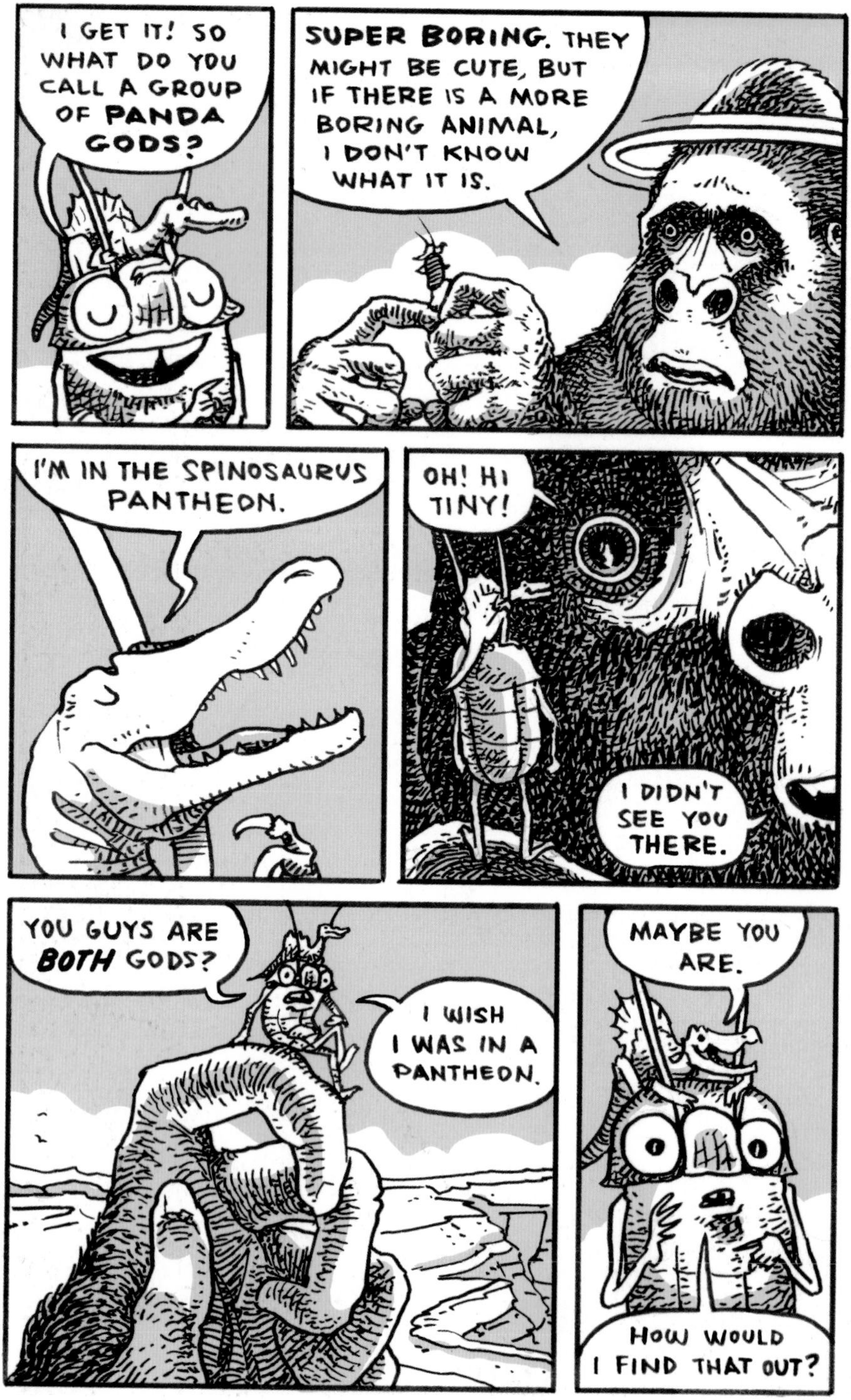
I GET IT! SO WHAT DO YOU CALL A GROUP OF **PANDA GODS**?
SUPER BORING. THEY MIGHT BE CUTE, BUT IF THERE IS A MORE BORING ANIMAL, I DON'T KNOW WHAT IT IS.
I'M IN THE SPINOSAURUS PANTHEON.
OH! HI TINY!
I DIDN'T SEE YOU THERE.
YOU GUYS ARE ***BOTH*** GODS?
I WISH I WAS IN A PANTHEON.
MAYBE YOU ARE.
HOW WOULD I FIND THAT OUT?

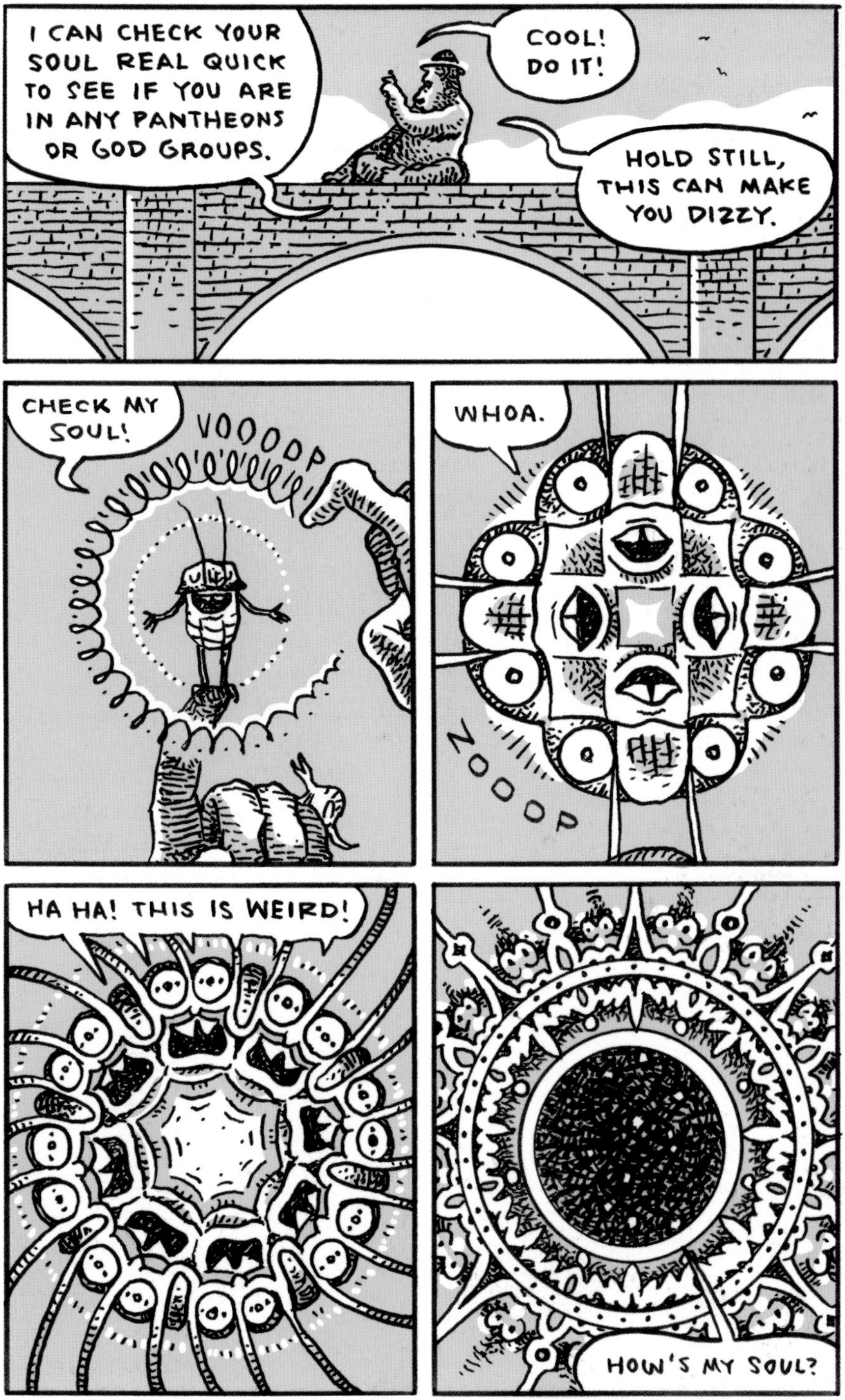
I CAN CHECK YOUR SOUL REAL QUICK TO SEE IF YOU ARE IN ANY PANTHEONS OR GOD GROUPS.
COOL! DO IT!
HOLD STILL, THIS CAN MAKE YOU DIZZY.
CHECK MY SOUL!
VOOOOOP
WHOA.
ZOOOOP
HA HA! THIS IS WEIRD!
HOW'S MY SOUL?

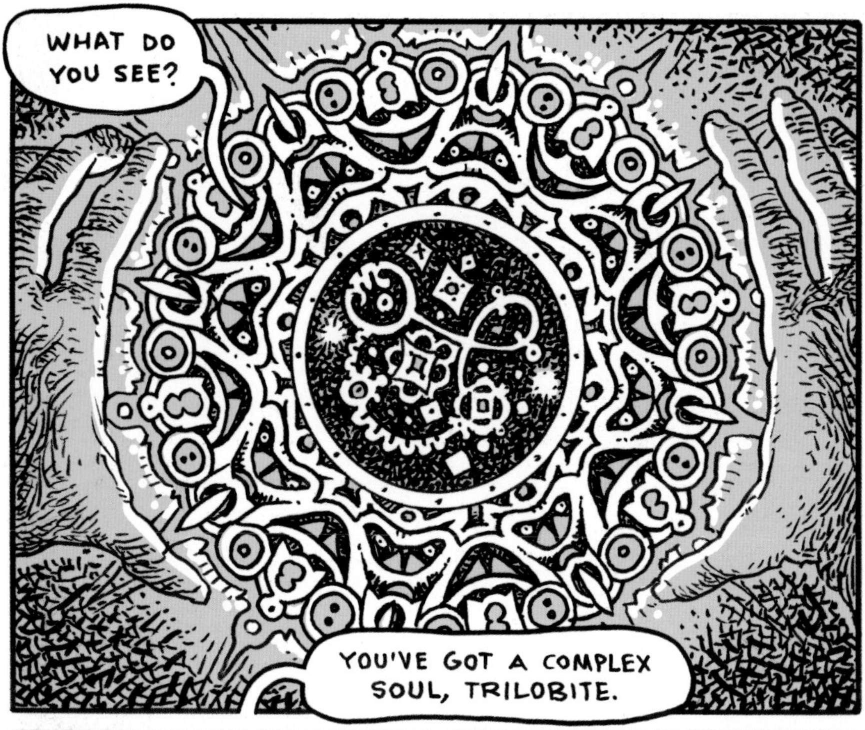
WHAT DO YOU SEE?
YOU'VE GOT A COMPLEX SOUL, TRILOBITE.

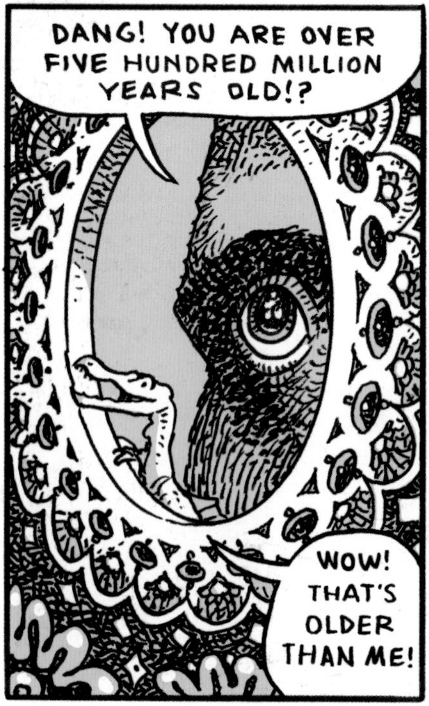
DANG! YOU ARE OVER FIVE HUNDRED MILLION YEARS OLD!?
WOW! THAT'S OLDER THAN ME!

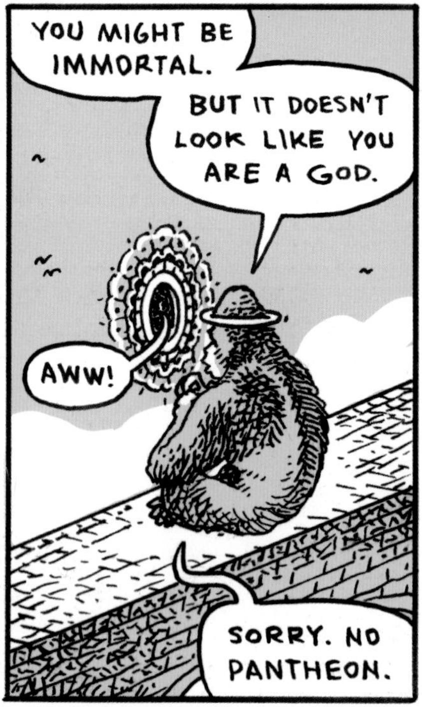
YOU MIGHT BE IMMORTAL.
BUT IT DOESN'T LOOK LIKE YOU ARE A GOD.
AWW!
SORRY. NO PANTHEON.

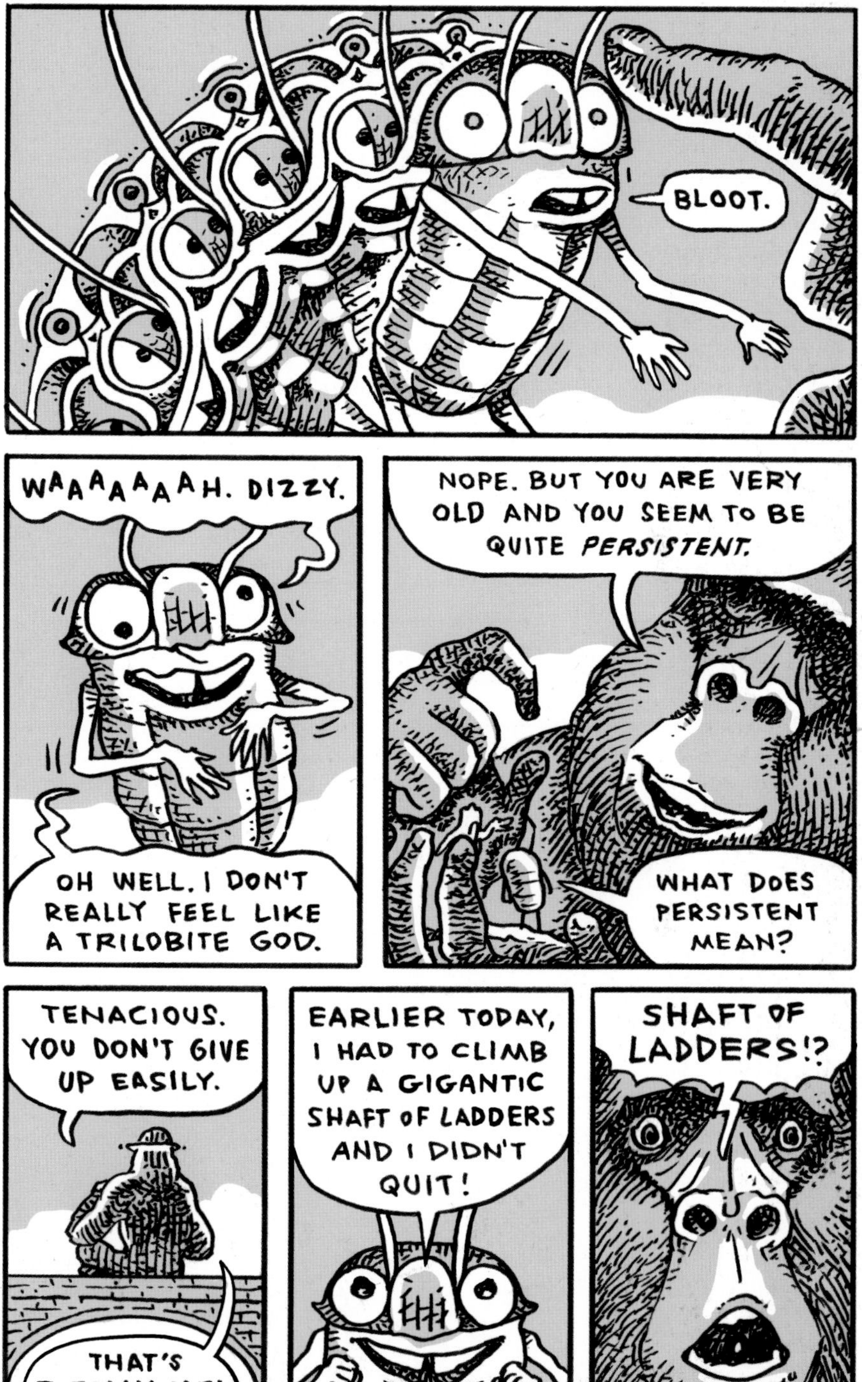
BLOOT.
WAAAAAAAH. DIZZY.
OH WELL. I DON'T REALLY FEEL LIKE A TRILOBITE GOD.
NOPE. BUT YOU ARE VERY OLD AND YOU SEEM TO BE QUITE *PERSISTENT*.
WHAT DOES PERSISTENT MEAN?
TENACIOUS. YOU DON'T GIVE UP EASILY.
THAT'S TOTALLY ME!
EARLIER TODAY, I HAD TO CLIMB UP A GIGANTIC SHAFT OF LADDERS AND I DIDN'T QUIT!
SHAFT OF LADDERS!?

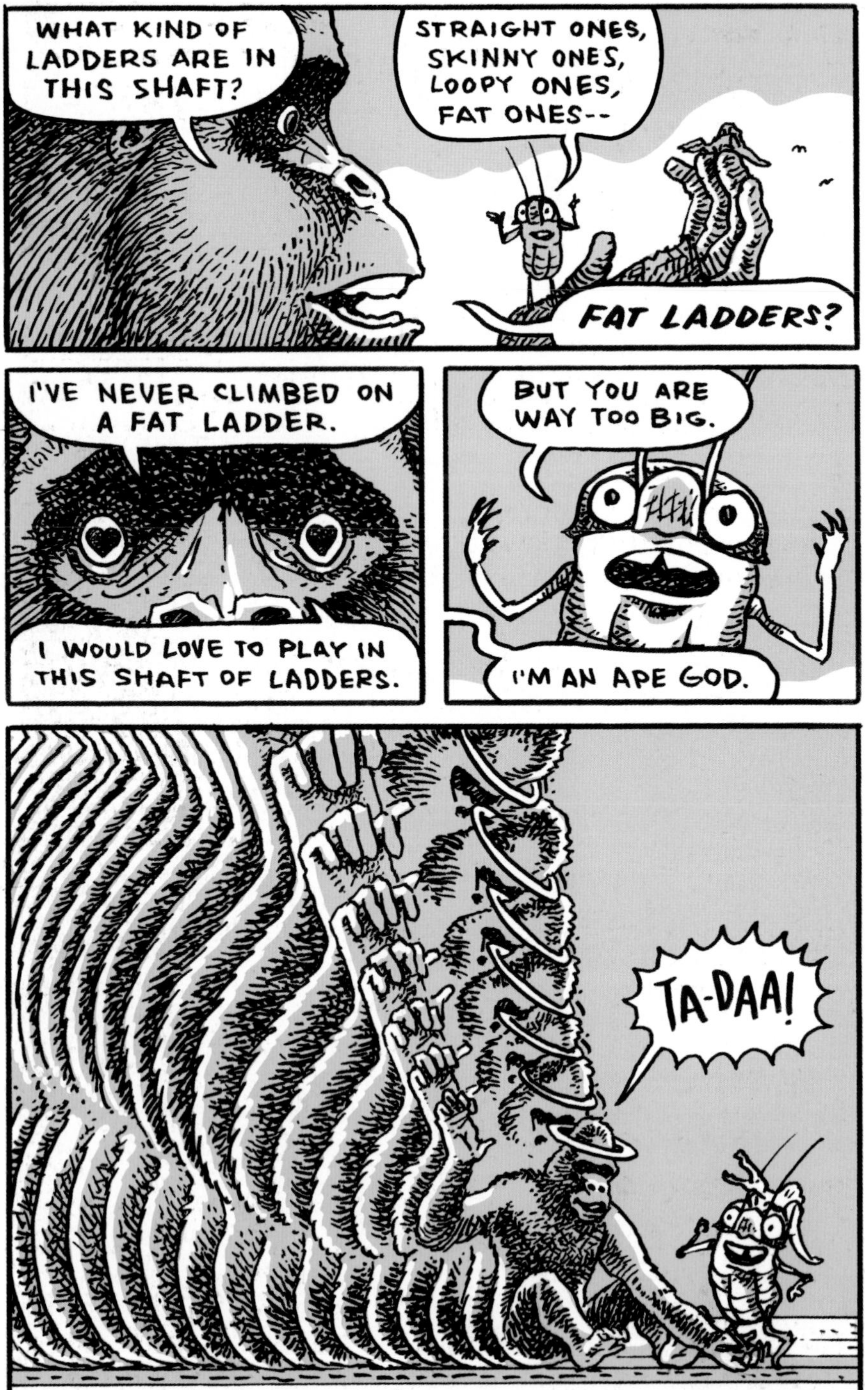
WHAT KIND OF LADDERS ARE IN THIS SHAFT?
STRAIGHT ONES, SKINNY ONES, LOOPY ONES, FAT ONES--
FAT LADDERS?
I'VE NEVER CLIMBED ON A FAT LADDER.
I WOULD LOVE TO PLAY IN THIS SHAFT OF LADDERS.
BUT YOU ARE WAY TOO BIG.
I'M AN APE GOD.
TA-DAA!

LET'S MAKE A *TRADE*.

I'LL TELL YOU WHERE THE LADDERS ARE IF YOU HELP ME FIND MY AMBULOCETUS.

YOUR FRIEND IS A WALKING WHALE?

YUP.

WE'VE BEEN BEST BUDDIES FOR YEARS. BUT SHE RAN OFF WITH A PALEO-NEWSCASTER.

WAIT! WAS IT **TIFFANY TIMBER**? I LOVE HER!

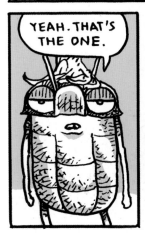

YEAH. THAT'S THE ONE.

WOOHOO! FAT LADDERS AND A CHANCE TO MEET TIFFANY TIMBER!

THUMP
THUMP
THUMP

IT'S A FUN DAY TO BE AN APE GOD!

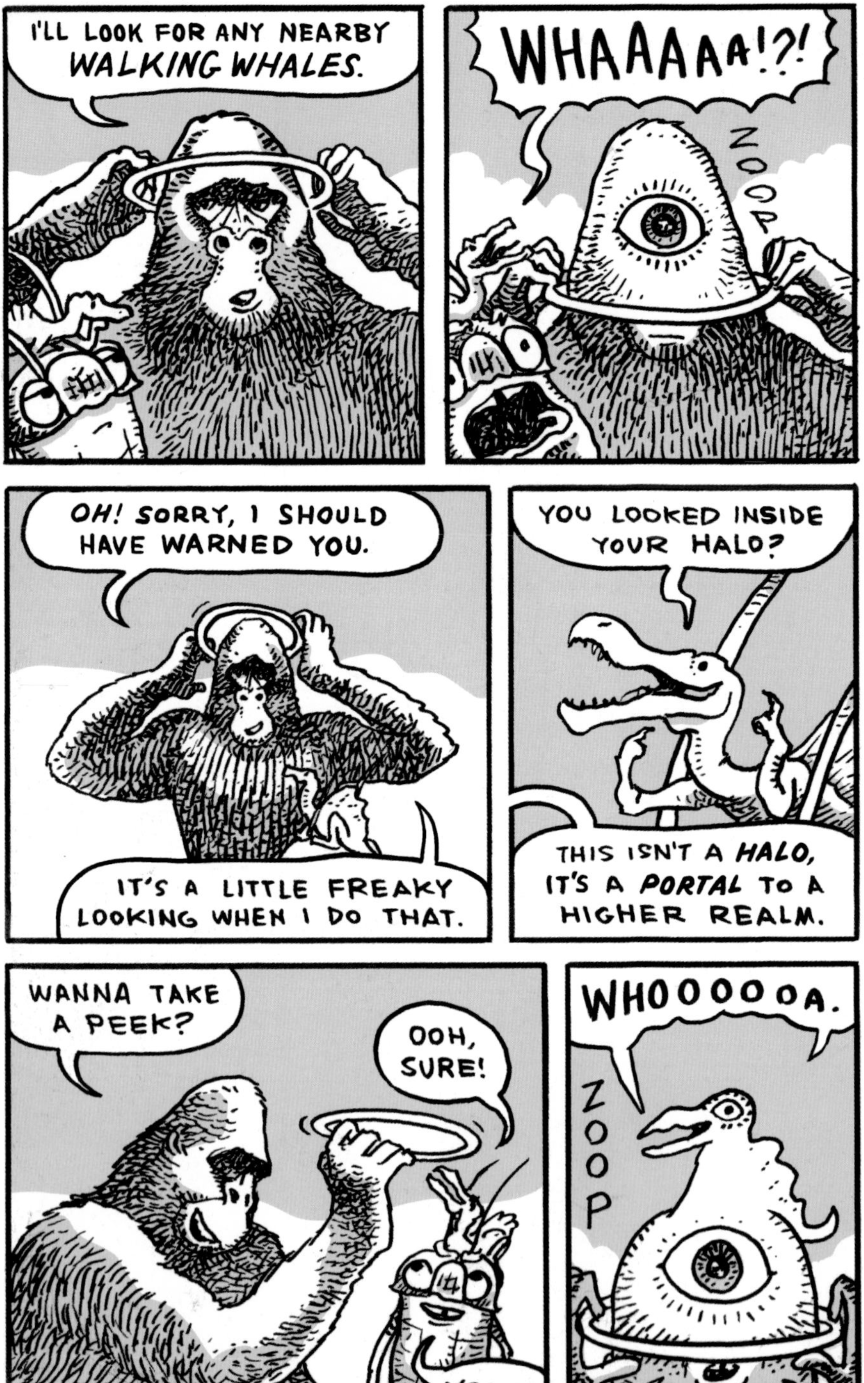
I'LL LOOK FOR ANY NEARBY WALKING WHALES.
WHAAAAA!?!
ZOOP
OH! SORRY, I SHOULD HAVE WARNED YOU.
IT'S A LITTLE FREAKY LOOKING WHEN I DO THAT.
YOU LOOKED INSIDE YOUR HALO?
THIS ISN'T A HALO, IT'S A PORTAL TO A HIGHER REALM.
WANNA TAKE A PEEK?
OOH, SURE!
YEAH!
WHOOOOOA.
ZOOP

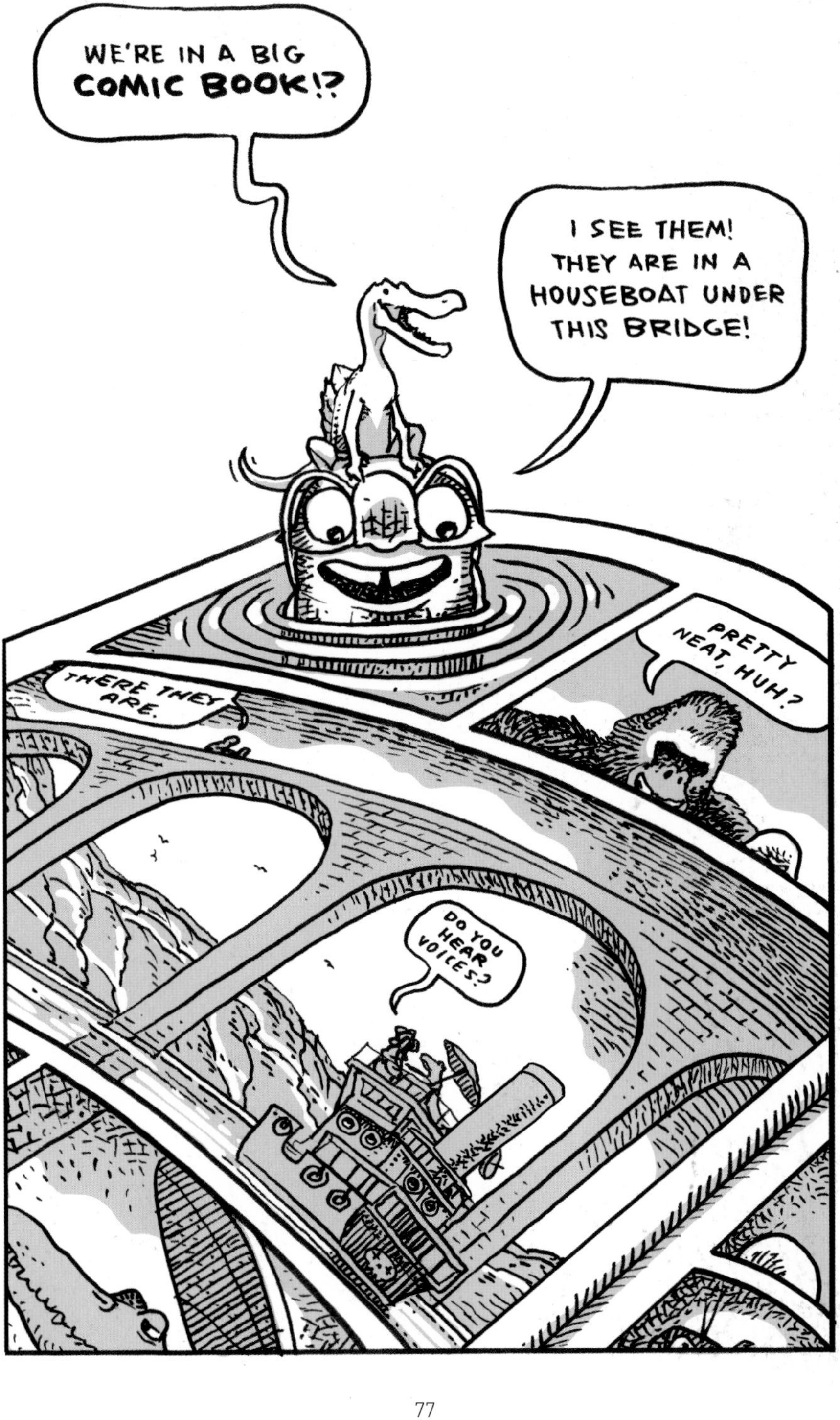
WE'RE IN A BIG COMIC BOOK!?
I SEE THEM! THEY ARE IN A HOUSEBOAT UNDER THIS BRIDGE!
THERE THEY ARE.
PRETTY NEAT, HUH?
DO YOU HEAR VOICES?

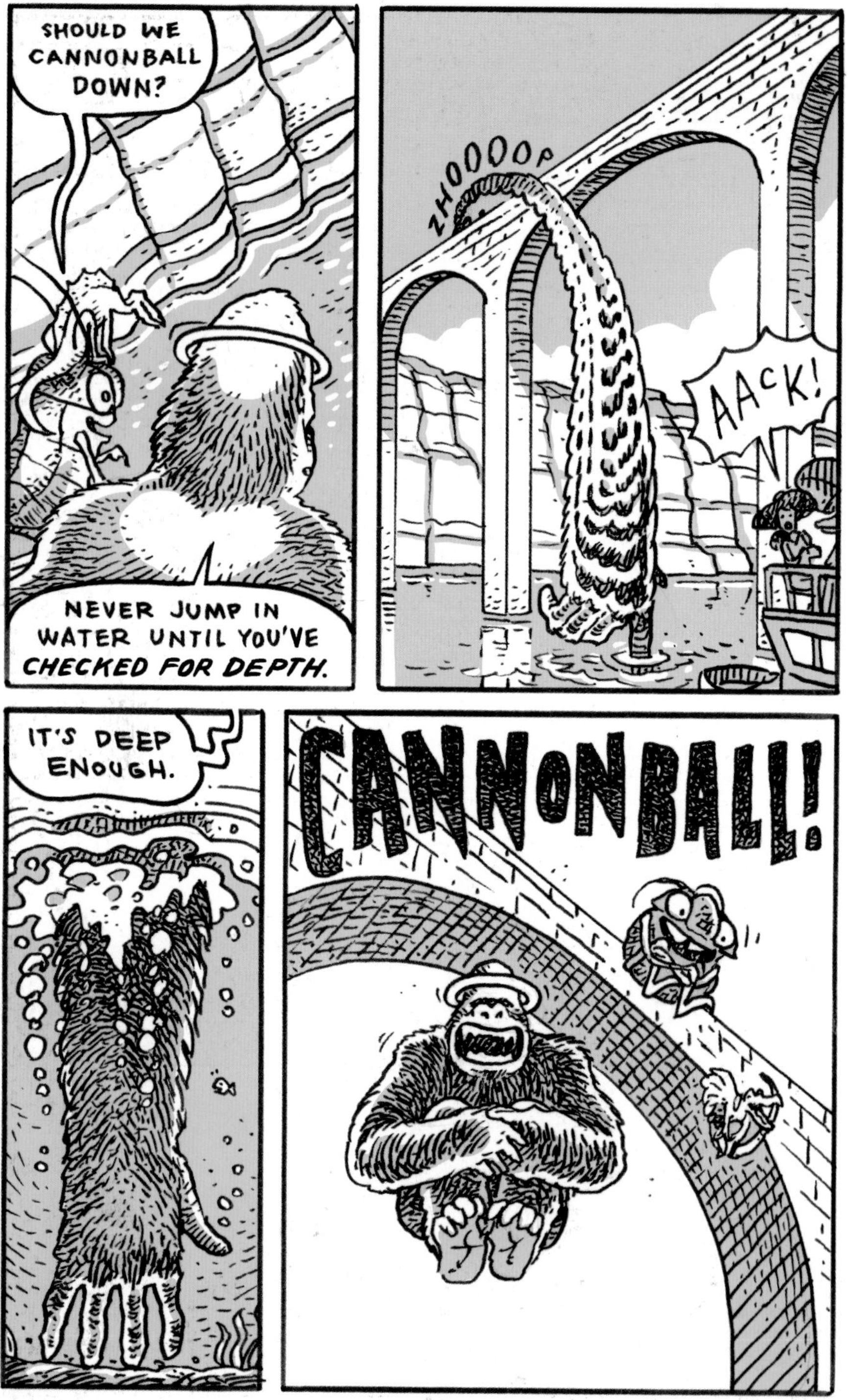
SHOULD WE CANNONBALL DOWN?
NEVER JUMP IN WATER UNTIL YOU'VE CHECKED FOR DEPTH.
ZHOOOOP
AACK!
IT'S DEEP ENOUGH.
CANNONBALL!

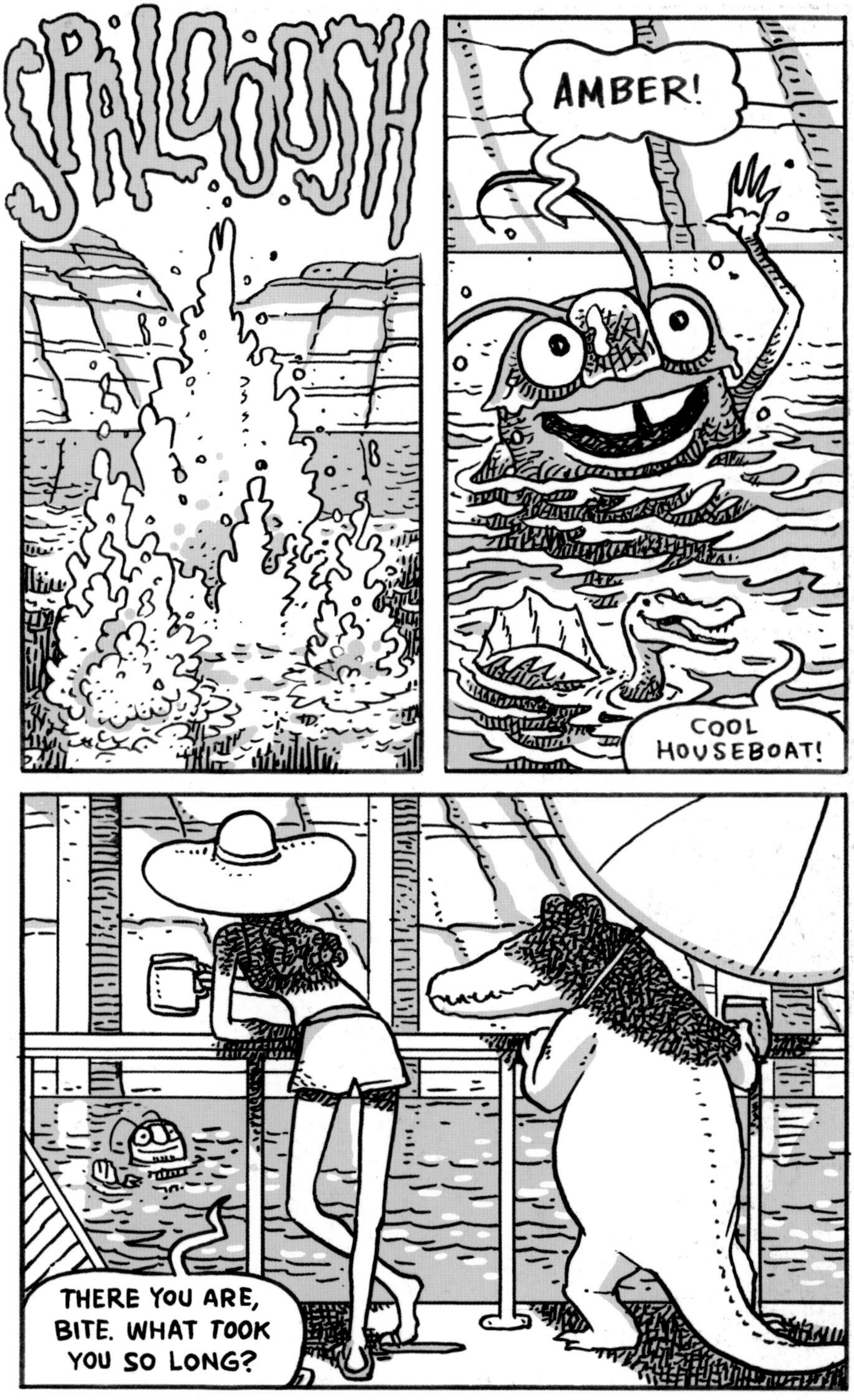
SPALOOOSH
AMBER!
COOL HOUSEBOAT!
THERE YOU ARE, BITE. WHAT TOOK YOU SO LONG?

CHAPTER 4

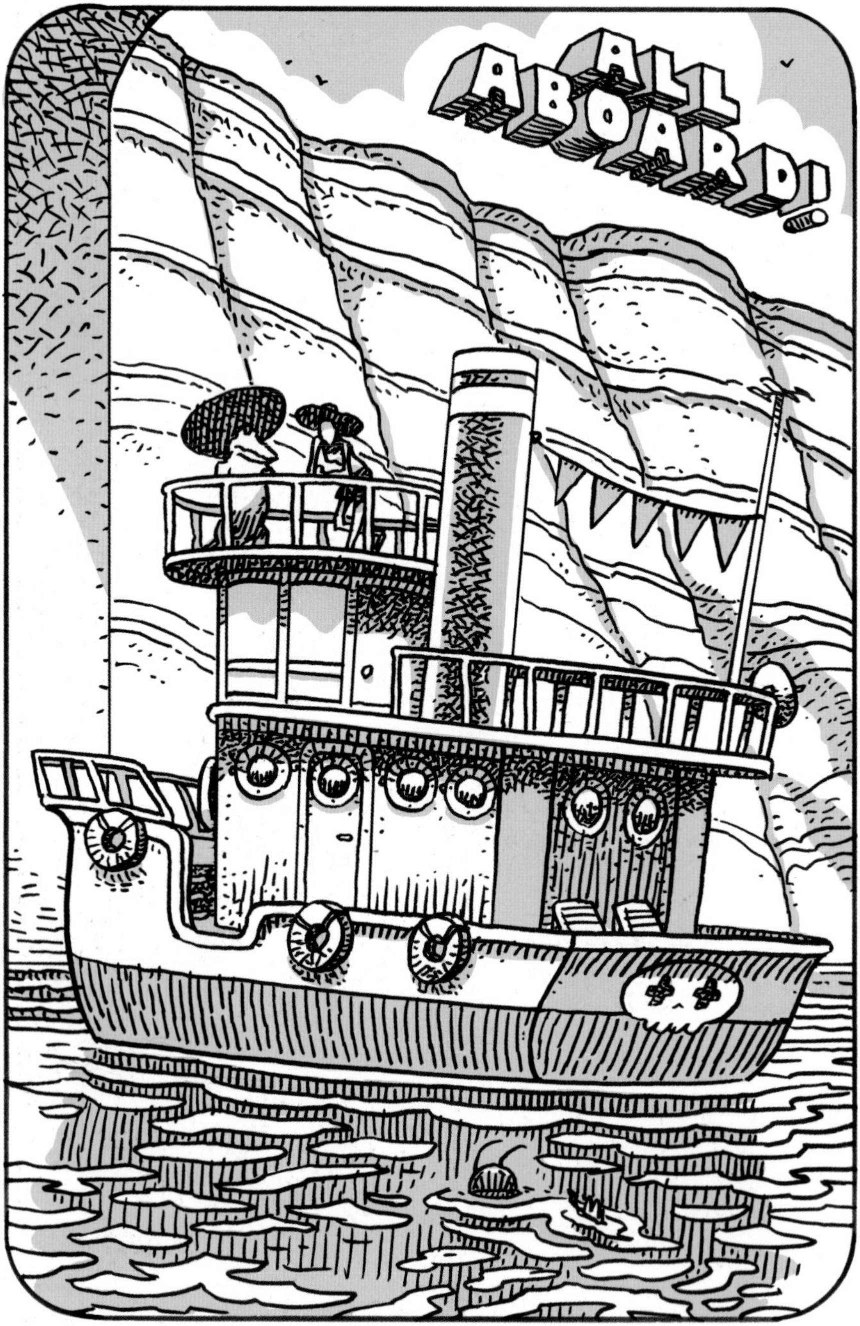
ALL ABOARD!

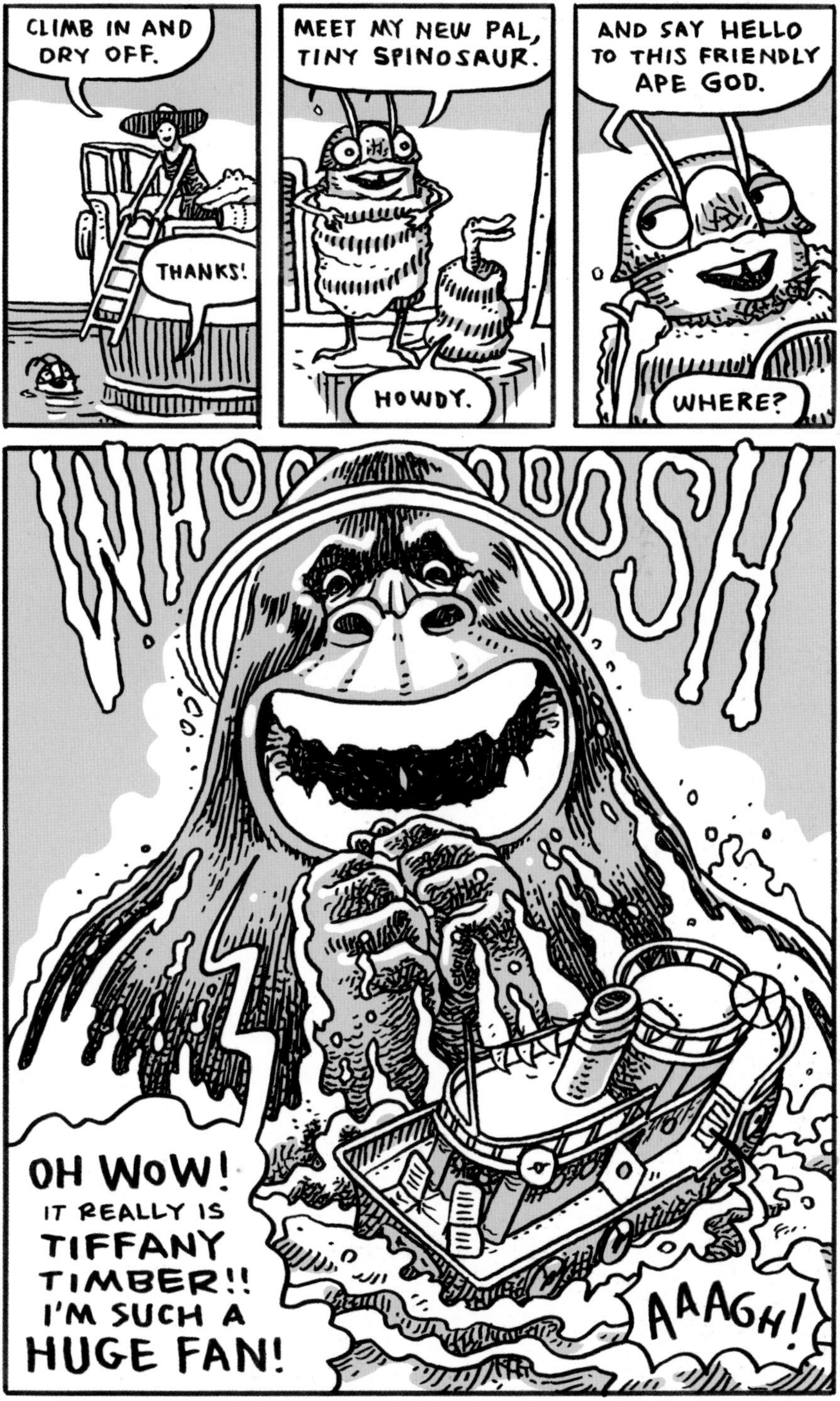
CLIMB IN AND DRY OFF.
THANKS!
MEET MY NEW PAL, TINY SPINOSAUR.
HOWDY.
AND SAY HELLO TO THIS FRIENDLY APE GOD.
WHERE?
WHOOOOOOOSH!
OH WOW! IT REALLY IS TIFFANY TIMBER!! I'M SUCH A HUGE FAN!
AAAGH!

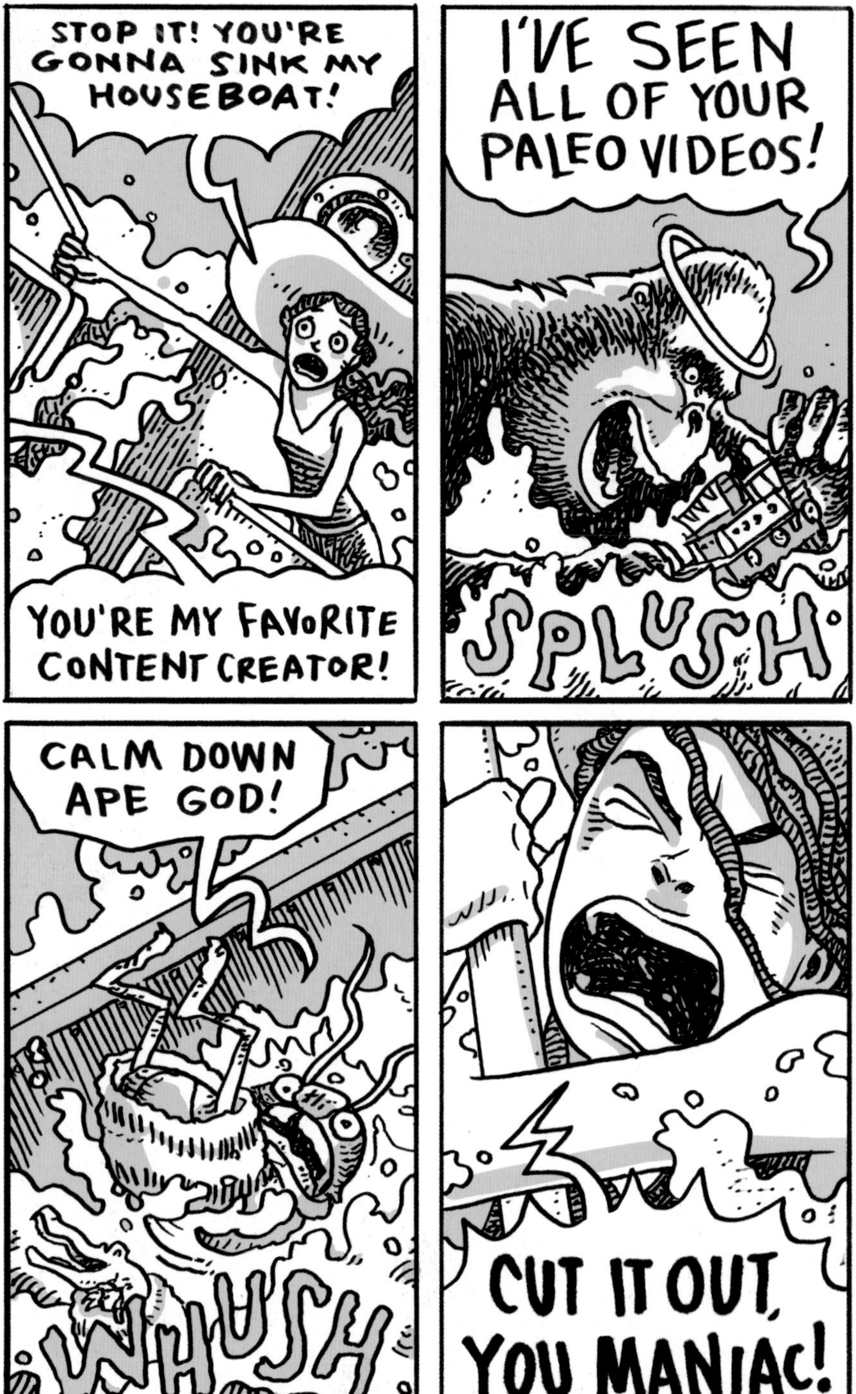
STOP IT! YOU'RE GONNA SINK MY HOUSEBOAT!
YOU'RE MY FAVORITE CONTENT CREATOR!
I'VE SEEN ALL OF YOUR PALEO VIDEOS!
SPLUSH
CALM DOWN APE GOD!
WHUSH
CUT IT OUT, YOU MANIAC!

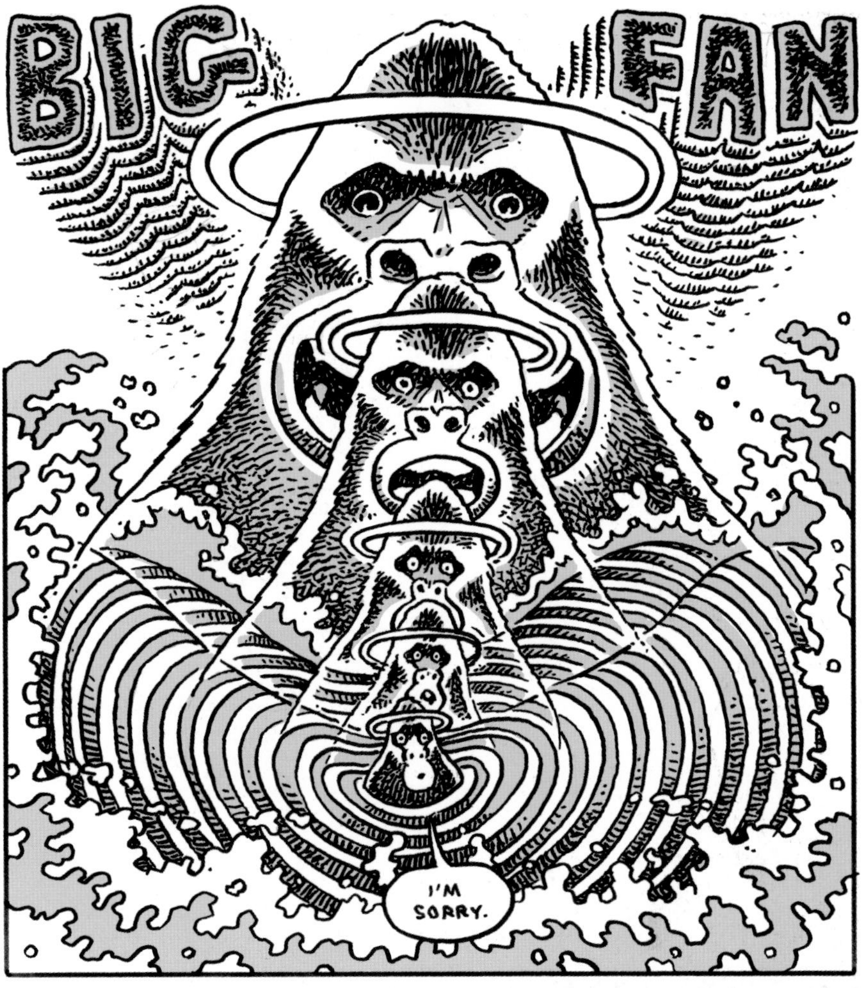
BIG FAN
I'M SORRY.

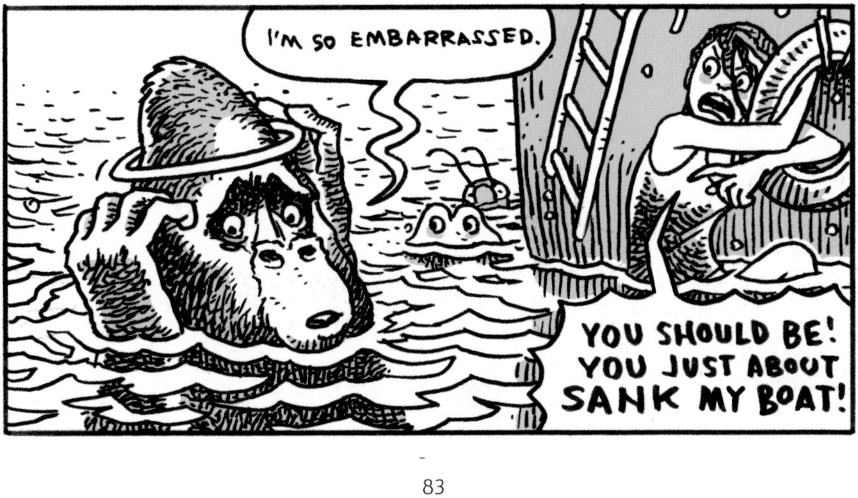
I'M SO EMBARRASSED.
YOU SHOULD BE! YOU JUST ABOUT SANK MY BOAT!

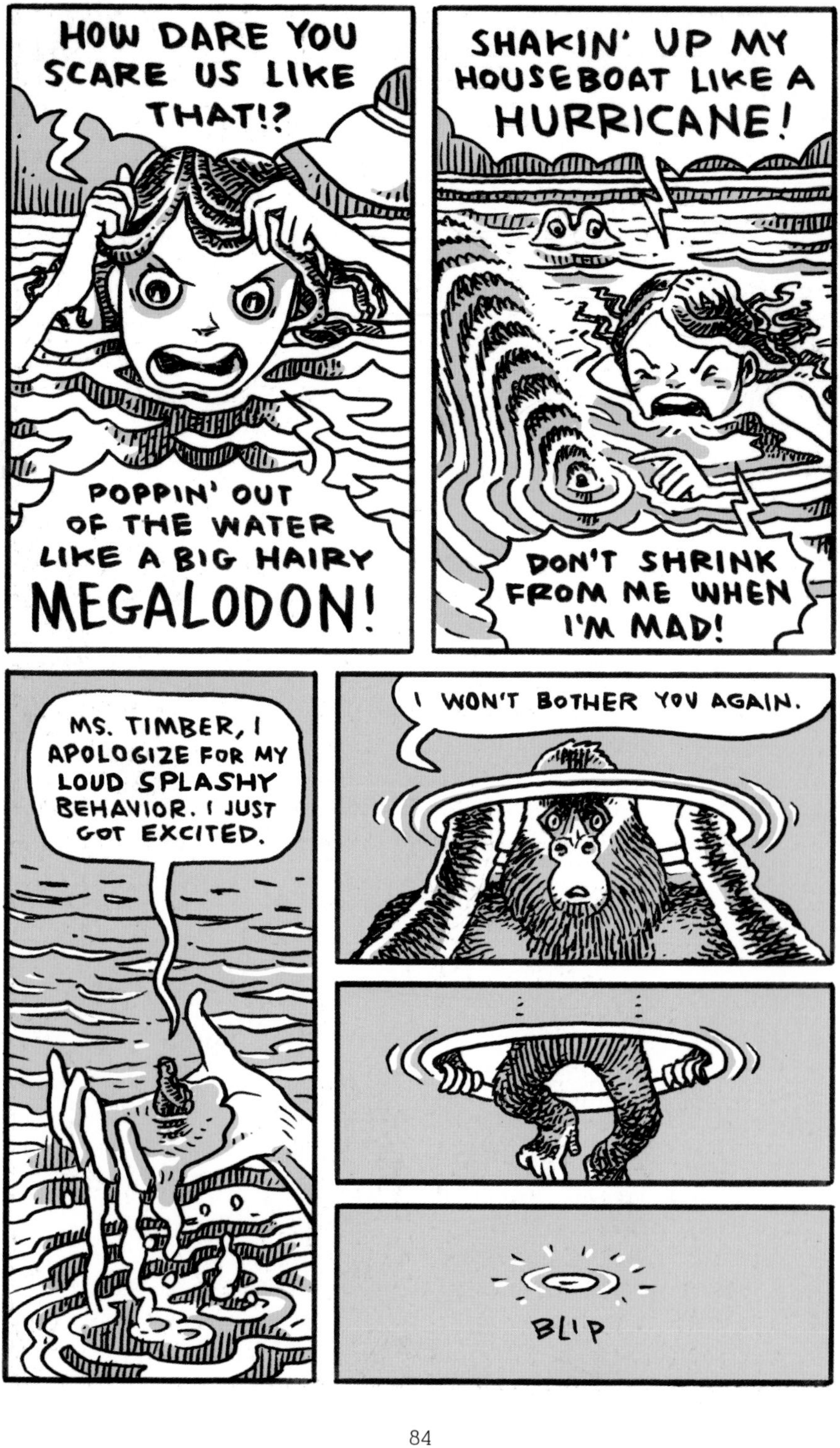
HOW DARE YOU SCARE US LIKE THAT!?
POPPIN' OUT OF THE WATER LIKE A BIG HAIRY MEGALODON!
SHAKIN' UP MY HOUSEBOAT LIKE A HURRICANE!
DON'T SHRINK FROM ME WHEN I'M MAD!
MS. TIMBER, I APOLOGIZE FOR MY LOUD SPLASHY BEHAVIOR. I JUST GOT EXCITED.
I WON'T BOTHER YOU AGAIN.
BLIP

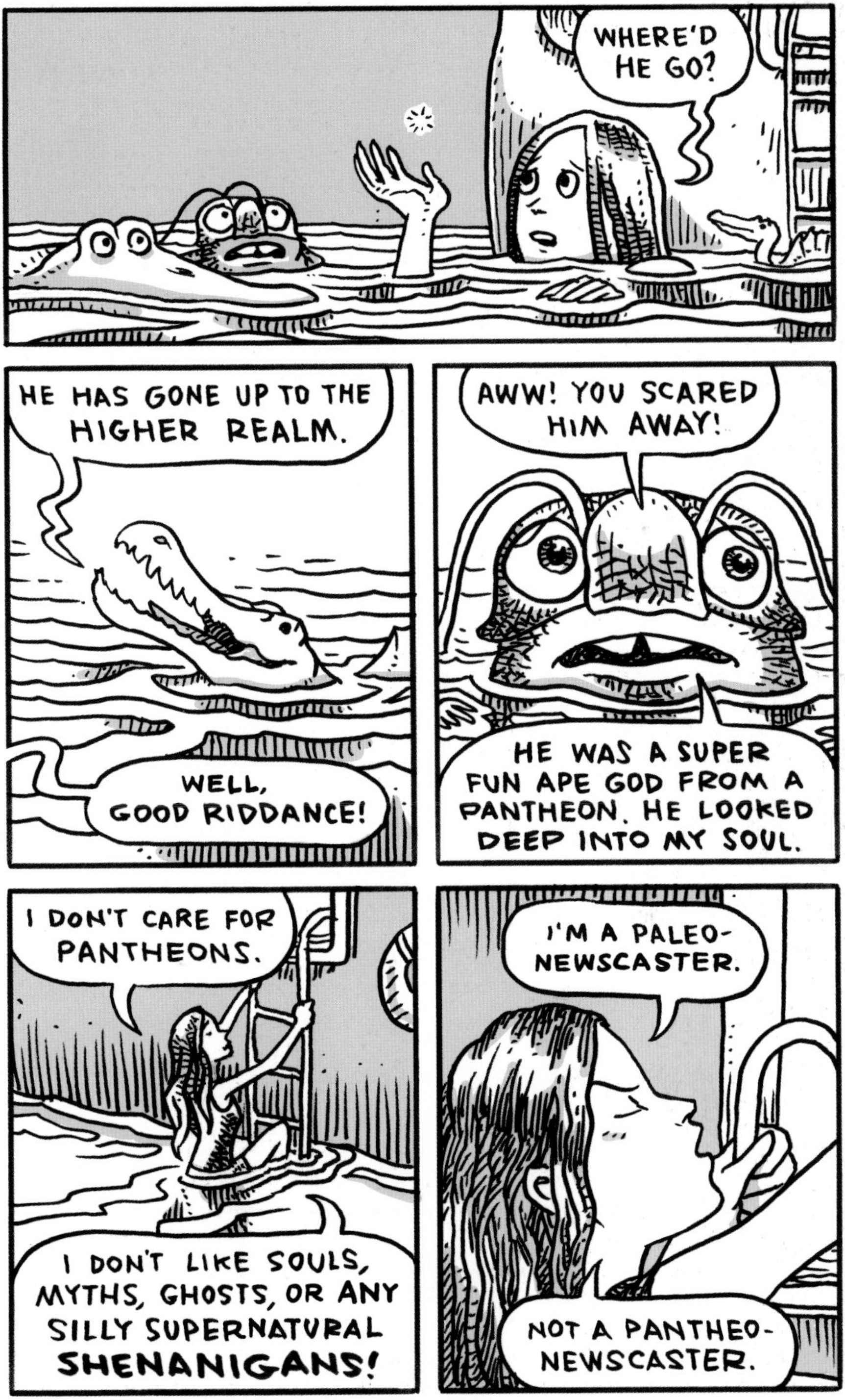
WHERE'D HE GO?
HE HAS GONE UP TO THE HIGHER REALM.
WELL, GOOD RIDDANCE!
AWW! YOU SCARED HIM AWAY!
HE WAS A SUPER FUN APE GOD FROM A PANTHEON. HE LOOKED DEEP INTO MY SOUL.
I DON'T CARE FOR PANTHEONS.
I DON'T LIKE SOULS, MYTHS, GHOSTS, OR ANY SILLY SUPERNATURAL SHENANIGANS!
I'M A PALEO-NEWSCASTER.
NOT A PANTHEO-NEWSCASTER.

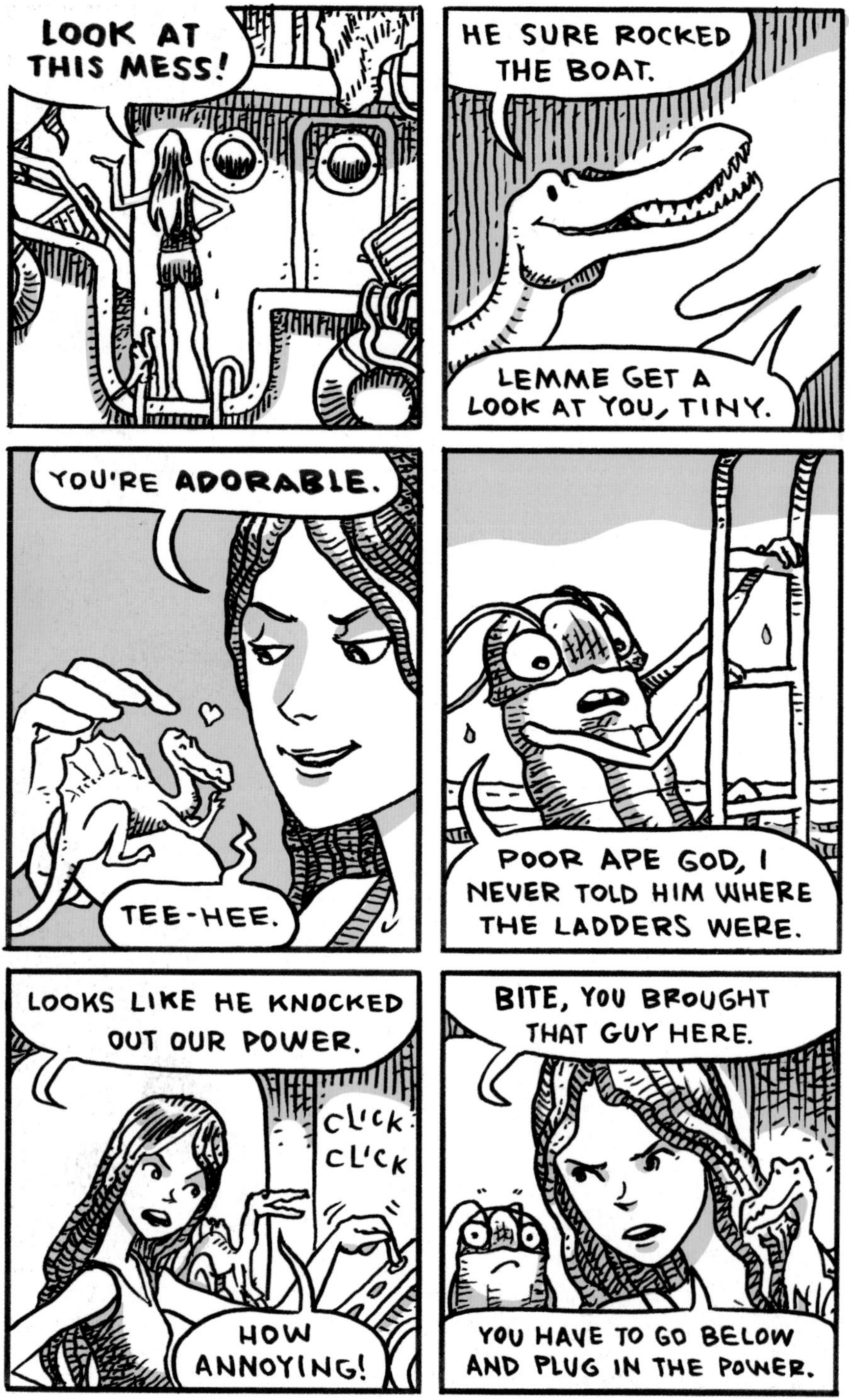
LOOK AT THIS MESS!
HE SURE ROCKED THE BOAT.
LEMME GET A LOOK AT YOU, TINY.
YOU'RE ADORABLE.
TEE-HEE.
POOR APE GOD, I NEVER TOLD HIM WHERE THE LADDERS WERE.
LOOKS LIKE HE KNOCKED OUT OUR POWER.
CLICK CLICK
HOW ANNOYING!
BITE, YOU BROUGHT THAT GUY HERE.
YOU HAVE TO GO BELOW AND PLUG IN THE POWER.

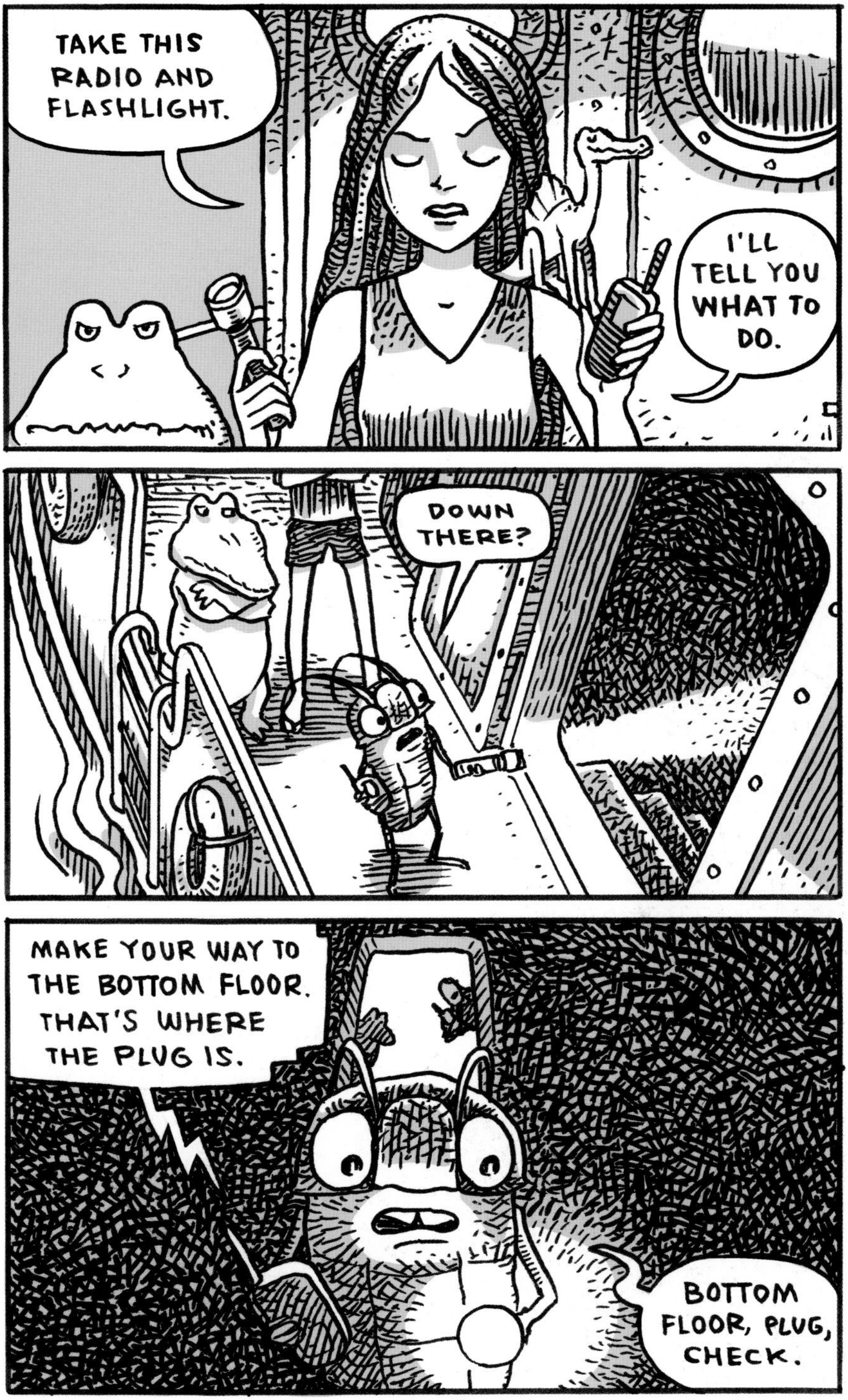

TAKE THIS RADIO AND FLASHLIGHT.
I'LL TELL YOU WHAT TO DO.
DOWN THERE?
MAKE YOUR WAY TO THE BOTTOM FLOOR. THAT'S WHERE THE PLUG IS.
BOTTOM FLOOR, PLUG, CHECK.

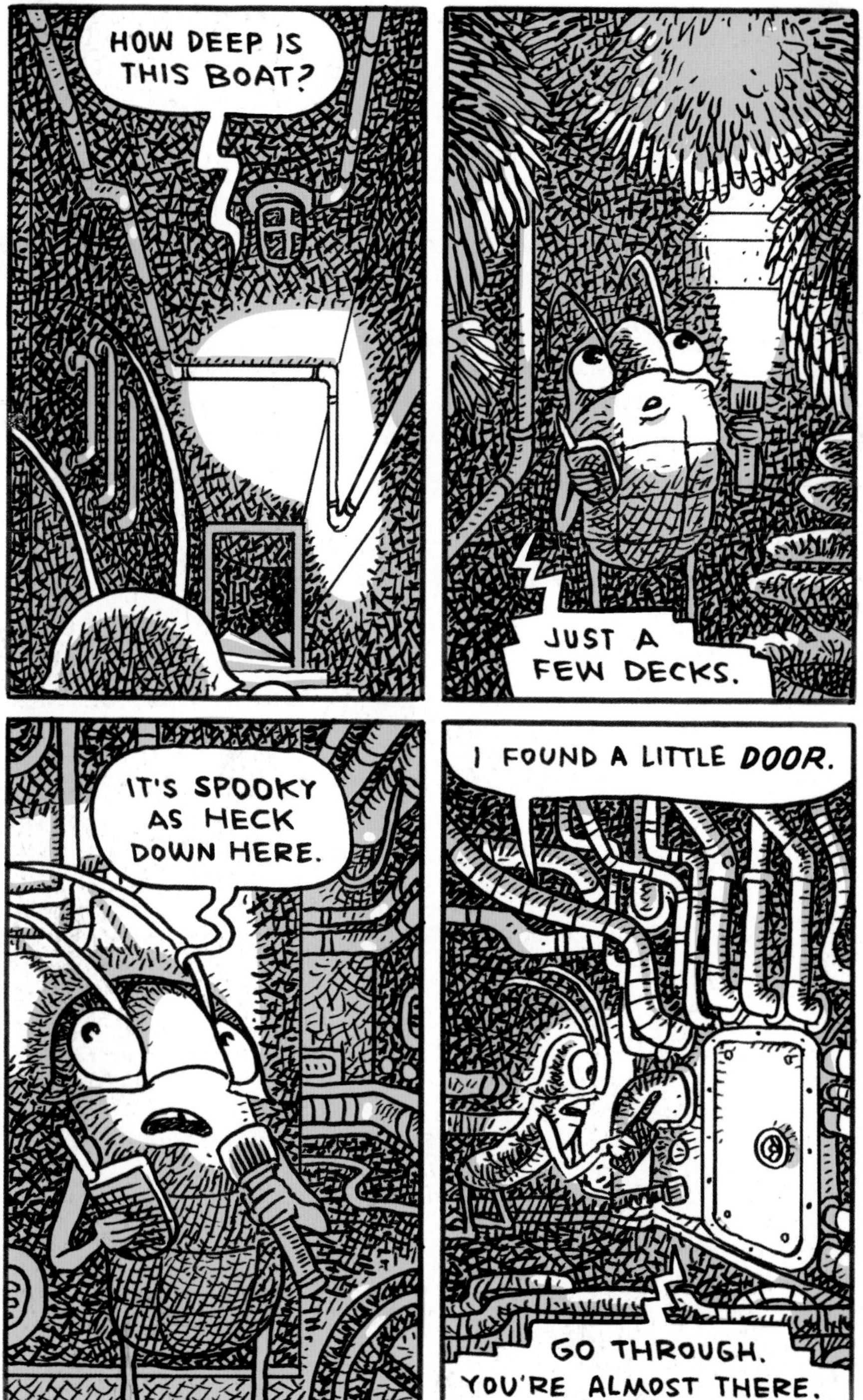
HOW DEEP IS THIS BOAT?
JUST A FEW DECKS.
IT'S SPOOKY AS HECK DOWN HERE.
I FOUND A LITTLE DOOR.
GO THROUGH. YOU'RE ALMOST THERE.

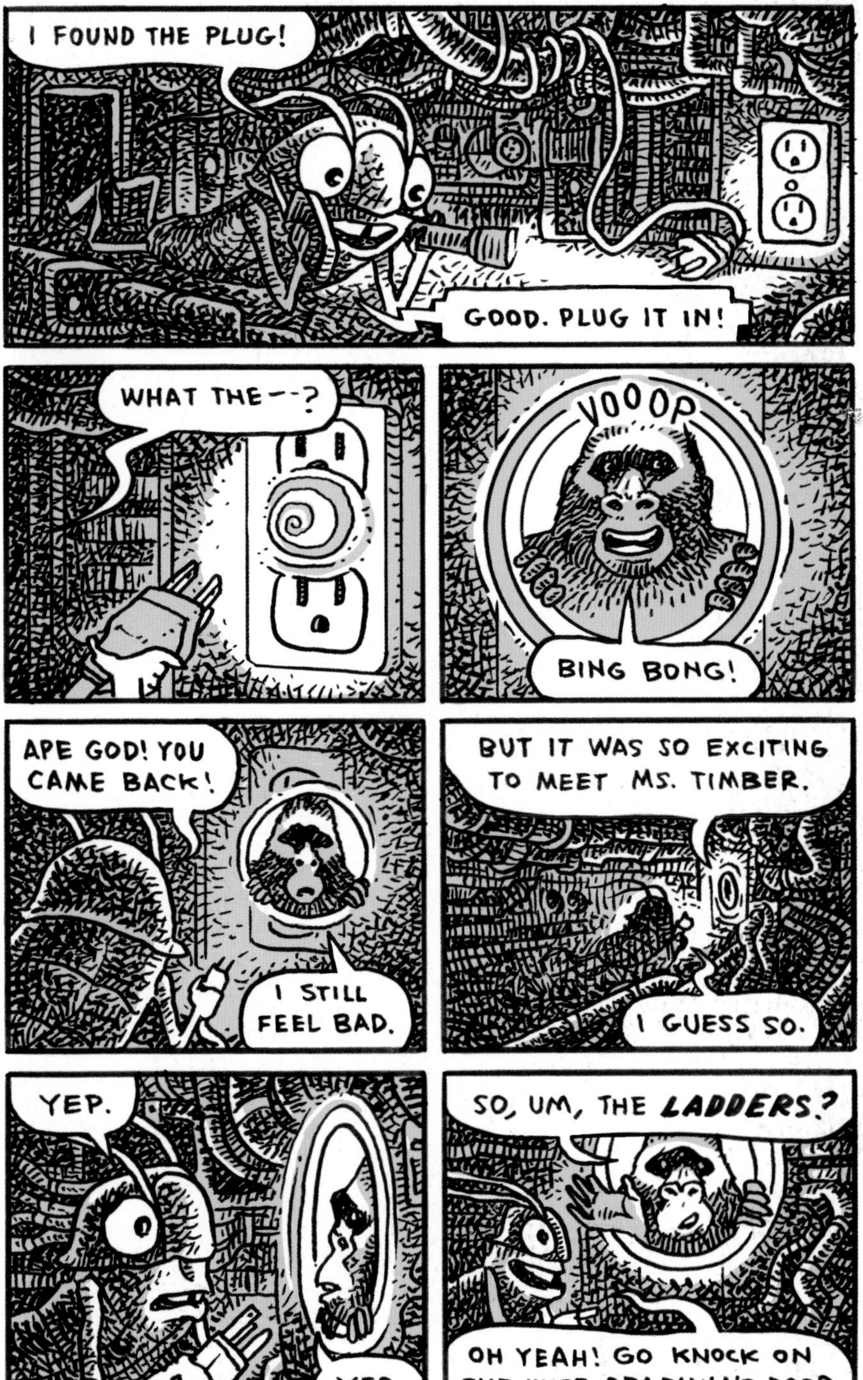
I FOUND THE PLUG!
GOOD. PLUG IT IN!
WHAT THE--?
VOOOP
BING BONG!
APE GOD! YOU CAME BACK!
I STILL FEEL BAD.
BUT IT WAS SO EXCITING TO MEET MS. TIMBER.
I GUESS SO.
YEP.
YEP.
SO, UM, THE *LADDERS*?
OH YEAH! GO KNOCK ON THE WISE OPABINIA'S DOOR.

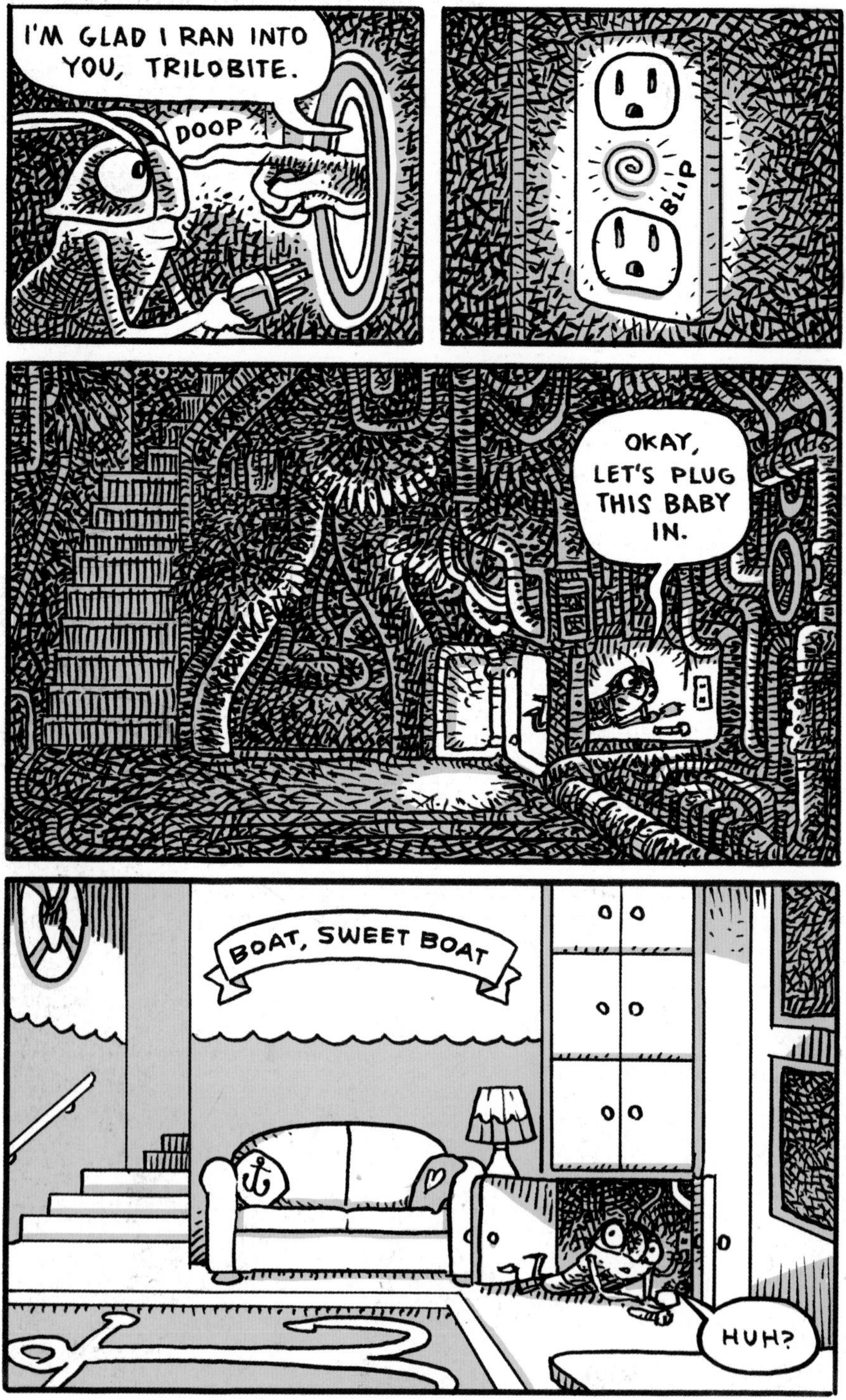
I'M GLAD I RAN INTO YOU, TRILOBITE.
DOOP
BLIP
OKAY, LET'S PLUG THIS BABY IN.
BOAT, SWEET BOAT
HUH?

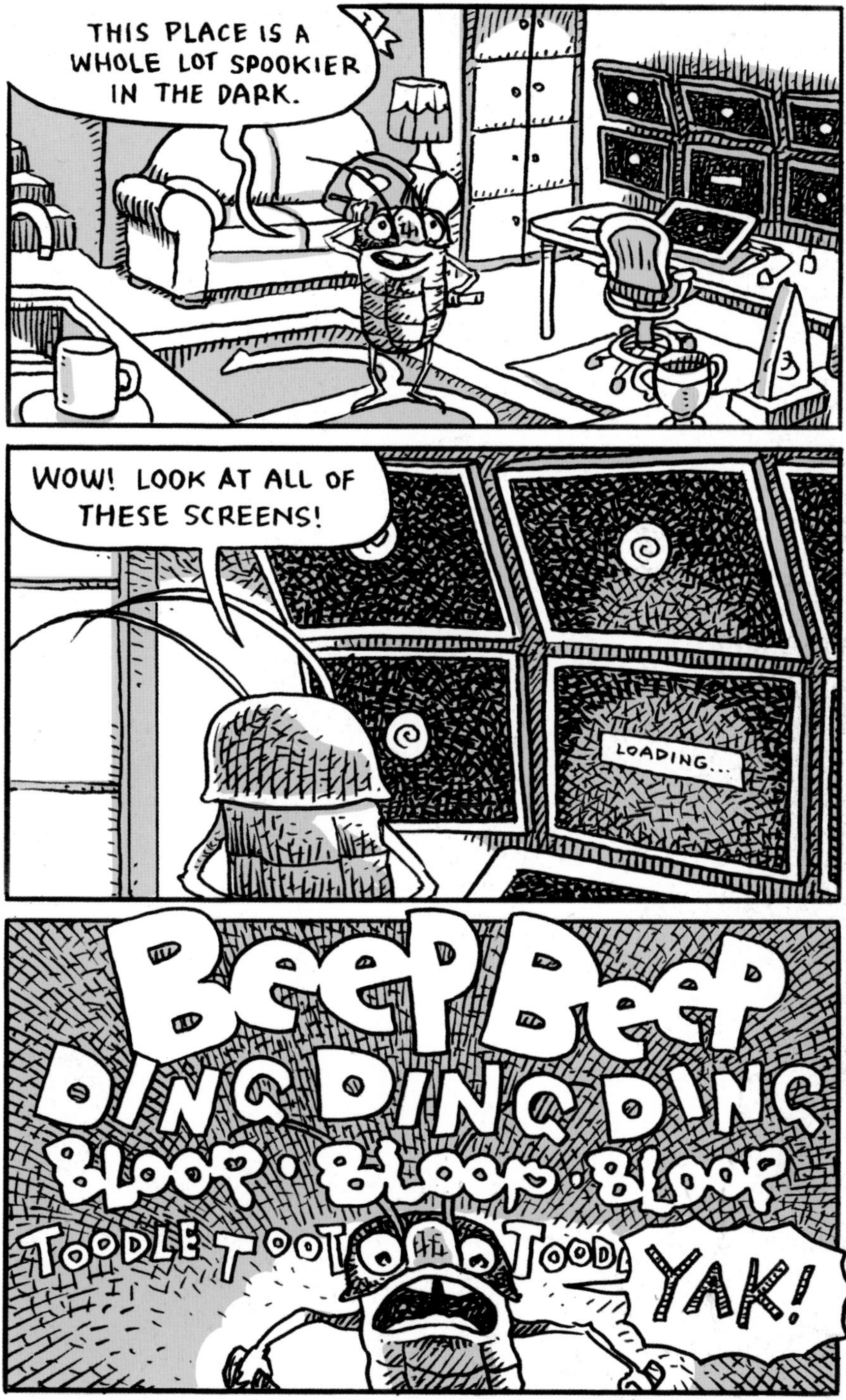
THIS PLACE IS A WHOLE LOT SPOOKIER IN THE DARK.
WOW! LOOK AT ALL OF THESE SCREENS!
LOADING...
BEEP BEEP
DING DING DING
BLOOP BLOOP BLOOP
TOODLE TOOT TOODL
YAK!

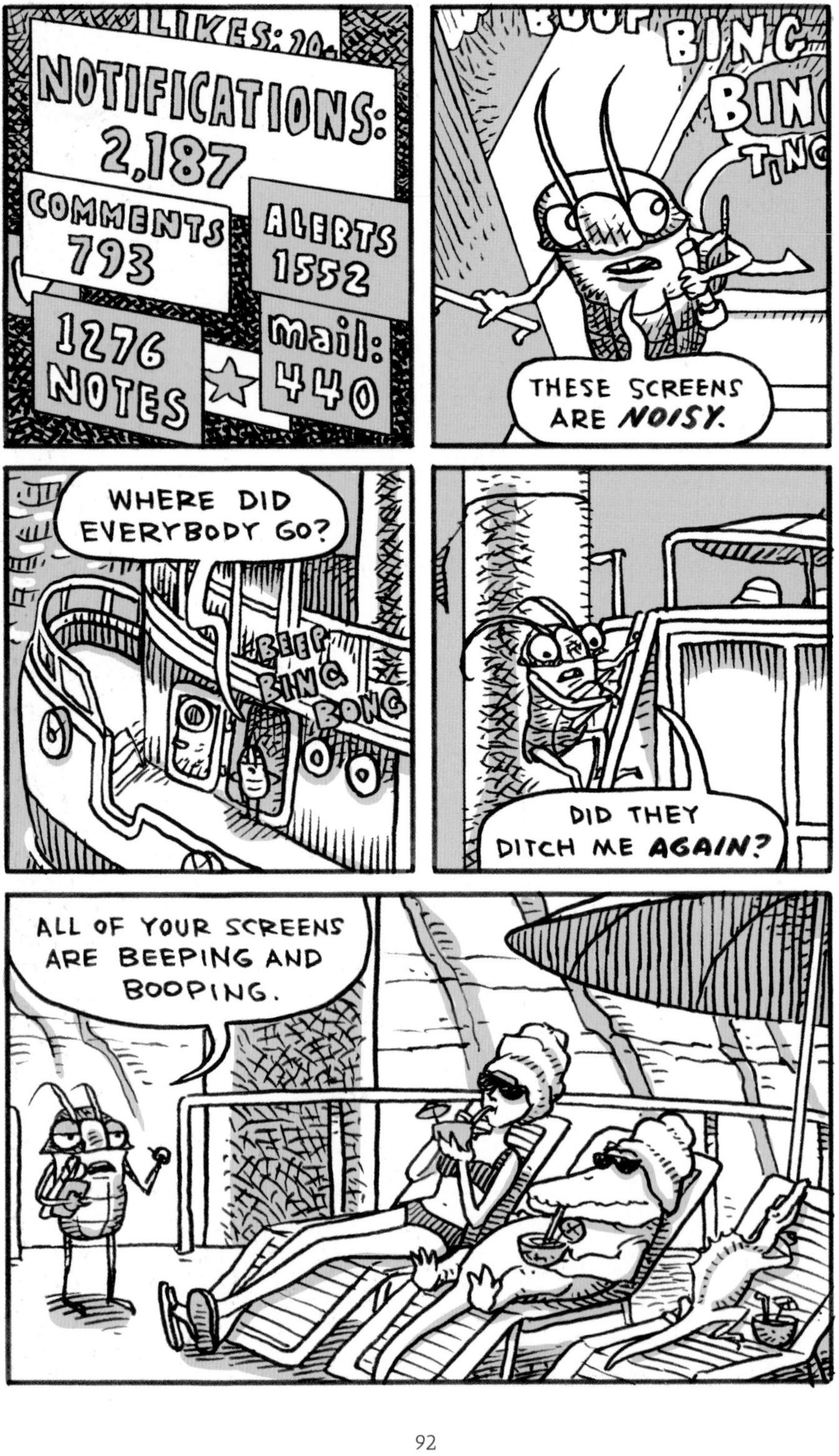
LIKES: 20
NOTIFICATIONS: 2,187
COMMENTS 793
ALERTS 1552
1276 NOTES
mail: 440
BING
BIN
TING
THESE SCREENS ARE NOISY.
WHERE DID EVERYBODY GO?
BEEP BING BONG
DID THEY DITCH ME AGAIN?
ALL OF YOUR SCREENS ARE BEEPING AND BOOPING.

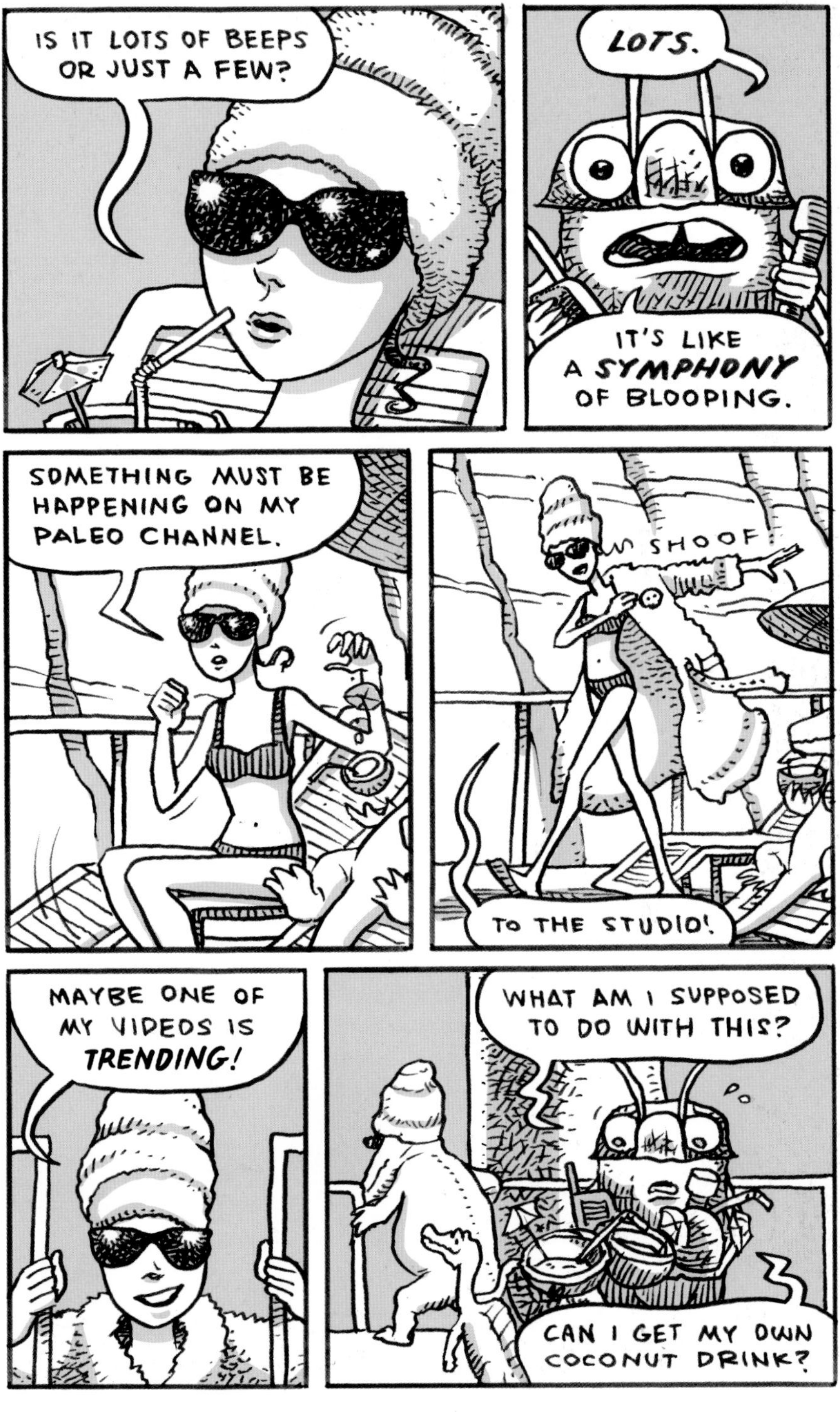
IS IT LOTS OF BEEPS OR JUST A FEW?
LOTS.
IT'S LIKE A SYMPHONY OF BLOOPING.
SOMETHING MUST BE HAPPENING ON MY PALEO CHANNEL.
SHOOF
TO THE STUDIO!
MAYBE ONE OF MY VIDEOS IS TRENDING!
WHAT AM I SUPPOSED TO DO WITH THIS?
CAN I GET MY OWN COCONUT DRINK?

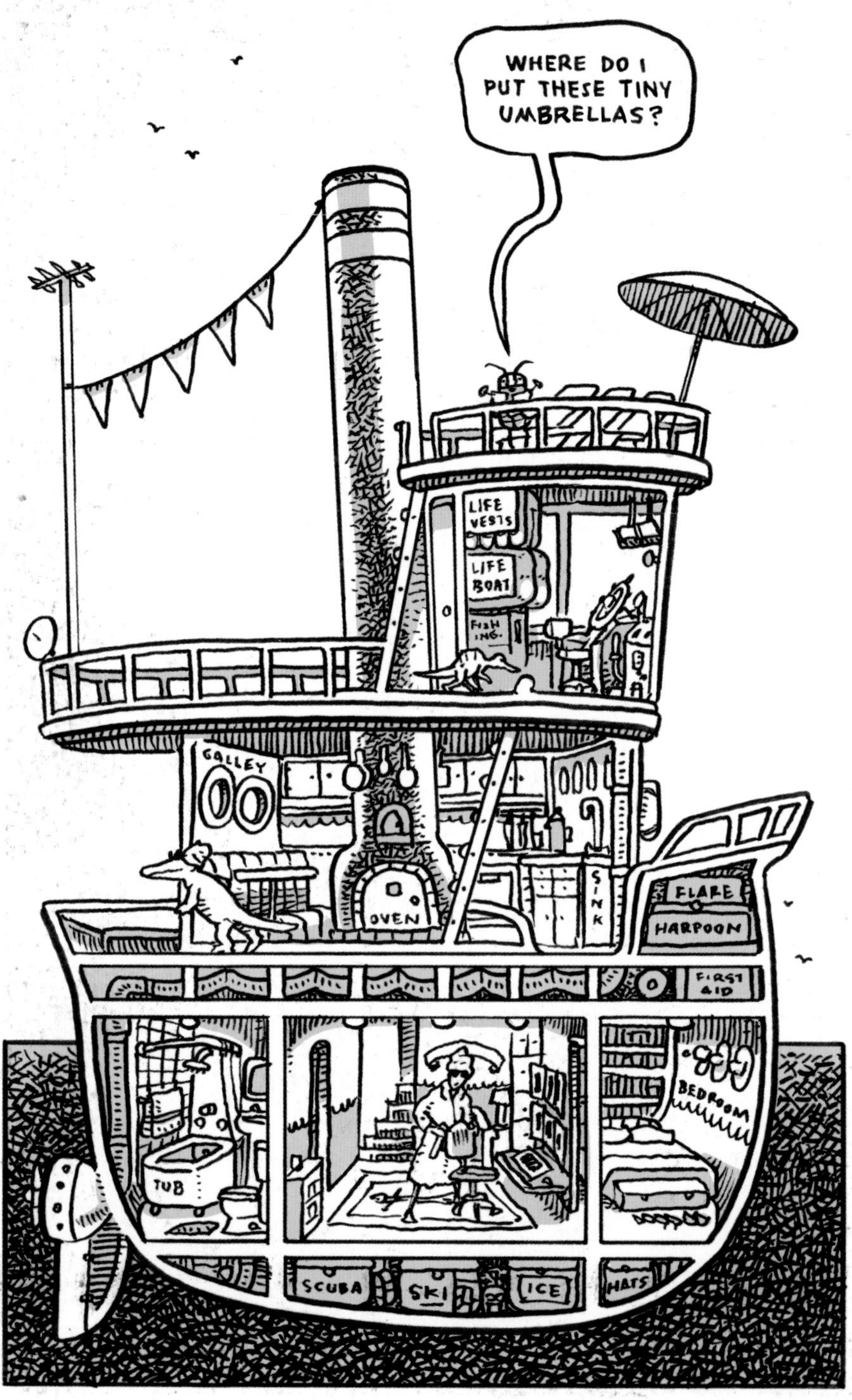
WHERE DO I PUT THESE TINY UMBRELLAS?
LIFE VESTS
LIFE BOAT
FISHING
GALLEY
OVEN
SINK
FLARE
HARPOON
FIRST AID
BEDROOM
TUB
SCUBA
SKI
ICE
HATS

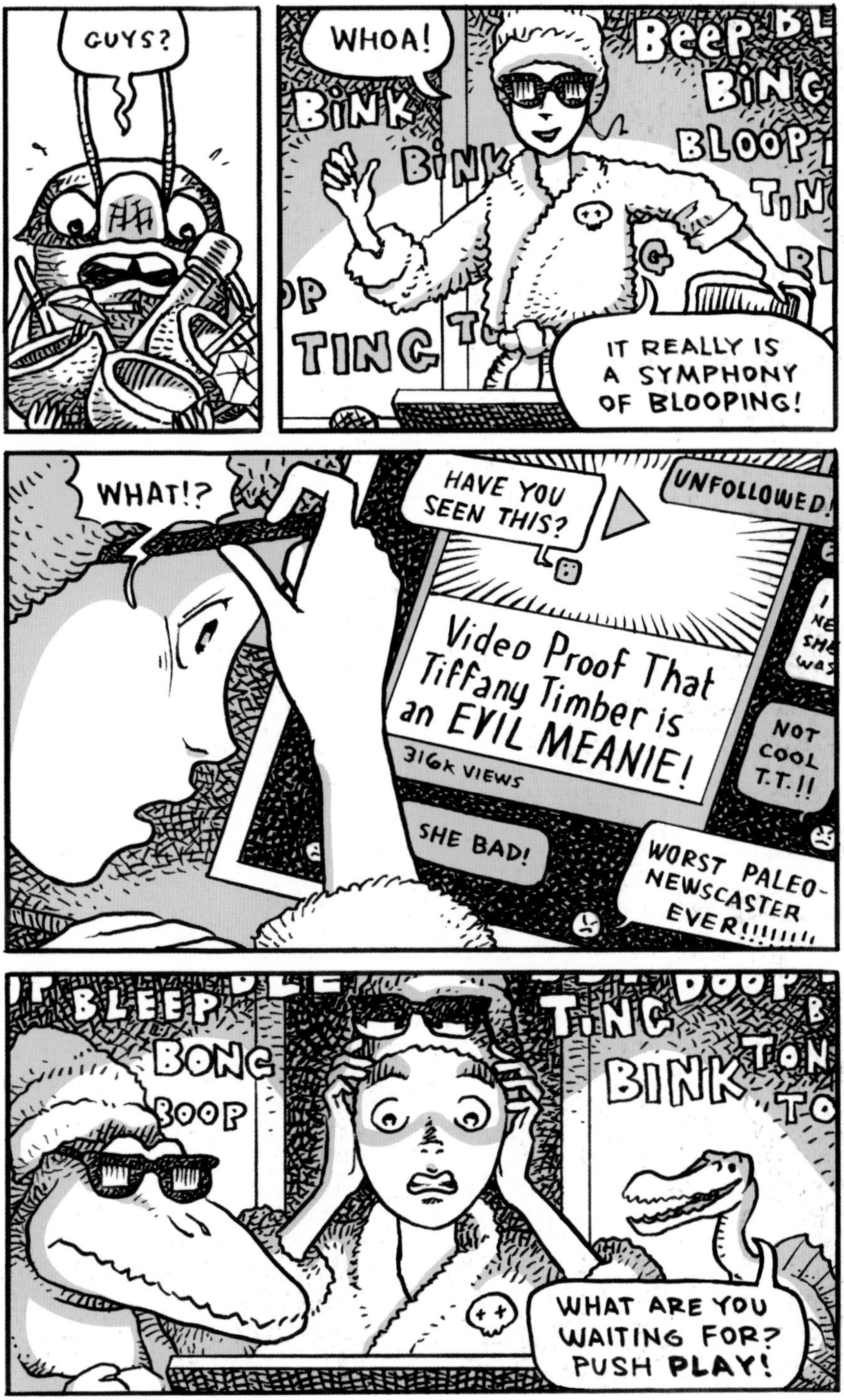
GUYS?
WHOA!
BINK
BINK
Beep
BING
BLOOP
TING
TING
IT REALLY IS A SYMPHONY OF BLOOPING!
WHAT!?
HAVE YOU SEEN THIS?
UNFOLLOWED!
Video Proof That Tiffany Timber is an EVIL MEANIE!
316K VIEWS
NOT COOL T.T.!!
SHE BAD!
WORST PALEO-NEWSCASTER EVER!!!!!!!
BLEEP
BONG
BOOP
TING
BINK
WHAT ARE YOU WAITING FOR? PUSH PLAY!

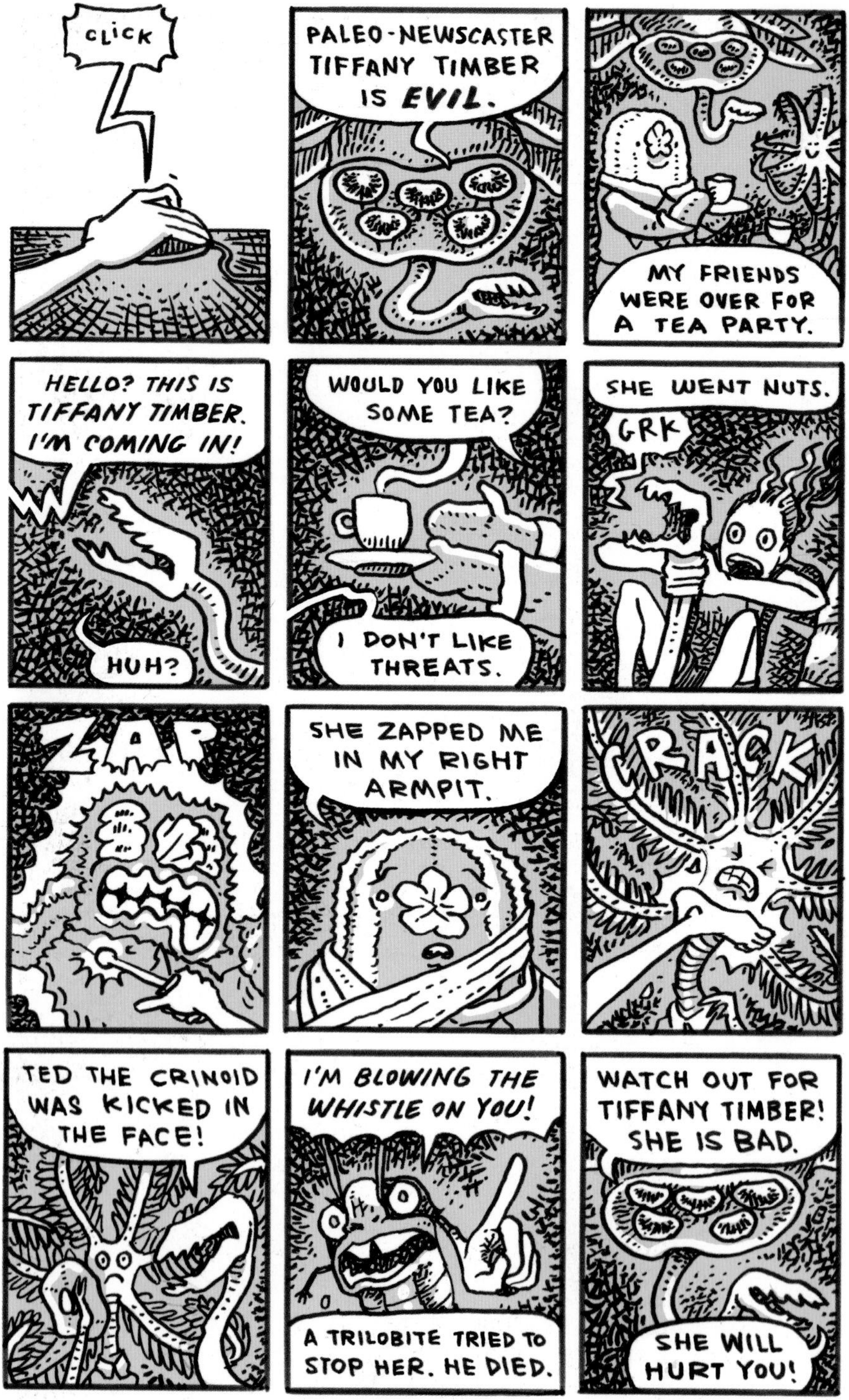
CLICK
PALEO-NEWSCASTER TIFFANY TIMBER IS EVIL.
MY FRIENDS WERE OVER FOR A TEA PARTY.
HELLO? THIS IS TIFFANY TIMBER. I'M COMING IN!
HUH?
WOULD YOU LIKE SOME TEA?
I DON'T LIKE THREATS.
SHE WENT NUTS.
GRK
ZAP
SHE ZAPPED ME IN MY RIGHT ARMPIT.
CRACK
TED THE CRINOID WAS KICKED IN THE FACE!
I'M BLOWING THE WHISTLE ON YOU!
A TRILOBITE TRIED TO STOP HER. HE DIED.
WATCH OUT FOR TIFFANY TIMBER! SHE IS BAD.
SHE WILL HURT YOU!

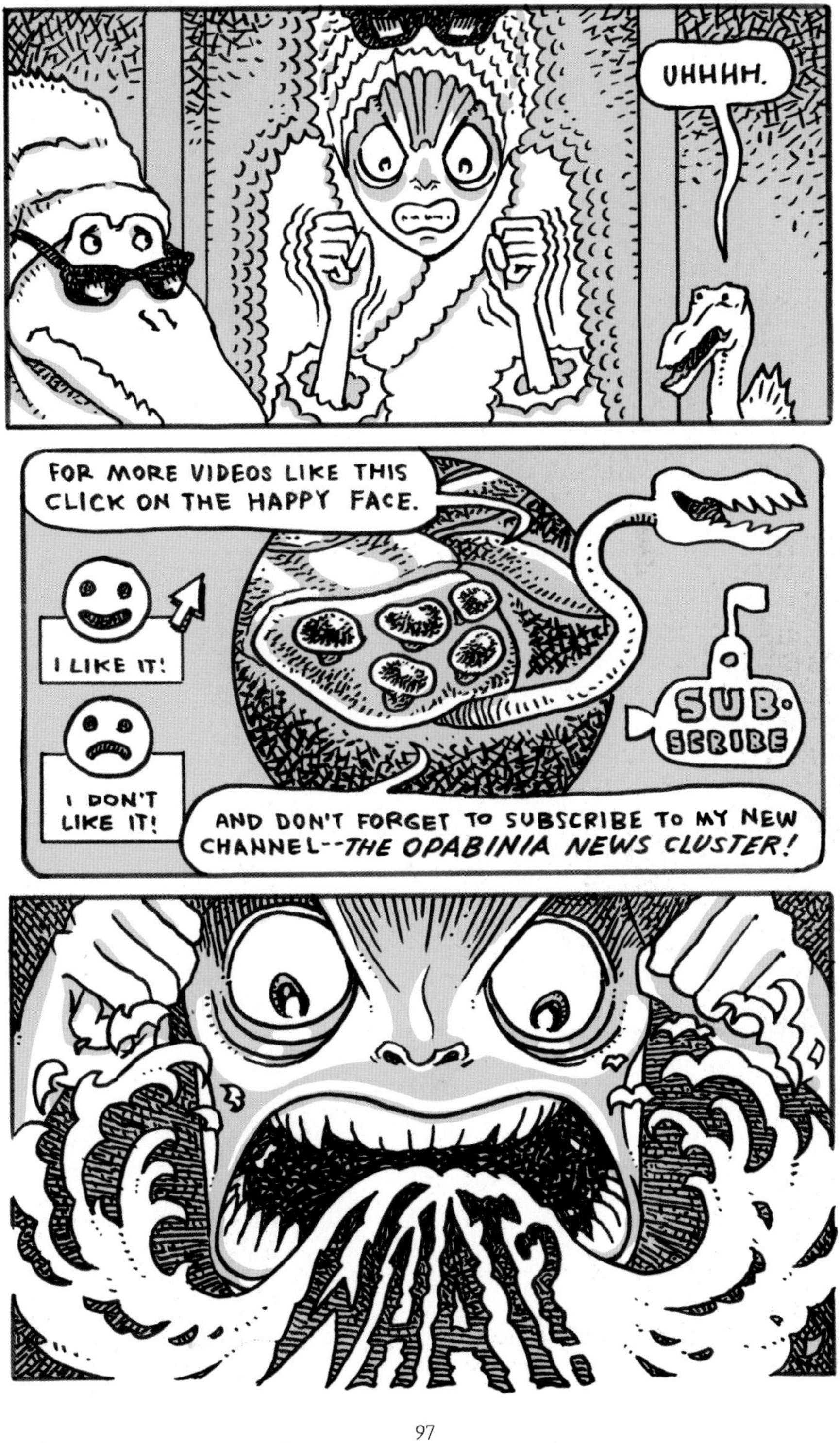
UHHHH.
FOR MORE VIDEOS LIKE THIS CLICK ON THE HAPPY FACE.
I LIKE IT!
I DON'T LIKE IT!
SUB-SCRIBE
AND DON'T FORGET TO SUBSCRIBE TO MY NEW CHANNEL--*THE OPABINIA NEWS CLUSTER!*
WHAT?!

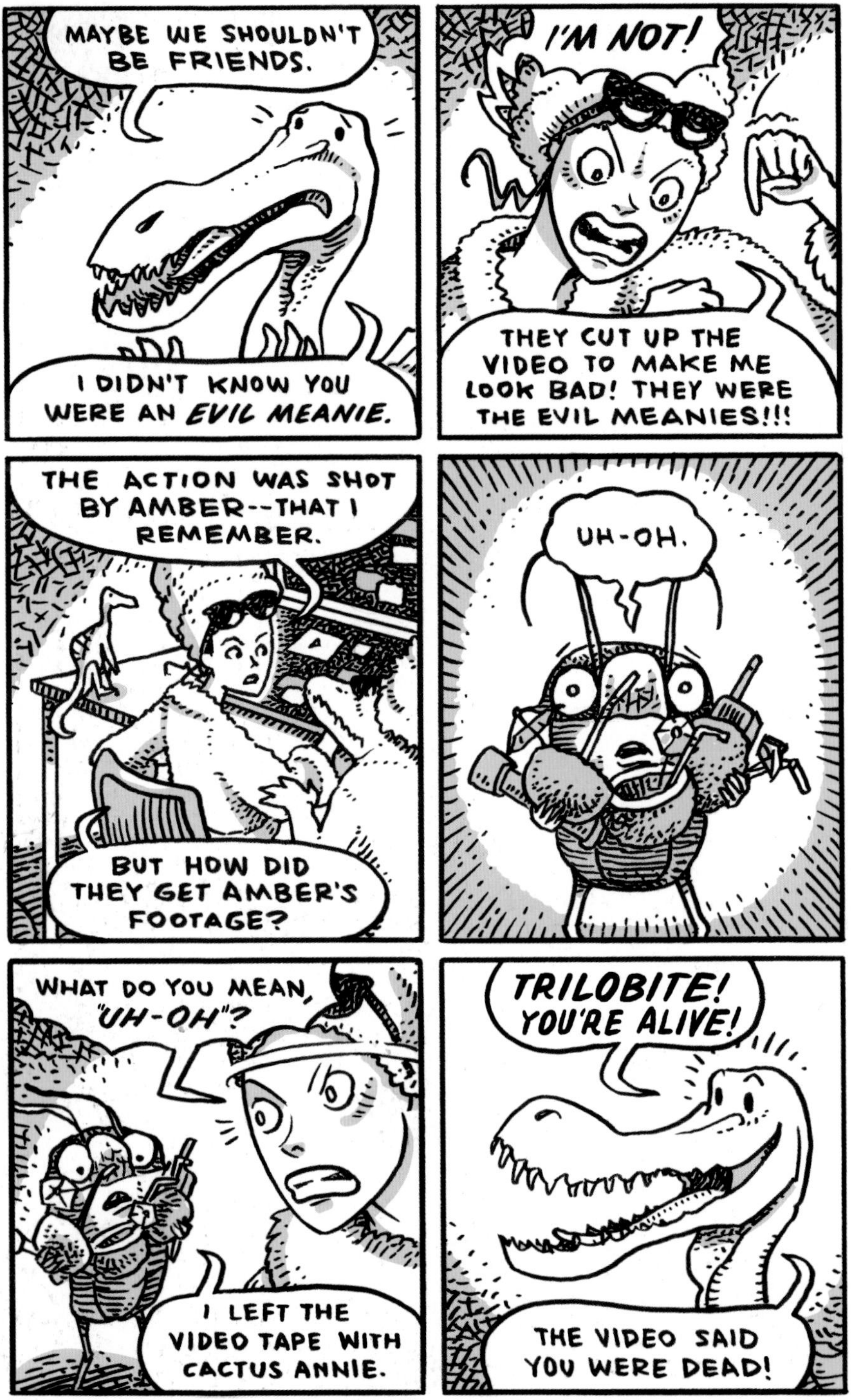
MAYBE WE SHOULDN'T BE FRIENDS.
I DIDN'T KNOW YOU WERE AN *EVIL MEANIE.*
I'M NOT!
THEY CUT UP THE VIDEO TO MAKE ME LOOK BAD! THEY WERE THE EVIL MEANIES!!!
THE ACTION WAS SHOT BY AMBER--THAT I REMEMBER.
BUT HOW DID THEY GET AMBER'S FOOTAGE?
UH-OH.
WHAT DO YOU MEAN, *"UH-OH"?*
I LEFT THE VIDEO TAPE WITH CACTUS ANNIE.
TRILOBITE! YOU'RE ALIVE!
THE VIDEO SAID YOU WERE DEAD!

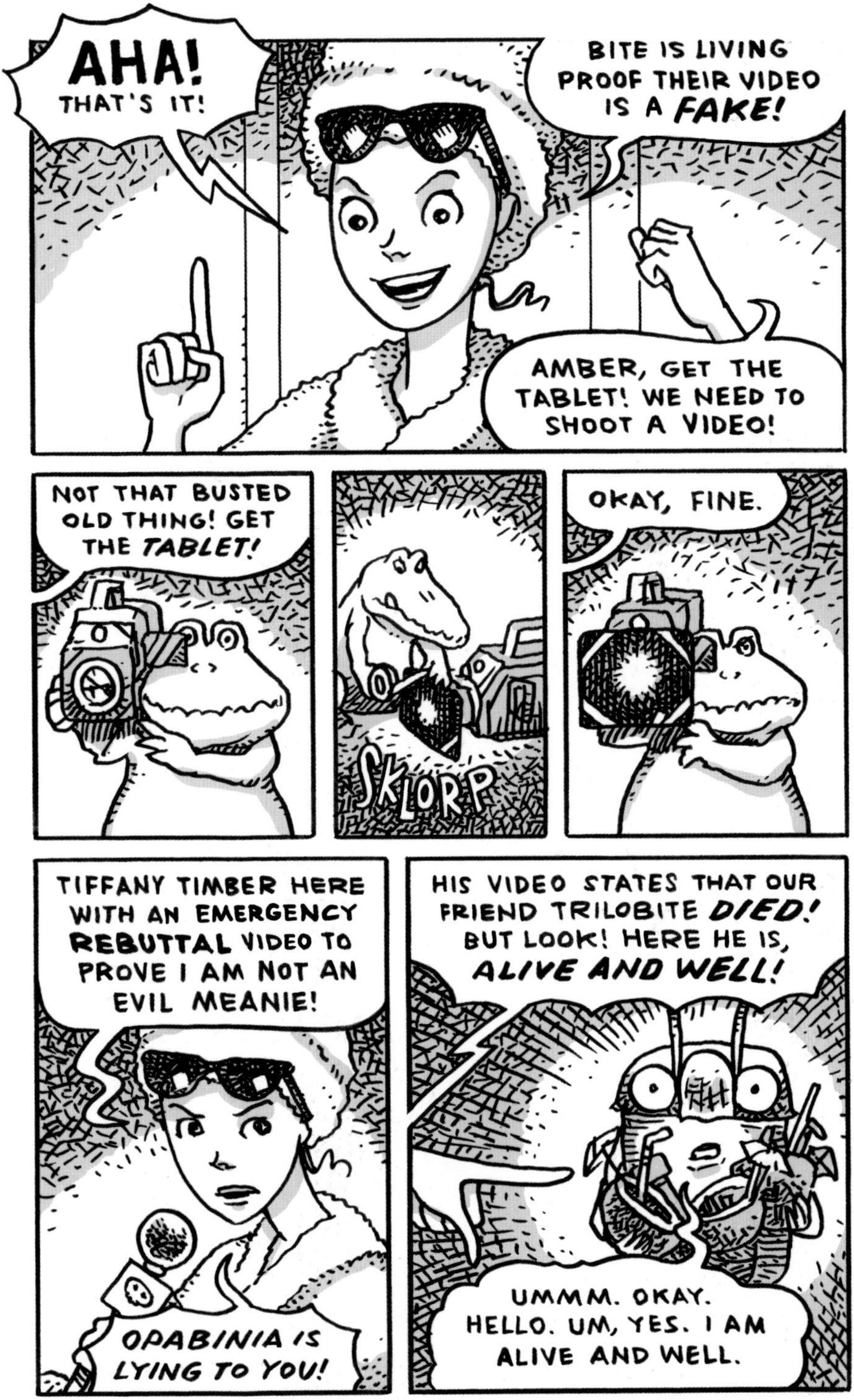
AHA! THAT'S IT!
BITE IS LIVING PROOF THEIR VIDEO IS A FAKE!
AMBER, GET THE TABLET! WE NEED TO SHOOT A VIDEO!
NOT THAT BUSTED OLD THING! GET THE TABLET!
SKLORP
OKAY, FINE.
TIFFANY TIMBER HERE WITH AN EMERGENCY REBUTTAL VIDEO TO PROVE I AM NOT AN EVIL MEANIE!
OPABINIA IS LYING TO YOU!
HIS VIDEO STATES THAT OUR FRIEND TRILOBITE DIED! BUT LOOK! HERE HE IS, ALIVE AND WELL!
UMMM. OKAY. HELLO. UM, YES. I AM ALIVE AND WELL.

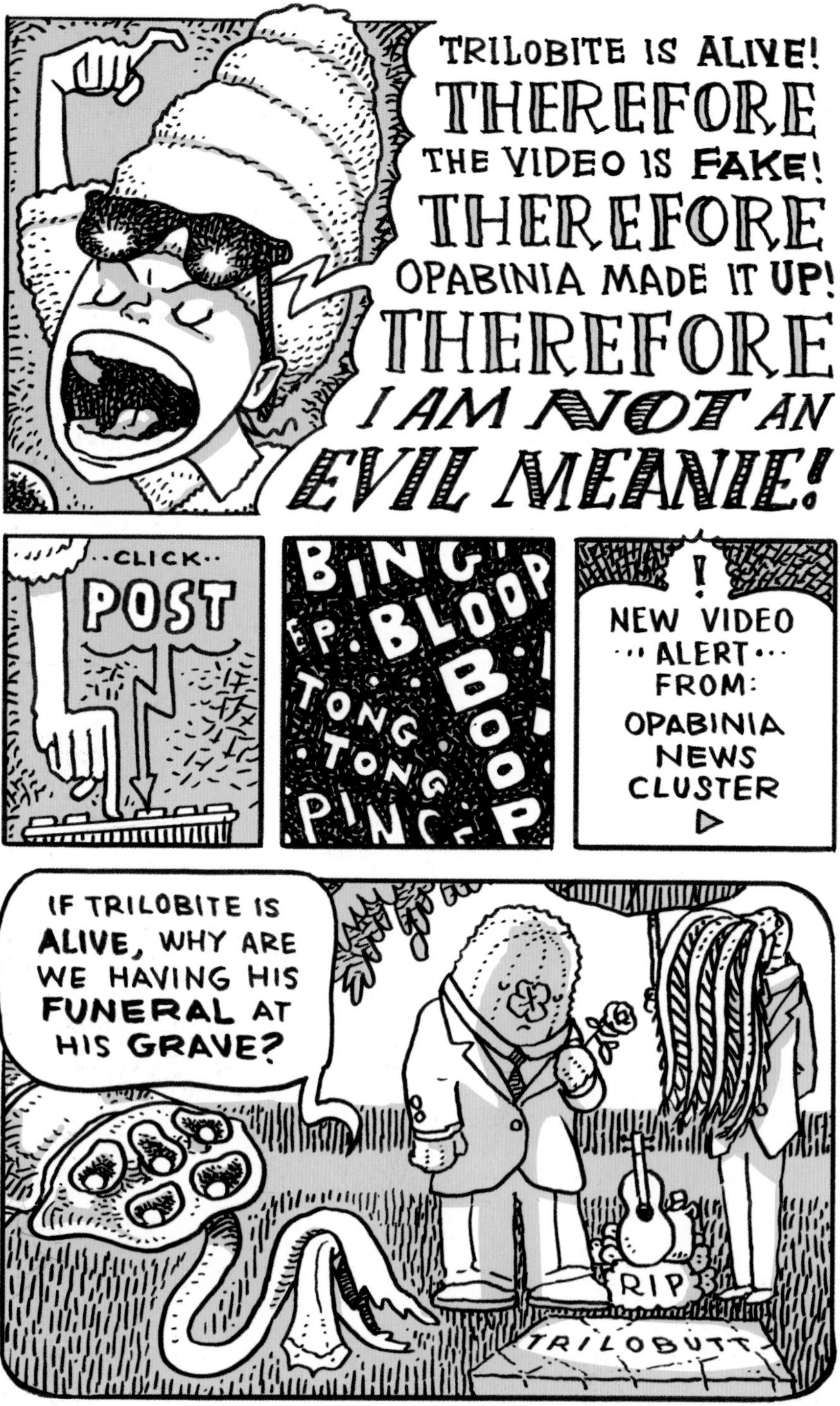
TRILOBITE IS ALIVE! THEREFORE THE VIDEO IS FAKE! THEREFORE OPABINIA MADE IT UP! THEREFORE I AM NOT AN EVIL MEANIE!
CLICK
POST
BING
BLOOP
B
TONG
TONG
BOOP
PING
!
NEW VIDEO ALERT FROM: OPABINIA NEWS CLUSTER
IF TRILOBITE IS ALIVE, WHY ARE WE HAVING HIS FUNERAL AT HIS GRAVE?
RIP
TRILOBUTT

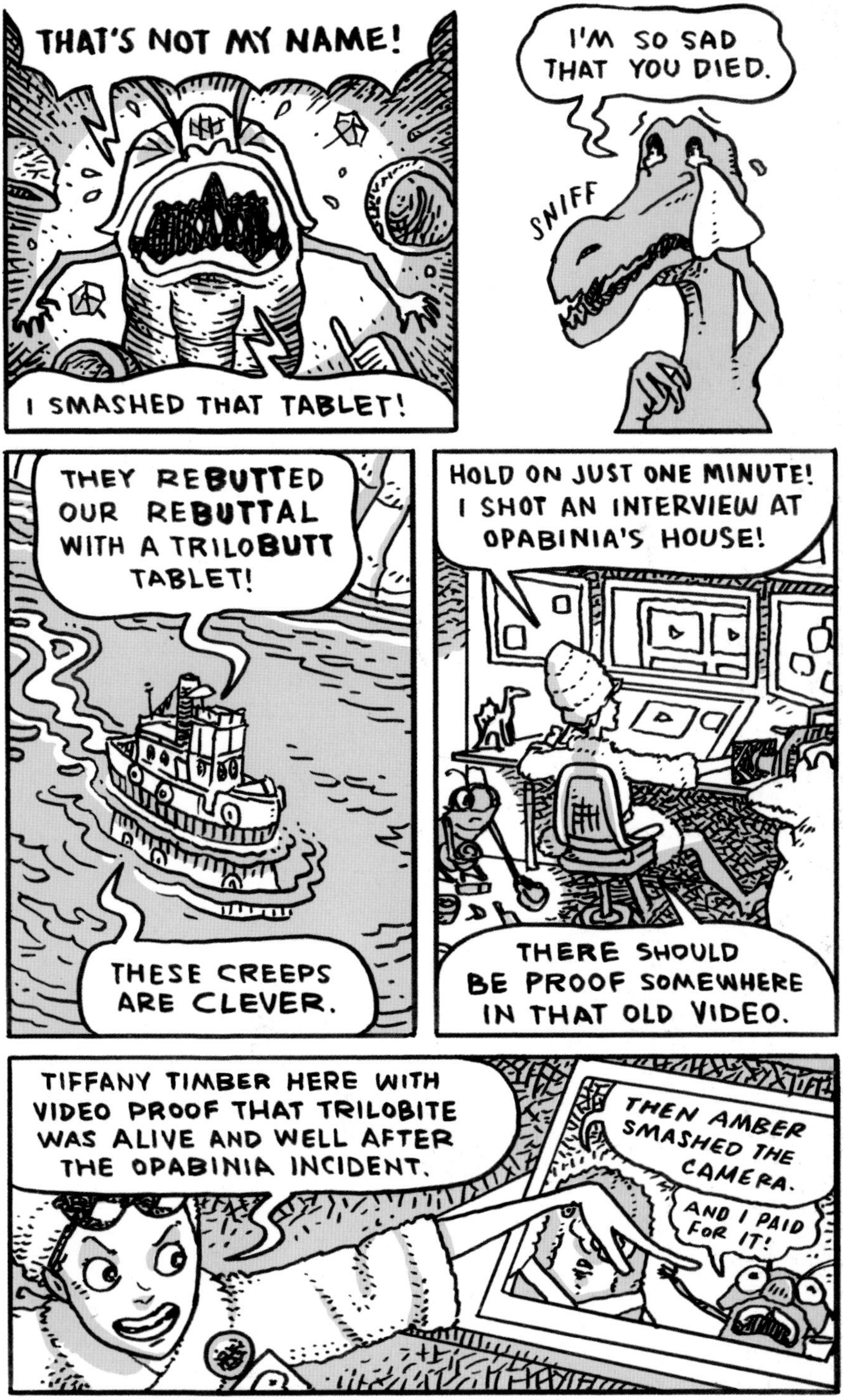
THAT'S NOT MY NAME!
I SMASHED THAT TABLET!
I'M SO SAD THAT YOU DIED.
SNIFF
THEY REBUTTED OUR REBUTTAL WITH A TRILOBUTT TABLET!
THESE CREEPS ARE CLEVER.
HOLD ON JUST ONE MINUTE! I SHOT AN INTERVIEW AT OPABINIA'S HOUSE!
THERE SHOULD BE PROOF SOMEWHERE IN THAT OLD VIDEO.
TIFFANY TIMBER HERE WITH VIDEO PROOF THAT TRILOBITE WAS ALIVE AND WELL AFTER THE OPABINIA INCIDENT.
THEN AMBER SMASHED THE CAMERA.
AND I PAID FOR IT!

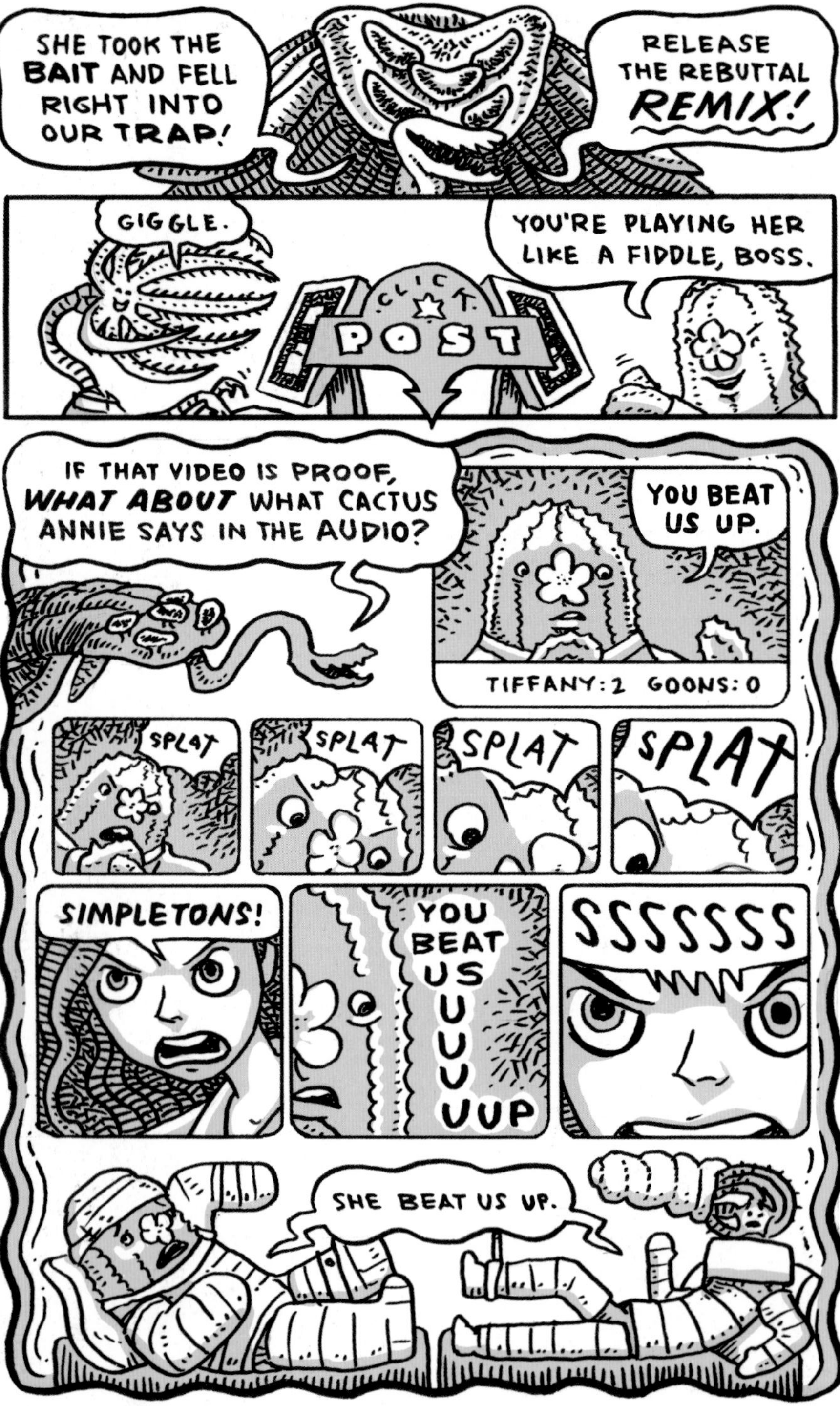
SHE TOOK THE BAIT AND FELL RIGHT INTO OUR TRAP!
RELEASE THE REBUTTAL REMIX!
GIGGLE.
YOU'RE PLAYING HER LIKE A FIDDLE, BOSS.
CLICK
POST
IF THAT VIDEO IS PROOF, WHAT ABOUT WHAT CACTUS ANNIE SAYS IN THE AUDIO?
YOU BEAT US UP.
TIFFANY: 2 GOONS: 0
SPLAT
SPLAT
SPLAT
SPLAT
SIMPLETONS!
YOU BEAT US UUUUUP
SSSSSSS
SHE BEAT US UP.

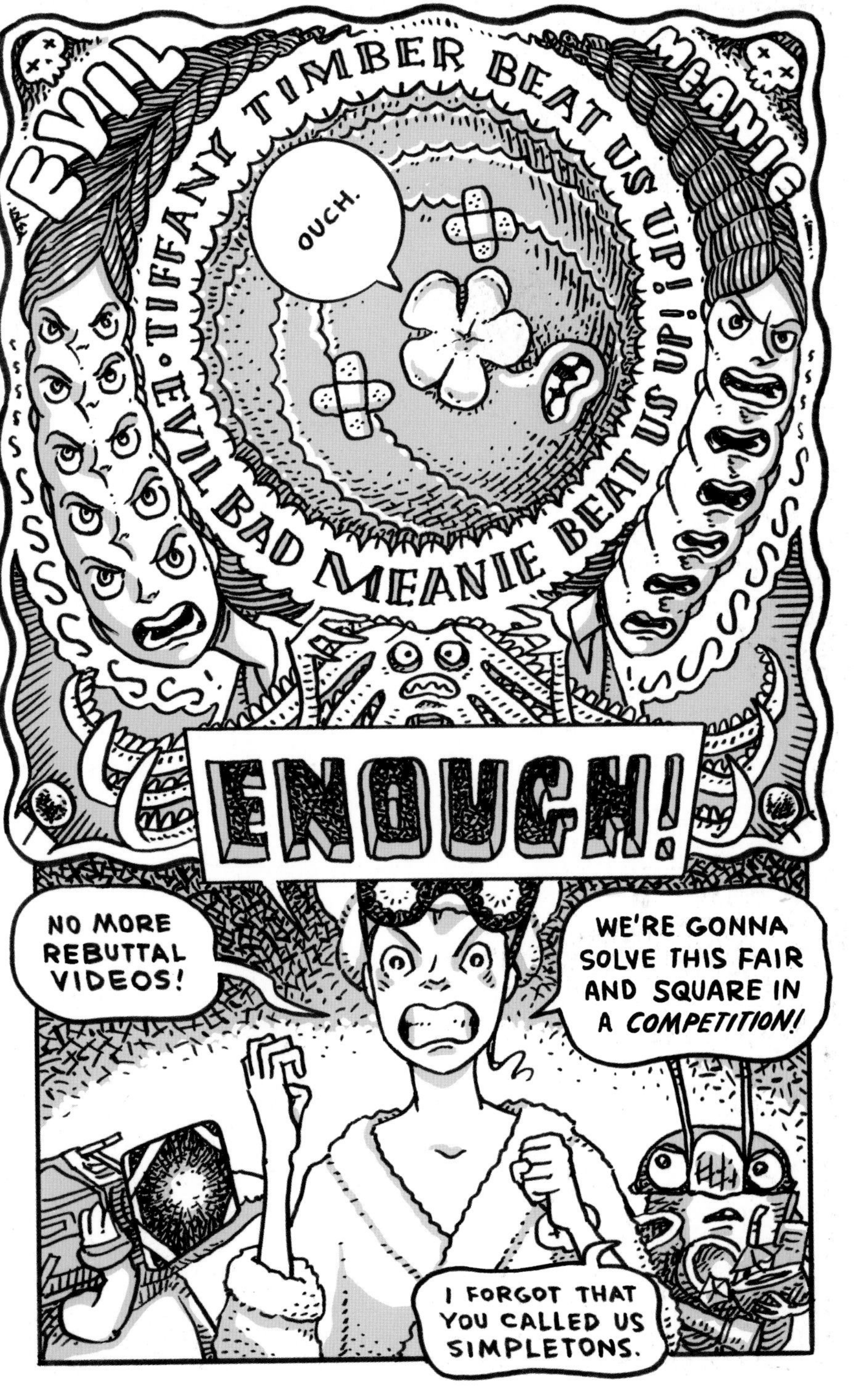
EVIL MEANIE
TIFFANY TIMBER BEAT US UP! • EVIL BAD MEANIE BEAT US UP!
OUCH.
ENOUGH!
NO MORE REBUTTAL VIDEOS!
WE'RE GONNA SOLVE THIS FAIR AND SQUARE IN A *COMPETITION!*
I FORGOT THAT YOU CALLED US SIMPLETONS.

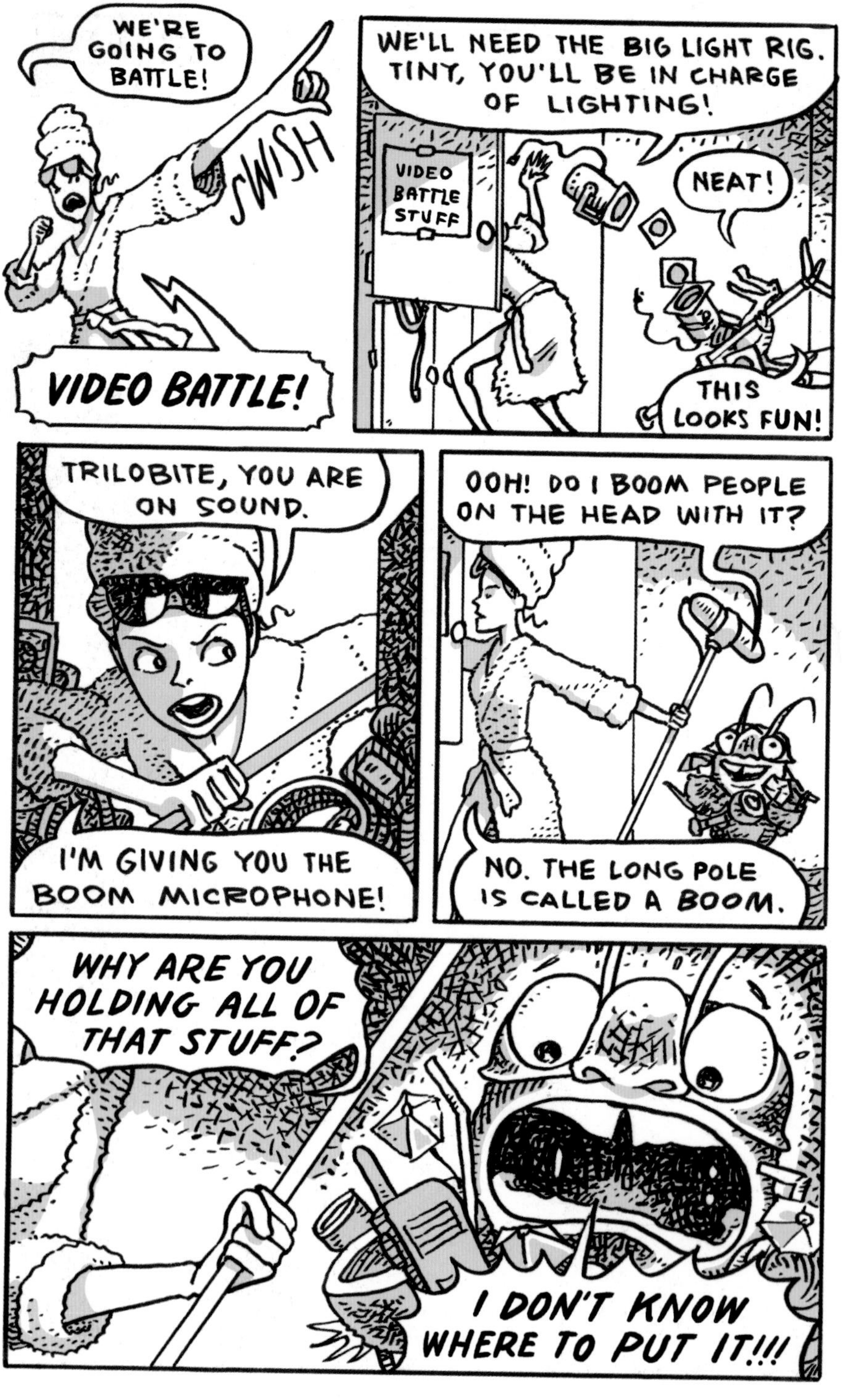
WE'RE GOING TO BATTLE!
SWISH
VIDEO BATTLE!
WE'LL NEED THE BIG LIGHT RIG. TINY, YOU'LL BE IN CHARGE OF LIGHTING!
VIDEO BATTLE STUFF
NEAT!
THIS LOOKS FUN!
TRILOBITE, YOU ARE ON SOUND.
I'M GIVING YOU THE BOOM MICROPHONE!
OOH! DO I BOOM PEOPLE ON THE HEAD WITH IT?
NO. THE LONG POLE IS CALLED A BOOM.
WHY ARE YOU HOLDING ALL OF THAT STUFF?
I DON'T KNOW WHERE TO PUT IT!!!

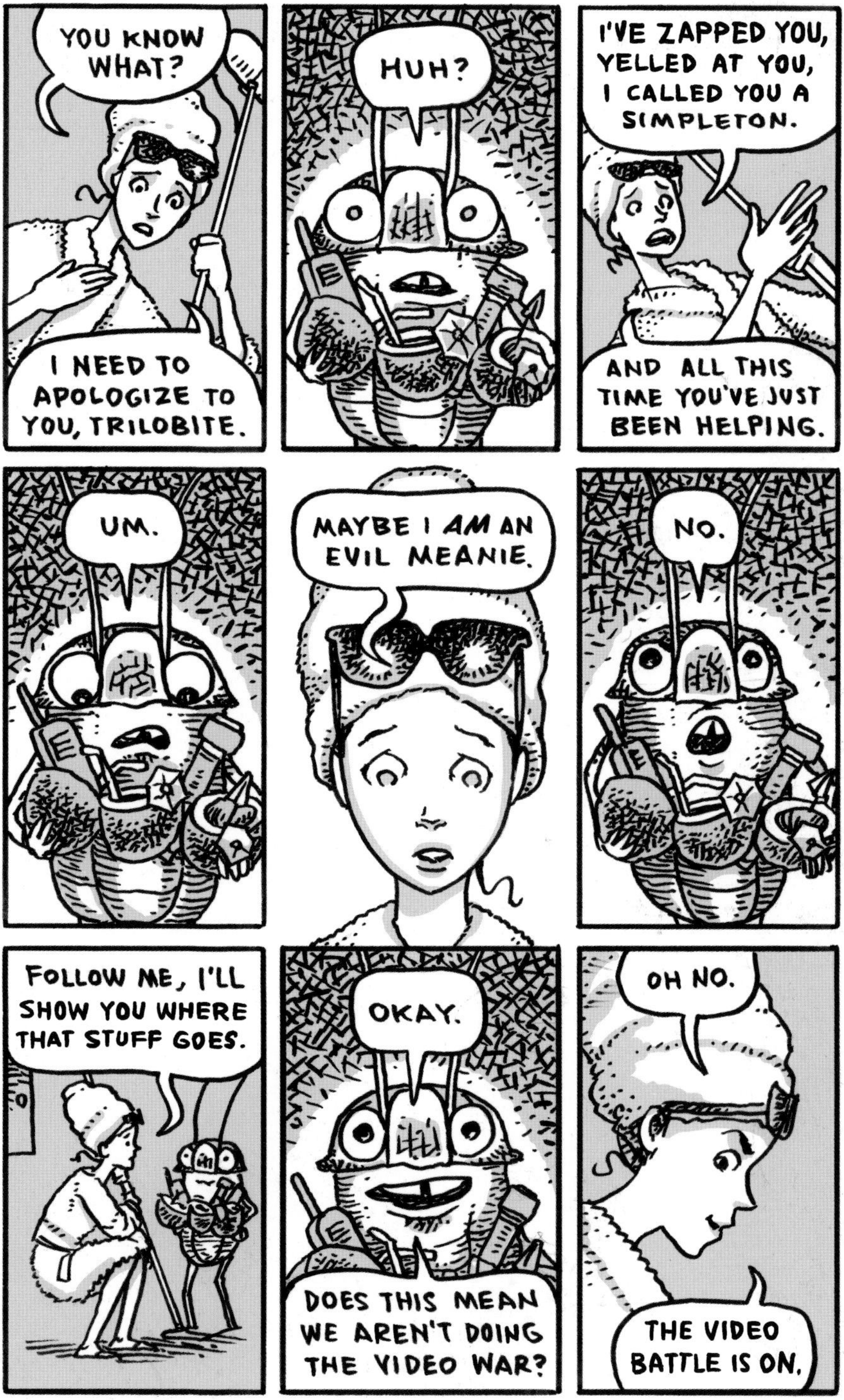
YOU KNOW WHAT?
I NEED TO APOLOGIZE TO YOU, TRILOBITE.
HUH?
I'VE ZAPPED YOU, YELLED AT YOU, I CALLED YOU A SIMPLETON.
AND ALL THIS TIME YOU'VE JUST BEEN HELPING.
UM.
MAYBE I *AM* AN EVIL MEANIE.
NO.
FOLLOW ME, I'LL SHOW YOU WHERE THAT STUFF GOES.
OKAY.
DOES THIS MEAN WE AREN'T DOING THE VIDEO WAR?
OH NO.
THE VIDEO BATTLE IS ON.

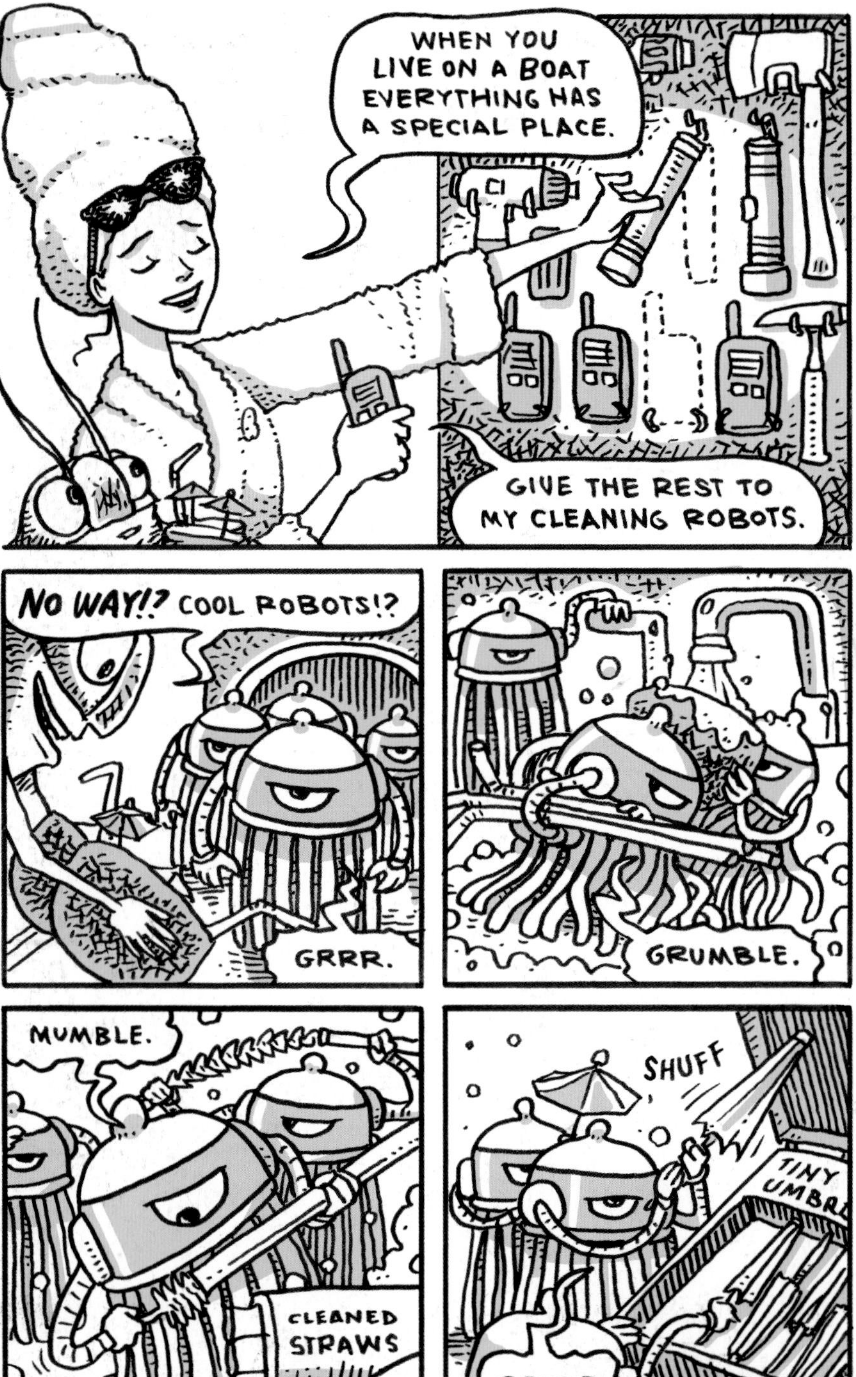
WHEN YOU LIVE ON A BOAT EVERYTHING HAS A SPECIAL PLACE.
GIVE THE REST TO MY CLEANING ROBOTS.
NO WAY!? COOL ROBOTS!?
GRRR.
GRUMBLE.
MUMBLE.
CLEANED STRAWS
SHUFF
TINY UMBR
GRUNT.

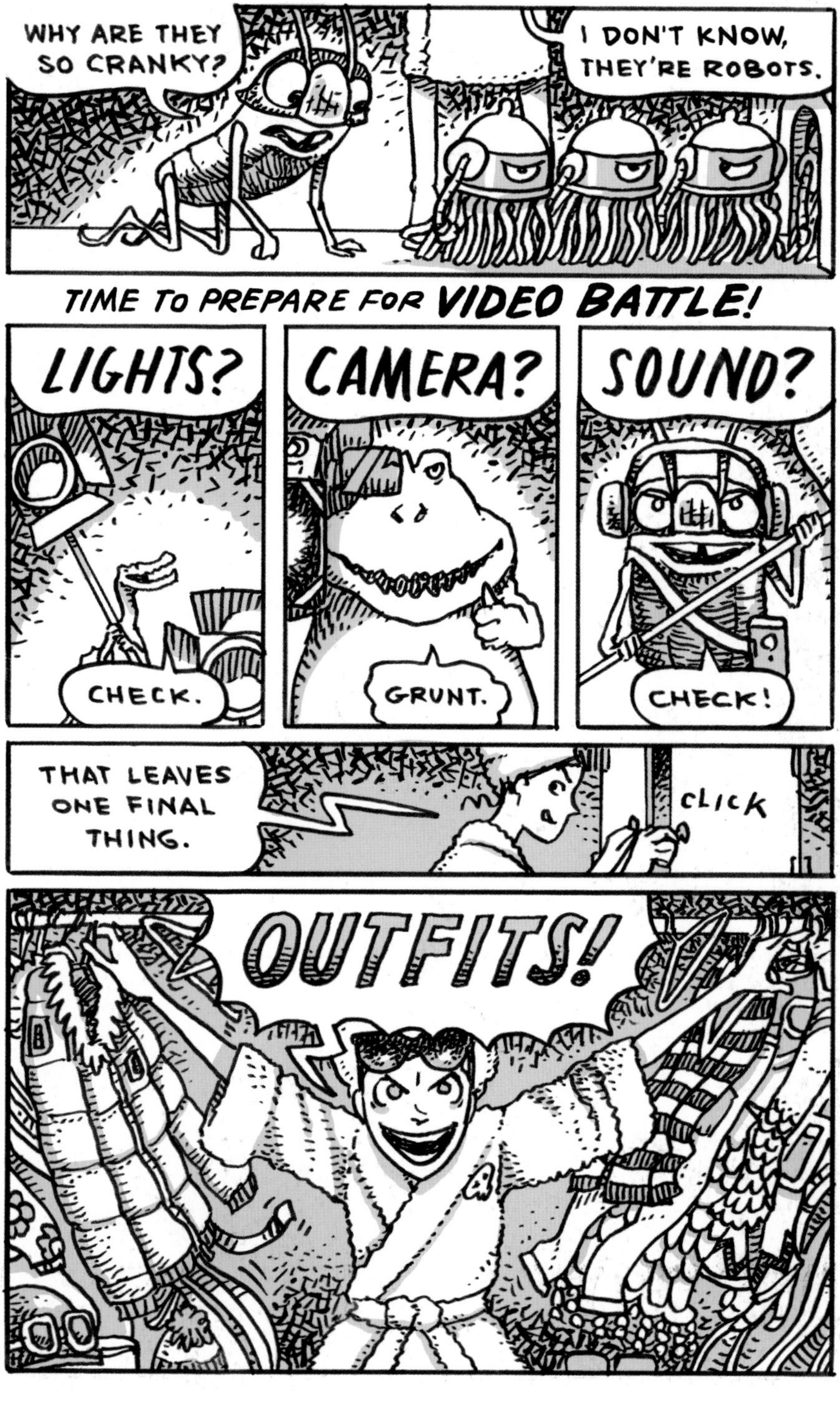
WHY ARE THEY SO CRANKY?
I DON'T KNOW, THEY'RE ROBOTS.
TIME TO PREPARE FOR VIDEO BATTLE!
LIGHTS?
CHECK.
CAMERA?
GRUNT.
SOUND?
CHECK!
THAT LEAVES ONE FINAL THING.
CLICK
OUTFITS!

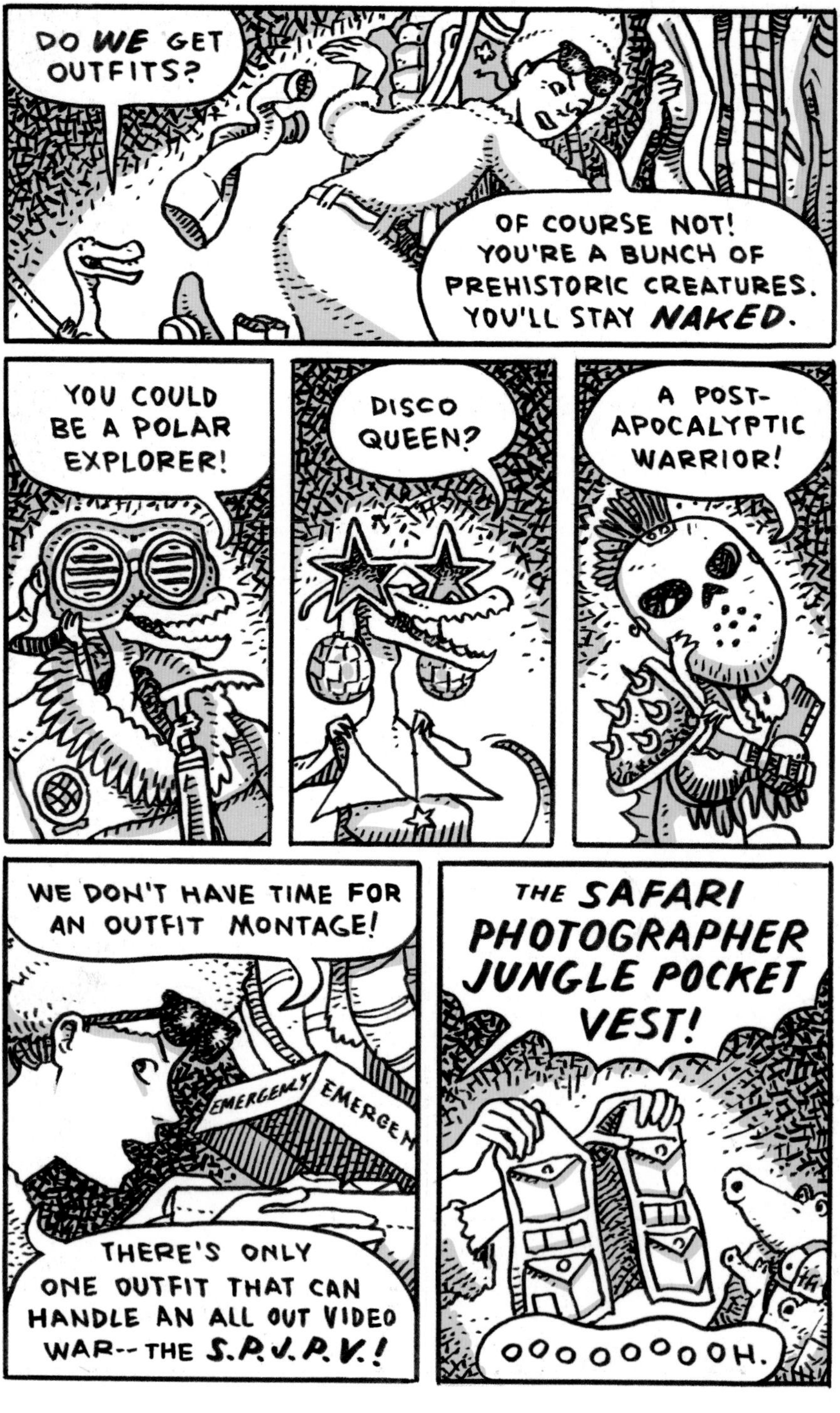
DO WE GET OUTFITS?
OF COURSE NOT! YOU'RE A BUNCH OF PREHISTORIC CREATURES. YOU'LL STAY NAKED.
YOU COULD BE A POLAR EXPLORER!
DISCO QUEEN?
A POST-APOCALYPTIC WARRIOR!
WE DON'T HAVE TIME FOR AN OUTFIT MONTAGE!
EMERGENCY
EMERGEN
THERE'S ONLY ONE OUTFIT THAT CAN HANDLE AN ALL OUT VIDEO WAR-- THE S.P.J.P.V.!
THE SAFARI PHOTOGRAPHER JUNGLE POCKET VEST!
OOOOOOOOOH.

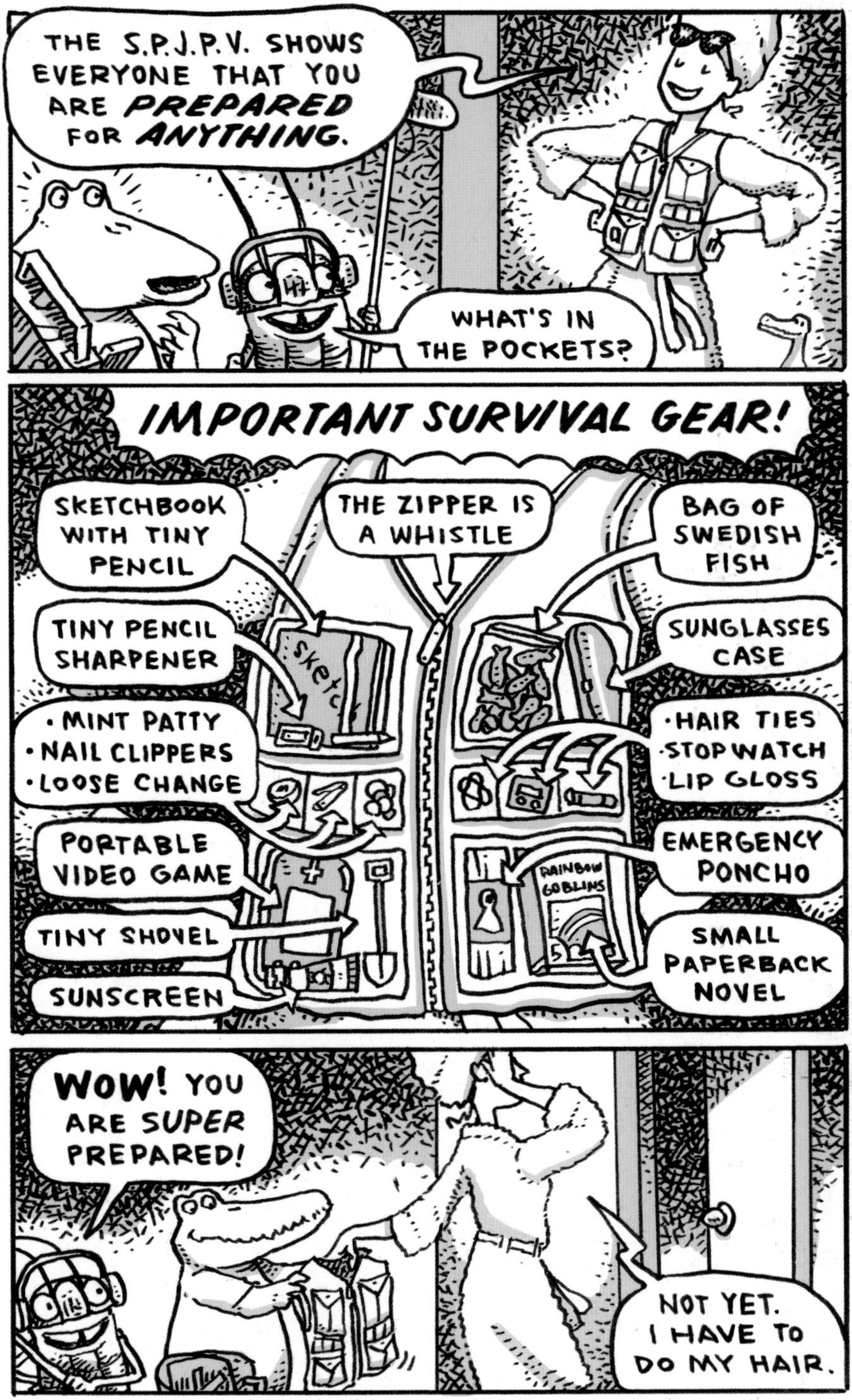
THE S.P.J.P.V. SHOWS EVERYONE THAT YOU ARE *PREPARED* FOR *ANYTHING*.
WHAT'S IN THE POCKETS?
IMPORTANT SURVIVAL GEAR!
SKETCHBOOK WITH TINY PENCIL
THE ZIPPER IS A WHISTLE
BAG OF SWEDISH FISH
TINY PENCIL SHARPENER
SKETCH
SUNGLASSES CASE
• MINT PATTY
• NAIL CLIPPERS
• LOOSE CHANGE
• HAIR TIES
• STOP WATCH
• LIP GLOSS
PORTABLE VIDEO GAME
EMERGENCY PONCHO
RAINBOW GOBLINS
TINY SHOVEL
SMALL PAPERBACK NOVEL
SUNSCREEN
WOW! YOU ARE SUPER PREPARED!
NOT YET. I HAVE TO DO MY HAIR.

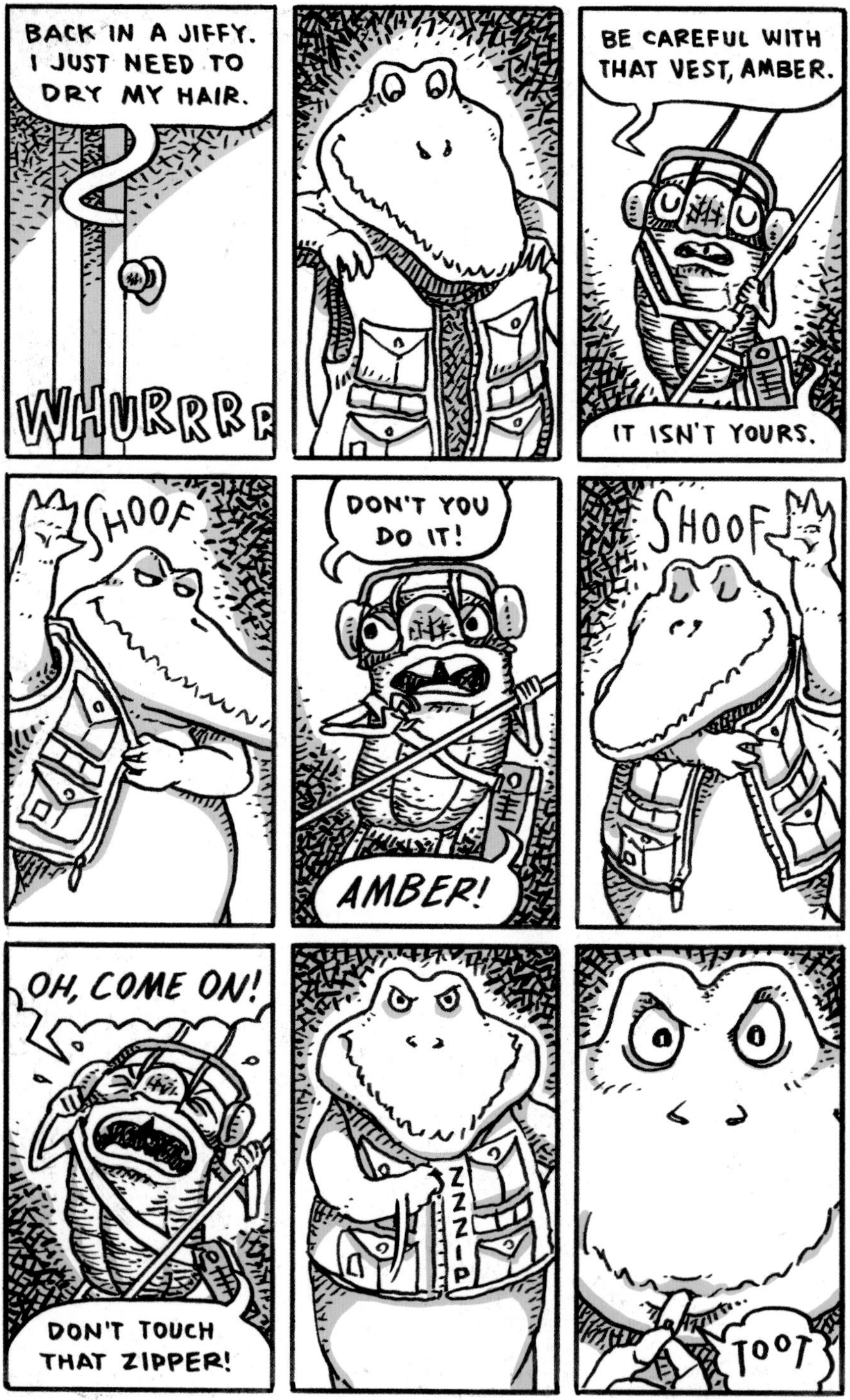
BACK IN A JIFFY. I JUST NEED TO DRY MY HAIR.
WHURRRR
BE CAREFUL WITH THAT VEST, AMBER.
IT ISN'T YOURS.
SHOOF
DON'T YOU DO IT!
AMBER!
SHOOF
OH, COME ON!
DON'T TOUCH THAT ZIPPER!
ZZZIP
TOOT

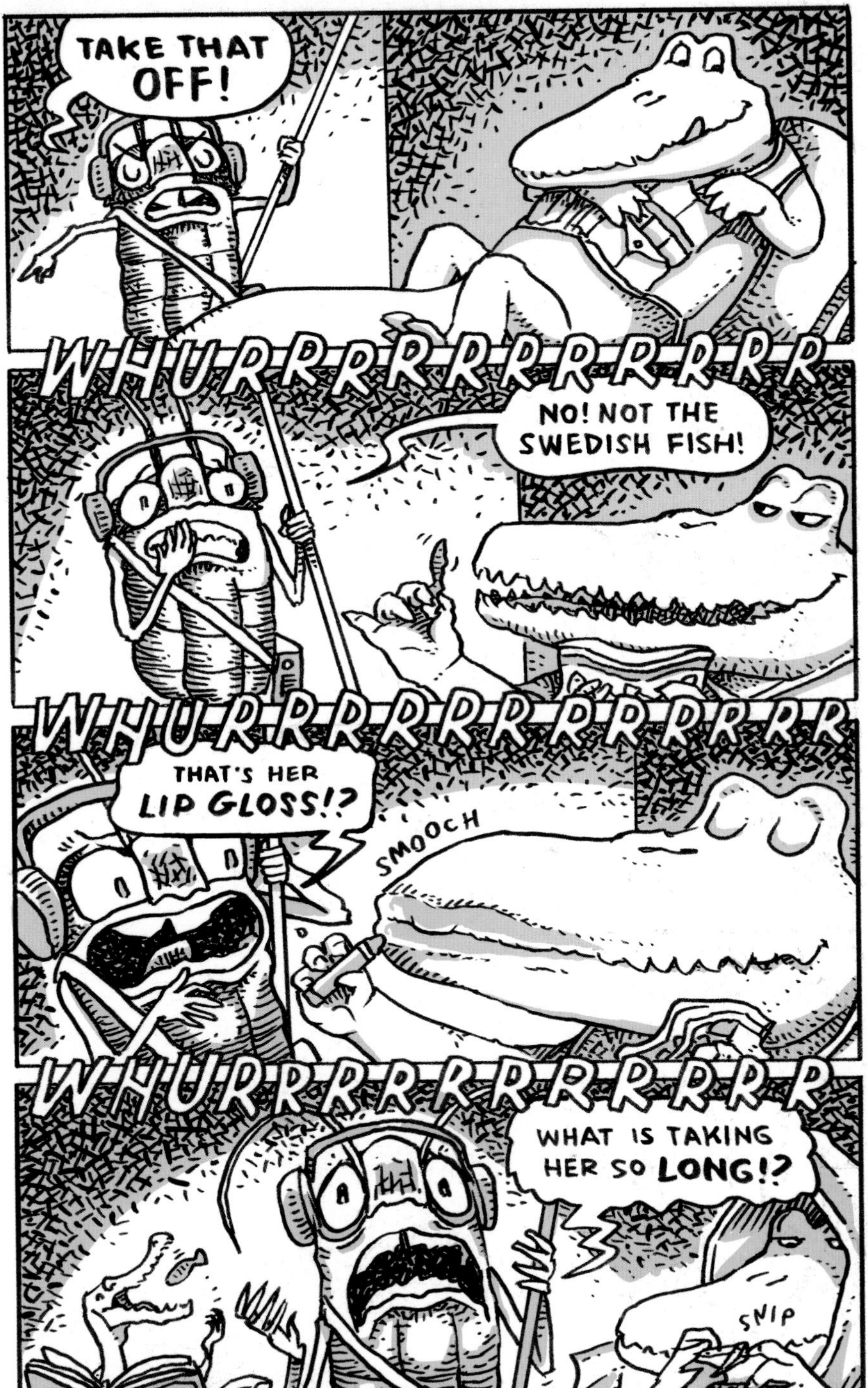
TAKE THAT OFF!
WHURRRRRRRRRRR
NO! NOT THE SWEDISH FISH!
WHURRRRRRRRRRRRR
THAT'S HER LIP GLOSS!?
SMOOCH
WHURRRRRRRRRRR
WHAT IS TAKING HER SO LONG!?
SNIP

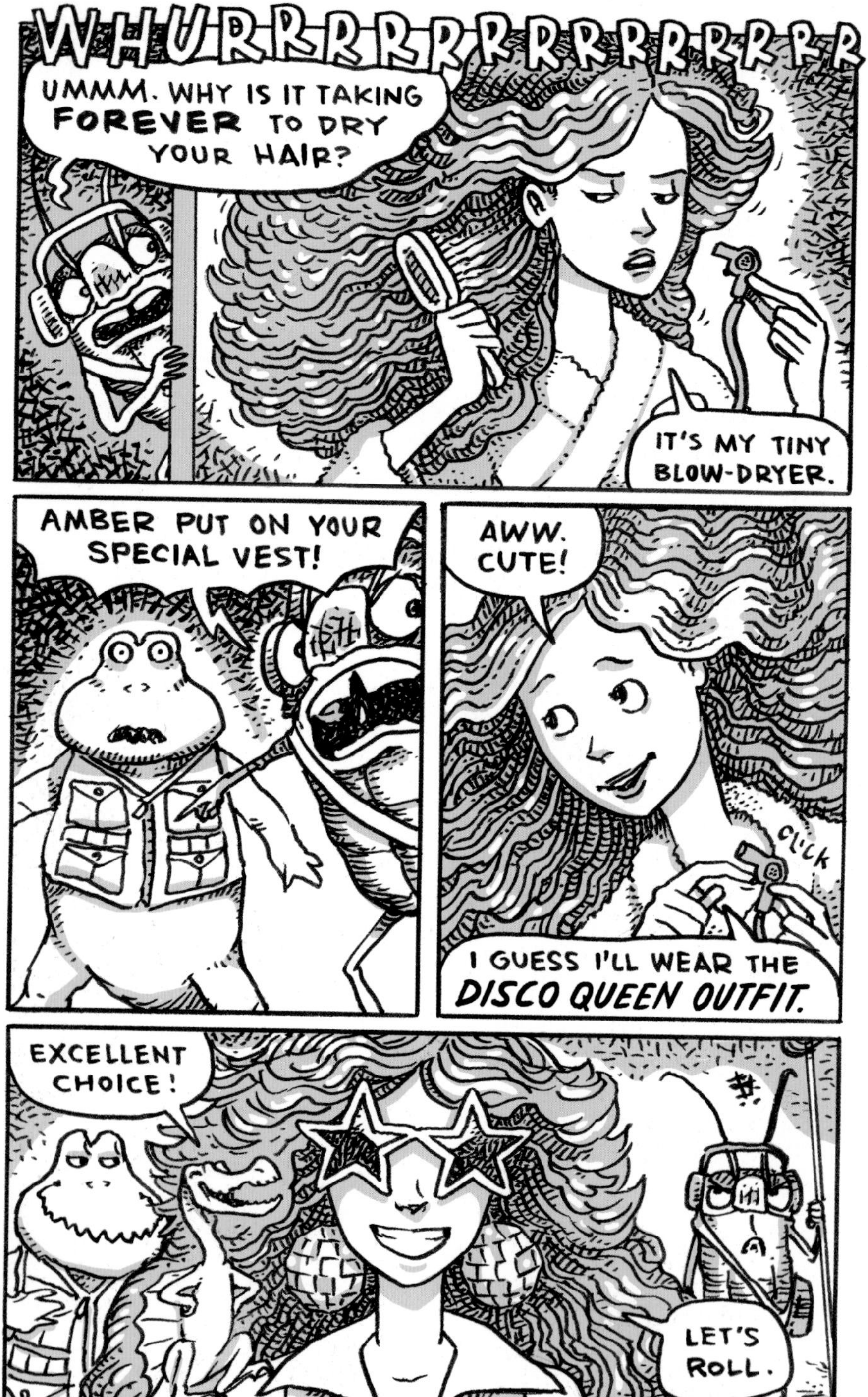
WHURRRRRRRRRRRRR
UMMM. WHY IS IT TAKING FOREVER TO DRY YOUR HAIR?
IT'S MY TINY BLOW-DRYER.
AMBER PUT ON YOUR SPECIAL VEST!
AWW. CUTE!
CLICK
I GUESS I'LL WEAR THE DISCO QUEEN OUTFIT.
EXCELLENT CHOICE!
LET'S ROLL.

CHAPTER 5

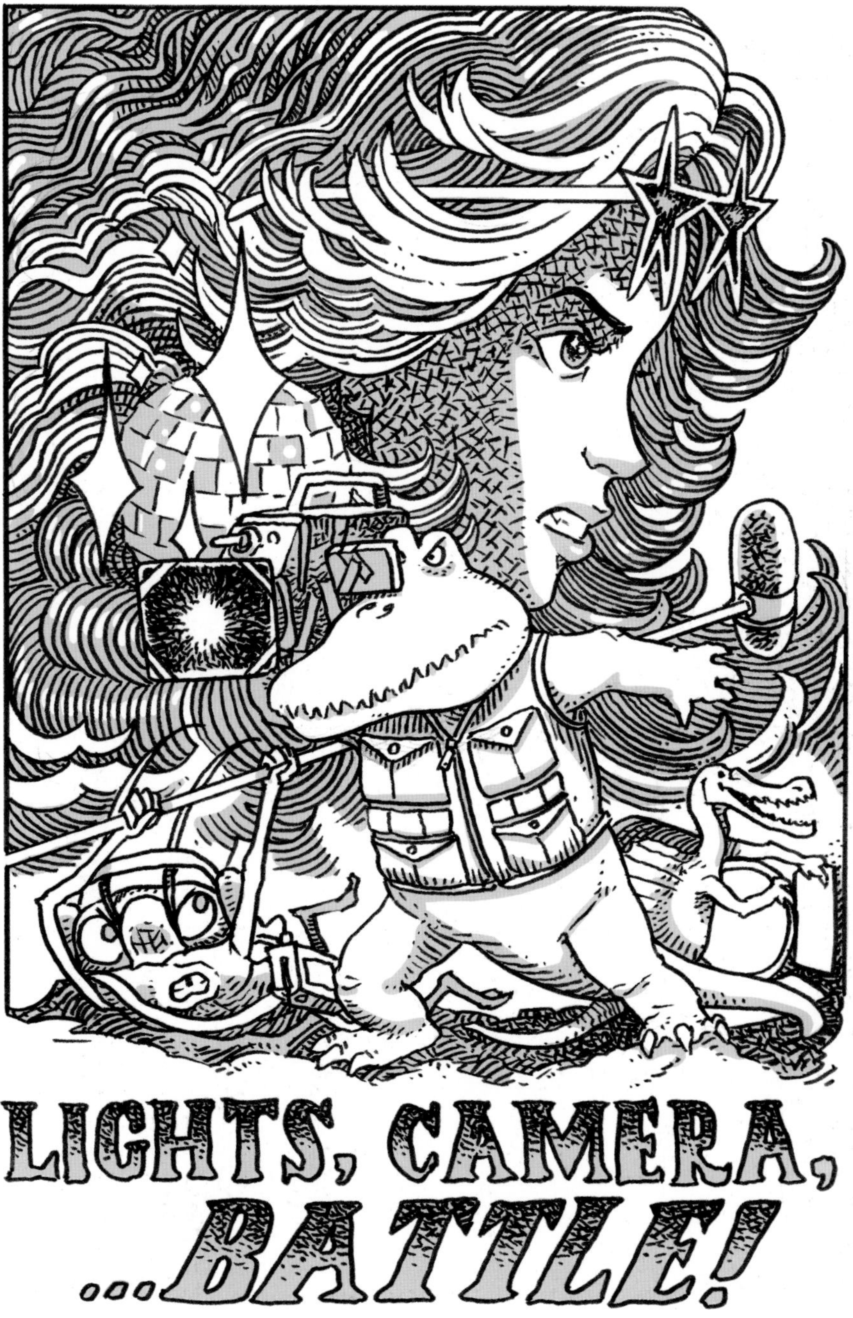

LIGHTS, CAMERA, ...BATTLE!

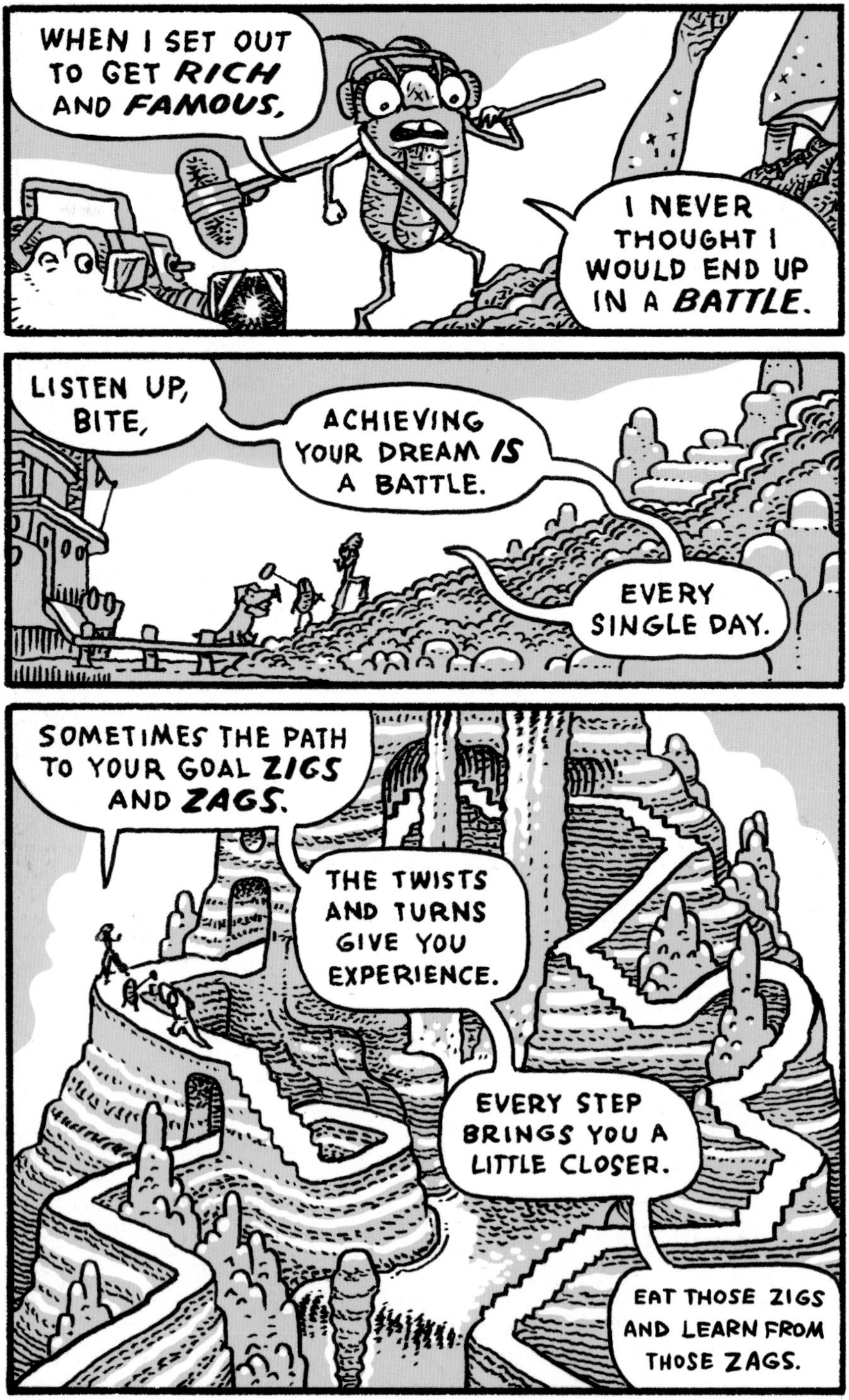
WHEN I SET OUT TO GET RICH AND FAMOUS,
I NEVER THOUGHT I WOULD END UP IN A BATTLE.
LISTEN UP, BITE,
ACHIEVING YOUR DREAM IS A BATTLE.
EVERY SINGLE DAY.
SOMETIMES THE PATH TO YOUR GOAL ZIGS AND ZAGS.
THE TWISTS AND TURNS GIVE YOU EXPERIENCE.
EVERY STEP BRINGS YOU A LITTLE CLOSER.
EAT THOSE ZIGS AND LEARN FROM THOSE ZAGS.

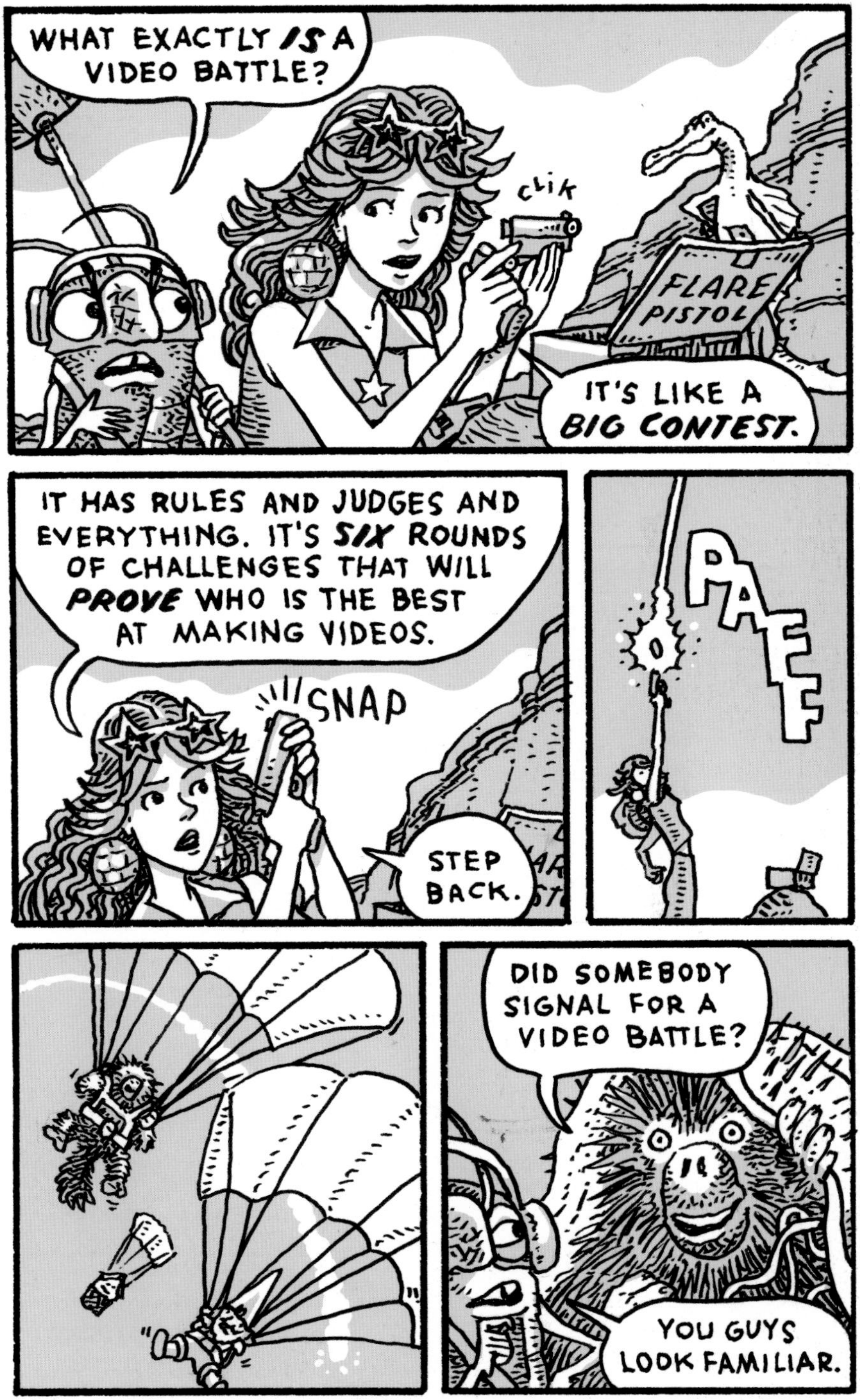
WHAT EXACTLY IS A VIDEO BATTLE?
CLIK
FLARE PISTOL
IT'S LIKE A BIG CONTEST.
IT HAS RULES AND JUDGES AND EVERYTHING. IT'S SIX ROUNDS OF CHALLENGES THAT WILL PROVE WHO IS THE BEST AT MAKING VIDEOS.
SNAP
STEP BACK.
PAFF
DID SOMEBODY SIGNAL FOR A VIDEO BATTLE?
YOU GUYS LOOK FAMILIAR.

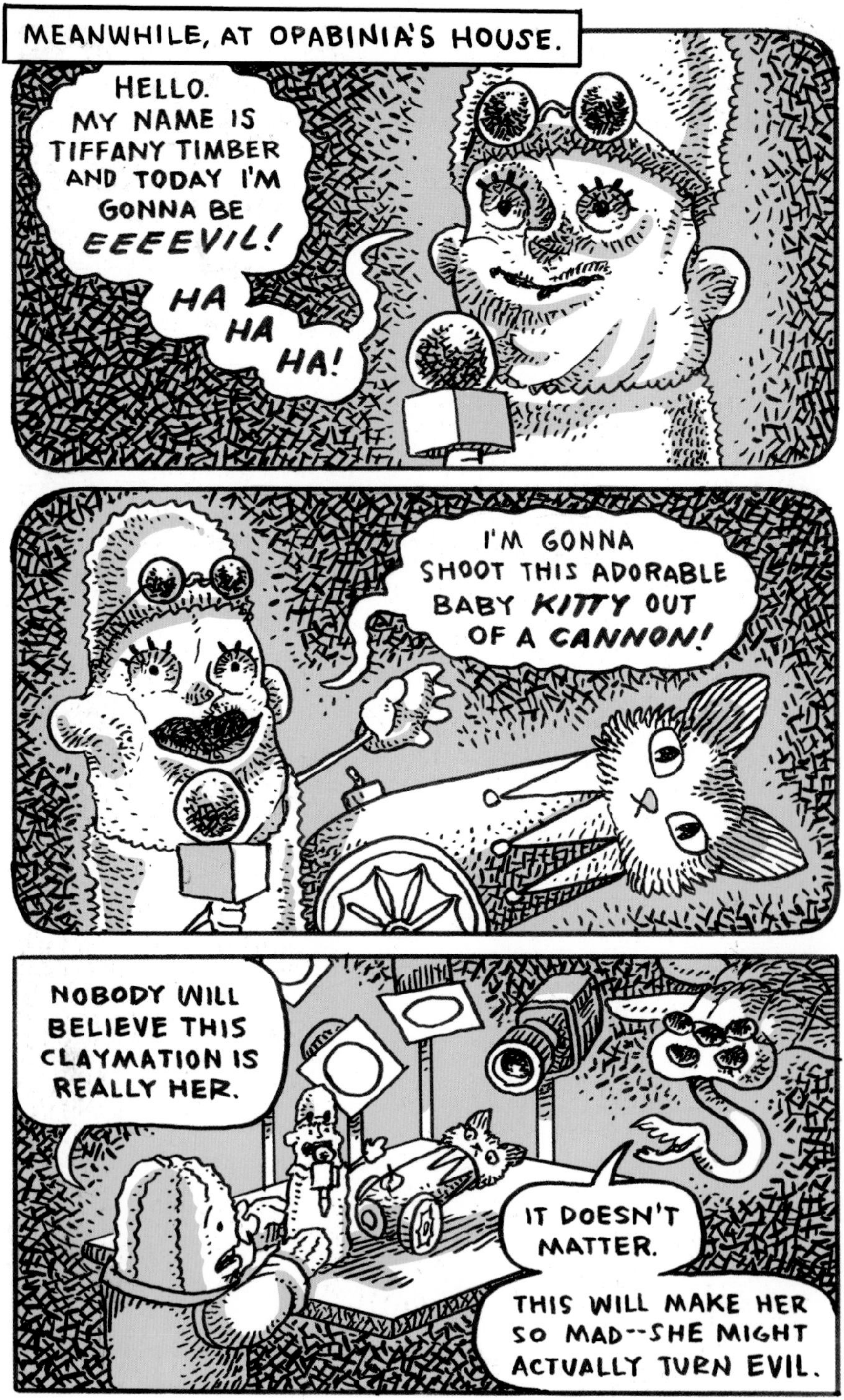
MEANWHILE, AT OPABINIA'S HOUSE.
HELLO. MY NAME IS TIFFANY TIMBER AND TODAY I'M GONNA BE EEEEVIL!
HA HA HA!
I'M GONNA SHOOT THIS ADORABLE BABY KITTY OUT OF A CANNON!
NOBODY WILL BELIEVE THIS CLAYMATION IS REALLY HER.
IT DOESN'T MATTER.
THIS WILL MAKE HER SO MAD--SHE MIGHT ACTUALLY TURN EVIL.

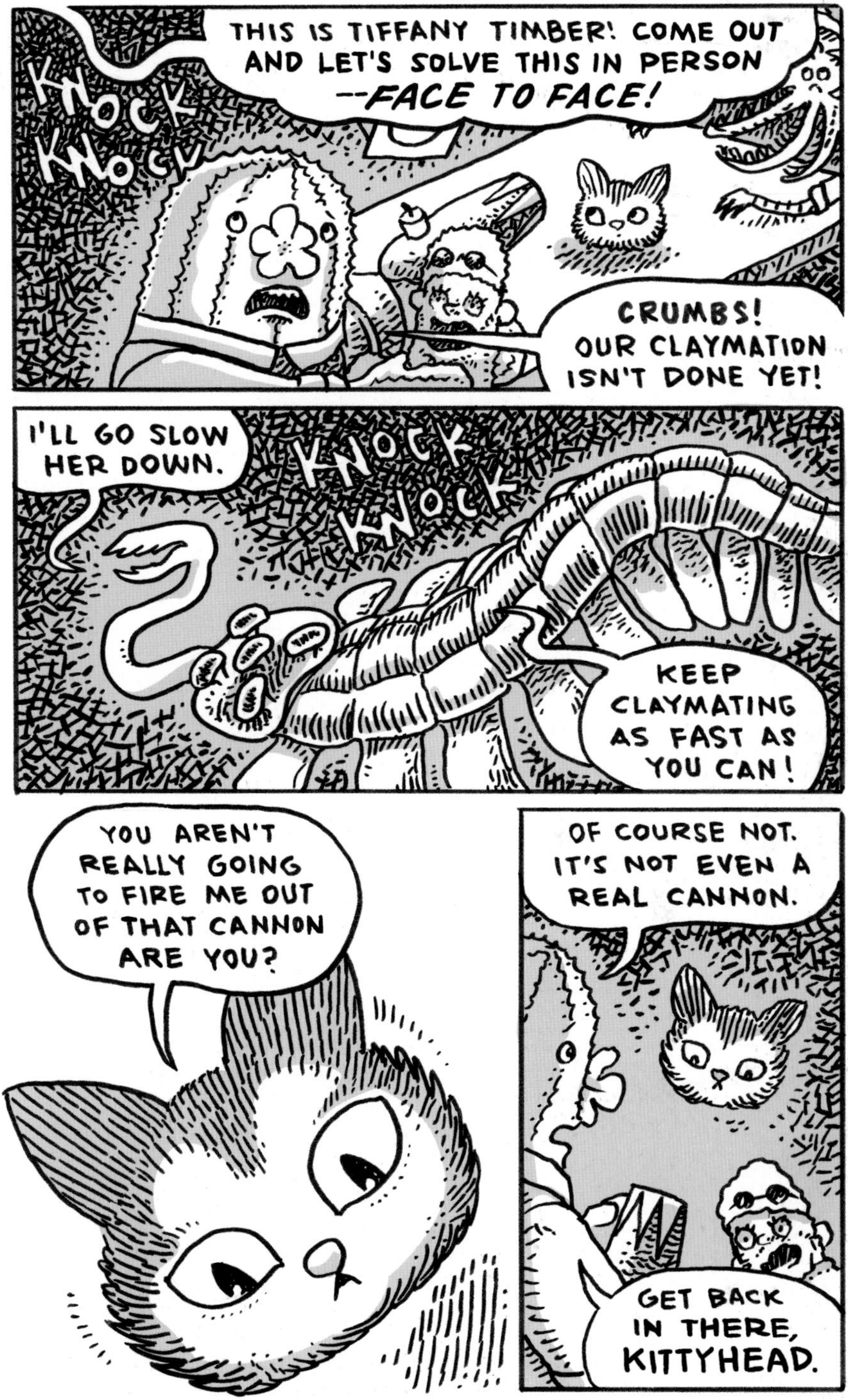
THIS IS TIFFANY TIMBER! COME OUT AND LET'S SOLVE THIS IN PERSON --FACE TO FACE!
KNOCK KNOCK
CRUMBS! OUR CLAYMATION ISN'T DONE YET!
I'LL GO SLOW HER DOWN.
KNOCK KNOCK
KEEP CLAYMATING AS FAST AS YOU CAN!
YOU AREN'T REALLY GOING TO FIRE ME OUT OF THAT CANNON ARE YOU?
OF COURSE NOT. IT'S NOT EVEN A REAL CANNON.
GET BACK IN THERE, KITTYHEAD.

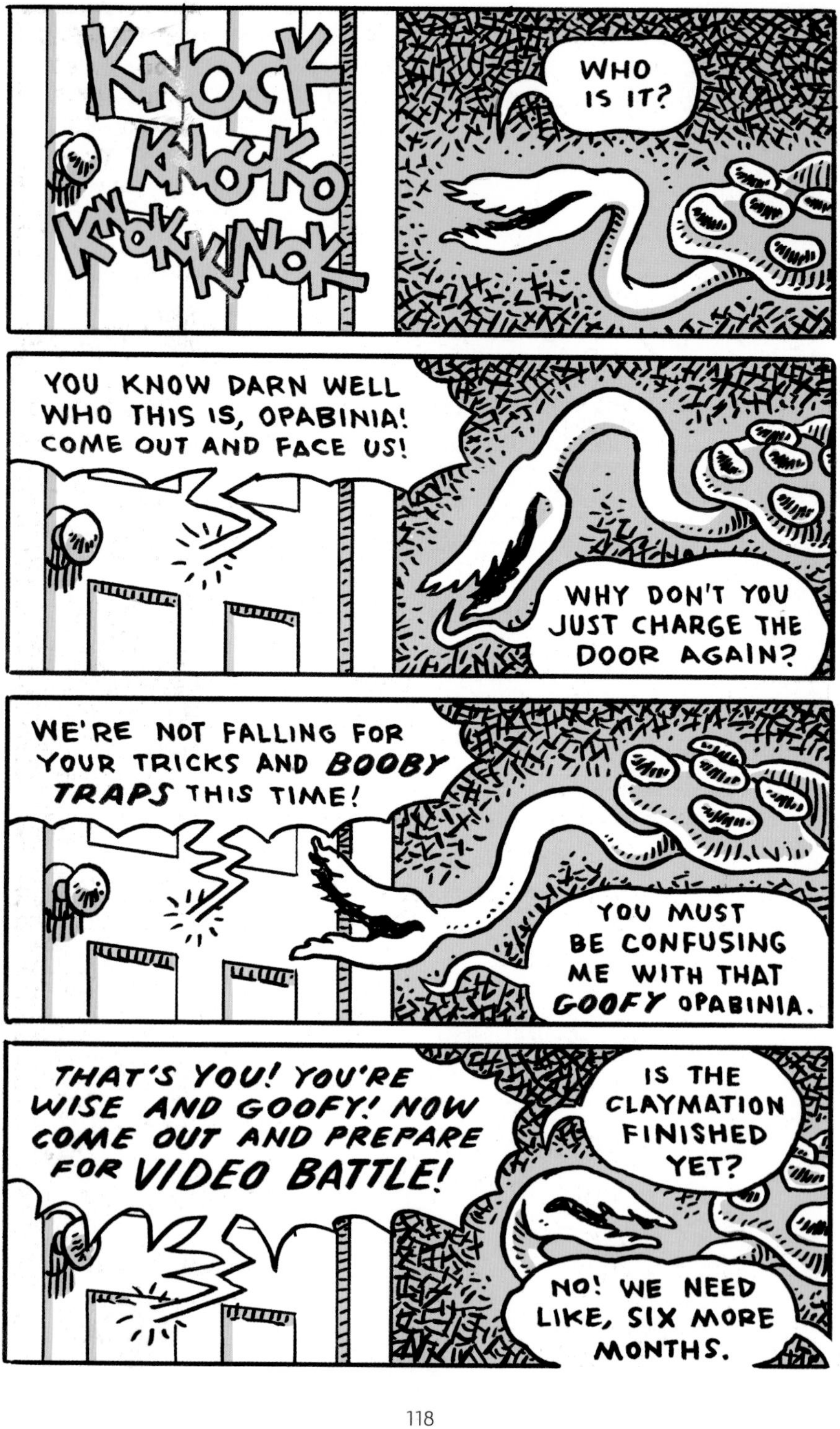
KNOCK KNOCK KNOCK KNOCK
WHO IS IT?
YOU KNOW DARN WELL WHO THIS IS, OPABINIA! COME OUT AND FACE US!
WHY DON'T YOU JUST CHARGE THE DOOR AGAIN?
WE'RE NOT FALLING FOR YOUR TRICKS AND *BOOBY TRAPS* THIS TIME!
YOU MUST BE CONFUSING ME WITH THAT *GOOFY* OPABINIA.
THAT'S YOU! YOU'RE WISE AND GOOFY! NOW COME OUT AND PREPARE FOR VIDEO BATTLE!
IS THE CLAYMATION FINISHED YET?
NO! WE NEED LIKE, SIX MORE MONTHS.

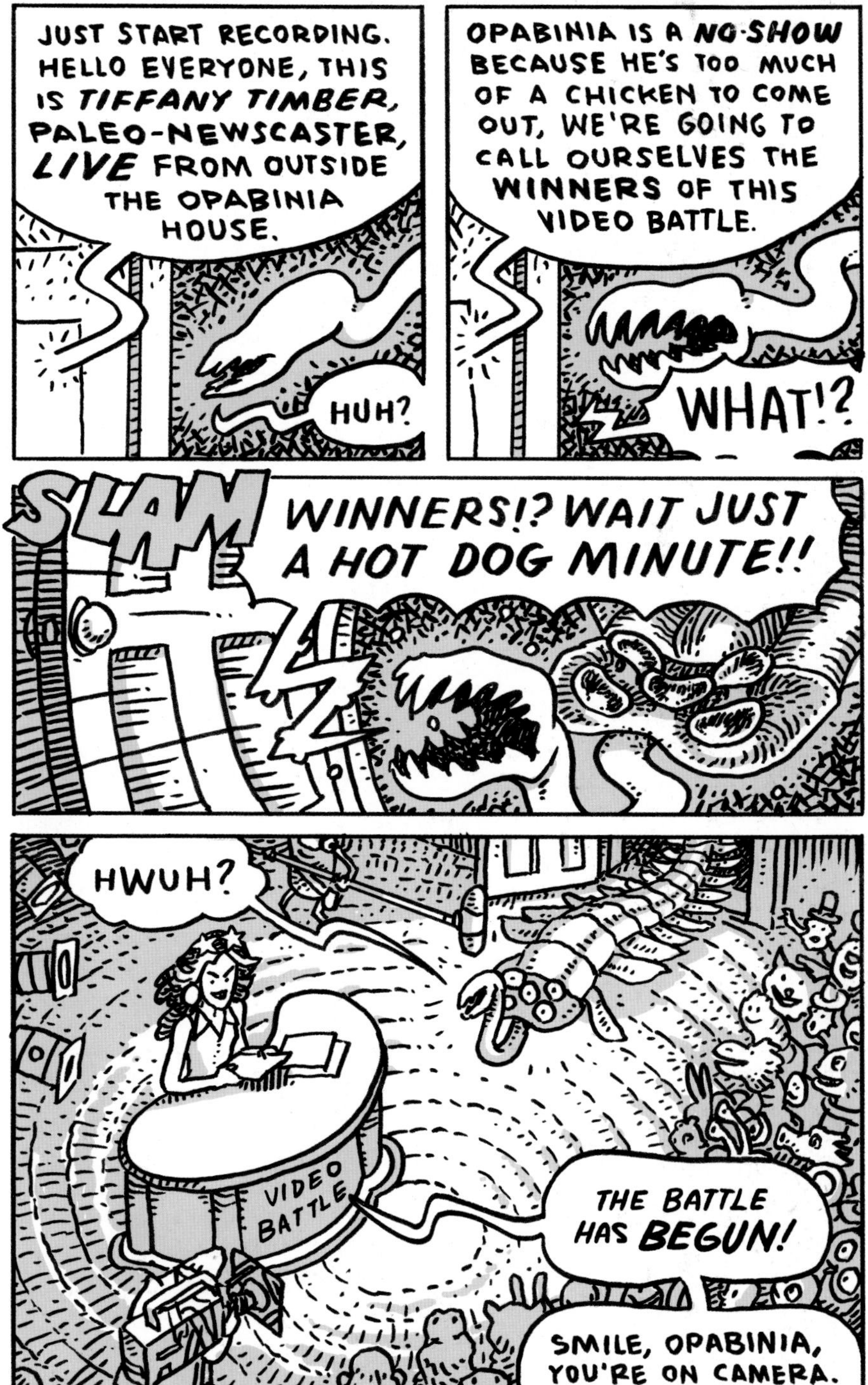
JUST START RECORDING. HELLO EVERYONE, THIS IS TIFFANY TIMBER, PALEO-NEWSCASTER, LIVE FROM OUTSIDE THE OPABINIA HOUSE.
HUH?
OPABINIA IS A NO-SHOW BECAUSE HE'S TOO MUCH OF A CHICKEN TO COME OUT, WE'RE GOING TO CALL OURSELVES THE WINNERS OF THIS VIDEO BATTLE.
WHAT!?
SLAM
WINNERS!? WAIT JUST A HOT DOG MINUTE!!
HWUH?
VIDEO BATTLE
THE BATTLE HAS BEGUN!
SMILE, OPABINIA, YOU'RE ON CAMERA.

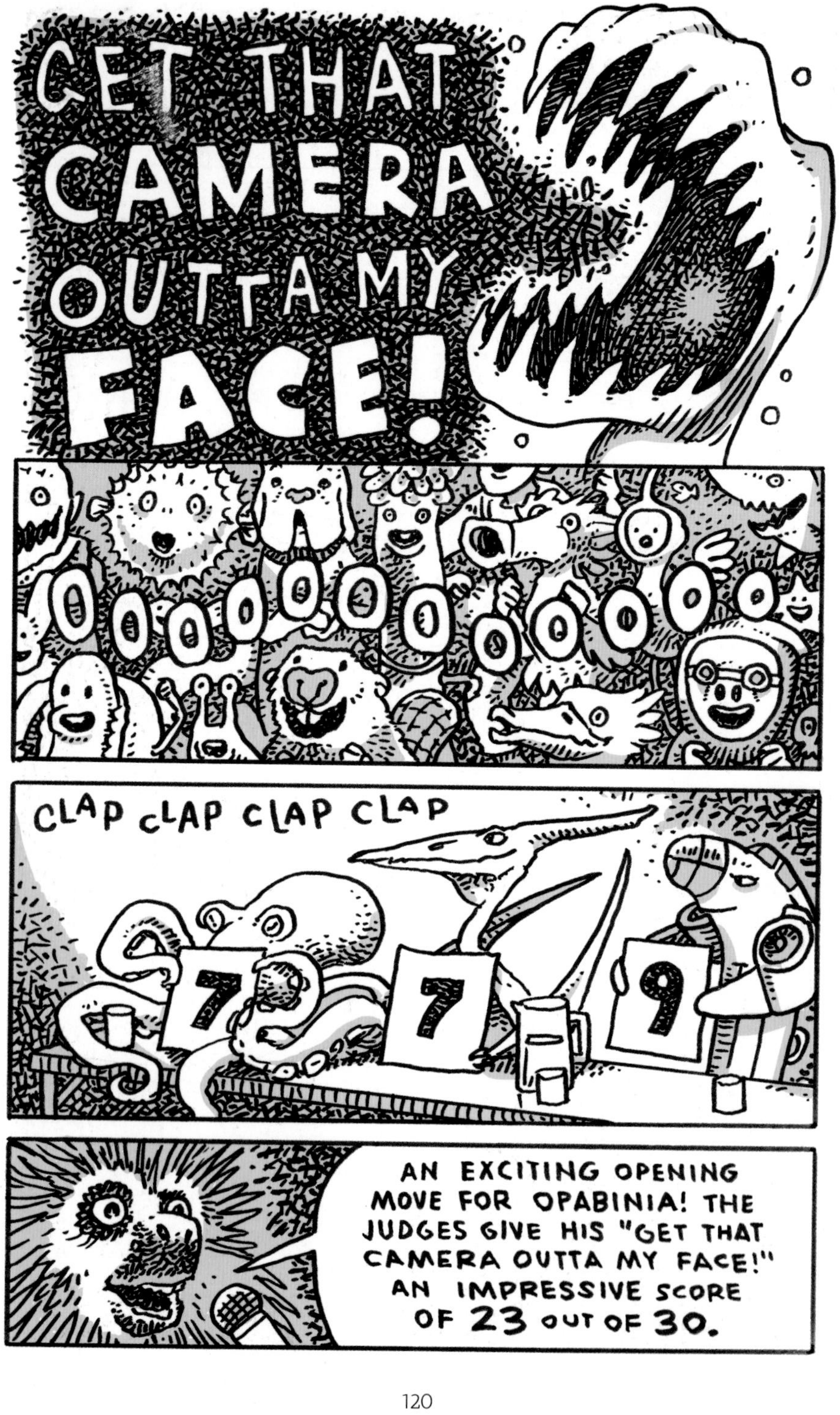
GET THAT CAMERA OUTTA MY FACE!
OOOOOOOOOOOOOO
CLAP CLAP CLAP CLAP
7
7
9
AN EXCITING OPENING MOVE FOR OPABINIA! THE JUDGES GIVE HIS "GET THAT CAMERA OUTTA MY FACE!" AN IMPRESSIVE SCORE OF 23 OUT OF 30.

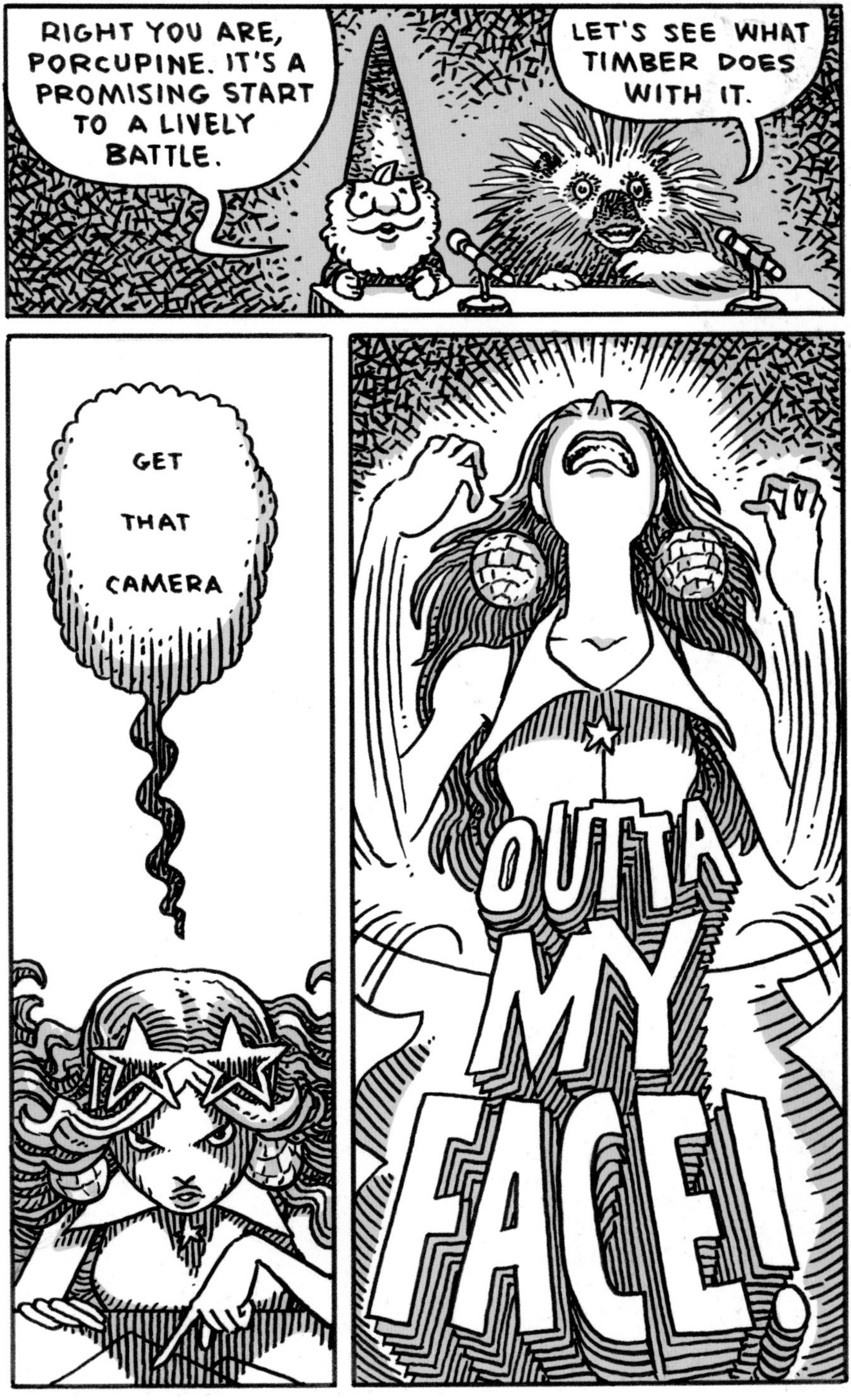
RIGHT YOU ARE, PORCUPINE. IT'S A PROMISING START TO A LIVELY BATTLE.
LET'S SEE WHAT TIMBER DOES WITH IT.
GET THAT CAMERA
OUTTA MY FACE!

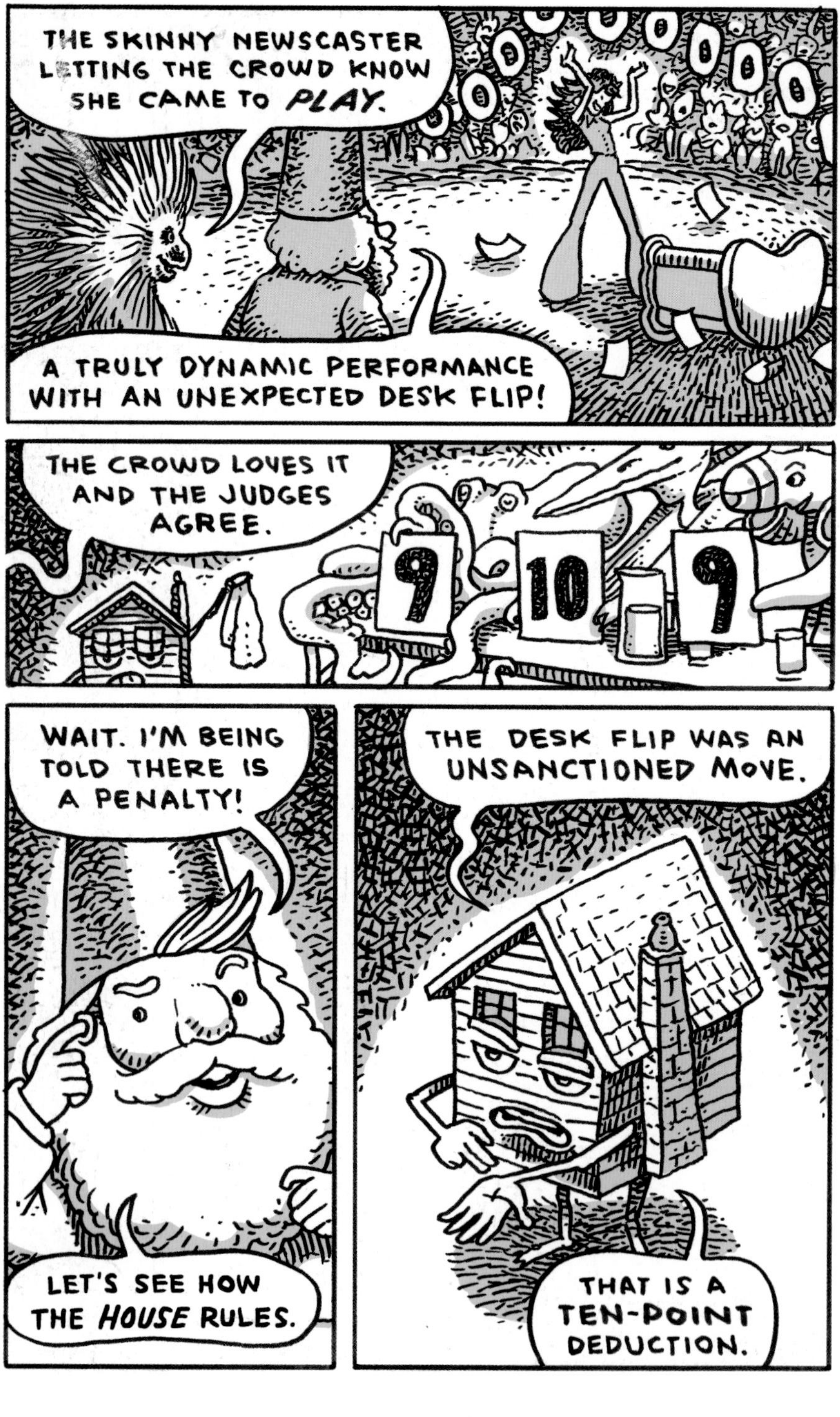
THE SKINNY NEWSCASTER LETTING THE CROWD KNOW SHE CAME TO *PLAY*.
A TRULY DYNAMIC PERFORMANCE WITH AN UNEXPECTED DESK FLIP!
THE CROWD LOVES IT AND THE JUDGES AGREE.
9
10
9
WAIT. I'M BEING TOLD THERE IS A PENALTY!
LET'S SEE HOW THE *HOUSE* RULES.
THE DESK FLIP WAS AN UNSANCTIONED MOVE.
THAT IS A TEN-POINT DEDUCTION.

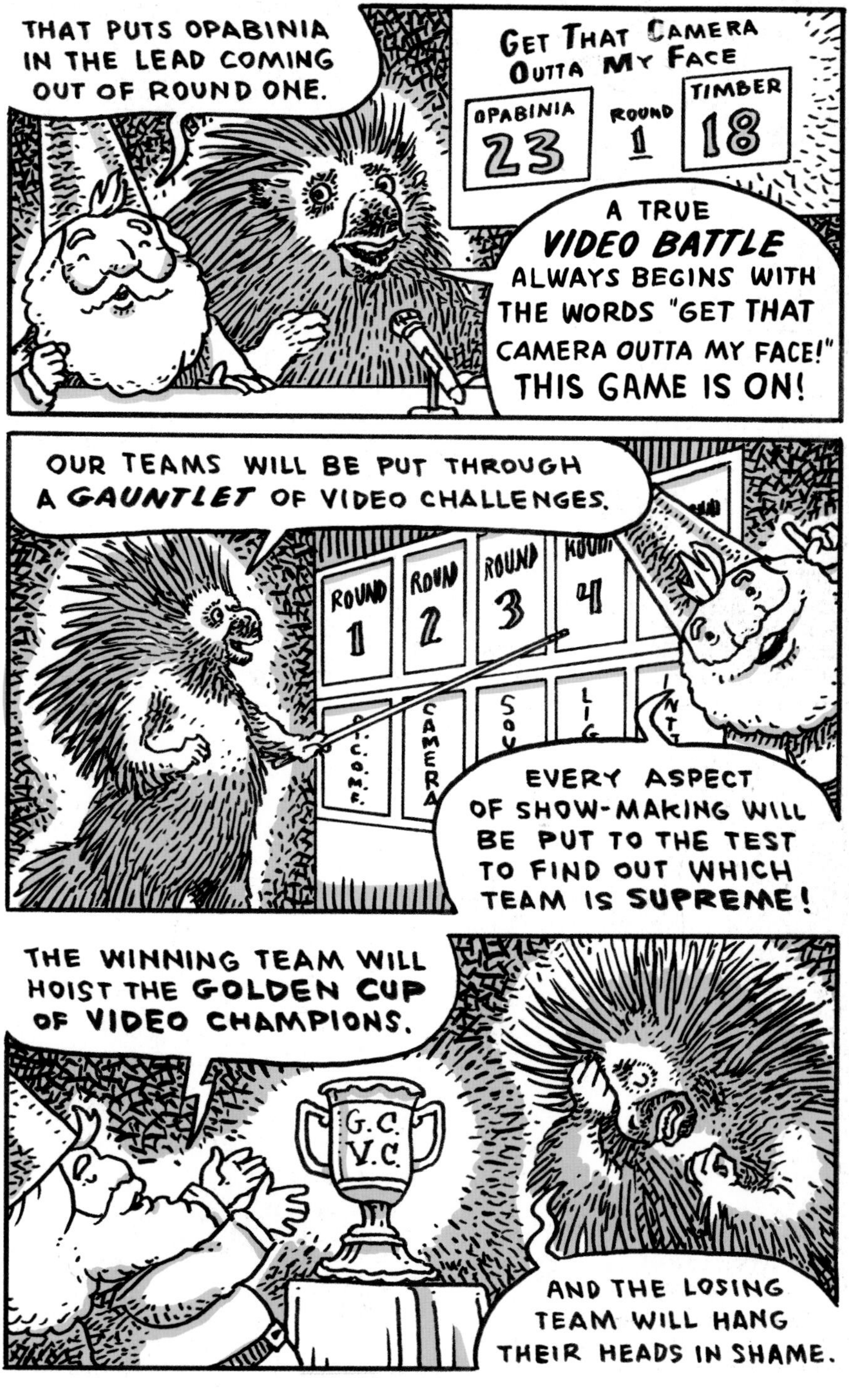
THAT PUTS OPABINIA IN THE LEAD COMING OUT OF ROUND ONE.
GET THAT CAMERA OUTTA MY FACE
OPABINIA 23
ROUND 1
TIMBER 18
A TRUE *VIDEO BATTLE* ALWAYS BEGINS WITH THE WORDS "GET THAT CAMERA OUTTA MY FACE!" THIS GAME IS ON!
OUR TEAMS WILL BE PUT THROUGH A *GAUNTLET* OF VIDEO CHALLENGES.
ROUND 1
ROUND 3
CAMERA
EVERY ASPECT OF SHOW-MAKING WILL BE PUT TO THE TEST TO FIND OUT WHICH TEAM IS **SUPREME!**
THE WINNING TEAM WILL HOIST THE **GOLDEN CUP** OF **VIDEO CHAMPIONS.**
G.C. V.C.
AND THE LOSING TEAM WILL HANG THEIR HEADS IN SHAME.

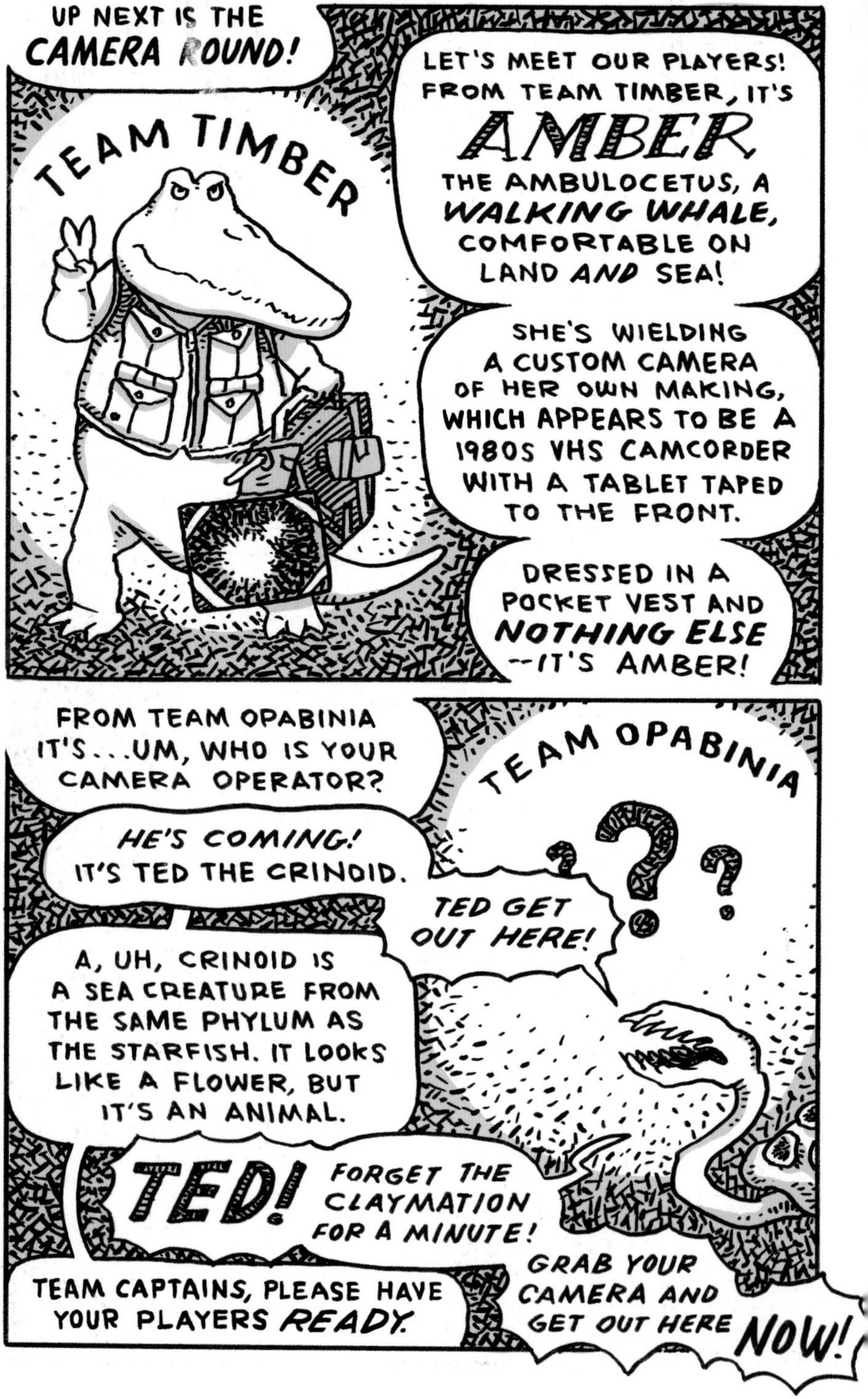
UP NEXT IS THE CAMERA ROUND!
LET'S MEET OUR PLAYERS! FROM TEAM TIMBER, IT'S AMBER THE AMBULOCETUS, A WALKING WHALE, COMFORTABLE ON LAND AND SEA!
TEAM TIMBER
SHE'S WIELDING A CUSTOM CAMERA OF HER OWN MAKING, WHICH APPEARS TO BE A 1980S VHS CAMCORDER WITH A TABLET TAPED TO THE FRONT.
DRESSED IN A POCKET VEST AND NOTHING ELSE --IT'S AMBER!
FROM TEAM OPABINIA IT'S...UM, WHO IS YOUR CAMERA OPERATOR?
TEAM OPABINIA
HE'S COMING! IT'S TED THE CRINOID.
TED GET OUT HERE!
A, UH, CRINOID IS A SEA CREATURE FROM THE SAME PHYLUM AS THE STARFISH. IT LOOKS LIKE A FLOWER, BUT IT'S AN ANIMAL.
TED! FORGET THE CLAYMATION FOR A MINUTE!
TEAM CAPTAINS, PLEASE HAVE YOUR PLAYERS READY.
GRAB YOUR CAMERA AND GET OUT HERE NOW!

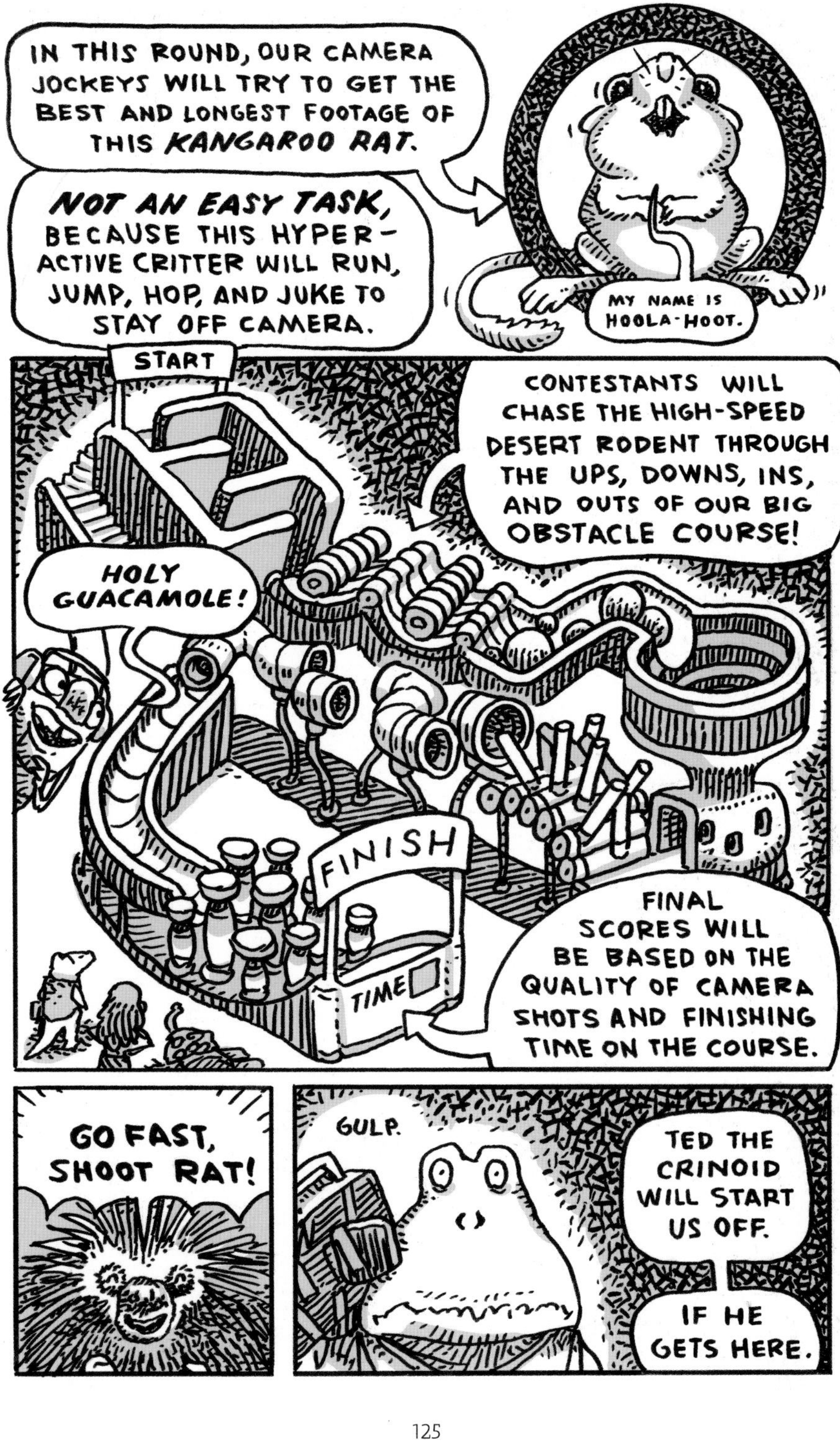
IN THIS ROUND, OUR CAMERA JOCKEYS WILL TRY TO GET THE BEST AND LONGEST FOOTAGE OF THIS KANGAROO RAT.
NOT AN EASY TASK, BECAUSE THIS HYPER-ACTIVE CRITTER WILL RUN, JUMP, HOP, AND JUKE TO STAY OFF CAMERA.
MY NAME IS HOOLA-HOOT.
START
CONTESTANTS WILL CHASE THE HIGH-SPEED DESERT RODENT THROUGH THE UPS, DOWNS, INS, AND OUTS OF OUR BIG OBSTACLE COURSE!
HOLY GUACAMOLE!
FINISH
TIME
FINAL SCORES WILL BE BASED ON THE QUALITY OF CAMERA SHOTS AND FINISHING TIME ON THE COURSE.
GO FAST, SHOOT RAT!
GULP.
TED THE CRINOID WILL START US OFF.
IF HE GETS HERE.

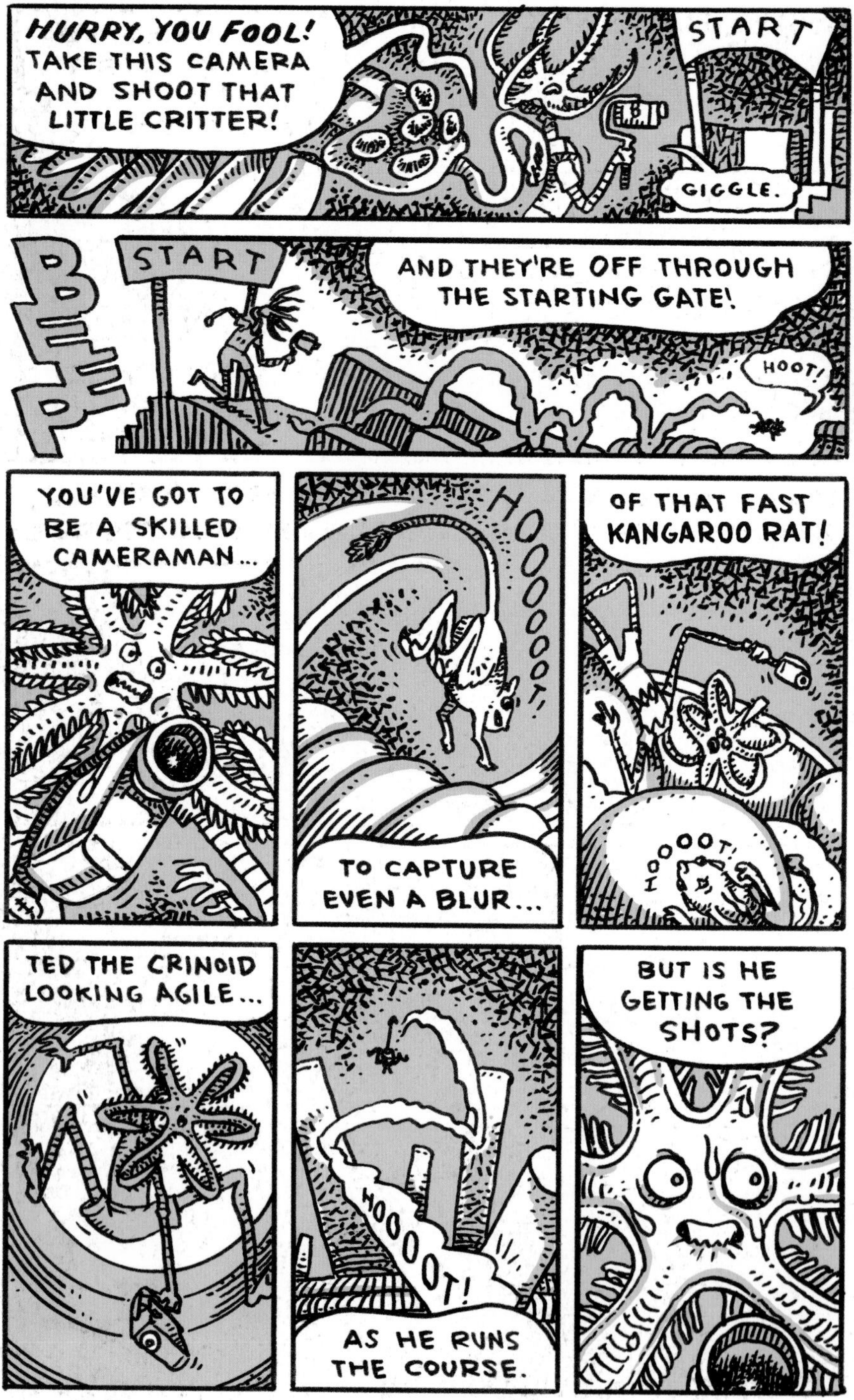
HURRY, YOU FOOL! TAKE THIS CAMERA AND SHOOT THAT LITTLE CRITTER!
START
GIGGLE.
BEEP
START
AND THEY'RE OFF THROUGH THE STARTING GATE!
HOOT!
YOU'VE GOT TO BE A SKILLED CAMERAMAN...
HOOOOOOOOT!
TO CAPTURE EVEN A BLUR...
OF THAT FAST KANGAROO RAT!
HOOOOT!
TED THE CRINOID LOOKING AGILE...
HOOOOOT!
AS HE RUNS THE COURSE.
BUT IS HE GETTING THE SHOTS?

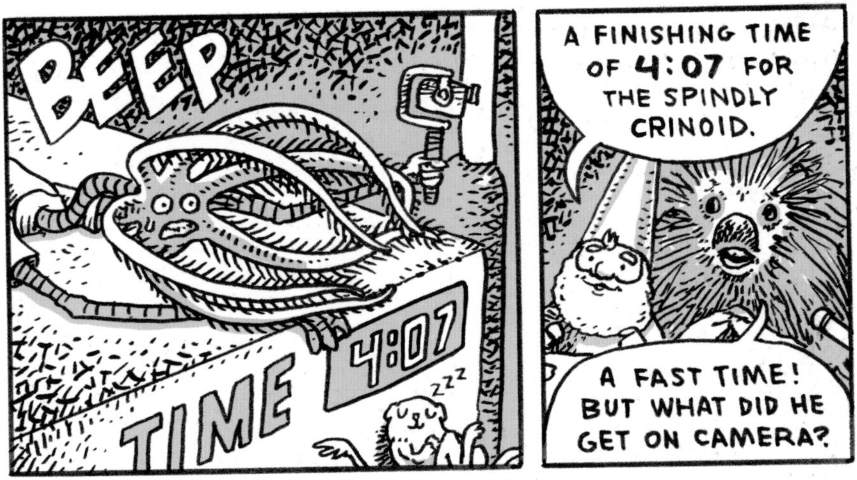
BEEP
TIME 4:07
ZZZ
A FINISHING TIME OF 4:07 FOR THE SPINDLY CRINOID.
A FAST TIME! BUT WHAT DID HE GET ON CAMERA?

IT ALL COMES DOWN TO THE **RECORDED FOOTAGE.**
LET'S TAKE A LOOK AT TED'S BEST SHOTS FROM HIS RUN.

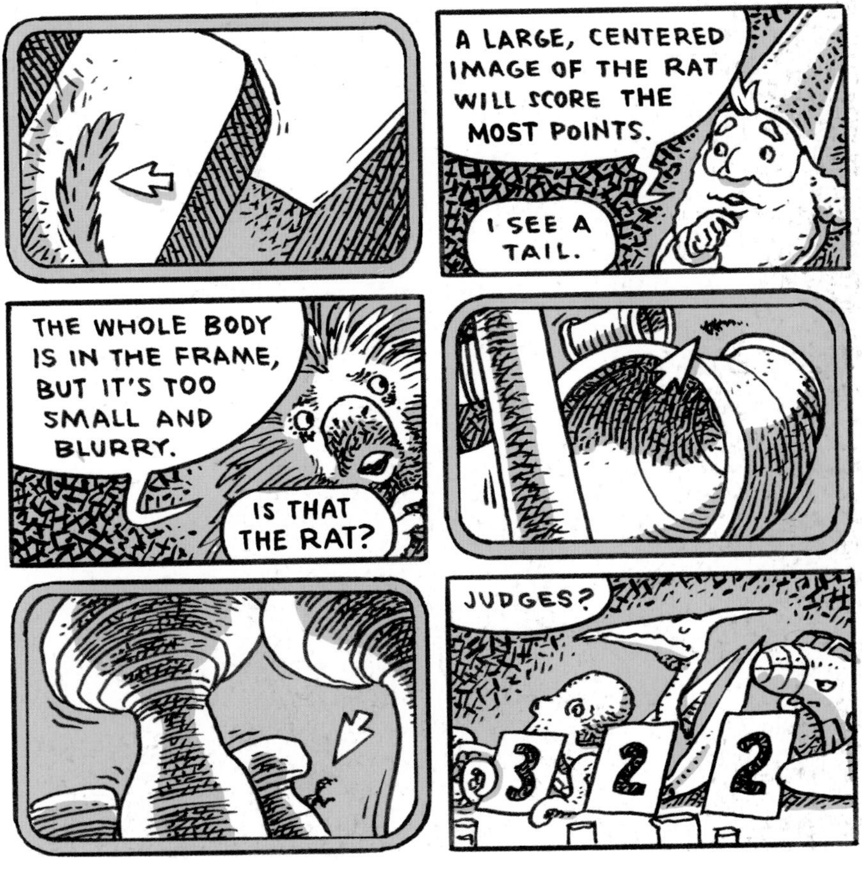
A LARGE, CENTERED IMAGE OF THE RAT WILL SCORE THE MOST POINTS.
I SEE A TAIL.
THE WHOLE BODY IS IN THE FRAME, BUT IT'S TOO SMALL AND BLURRY.
IS THAT THE RAT?
JUDGES?
3
2
2

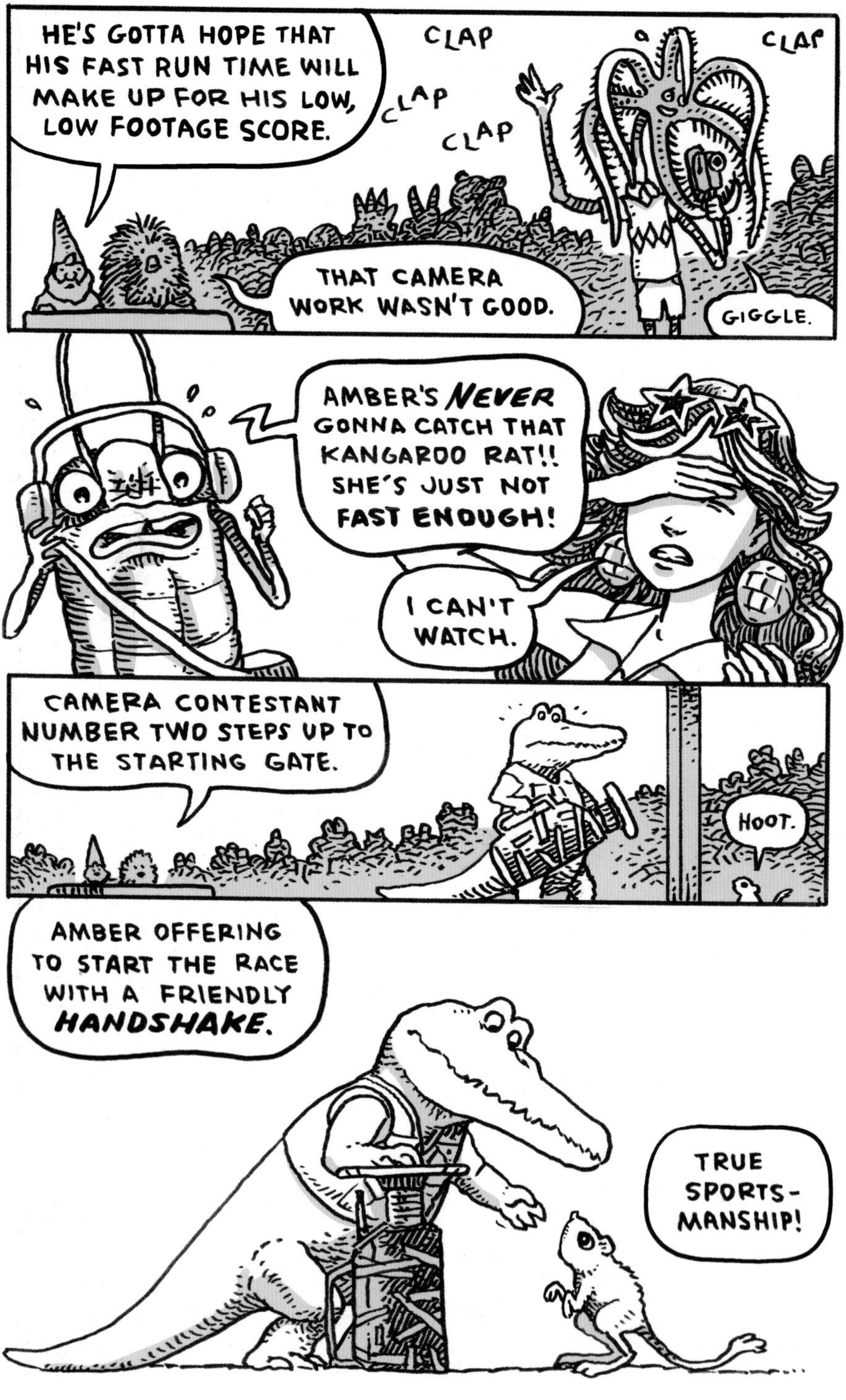
HE'S GOTTA HOPE THAT HIS FAST RUN TIME WILL MAKE UP FOR HIS LOW, LOW FOOTAGE SCORE.
CLAP
CLAP
CLAP
CLAP
THAT CAMERA WORK WASN'T GOOD.
GIGGLE.
AMBER'S NEVER GONNA CATCH THAT KANGAROO RAT!! SHE'S JUST NOT FAST ENOUGH!
I CAN'T WATCH.
CAMERA CONTESTANT NUMBER TWO STEPS UP TO THE STARTING GATE.
HOOT.
AMBER OFFERING TO START THE RACE WITH A FRIENDLY HANDSHAKE.
TRUE SPORTS-MANSHIP!

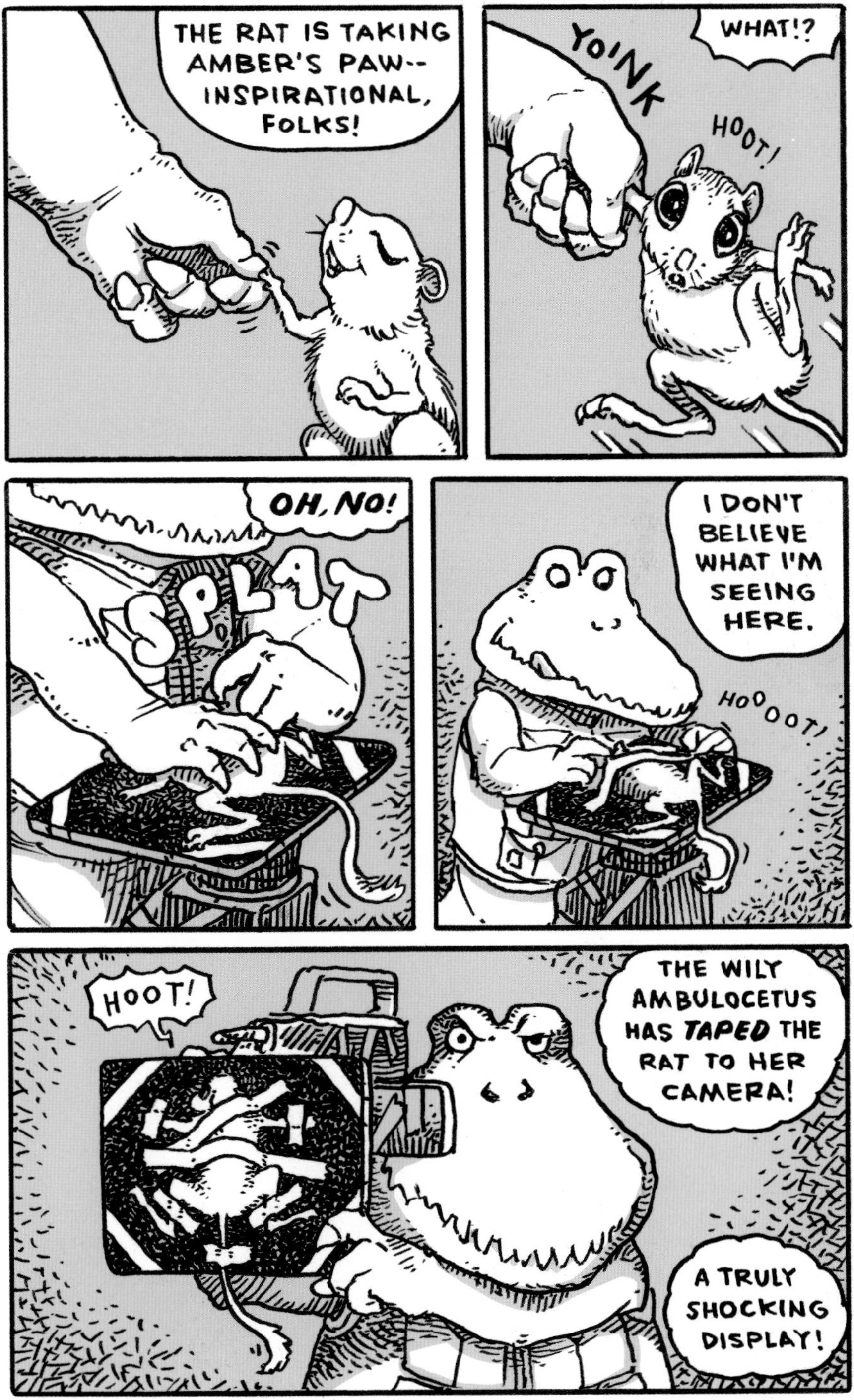
THE RAT IS TAKING AMBER'S PAW-- INSPIRATIONAL, FOLKS!
YOINK
WHAT!?
HOOT!
OH, NO!
SPLAT
I DON'T BELIEVE WHAT I'M SEEING HERE.
HOOOOT!
HOOT!
THE WILY AMBULOCETUS HAS TAPED THE RAT TO HER CAMERA!
A TRULY SHOCKING DISPLAY!

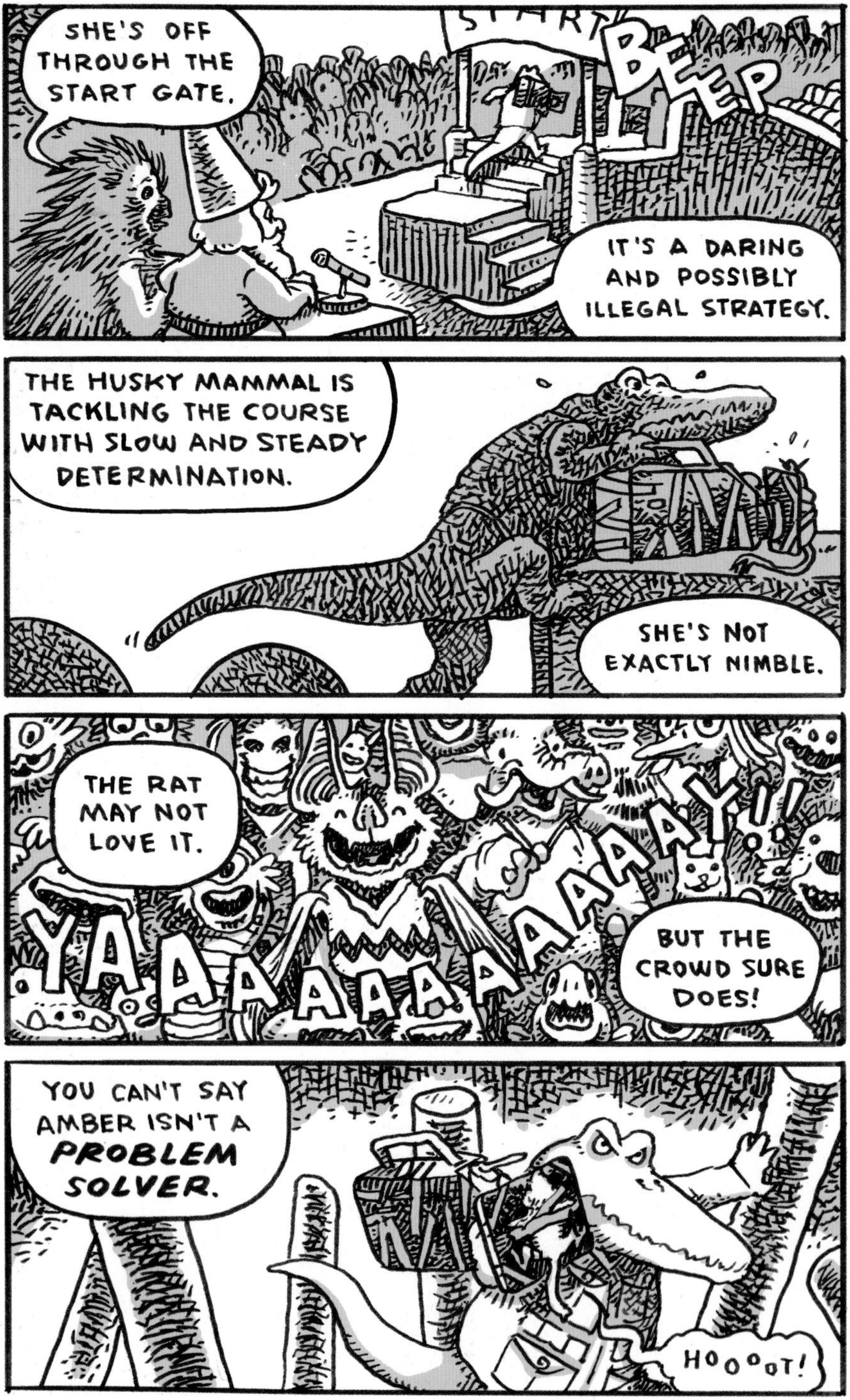
SHE'S OFF THROUGH THE START GATE.
START
BEEP
IT'S A DARING AND POSSIBLY ILLEGAL STRATEGY.
THE HUSKY MAMMAL IS TACKLING THE COURSE WITH SLOW AND STEADY DETERMINATION.
SHE'S NOT EXACTLY NIMBLE.
THE RAT MAY NOT LOVE IT.
YAAAAAAAAAAAAY!!
BUT THE CROWD SURE DOES!
YOU CAN'T SAY AMBER ISN'T A ***PROBLEM SOLVER***.
HOOOOT!

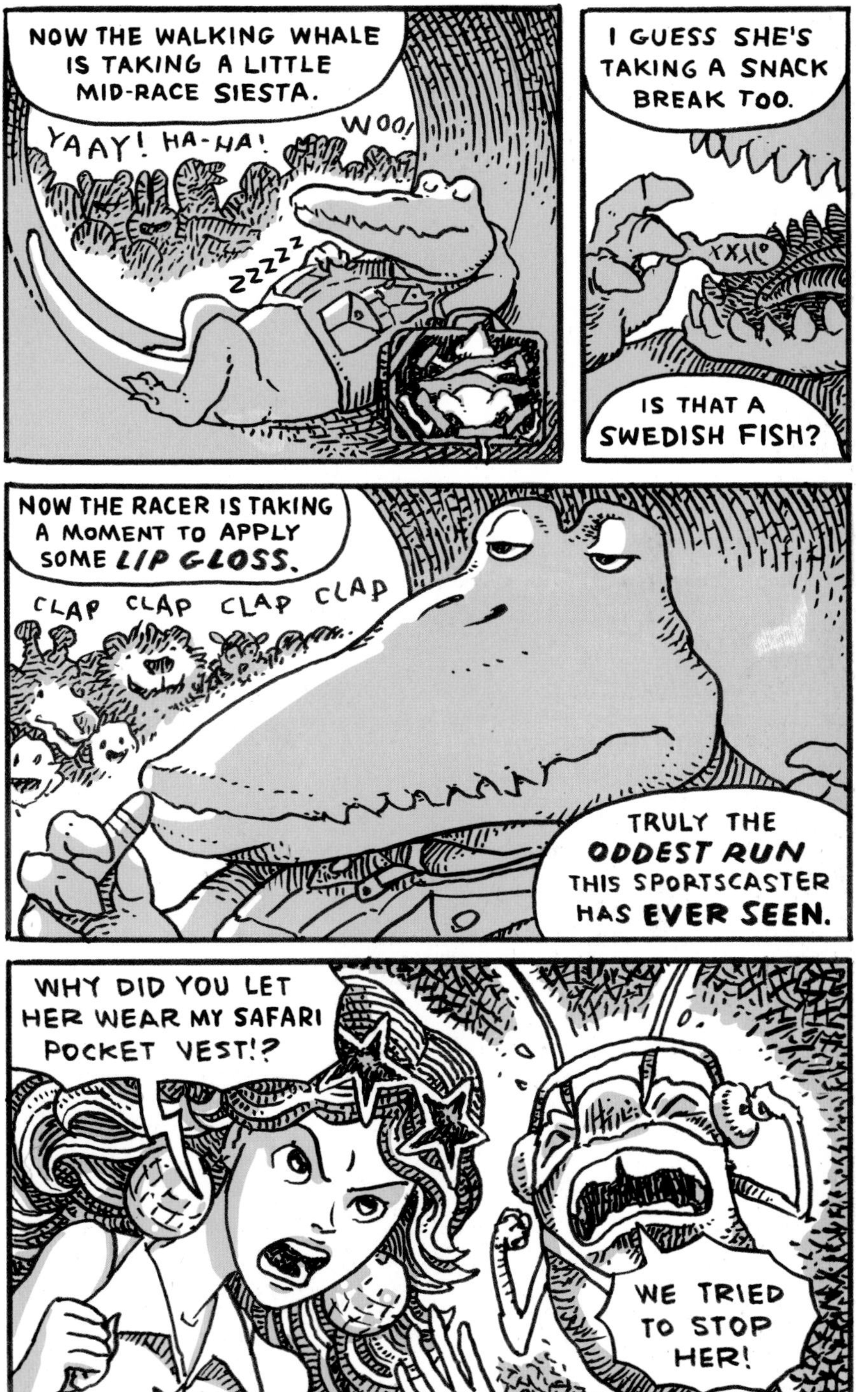
NOW THE WALKING WHALE IS TAKING A LITTLE MID-RACE SIESTA.
YAAY! HA-HA!
WOO!
ZZZZZ
I GUESS SHE'S TAKING A SNACK BREAK TOO.
IS THAT A SWEDISH FISH?
NOW THE RACER IS TAKING A MOMENT TO APPLY SOME LIP GLOSS.
CLAP CLAP CLAP CLAP
TRULY THE ODDEST RUN THIS SPORTSCASTER HAS EVER SEEN.
WHY DID YOU LET HER WEAR MY SAFARI POCKET VEST!?
WE TRIED TO STOP HER!

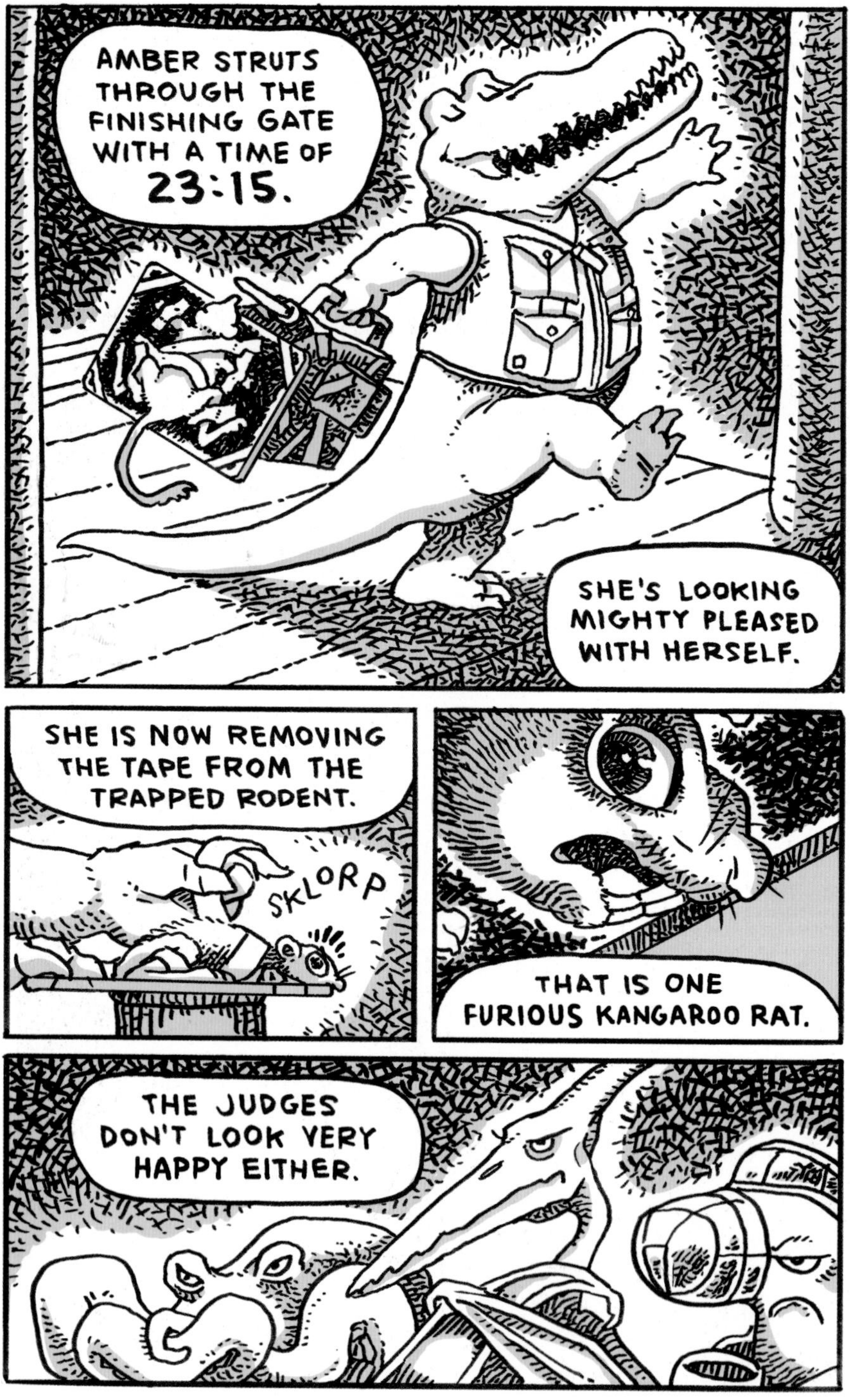
AMBER STRUTS THROUGH THE FINISHING GATE WITH A TIME OF 23:15.
SHE'S LOOKING MIGHTY PLEASED WITH HERSELF.
SHE IS NOW REMOVING THE TAPE FROM THE TRAPPED RODENT.
SKLORP
THAT IS ONE FURIOUS KANGAROO RAT.
THE JUDGES DON'T LOOK VERY HAPPY EITHER.

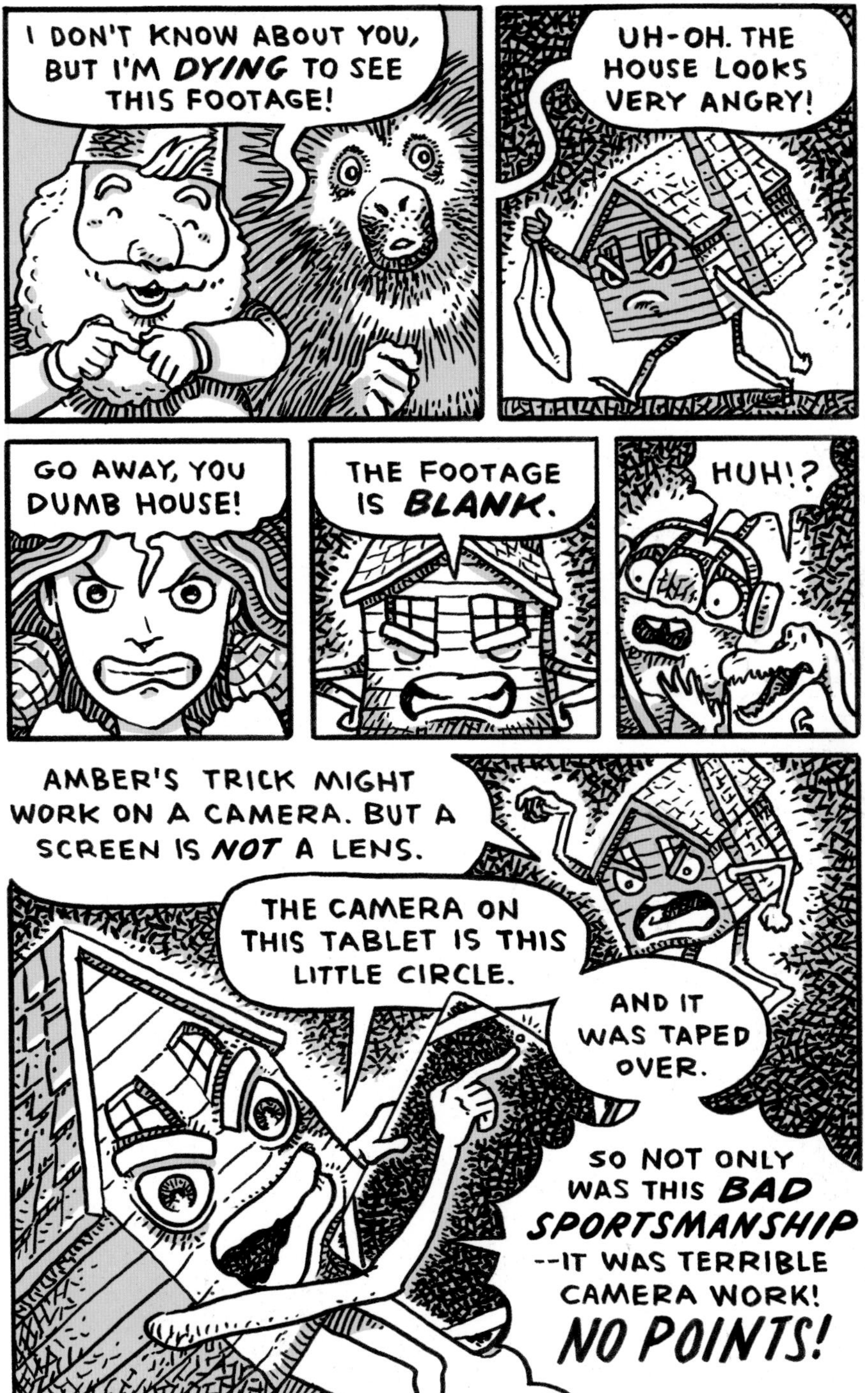
I DON'T KNOW ABOUT YOU, BUT I'M DYING TO SEE THIS FOOTAGE!
UH-OH. THE HOUSE LOOKS VERY ANGRY!
GO AWAY, YOU DUMB HOUSE!
THE FOOTAGE IS BLANK.
HUH!?
AMBER'S TRICK MIGHT WORK ON A CAMERA. BUT A SCREEN IS NOT A LENS.
THE CAMERA ON THIS TABLET IS THIS LITTLE CIRCLE.
AND IT WAS TAPED OVER.
SO NOT ONLY WAS THIS BAD SPORTSMANSHIP --IT WAS TERRIBLE CAMERA WORK! NO POINTS!

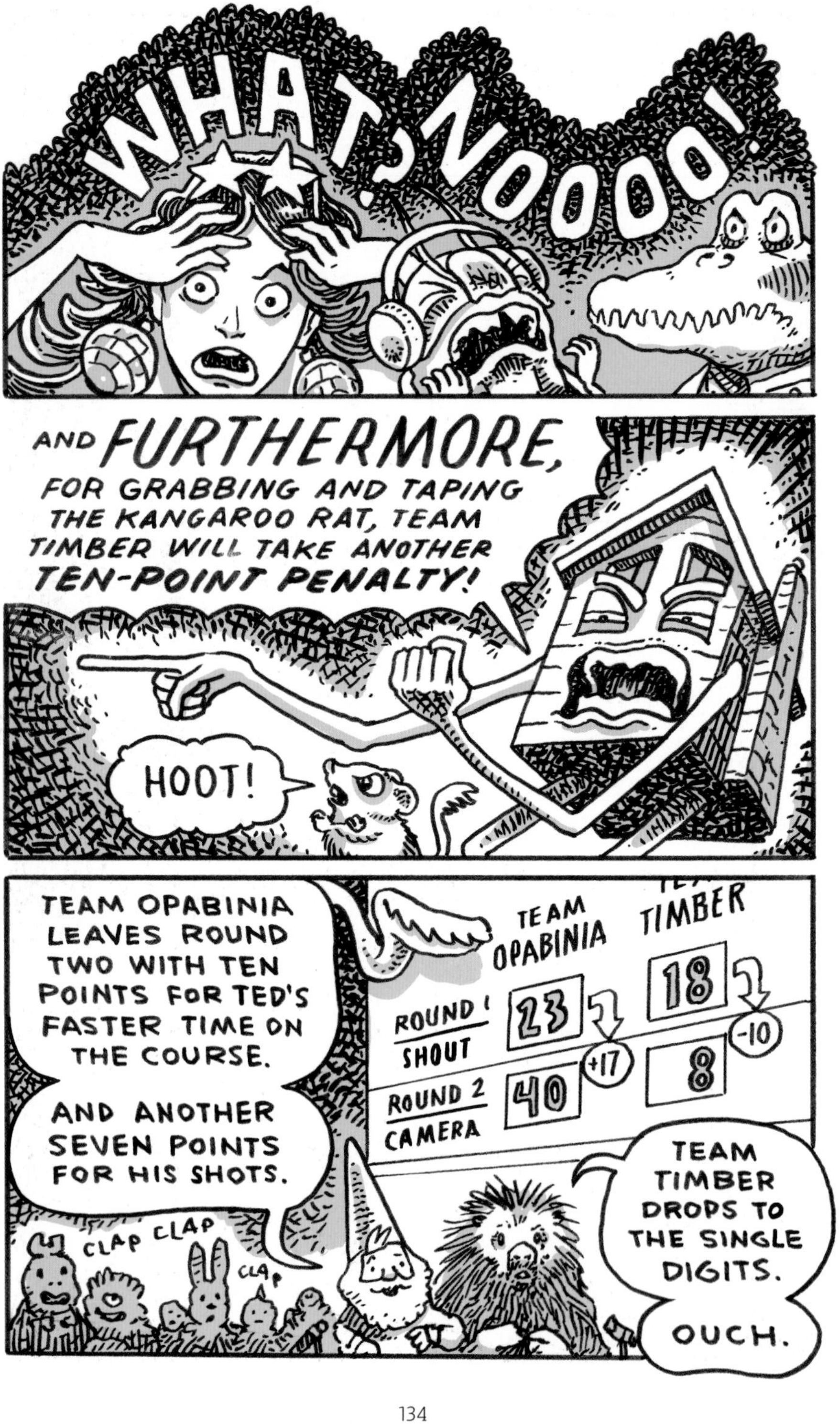
WHAT? NOOOO!
AND FURTHERMORE, FOR GRABBING AND TAPING THE KANGAROO RAT, TEAM TIMBER WILL TAKE ANOTHER TEN-POINT PENALTY!
HOOT!
TEAM OPABINIA LEAVES ROUND TWO WITH TEN POINTS FOR TED'S FASTER TIME ON THE COURSE.
AND ANOTHER SEVEN POINTS FOR HIS SHOTS.
TEAM OPABINIA
TEAM TIMBER
ROUND 1 SHOUT
ROUND 2 CAMERA
23
18
40
8
+17
-10
CLAP CLAP
CLAP
TEAM TIMBER DROPS TO THE SINGLE DIGITS.
OUCH.

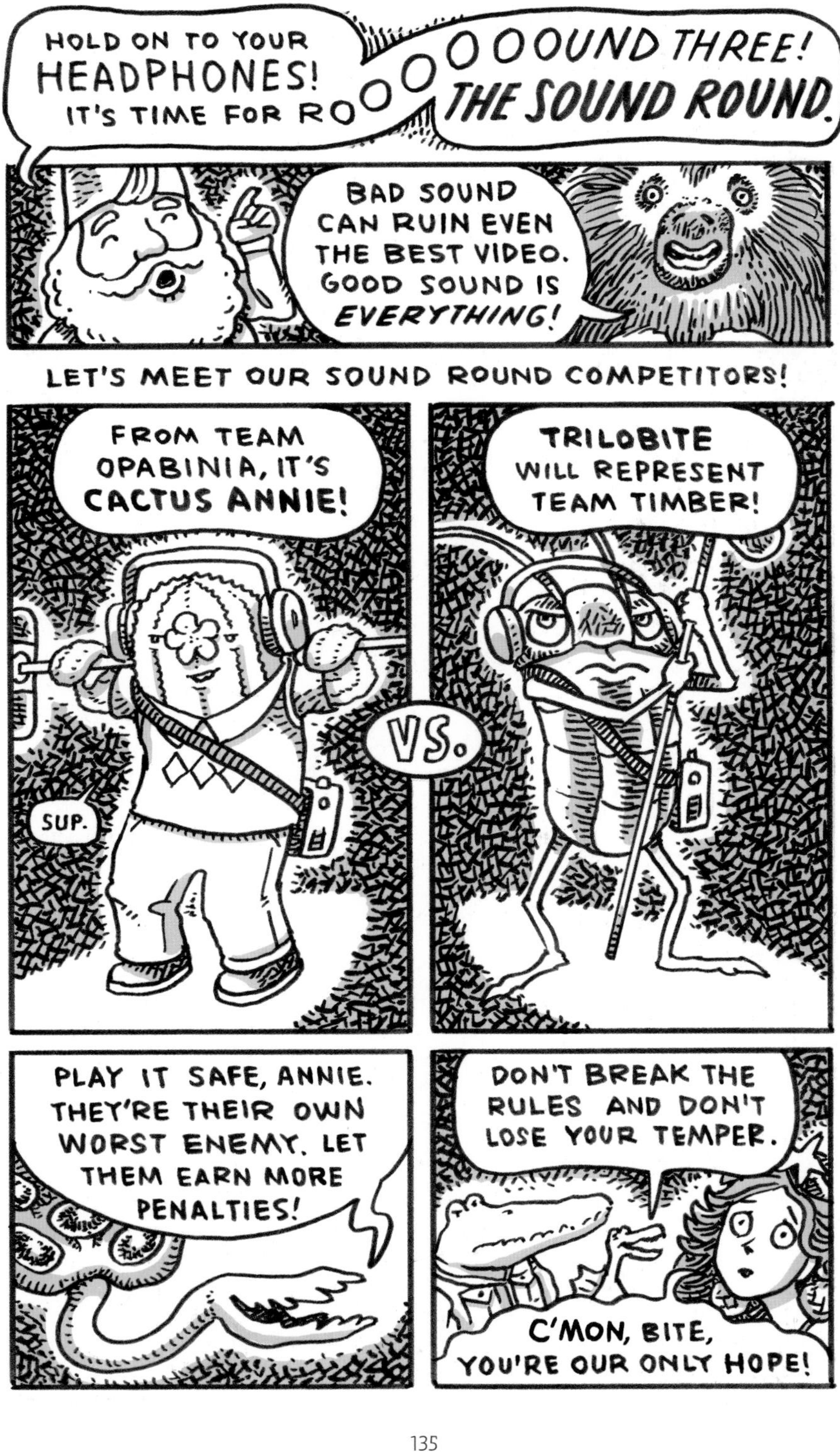

HOLD ON TO YOUR HEADPHONES! IT'S TIME FOR ROOOOOOOOUND THREE! THE SOUND ROUND.
BAD SOUND CAN RUIN EVEN THE BEST VIDEO. GOOD SOUND IS EVERYTHING!
LET'S MEET OUR SOUND ROUND COMPETITORS!
FROM TEAM OPABINIA, IT'S CACTUS ANNIE!
SUP.
VS.
TRILOBITE WILL REPRESENT TEAM TIMBER!
PLAY IT SAFE, ANNIE. THEY'RE THEIR OWN WORST ENEMY. LET THEM EARN MORE PENALTIES!
DON'T BREAK THE RULES AND DON'T LOSE YOUR TEMPER.
C'MON, BITE, YOU'RE OUR ONLY HOPE!

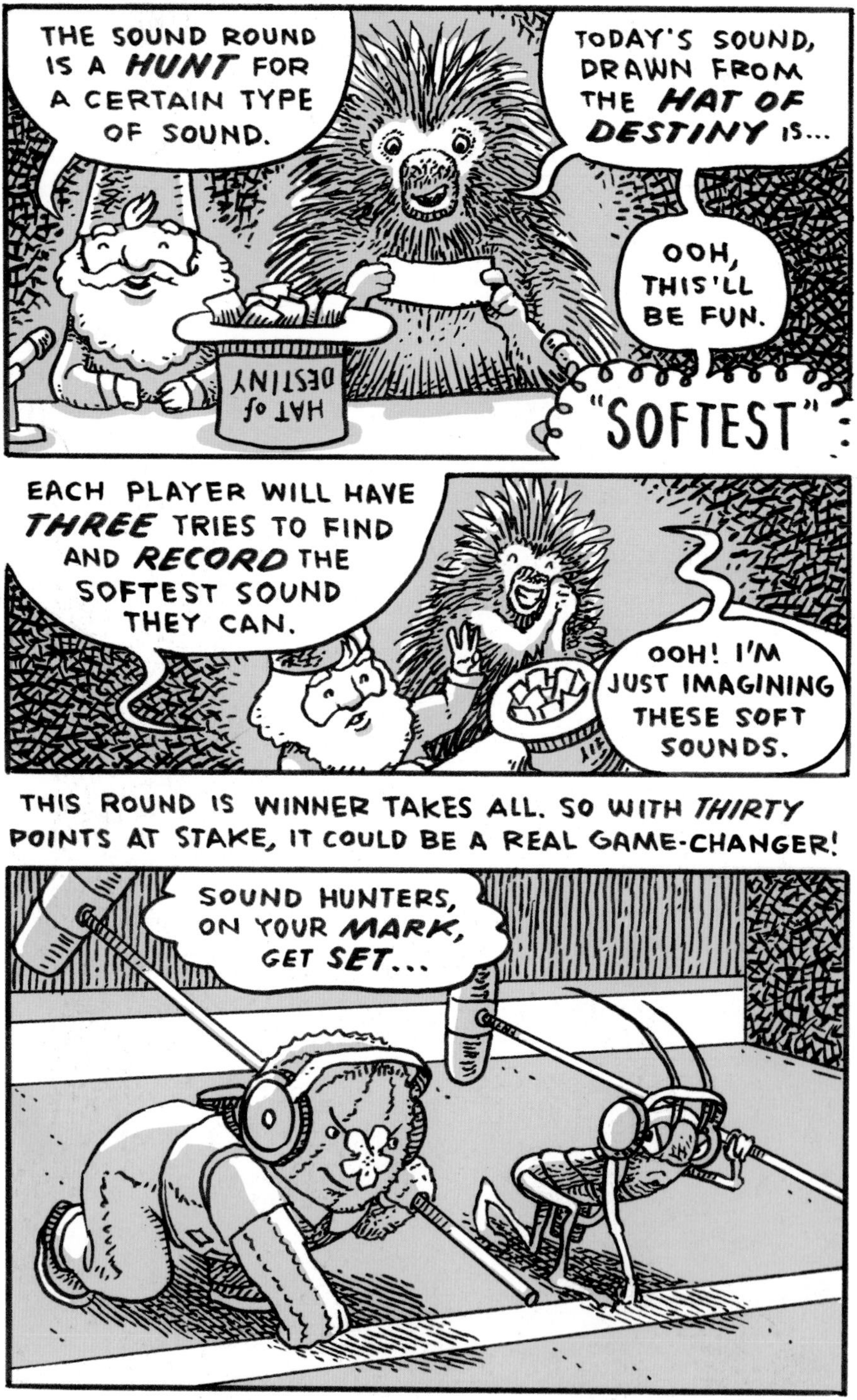
THE SOUND ROUND IS A ***HUNT*** FOR A CERTAIN TYPE OF SOUND.
TODAY'S SOUND, DRAWN FROM THE ***HAT OF DESTINY*** IS...
OOH, THIS'LL BE FUN.
"SOFTEST"
EACH PLAYER WILL HAVE ***THREE*** TRIES TO FIND AND ***RECORD*** THE SOFTEST SOUND THEY CAN.
OOH! I'M JUST IMAGINING THESE SOFT SOUNDS.
THIS ROUND IS WINNER TAKES ALL. SO WITH *THIRTY* POINTS AT STAKE, IT COULD BE A REAL GAME-CHANGER!
SOUND HUNTERS, ON YOUR ***MARK***, GET ***SET***...

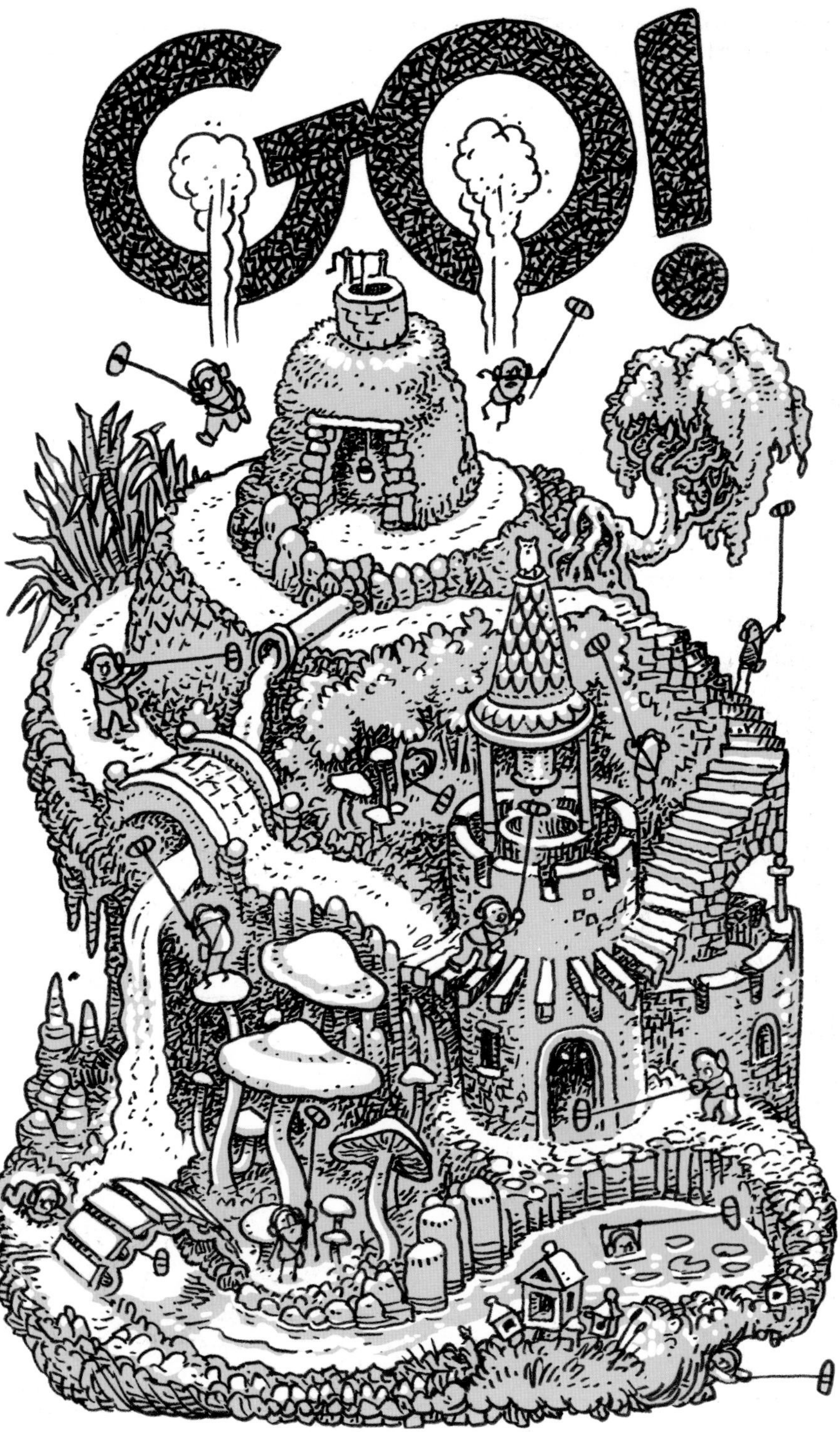
GO!

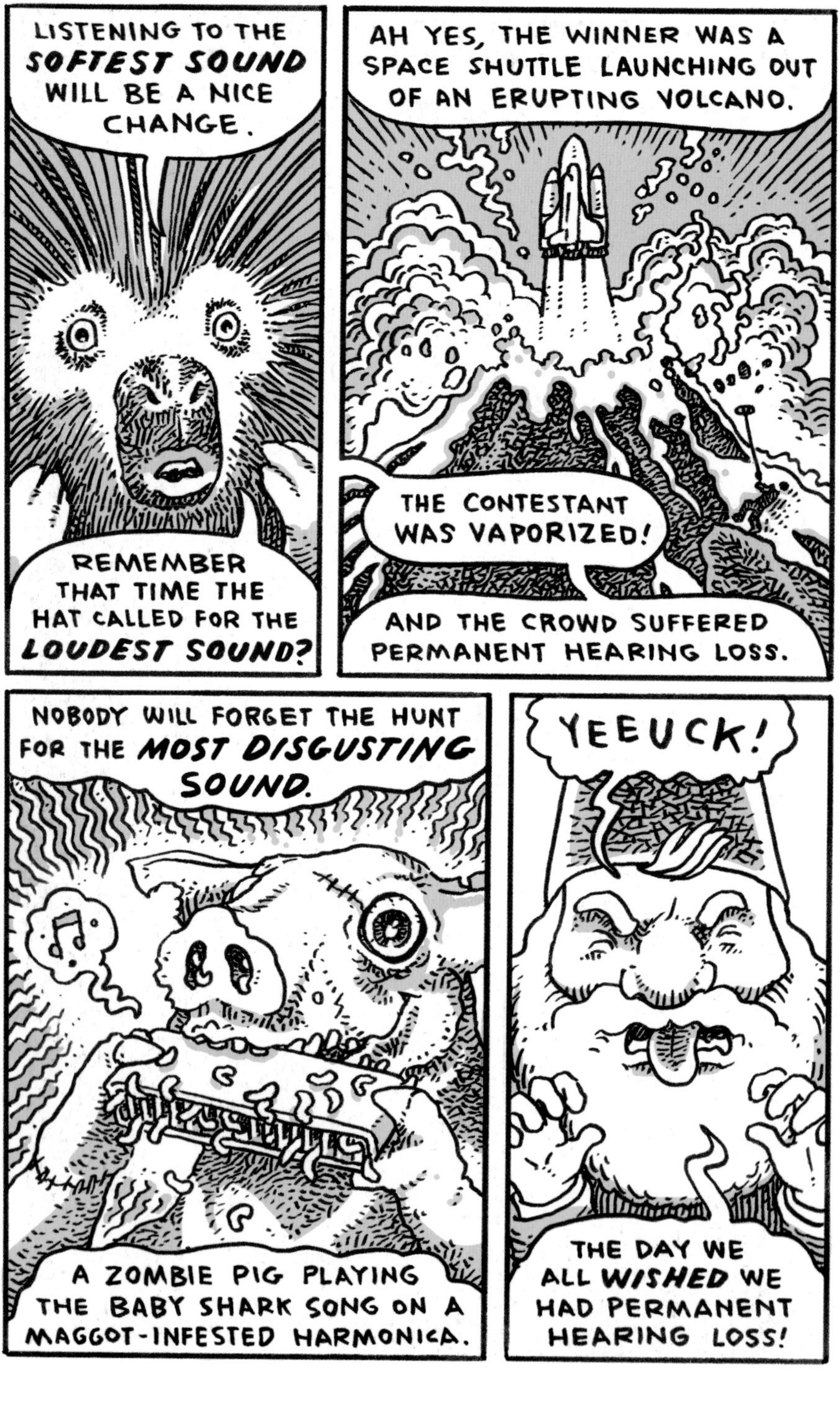
LISTENING TO THE SOFTEST SOUND WILL BE A NICE CHANGE.
REMEMBER THAT TIME THE HAT CALLED FOR THE LOUDEST SOUND?
AH YES, THE WINNER WAS A SPACE SHUTTLE LAUNCHING OUT OF AN ERUPTING VOLCANO.
THE CONTESTANT WAS VAPORIZED!
AND THE CROWD SUFFERED PERMANENT HEARING LOSS.
NOBODY WILL FORGET THE HUNT FOR THE MOST DISGUSTING SOUND.
A ZOMBIE PIG PLAYING THE BABY SHARK SONG ON A MAGGOT-INFESTED HARMONICA.
YEEUCK!
THE DAY WE ALL WISHED WE HAD PERMANENT HEARING LOSS!

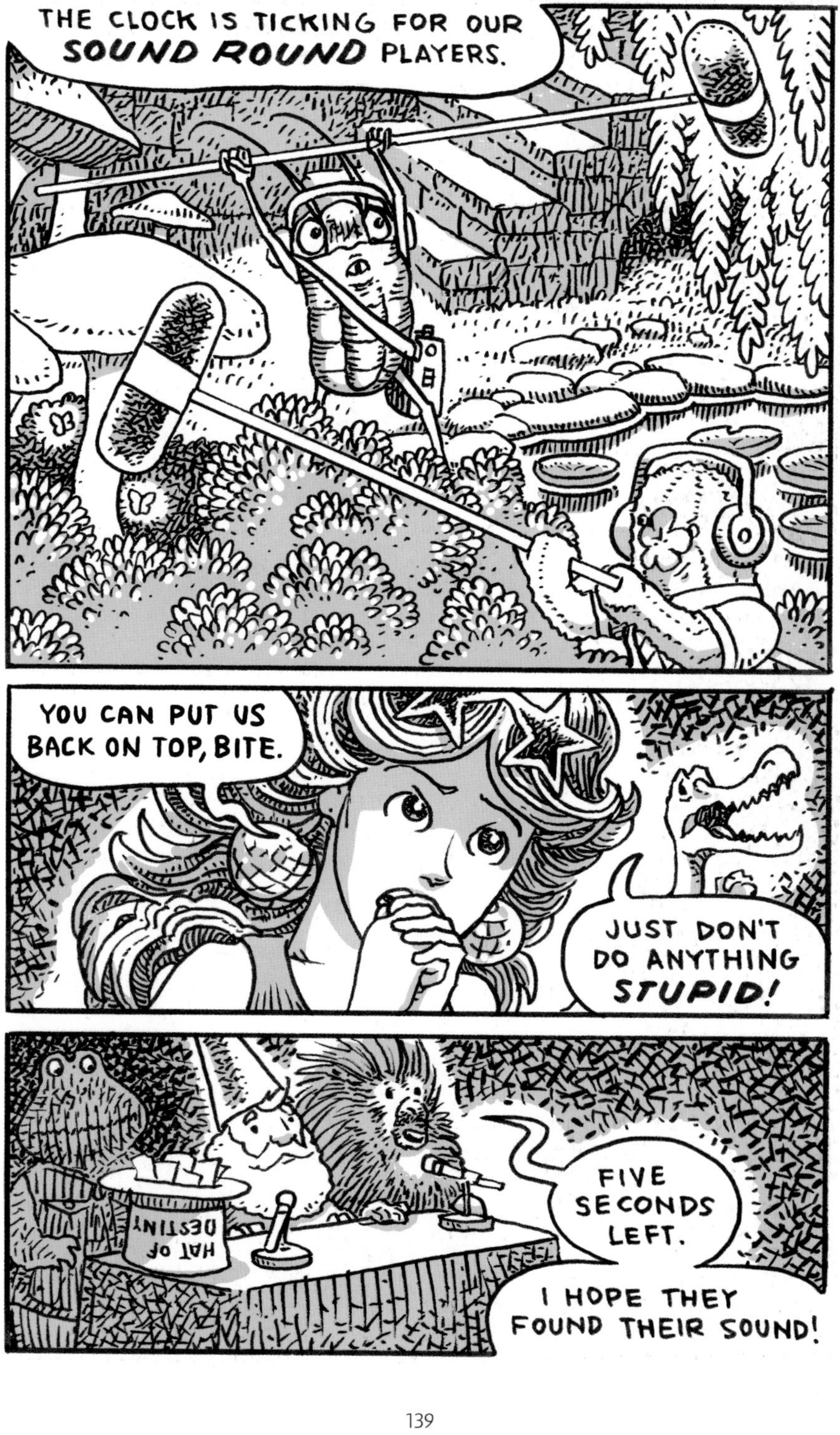
THE CLOCK IS TICKING FOR OUR SOUND ROUND PLAYERS.
YOU CAN PUT US BACK ON TOP, BITE.
JUST DON'T DO ANYTHING STUPID!
FIVE SECONDS LEFT.
I HOPE THEY FOUND THEIR SOUND!

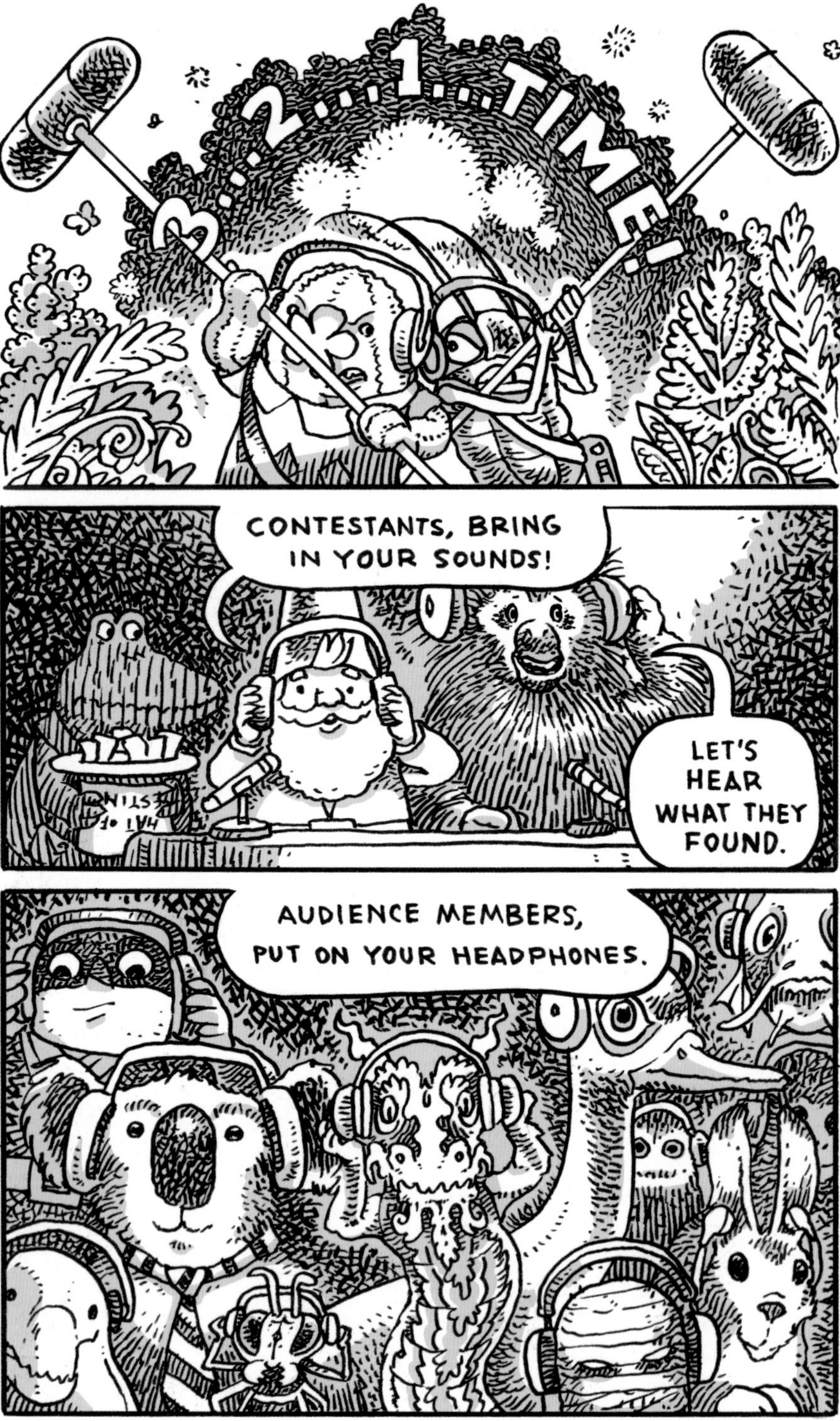
3...2...1...TIME!
CONTESTANTS, BRING IN YOUR SOUNDS!
LET'S HEAR WHAT THEY FOUND.
AUDIENCE MEMBERS, PUT ON YOUR HEADPHONES.

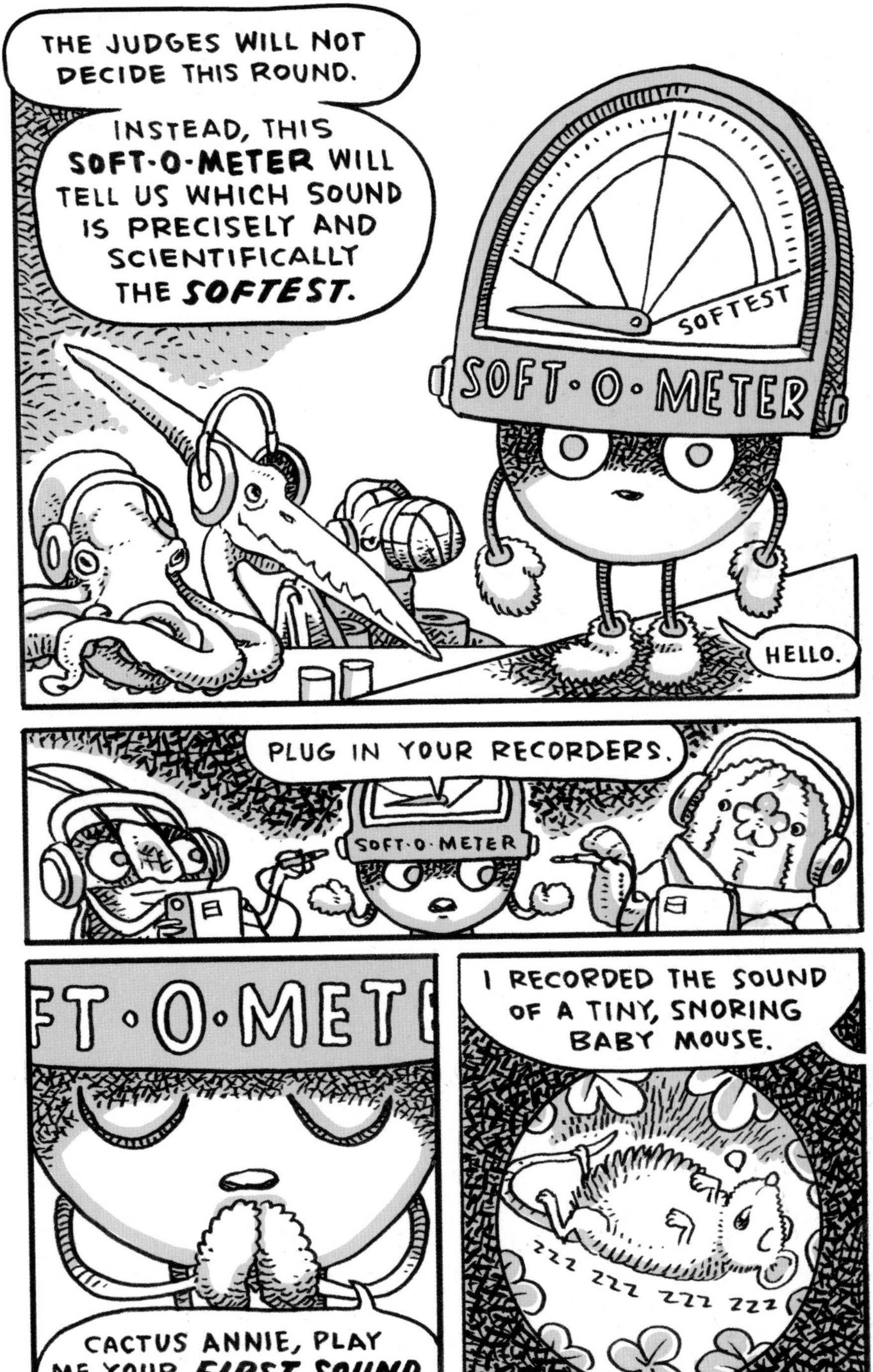
THE JUDGES WILL NOT DECIDE THIS ROUND.
INSTEAD, THIS **SOFT-O-METER** WILL TELL US WHICH SOUND IS PRECISELY AND SCIENTIFICALLY THE ***SOFTEST.***
SOFTEST
SOFT·O·METER
HELLO.
PLUG IN YOUR RECORDERS.
SOFT·O·METER
FT·O·METE
CACTUS ANNIE, PLAY ME YOUR ***FIRST SOUND.***
I RECORDED THE SOUND OF A TINY, SNORING BABY MOUSE.
ZZZ ZZZ ZZZ ZZZ

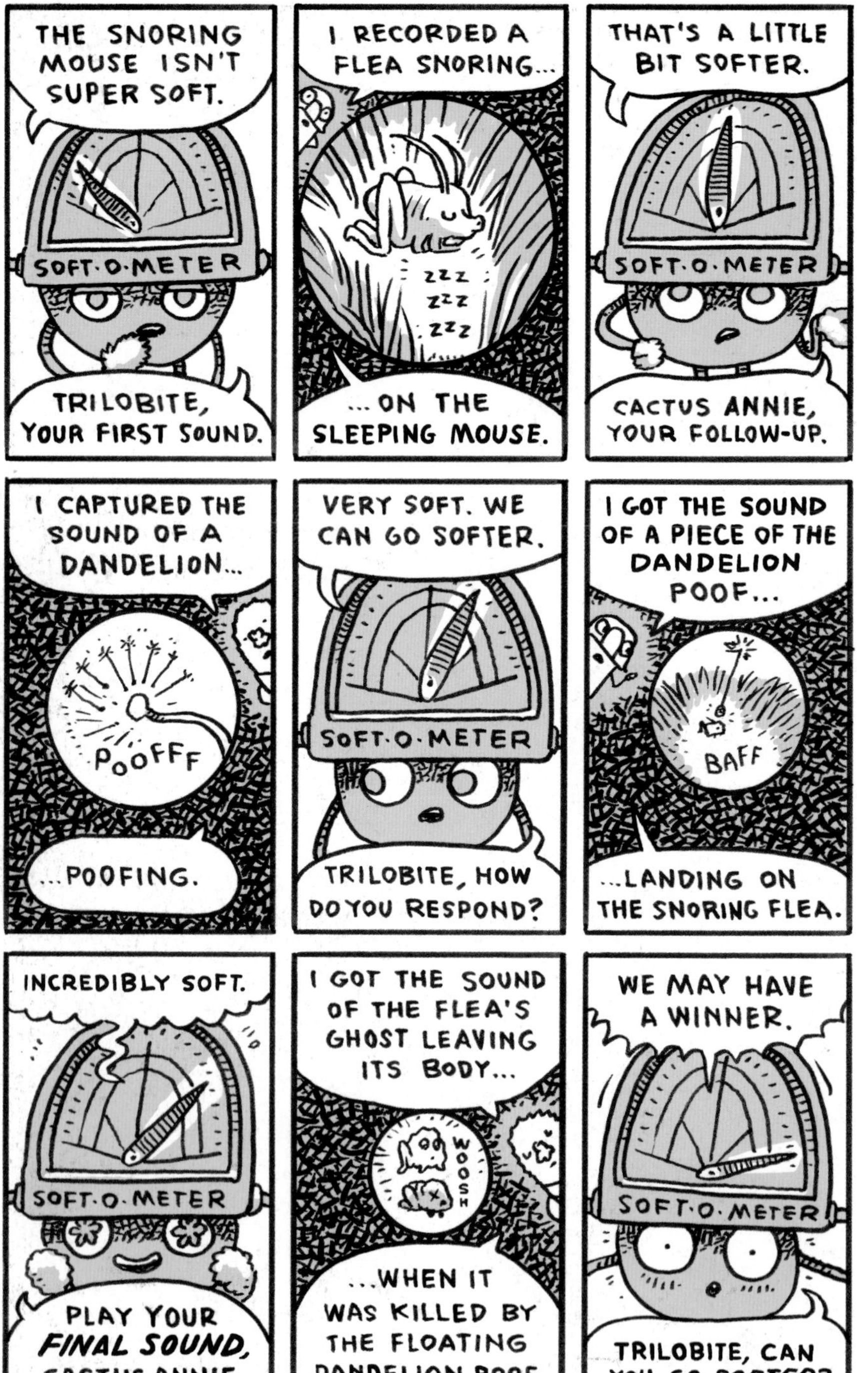
THE SNORING MOUSE ISN'T SUPER SOFT.
SOFT-O-METER
TRILOBITE, YOUR FIRST SOUND.
I RECORDED A FLEA SNORING...
ZZZ ZZZ ZZZ
...ON THE SLEEPING MOUSE.
THAT'S A LITTLE BIT SOFTER.
SOFT-O-METER
CACTUS ANNIE, YOUR FOLLOW-UP.
I CAPTURED THE SOUND OF A DANDELION...
POOFFF
...POOFING.
VERY SOFT. WE CAN GO SOFTER.
SOFT-O-METER
TRILOBITE, HOW DO YOU RESPOND?
I GOT THE SOUND OF A PIECE OF THE DANDELION POOF...
BAFF
...LANDING ON THE SNORING FLEA.
INCREDIBLY SOFT.
SOFT-O-METER
PLAY YOUR *FINAL SOUND,* CACTUS ANNIE.
I GOT THE SOUND OF THE FLEA'S GHOST LEAVING ITS BODY...
WOOSH
...WHEN IT WAS KILLED BY THE FLOATING DANDELION POOF.
WE MAY HAVE A WINNER.
SOFT-O-METER
TRILOBITE, CAN YOU GO *SOFTER?*

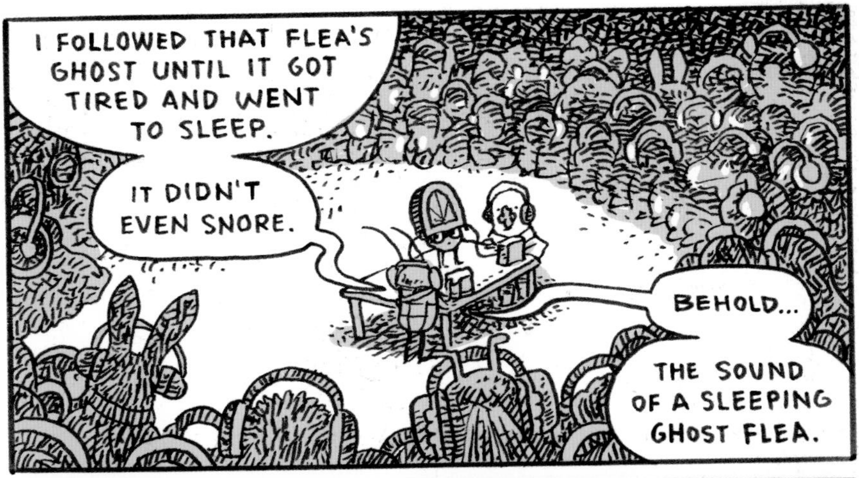
I FOLLOWED THAT FLEA'S GHOST UNTIL IT GOT TIRED AND WENT TO SLEEP.
IT DIDN'T EVEN SNORE.
BEHOLD...
THE SOUND OF A SLEEPING GHOST FLEA.

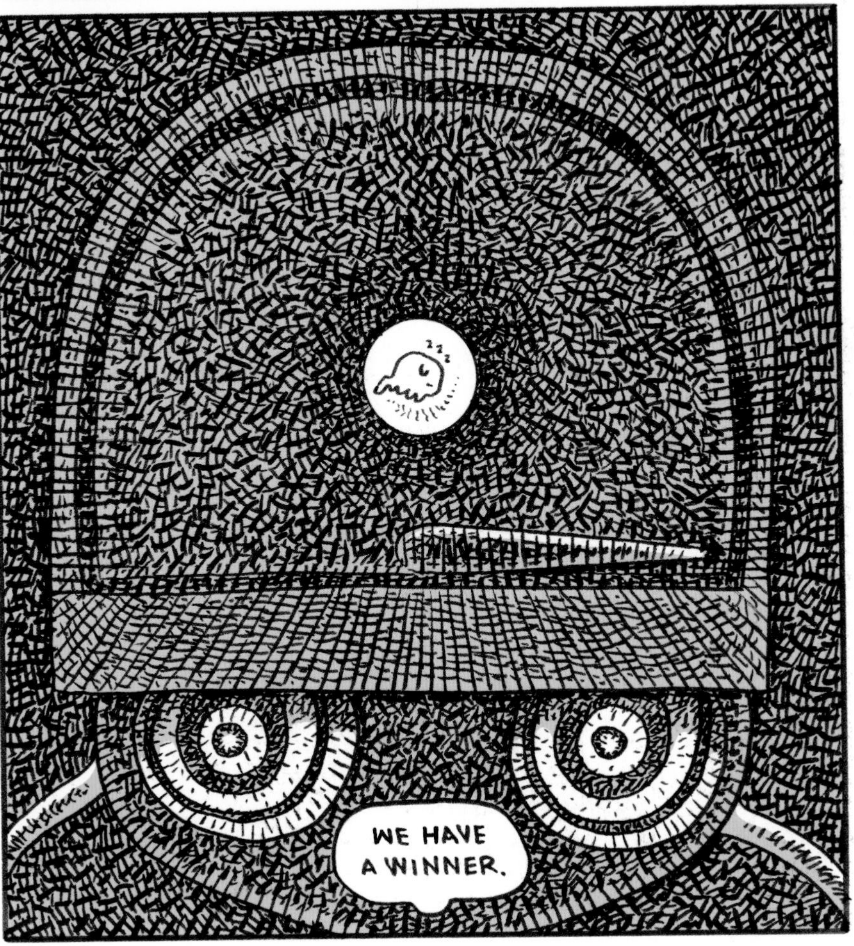
WE HAVE A WINNER.

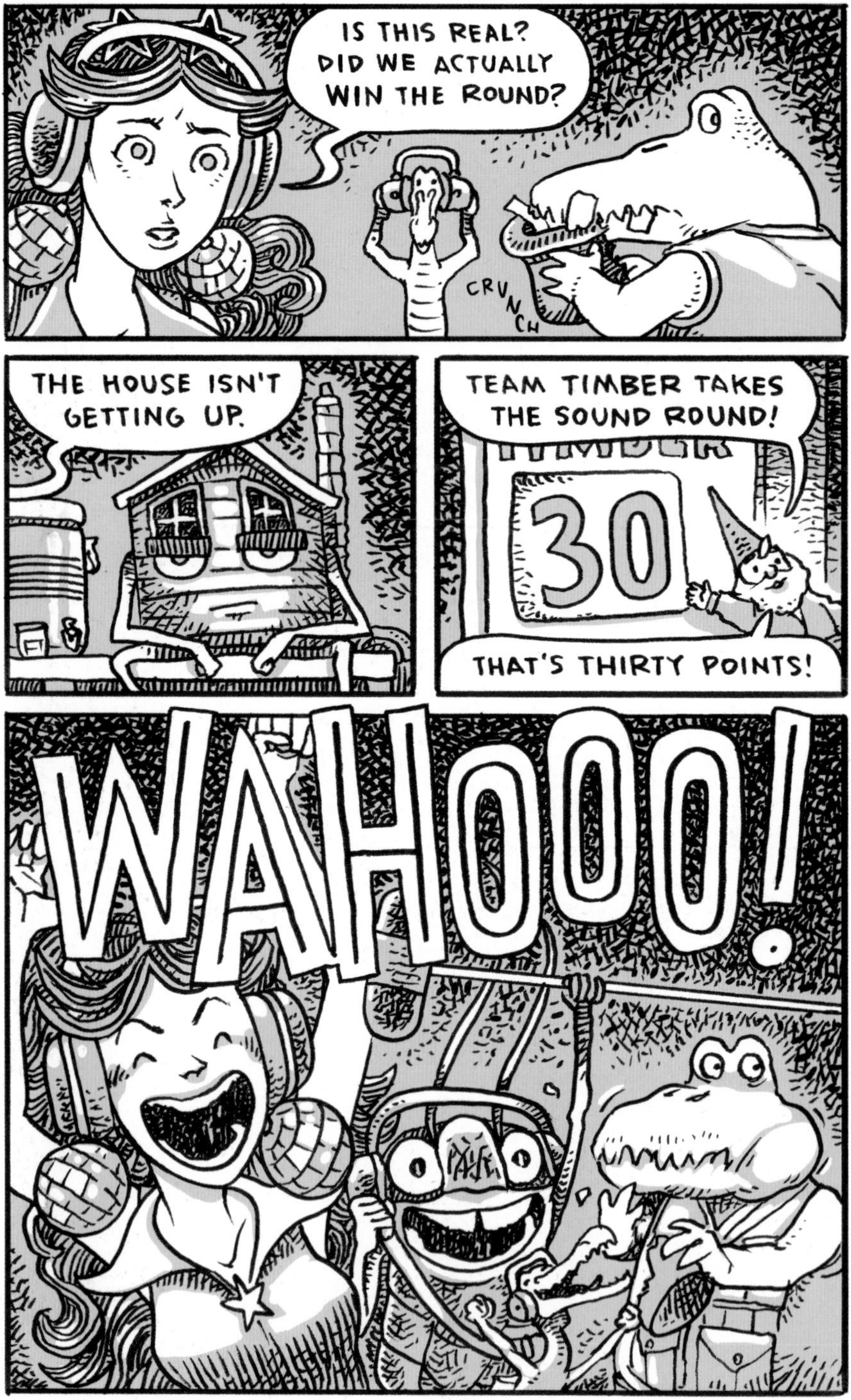
IS THIS REAL? DID WE ACTUALLY WIN THE ROUND?
CRUNCH
THE HOUSE ISN'T GETTING UP.
TEAM TIMBER TAKES THE SOUND ROUND!
30
THAT'S THIRTY POINTS!
WAHOOO!

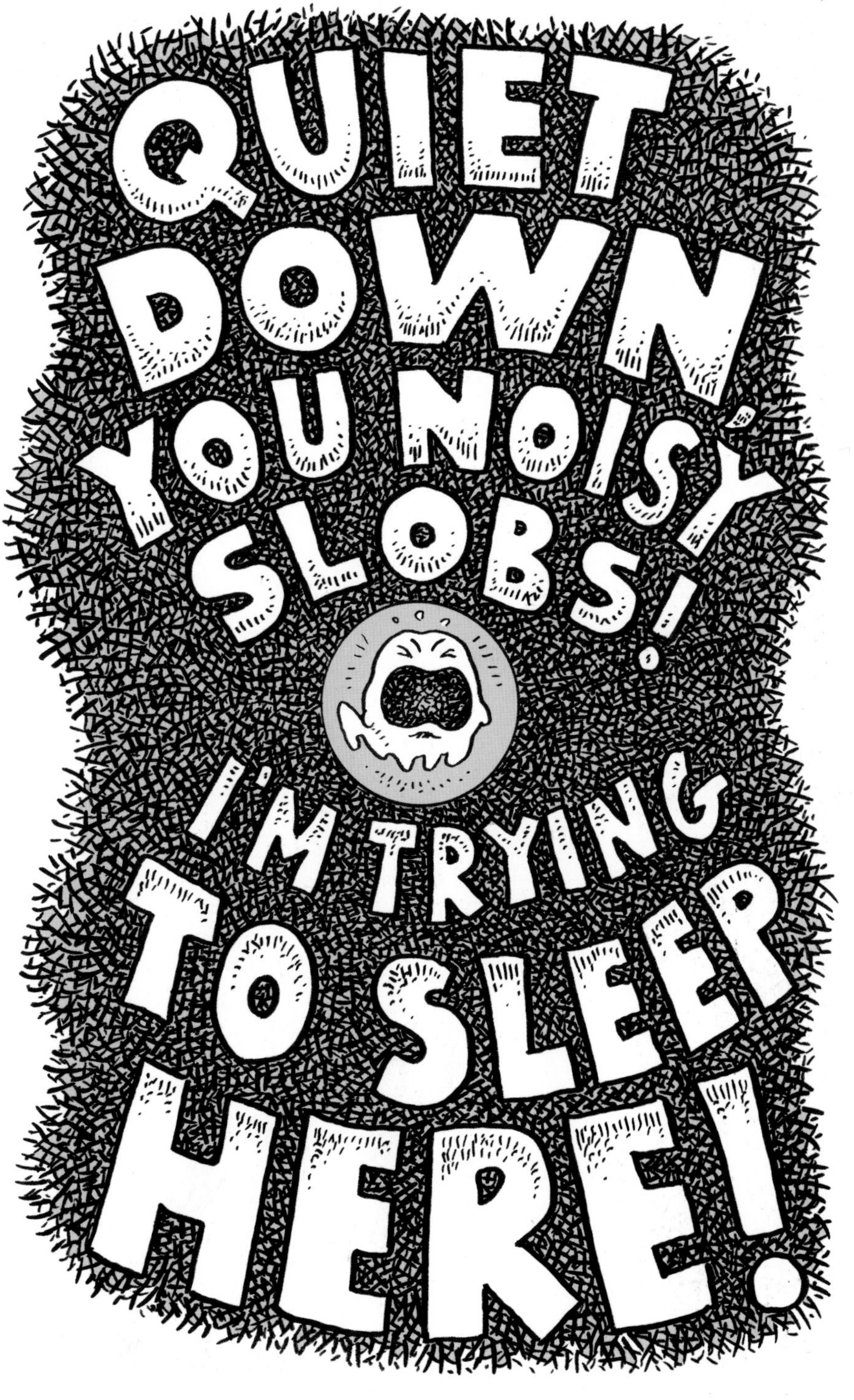
QUIET DOWN YOU NOISY SLOBS!
I'M TRYING TO SLEEP HERE!

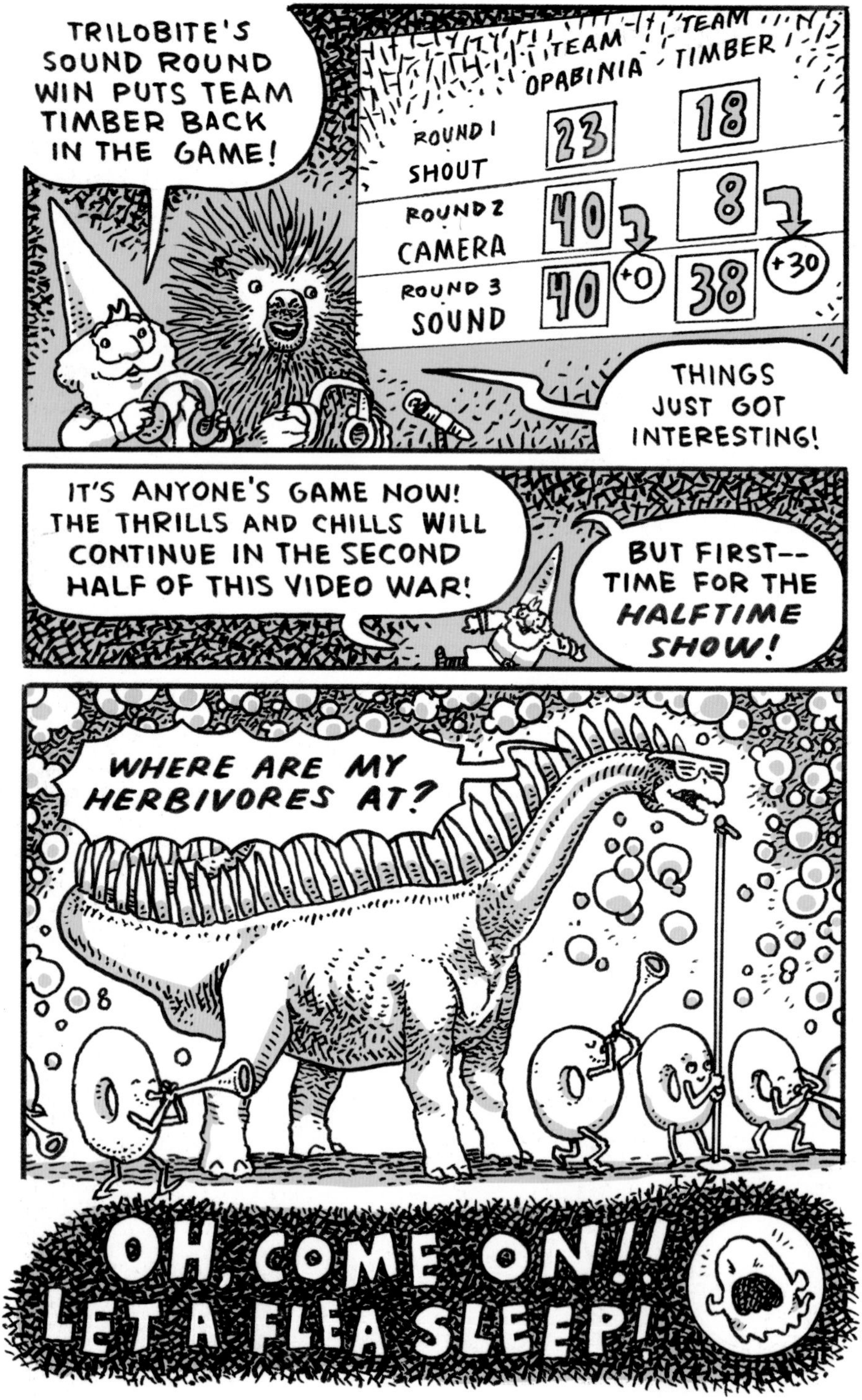
TRILOBITE'S SOUND ROUND WIN PUTS TEAM TIMBER BACK IN THE GAME!
TEAM OPABINIA
TEAM TIMBER
ROUND 1 SHOUT
23
18
ROUND 2 CAMERA
40
8
ROUND 3 SOUND
40
+0
38
+30
THINGS JUST GOT INTERESTING!
IT'S ANYONE'S GAME NOW! THE THRILLS AND CHILLS WILL CONTINUE IN THE SECOND HALF OF THIS VIDEO WAR!
BUT FIRST-- TIME FOR THE *HALFTIME SHOW!*
WHERE ARE MY HERBIVORES AT?
OH, COME ON!! LET A FLEA SLEEP!

CHAPTER 6

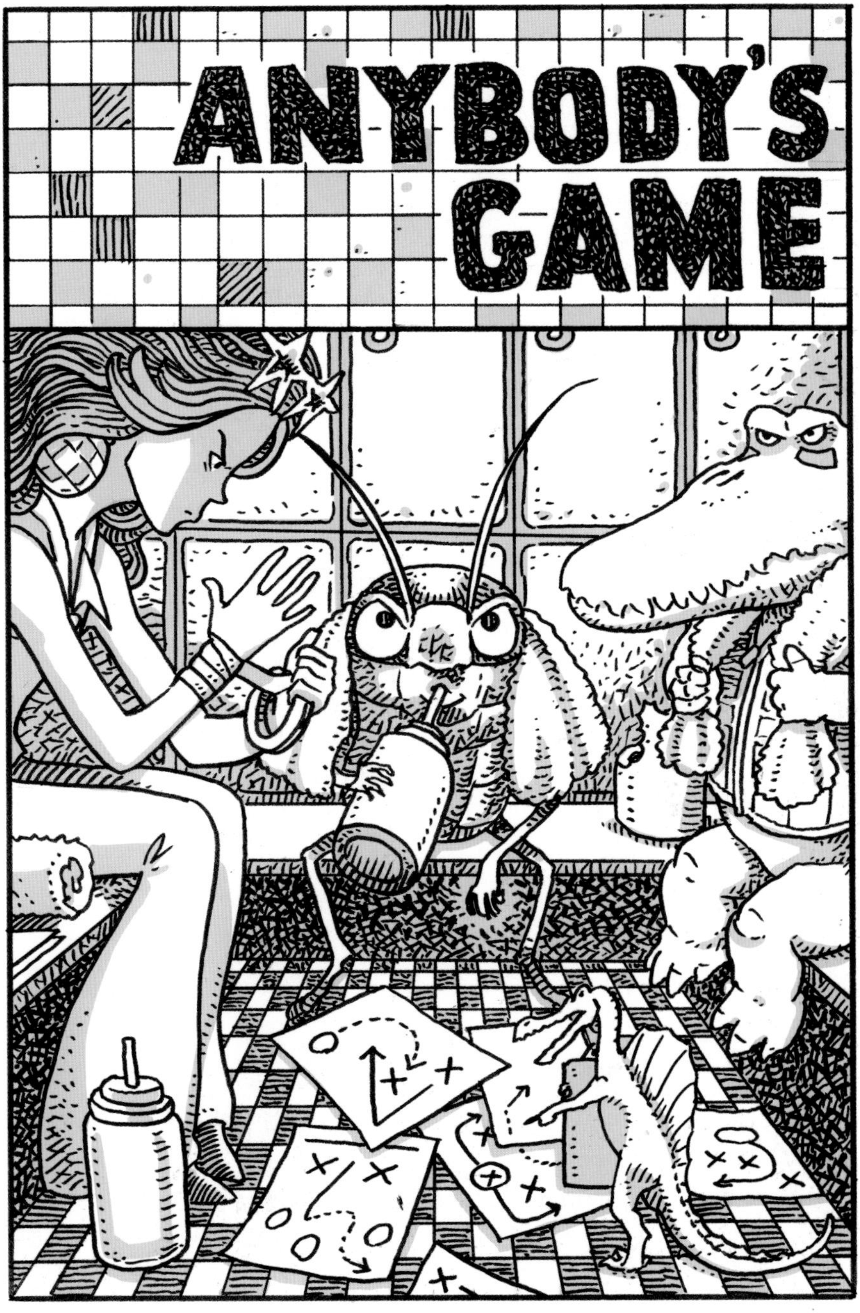
ANYBODY'S GAME

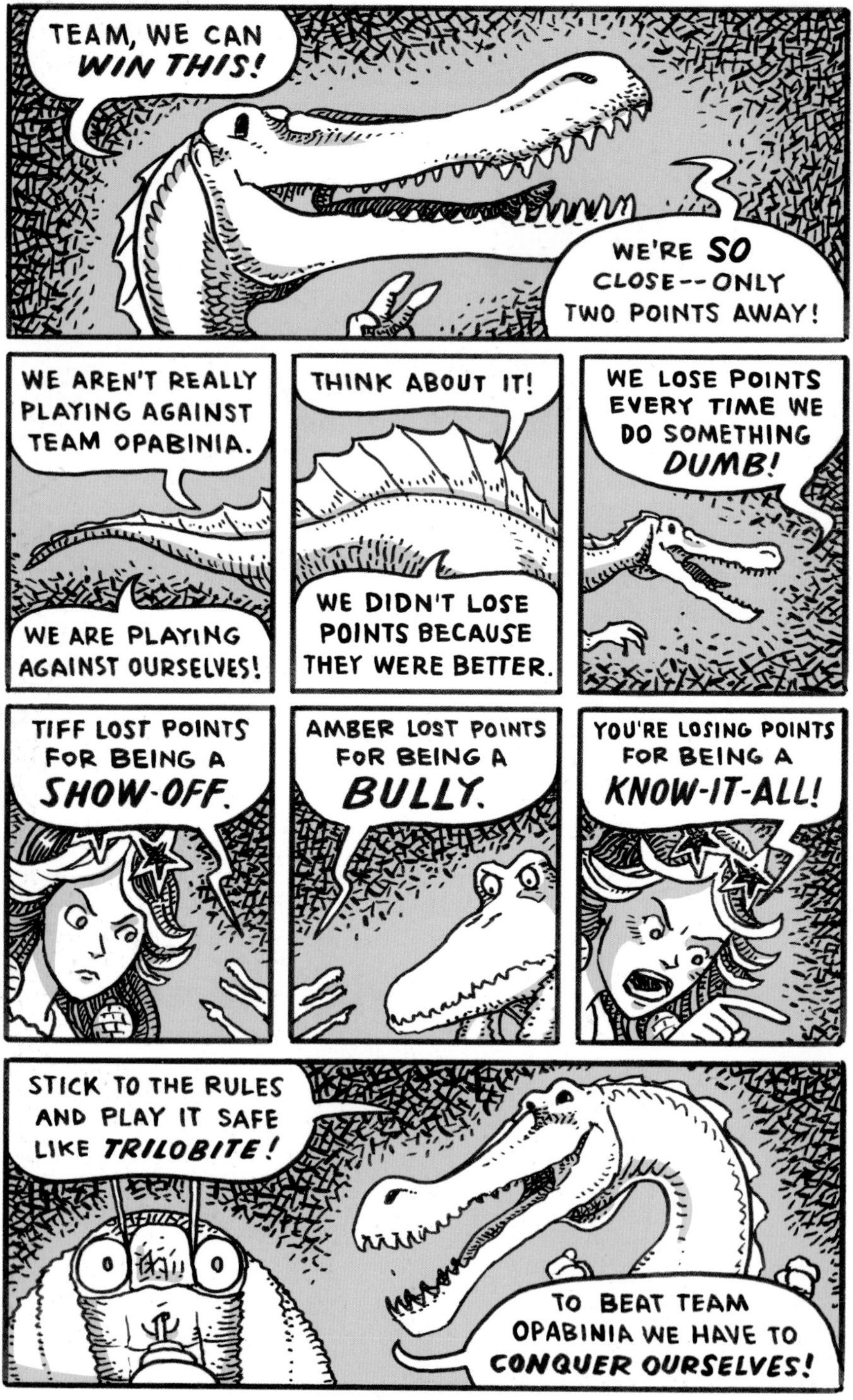
TEAM, WE CAN WIN THIS!
WE'RE SO CLOSE--ONLY TWO POINTS AWAY!
WE AREN'T REALLY PLAYING AGAINST TEAM OPABINIA.
WE ARE PLAYING AGAINST OURSELVES!
THINK ABOUT IT!
WE DIDN'T LOSE POINTS BECAUSE THEY WERE BETTER.
WE LOSE POINTS EVERY TIME WE DO SOMETHING DUMB!
TIFF LOST POINTS FOR BEING A SHOW-OFF.
AMBER LOST POINTS FOR BEING A BULLY.
YOU'RE LOSING POINTS FOR BEING A KNOW-IT-ALL!
STICK TO THE RULES AND PLAY IT SAFE LIKE TRILOBITE!
TO BEAT TEAM OPABINIA WE HAVE TO CONQUER OURSELVES!

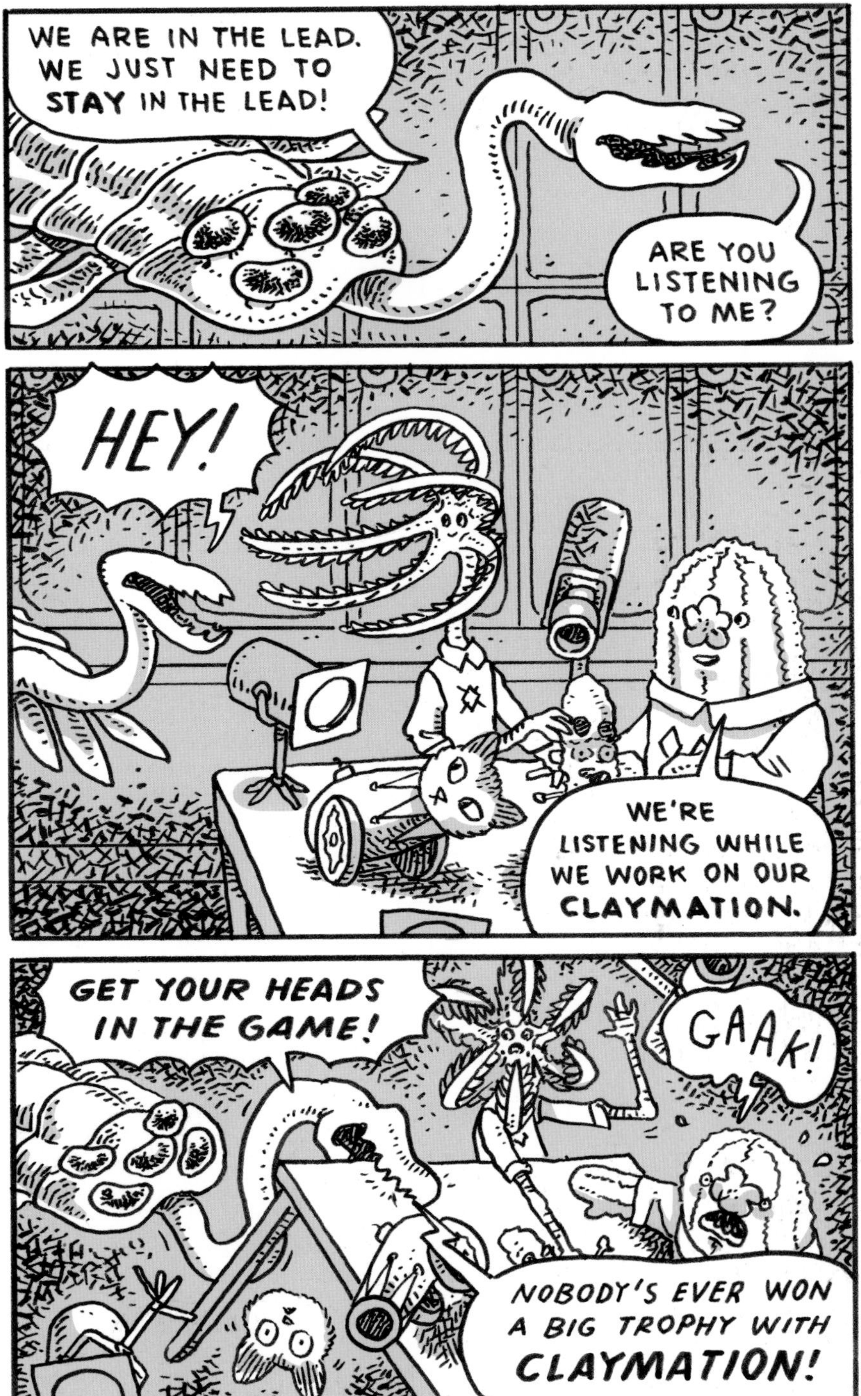
WE ARE IN THE LEAD. WE JUST NEED TO STAY IN THE LEAD!
ARE YOU LISTENING TO ME?
HEY!
WE'RE LISTENING WHILE WE WORK ON OUR CLAYMATION.
GET YOUR HEADS IN THE GAME!
GAAK!
NOBODY'S EVER WON A BIG TROPHY WITH CLAYMATION!

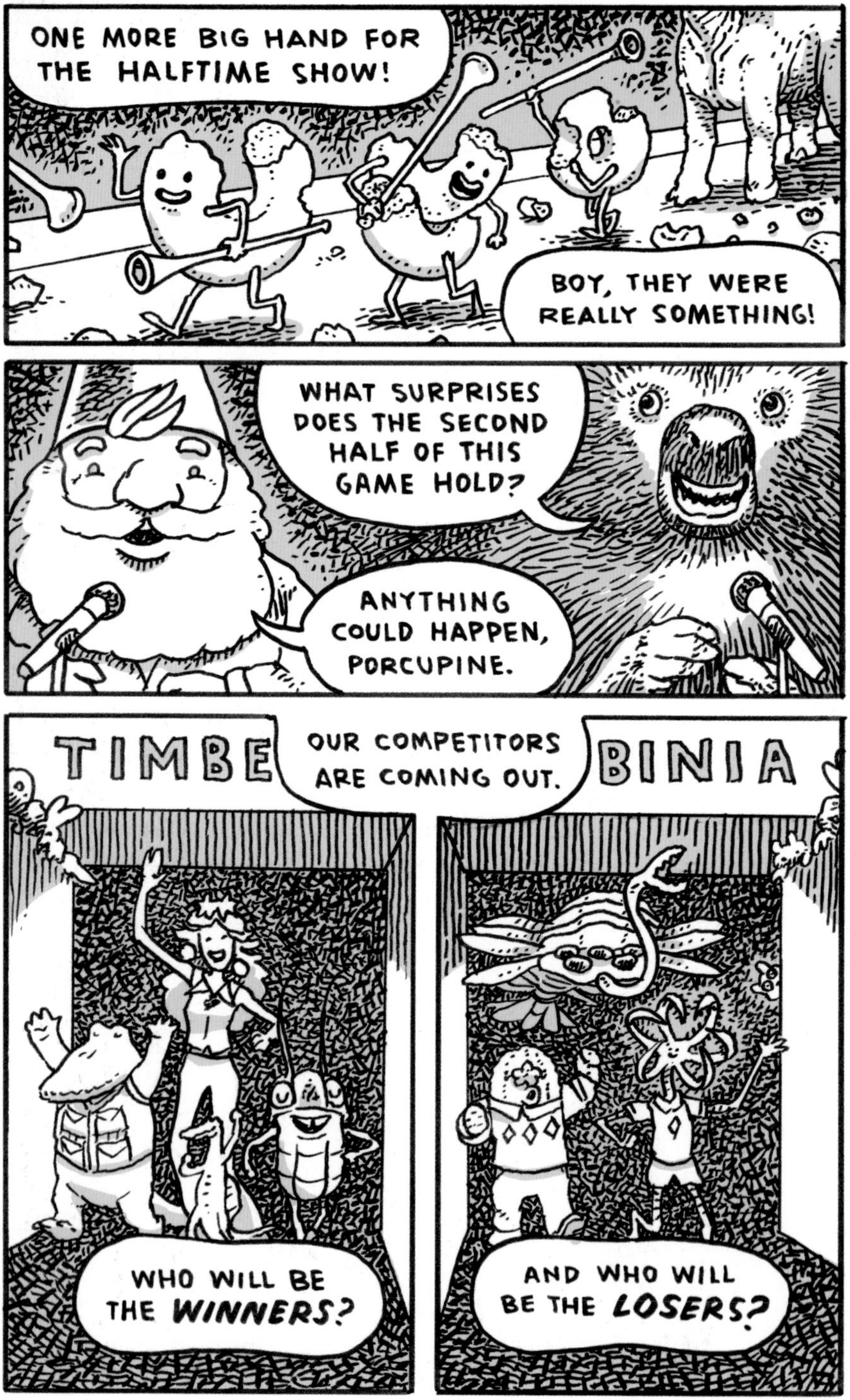
ONE MORE BIG HAND FOR THE HALFTIME SHOW!
BOY, THEY WERE REALLY SOMETHING!
WHAT SURPRISES DOES THE SECOND HALF OF THIS GAME HOLD?
ANYTHING COULD HAPPEN, PORCUPINE.
TIMBE
OUR COMPETITORS ARE COMING OUT.
BINIA
WHO WILL BE THE WINNERS?
AND WHO WILL BE THE LOSERS?

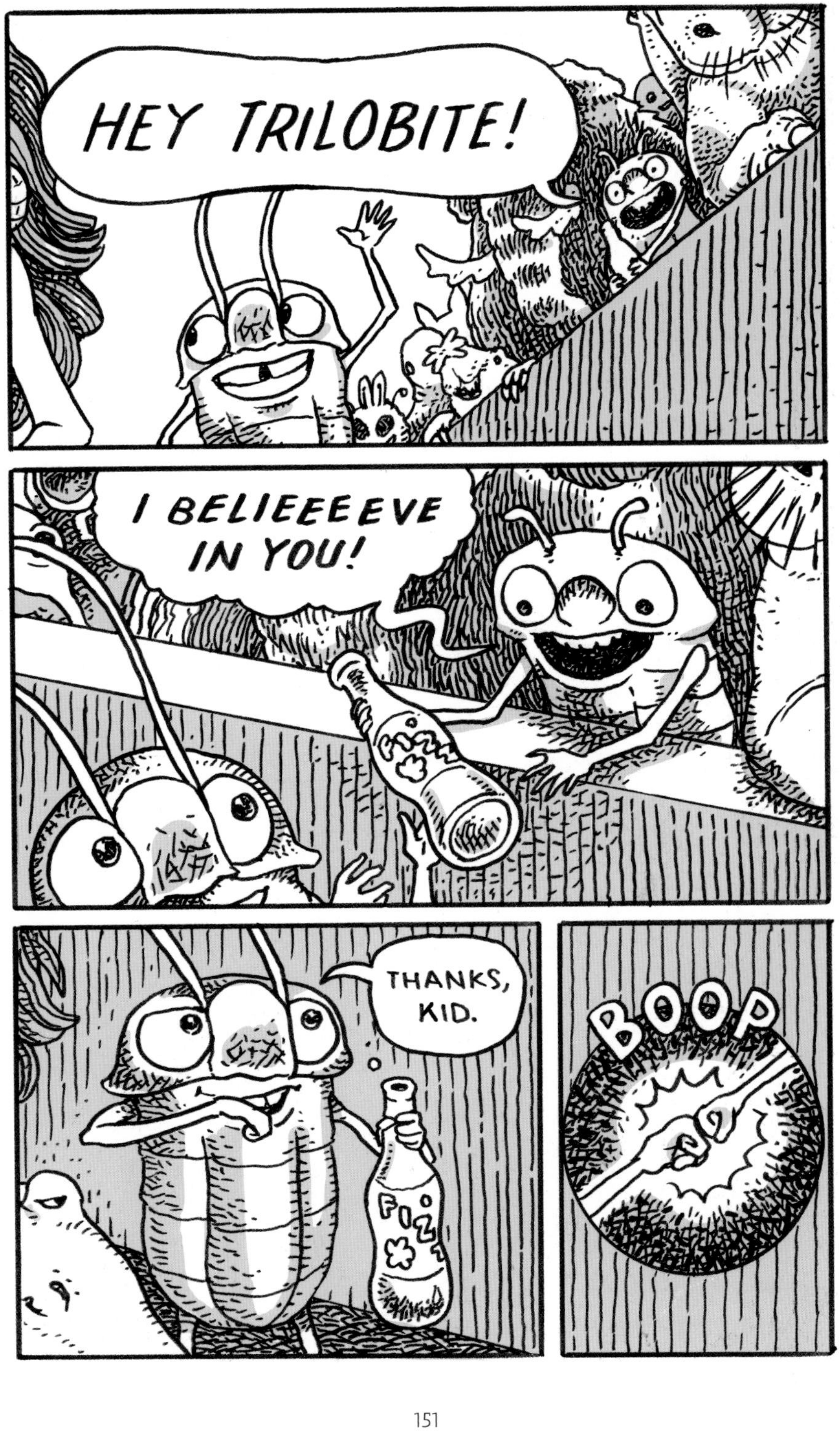
HEY TRILOBITE!
I BELIEEEEVE IN YOU!
THANKS, KID.
BOOP

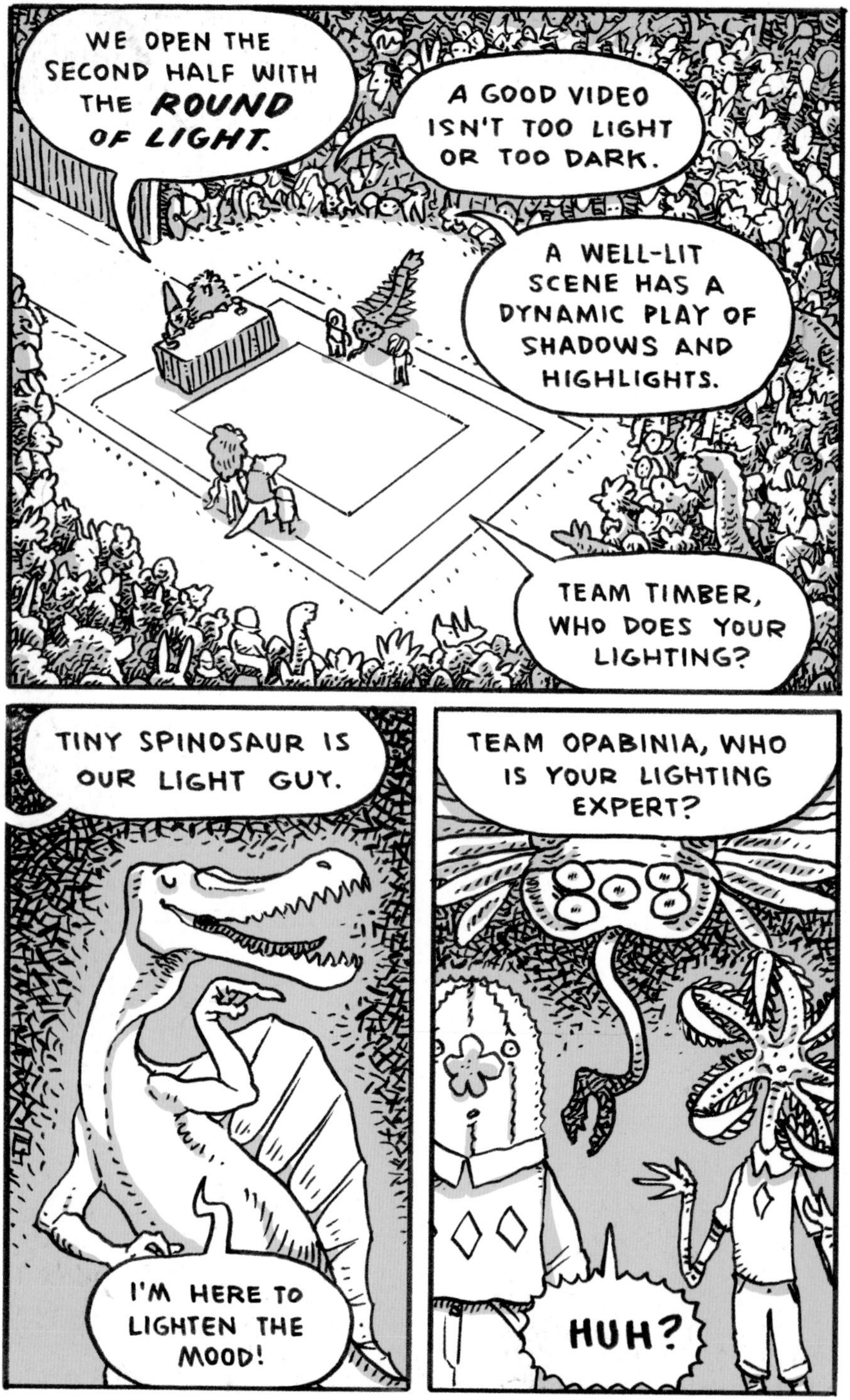
WE OPEN THE SECOND HALF WITH THE ROUND OF LIGHT.
A GOOD VIDEO ISN'T TOO LIGHT OR TOO DARK.
A WELL-LIT SCENE HAS A DYNAMIC PLAY OF SHADOWS AND HIGHLIGHTS.
TEAM TIMBER, WHO DOES YOUR LIGHTING?
TINY SPINOSAUR IS OUR LIGHT GUY.
I'M HERE TO LIGHTEN THE MOOD!
TEAM OPABINIA, WHO IS YOUR LIGHTING EXPERT?
HUH?

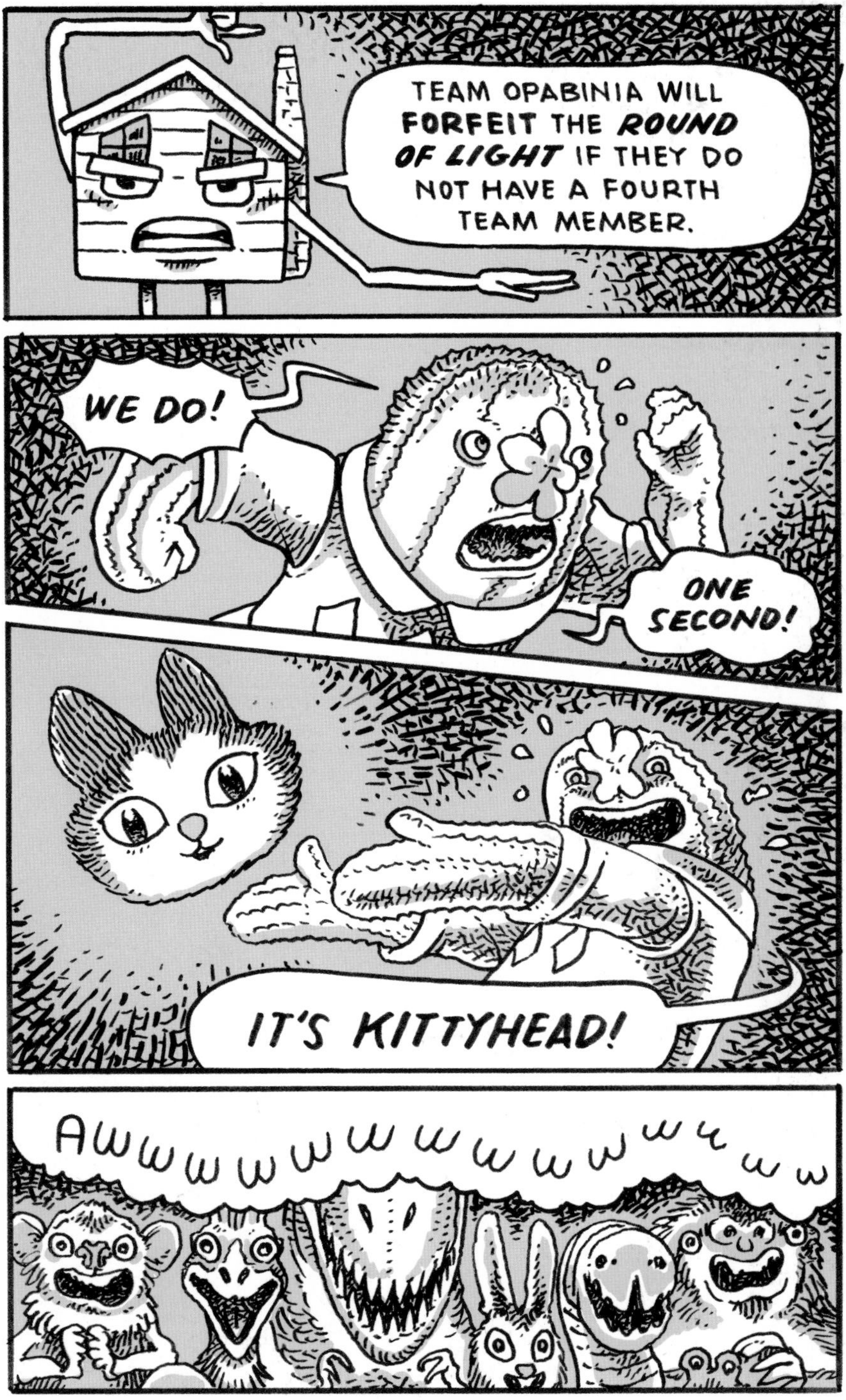
TEAM OPABINIA WILL **FORFEIT** THE ***ROUND OF LIGHT*** IF THEY DO NOT HAVE A FOURTH TEAM MEMBER.
WE DO!
ONE SECOND!
IT'S KITTYHEAD!
AWWWWWWWWWWWWWWWWW

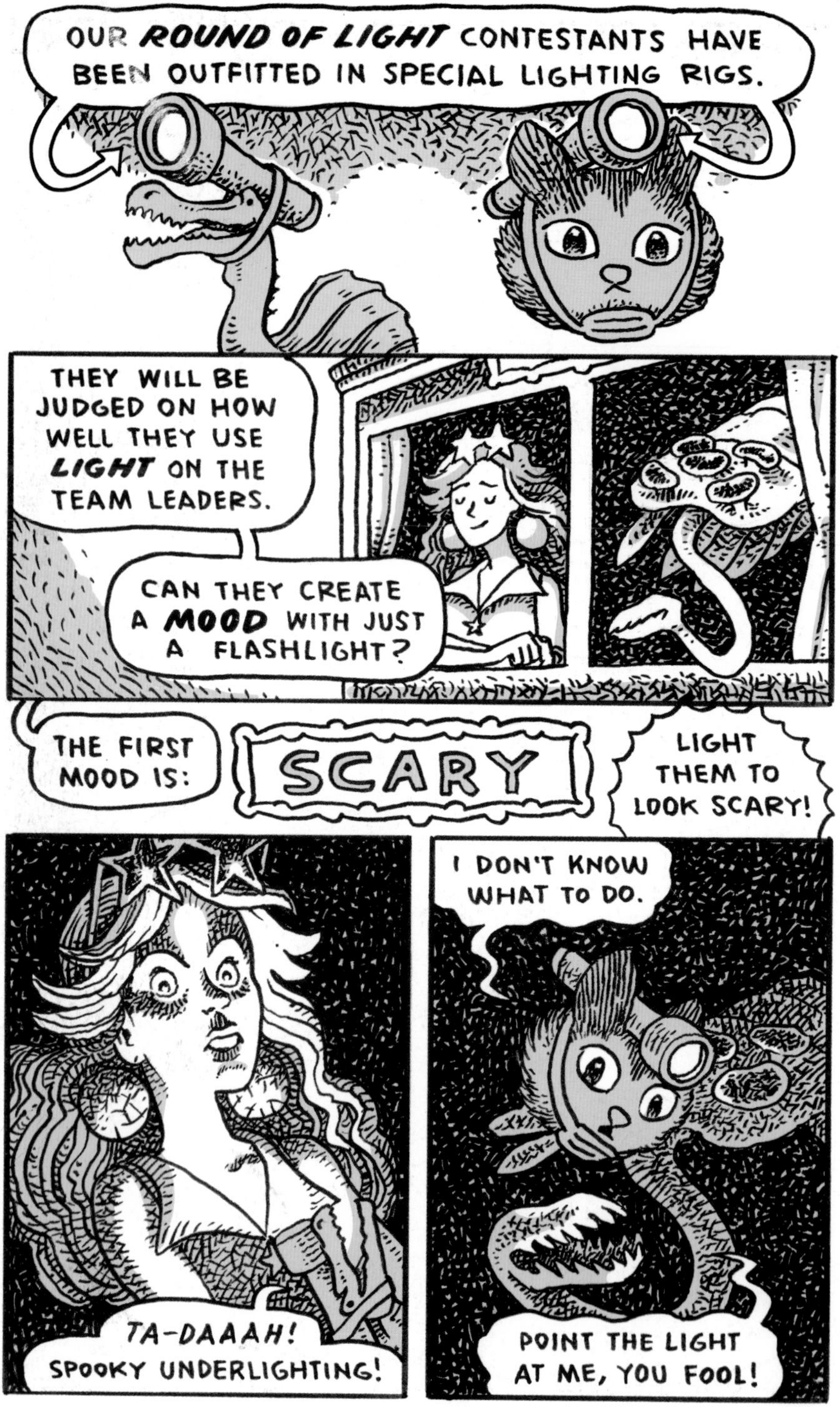
OUR ROUND OF LIGHT CONTESTANTS HAVE BEEN OUTFITTED IN SPECIAL LIGHTING RIGS.
THEY WILL BE JUDGED ON HOW WELL THEY USE LIGHT ON THE TEAM LEADERS.
CAN THEY CREATE A MOOD WITH JUST A FLASHLIGHT?
THE FIRST MOOD IS:
SCARY
LIGHT THEM TO LOOK SCARY!
TA-DAAAH! SPOOKY UNDERLIGHTING!
I DON'T KNOW WHAT TO DO.
POINT THE LIGHT AT ME, YOU FOOL!

THE NEXT MOOD IS GONNA BE...

SAD

SAD LIGHT!

DO A SAD FACE.

THIS IS MY SAD FACE!

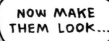

NOW MAKE THEM LOOK...

ANGRY

GRRR!

UM.

I'M ANGRY!

TEAM OPABINIA IS *REALLY* STRUGGLING WITH THIS ROUND.

SPIN

THERE'S ONE MOOD LEFT. CAN KITTYHEAD DO IT?

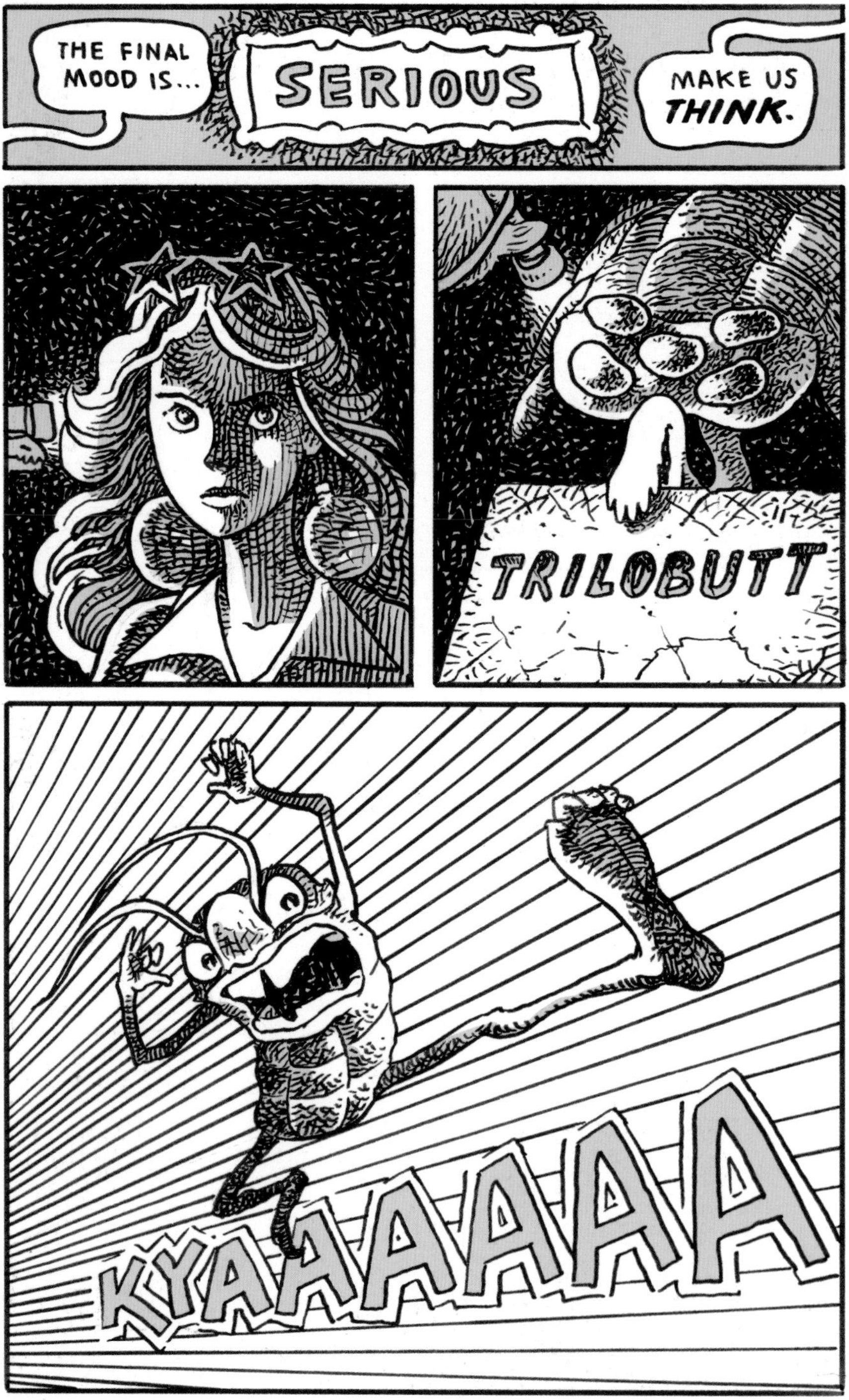
THE FINAL MOOD IS...
SERIOUS
MAKE US THINK.
TRILOBUTT
KYAAAAAAA

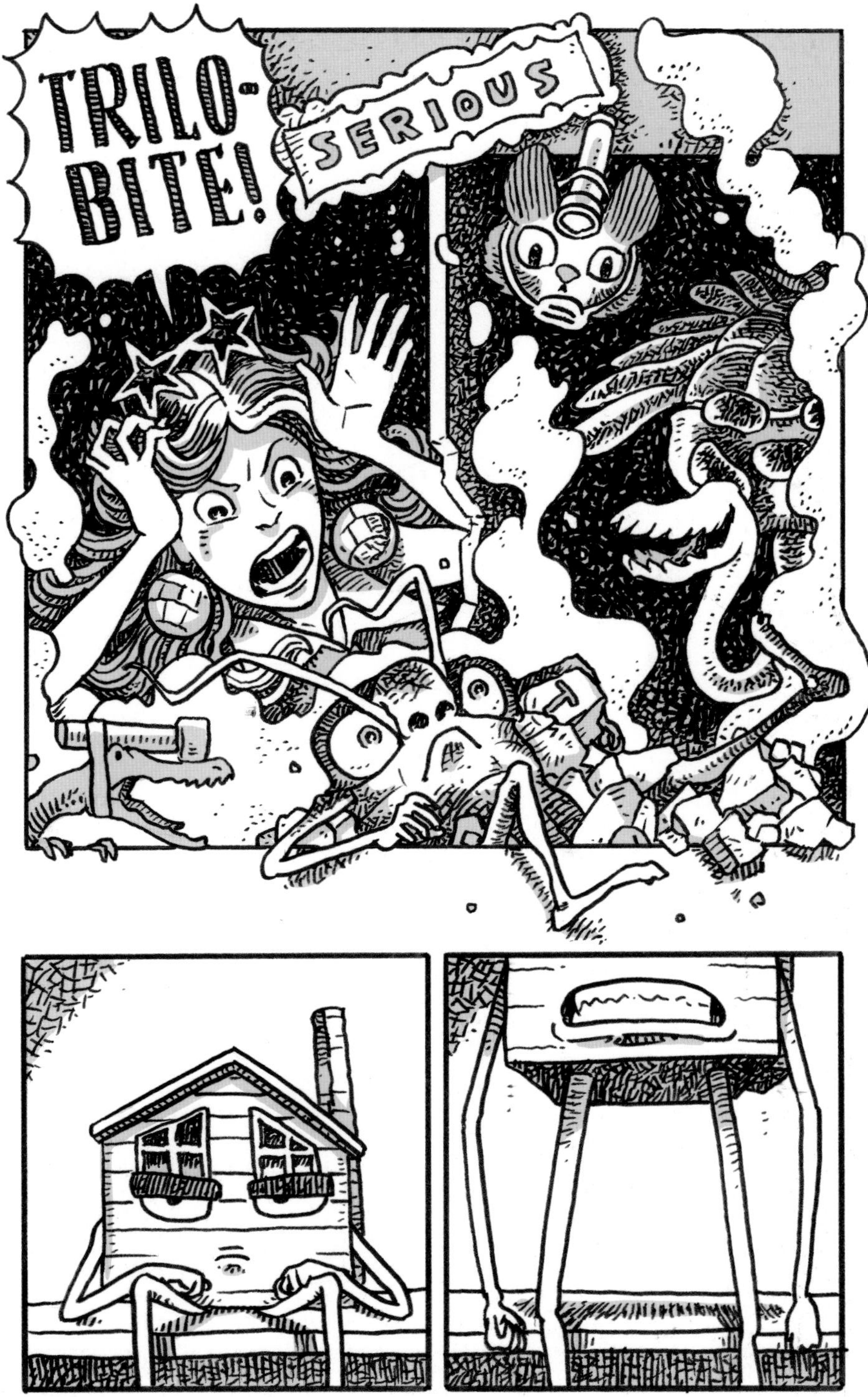
TRILO-BITE!
SERIOUS

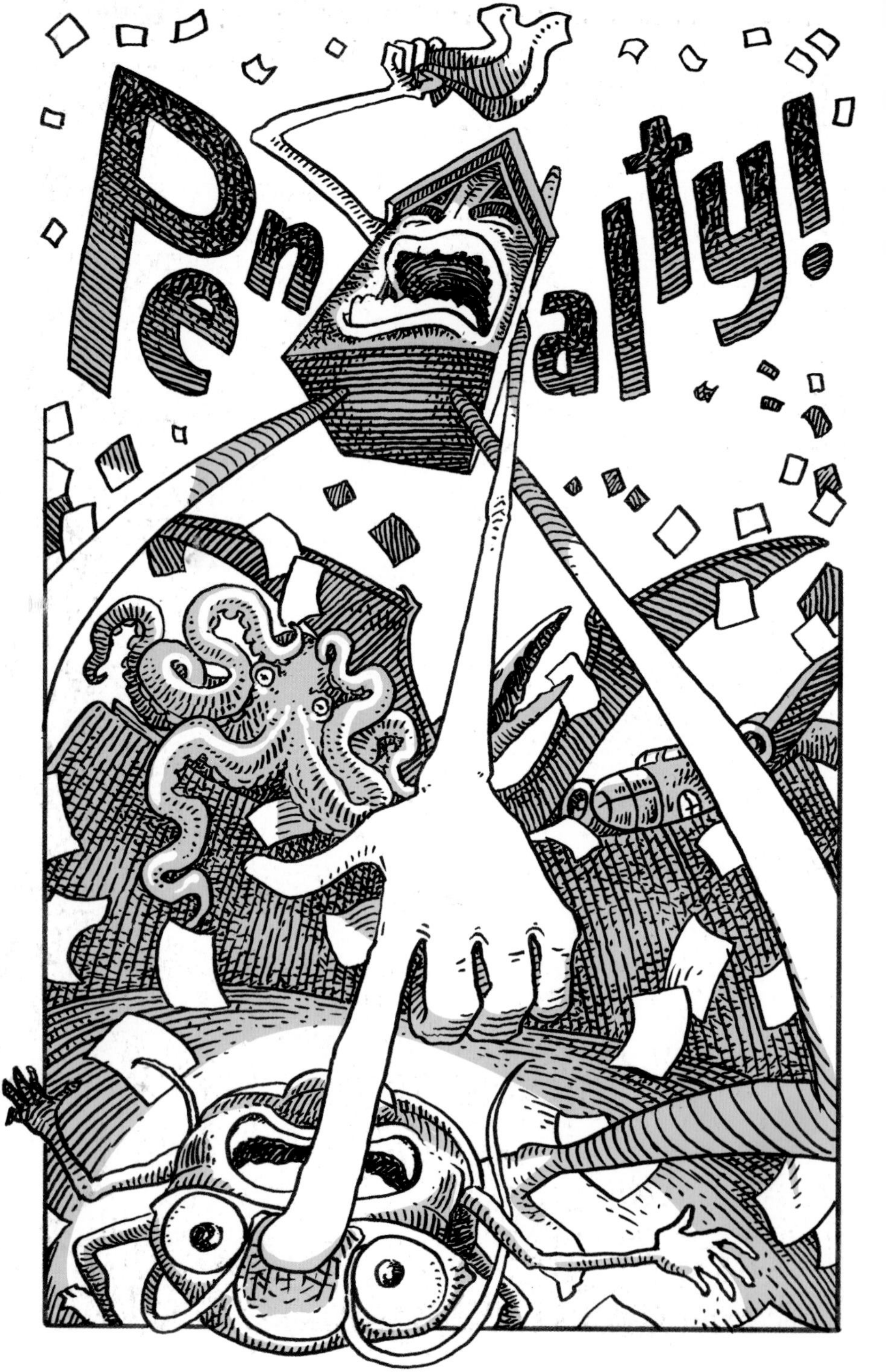
Penalty!

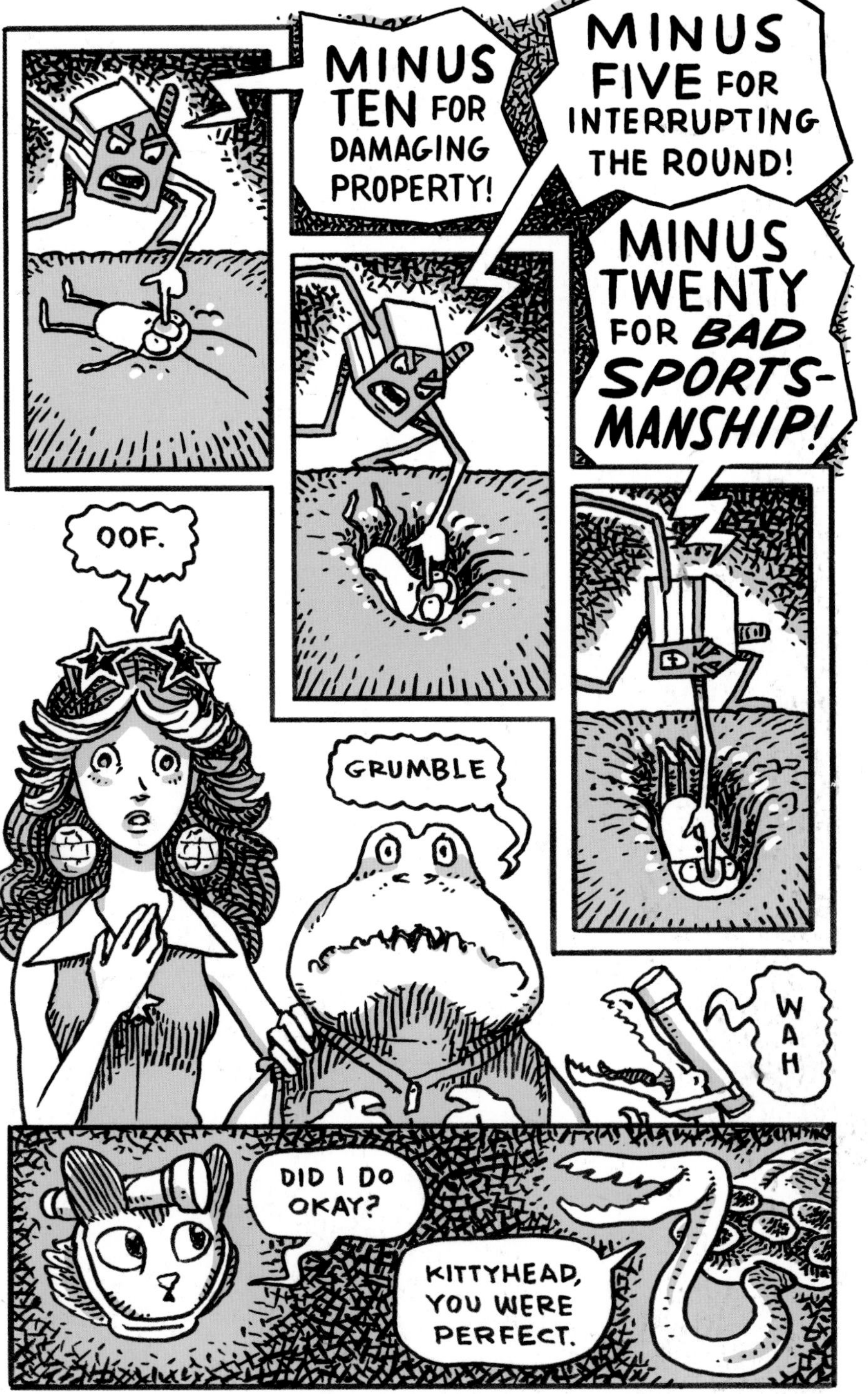
MINUS TEN FOR DAMAGING PROPERTY!
MINUS FIVE FOR INTERRUPTING THE ROUND!
MINUS TWENTY FOR BAD SPORTS-MANSHIP!
OOF.
GRUMBLE
WAH
DID I DO OKAY?
KITTYHEAD, YOU WERE PERFECT.

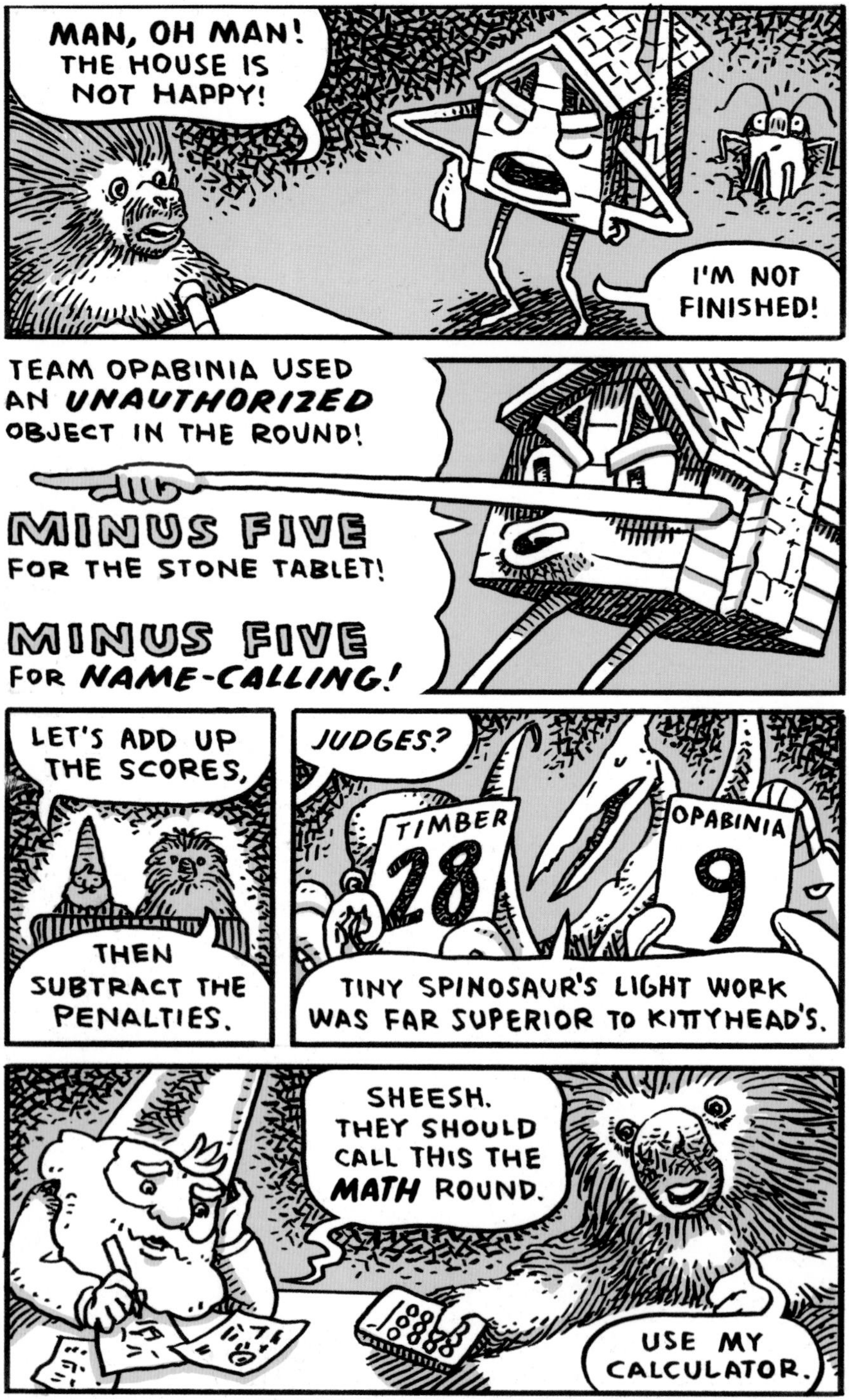
MAN, OH MAN! THE HOUSE IS NOT HAPPY!
I'M NOT FINISHED!
TEAM OPABINIA USED AN *UNAUTHORIZED* OBJECT IN THE ROUND!
MINUS FIVE FOR THE STONE TABLET!
MINUS FIVE FOR *NAME-CALLING!*
LET'S ADD UP THE SCORES,
THEN SUBTRACT THE PENALTIES.
JUDGES?
TIMBER
28
OPABINIA
9
TINY SPINOSAUR'S LIGHT WORK WAS FAR SUPERIOR TO KITTYHEAD'S.
SHEESH. THEY SHOULD CALL THIS THE *MATH* ROUND.
USE MY CALCULATOR.

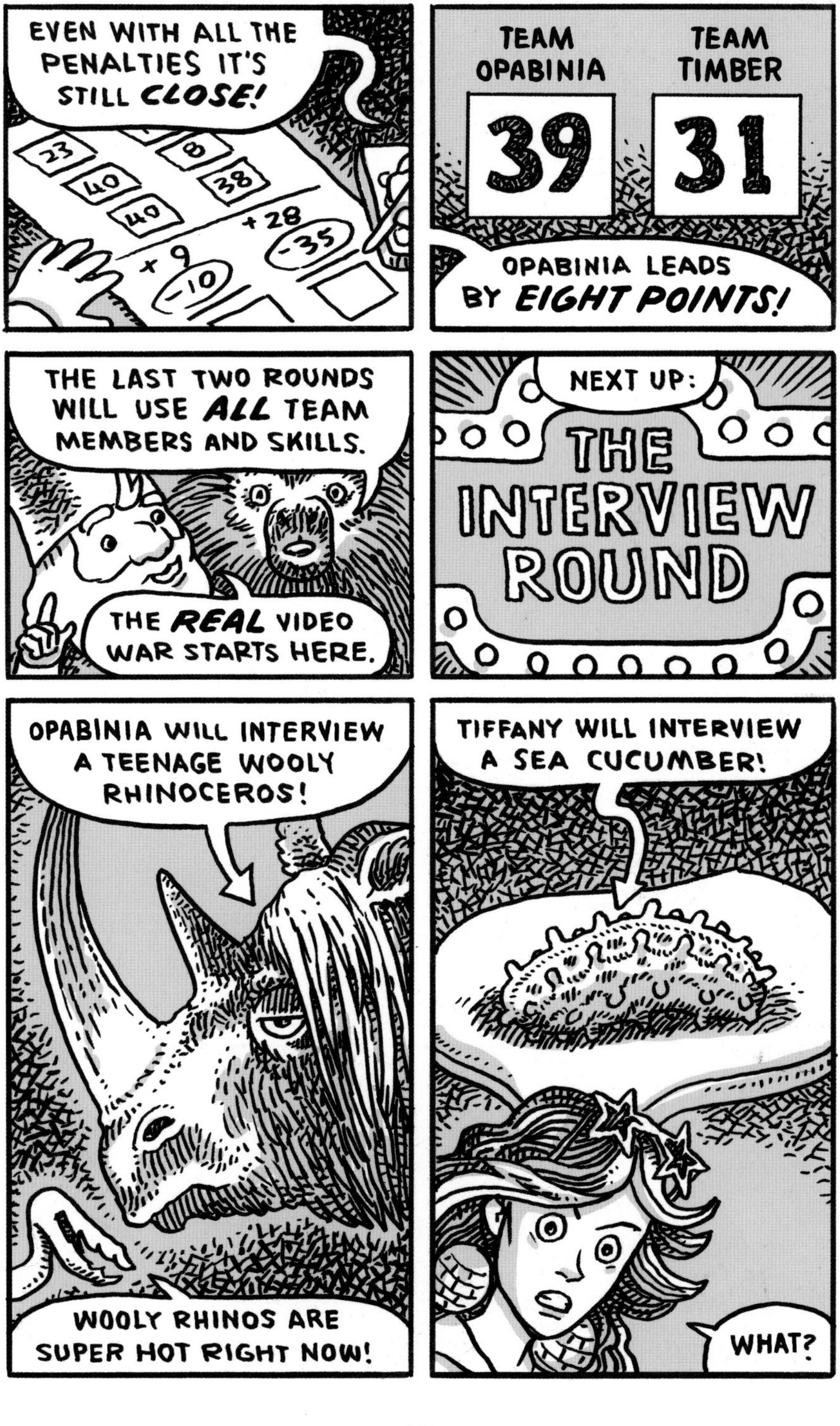
EVEN WITH ALL THE PENALTIES IT'S STILL *CLOSE!*
23
40
40
8
38
+28
-35
+9
-10
TEAM OPABINIA
TEAM TIMBER
39
31
OPABINIA LEADS BY *EIGHT POINTS!*
THE LAST TWO ROUNDS WILL USE *ALL* TEAM MEMBERS AND SKILLS.
THE *REAL* VIDEO WAR STARTS HERE.
NEXT UP:
THE INTERVIEW ROUND
OPABINIA WILL INTERVIEW A TEENAGE WOOLY RHINOCEROS!
WOOLY RHINOS ARE SUPER HOT RIGHT NOW!
TIFFANY WILL INTERVIEW A SEA CUCUMBER!
WHAT?

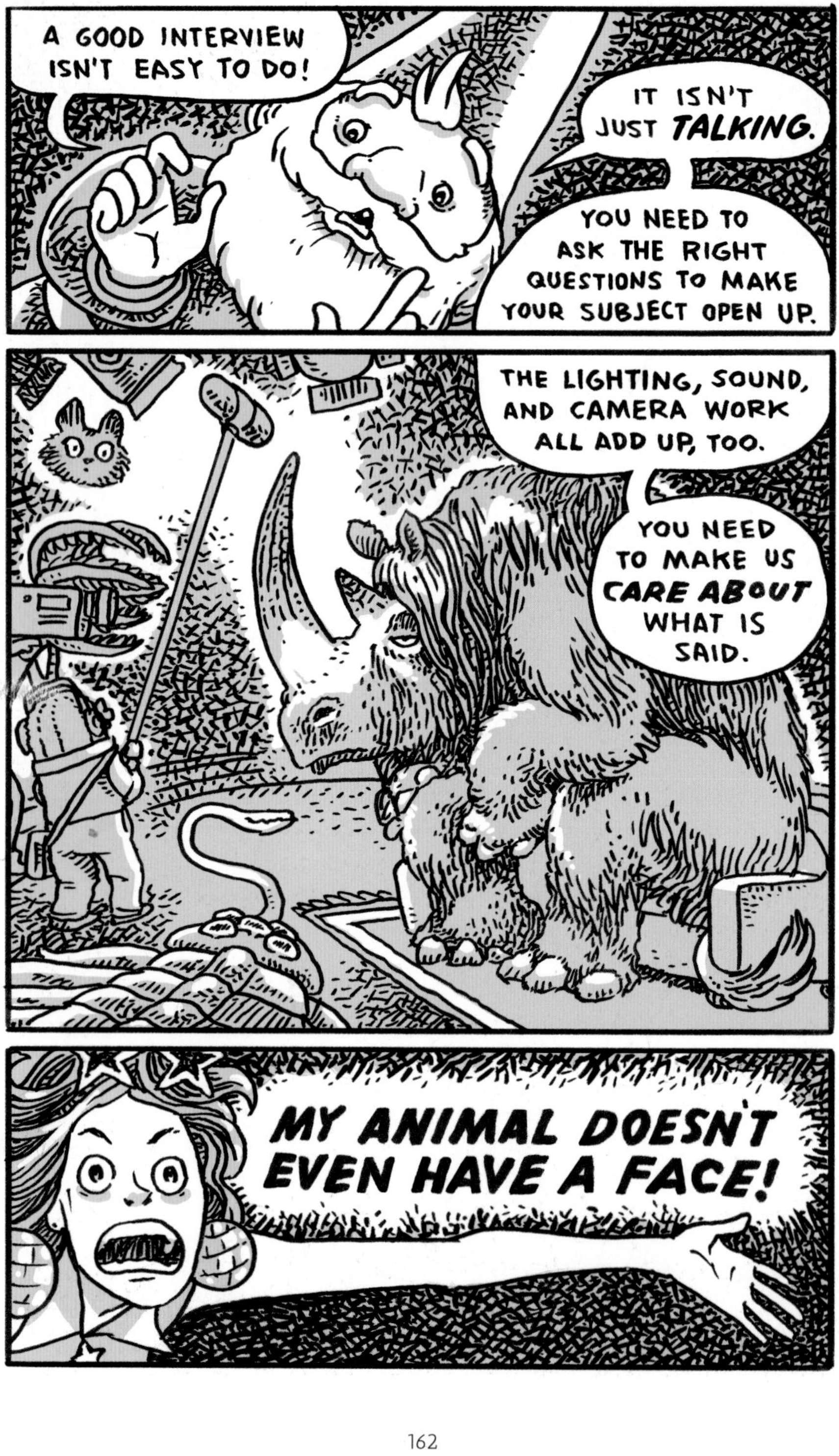
A GOOD INTERVIEW ISN'T EASY TO DO!
IT ISN'T JUST TALKING.
YOU NEED TO ASK THE RIGHT QUESTIONS TO MAKE YOUR SUBJECT OPEN UP.
THE LIGHTING, SOUND, AND CAMERA WORK ALL ADD UP, TOO.
YOU NEED TO MAKE US CARE ABOUT WHAT IS SAID.
MY ANIMAL DOESN'T EVEN HAVE A FACE!

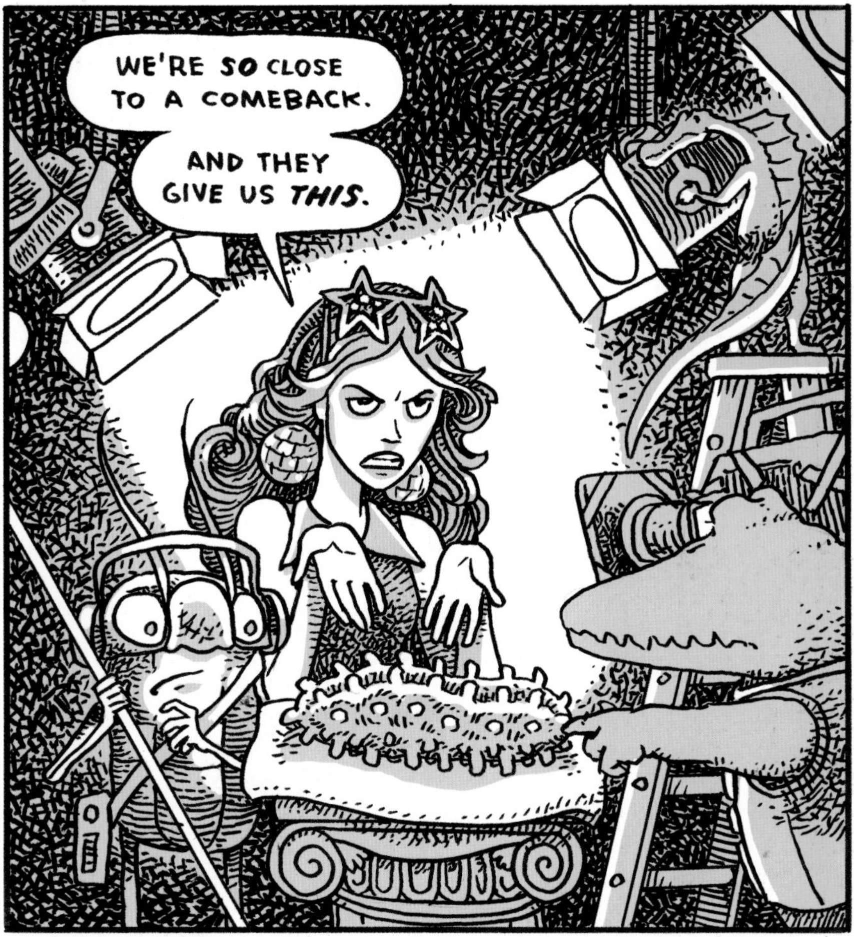
WE'RE SO CLOSE TO A COMEBACK.
AND THEY GIVE US THIS.

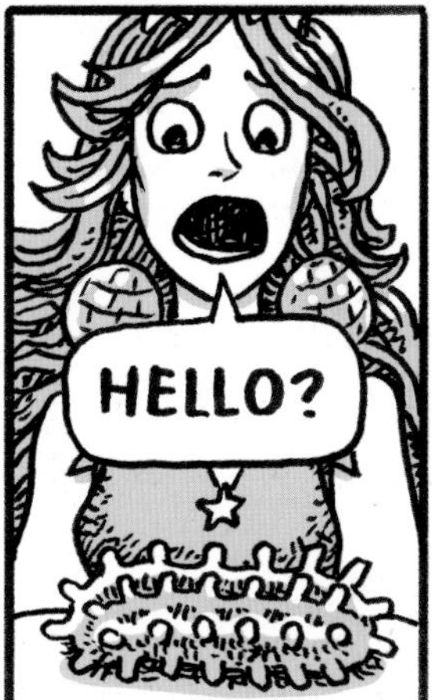
HELLO?

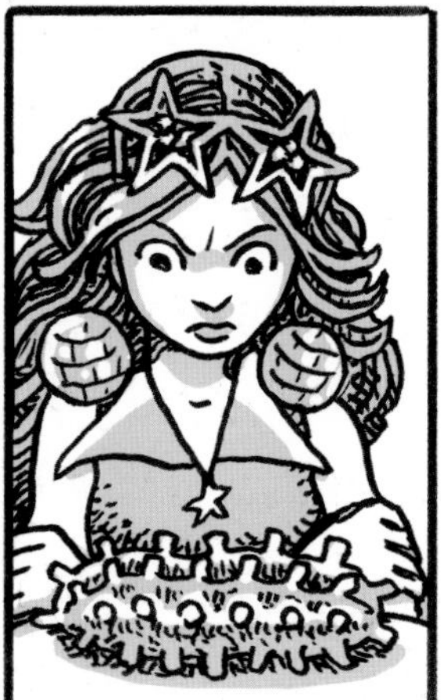

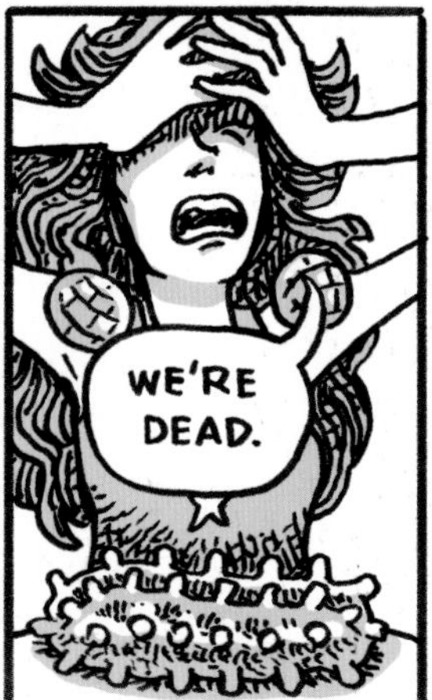
WE'RE DEAD.

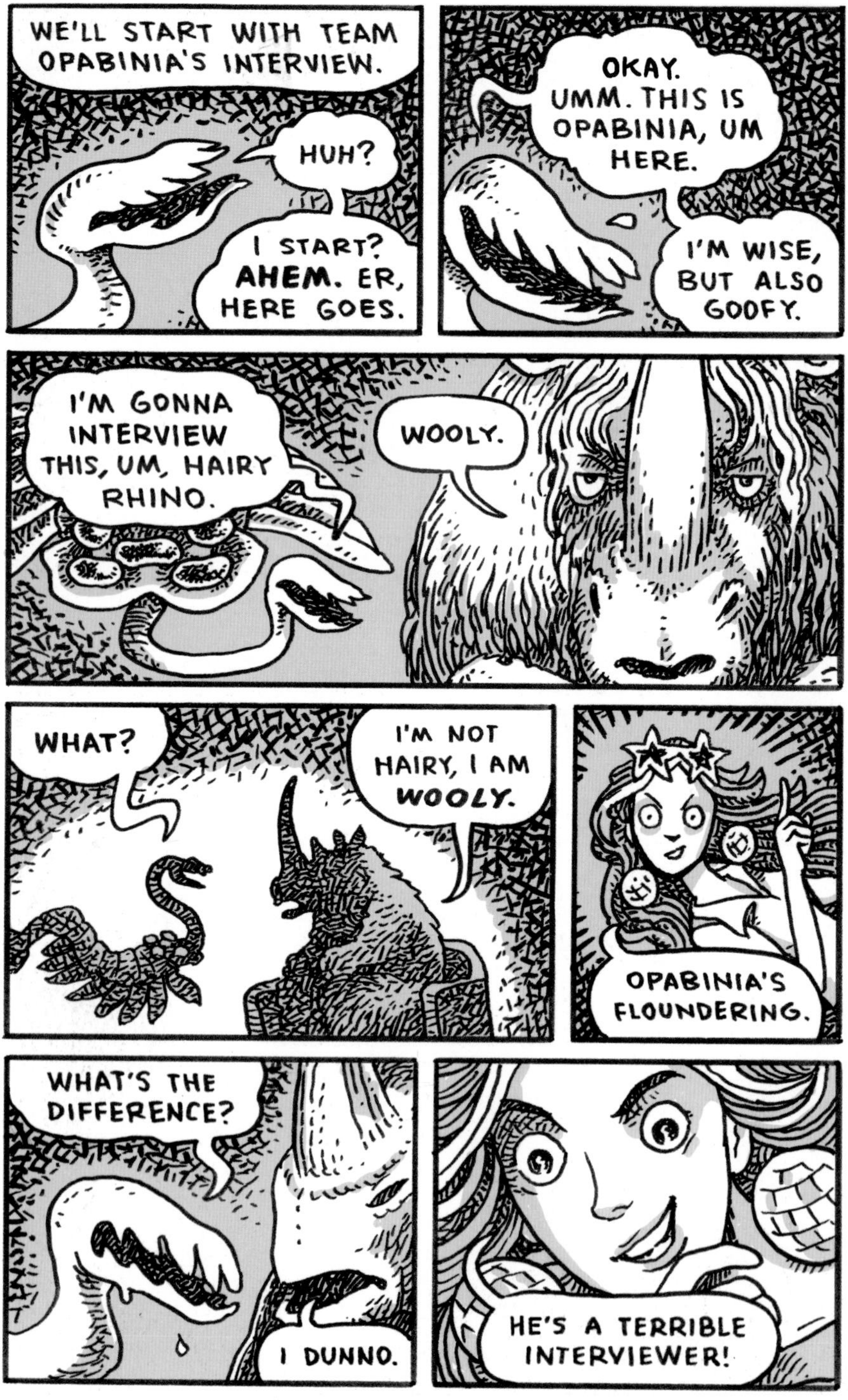
WE'LL START WITH TEAM OPABINIA'S INTERVIEW.
HUH?
I START? AHEM. ER, HERE GOES.
OKAY. UMM. THIS IS OPABINIA, UM HERE.
I'M WISE, BUT ALSO GOOFY.
I'M GONNA INTERVIEW THIS, UM, HAIRY RHINO.
WOOLY.
WHAT?
I'M NOT HAIRY, I AM WOOLY.
OPABINIA'S FLOUNDERING.
WHAT'S THE DIFFERENCE?
I DUNNO.
HE'S A TERRIBLE INTERVIEWER!

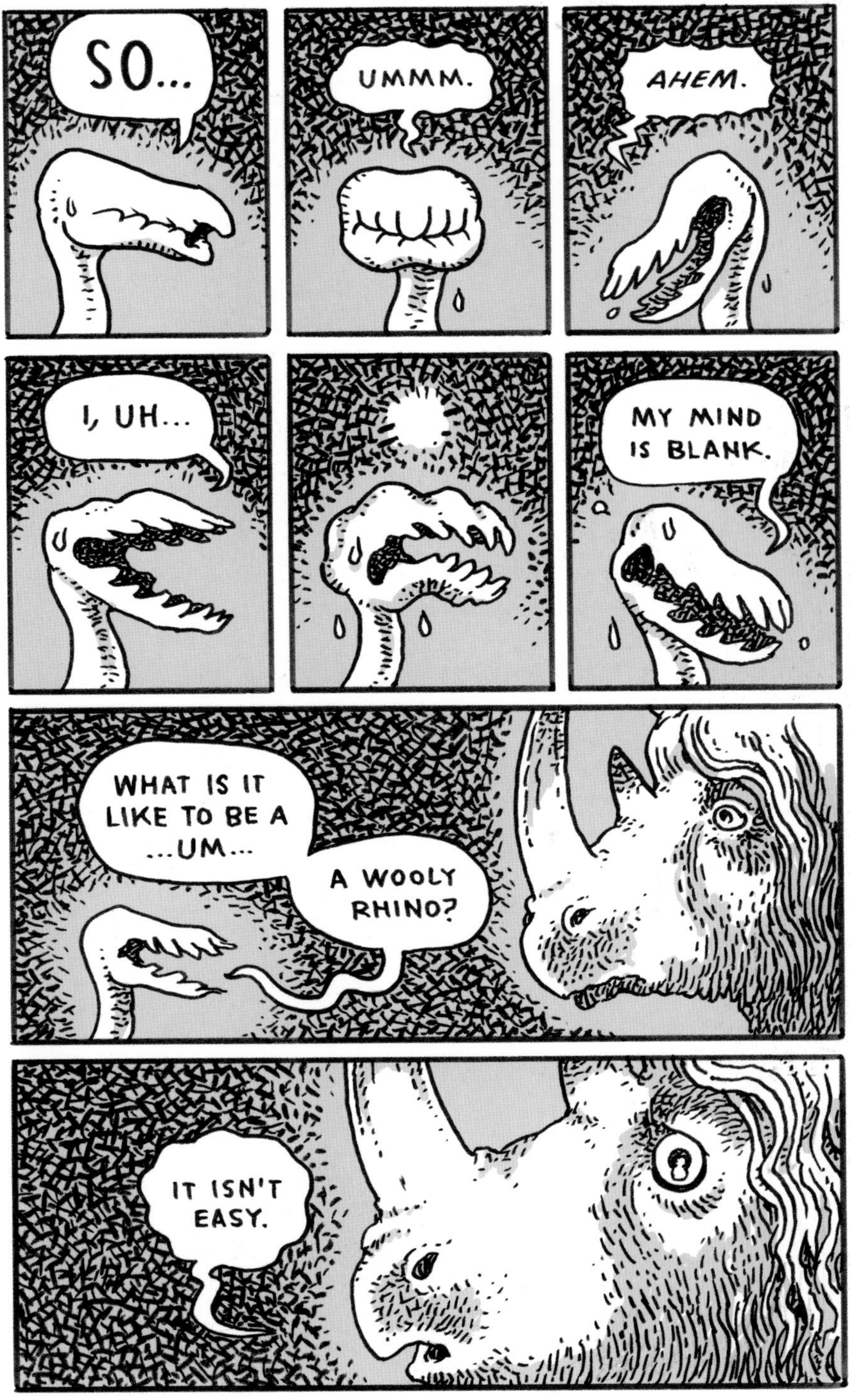
SO...
UMMM.
AHEM.
I, UH...
MY MIND IS BLANK.
WHAT IS IT LIKE TO BE A ...UM...
A WOOLY RHINO?
IT ISN'T EASY.

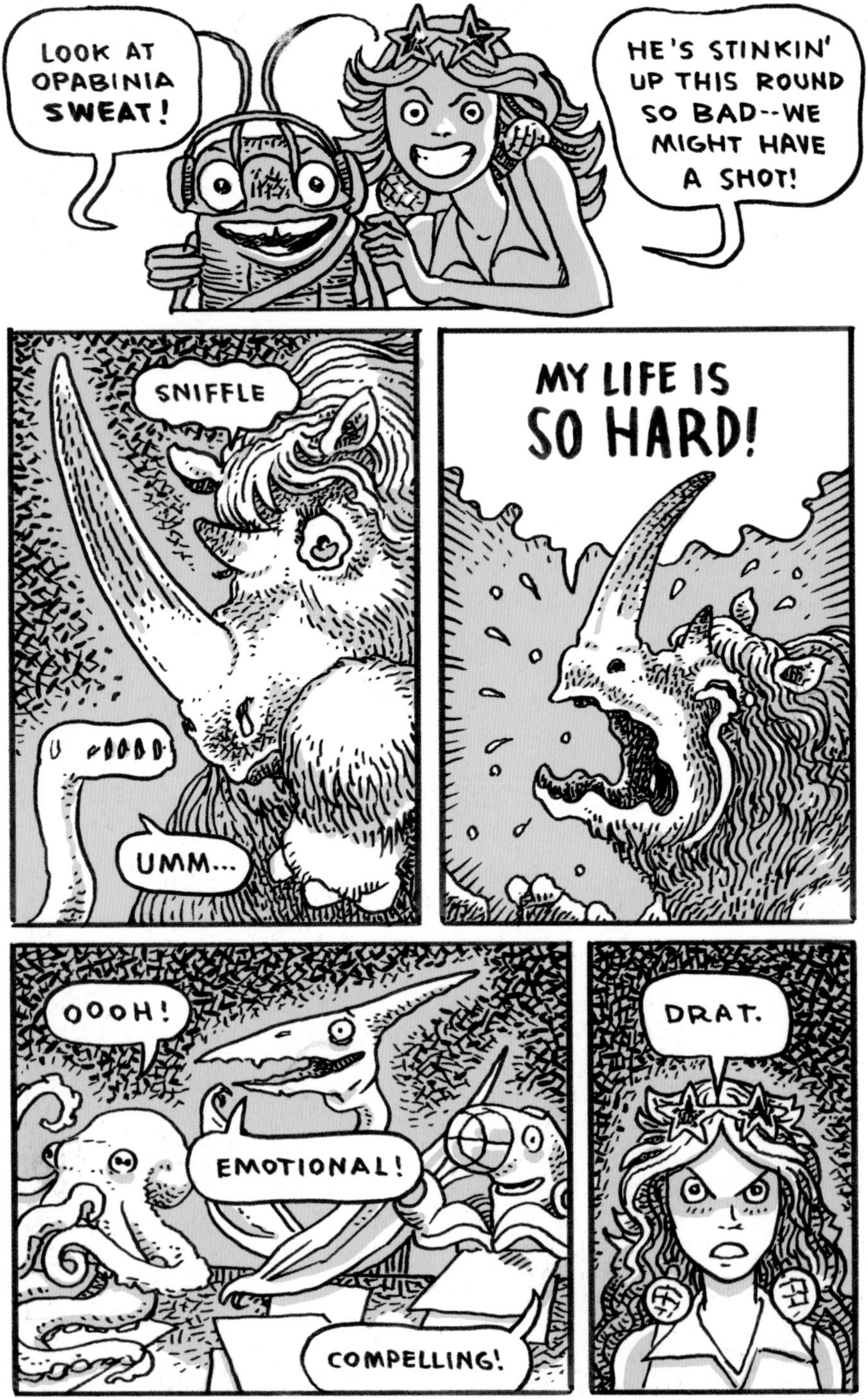
LOOK AT OPABINIA SWEAT!
HE'S STINKIN' UP THIS ROUND SO BAD--WE MIGHT HAVE A SHOT!
SNIFFLE
UMM...
MY LIFE IS SO HARD!
OOOH!
EMOTIONAL!
COMPELLING!
DRAT.

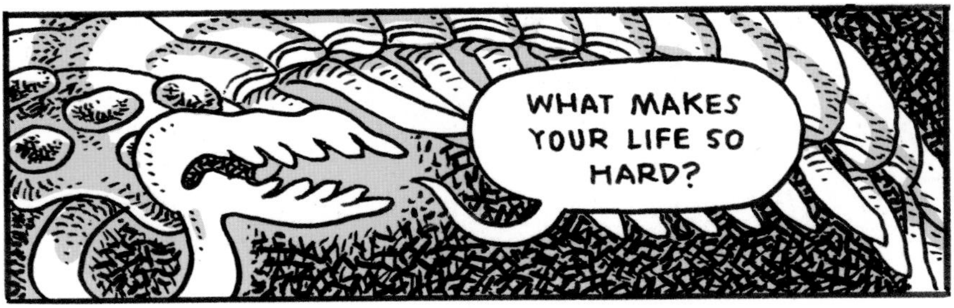
WHAT MAKES YOUR LIFE SO HARD?

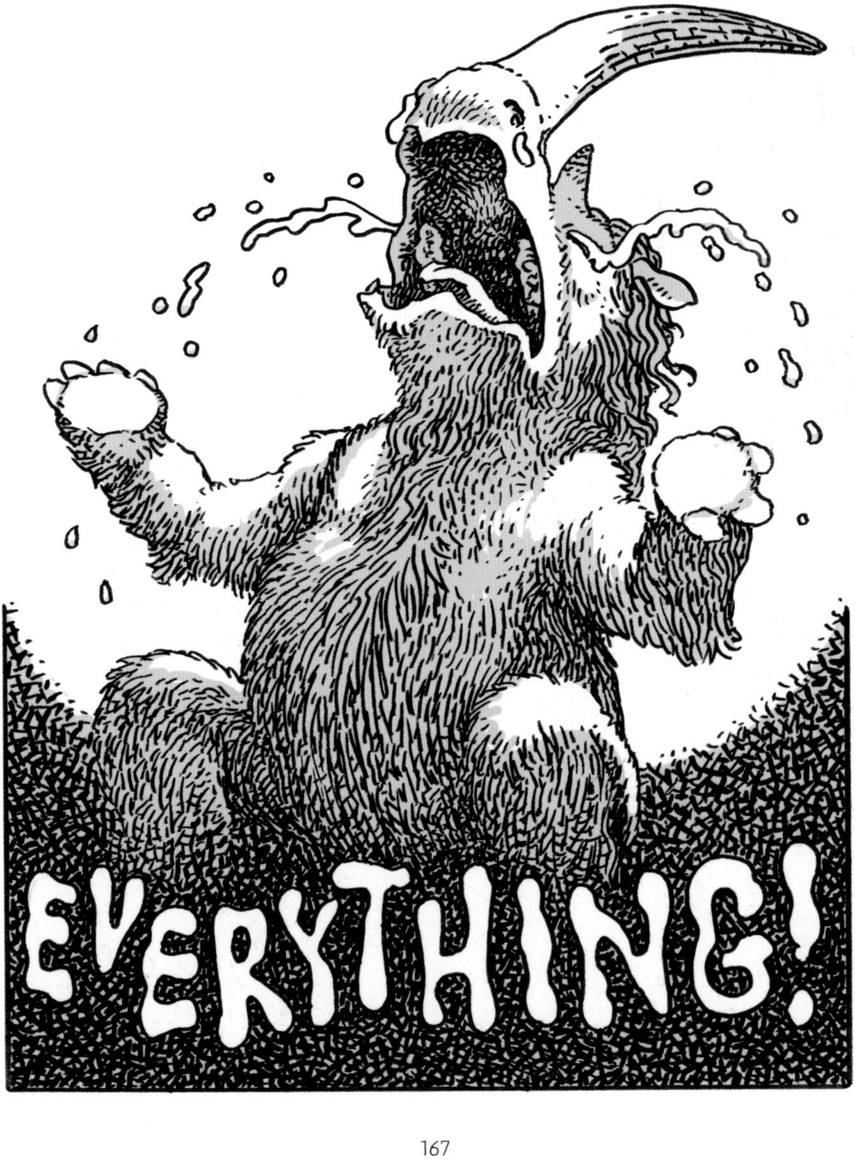
EVERYTHING!

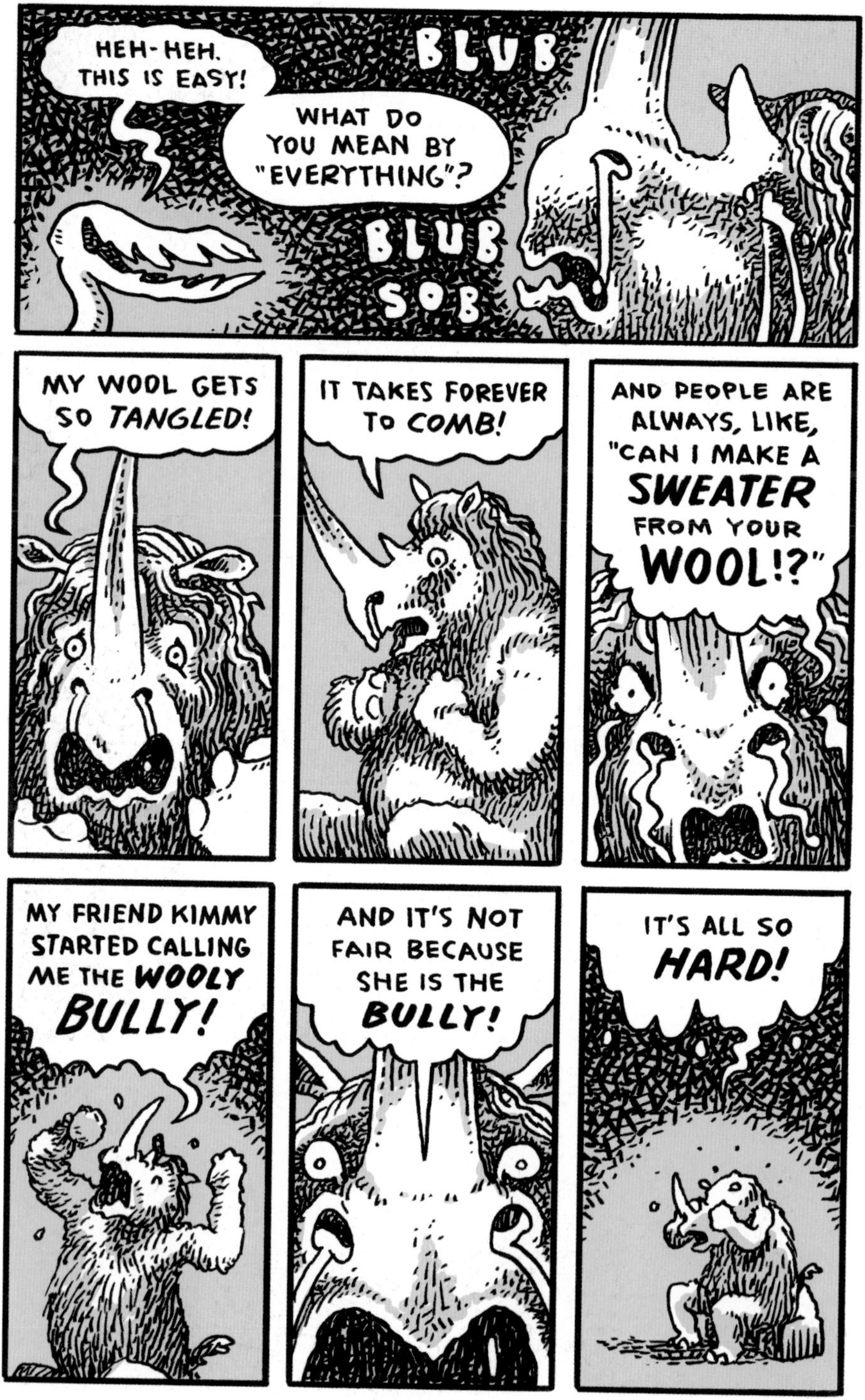
HEH-HEH. THIS IS EASY!
BLUB
WHAT DO YOU MEAN BY "EVERYTHING"?
BLUB
SOB
MY WOOL GETS SO TANGLED!
IT TAKES FOREVER TO COMB!
AND PEOPLE ARE ALWAYS, LIKE, "CAN I MAKE A SWEATER FROM YOUR WOOL!?"
MY FRIEND KIMMY STARTED CALLING ME THE WOOLY BULLY!
AND IT'S NOT FAIR BECAUSE SHE IS THE BULLY!
IT'S ALL SO HARD!

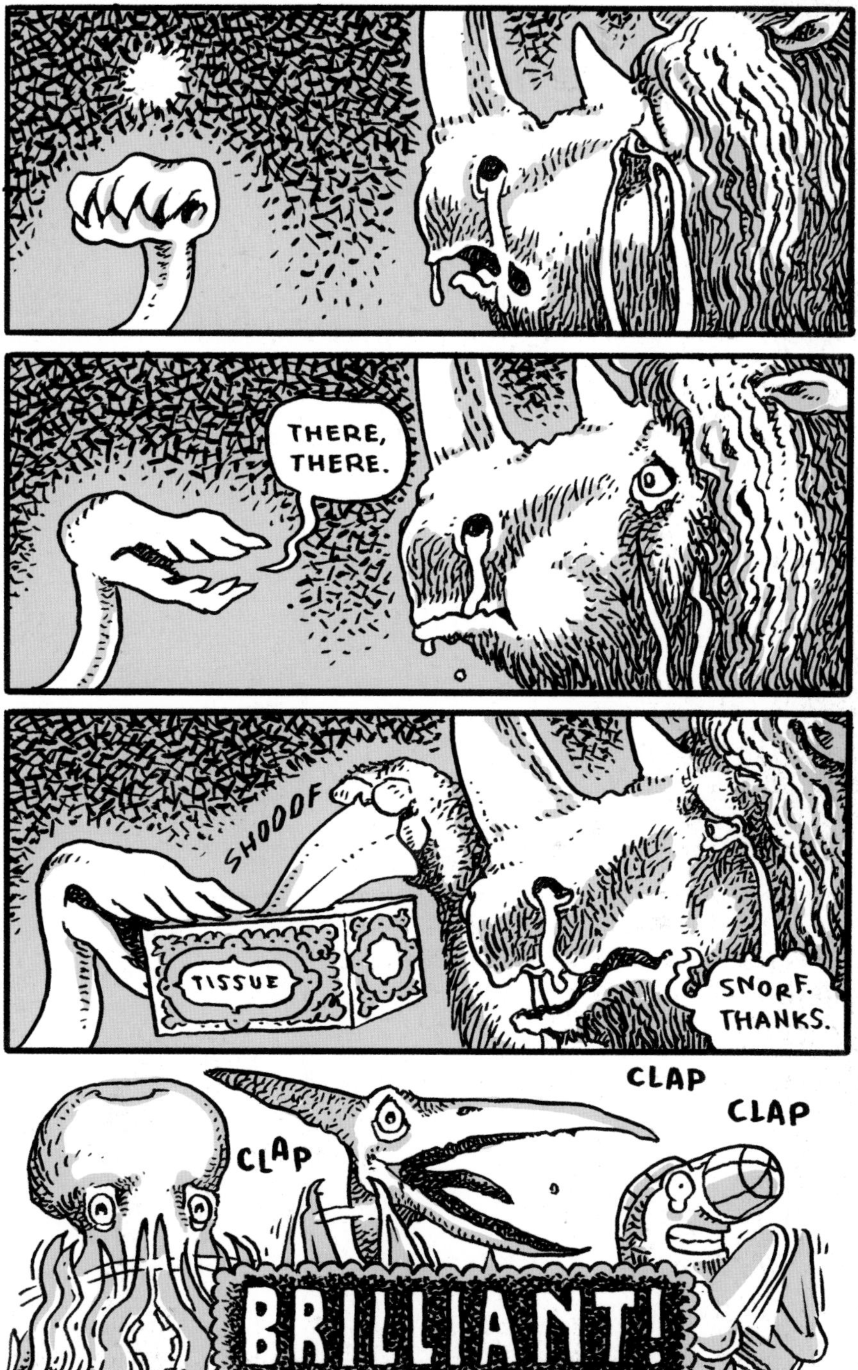
THERE, THERE.
SHOOOF
TISSUE
SNORF. THANKS.
CLAP
CLAP
CLAP
BRILLIANT!

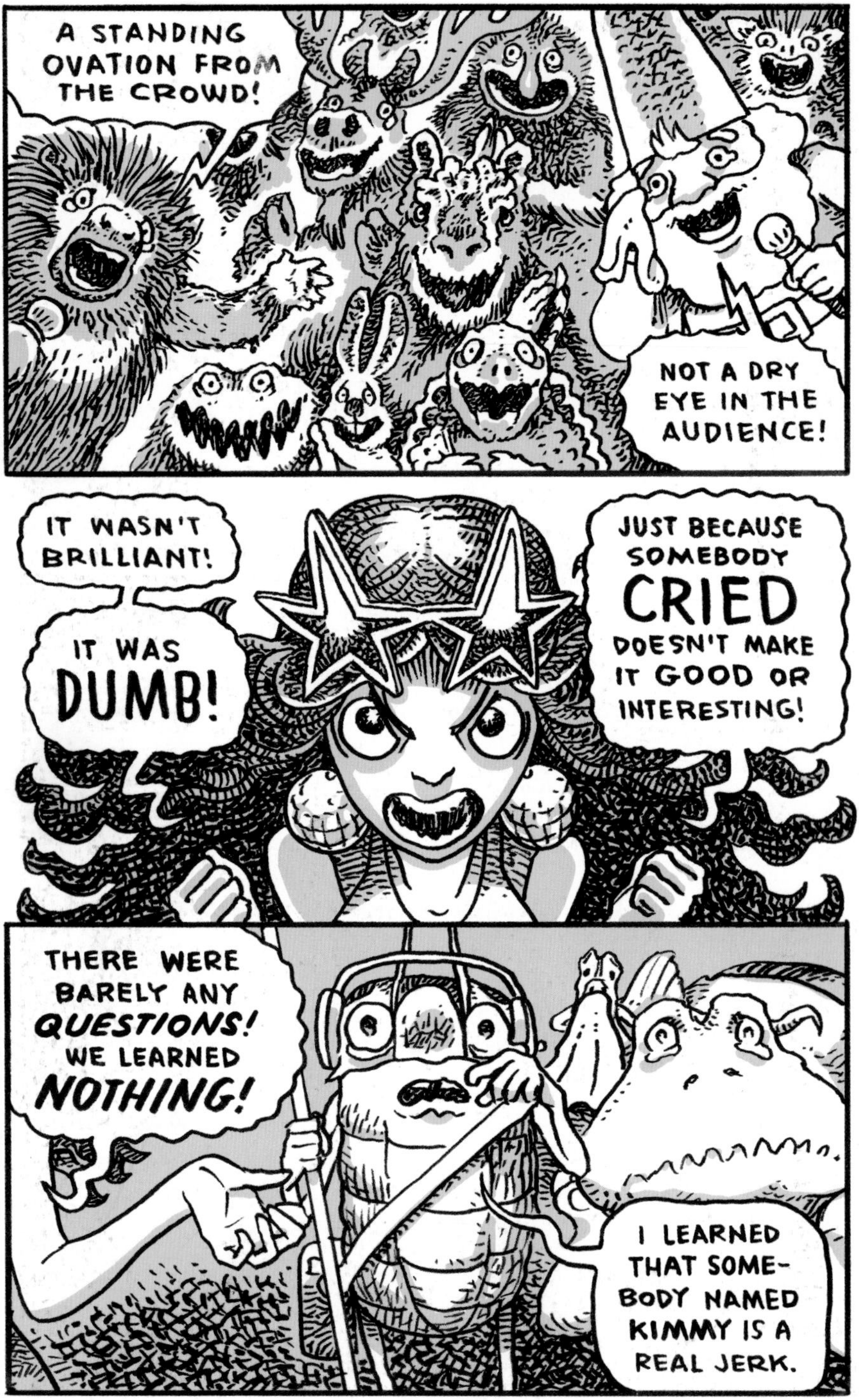
A STANDING OVATION FROM THE CROWD!
NOT A DRY EYE IN THE AUDIENCE!
IT WASN'T BRILLIANT!
IT WAS DUMB!
JUST BECAUSE SOMEBODY CRIED DOESN'T MAKE IT GOOD OR INTERESTING!
THERE WERE BARELY ANY QUESTIONS! WE LEARNED NOTHING!
I LEARNED THAT SOMEBODY NAMED KIMMY IS A REAL JERK.

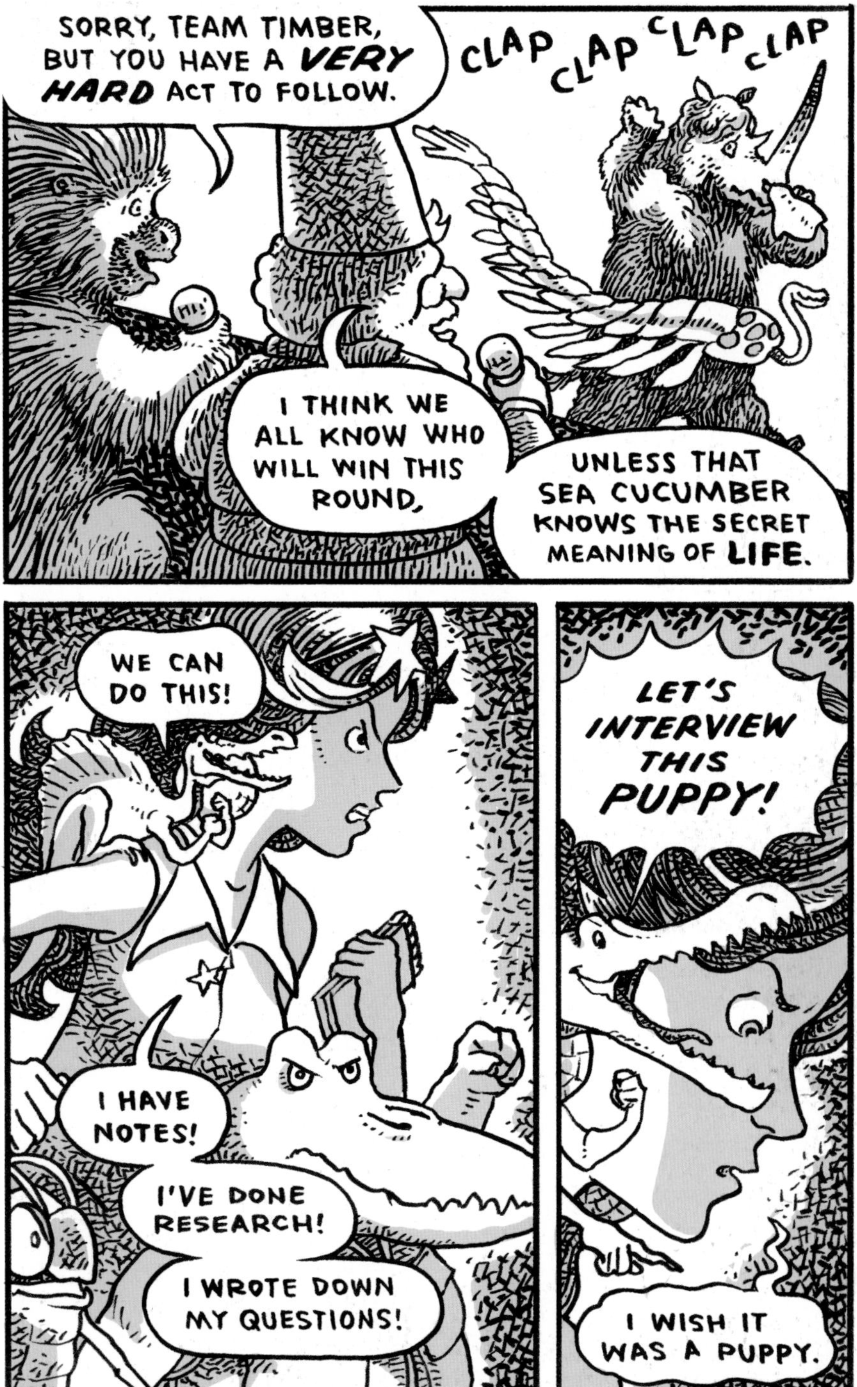
SORRY, TEAM TIMBER, BUT YOU HAVE A VERY HARD ACT TO FOLLOW.
CLAP CLAP CLAP CLAP
I THINK WE ALL KNOW WHO WILL WIN THIS ROUND,
UNLESS THAT SEA CUCUMBER KNOWS THE SECRET MEANING OF LIFE.
WE CAN DO THIS!
I HAVE NOTES!
I'VE DONE RESEARCH!
I WROTE DOWN MY QUESTIONS!
LET'S INTERVIEW THIS PUPPY!
I WISH IT WAS A PUPPY.

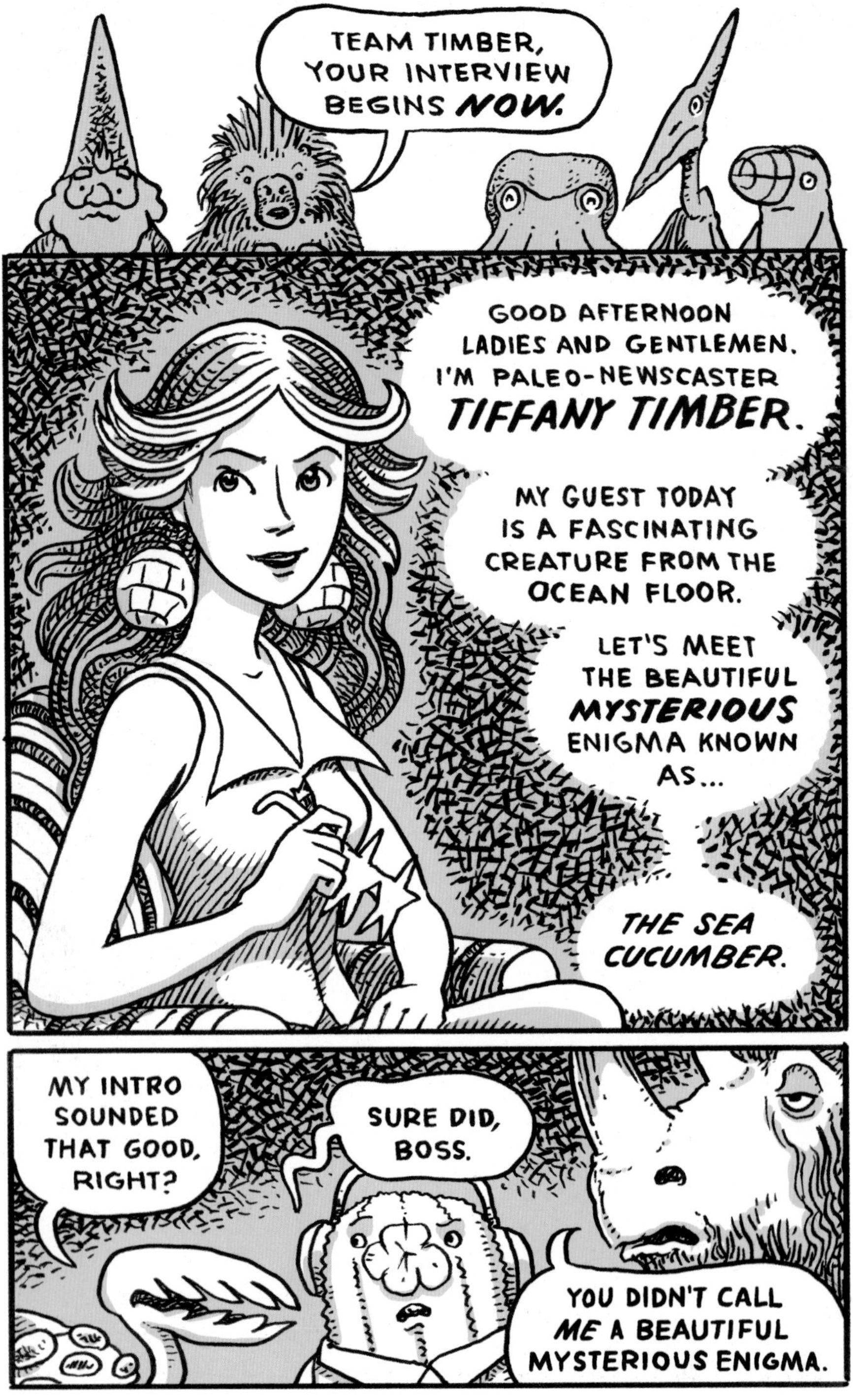
TEAM TIMBER,
YOUR INTERVIEW
BEGINS NOW.
GOOD AFTERNOON
LADIES AND GENTLEMEN.
I'M PALEO-NEWSCASTER
TIFFANY TIMBER.
MY GUEST TODAY
IS A FASCINATING
CREATURE FROM THE
OCEAN FLOOR.
LET'S MEET
THE BEAUTIFUL
MYSTERIOUS
ENIGMA KNOWN
AS...
THE SEA
CUCUMBER.
MY INTRO
SOUNDED
THAT GOOD,
RIGHT?
SURE DID,
BOSS.
YOU DIDN'T CALL
ME A BEAUTIFUL
MYSTERIOUS ENIGMA.

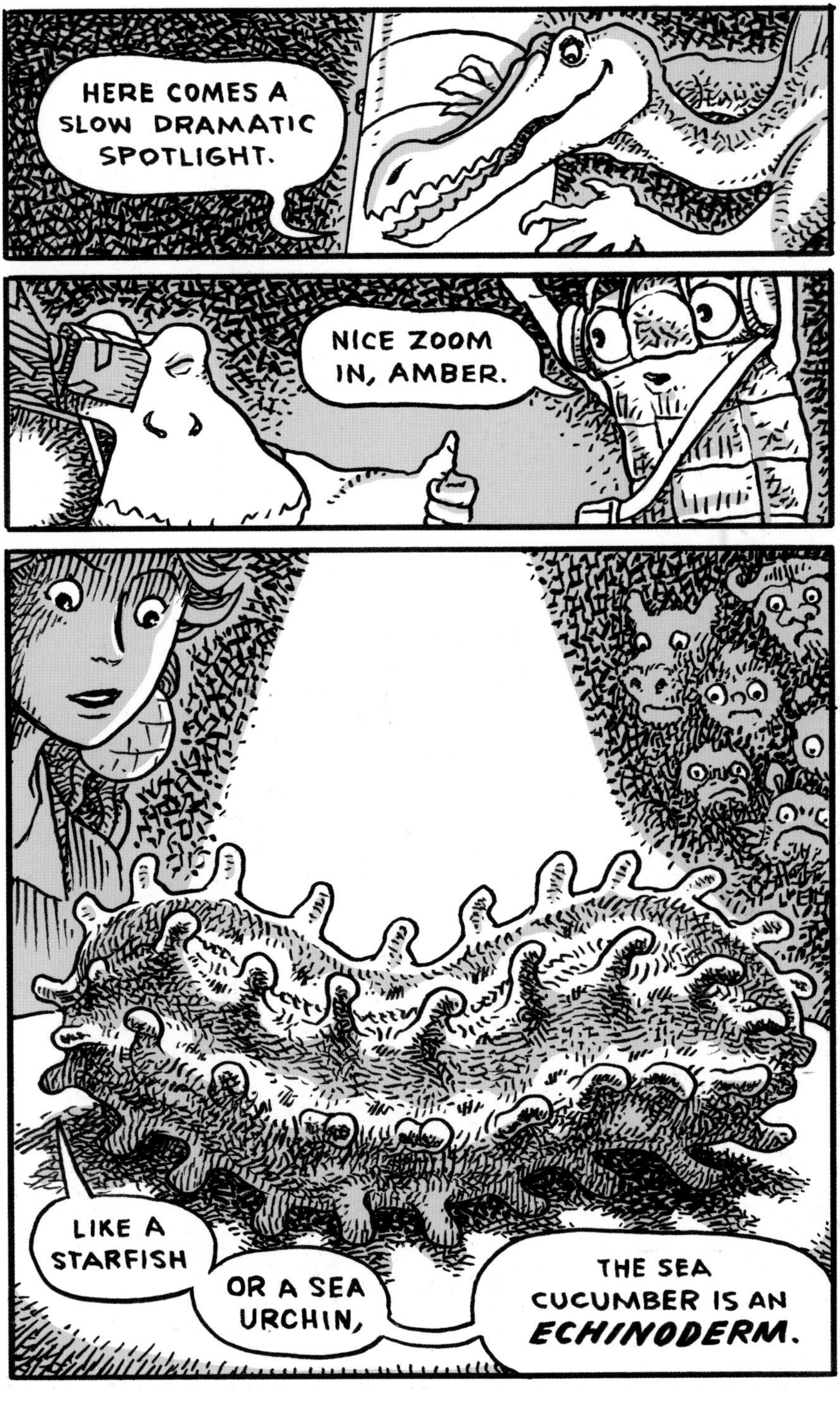
HERE COMES A SLOW DRAMATIC SPOTLIGHT.
NICE ZOOM IN, AMBER.
LIKE A STARFISH
OR A SEA URCHIN,
THE SEA CUCUMBER IS AN ECHINODERM.

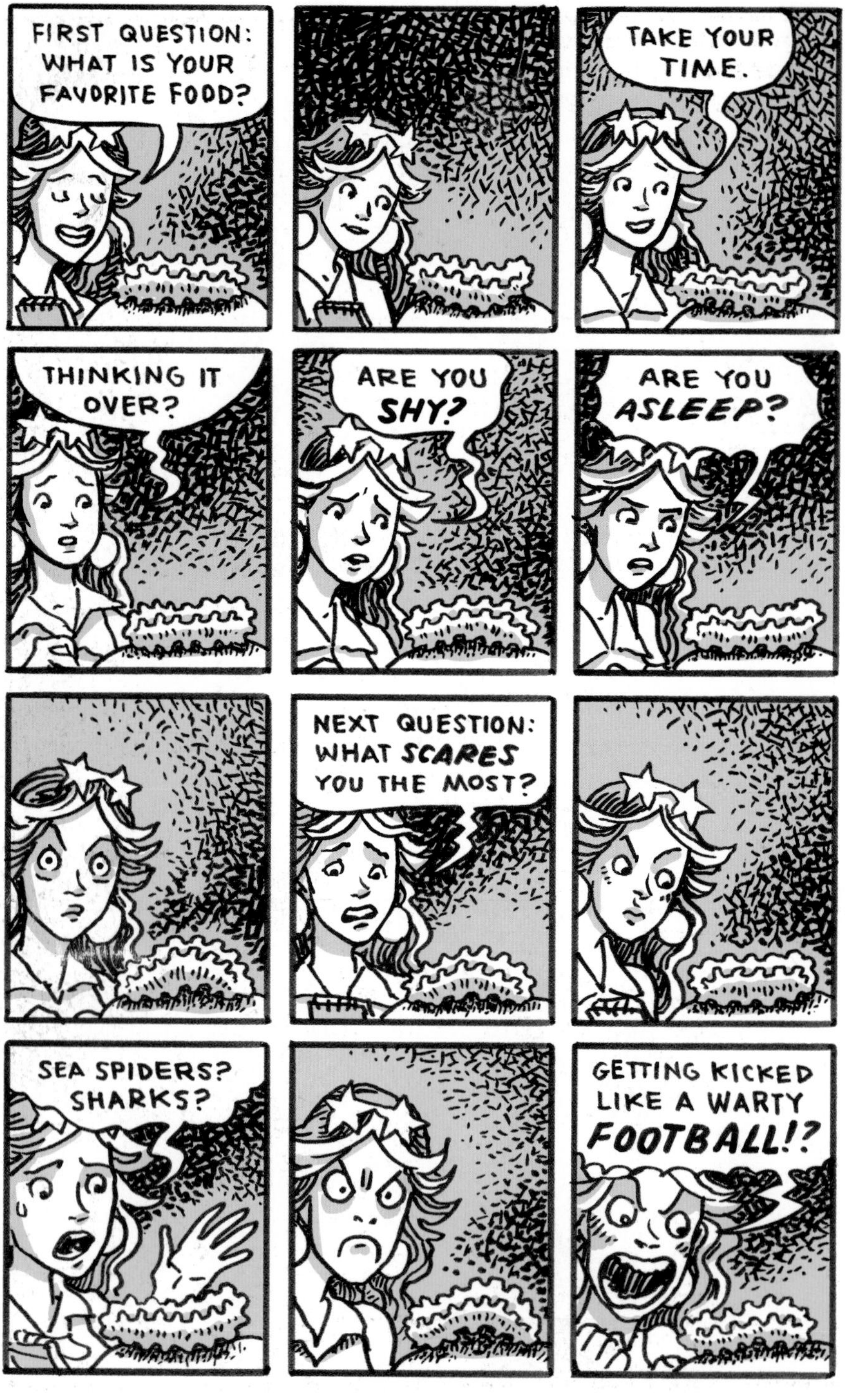
FIRST QUESTION: WHAT IS YOUR FAVORITE FOOD?
TAKE YOUR TIME.
THINKING IT OVER?
ARE YOU SHY?
ARE YOU ASLEEP?
NEXT QUESTION: WHAT SCARES YOU THE MOST?
SEA SPIDERS? SHARKS?
GETTING KICKED LIKE A WARTY FOOTBALL!?

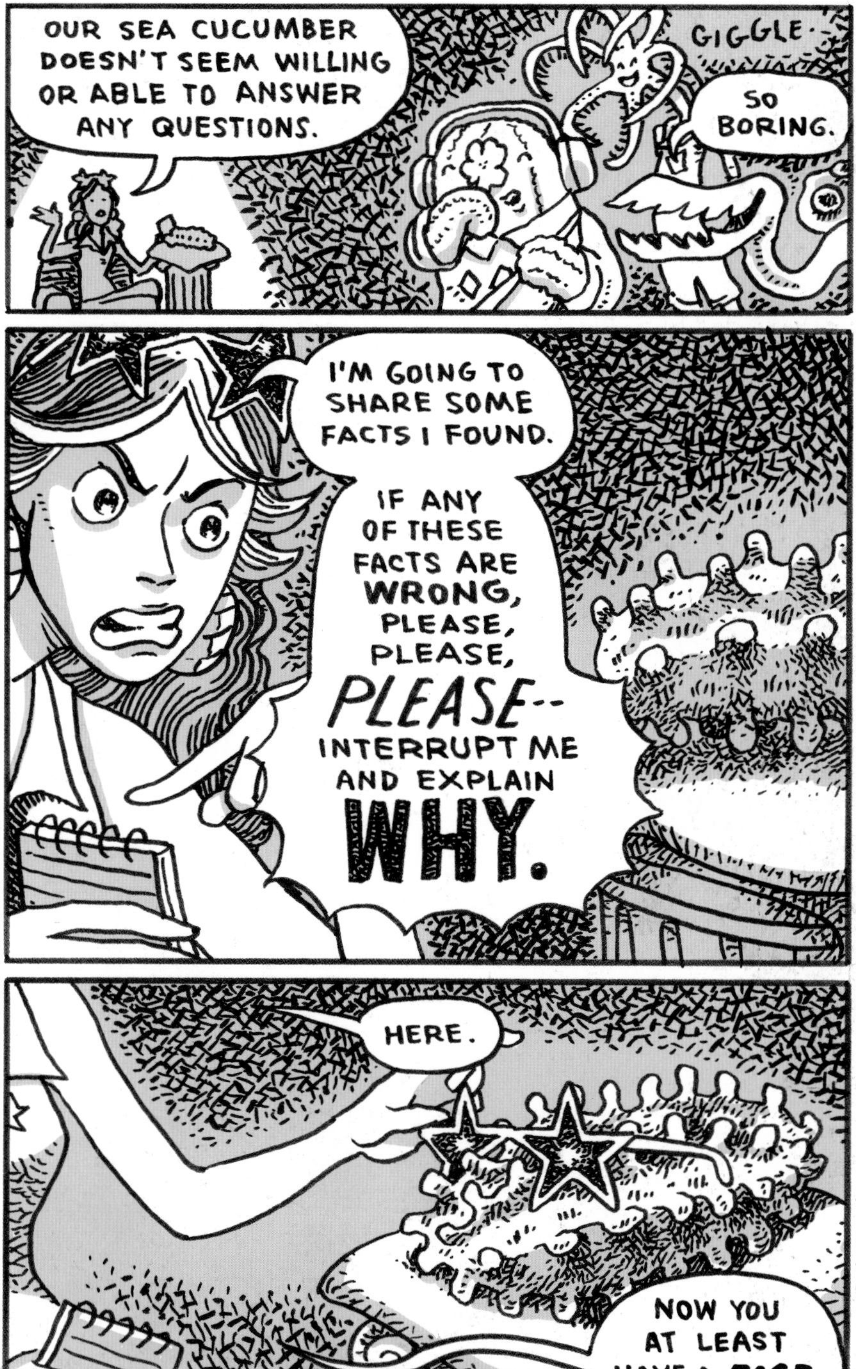
OUR SEA CUCUMBER DOESN'T SEEM WILLING OR ABLE TO ANSWER ANY QUESTIONS.
GIGGLE.
SO BORING.
I'M GOING TO SHARE SOME FACTS I FOUND.
IF ANY OF THESE FACTS ARE WRONG, PLEASE, PLEASE, PLEASE-- INTERRUPT ME AND EXPLAIN WHY.
HERE.
NOW YOU AT LEAST HAVE A FACE.

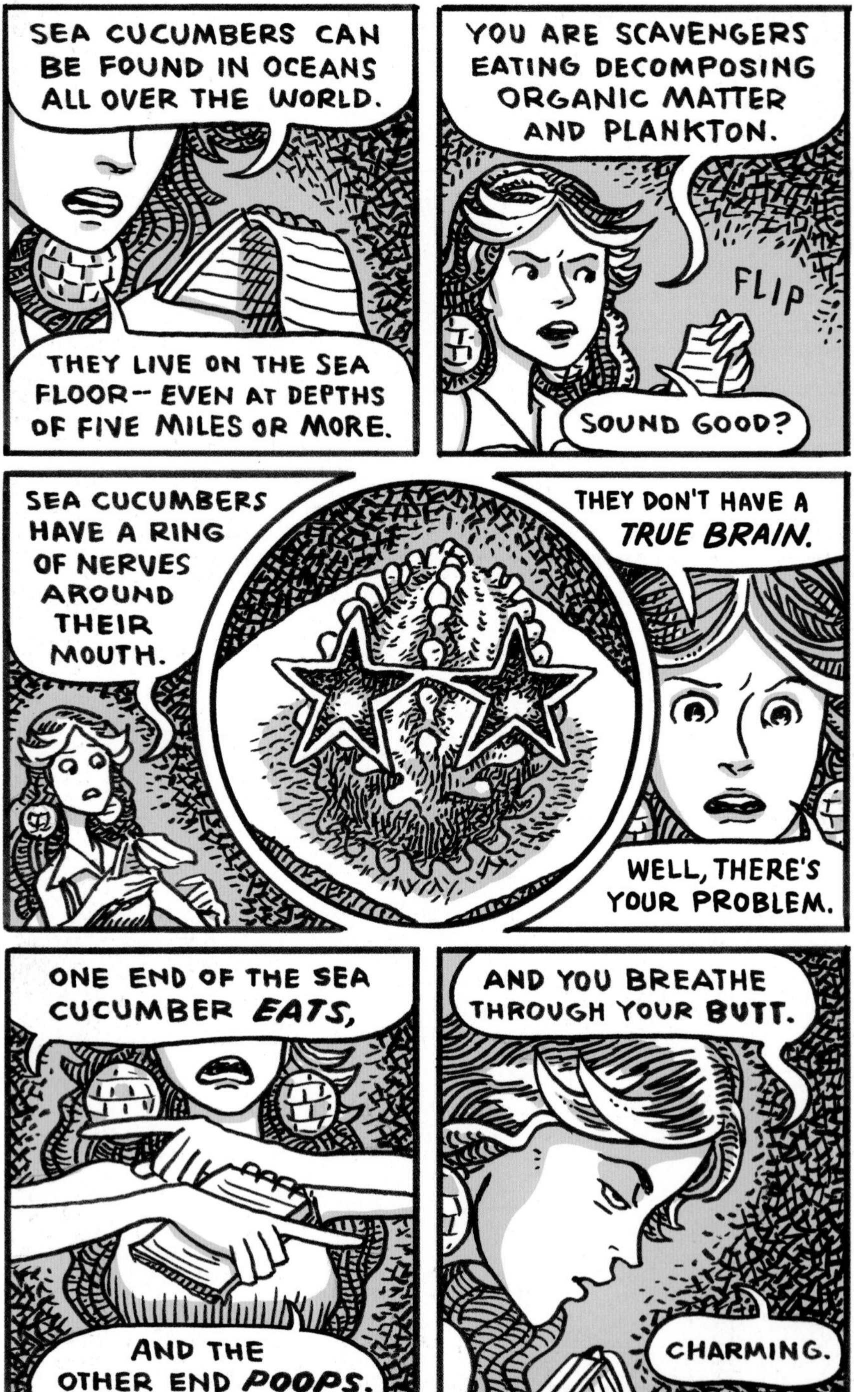
SEA CUCUMBERS CAN BE FOUND IN OCEANS ALL OVER THE WORLD.
THEY LIVE ON THE SEA FLOOR-- EVEN AT DEPTHS OF FIVE MILES OR MORE.
YOU ARE SCAVENGERS EATING DECOMPOSING ORGANIC MATTER AND PLANKTON.
FLIP
SOUND GOOD?
SEA CUCUMBERS HAVE A RING OF NERVES AROUND THEIR MOUTH.
THEY DON'T HAVE A *TRUE BRAIN.*
WELL, THERE'S YOUR PROBLEM.
ONE END OF THE SEA CUCUMBER *EATS,*
AND THE OTHER END *POOPS.*
AND YOU BREATHE THROUGH YOUR BUTT.
CHARMING.

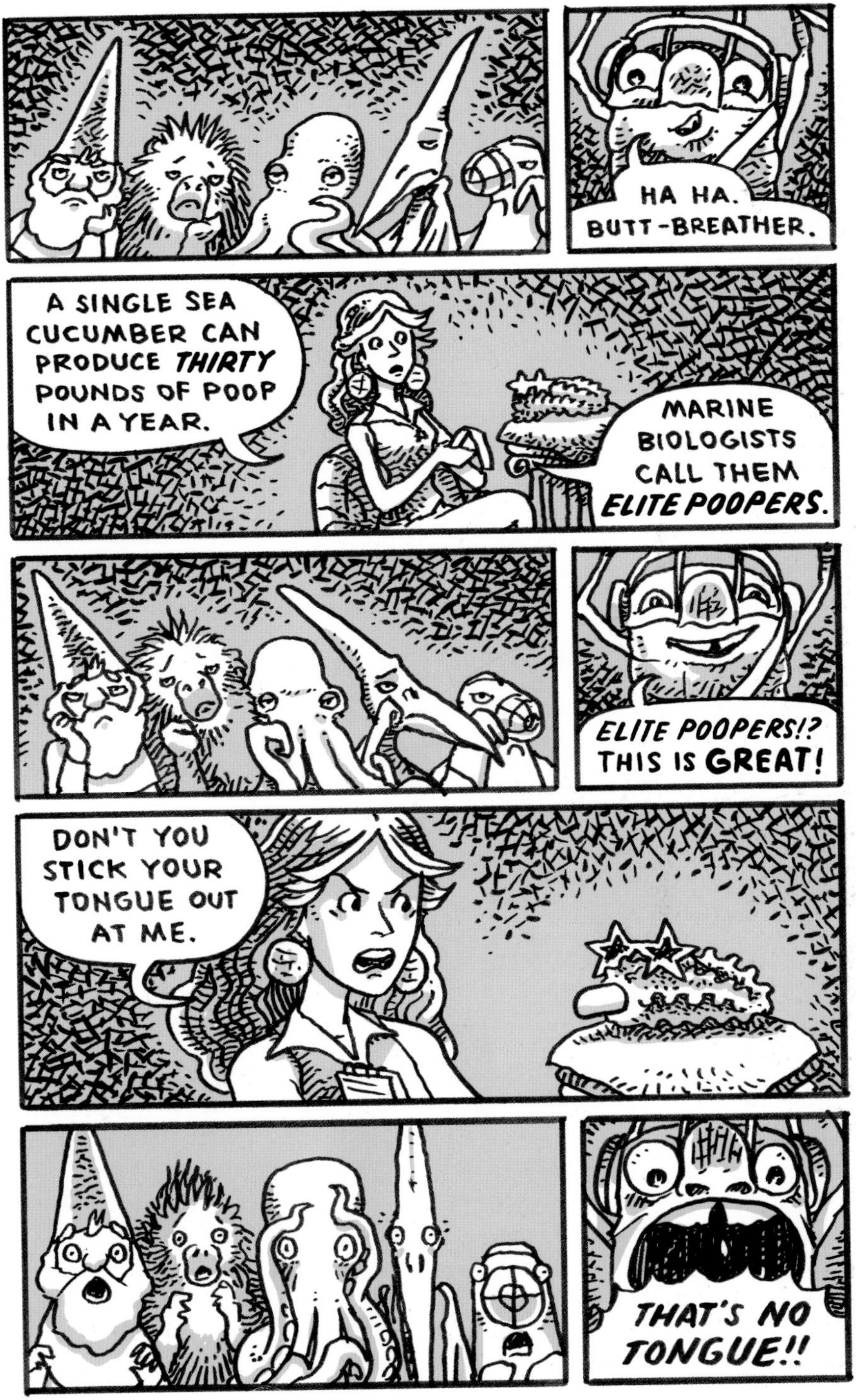
HA HA.
BUTT-BREATHER.
A SINGLE SEA CUCUMBER CAN PRODUCE *THIRTY* POUNDS OF POOP IN A YEAR.
MARINE BIOLOGISTS CALL THEM *ELITE POOPERS*.
ELITE POOPERS!? THIS IS **GREAT**!
DON'T YOU STICK YOUR TONGUE OUT AT ME.
THAT'S NO TONGUE!!

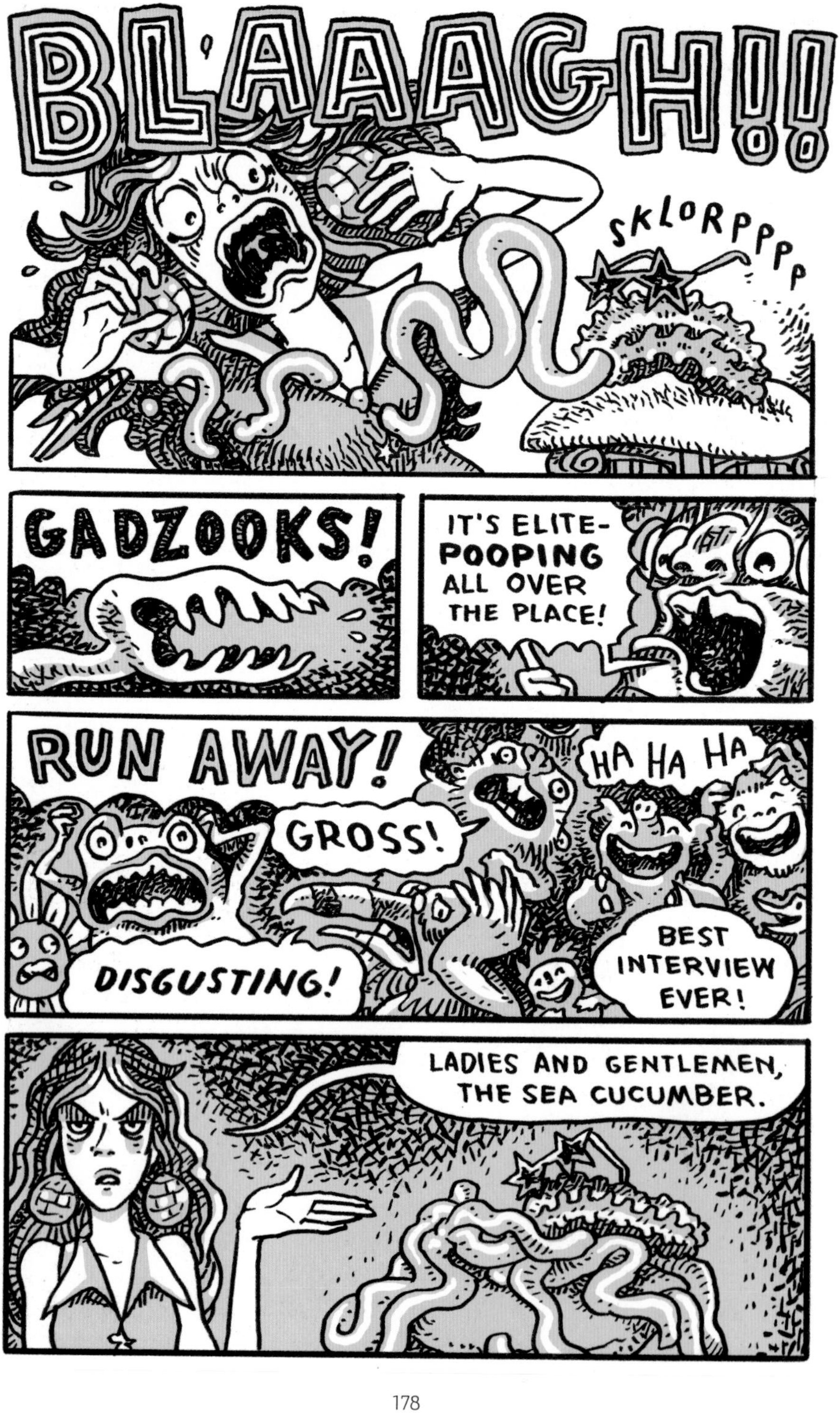
BLAAAGH!!
SKLORPPPPP
GADZOOKS!
IT'S ELITE-POOPING ALL OVER THE PLACE!
RUN AWAY!
GROSS!
HA HA HA
DISGUSTING!
BEST INTERVIEW EVER!
LADIES AND GENTLEMEN, THE SEA CUCUMBER.

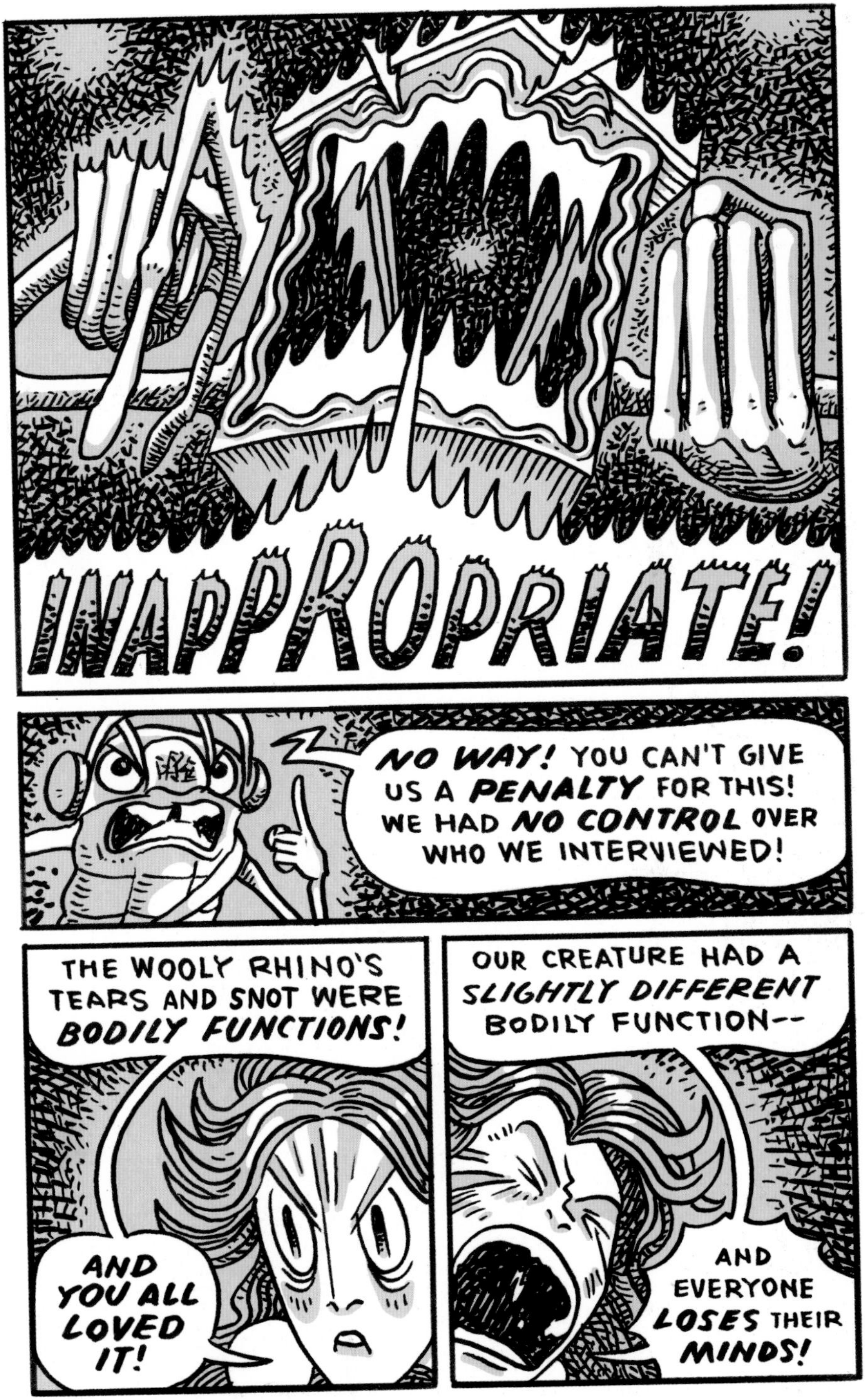
INAPPROPRIATE!
NO WAY! YOU CAN'T GIVE US A PENALTY FOR THIS! WE HAD NO CONTROL OVER WHO WE INTERVIEWED!
THE WOOLY RHINO'S TEARS AND SNOT WERE BODILY FUNCTIONS!
AND YOU ALL LOVED IT!
OUR CREATURE HAD A SLIGHTLY DIFFERENT BODILY FUNCTION--
AND EVERYONE LOSES THEIR MINDS!

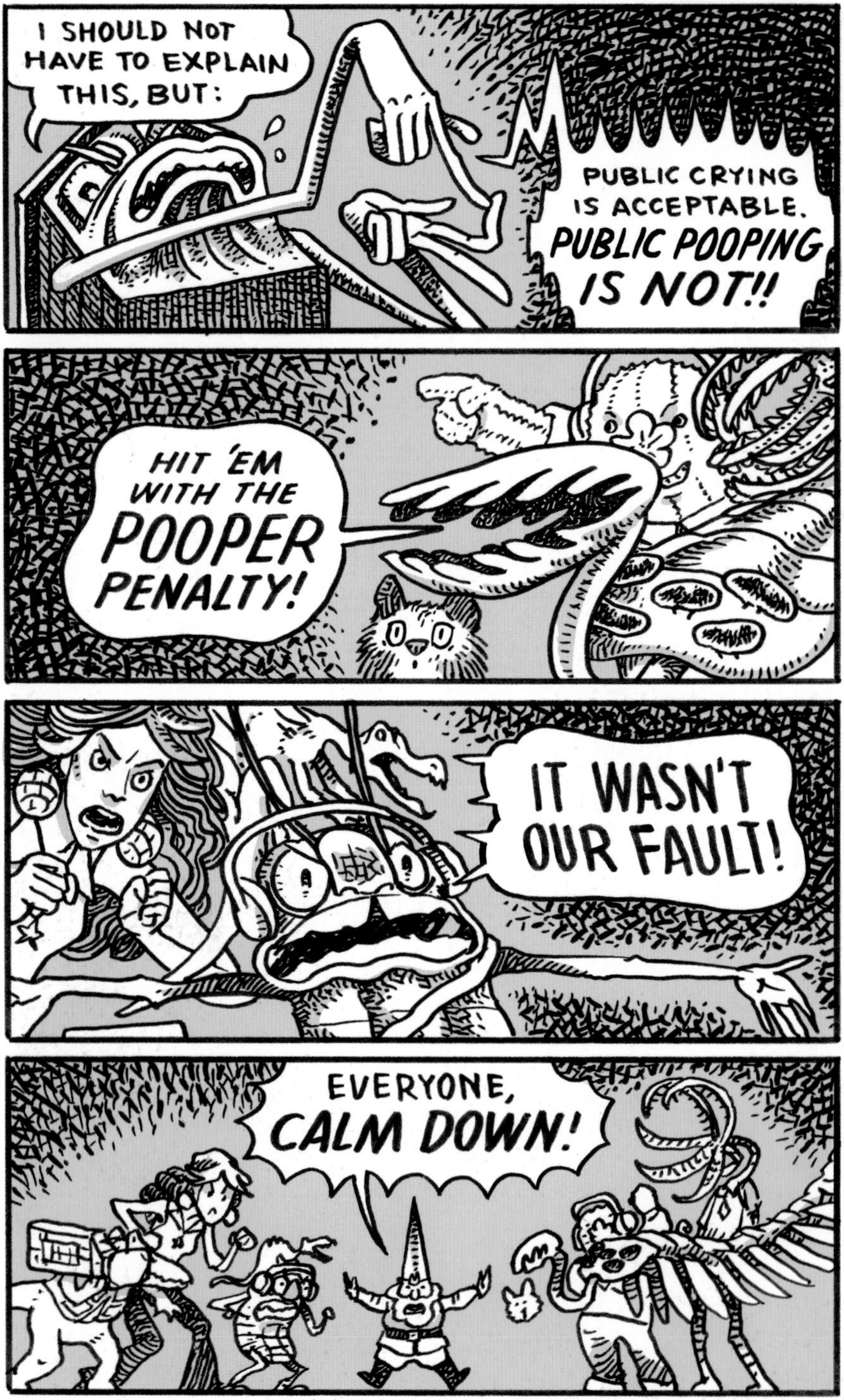
I SHOULD NOT HAVE TO EXPLAIN THIS, BUT:
PUBLIC CRYING IS ACCEPTABLE. PUBLIC POOPING IS NOT!!
HIT 'EM WITH THE POOPER PENALTY!
IT WASN'T OUR FAULT!
EVERYONE, CALM DOWN!

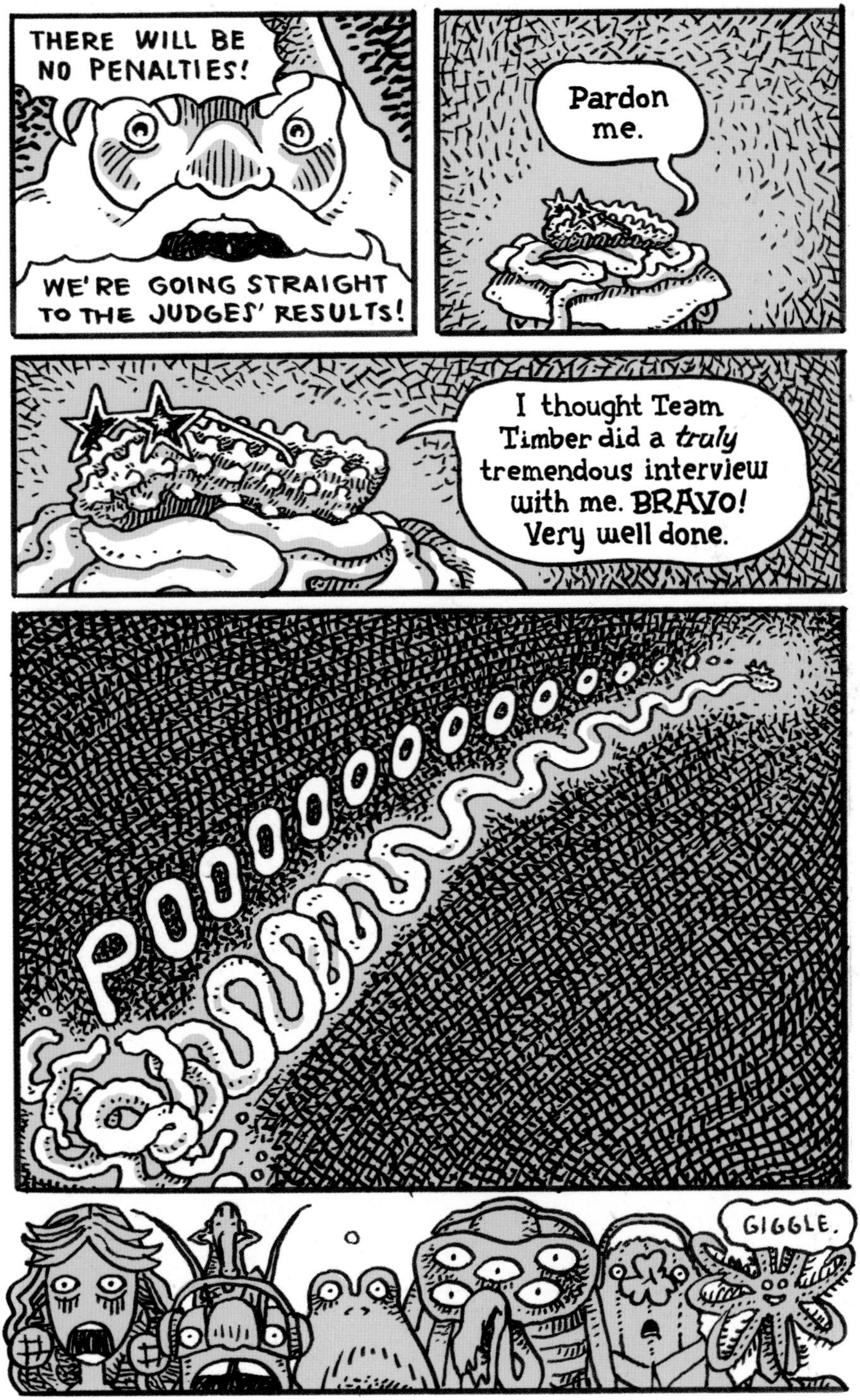
THERE WILL BE NO PENALTIES!
WE'RE GOING STRAIGHT TO THE JUDGES' RESULTS!
Pardon me.
I thought Team Timber did a *truly* tremendous interview with me. BRAVO! Very well done.
POOOOOOOOOOOOOOO...
GIGGLE.

GOODBYE, SEA CUCUMBER.

POOOOOOO

I NEED A DIFFERENT CAREER.

SERIOUSLY, WHO PUT THAT CREATURE ON THE INTERVIEW LIST?

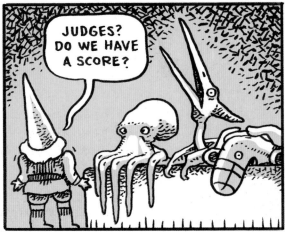

JUDGES? DO WE HAVE A SCORE?

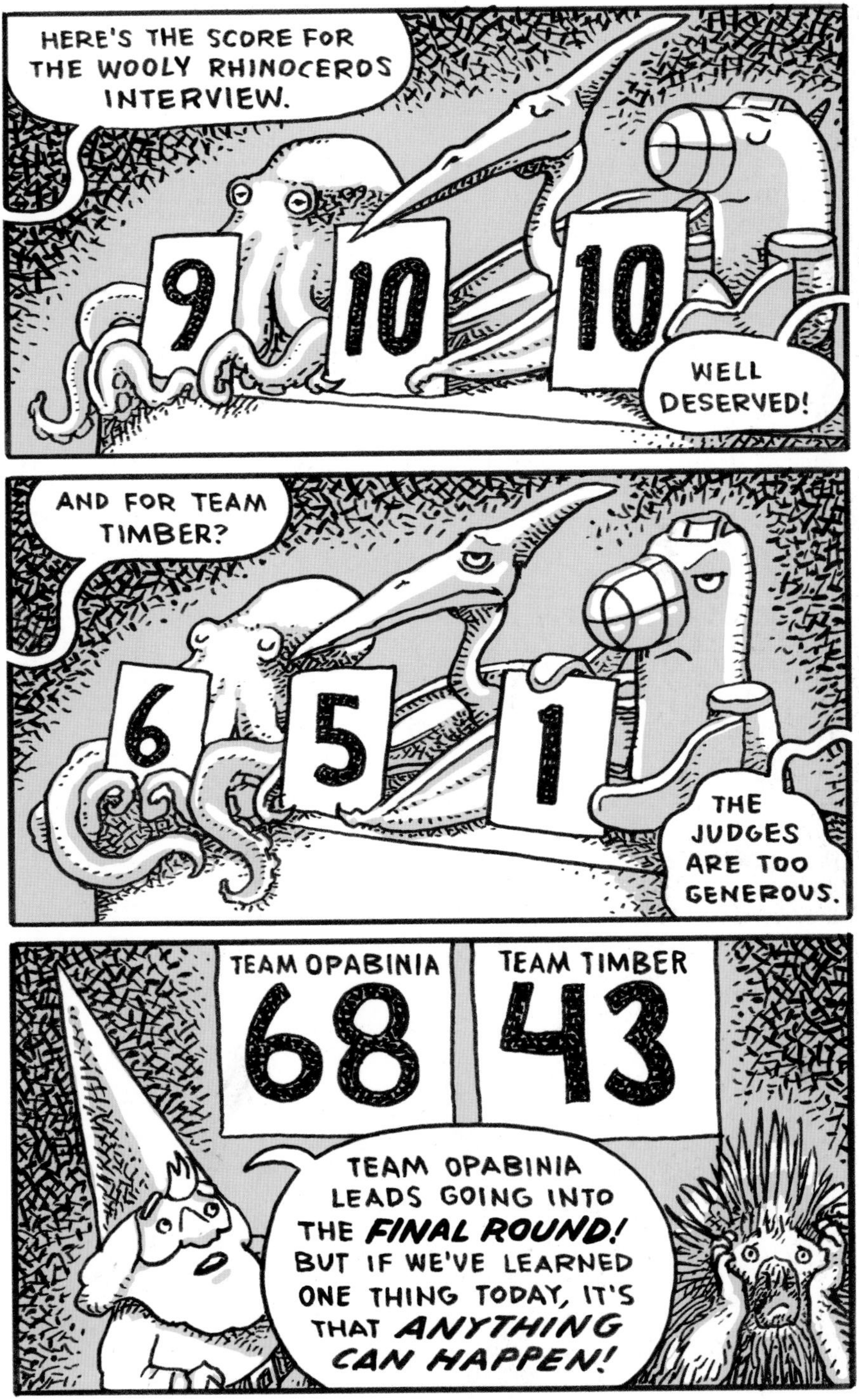

HERE'S THE SCORE FOR THE WOOLY RHINOCEROS INTERVIEW.
9
10
10
WELL DESERVED!
AND FOR TEAM TIMBER?
6
5
1
THE JUDGES ARE TOO GENEROUS.
TEAM OPABINIA
68
TEAM TIMBER
43
TEAM OPABINIA LEADS GOING INTO THE FINAL ROUND! BUT IF WE'VE LEARNED ONE THING TODAY, IT'S THAT ANYTHING CAN HAPPEN!

CHAPTER 7

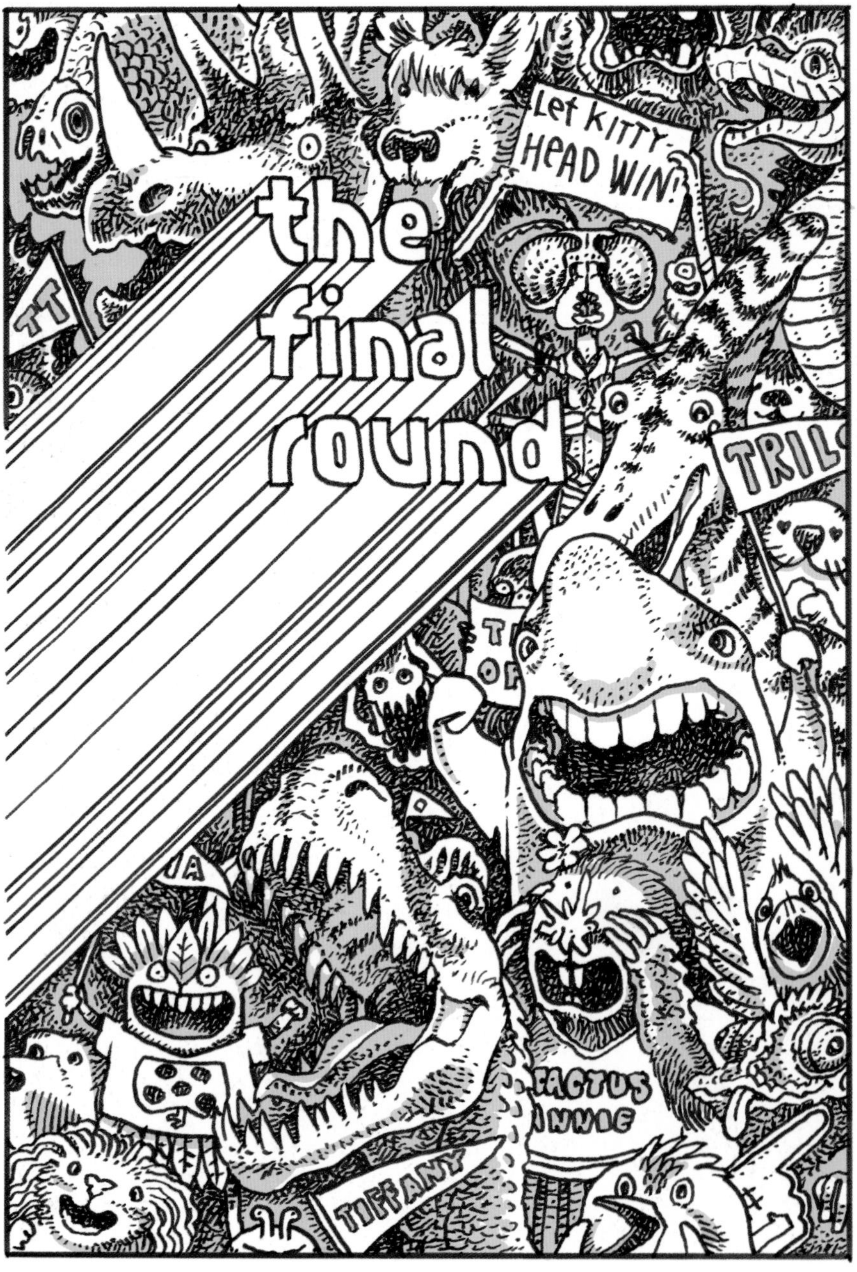

the final round
Let KITTY HEAD WIN!
TIFFANY

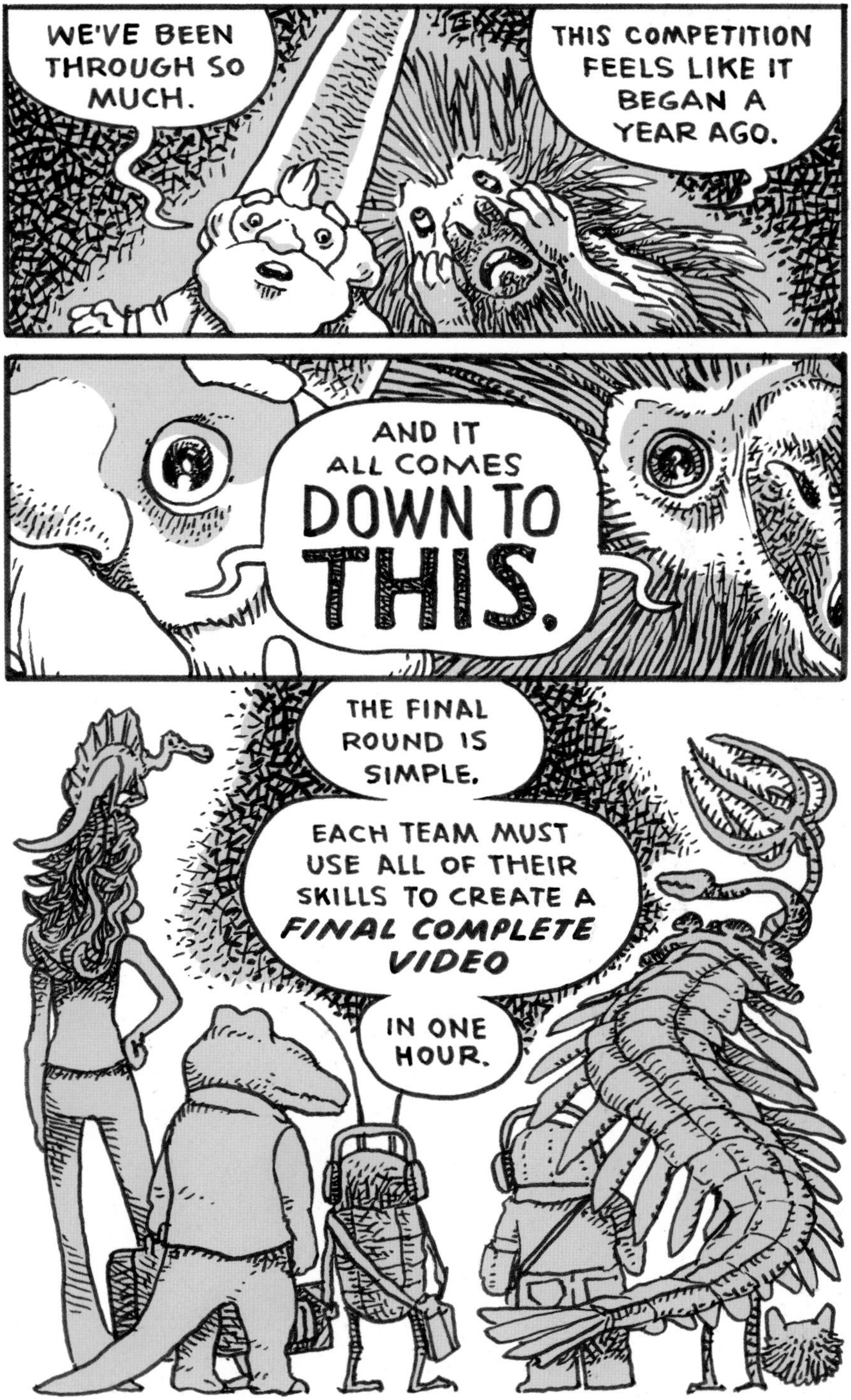
WE'VE BEEN THROUGH SO MUCH.
THIS COMPETITION FEELS LIKE IT BEGAN A YEAR AGO.
AND IT ALL COMES DOWN TO THIS.
THE FINAL ROUND IS SIMPLE.
EACH TEAM MUST USE ALL OF THEIR SKILLS TO CREATE A *FINAL COMPLETE VIDEO*
IN ONE HOUR.

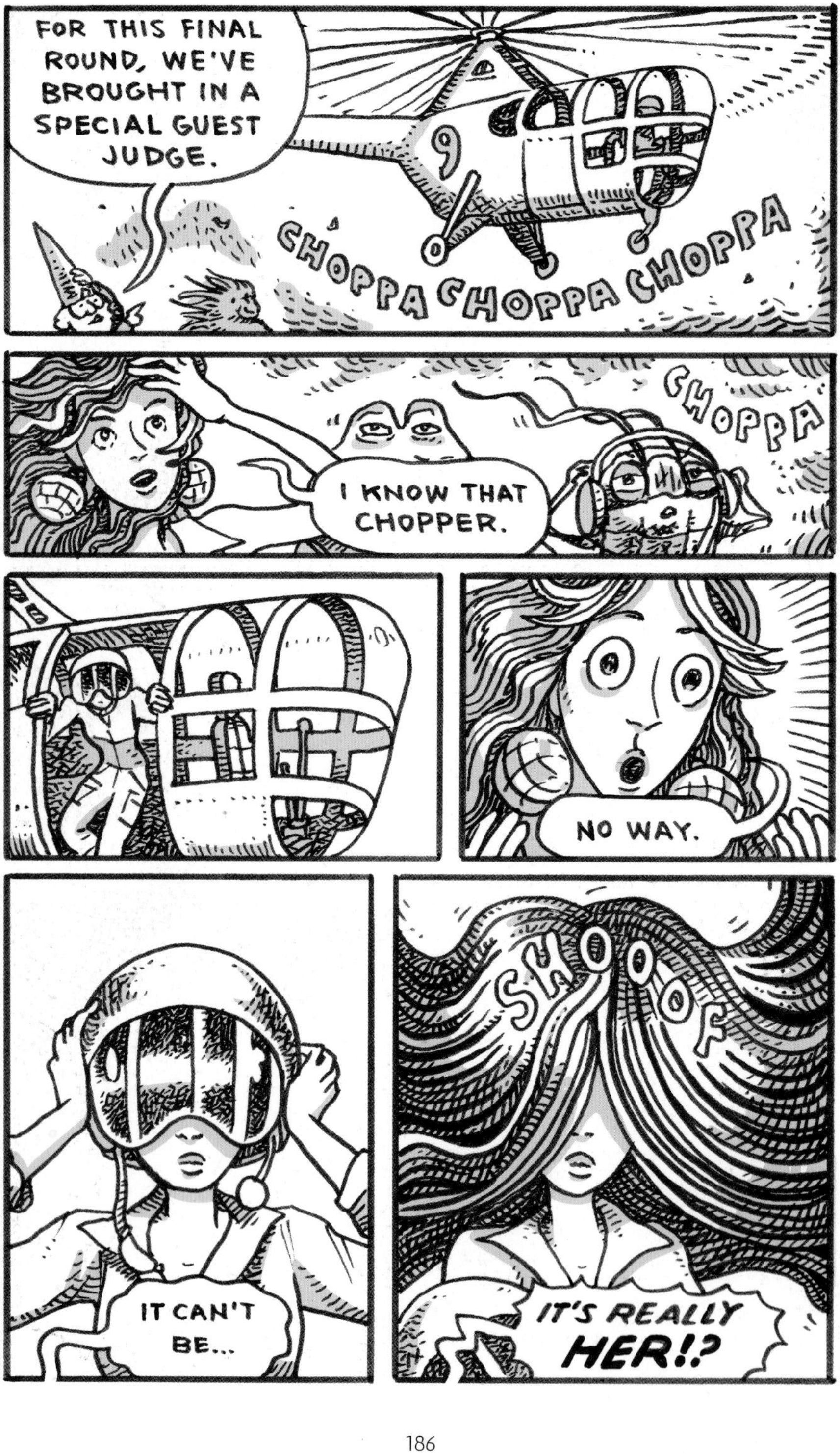
FOR THIS FINAL ROUND, WE'VE BROUGHT IN A SPECIAL GUEST JUDGE.
9
CHOPPA CHOPPA CHOPPA
CHOPPA
I KNOW THAT CHOPPER.
NO WAY.
IT CAN'T BE...
SHOOOF
IT'S REALLY HER!?

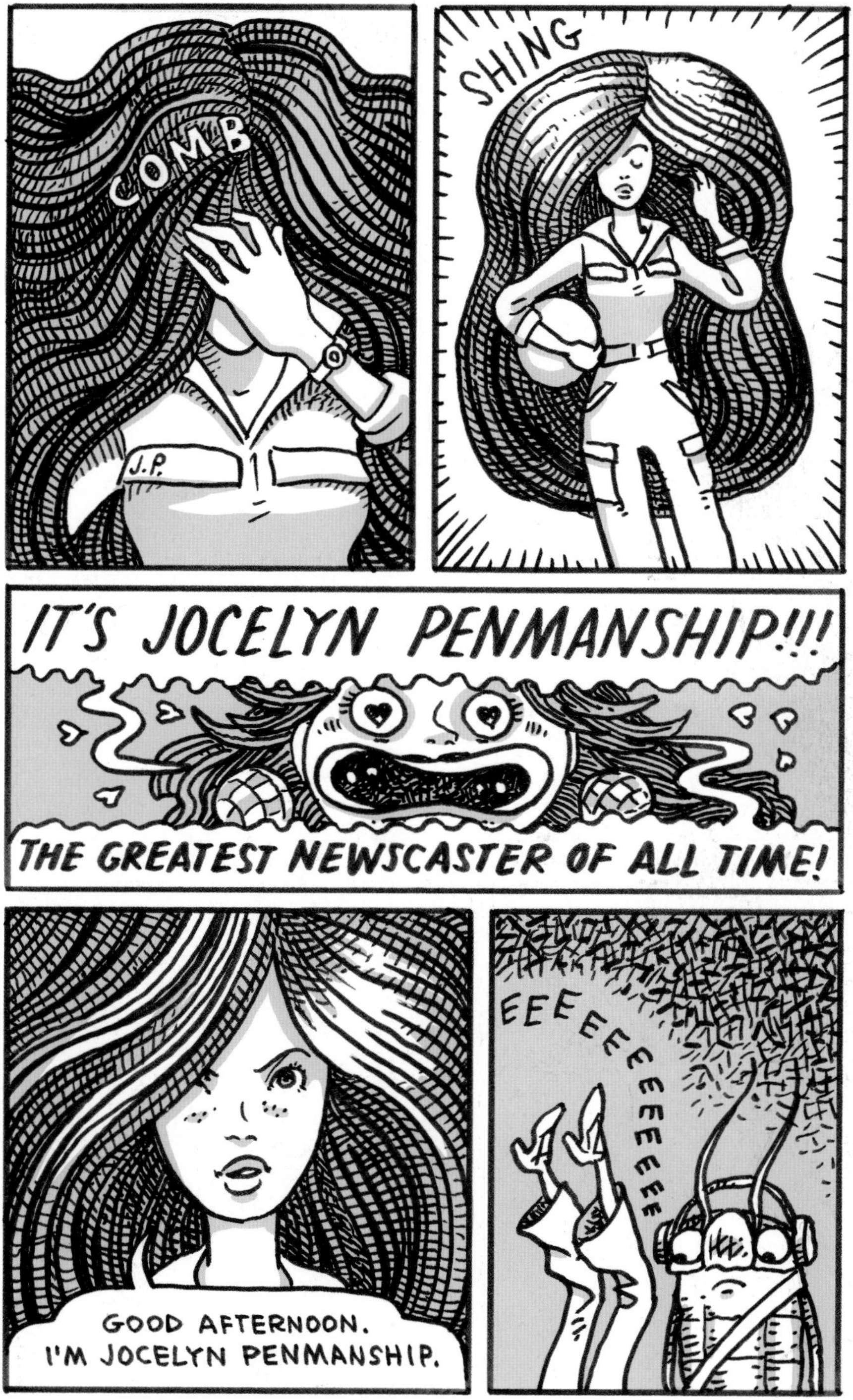
COMB
SHING
IT'S JOCELYN PENMANSHIP!!!
THE GREATEST NEWSCASTER OF ALL TIME!
GOOD AFTERNOON.
I'M JOCELYN PENMANSHIP.
EEEEEEEEEEEEEEEE

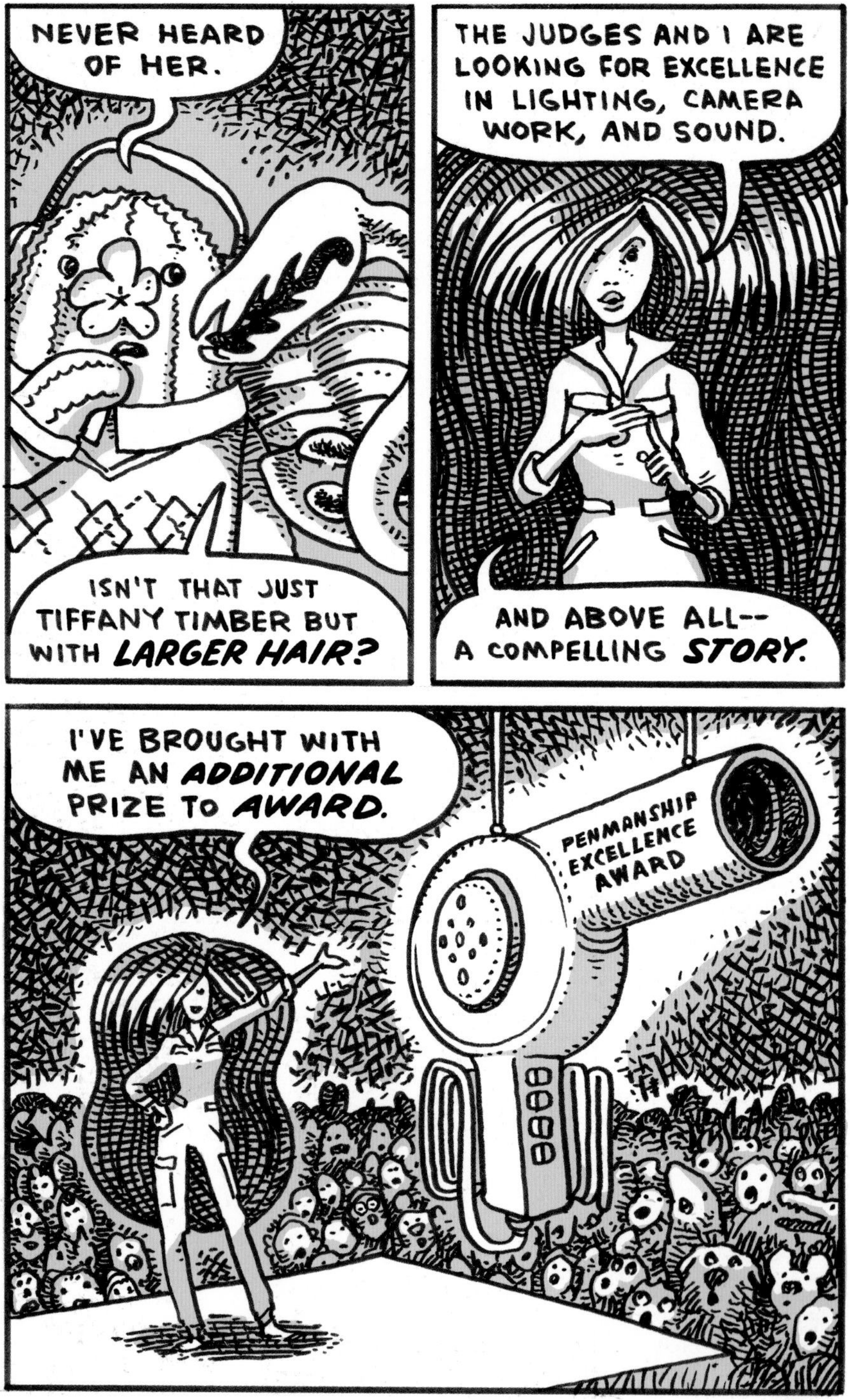
NEVER HEARD OF HER.
ISN'T THAT JUST TIFFANY TIMBER BUT WITH LARGER HAIR?
THE JUDGES AND I ARE LOOKING FOR EXCELLENCE IN LIGHTING, CAMERA WORK, AND SOUND.
AND ABOVE ALL-- A COMPELLING STORY.
I'VE BROUGHT WITH ME AN ADDITIONAL PRIZE TO AWARD.
PENMANSHIP EXCELLENCE AWARD

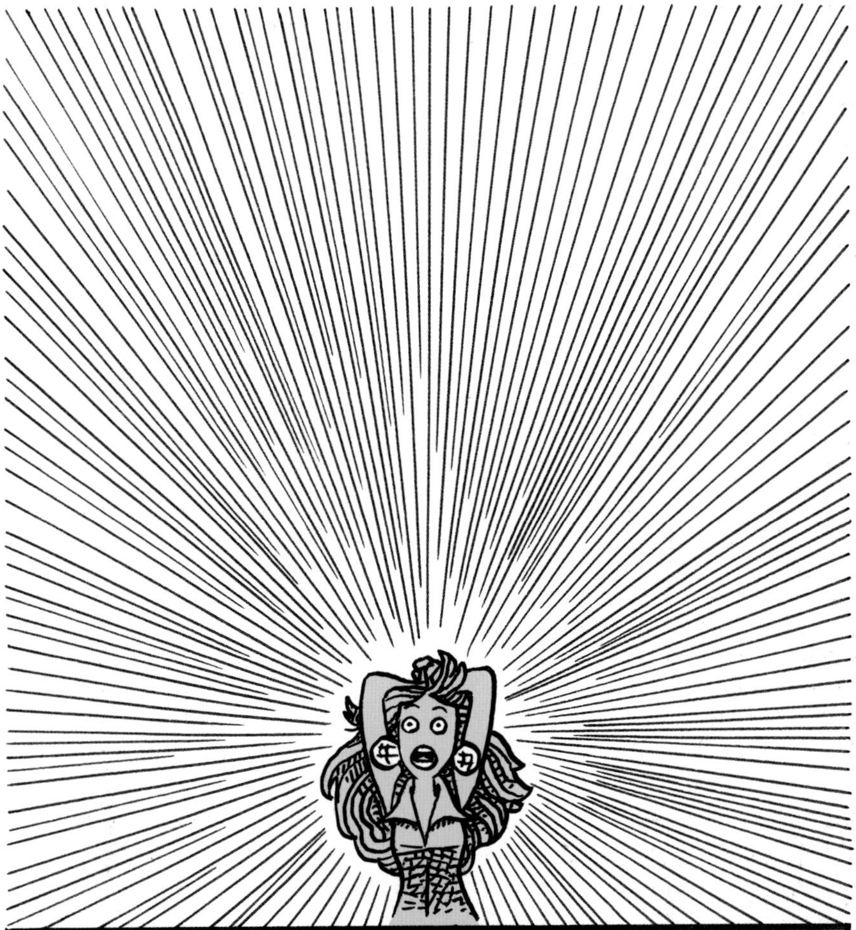

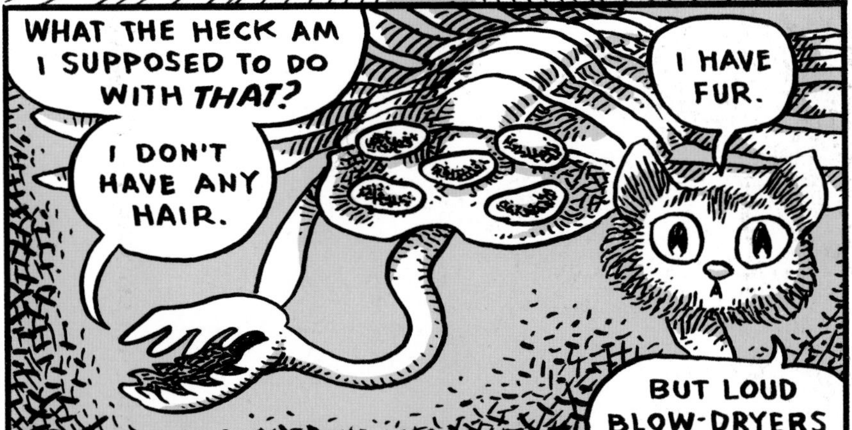
WHAT THE HECK AM I SUPPOSED TO DO WITH *THAT?*
I DON'T HAVE ANY HAIR.
I HAVE FUR.
BUT LOUD BLOW-DRYERS SCARE ME.

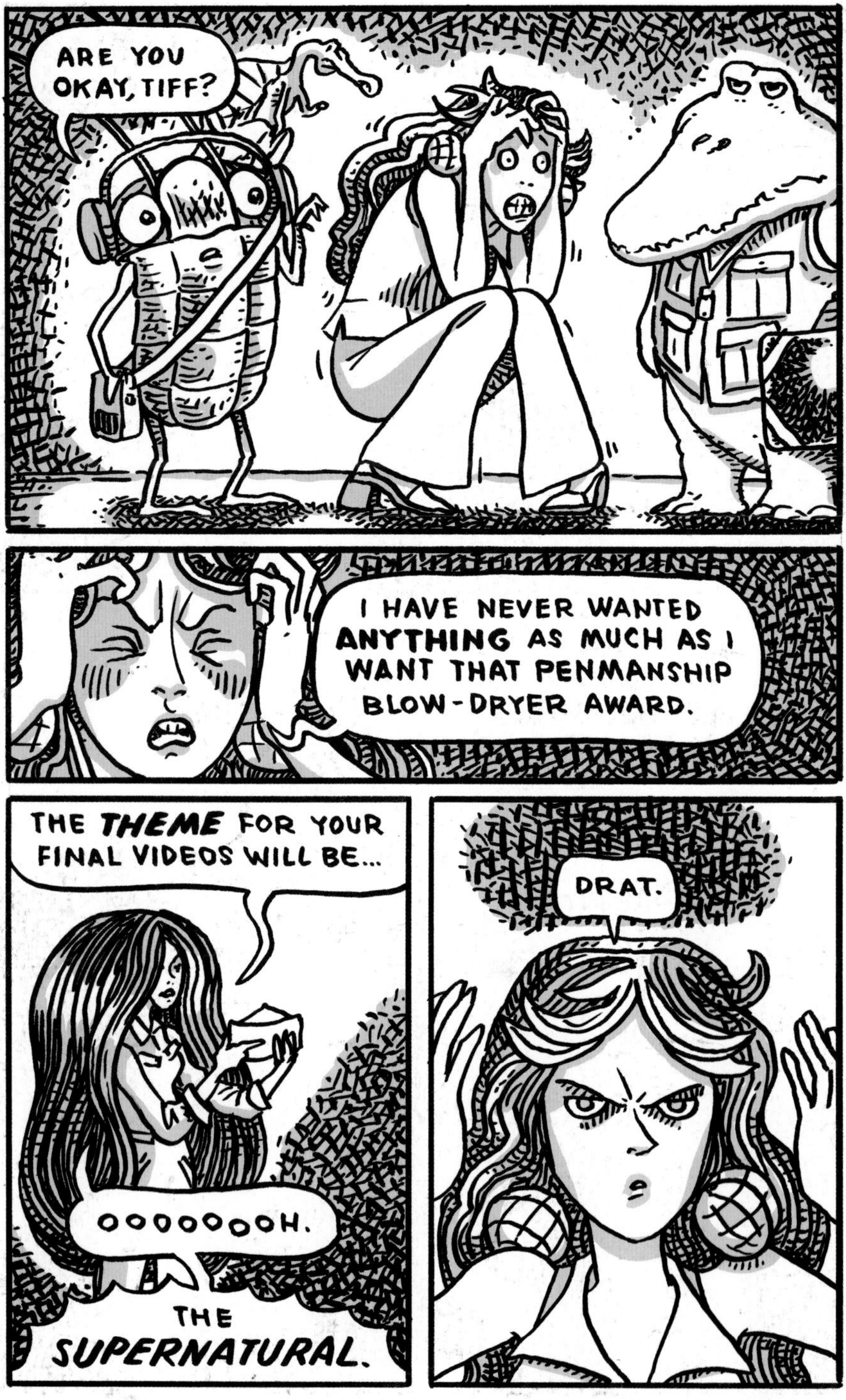
ARE YOU OKAY, TIFF?
I HAVE NEVER WANTED **ANYTHING** AS MUCH AS I WANT THAT PENMANSHIP BLOW-DRYER AWARD.
THE *THEME* FOR YOUR FINAL VIDEOS WILL BE...
OOOOOOOOH.
THE *SUPERNATURAL*.
DRAT.

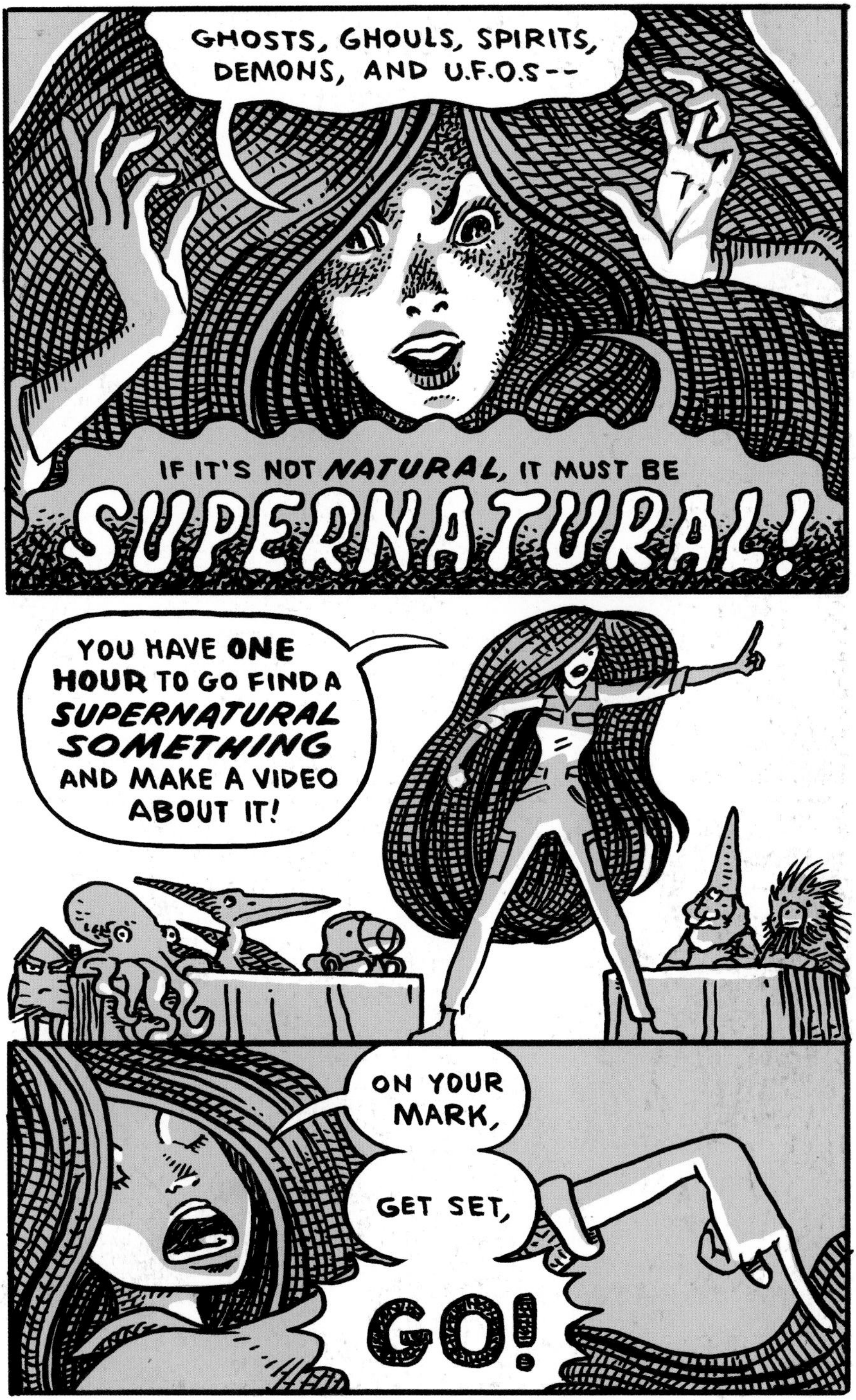

GHOSTS, GHOULS, SPIRITS, DEMONS, AND U.F.O.S--
IF IT'S NOT NATURAL, IT MUST BE
SUPERNATURAL!
YOU HAVE ONE HOUR TO GO FIND A SUPERNATURAL SOMETHING AND MAKE A VIDEO ABOUT IT!
ON YOUR MARK,
GET SET,
GO!

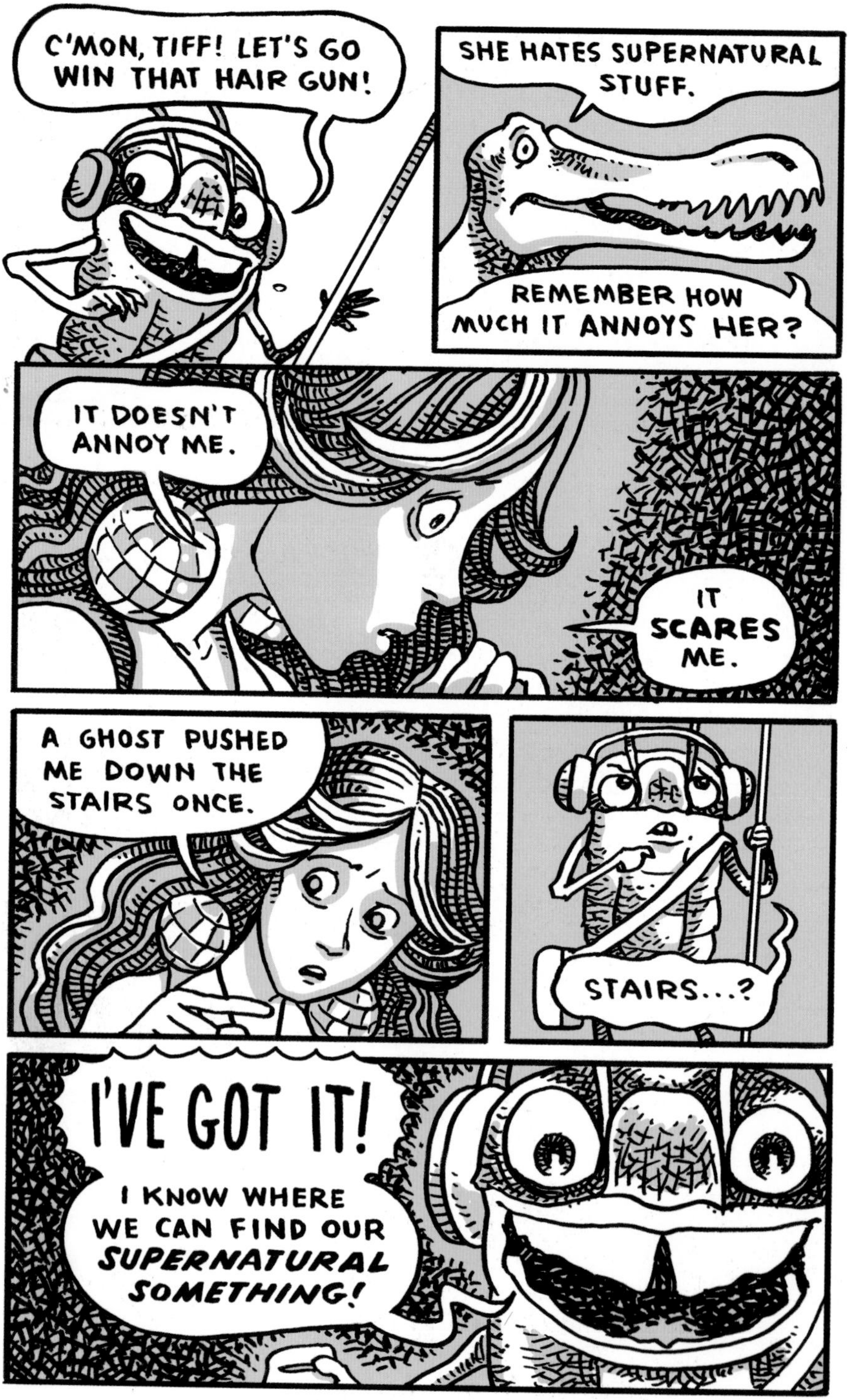
C'MON, TIFF! LET'S GO WIN THAT HAIR GUN!
SHE HATES SUPERNATURAL STUFF.
REMEMBER HOW MUCH IT ANNOYS HER?
IT DOESN'T ANNOY ME.
IT SCARES ME.
A GHOST PUSHED ME DOWN THE STAIRS ONCE.
STAIRS...?
I'VE GOT IT!
I KNOW WHERE WE CAN FIND OUR *SUPERNATURAL SOMETHING!*

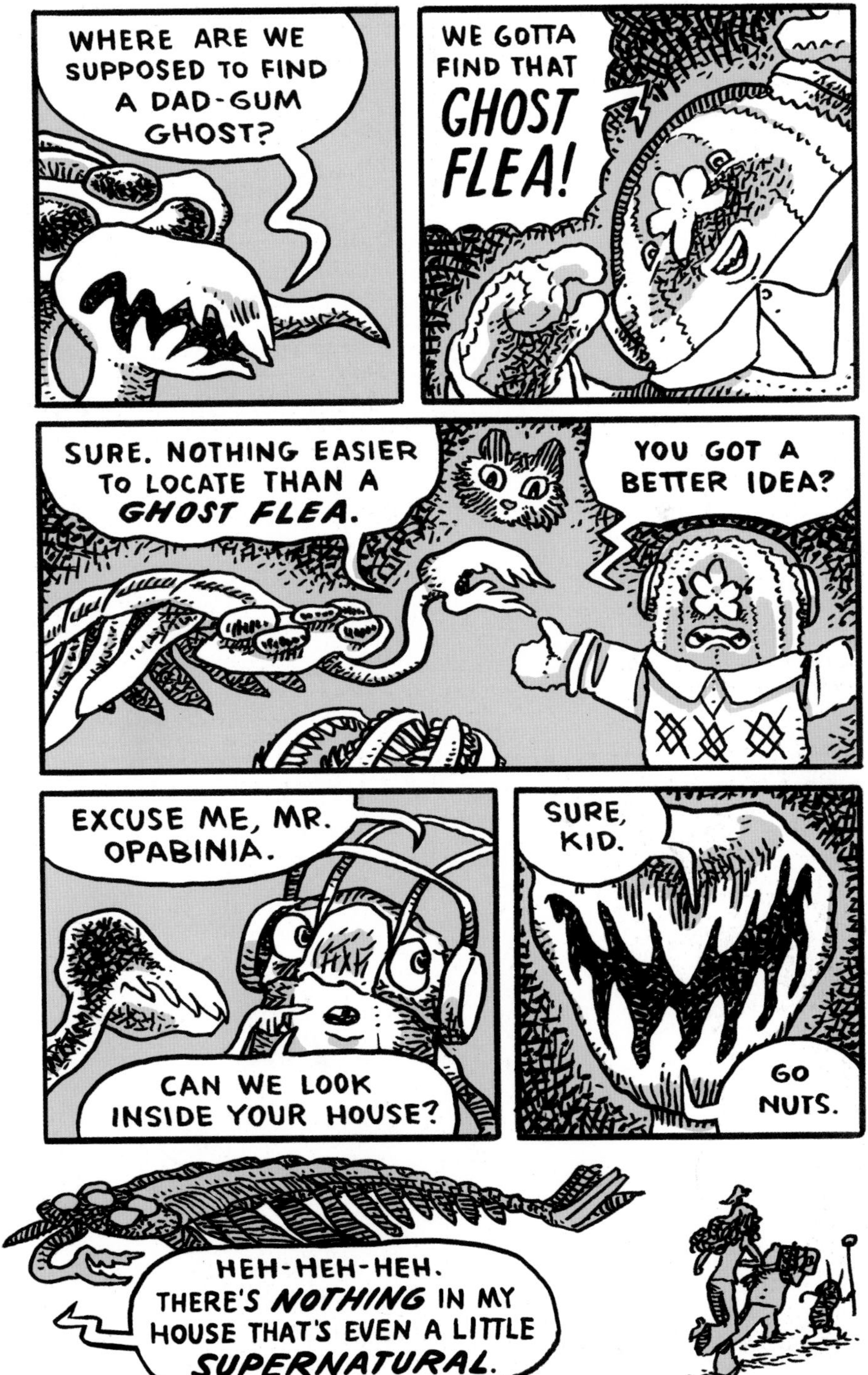
WHERE ARE WE SUPPOSED TO FIND A DAD-GUM GHOST?
WE GOTTA FIND THAT GHOST FLEA!
SURE. NOTHING EASIER TO LOCATE THAN A GHOST FLEA.
YOU GOT A BETTER IDEA?
EXCUSE ME, MR. OPABINIA.
CAN WE LOOK INSIDE YOUR HOUSE?
SURE, KID.
GO NUTS.
HEH-HEH-HEH. THERE'S NOTHING IN MY HOUSE THAT'S EVEN A LITTLE SUPERNATURAL.

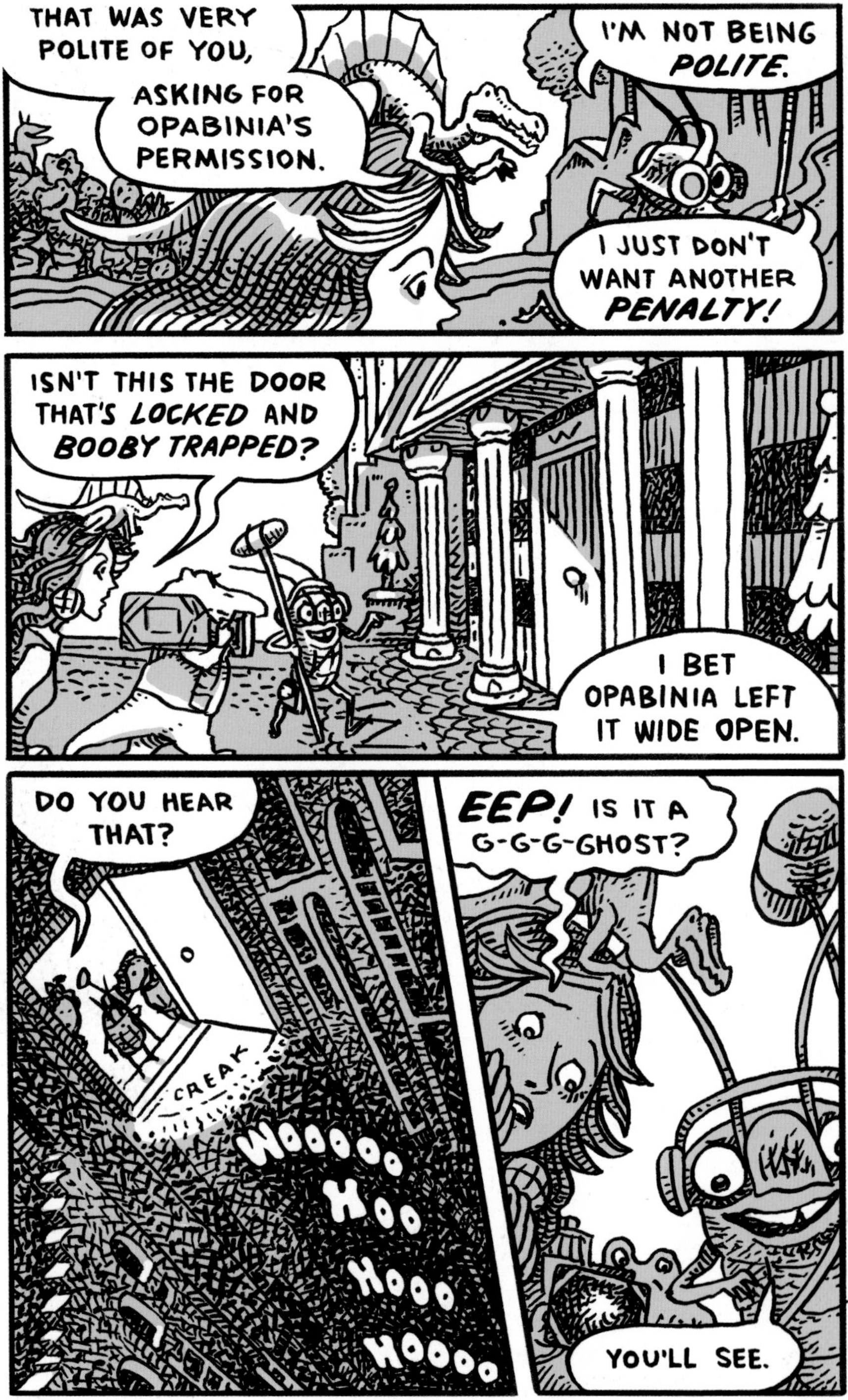
THAT WAS VERY POLITE OF YOU,
ASKING FOR OPABINIA'S PERMISSION.
I'M NOT BEING *POLITE*.
I JUST DON'T WANT ANOTHER *PENALTY*!
ISN'T THIS THE DOOR THAT'S *LOCKED* AND *BOOBY TRAPPED*?
I BET OPABINIA LEFT IT WIDE OPEN.
DO YOU HEAR THAT?
CREAK
WOOOOO HOO HOOO HOOOO
EEP! IS IT A G-G-G-GHOST?
YOU'LL SEE.

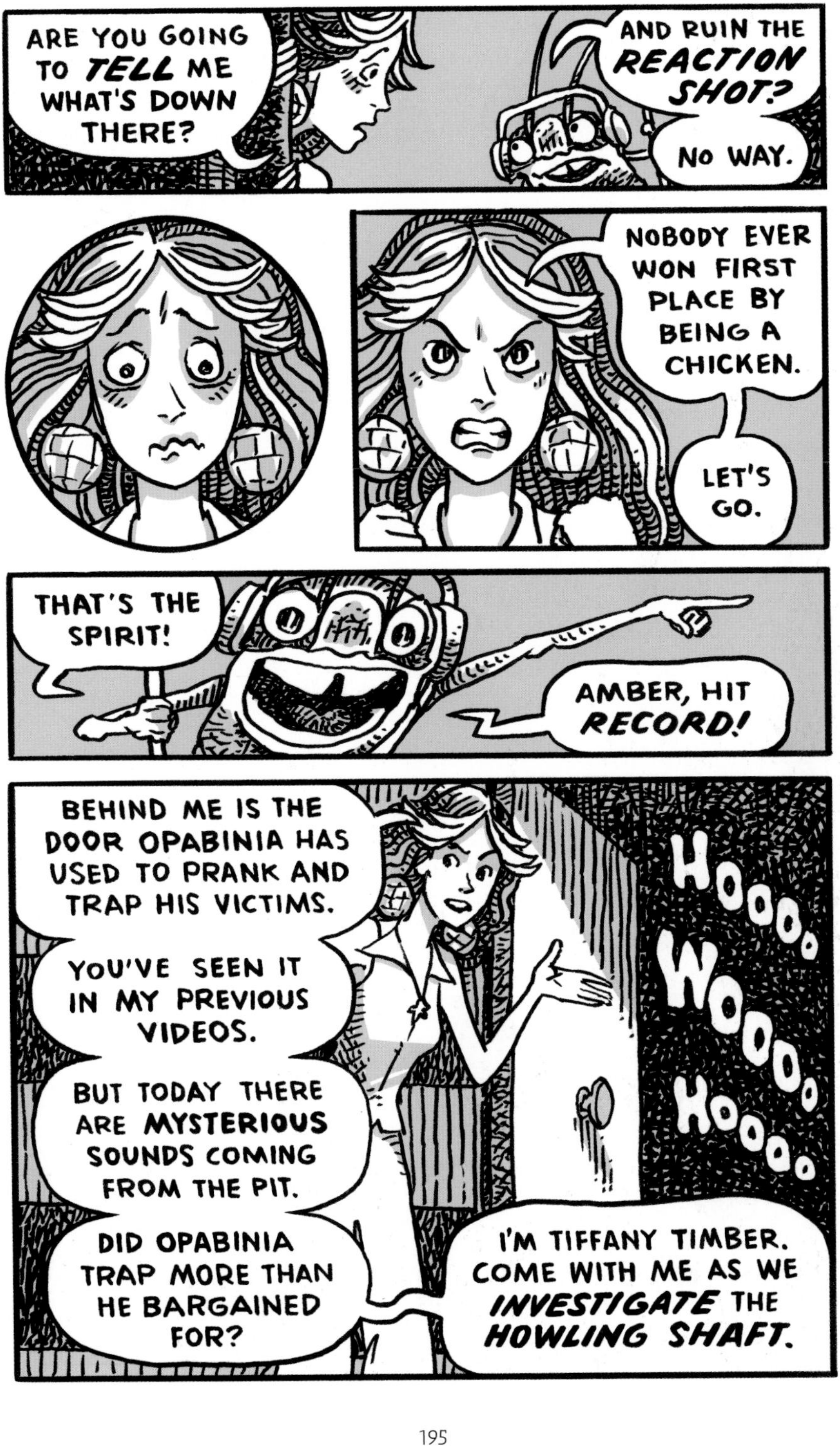
ARE YOU GOING TO *TELL* ME WHAT'S DOWN THERE?
AND RUIN THE *REACTION SHOT?*
NO WAY.
NOBODY EVER WON FIRST PLACE BY BEING A CHICKEN.
LET'S GO.
THAT'S THE SPIRIT!
AMBER, HIT *RECORD!*
BEHIND ME IS THE DOOR OPABINIA HAS USED TO PRANK AND TRAP HIS VICTIMS.
YOU'VE SEEN IT IN MY PREVIOUS VIDEOS.
BUT TODAY THERE ARE **MYSTERIOUS** SOUNDS COMING FROM THE PIT.
HOOOOO WOOOOO HOOOOO
DID OPABINIA TRAP MORE THAN HE BARGAINED FOR?
I'M TIFFANY TIMBER. COME WITH ME AS WE *INVESTIGATE* THE *HOWLING SHAFT.*

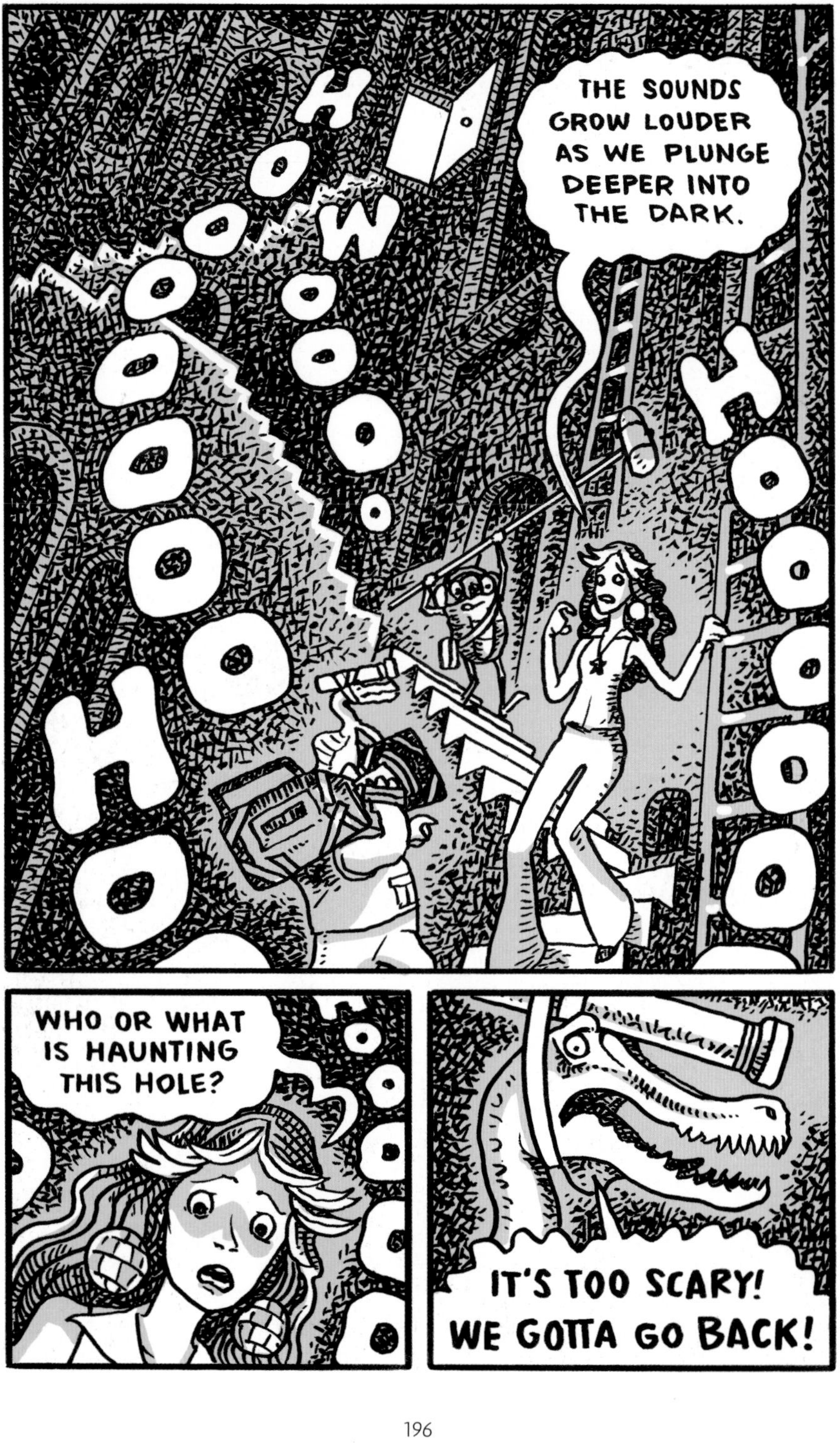
THE SOUNDS GROW LOUDER AS WE PLUNGE DEEPER INTO THE DARK.
WHO OR WHAT IS HAUNTING THIS HOLE?
IT'S TOO SCARY! WE GOTTA GO BACK!

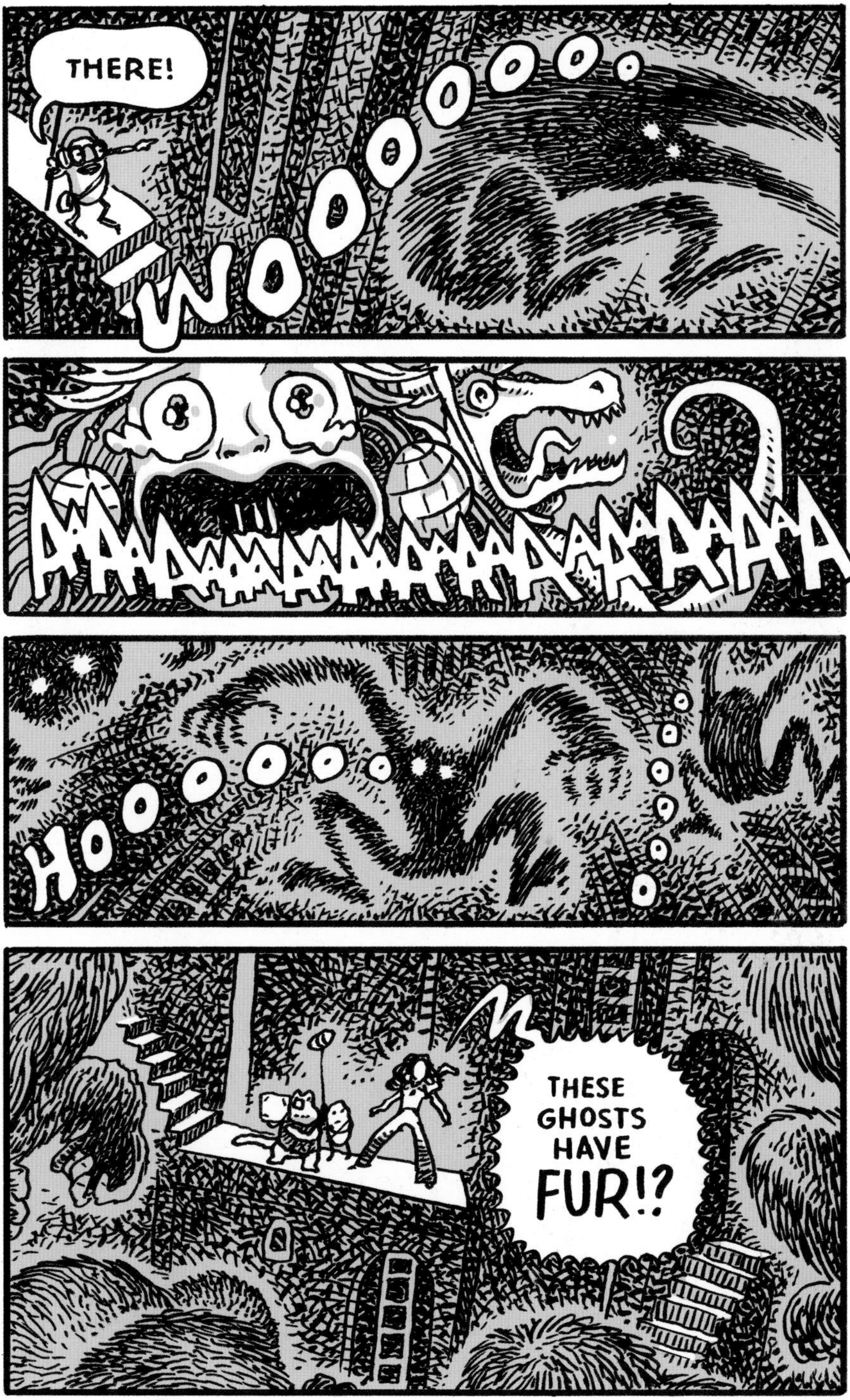
THERE!
WOOOOOOOO.
AAAAAAAAAAAAAAAAAAAAAAAAA
HOOOOOOOOOOOOOO
THESE GHOSTS HAVE FUR!?

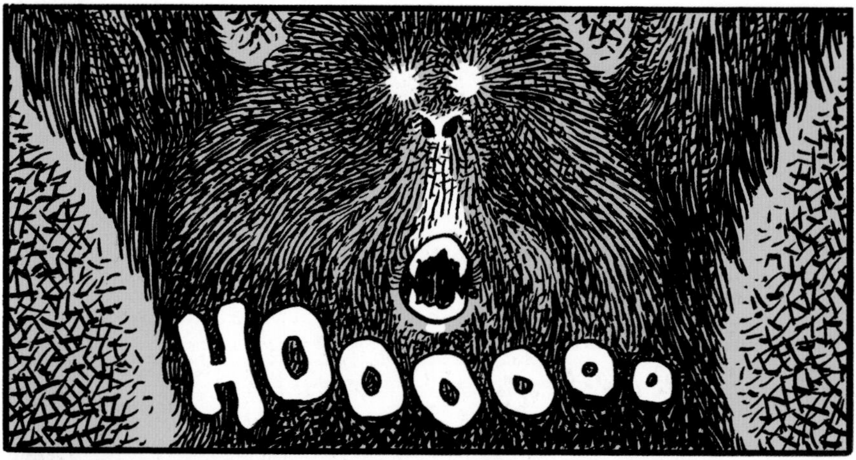
HOOOOOO

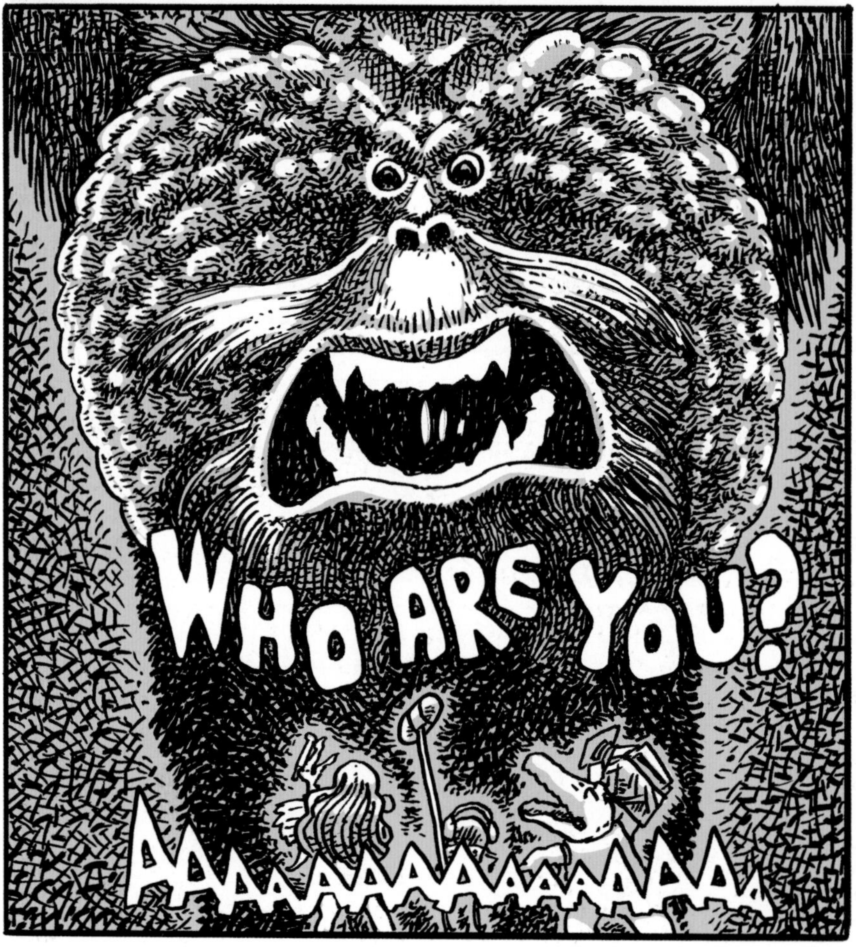
WHO ARE YOU?
AAAAAAAAAAAAA

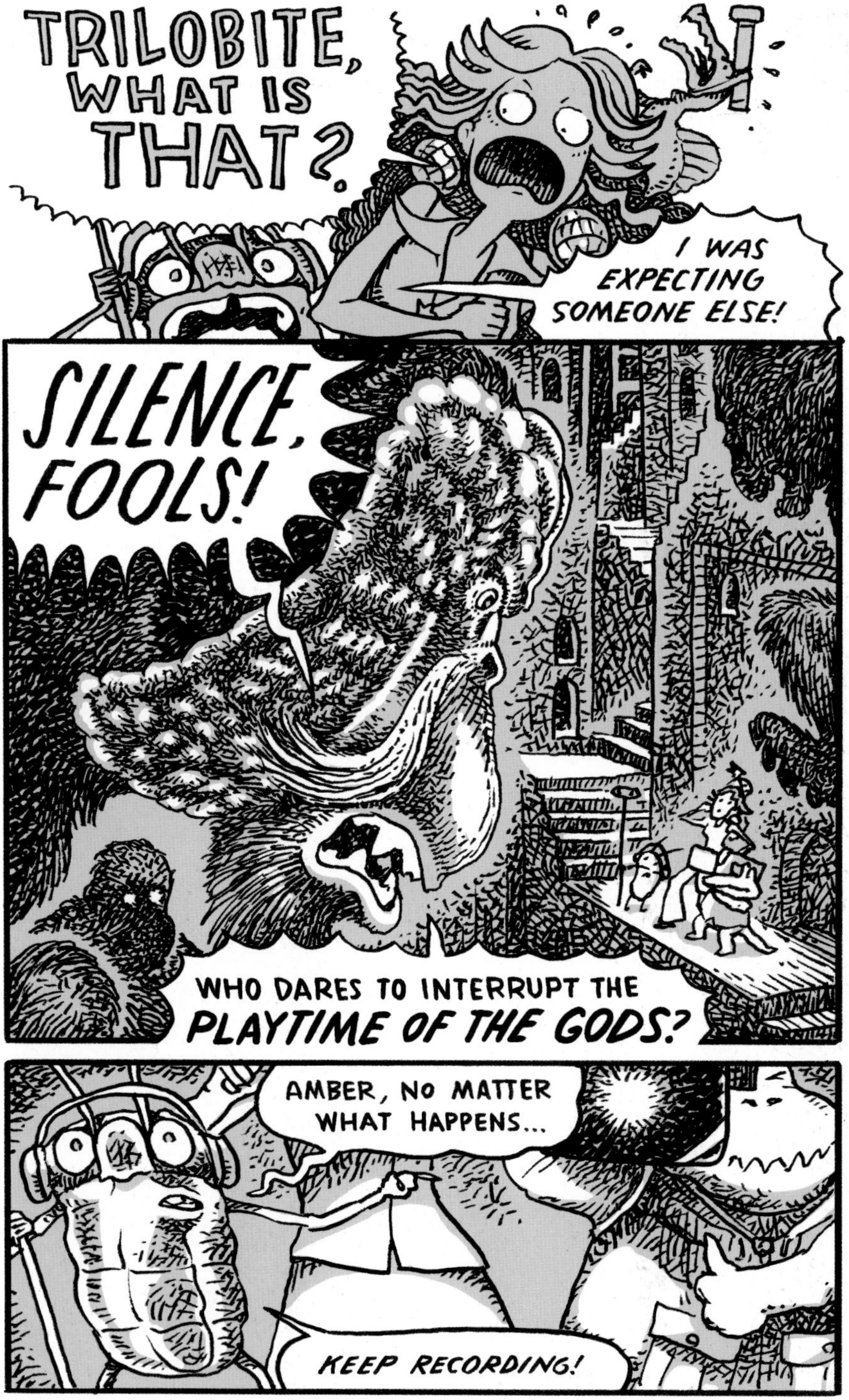
TRILOBITE, WHAT IS THAT?
I WAS EXPECTING SOMEONE ELSE!
SILENCE, FOOLS!
WHO DARES TO INTERRUPT THE PLAYTIME OF THE GODS?
AMBER, NO MATTER WHAT HAPPENS...
KEEP RECORDING!

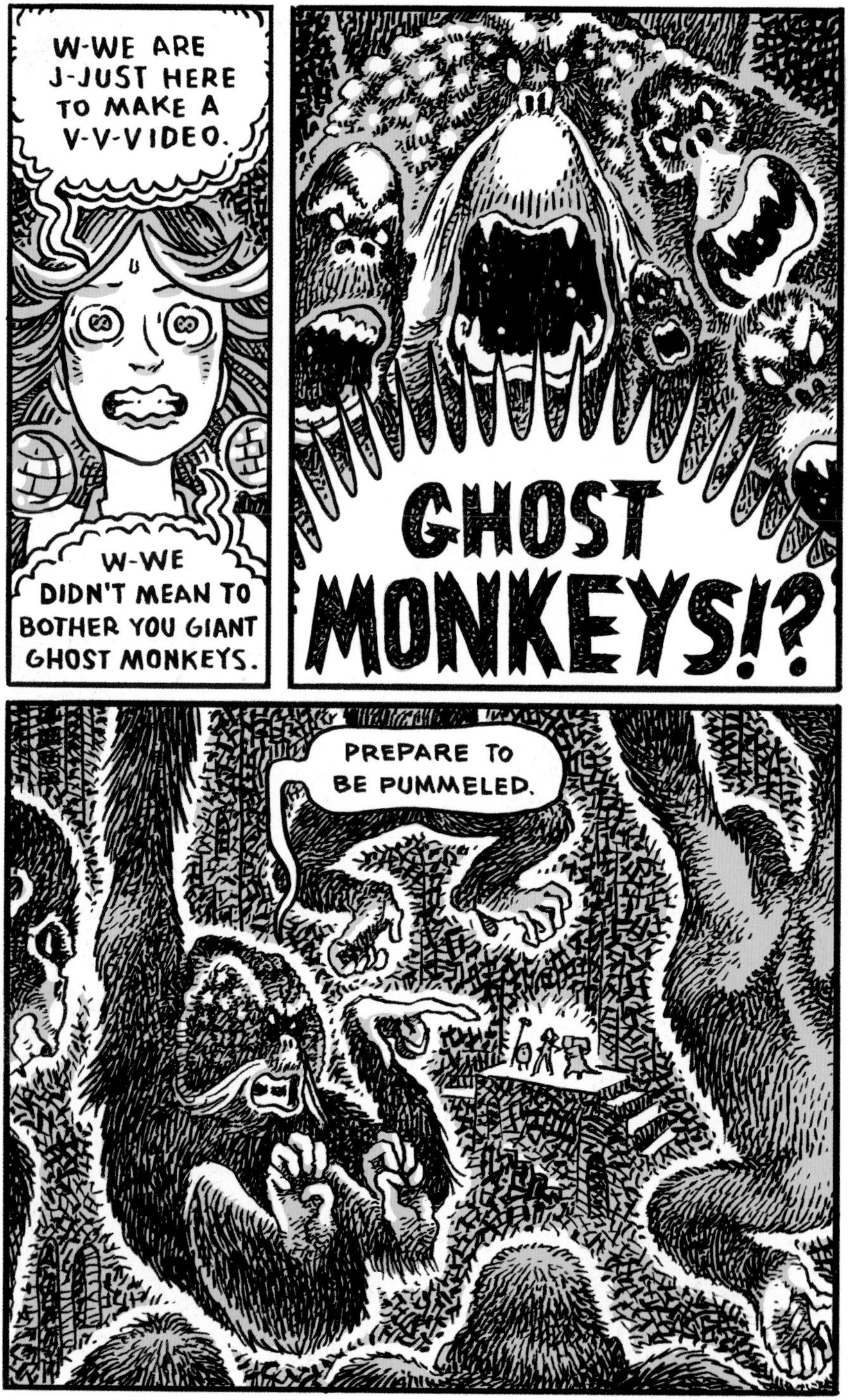
W-WE ARE J-JUST HERE TO MAKE A V-V-VIDEO.
W-WE DIDN'T MEAN TO BOTHER YOU GIANT GHOST MONKEYS.
GHOST MONKEYS!?
PREPARE TO BE PUMMELED.

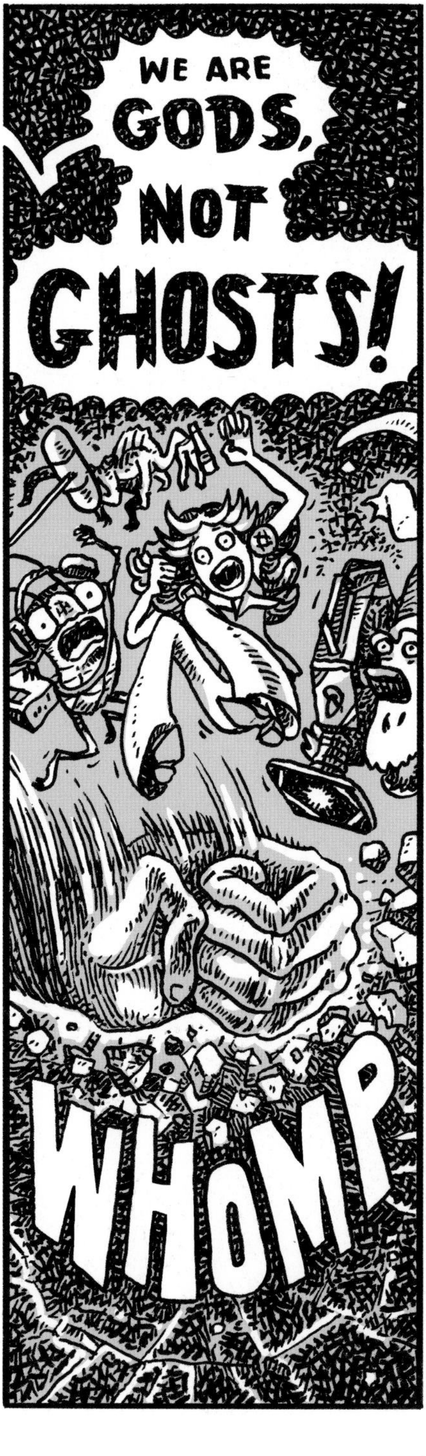
WE ARE GODS, NOT GHOSTS!
WHOMP

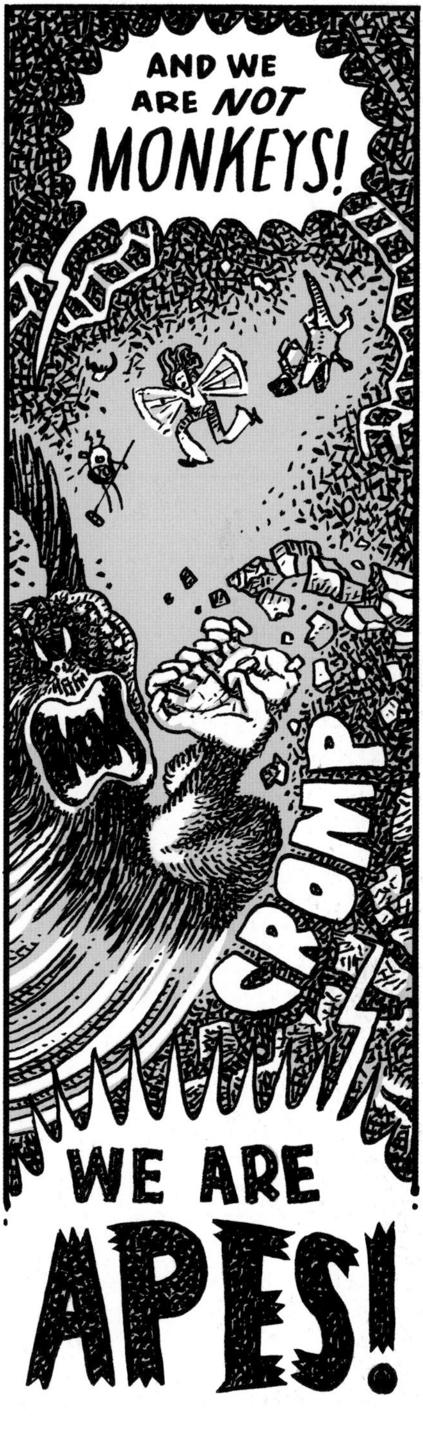
AND WE ARE *NOT* MONKEYS!
CROMP
WE ARE APES!

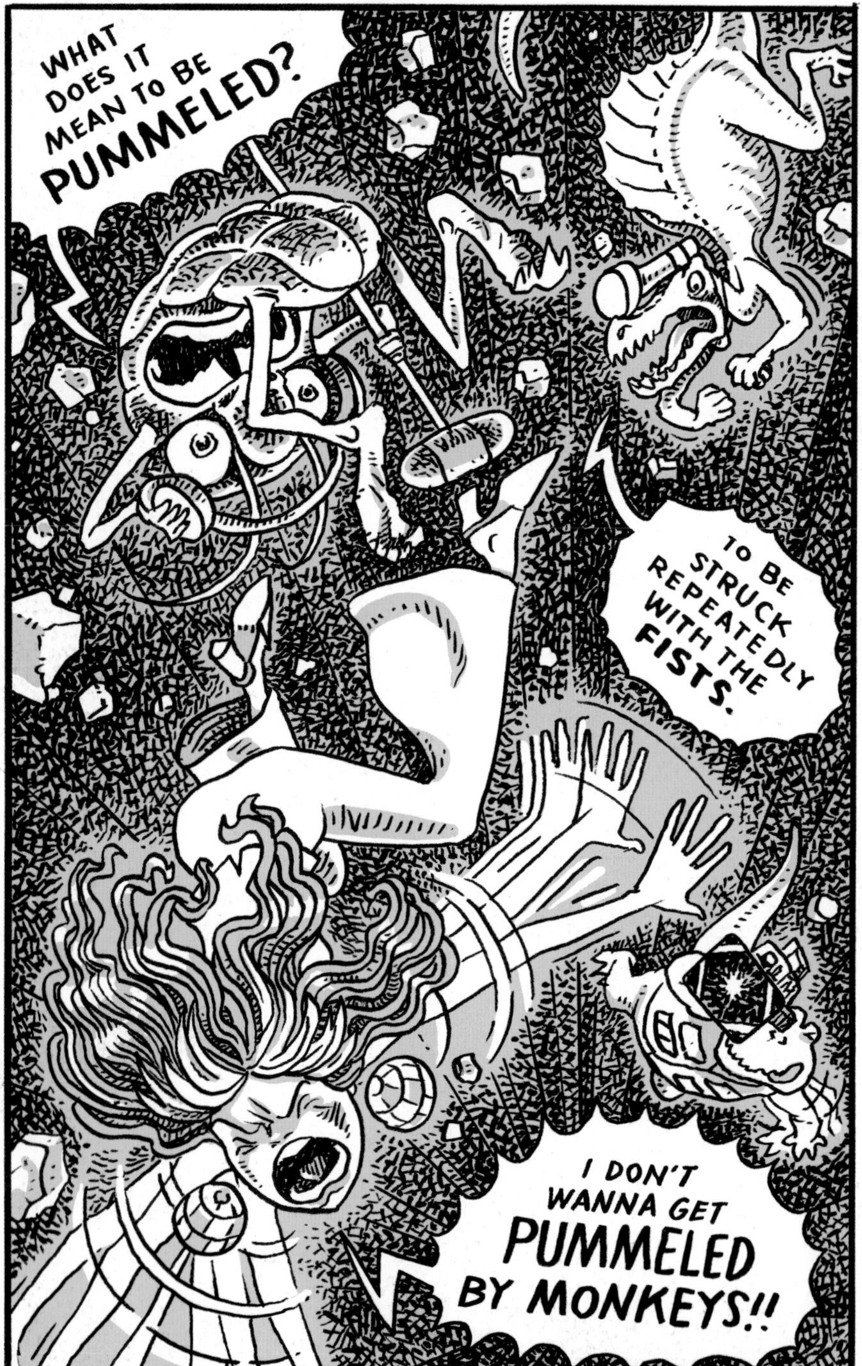
WHAT DOES IT MEAN TO BE PUMMELED?
TO BE STRUCK REPEATEDLY WITH THE FISTS.
I DON'T WANNA GET PUMMELED BY MONKEYS!!

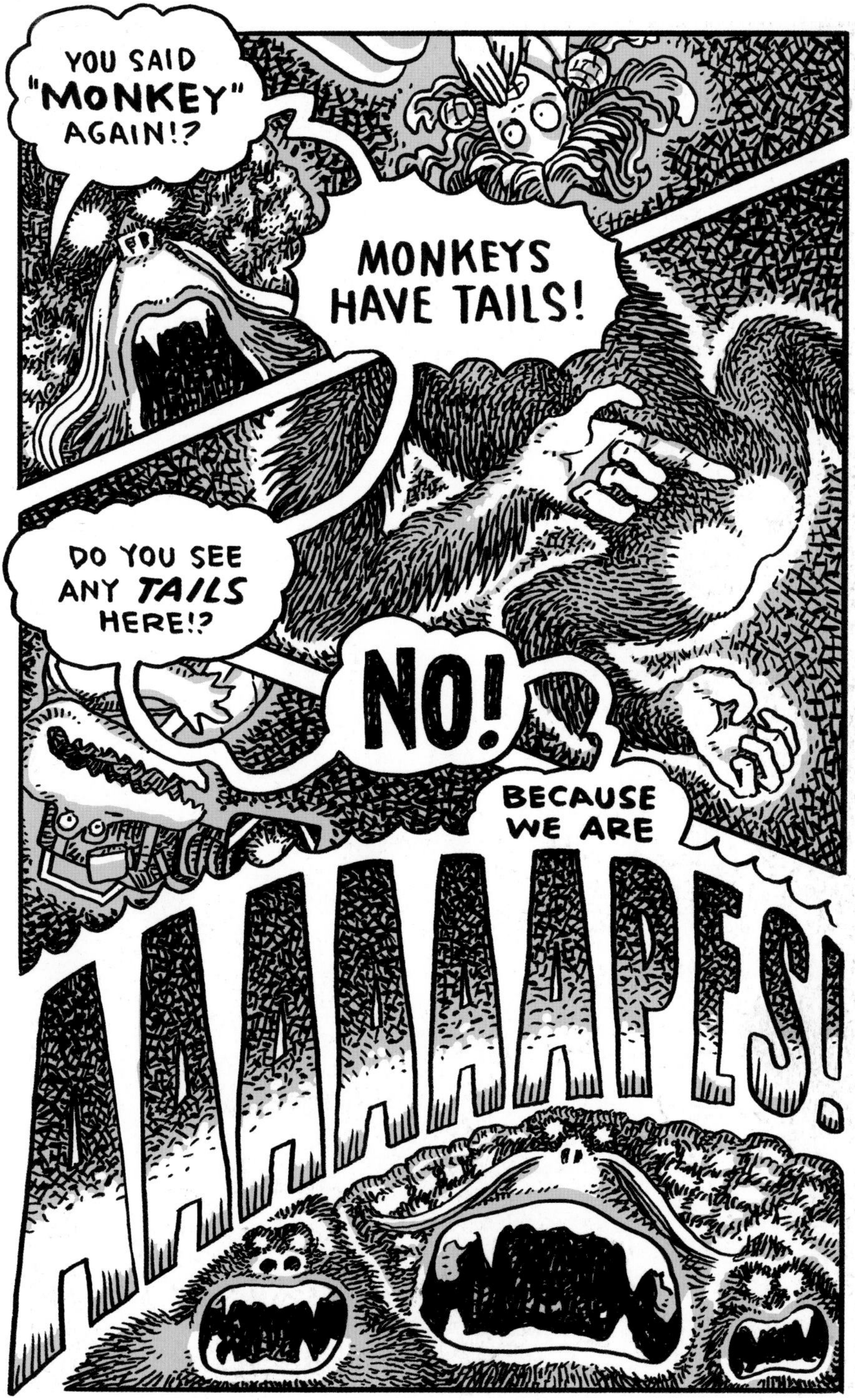
YOU SAID "MONKEY" AGAIN!?
MONKEYS HAVE TAILS!
DO YOU SEE ANY TAILS HERE!?
NO!
BECAUSE WE ARE
AAAAAAPES!

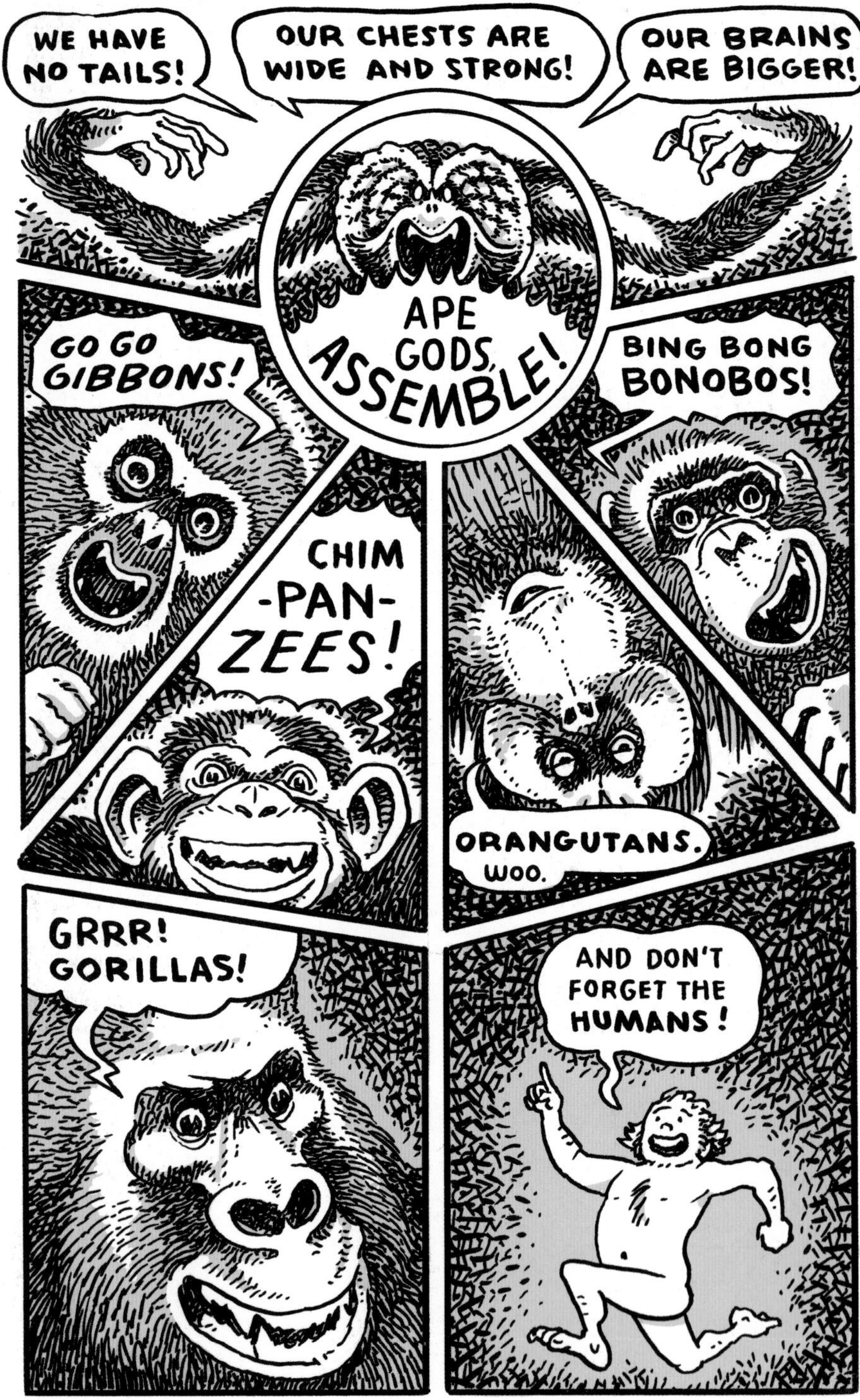
WE HAVE NO TAILS!
OUR CHESTS ARE WIDE AND STRONG!
OUR BRAINS ARE BIGGER!
APE GODS, ASSEMBLE!
GO GO GIBBONS!
BING BONG BONOBOS!
CHIM -PAN- ZEES!
ORANGUTANS. WOO.
GRRR! GORILLAS!
AND DON'T FORGET THE HUMANS!

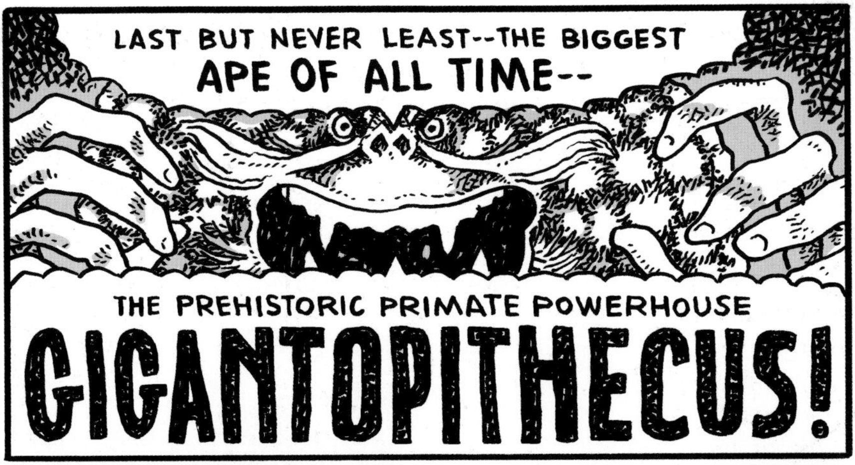
LAST BUT NEVER LEAST--THE BIGGEST APE OF ALL TIME--
THE PREHISTORIC PRIMATE POWERHOUSE
GIGANTOPITHECUS!

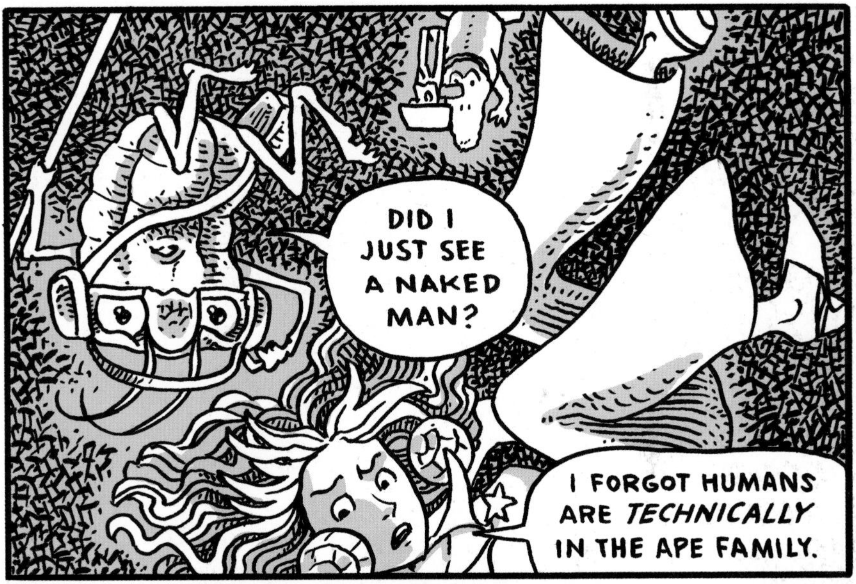
DID I JUST SEE A NAKED MAN?
I FORGOT HUMANS ARE *TECHNICALLY* IN THE APE FAMILY.

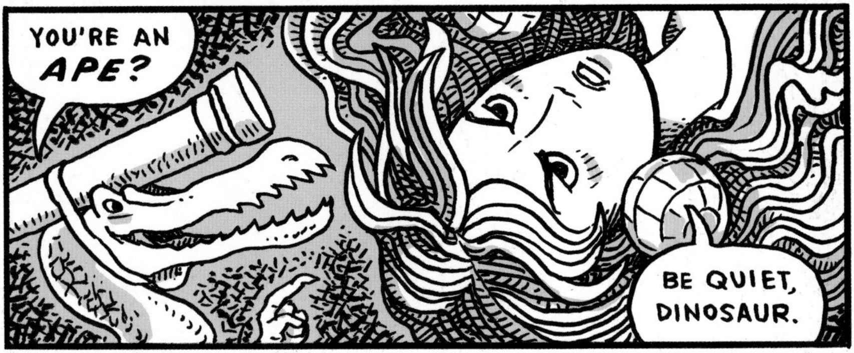
YOU'RE AN *APE?*
BE QUIET, DINOSAUR.

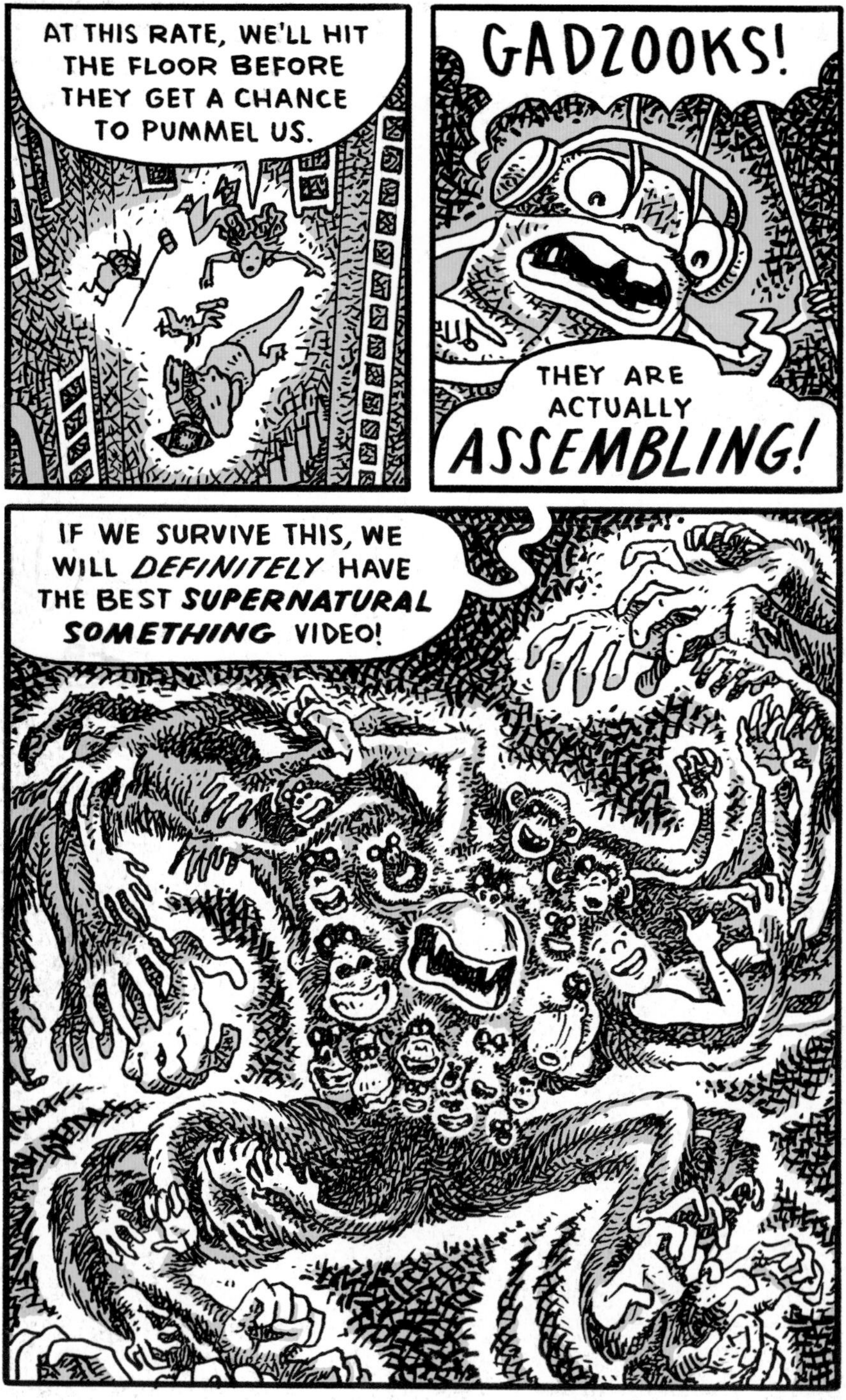
AT THIS RATE, WE'LL HIT THE FLOOR BEFORE THEY GET A CHANCE TO PUMMEL US.
GADZOOKS!
THEY ARE ACTUALLY ASSEMBLING!
IF WE SURVIVE THIS, WE WILL DEFINITELY HAVE THE BEST SUPERNATURAL SOMETHING VIDEO!

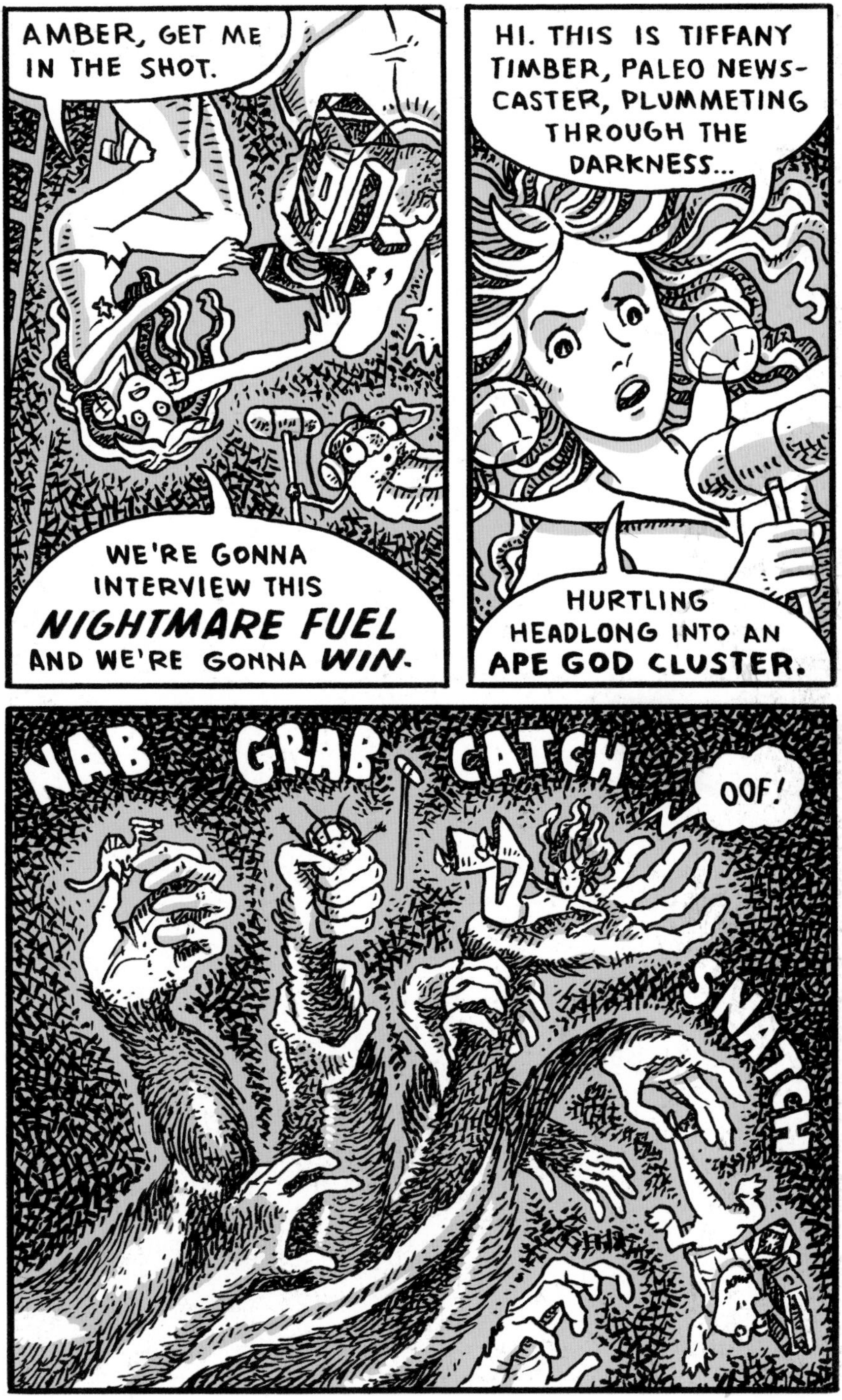
AMBER, GET ME IN THE SHOT.
WE'RE GONNA INTERVIEW THIS NIGHTMARE FUEL AND WE'RE GONNA WIN.
HI. THIS IS TIFFANY TIMBER, PALEO NEWS-CASTER, PLUMMETING THROUGH THE DARKNESS...
HURTLING HEADLONG INTO AN APE GOD CLUSTER.
NAB
GRAB
CATCH
OOF!
SNATCH

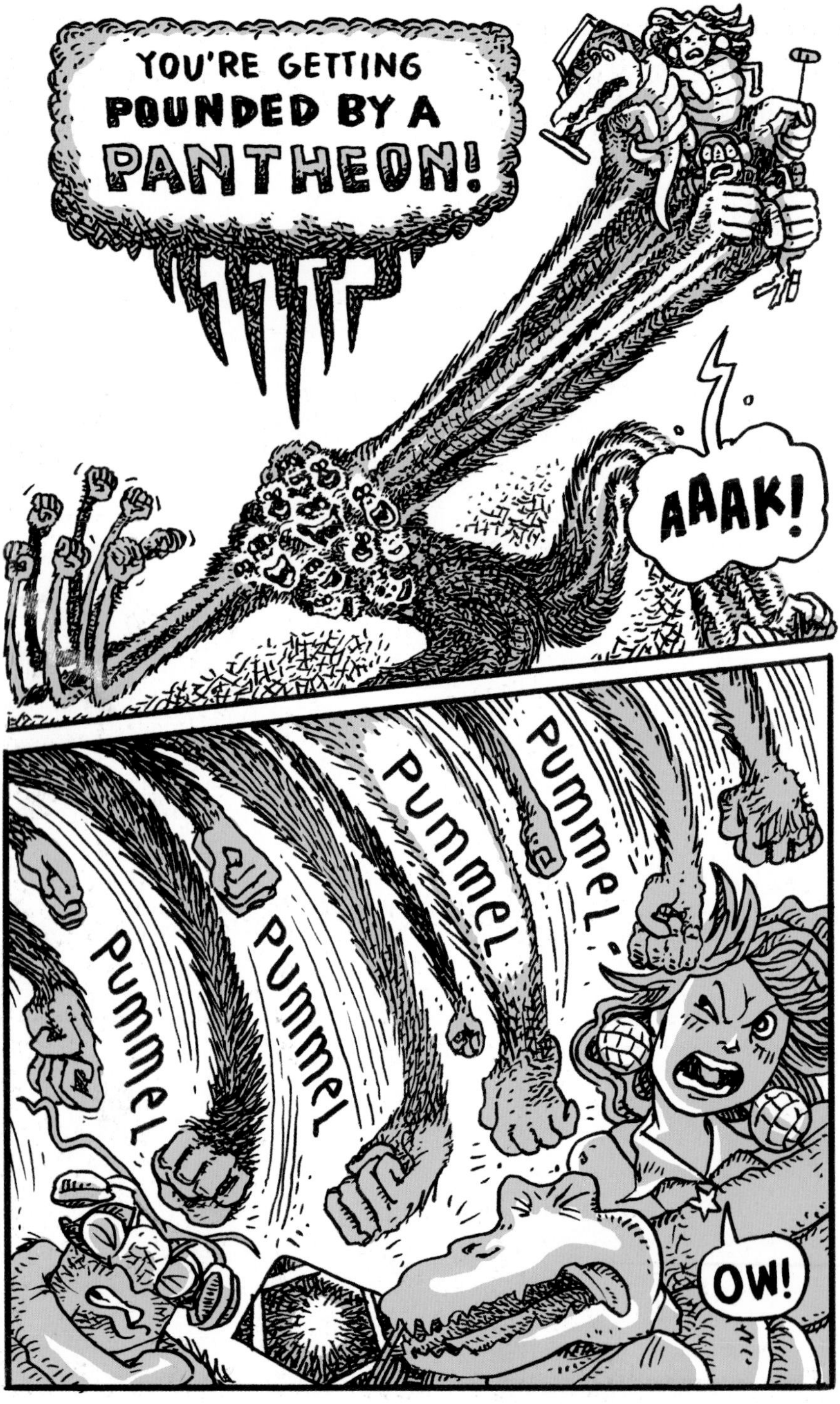

YOU'RE GETTING POUNDED BY A PANTHEON!
AAAK!
Pummel
Pummel
Pummel
Pummel
OW!

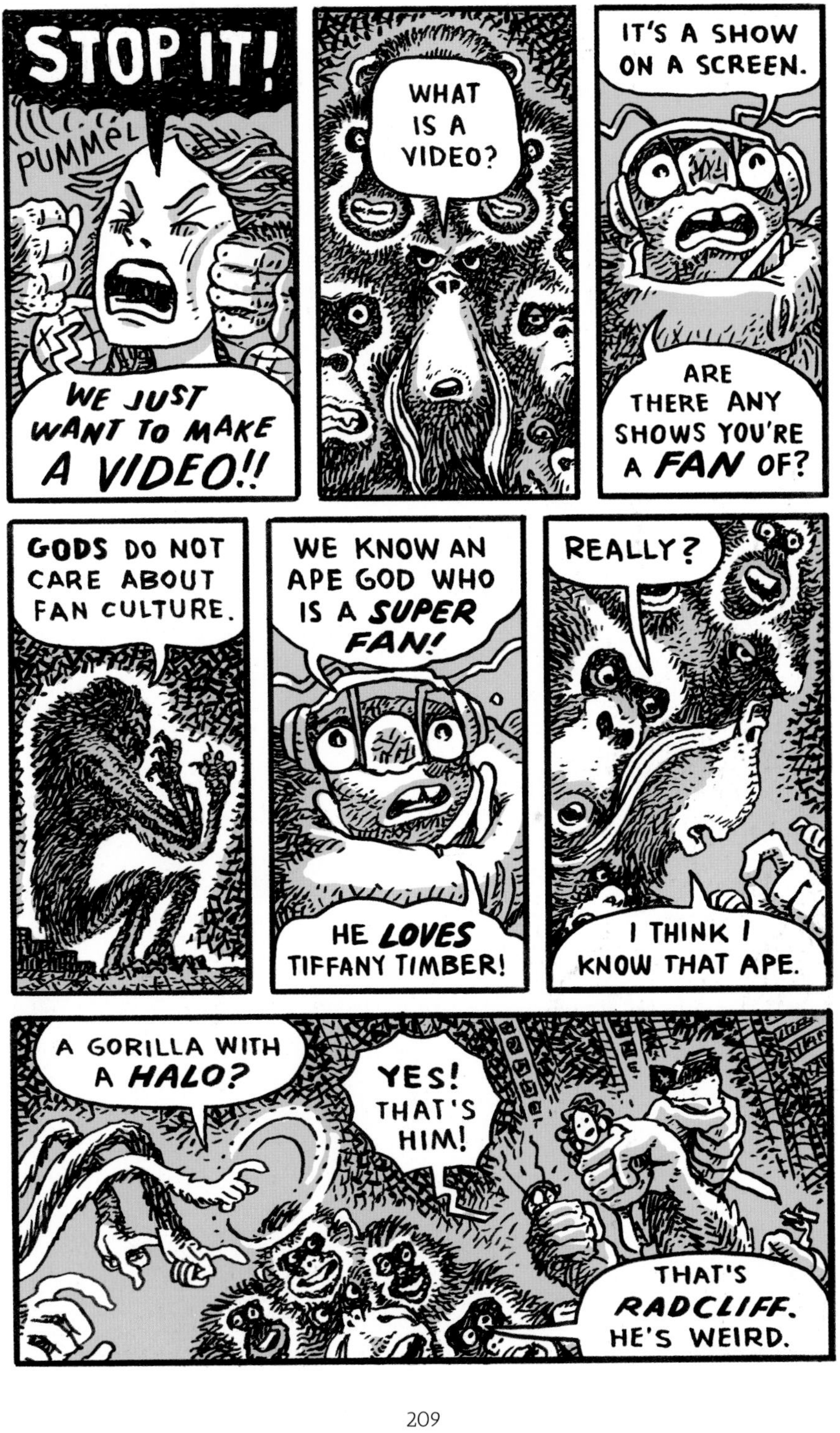
STOP IT!
PUMMEL
WE JUST WANT TO MAKE A VIDEO!!
WHAT IS A VIDEO?
IT'S A SHOW ON A SCREEN.
ARE THERE ANY SHOWS YOU'RE A FAN OF?
GODS DO NOT CARE ABOUT FAN CULTURE.
WE KNOW AN APE GOD WHO IS A SUPER FAN!
HE LOVES TIFFANY TIMBER!
REALLY?
I THINK I KNOW THAT APE.
A GORILLA WITH A HALO?
YES! THAT'S HIM!
THAT'S RADCLIFF. HE'S WEIRD.

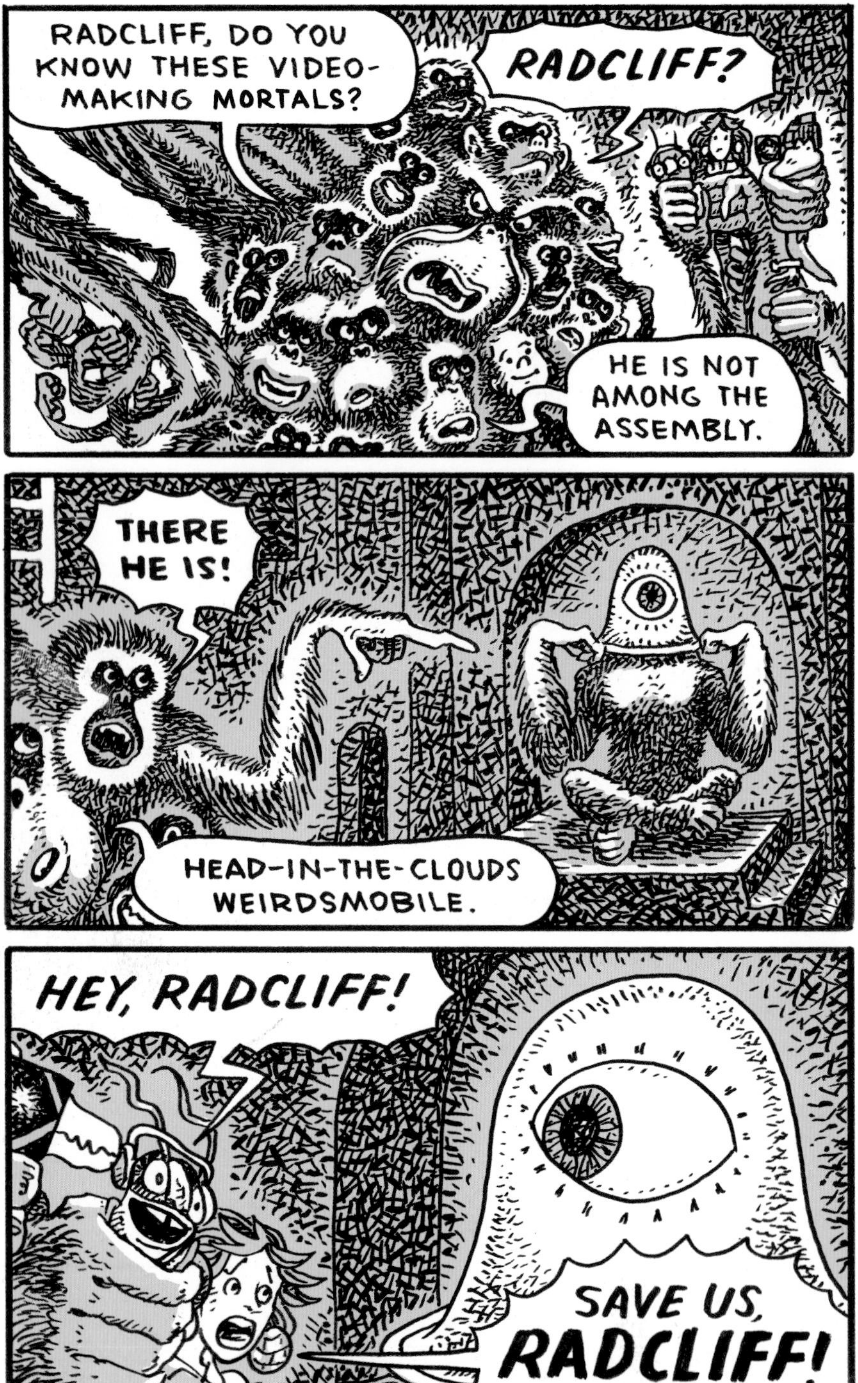

RADCLIFF, DO YOU KNOW THESE VIDEO-MAKING MORTALS?
RADCLIFF?
HE IS NOT AMONG THE ASSEMBLY.
THERE HE IS!
HEAD-IN-THE-CLOUDS WEIRDSMOBILE.
HEY, RADCLIFF!
SAVE US, RADCLIFF!

HOLD ON.
I'M LOOKING AHEAD TO THE END OF THE STORY.
THE ENDING IS RATHER...
...UNEXPECTED.
DO WE WIN?
I KNOW THAT VOICE!
TIFFANY TIMBER!?!
HEY, PANTHEON!
THUMPA
GET YOUR DIRTY HANDS OFF OF MY PALS!
THUMPA

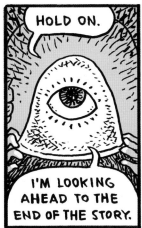

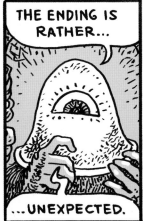

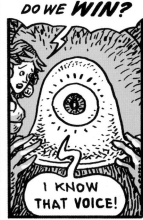

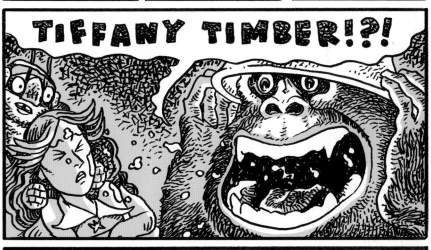

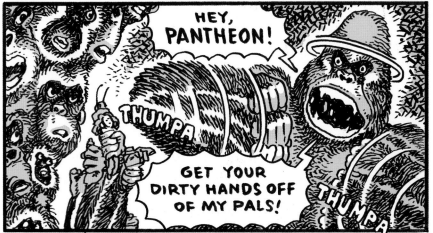

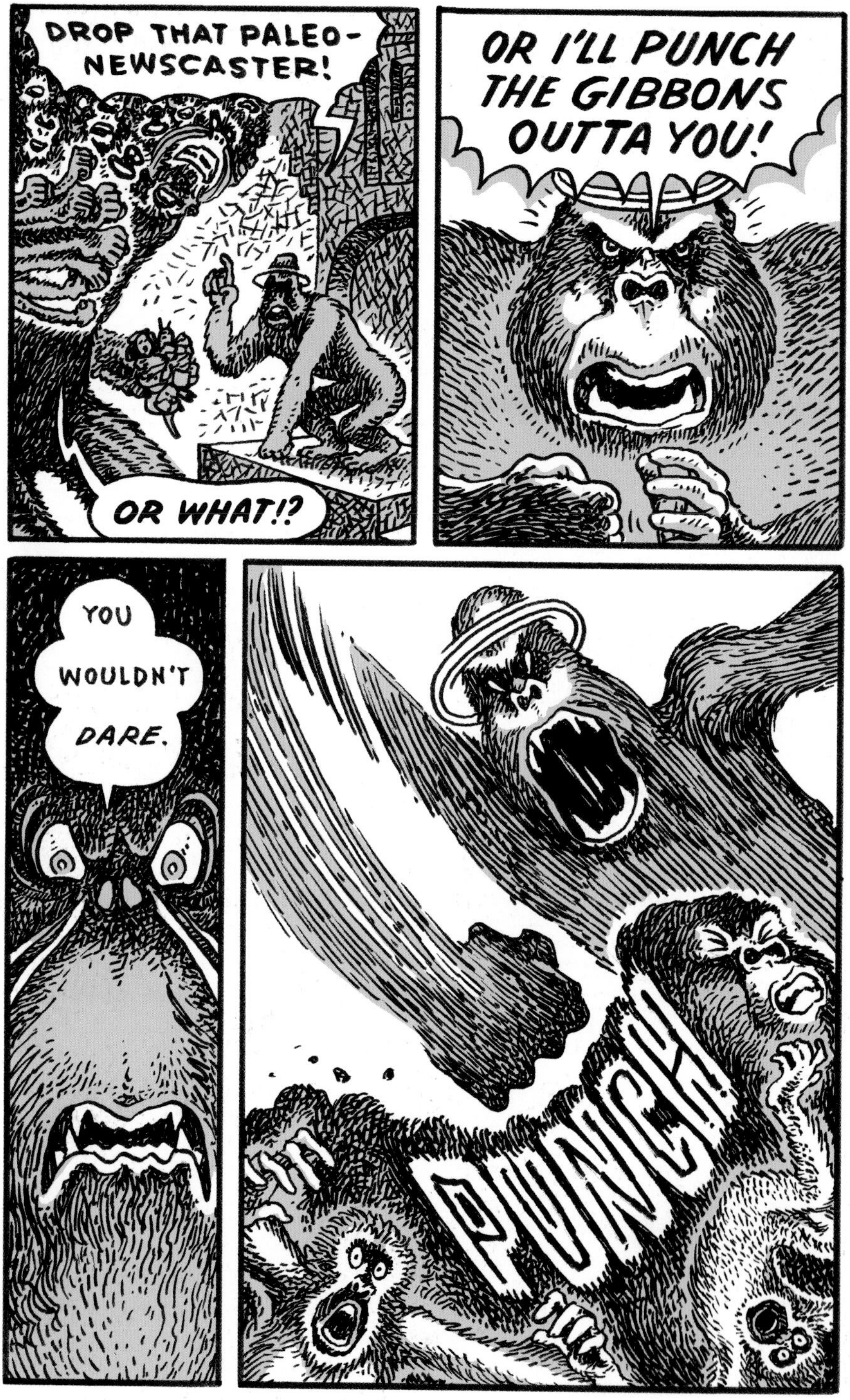
DROP THAT PALEO-NEWSCASTER!
OR WHAT!?
OR I'LL PUNCH THE GIBBONS OUTTA YOU!
YOU WOULDN'T DARE.
PUNCH!

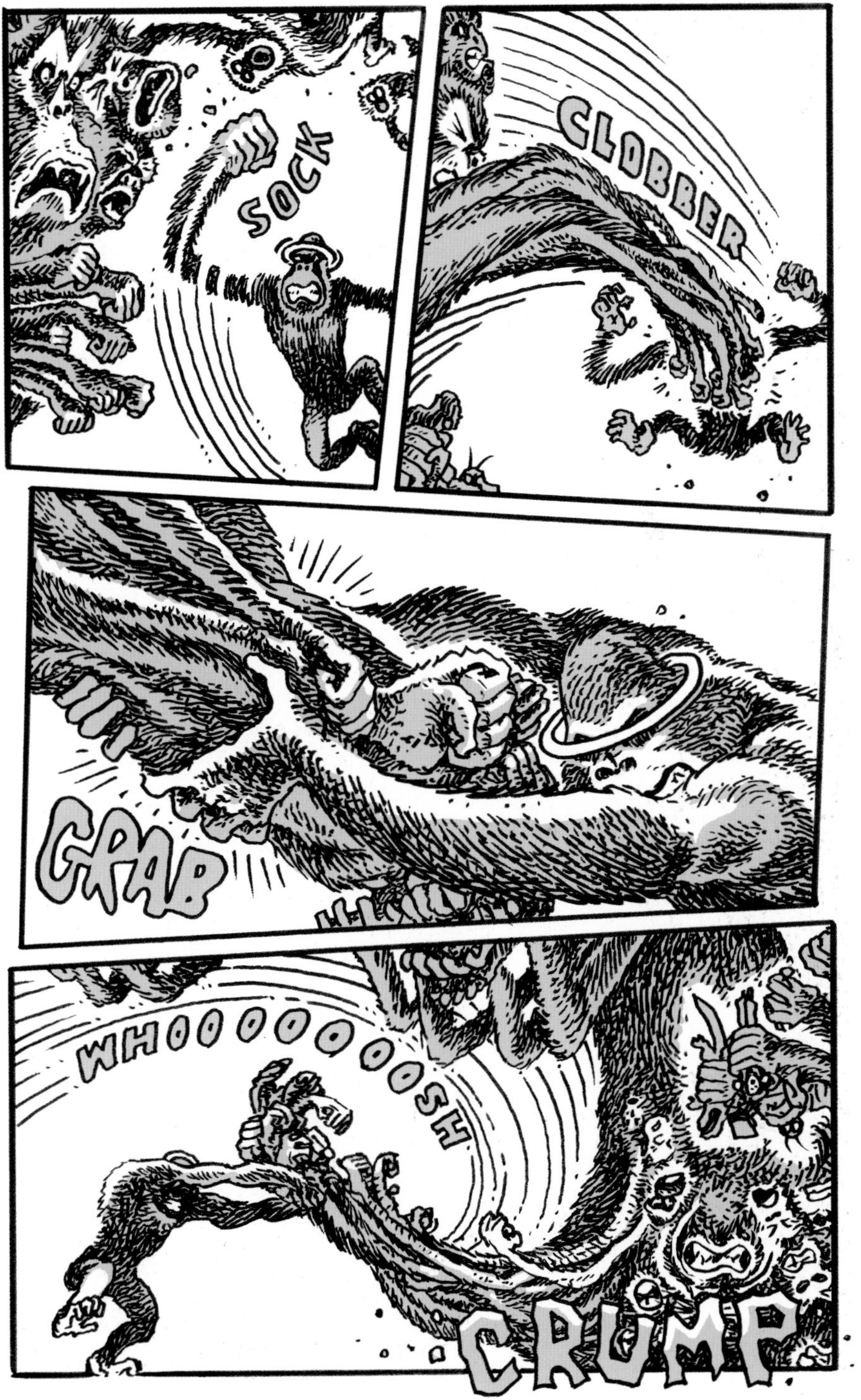
SOCK
CLOBBER
GRAB
WHOOOOOOOOSH
CRUMP

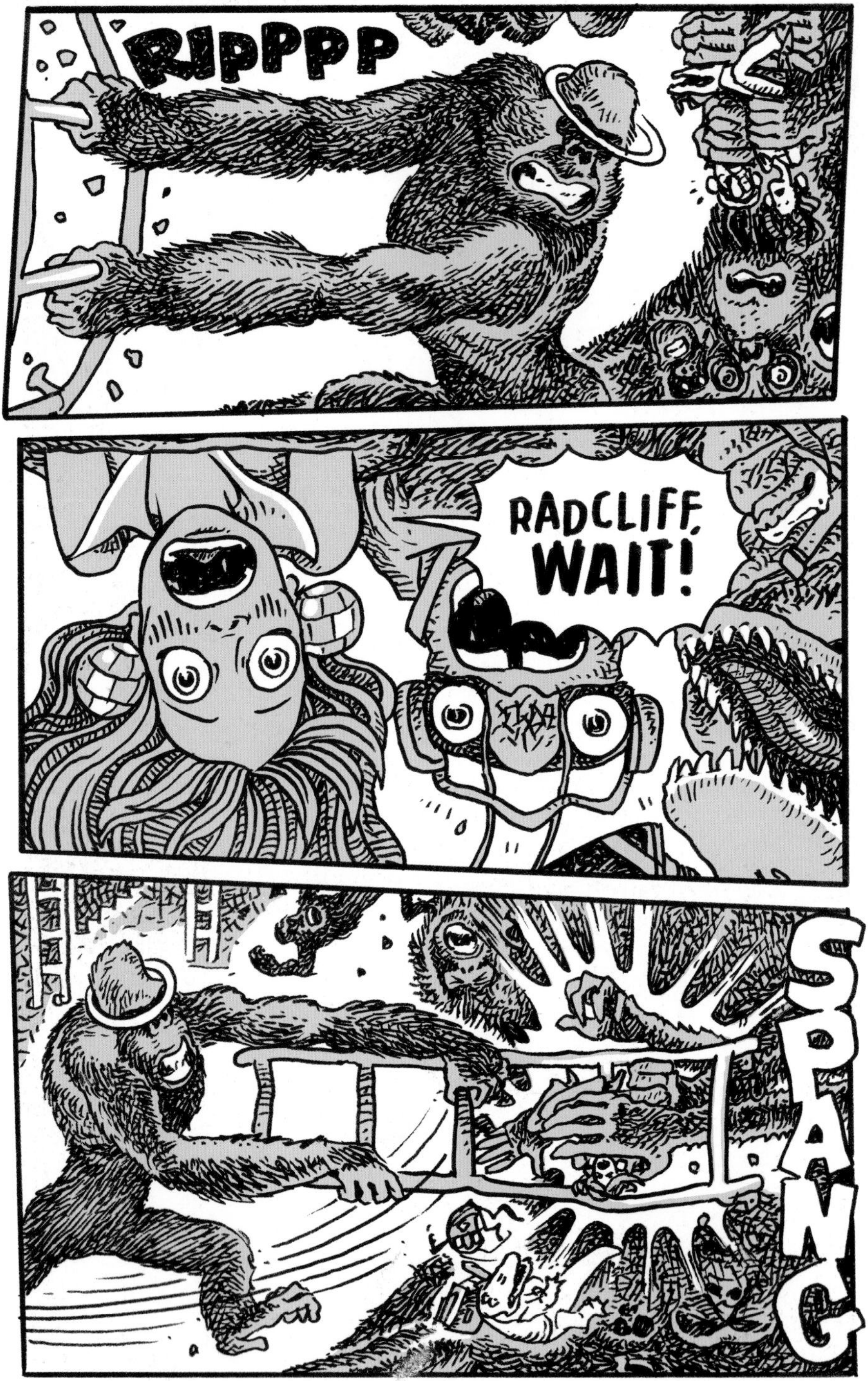
RIPPPP
RADCLIFF, WAIT!
SPANG

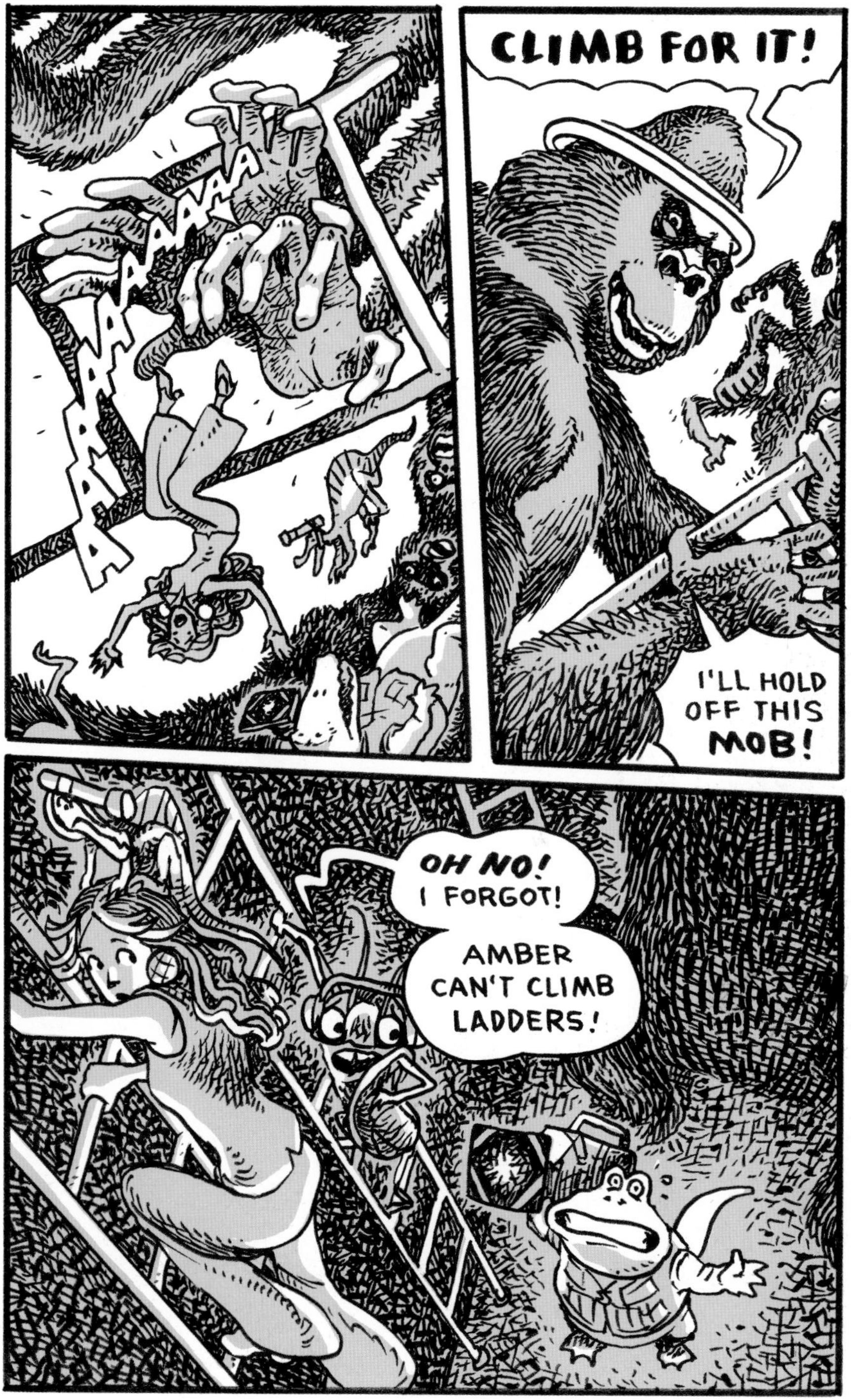
AAAAAAAAAAAAA
CLIMB FOR IT!
I'LL HOLD OFF THIS MOB!
OH NO! I FORGOT!
AMBER CAN'T CLIMB LADDERS!

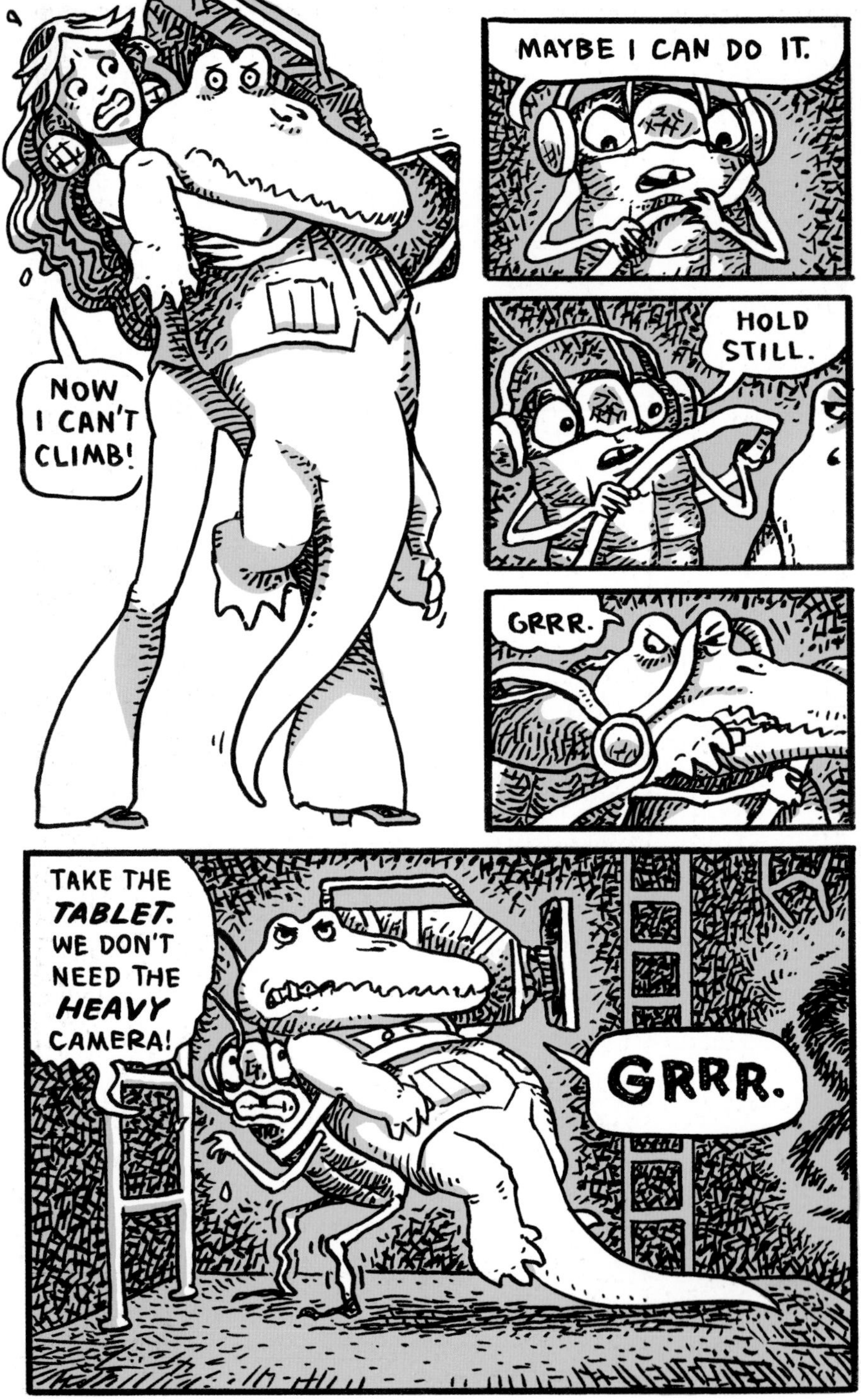
NOW I CAN'T CLIMB!
MAYBE I CAN DO IT.
HOLD STILL.
GRRR.
TAKE THE *TABLET.* WE DON'T NEED THE *HEAVY* CAMERA!
GRRR.

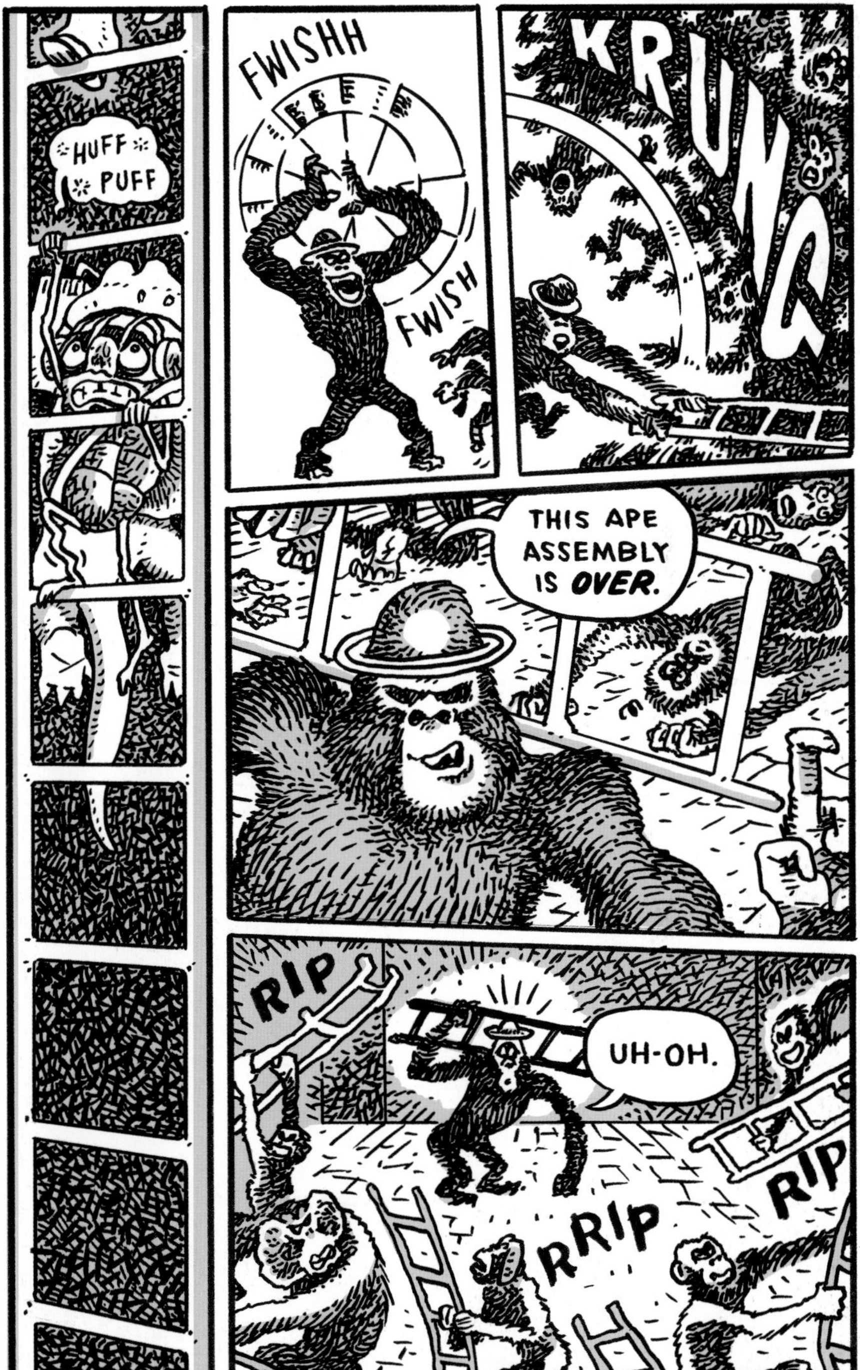

HUFF
PUFF
FWISHH
FWISH
KRUNCH
THIS APE ASSEMBLY IS *OVER*.
RIP
UH-OH.
RIP
RRIP

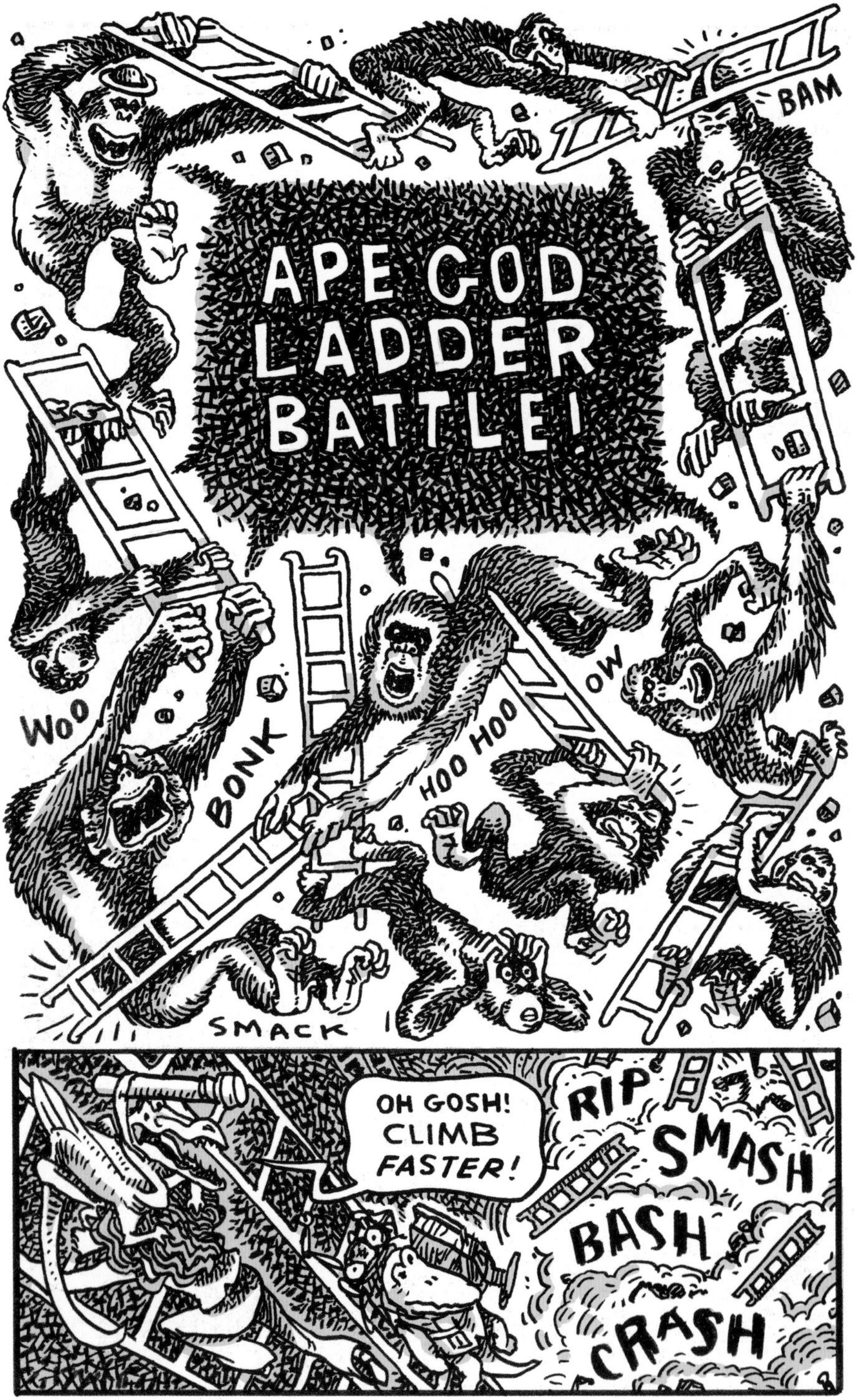
APE GOD LADDER BATTLE!
BAM
WOO
BONK
HOO HOO
OW
SMACK
OH GOSH! CLIMB FASTER!
RIP
SMASH
BASH
CRASH

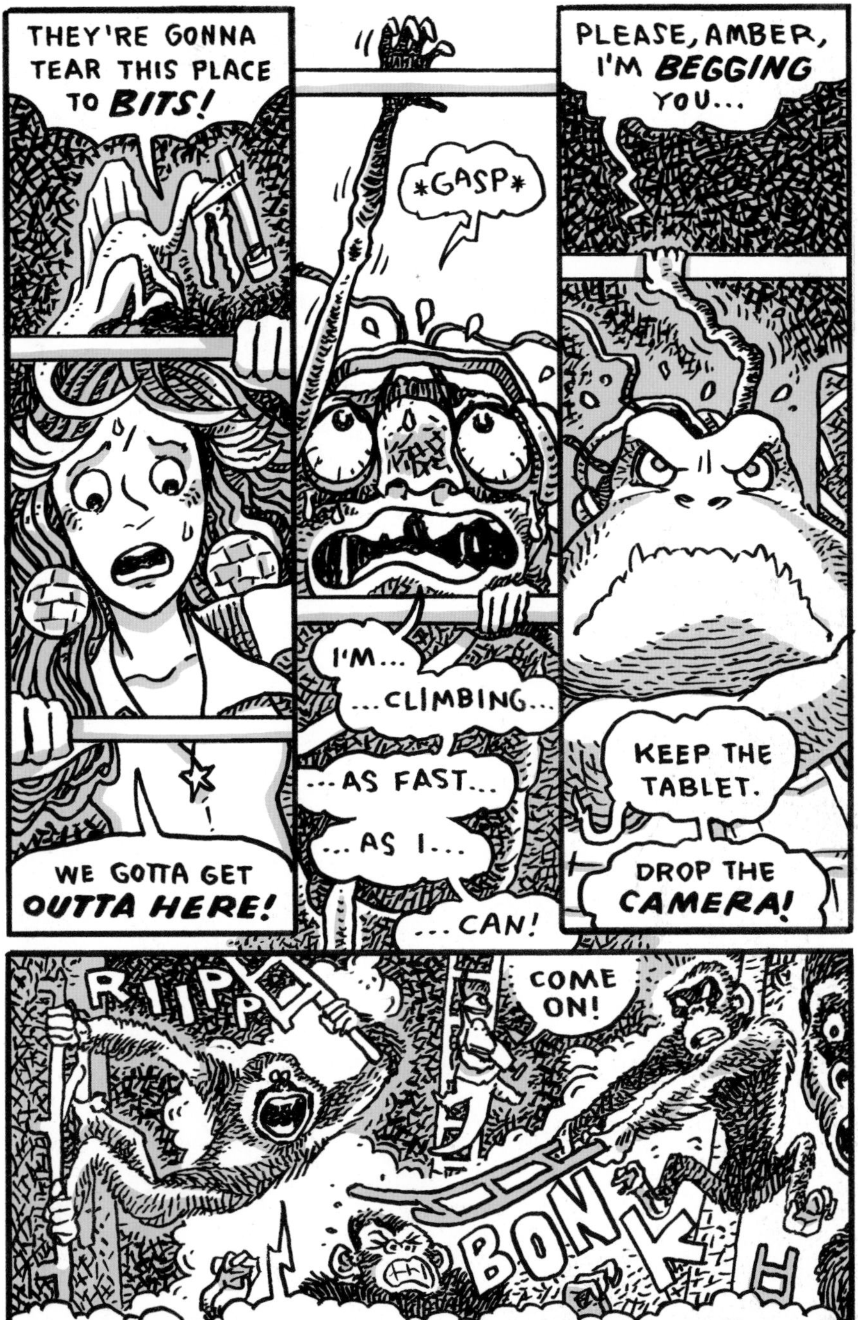

THEY'RE GONNA TEAR THIS PLACE TO BITS!
WE GOTTA GET OUTTA HERE!
GASP
I'M...
...CLIMBING...
...AS FAST...
...AS I...
...CAN!
PLEASE, AMBER, I'M BEGGING YOU...
KEEP THE TABLET.
DROP THE CAMERA!
RIIPP
COME ON!
BONK
GIBBONS RULE! BONOBOS DROOL!

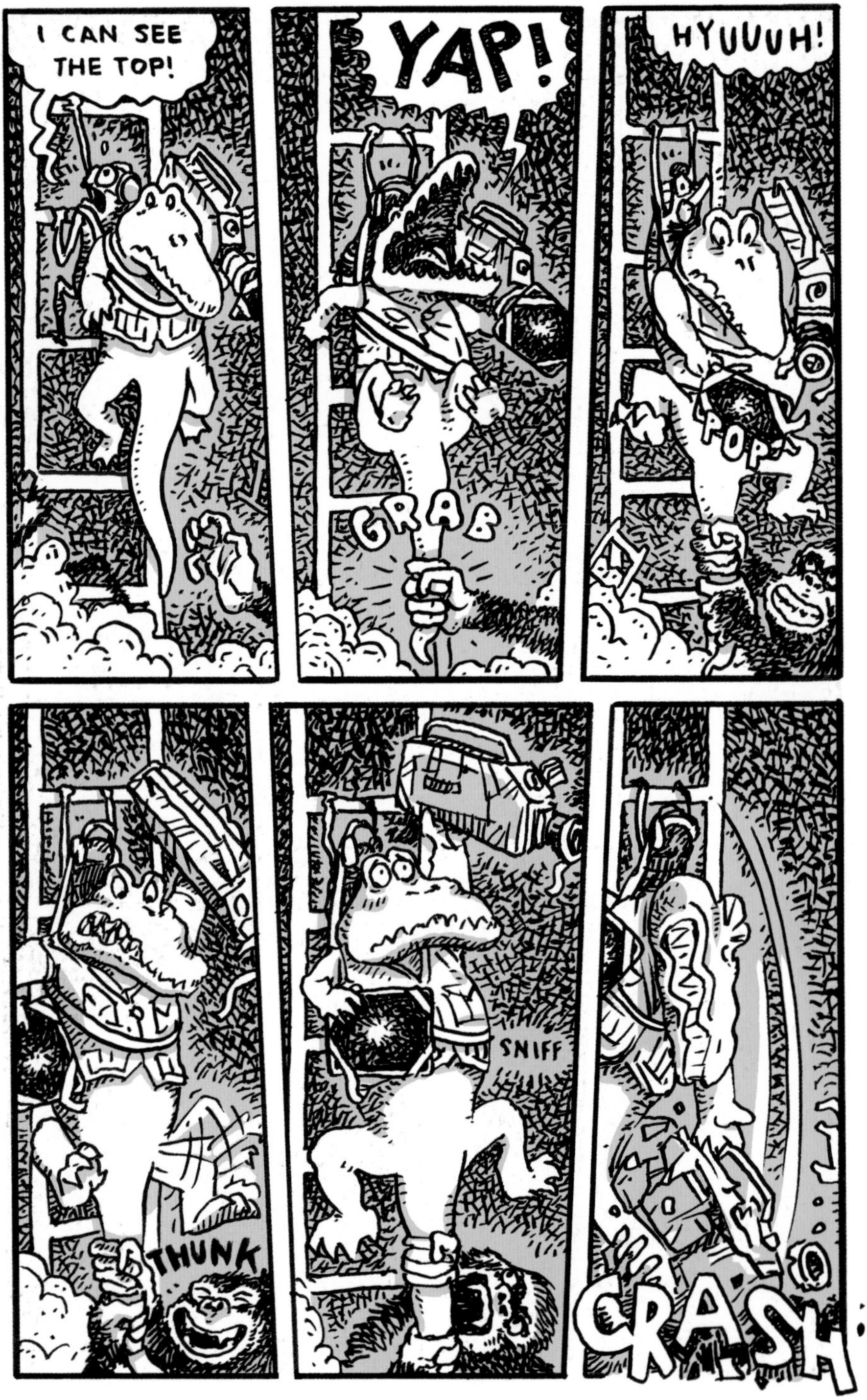
I CAN SEE THE TOP!
YAP!
GRAB
HYUUUH!
POP
THUNK
SNIFF
CRASH

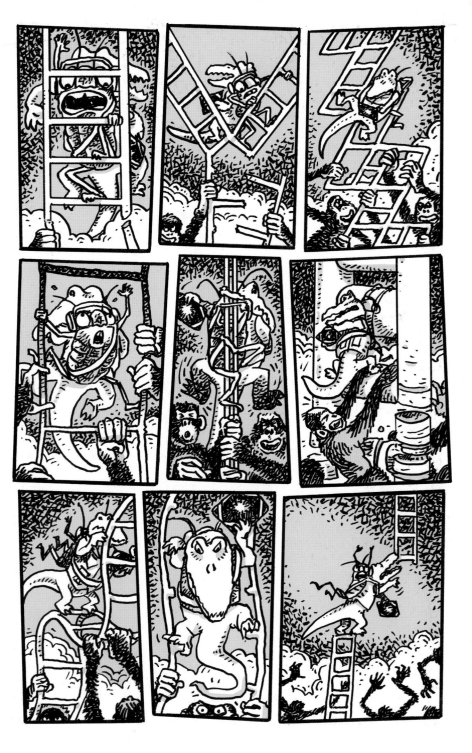

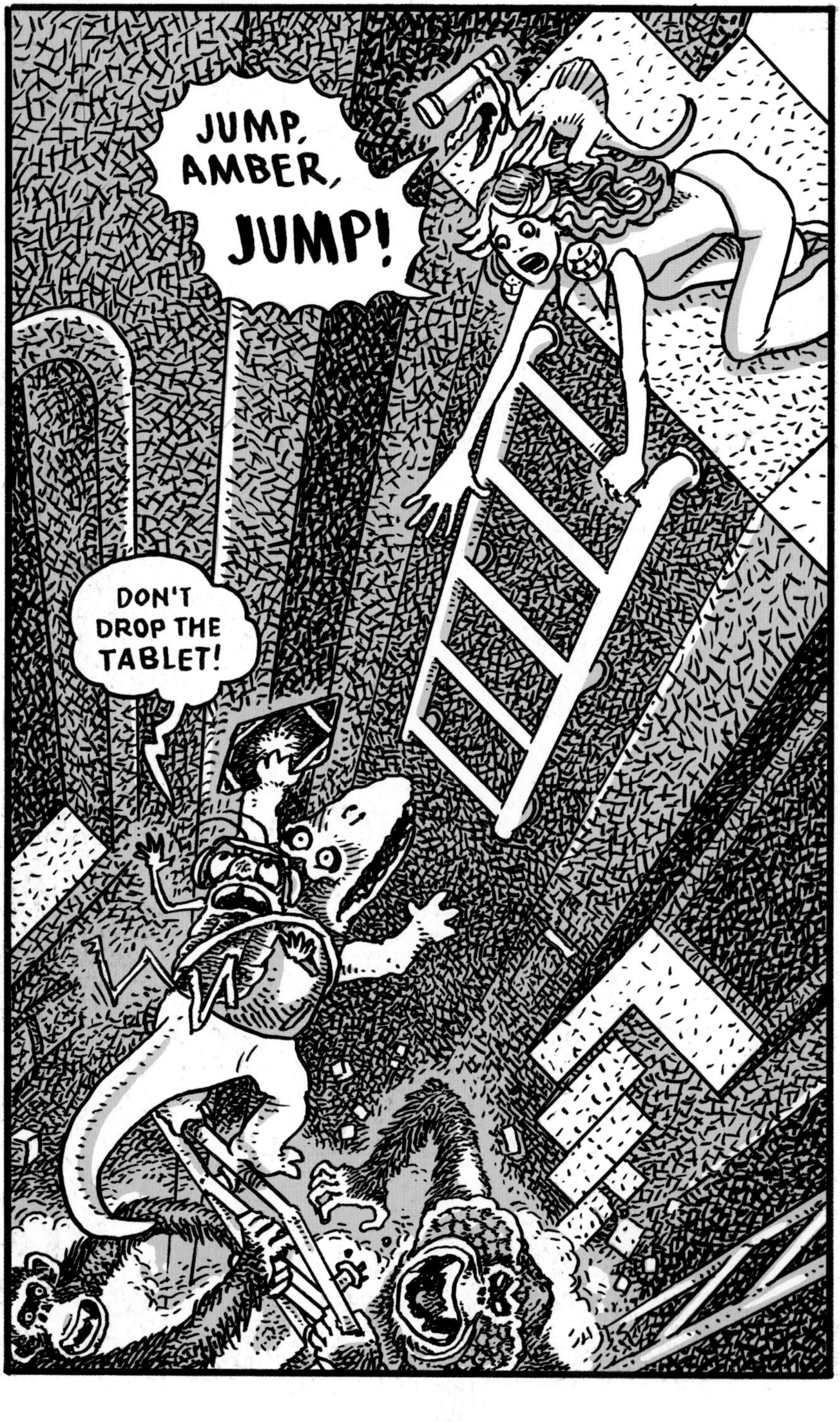
JUMP, AMBER, JUMP!
DON'T DROP THE TABLET!

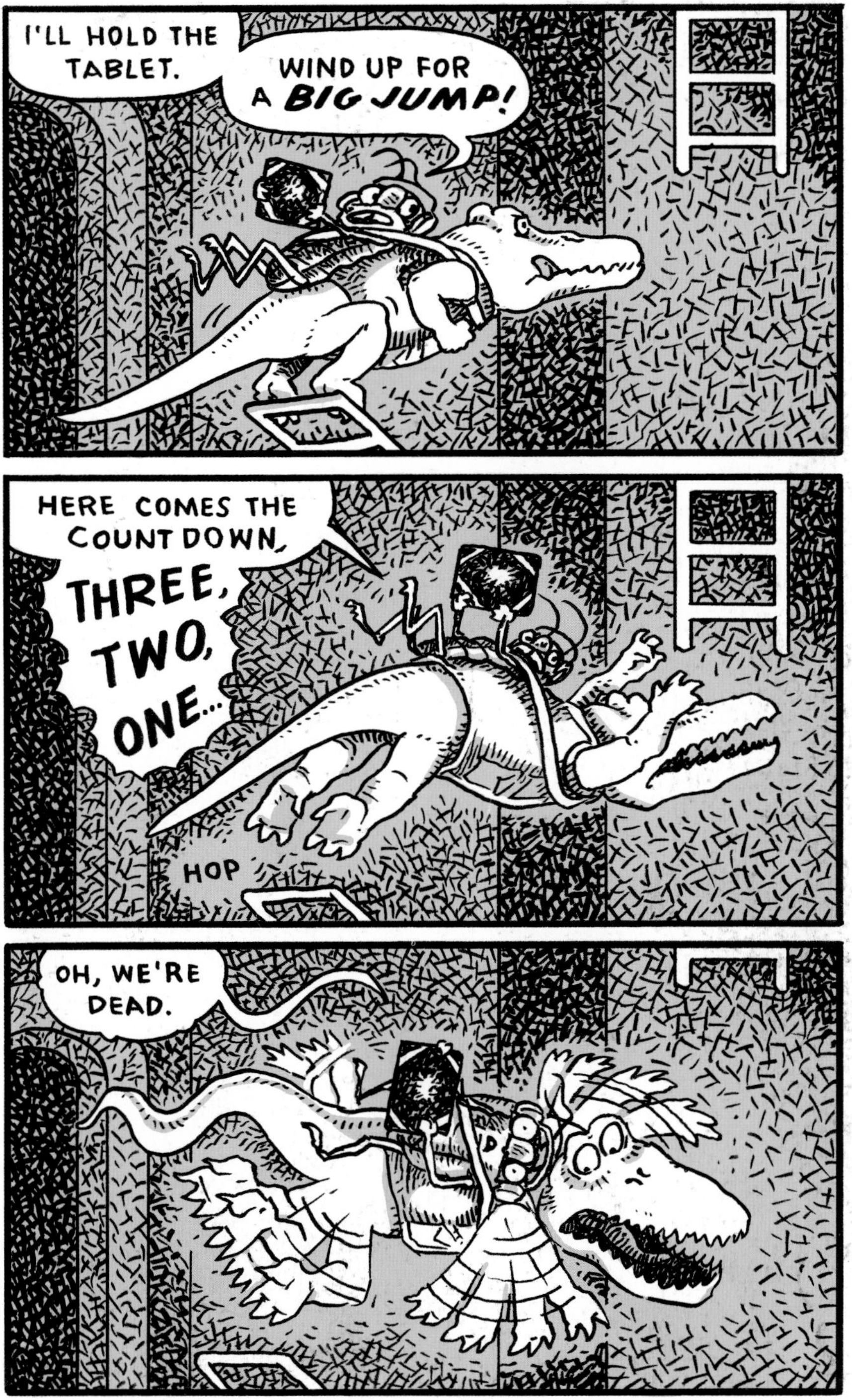
I'LL HOLD THE TABLET.
WIND UP FOR A BIG JUMP!
HERE COMES THE COUNT DOWN,
THREE, TWO, ONE...
HOP
OH, WE'RE DEAD.

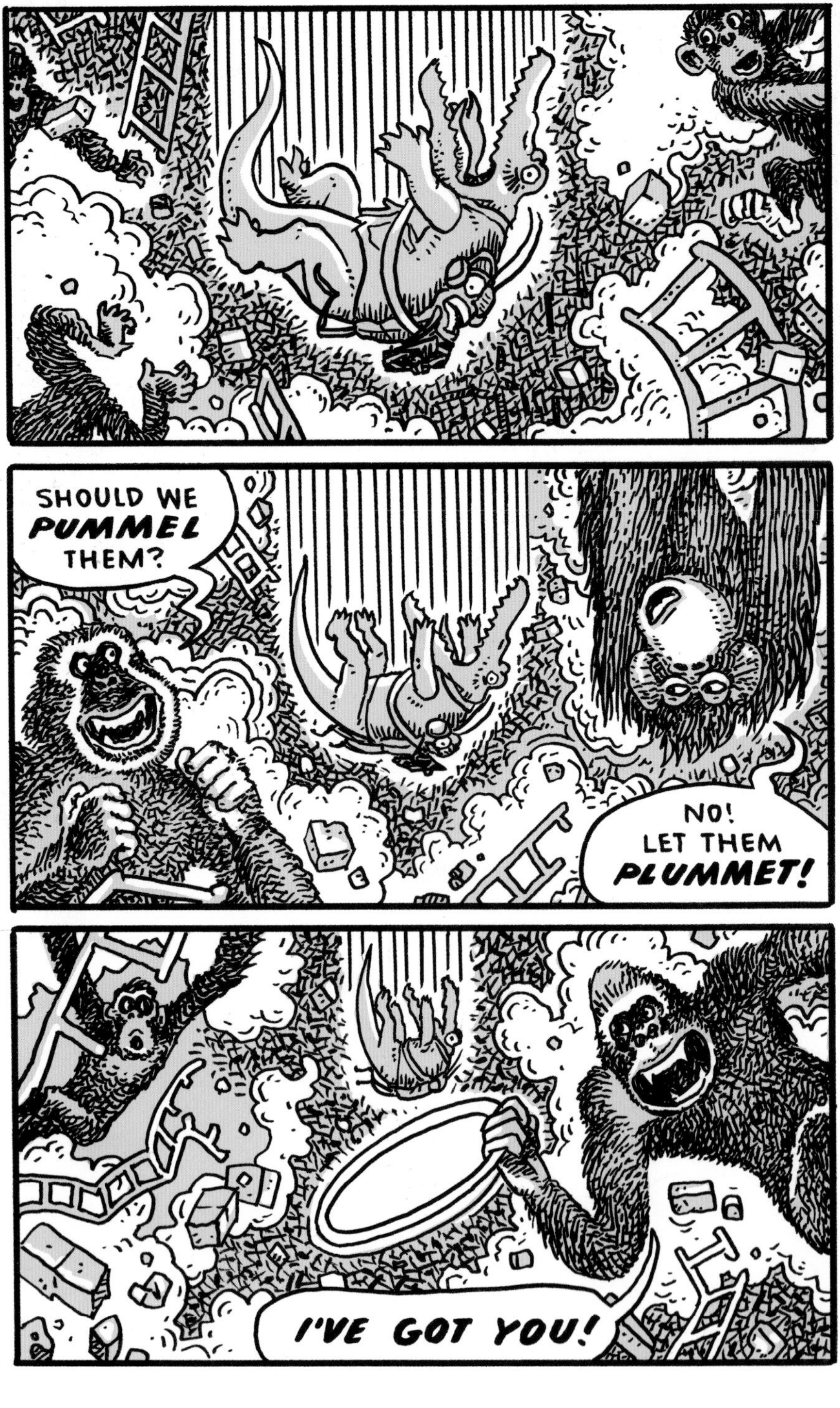
SHOULD WE PUMMEL THEM?
NO! LET THEM PLUMMET!
I'VE GOT YOU!

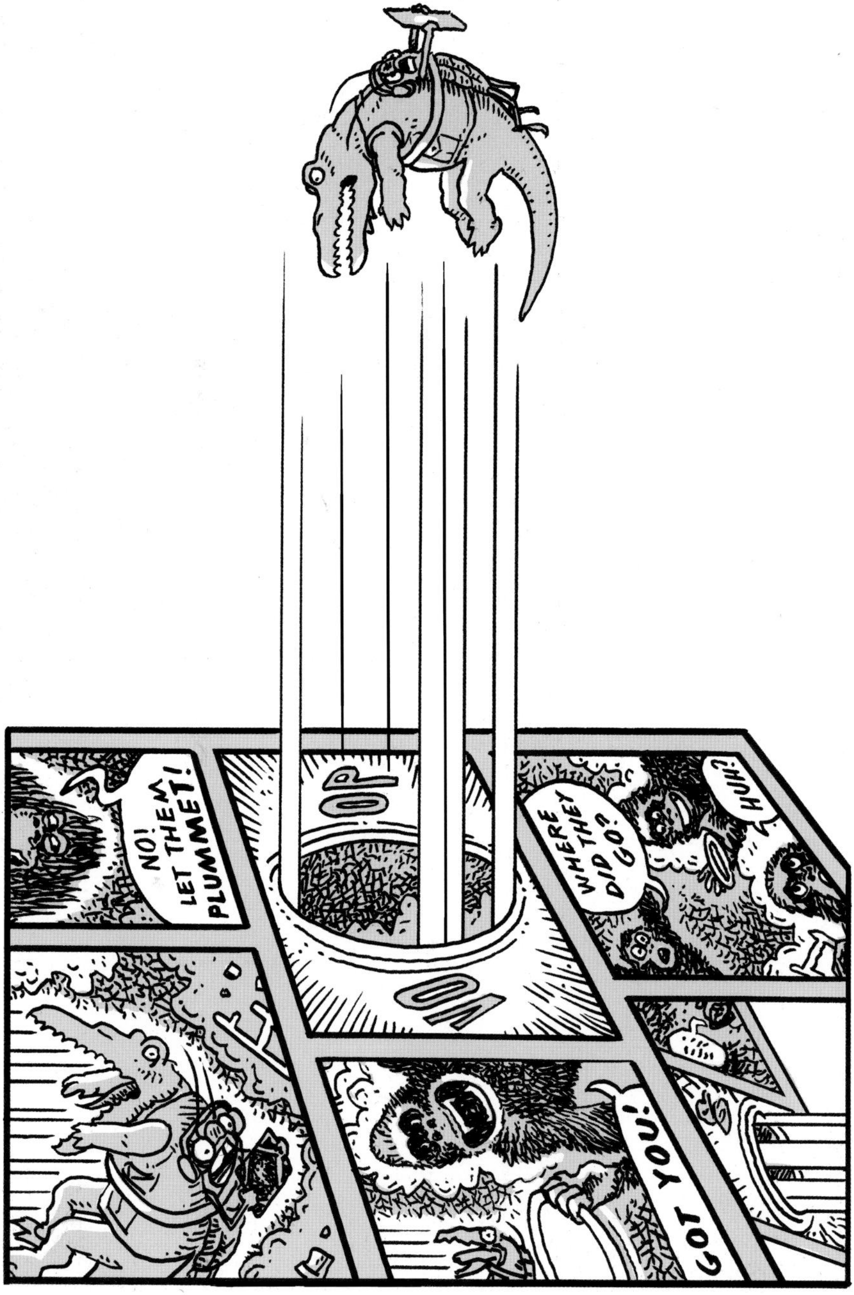

NO! LET THEM PLUMMET!
VOOP
WHERE DID THEY GO?
HUH?
GOT YOU!

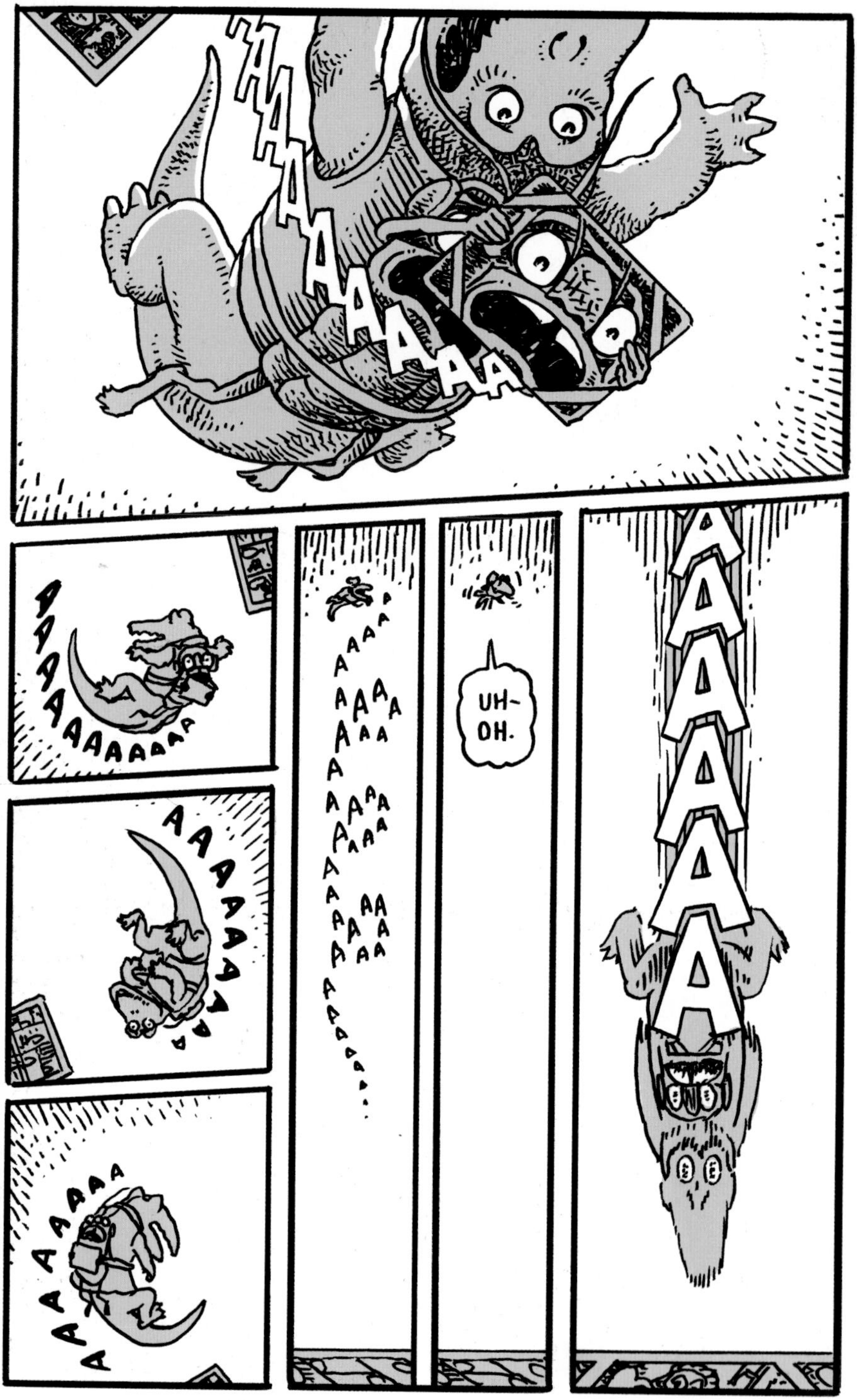
AAAAAAAAAAAA
AAAAAAAAAAAAAAA
AAAAAAAAAA
AAAAAAAAA
AAAAAAAAAAAAAAAAAAAAAAAAAAAAAAAA
UH-OH.
AAAAAAA

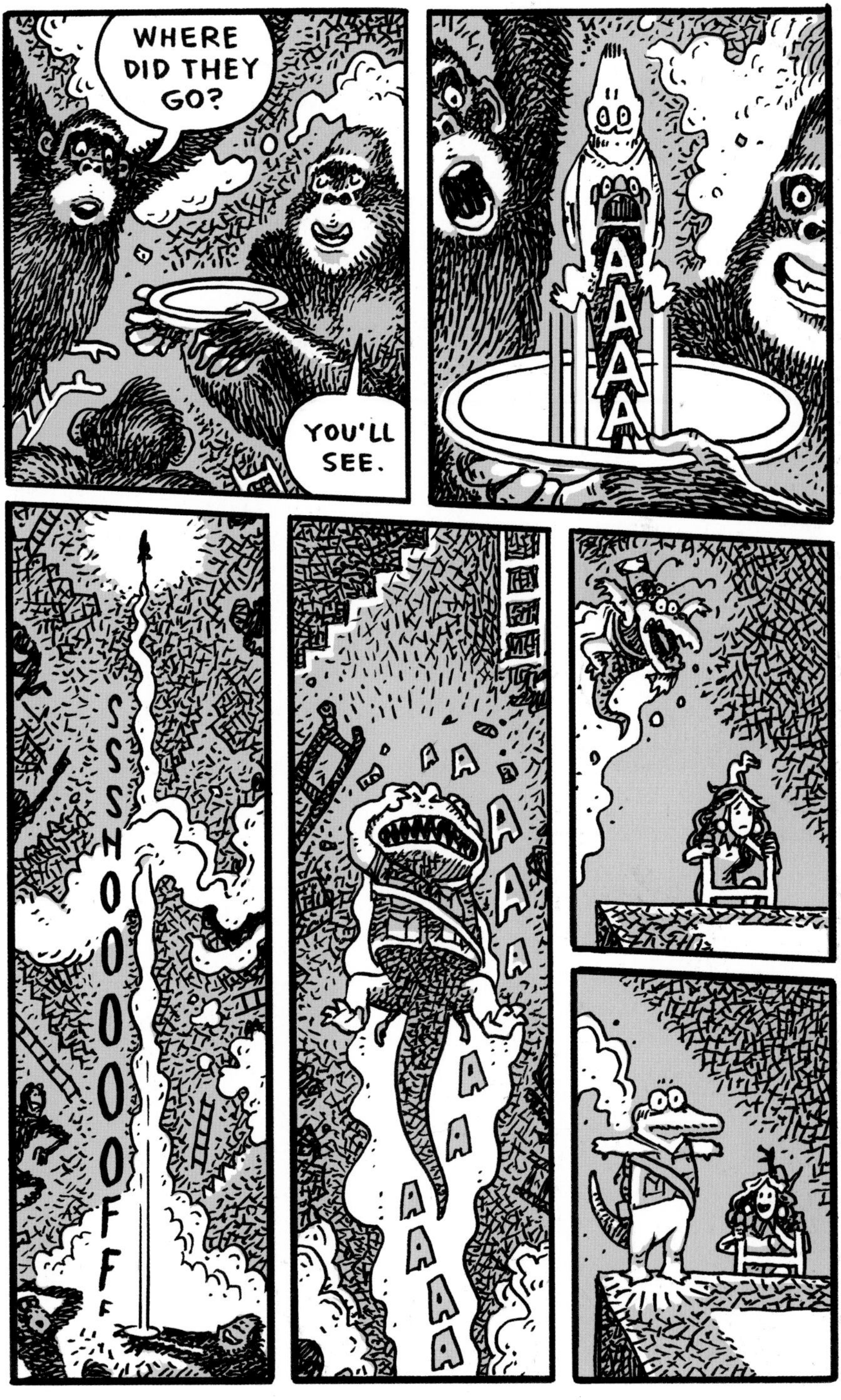
WHERE DID THEY GO?
YOU'LL SEE.
AAAA
SSHOOOOOFFF
AAAAAAAAAAAAAAA

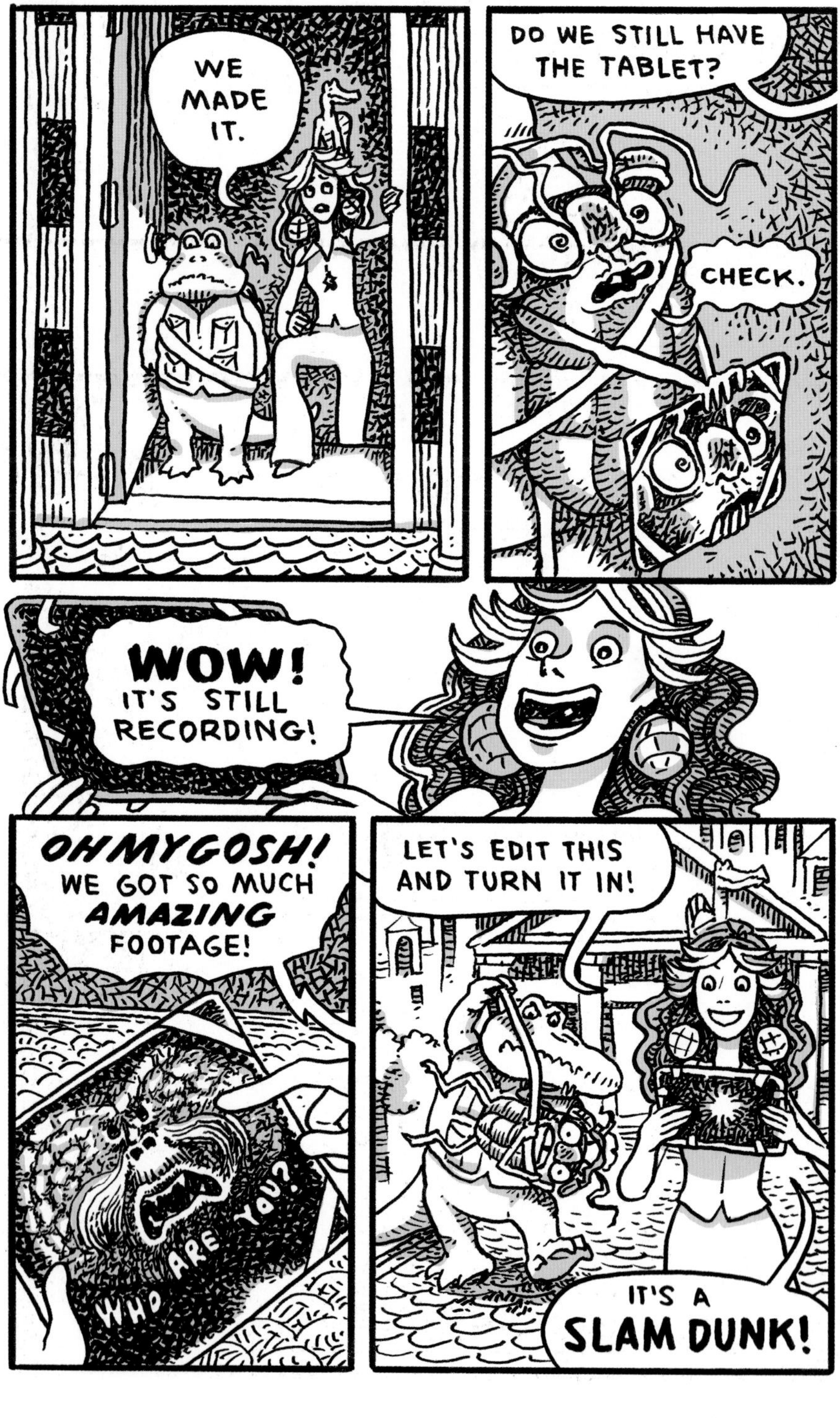
WE MADE IT.
DO WE STILL HAVE THE TABLET?
CHECK.
WOW! IT'S STILL RECORDING!
OHMYGOSH! WE GOT SO MUCH AMAZING FOOTAGE!
WHO ARE YOU?
LET'S EDIT THIS AND TURN IT IN!
IT'S A SLAM DUNK!

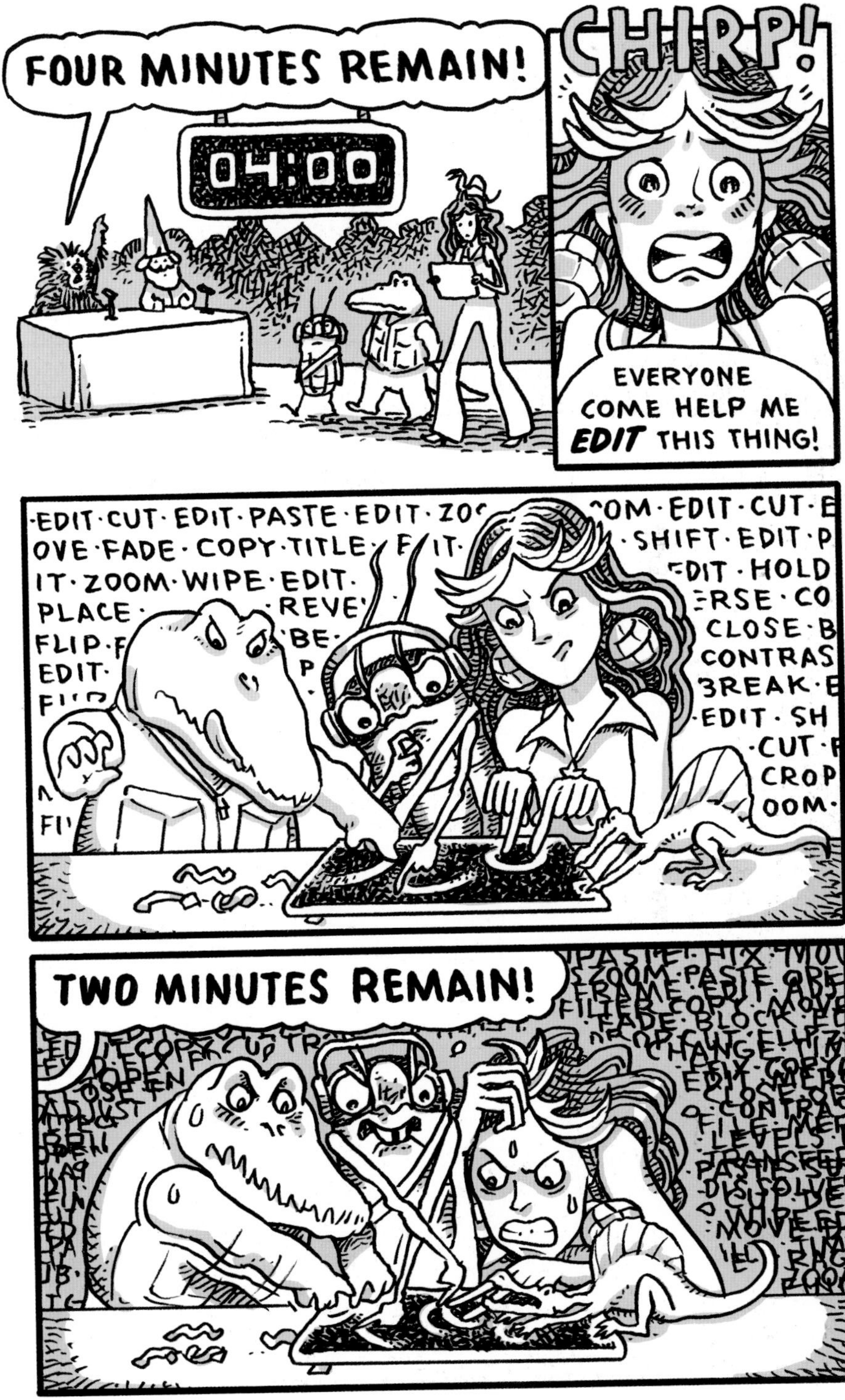
FOUR MINUTES REMAIN!
04:00
CHIRP!
EVERYONE COME HELP ME EDIT THIS THING!
TWO MINUTES REMAIN!

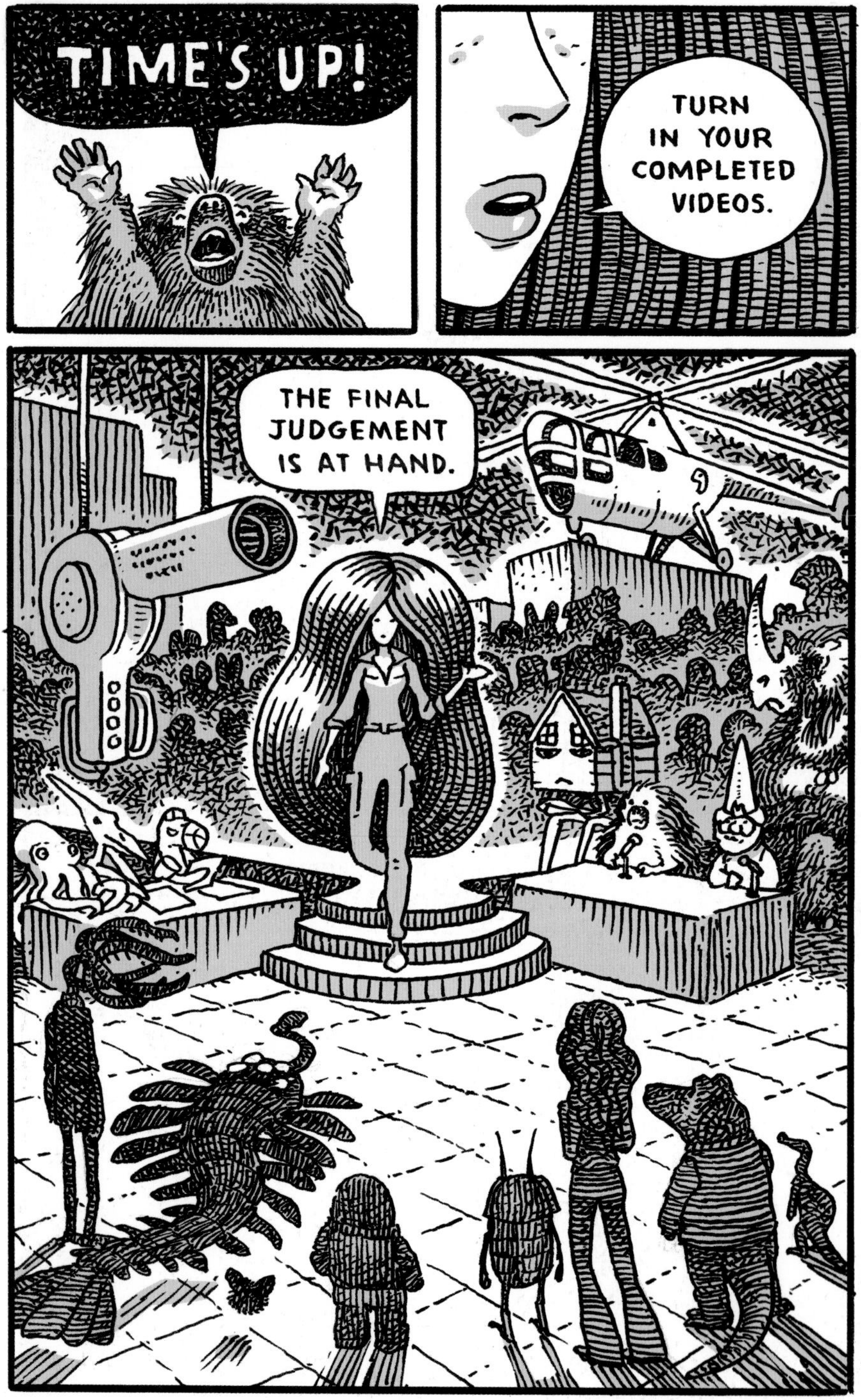
TIME'S UP!
TURN IN YOUR COMPLETED VIDEOS.
THE FINAL JUDGEMENT IS AT HAND.

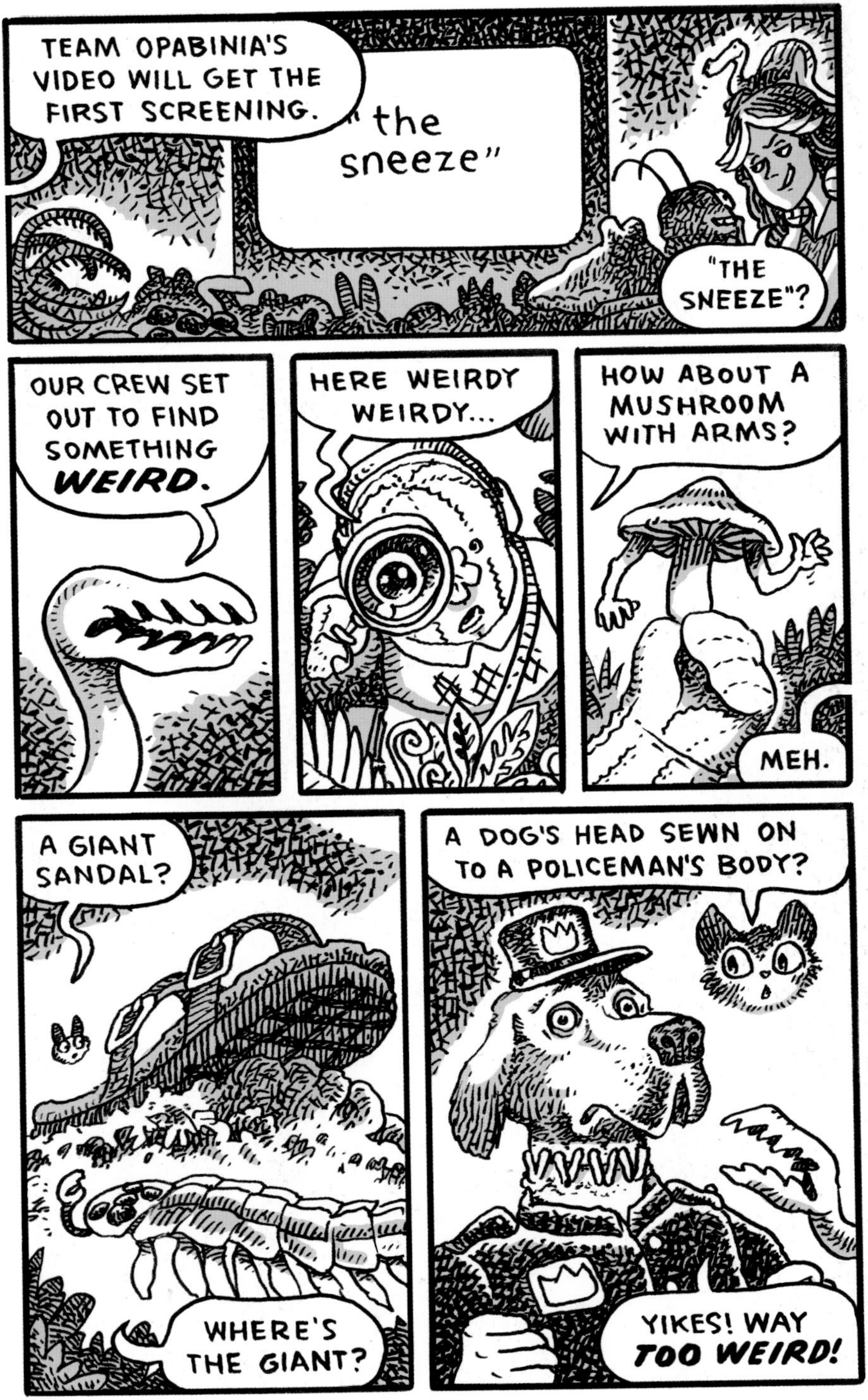
TEAM OPABINIA'S VIDEO WILL GET THE FIRST SCREENING.
"the sneeze"
"THE SNEEZE"?
OUR CREW SET OUT TO FIND SOMETHING **WEIRD.**
HERE WEIRDY WEIRDY...
HOW ABOUT A MUSHROOM WITH ARMS?
MEH.
A GIANT SANDAL?
WHERE'S THE GIANT?
A DOG'S HEAD SEWN ON TO A POLICEMAN'S BODY?
YIKES! WAY **TOO WEIRD!**

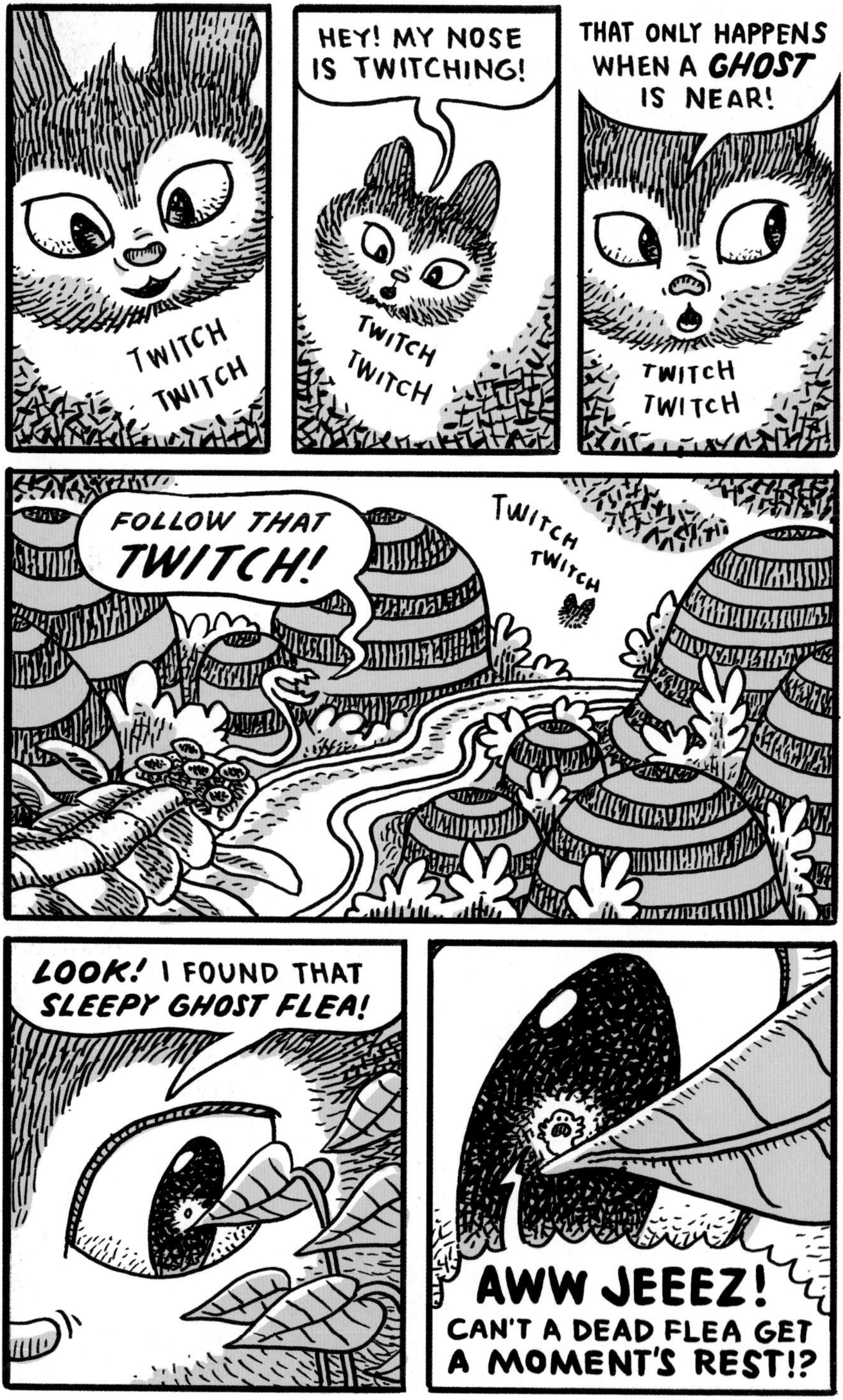
TWITCH
TWITCH
HEY! MY NOSE IS TWITCHING!
TWITCH
TWITCH
THAT ONLY HAPPENS WHEN A GHOST IS NEAR!
TWITCH
TWITCH
FOLLOW THAT TWITCH!
TWITCH
TWITCH
LOOK! I FOUND THAT SLEEPY GHOST FLEA!
AWW JEEEZ!
CAN'T A DEAD FLEA GET A MOMENT'S REST!?

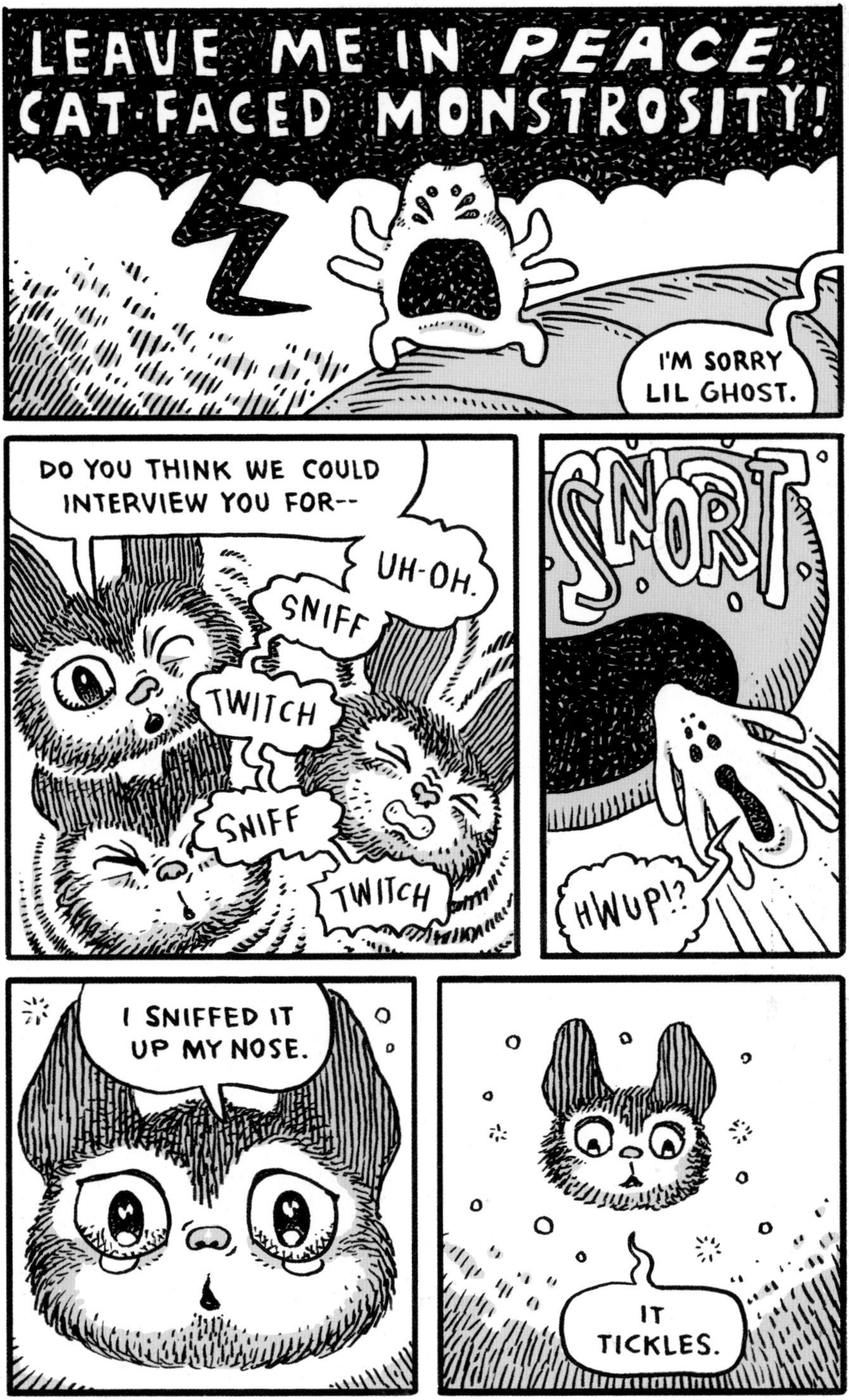
LEAVE ME IN PEACE, CAT-FACED MONSTROSITY!
I'M SORRY LIL GHOST.
DO YOU THINK WE COULD INTERVIEW YOU FOR--
UH-OH.
SNIFF
TWITCH
SNIFF
TWITCH
SNORT
HWUP!?
I SNIFFED IT UP MY NOSE.
IT TICKLES.

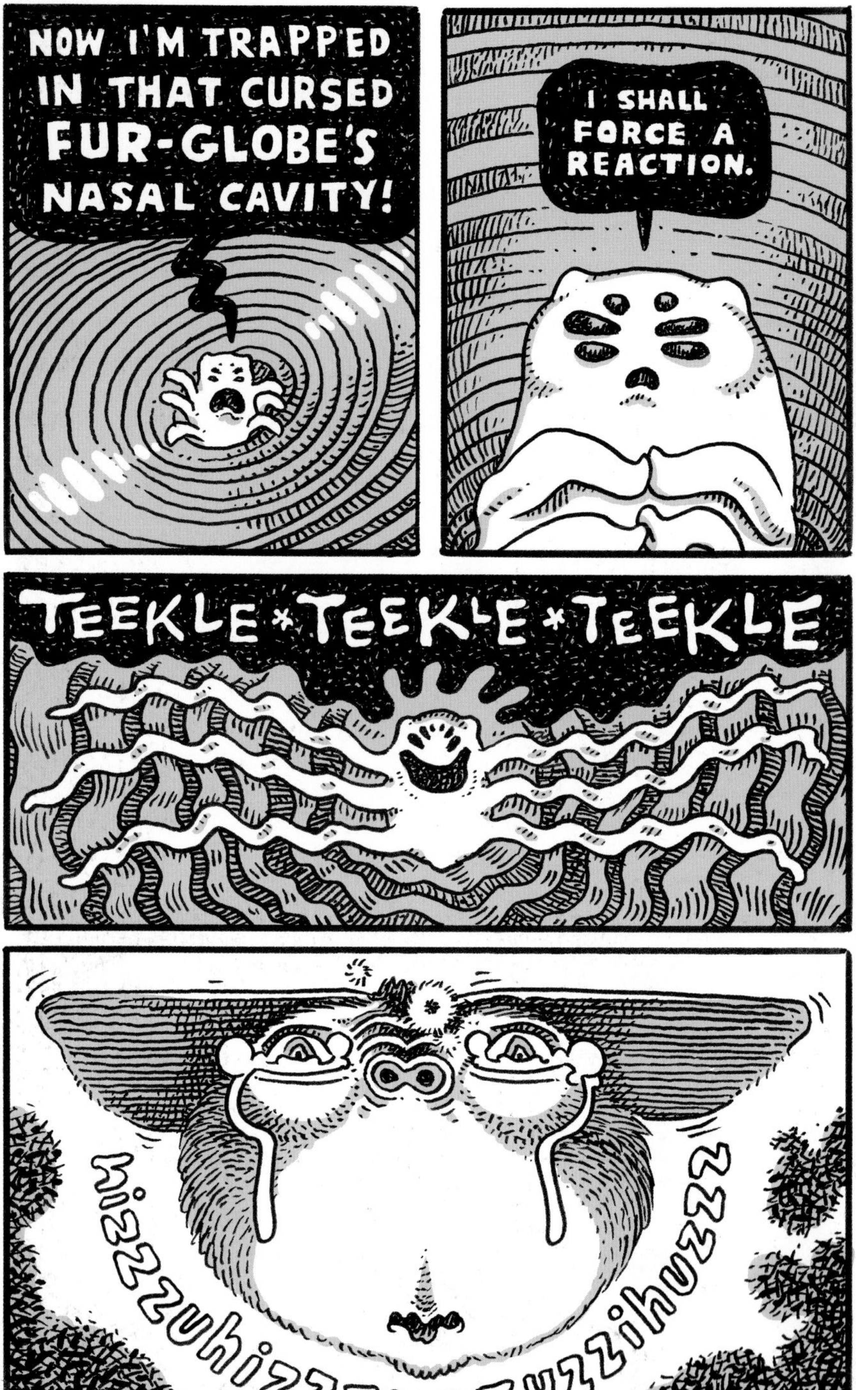
NOW I'M TRAPPED IN THAT CURSED FUR-GLOBE'S NASAL CAVITY!
I SHALL FORCE A REACTION.
TEEKLE * TEEKLE * TEEKLE
hizzzuhizzzzuzzzuzzzihuzzz

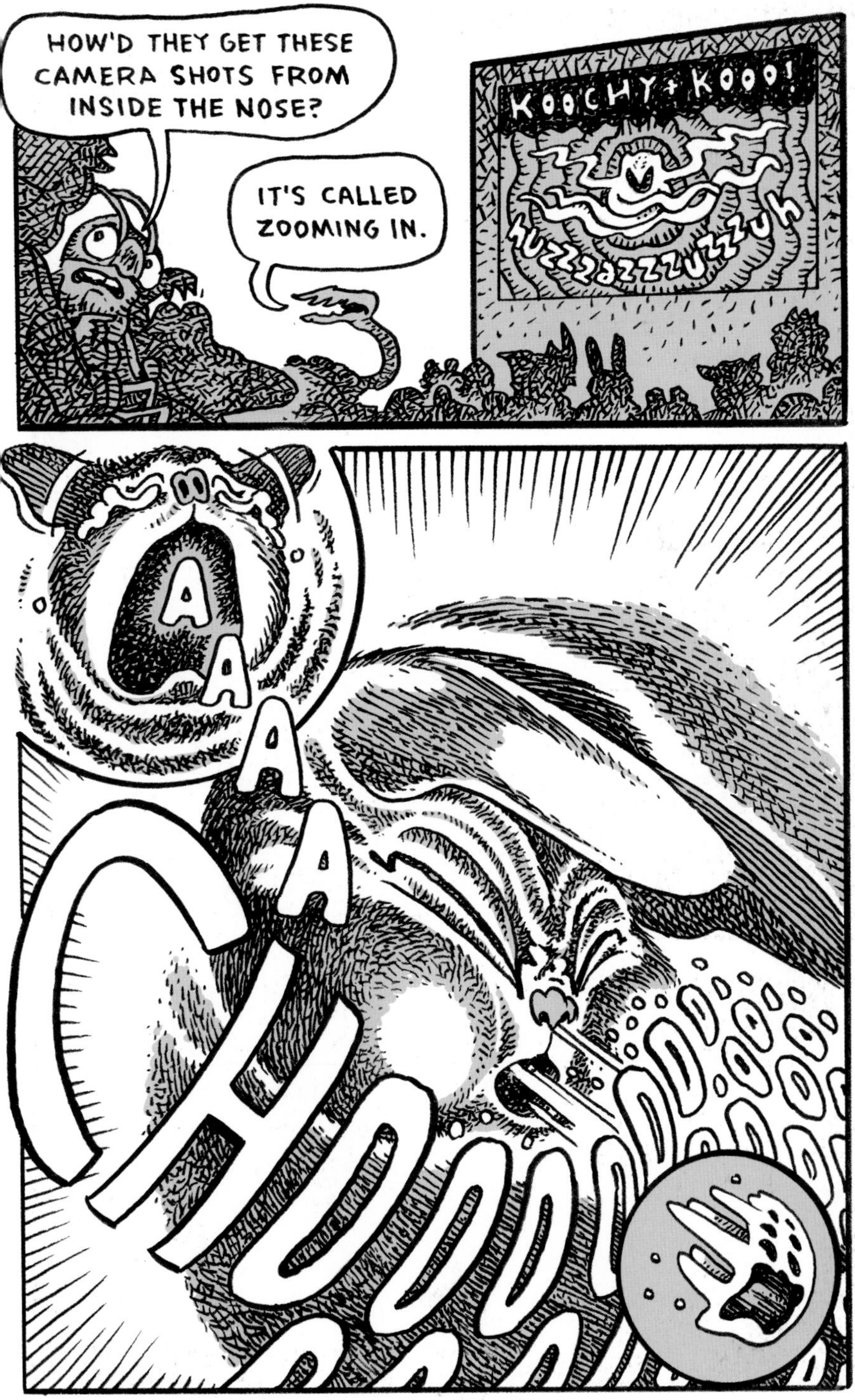
HOW'D THEY GET THESE CAMERA SHOTS FROM INSIDE THE NOSE?
IT'S CALLED ZOOMING IN.
KOOCHY + KOOO!
huzzzazzzzuzzzuh
AAAA
CHOOOOO

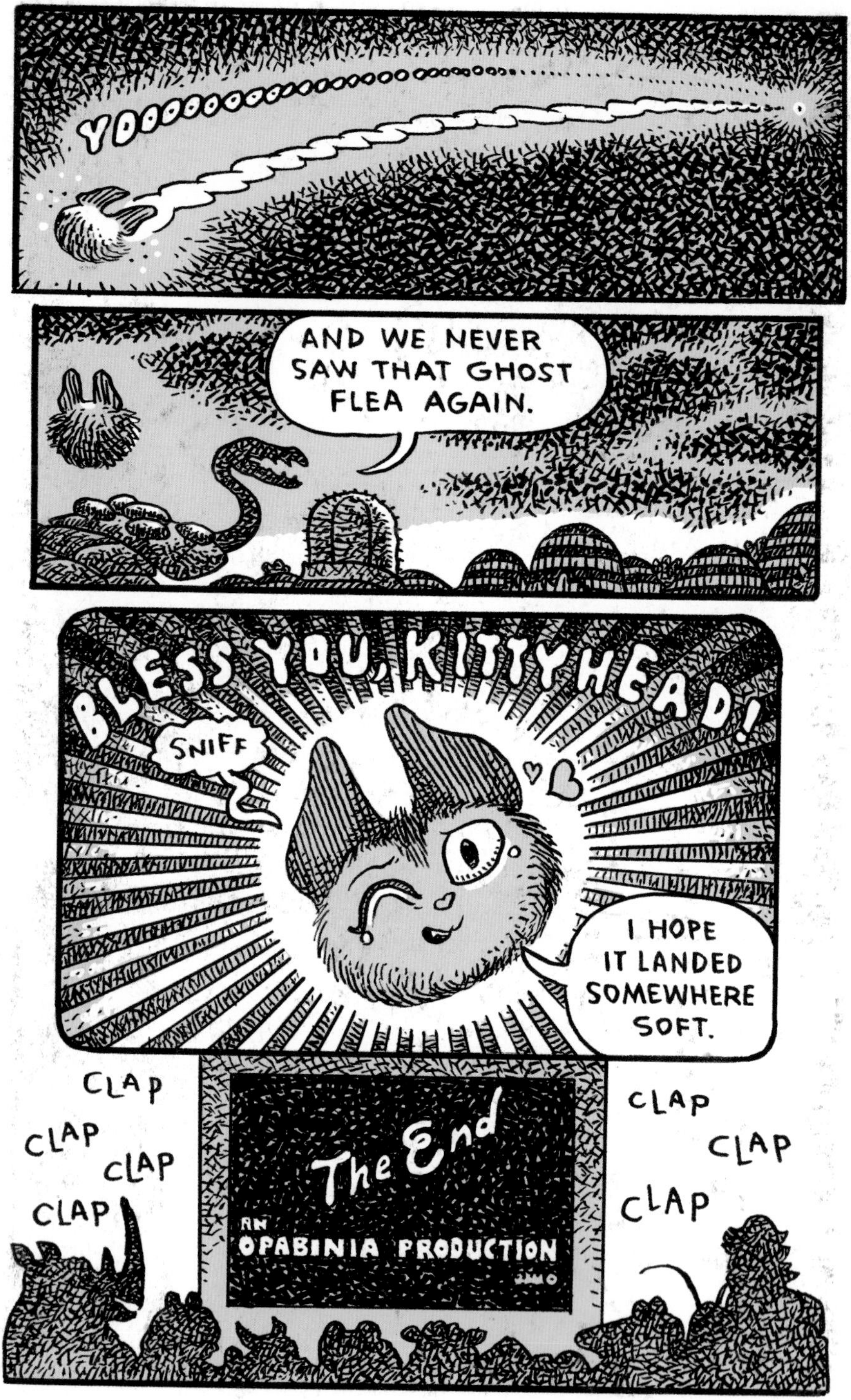
YOOOOOOOOOOOOOOOOOOOOO
AND WE NEVER SAW THAT GHOST FLEA AGAIN.
BLESS YOU, KITTY HEAD!
SNIFF
I HOPE IT LANDED SOMEWHERE SOFT.
CLAP
CLAP
CLAP
CLAP
CLAP
CLAP
CLAP
The End
AN OPABINIA PRODUCTION

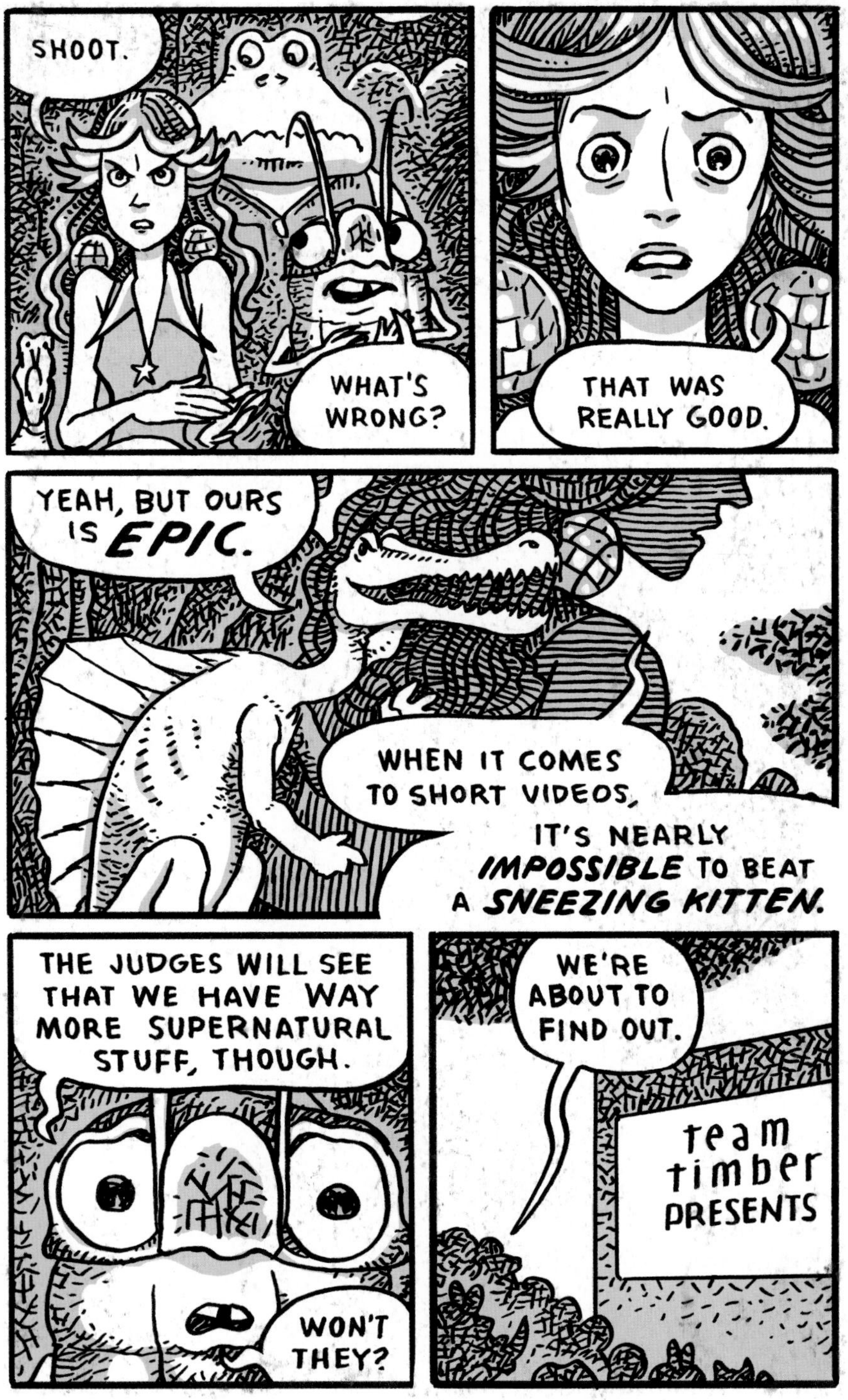
SHOOT.
WHAT'S WRONG?
THAT WAS REALLY GOOD.
YEAH, BUT OURS IS EPIC.
WHEN IT COMES TO SHORT VIDEOS,
IT'S NEARLY IMPOSSIBLE TO BEAT A SNEEZING KITTEN.
THE JUDGES WILL SEE THAT WE HAVE WAY MORE SUPERNATURAL STUFF, THOUGH.
WON'T THEY?
WE'RE ABOUT TO FIND OUT.
team timber PRESENTS

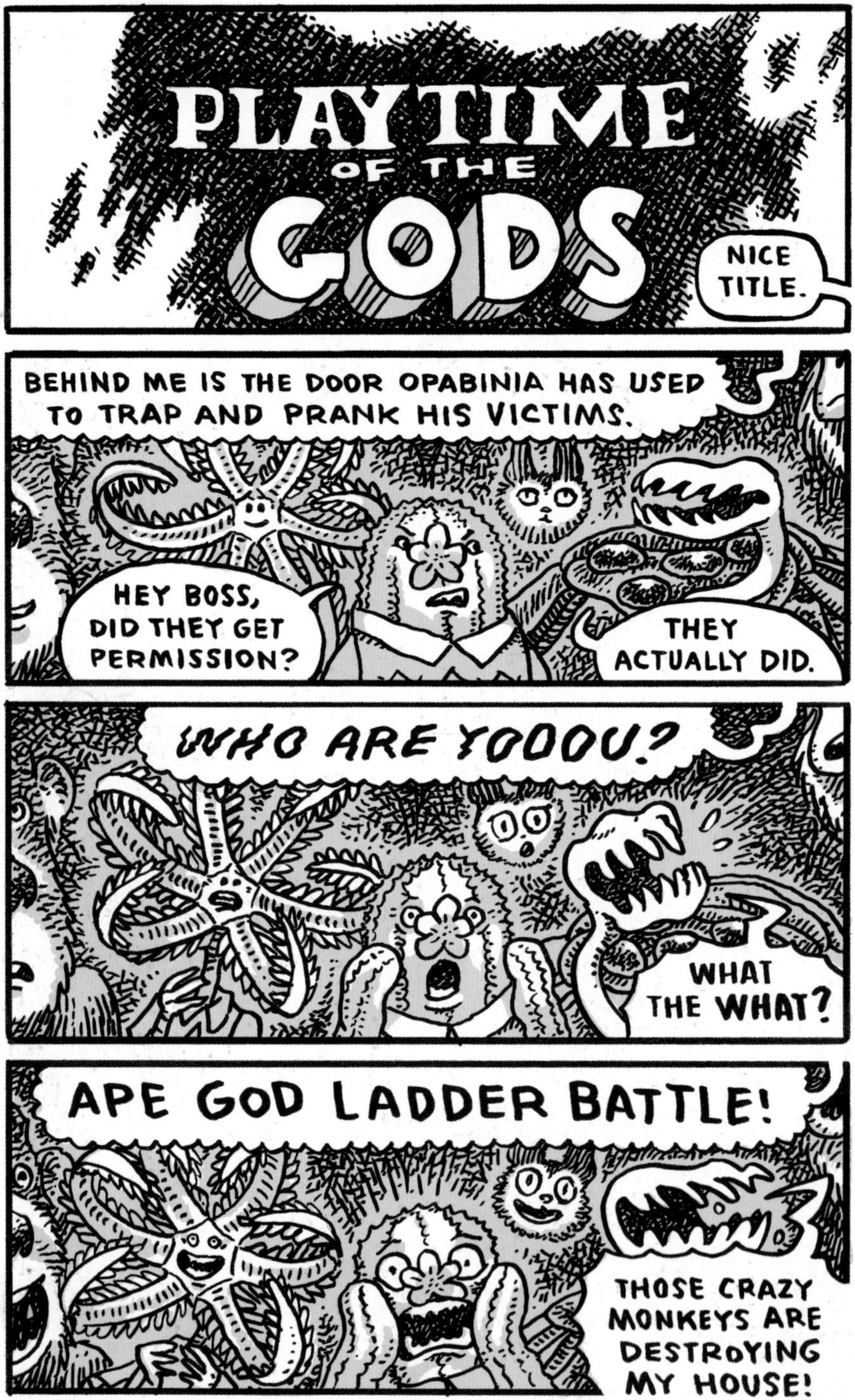
PLAYTIME OF THE GODS
NICE TITLE.
BEHIND ME IS THE DOOR OPABINIA HAS USED TO TRAP AND PRANK HIS VICTIMS.
HEY BOSS, DID THEY GET PERMISSION?
THEY ACTUALLY DID.
WHO ARE YOOOU?
WHAT THE WHAT?
APE GOD LADDER BATTLE!
THOSE CRAZY MONKEYS ARE DESTROYING MY HOUSE!

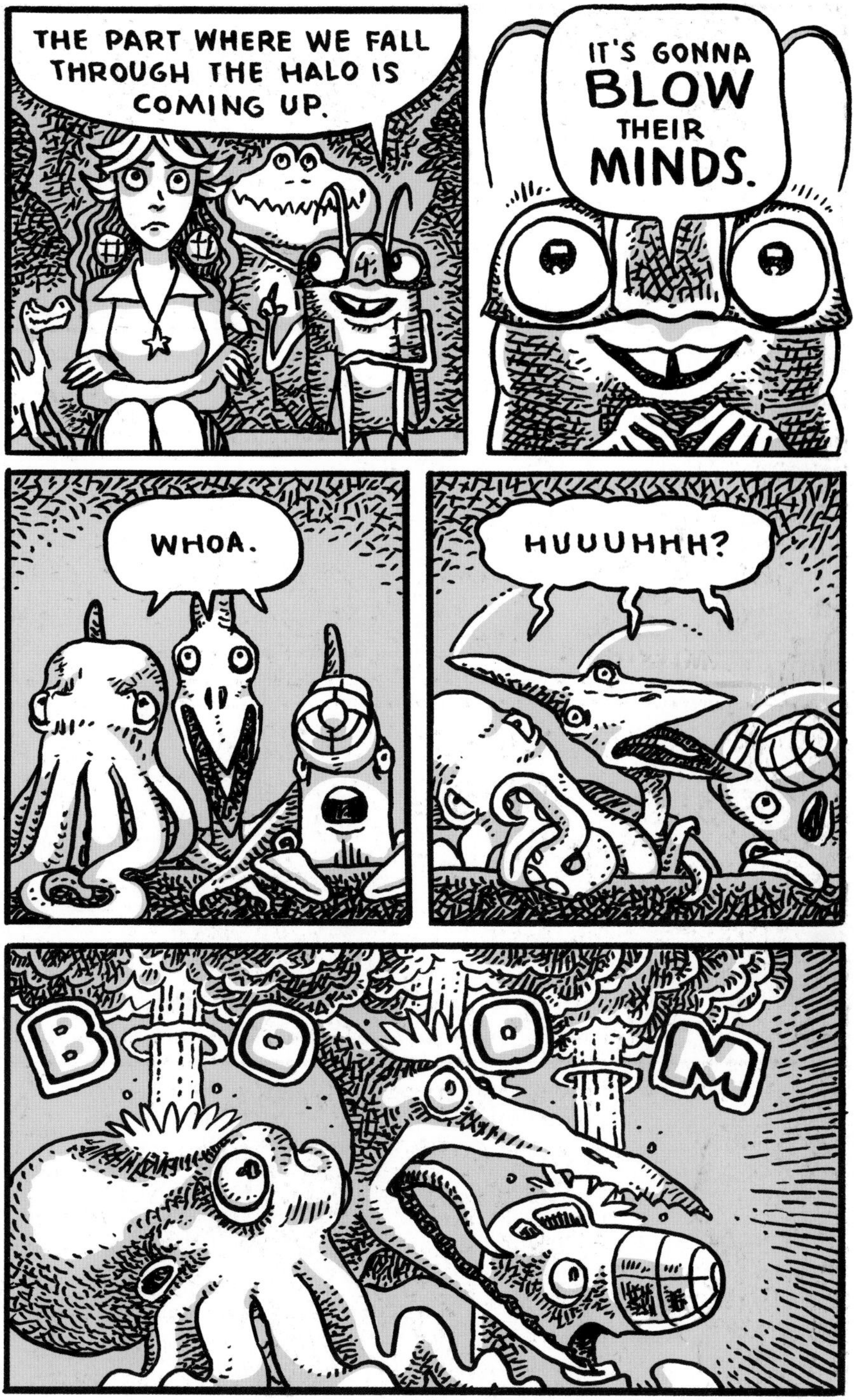
THE PART WHERE WE FALL THROUGH THE HALO IS COMING UP.
IT'S GONNA BLOW THEIR MINDS.
WHOA.
HUUUHHH?
BOOM

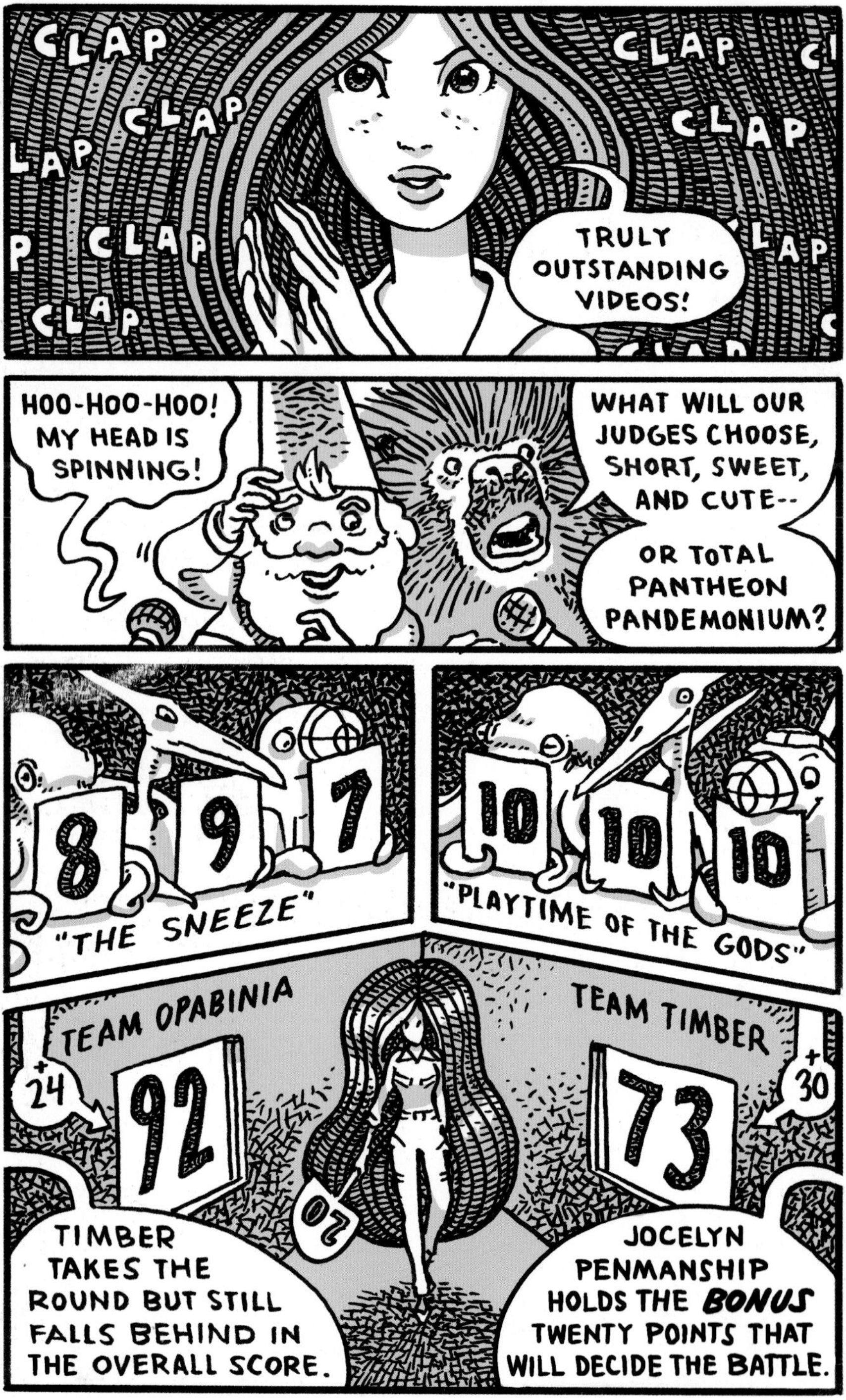
CLAP CLAP CLAP CLAP
TRULY OUTSTANDING VIDEOS!
HOO-HOO-HOO! MY HEAD IS SPINNING!
WHAT WILL OUR JUDGES CHOOSE, SHORT, SWEET, AND CUTE--
OR TOTAL PANTHEON PANDEMONIUM?
8 9 7
"THE SNEEZE"
10 10 10
"PLAYTIME OF THE GODS"
TEAM OPABINIA
+24
92
TEAM TIMBER
+30
73
20
TIMBER TAKES THE ROUND BUT STILL FALLS BEHIND IN THE OVERALL SCORE.
JOCELYN PENMANSHIP HOLDS THE *BONUS* TWENTY POINTS THAT WILL DECIDE THE BATTLE.

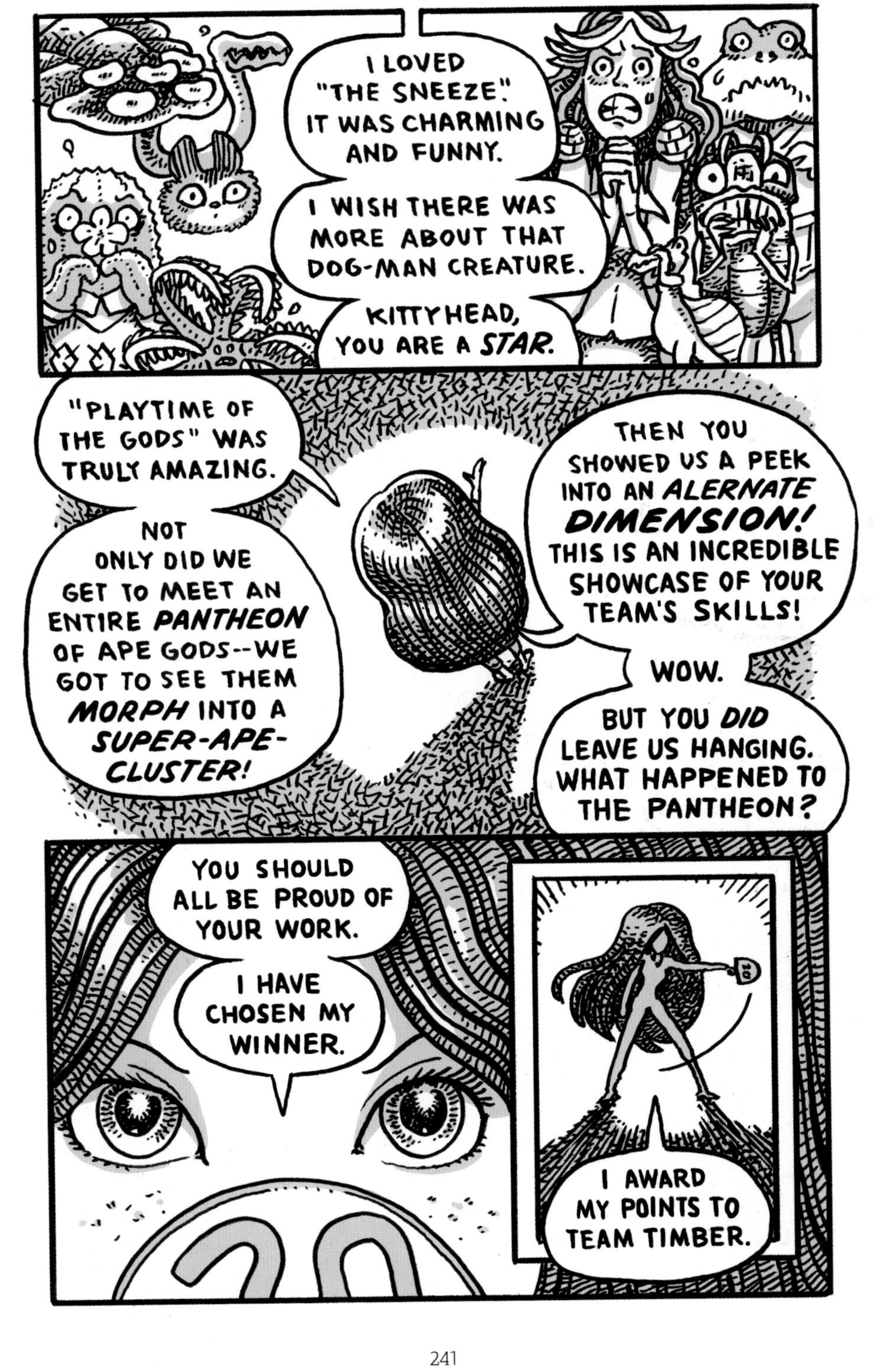
I LOVED "THE SNEEZE." IT WAS CHARMING AND FUNNY.
I WISH THERE WAS MORE ABOUT THAT DOG-MAN CREATURE.
KITTYHEAD, YOU ARE A *STAR.*
"PLAYTIME OF THE GODS" WAS TRULY AMAZING.
NOT ONLY DID WE GET TO MEET AN ENTIRE *PANTHEON* OF APE GODS--WE GOT TO SEE THEM *MORPH* INTO A *SUPER-APE-CLUSTER!*
THEN YOU SHOWED US A PEEK INTO AN *ALERNATE DIMENSION!* THIS IS AN INCREDIBLE SHOWCASE OF YOUR TEAM'S SKILLS!
WOW.
BUT YOU *DID* LEAVE US HANGING. WHAT HAPPENED TO THE PANTHEON?
YOU SHOULD ALL BE PROUD OF YOUR WORK.
I HAVE CHOSEN MY WINNER.
I AWARD MY POINTS TO TEAM TIMBER.

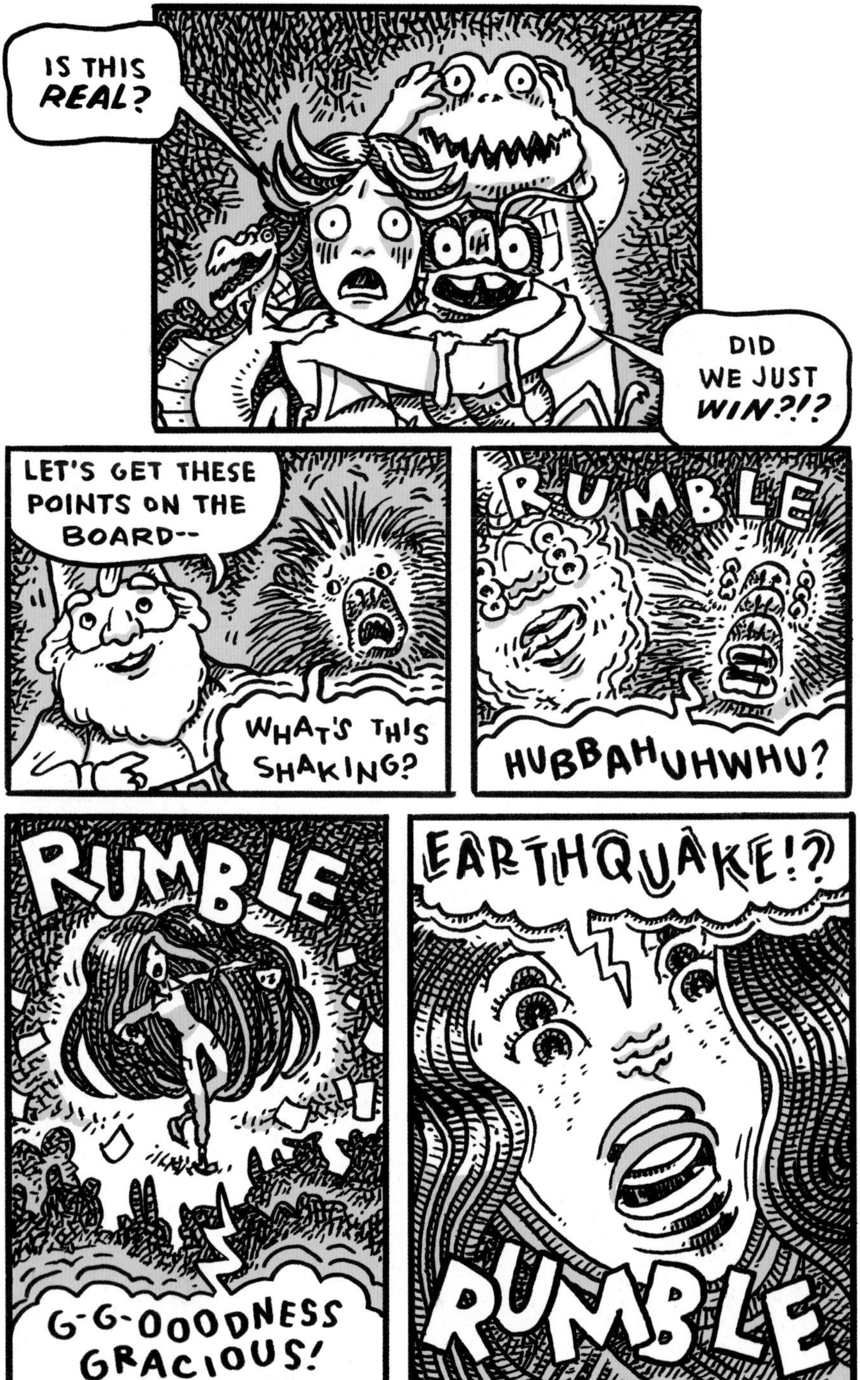
IS THIS *REAL?*
DID WE JUST *WIN?!?*
LET'S GET THESE POINTS ON THE BOARD--
WHAT'S THIS SHAKING?
RUMBLE
HUBBAH UHWHU?
RUMBLE
G-G-OOODNESS GRACIOUS!
EARTHQUAKE!?
RUMBLE

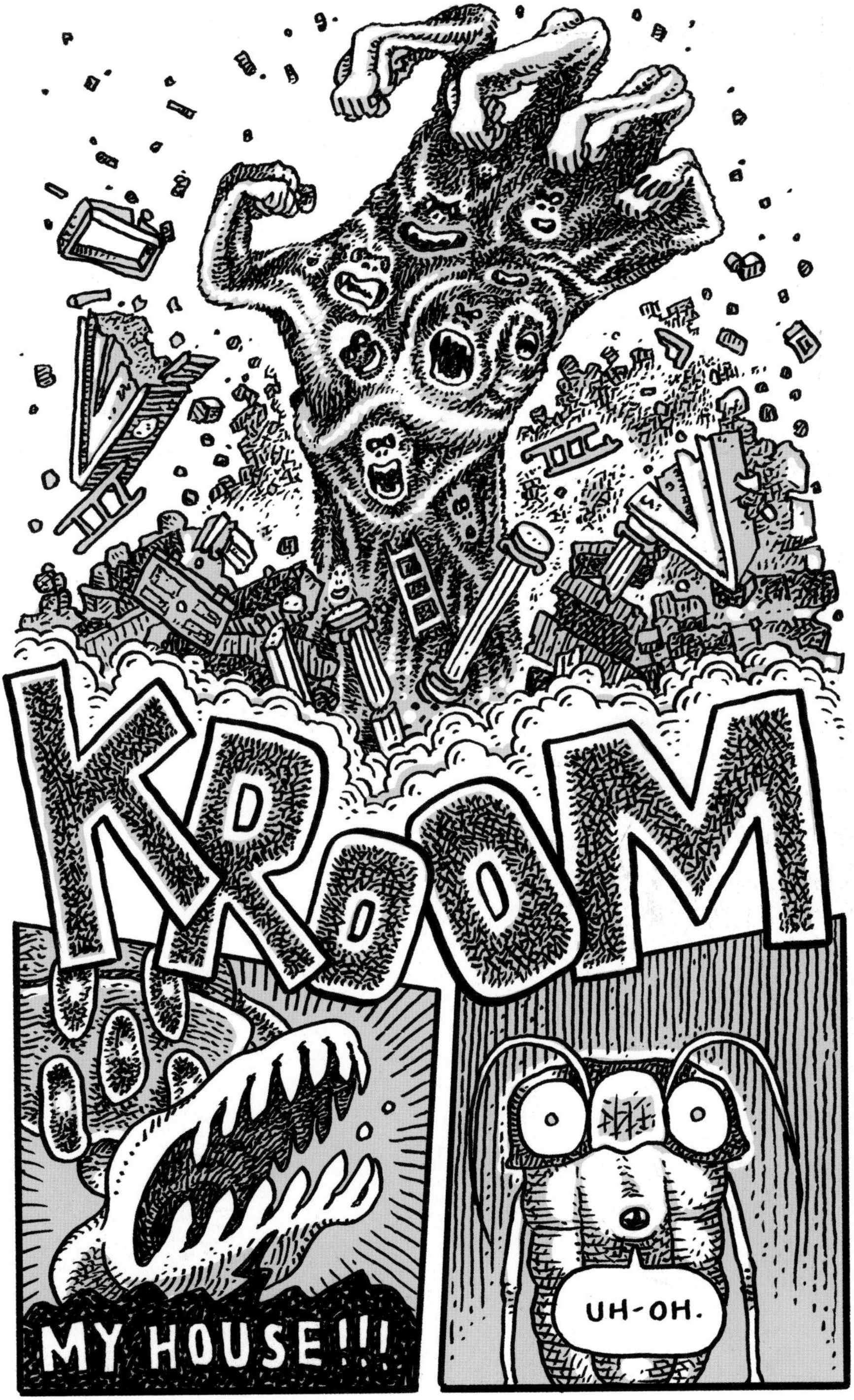
KROOM
MY HOUSE!!!
UH-OH.

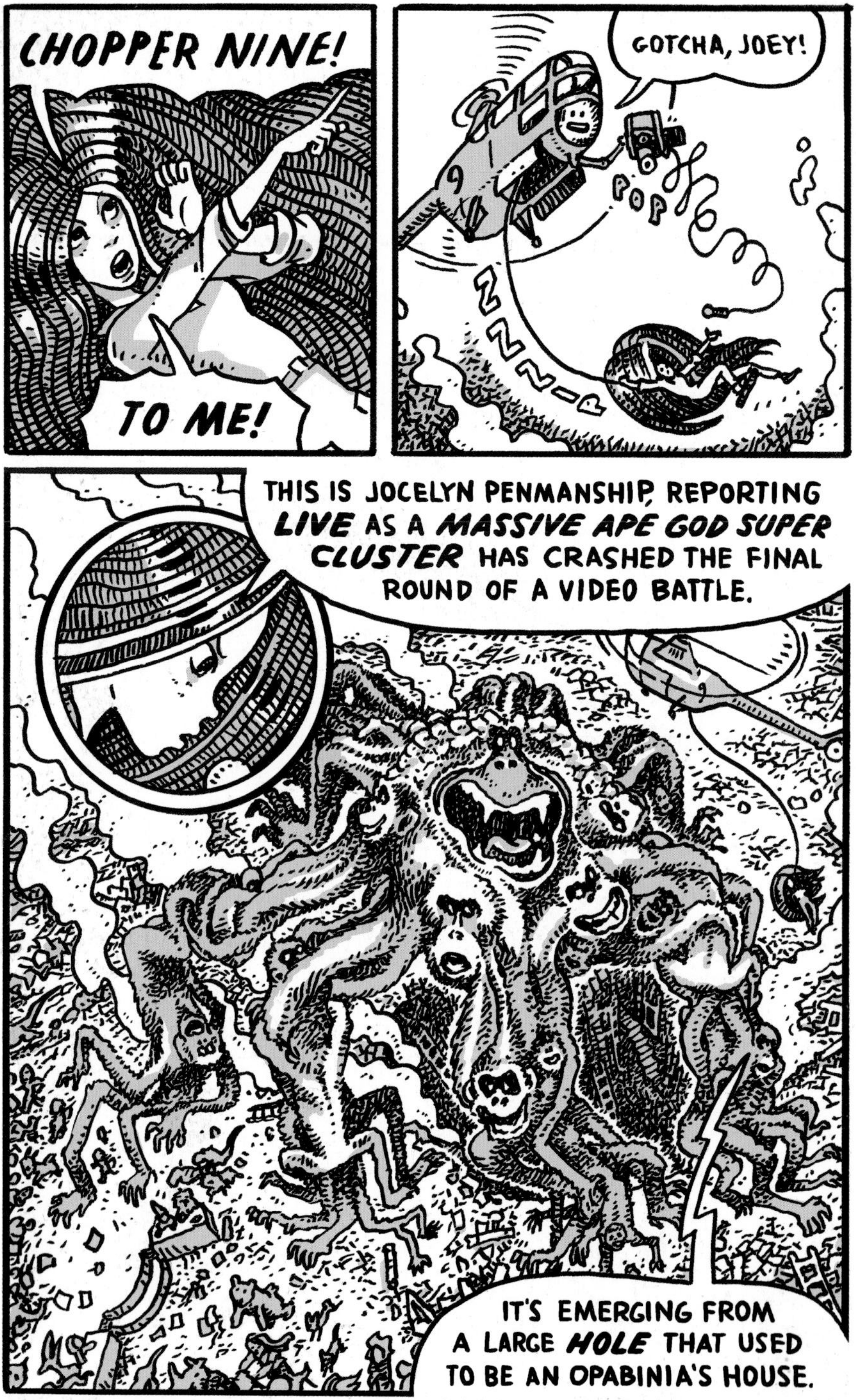

CHOPPER NINE!
TO ME!
GOTCHA, JOEY!
POP
ZZZZ-P
THIS IS JOCELYN PENMANSHIP, REPORTING LIVE AS A MASSIVE APE GOD SUPER CLUSTER HAS CRASHED THE FINAL ROUND OF A VIDEO BATTLE.
IT'S EMERGING FROM A LARGE HOLE THAT USED TO BE AN OPABINIA'S HOUSE.

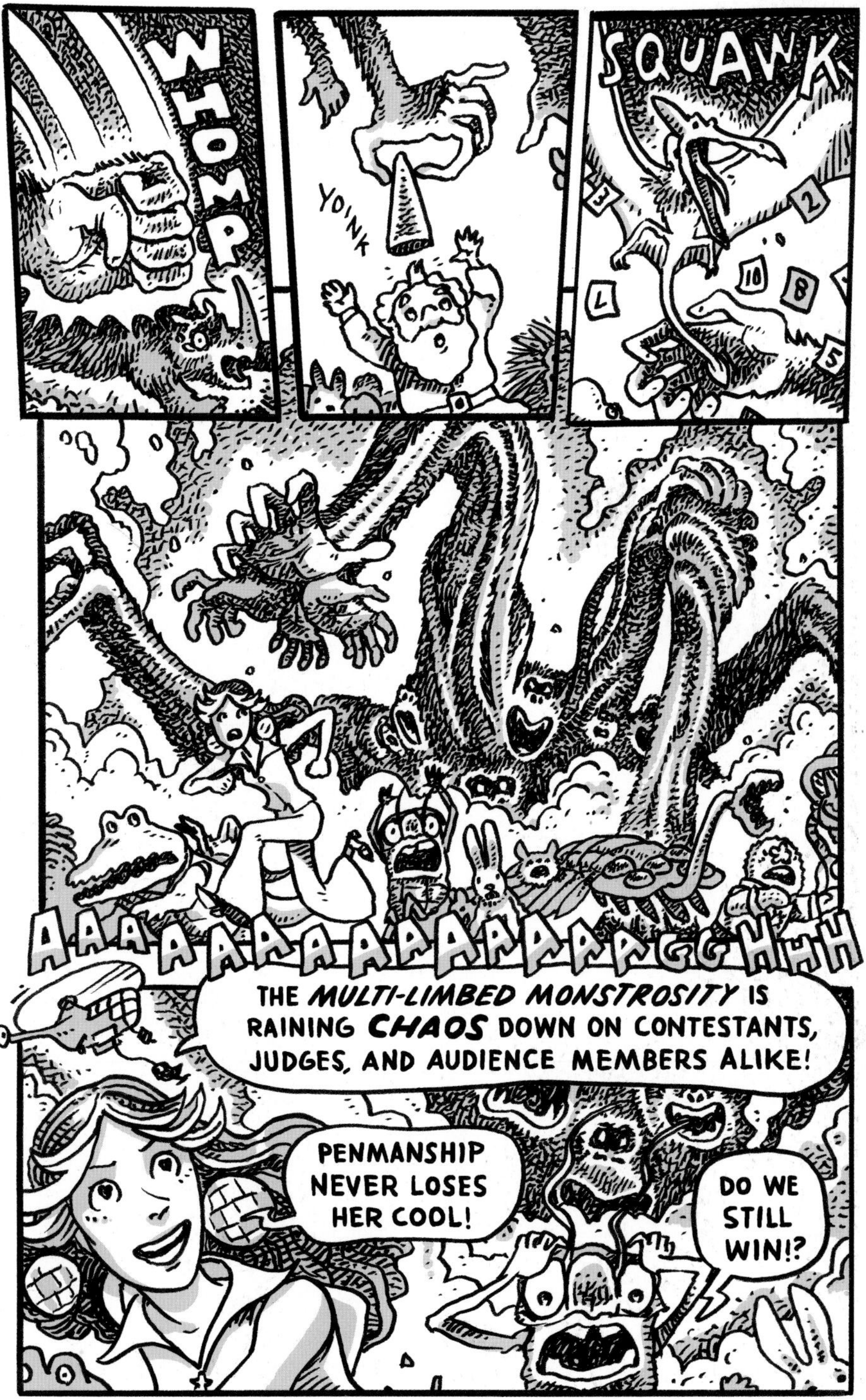
WHOMP
YOINK
SQUAWK
AAAAAAAAAAAAAAGGHHH
THE *MULTI-LIMBED MONSTROSITY* IS RAINING **CHAOS** DOWN ON CONTESTANTS, JUDGES, AND AUDIENCE MEMBERS ALIKE!
PENMANSHIP NEVER LOSES HER COOL!
DO WE STILL WIN!?

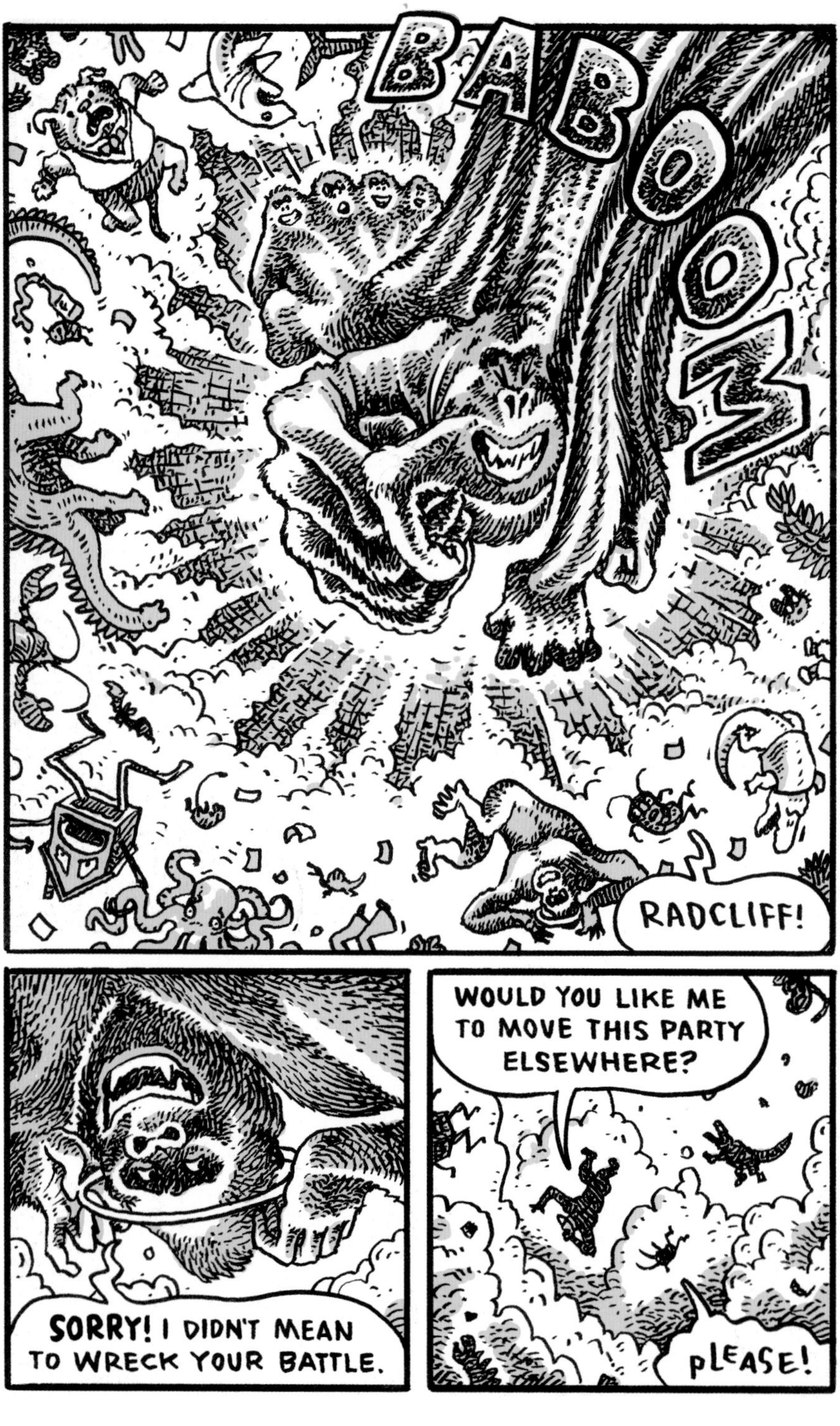
BABOOM
RADCLIFF!
SORRY! I DIDN'T MEAN TO WRECK YOUR BATTLE.
WOULD YOU LIKE ME TO MOVE THIS PARTY ELSEWHERE?
PLEASE!

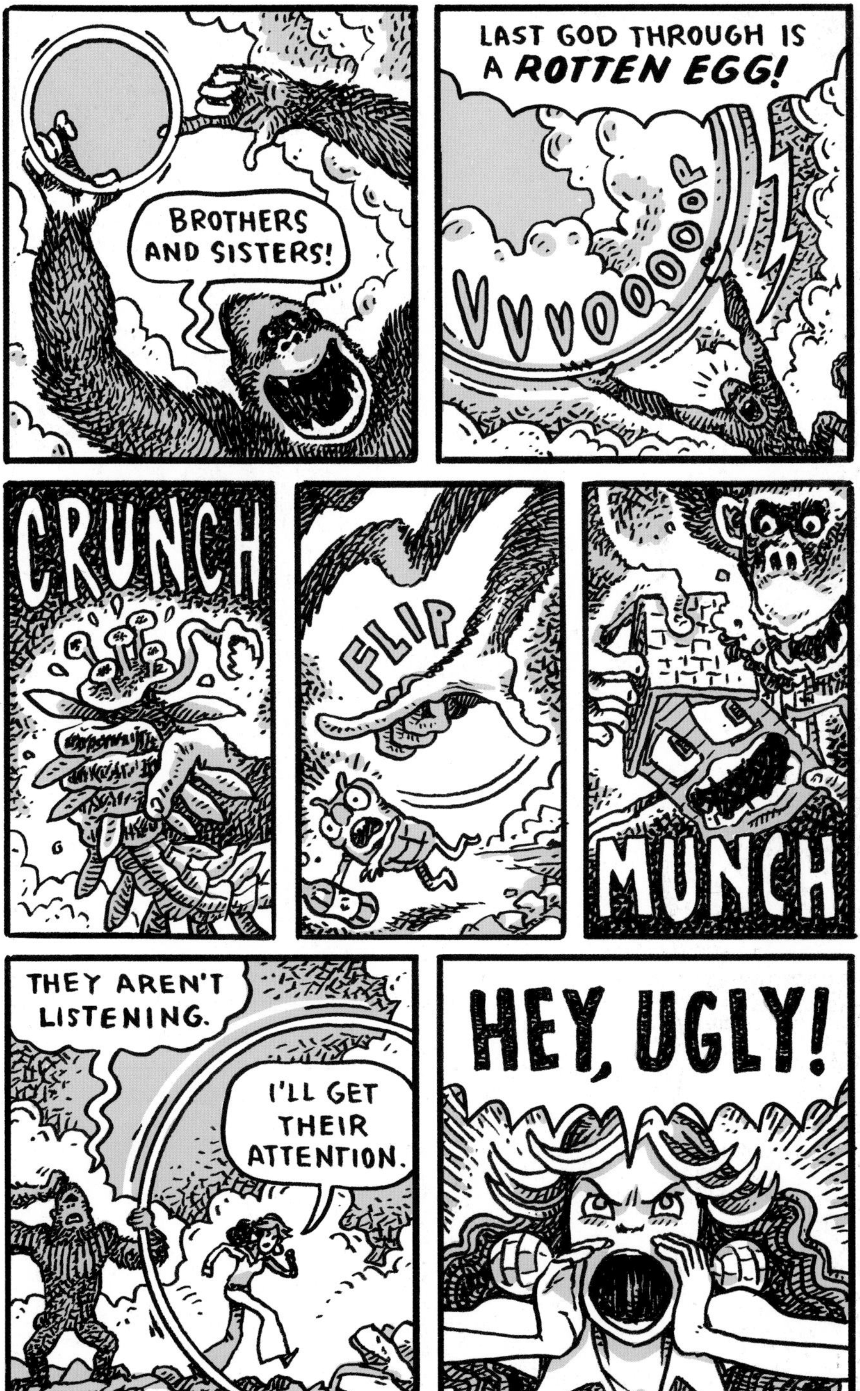
BROTHERS AND SISTERS!
LAST GOD THROUGH IS A ROTTEN EGG!
VVVOOOOOOR
CRUNCH
FLIP
MUNCH
THEY AREN'T LISTENING.
I'LL GET THEIR ATTENTION.
HEY, UGLY!

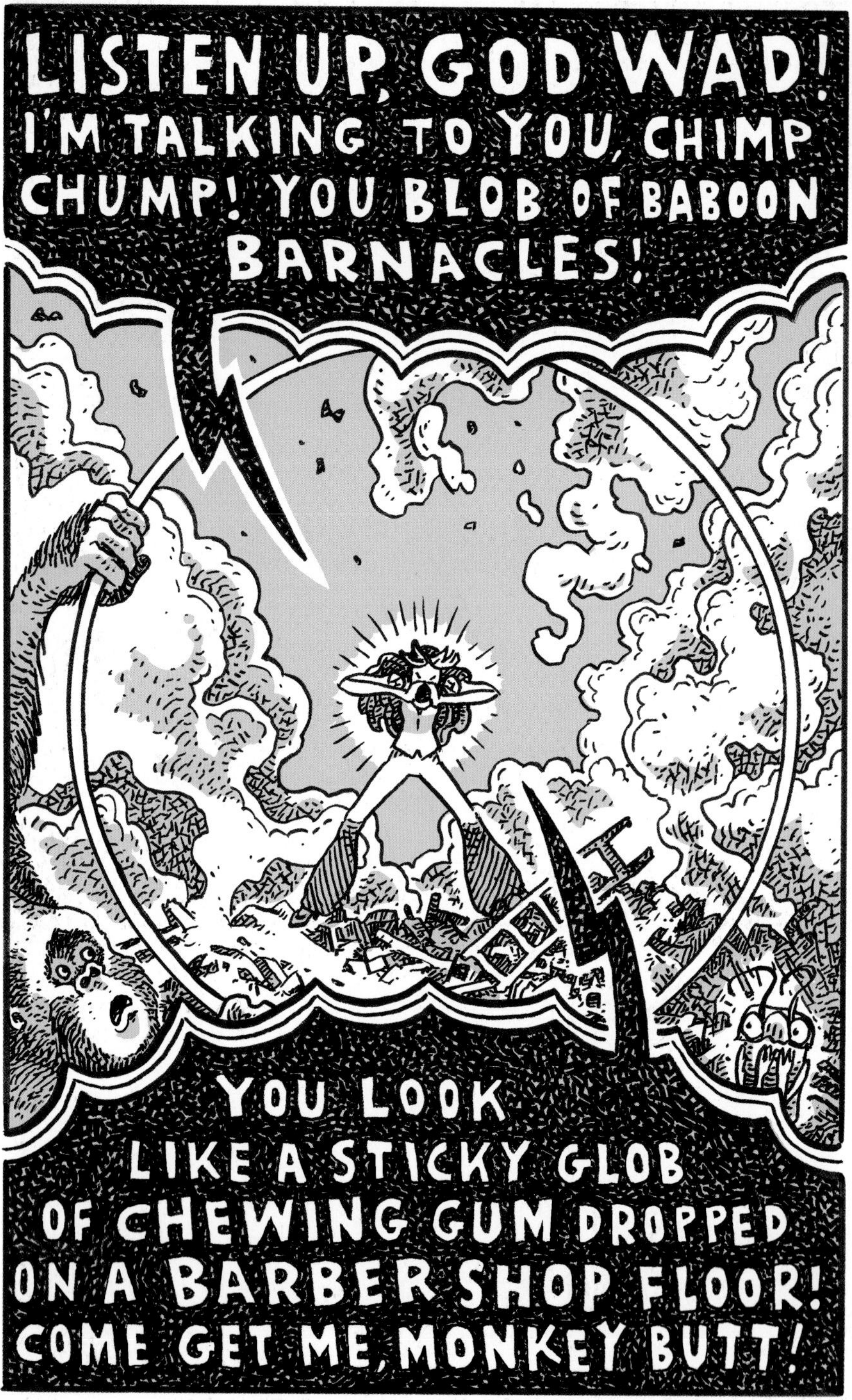
LISTEN UP, GOD WAD! I'M TALKING TO YOU, CHIMP CHUMP! YOU BLOB OF BABOON BARNACLES!
YOU LOOK LIKE A STICKY GLOB OF CHEWING GUM DROPPED ON A BARBER SHOP FLOOR! COME GET ME, MONKEY BUTT!

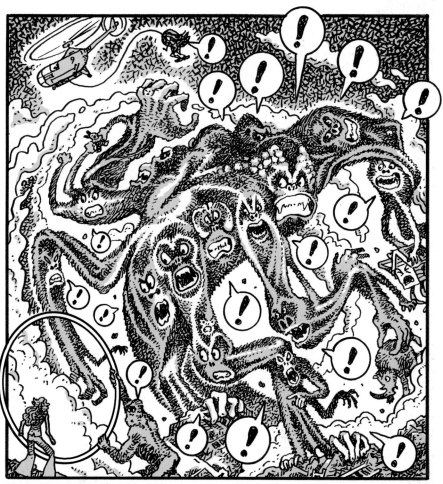

WELL, *THAT* GOT THEIR ATTENTION.

WOW, TIFFANY.

I DIDN'T KNOW YOU HAD IT IN YOU.

I'M JUST GETTING *REAL* TIRED OF THIS-- THIS--

APE SHOW.

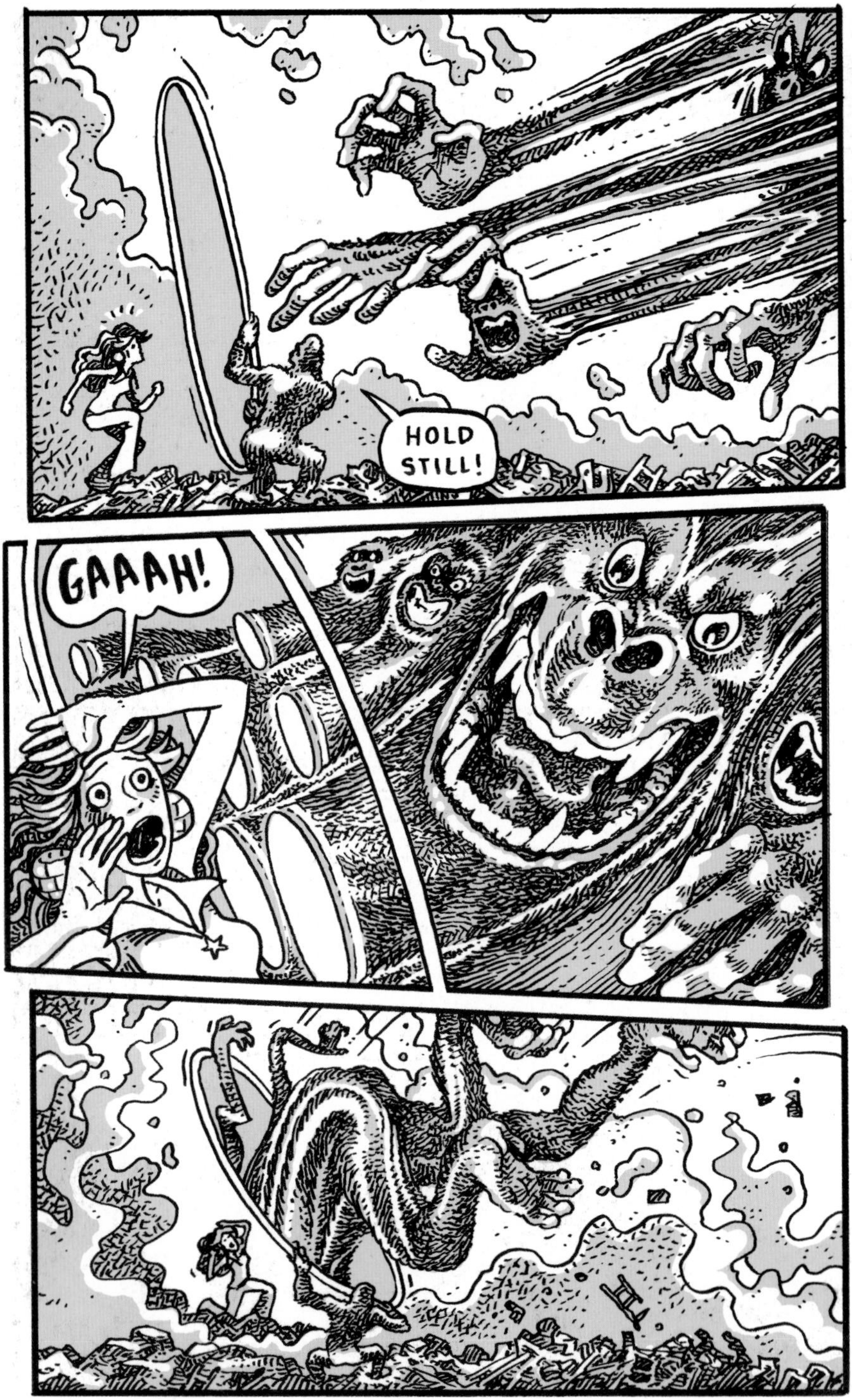
HOLD STILL!
GAAAH!

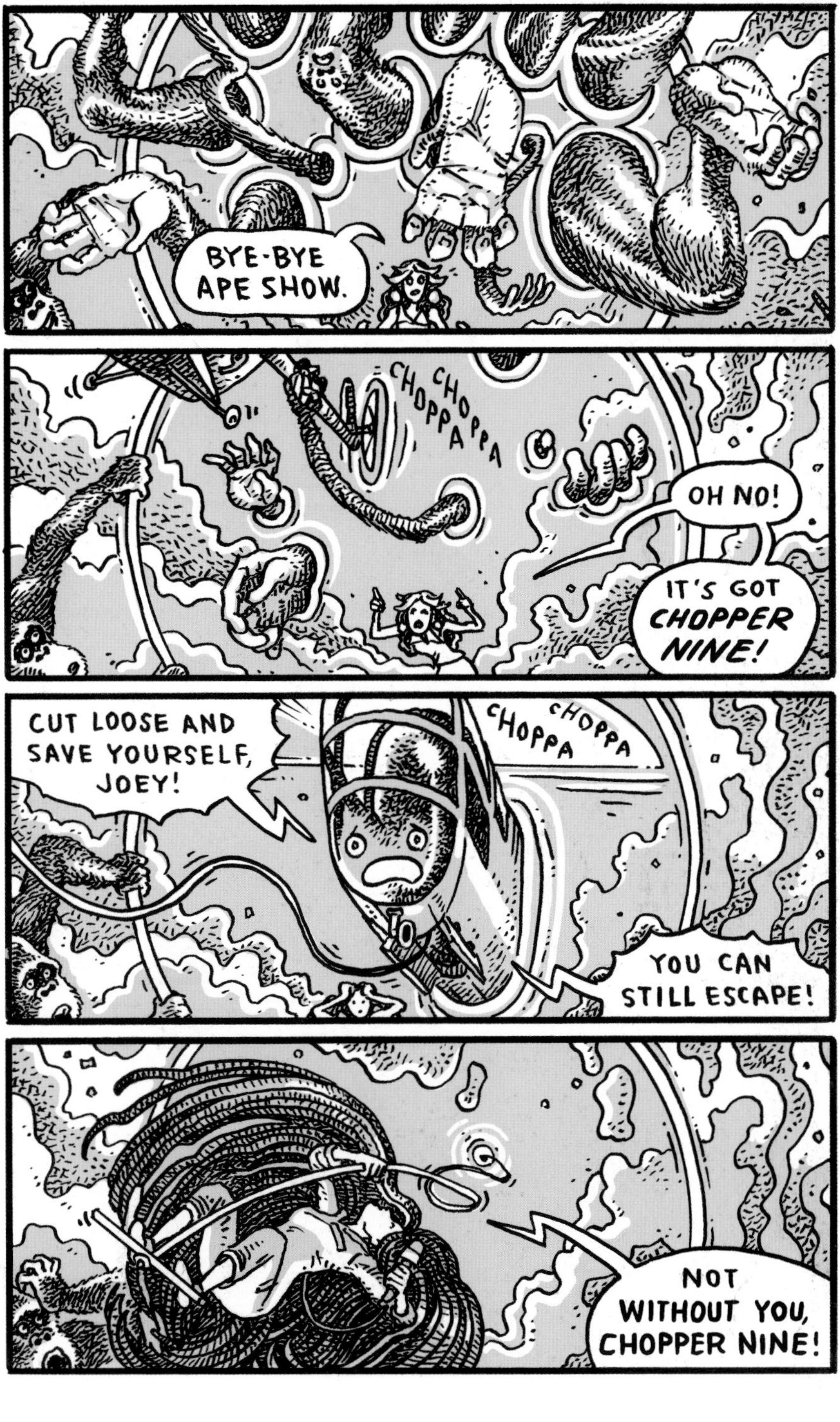
BYE-BYE APE SHOW.
CHOPPA CHOPPA
OH NO!
IT'S GOT CHOPPER NINE!
CUT LOOSE AND SAVE YOURSELF, JOEY!
CHOPPA CHOPPA
YOU CAN STILL ESCAPE!
NOT WITHOUT YOU, CHOPPER NINE!

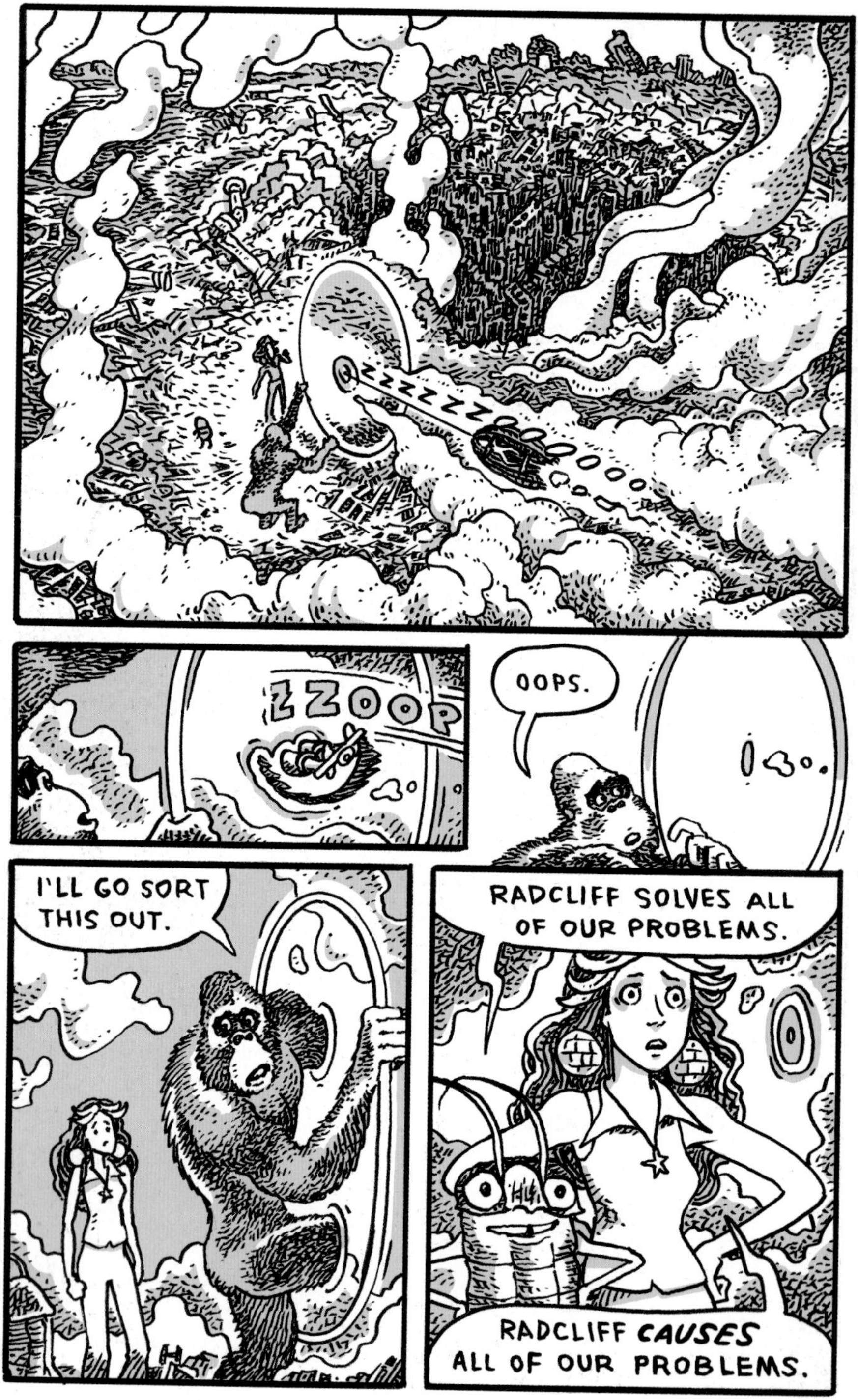
ZZZZZZZ
ZZOOP
OOPS.
I'LL GO SORT THIS OUT.
RADCLIFF SOLVES ALL OF OUR PROBLEMS.
RADCLIFF *CAUSES* ALL OF OUR PROBLEMS.

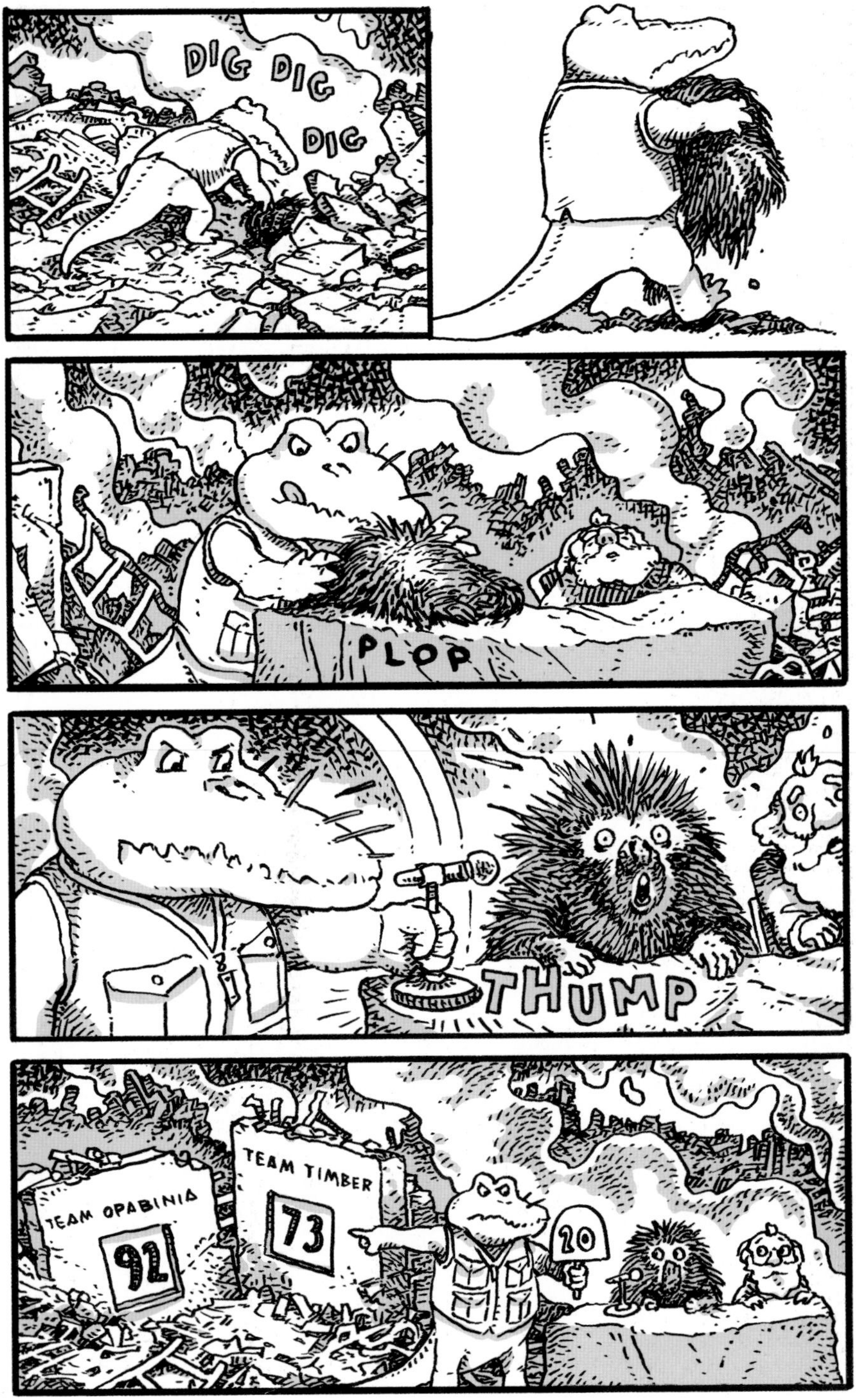
DIG DIG
DIG
PLOP
THUMP
TEAM OPABINIA
92
TEAM TIMBER
73
20

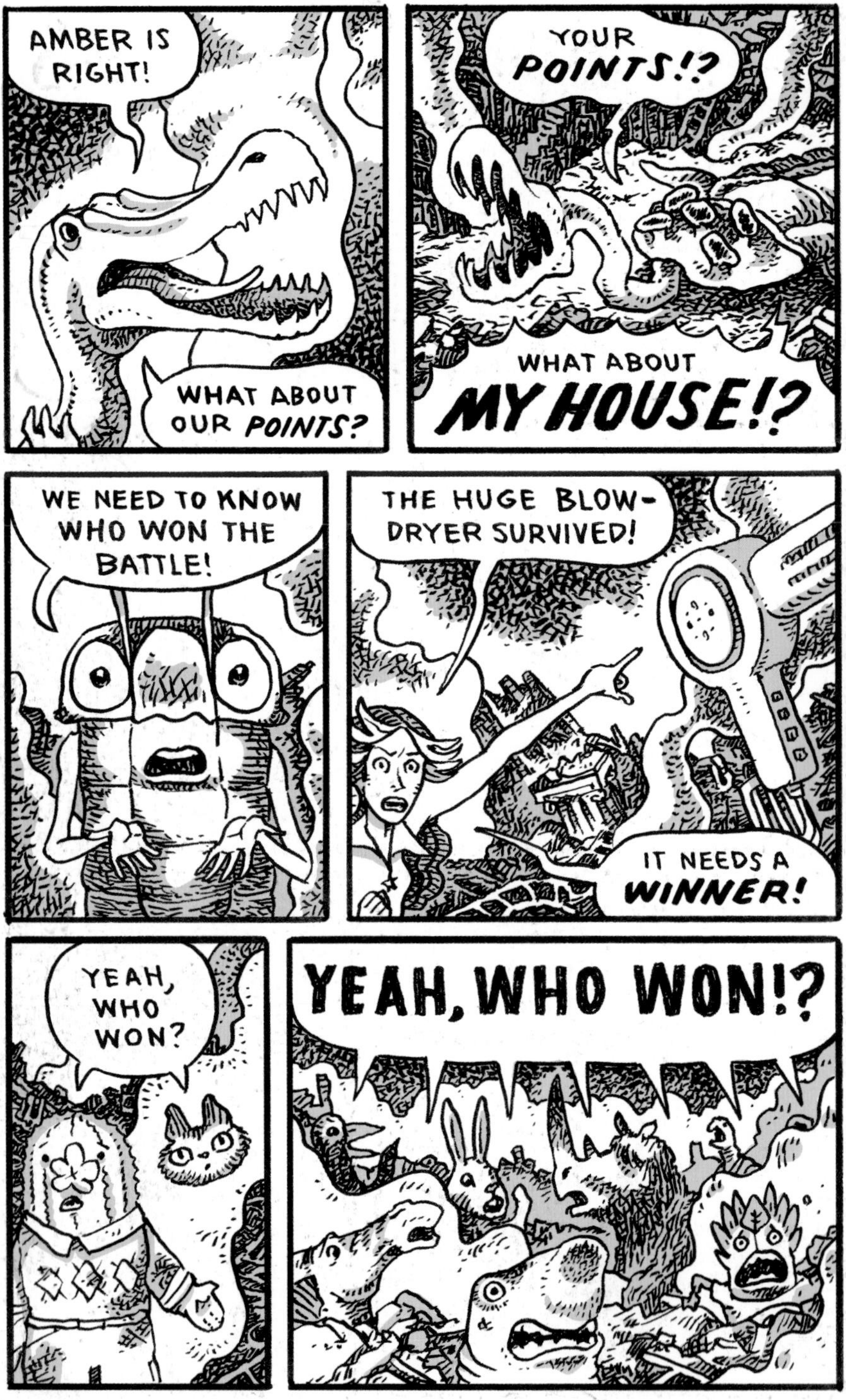
AMBER IS RIGHT!
WHAT ABOUT OUR POINTS?
YOUR POINTS!?
WHAT ABOUT MY HOUSE!?
WE NEED TO KNOW WHO WON THE BATTLE!
THE HUGE BLOW-DRYER SURVIVED!
IT NEEDS A WINNER!
YEAH, WHO WON?
YEAH, WHO WON!?

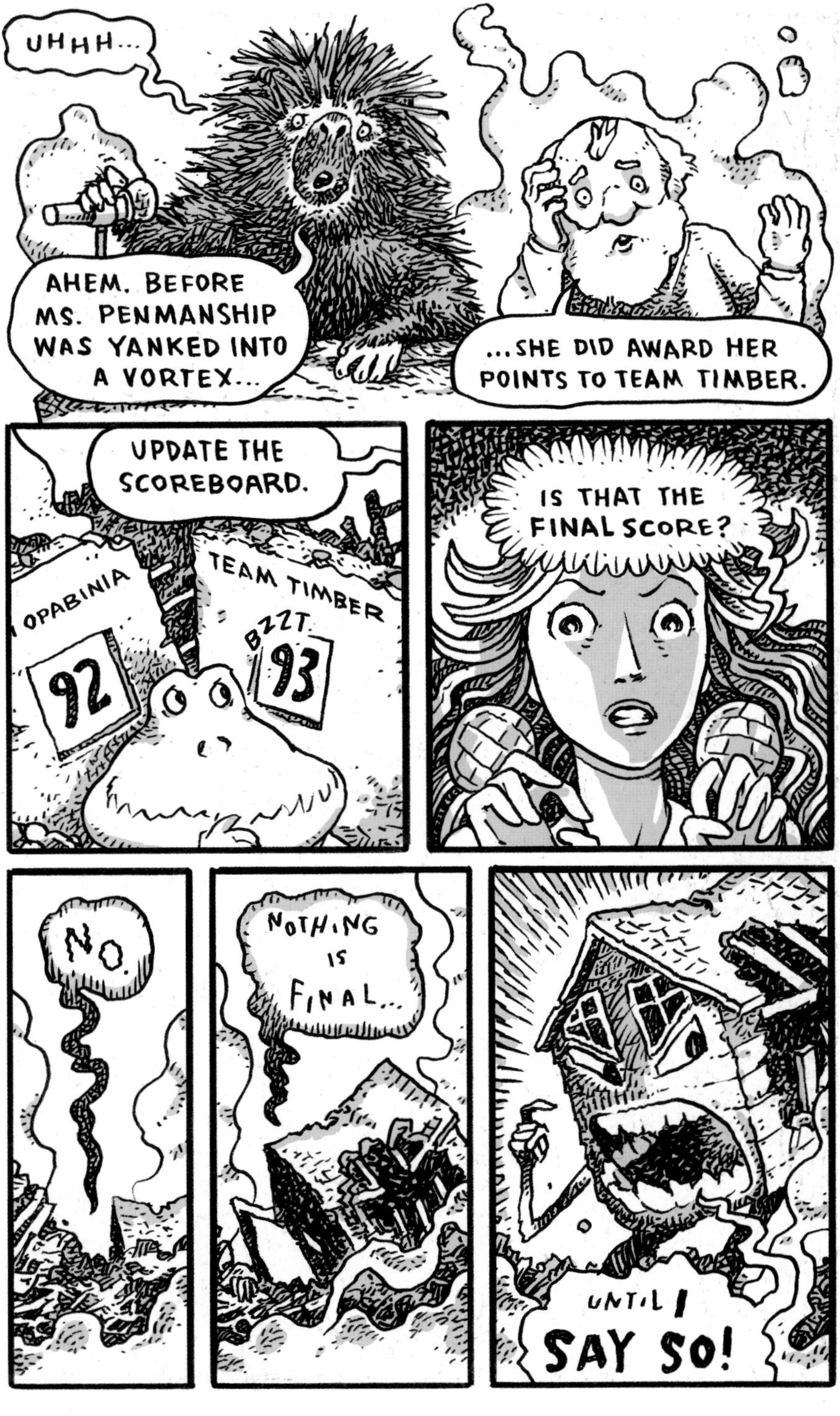

UHHH...
AHEM. BEFORE MS. PENMANSHIP WAS YANKED INTO A VORTEX...
...SHE DID AWARD HER POINTS TO TEAM TIMBER.
UPDATE THE SCOREBOARD.
OPABINIA
92
TEAM TIMBER
BZZT.
93
IS THAT THE FINAL SCORE?
NO.
NOTHING IS FINAL...
UNTIL I SAY SO!

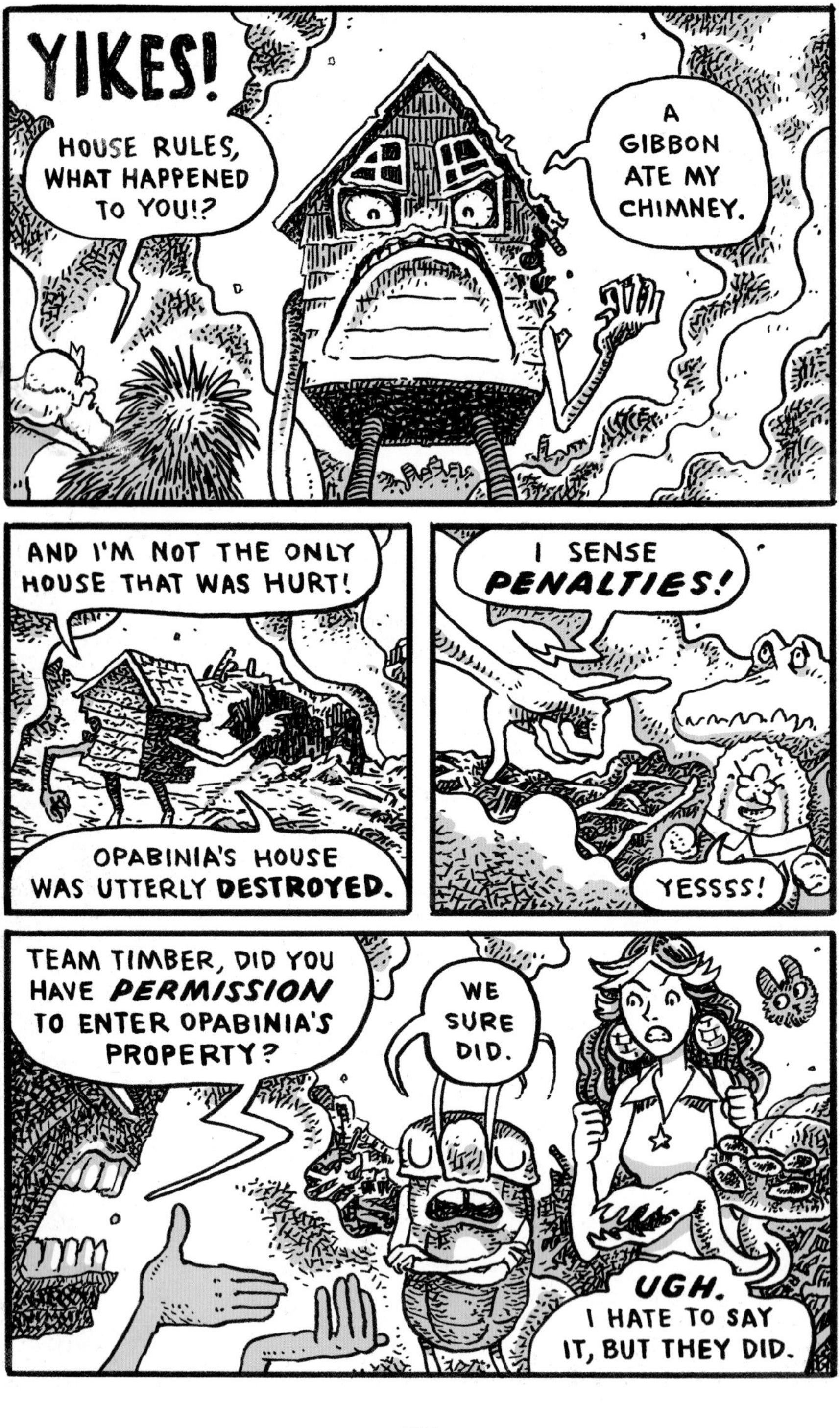
YIKES!
HOUSE RULES, WHAT HAPPENED TO YOU!?
A GIBBON ATE MY CHIMNEY.
AND I'M NOT THE ONLY HOUSE THAT WAS HURT!
OPABINIA'S HOUSE WAS UTTERLY DESTROYED.
I SENSE PENALTIES!
YESSSS!
TEAM TIMBER, DID YOU HAVE PERMISSION TO ENTER OPABINIA'S PROPERTY?
WE SURE DID.
UGH. I HATE TO SAY IT, BUT THEY DID.

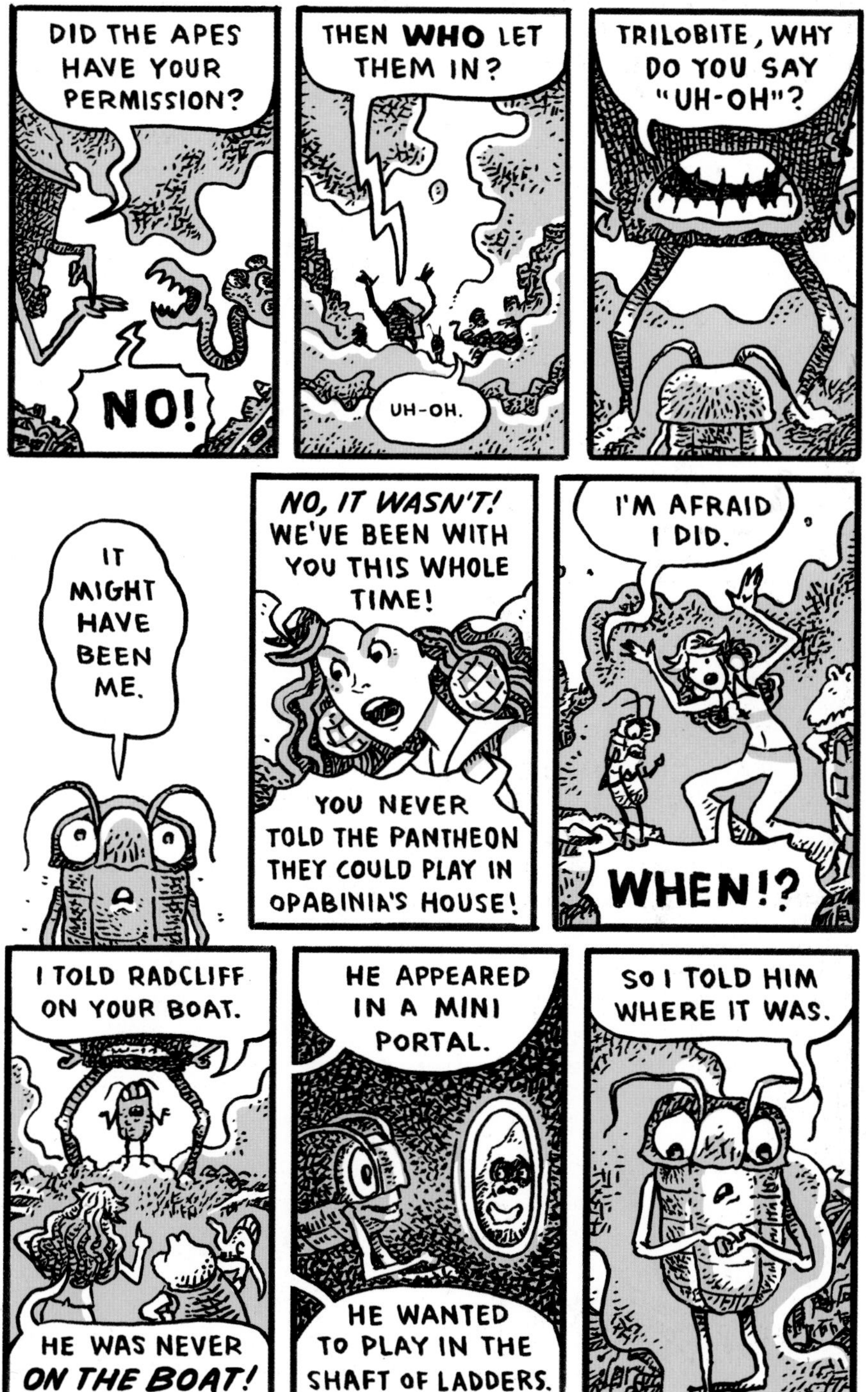
DID THE APES HAVE YOUR PERMISSION?
NO!
THEN **WHO** LET THEM IN?
UH-OH.
TRILOBITE, WHY DO YOU SAY "UH-OH"?
IT MIGHT HAVE BEEN ME.
NO, IT WASN'T! WE'VE BEEN WITH YOU THIS WHOLE TIME!
YOU NEVER TOLD THE PANTHEON THEY COULD PLAY IN OPABINIA'S HOUSE!
I'M AFRAID I DID.
WHEN!?
I TOLD RADCLIFF ON YOUR BOAT.
HE WAS NEVER *ON THE BOAT!*
HE APPEARED IN A MINI PORTAL.
HE WANTED TO PLAY IN THE SHAFT OF LADDERS.
SO I TOLD HIM WHERE IT WAS.

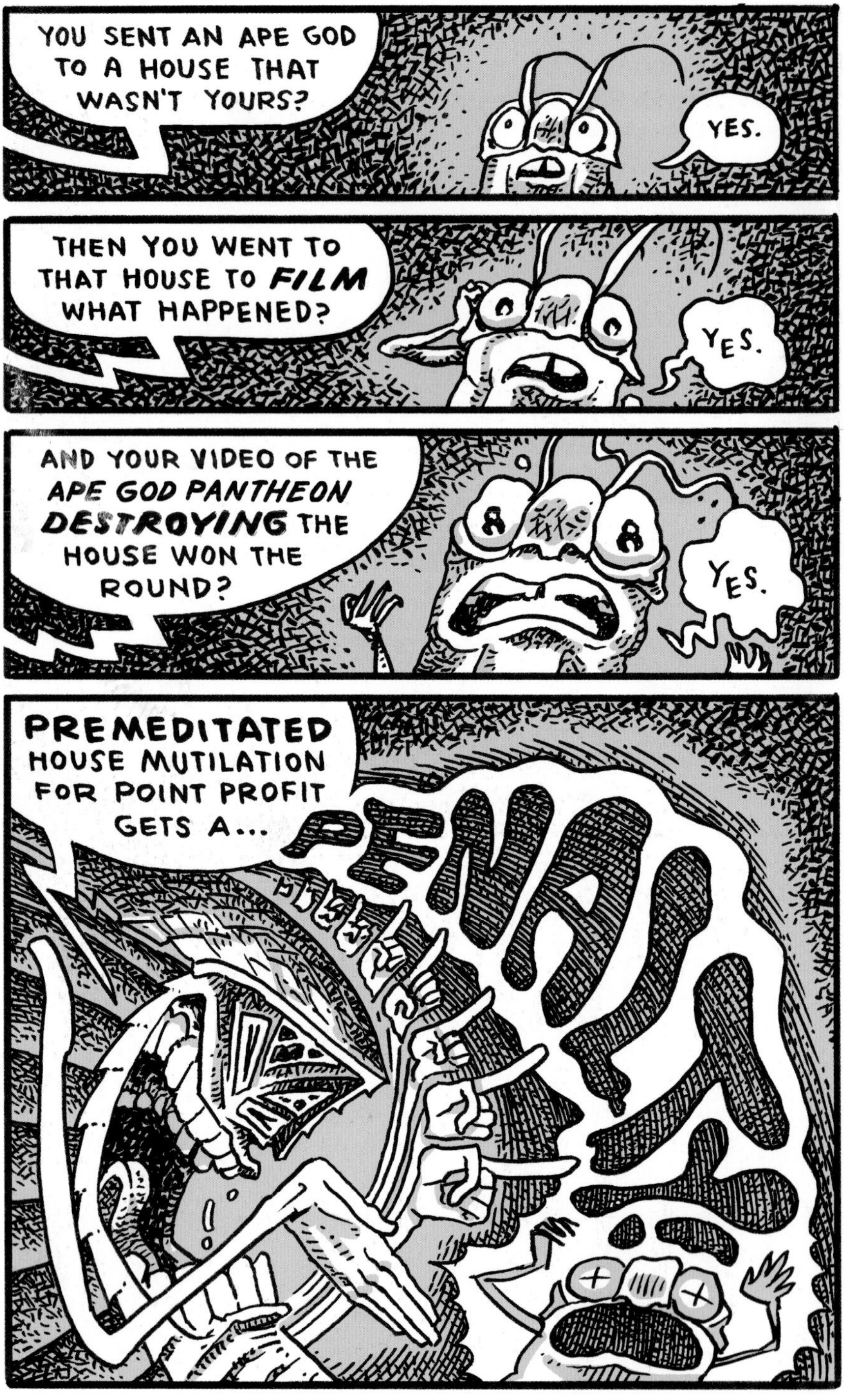
YOU SENT AN APE GOD TO A HOUSE THAT WASN'T YOURS?
YES.
THEN YOU WENT TO THAT HOUSE TO FILM WHAT HAPPENED?
YES.
AND YOUR VIDEO OF THE APE GOD PANTHEON DESTROYING THE HOUSE WON THE ROUND?
YES.
PREMEDITATED HOUSE MUTILATION FOR POINT PROFIT GETS A...
PENALTY

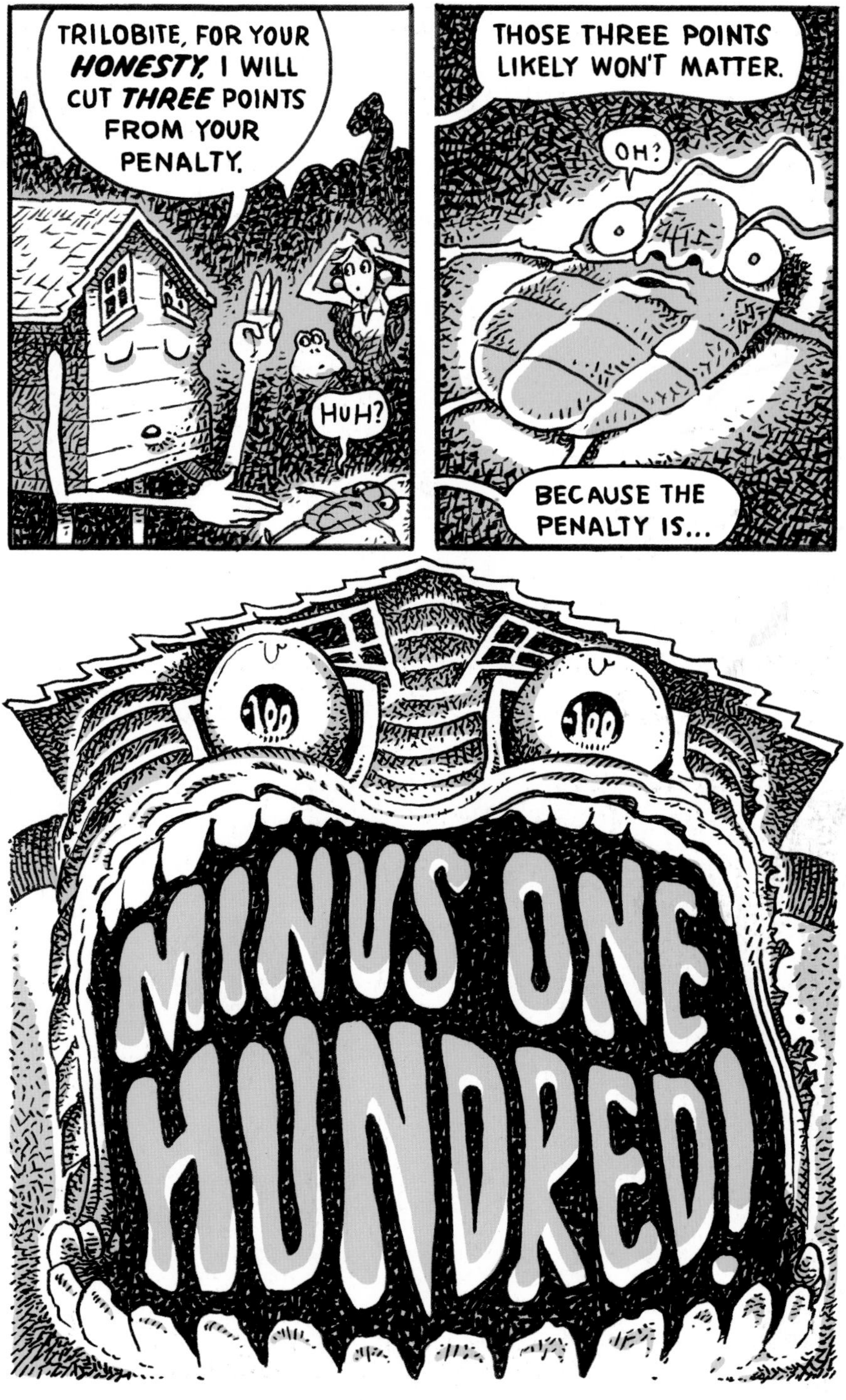
TRILOBITE, FOR YOUR *HONESTY,* I WILL CUT *THREE* POINTS FROM YOUR PENALTY.
HUH?
THOSE THREE POINTS LIKELY WON'T MATTER.
OH?
BECAUSE THE PENALTY IS...
-100
-100
MINUS ONE HUNDRED!

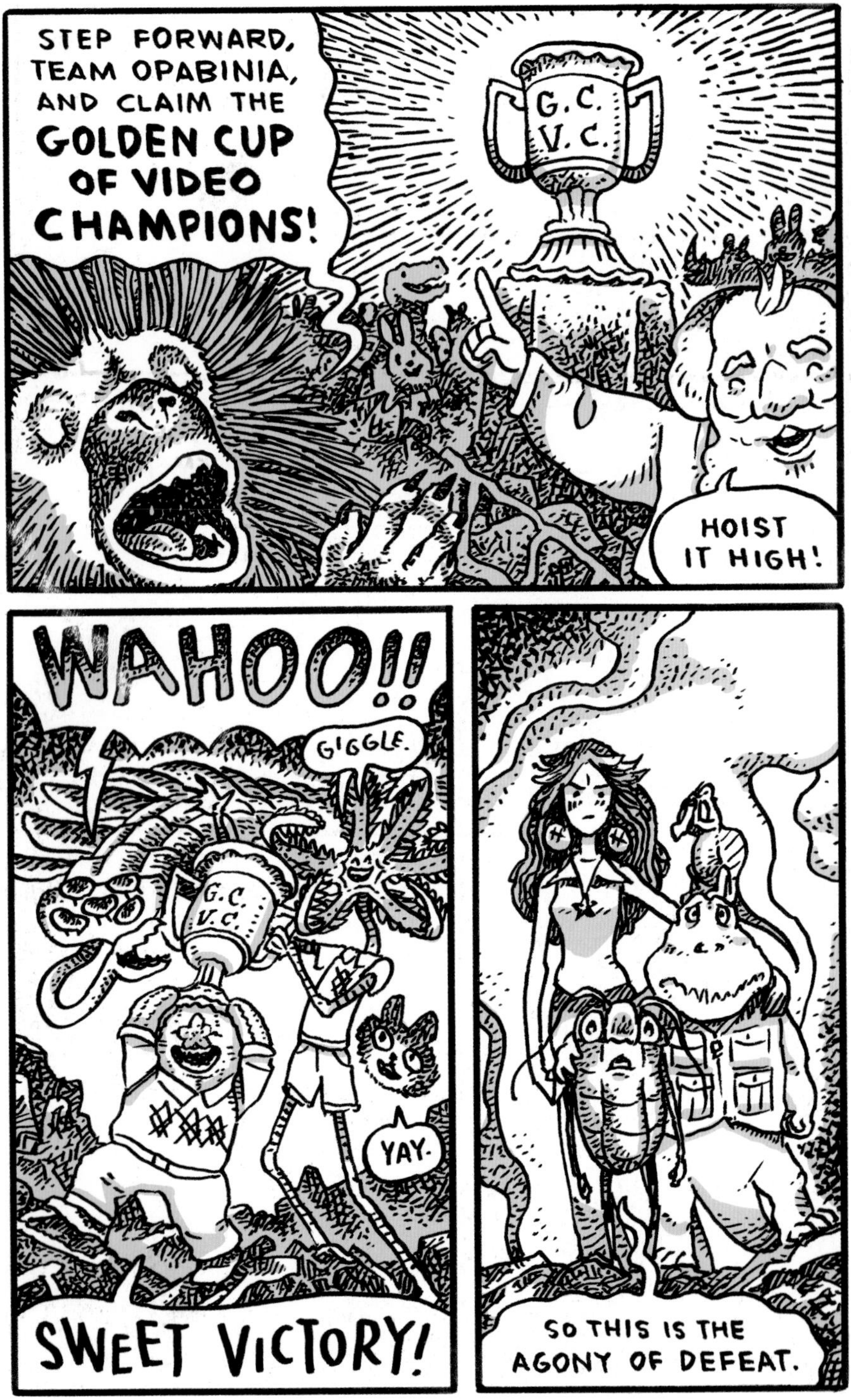
STEP FORWARD, TEAM OPABINIA, AND CLAIM THE GOLDEN CUP OF VIDEO CHAMPIONS!
G.C. V.C.
HOIST IT HIGH!
WAHOO!!
GIGGLE.
G.C. V.C.
YAY.
SWEET VICTORY!
SO THIS IS THE AGONY OF DEFEAT.

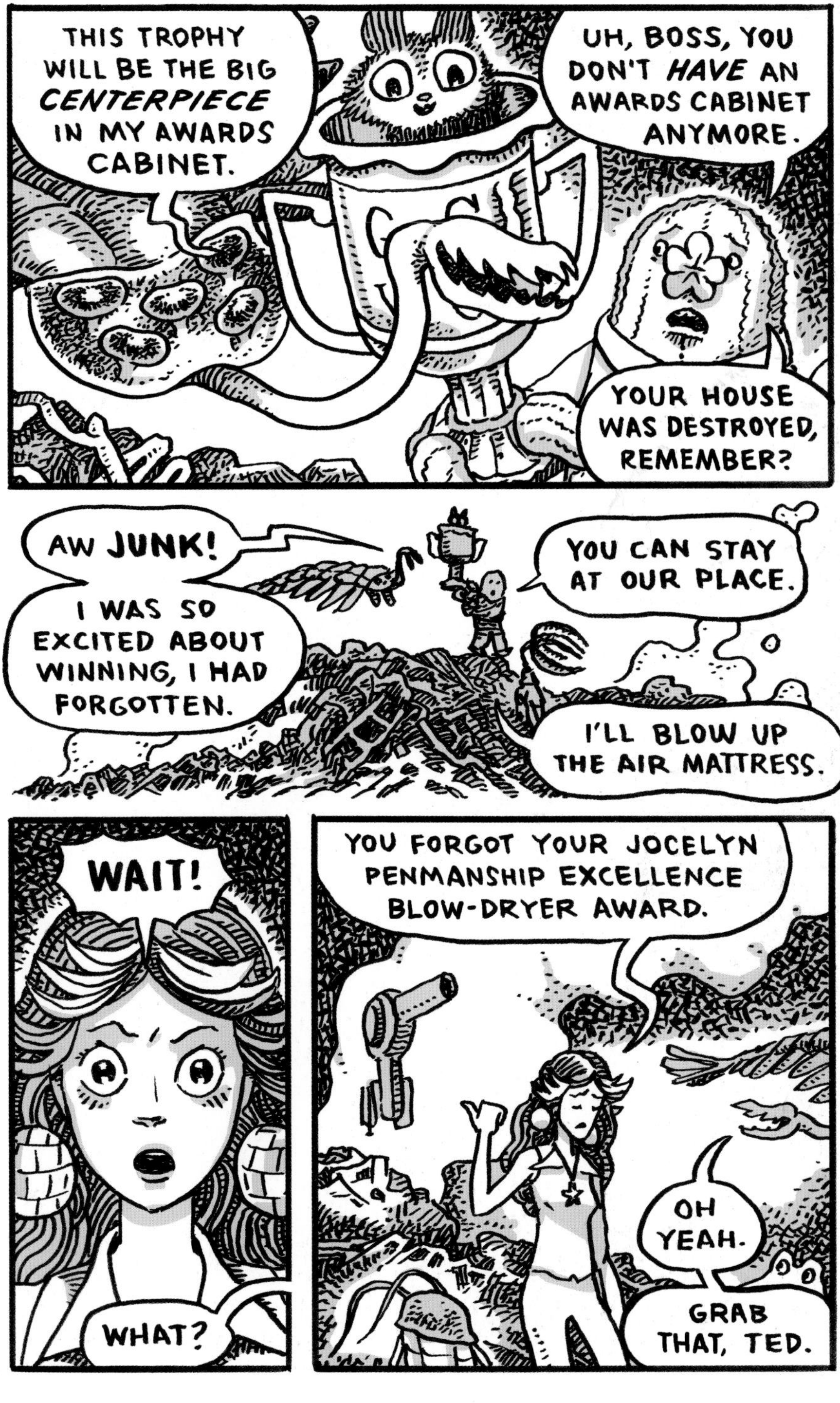
THIS TROPHY WILL BE THE BIG *CENTERPIECE* IN MY AWARDS CABINET.
UH, BOSS, YOU DON'T *HAVE* AN AWARDS CABINET ANYMORE.
YOUR HOUSE WAS DESTROYED, REMEMBER?
AW **JUNK!**
I WAS SO EXCITED ABOUT WINNING, I HAD FORGOTTEN.
YOU CAN STAY AT OUR PLACE.
I'LL BLOW UP THE AIR MATTRESS.
WAIT!
WHAT?
YOU FORGOT YOUR JOCELYN PENMANSHIP EXCELLENCE BLOW-DRYER AWARD.
OH YEAH.
GRAB THAT, TED.

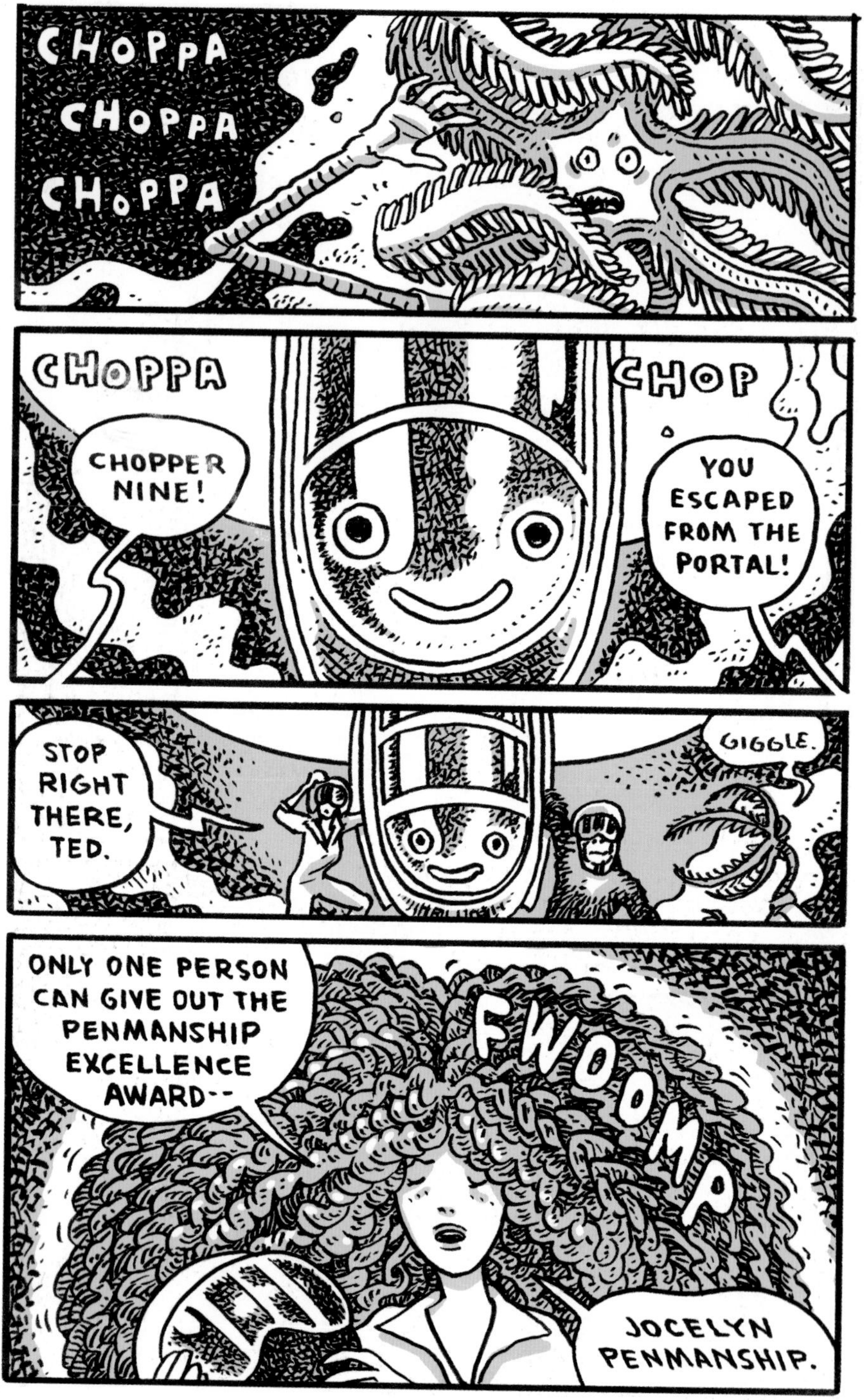
CHOPPA
CHOPPA
CHOPPA
CHOPPA
CHOPPER NINE!
CHOP
YOU ESCAPED FROM THE PORTAL!
STOP RIGHT THERE, TED.
GIGGLE.
ONLY ONE PERSON CAN GIVE OUT THE PENMANSHIP EXCELLENCE AWARD--
FWOOMP
JOCELYN PENMANSHIP.

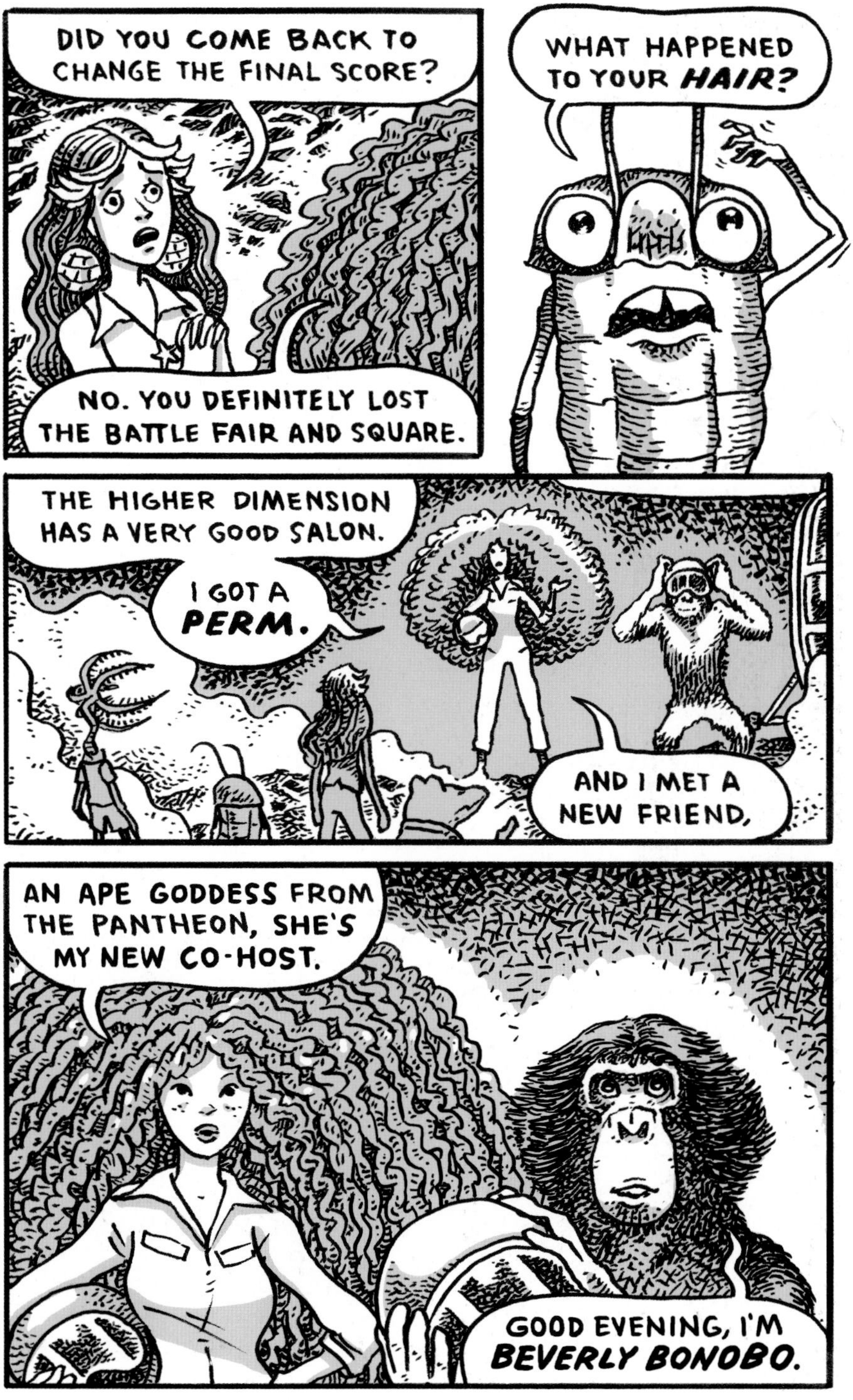
DID YOU COME BACK TO CHANGE THE FINAL SCORE?
NO. YOU DEFINITELY LOST THE BATTLE FAIR AND SQUARE.
WHAT HAPPENED TO YOUR *HAIR?*
THE HIGHER DIMENSION HAS A VERY GOOD SALON.
I GOT A **PERM.**
AND I MET A NEW FRIEND,
AN APE GODDESS FROM THE PANTHEON, SHE'S MY NEW CO-HOST.
GOOD EVENING, I'M ***BEVERLY BONOBO.***

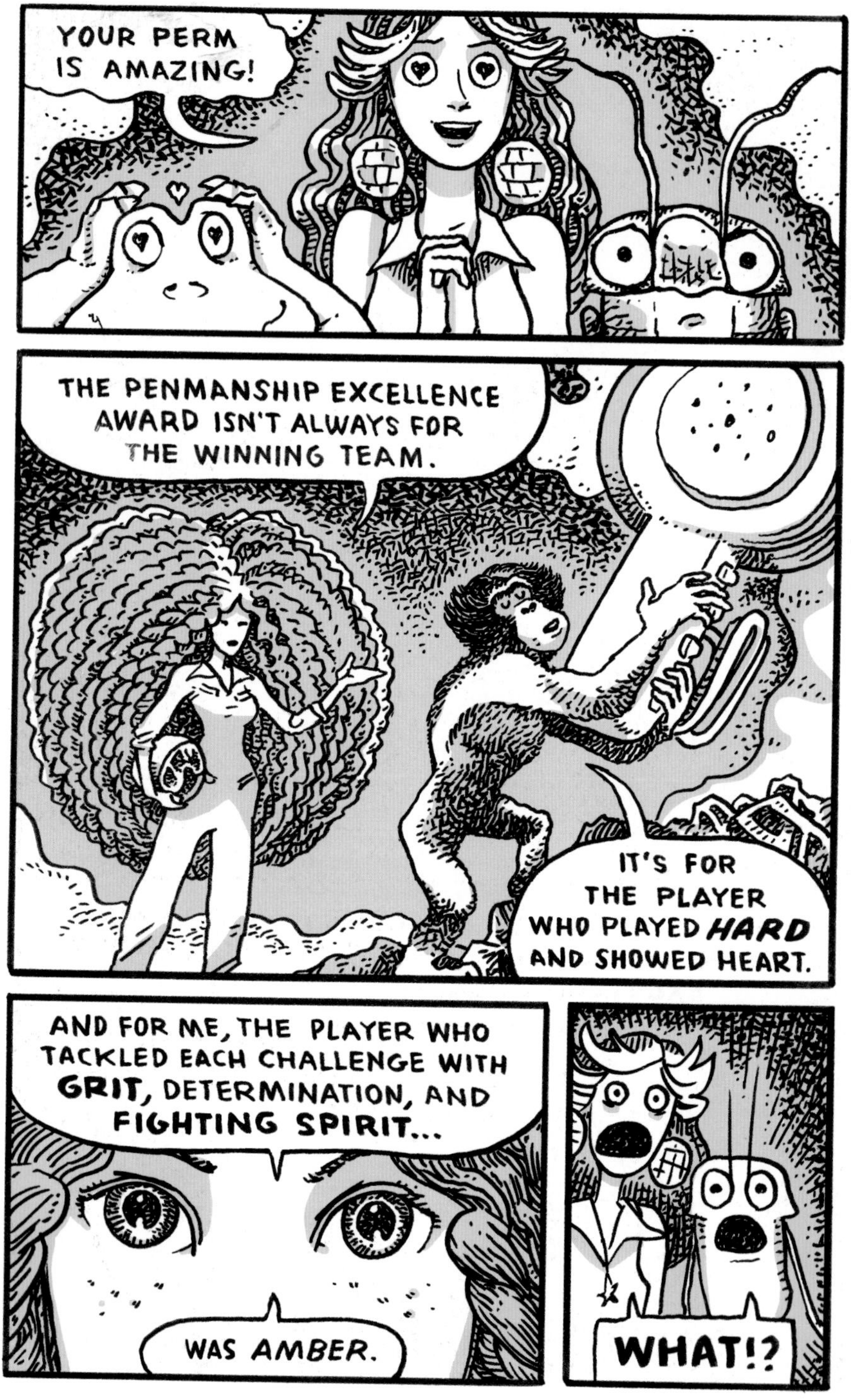
YOUR PERM IS AMAZING!
THE PENMANSHIP EXCELLENCE AWARD ISN'T ALWAYS FOR THE WINNING TEAM.
IT'S FOR THE PLAYER WHO PLAYED HARD AND SHOWED HEART.
AND FOR ME, THE PLAYER WHO TACKLED EACH CHALLENGE WITH GRIT, DETERMINATION, AND FIGHTING SPIRIT...
WAS AMBER.
WHAT!?

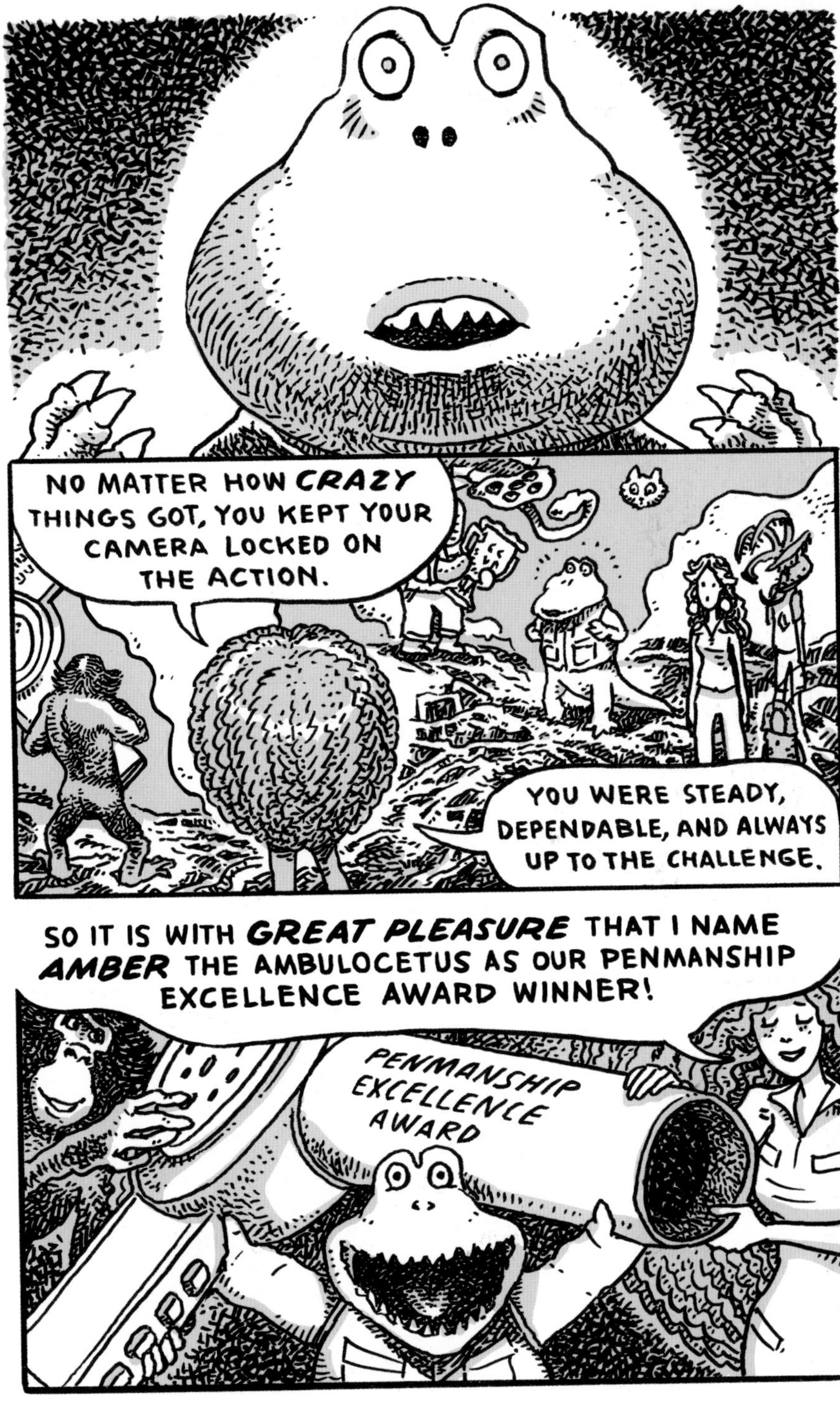
NO MATTER HOW CRAZY THINGS GOT, YOU KEPT YOUR CAMERA LOCKED ON THE ACTION.
YOU WERE STEADY, DEPENDABLE, AND ALWAYS UP TO THE CHALLENGE.
SO IT IS WITH GREAT PLEASURE THAT I NAME AMBER THE AMBULOCETUS AS OUR PENMANSHIP EXCELLENCE AWARD WINNER!
PENMANSHIP EXCELLENCE AWARD

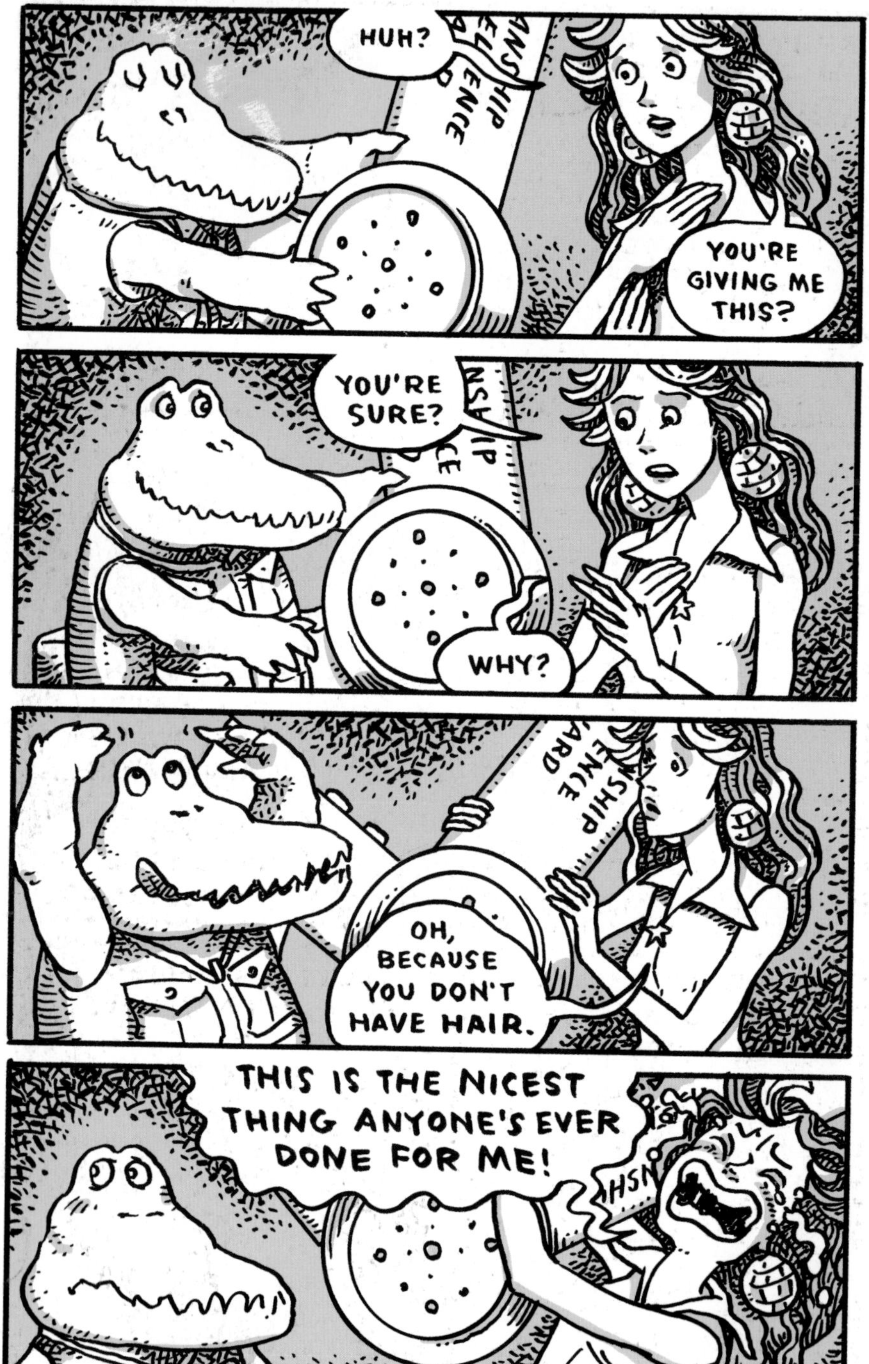
HUH?
YOU'RE GIVING ME THIS?
YOU'RE SURE?
WHY?
OH, BECAUSE YOU DON'T HAVE HAIR.
THIS IS THE NICEST THING ANYONE'S EVER DONE FOR ME!

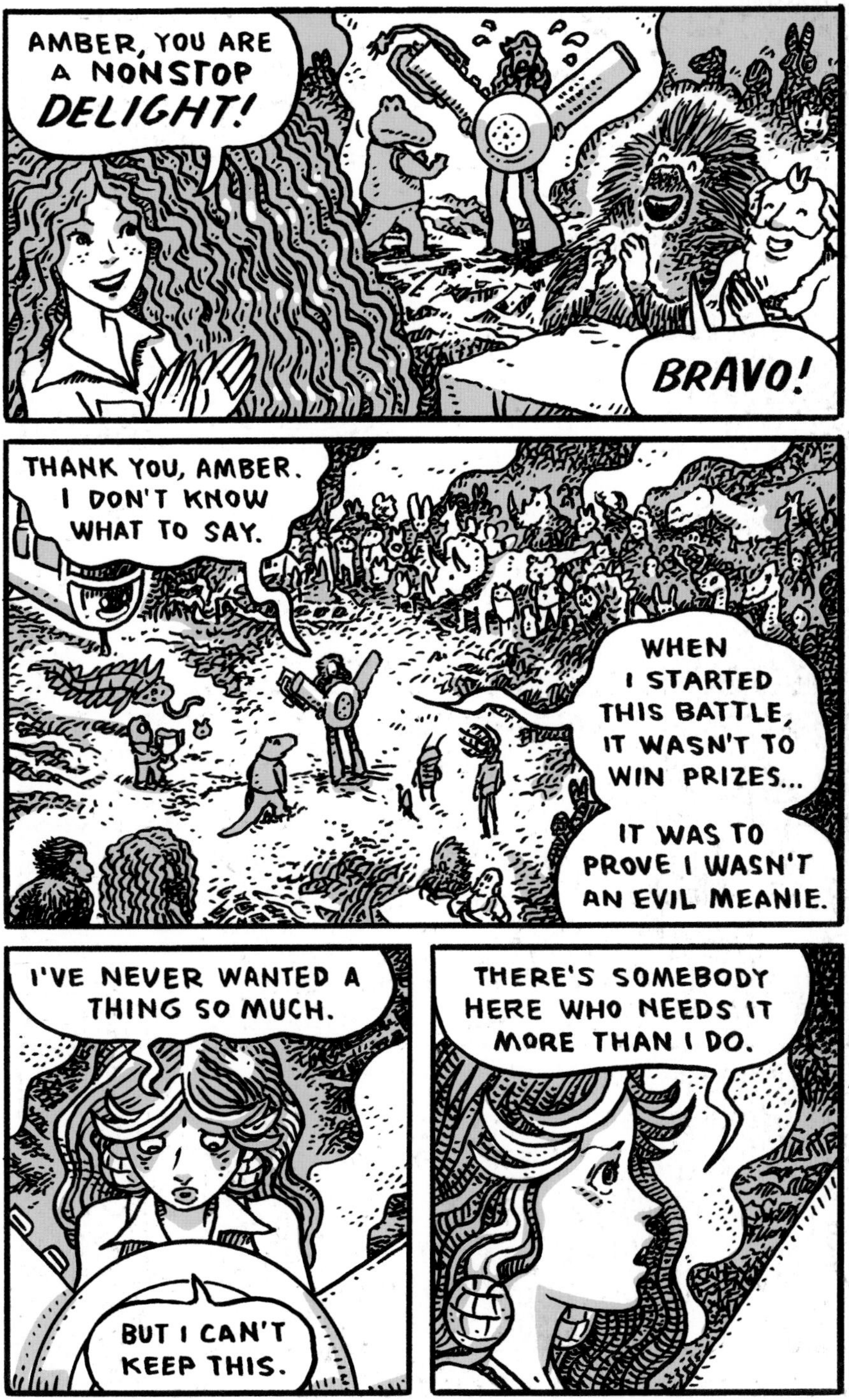
AMBER, YOU ARE A NONSTOP DELIGHT!
BRAVO!
THANK YOU, AMBER. I DON'T KNOW WHAT TO SAY.
WHEN I STARTED THIS BATTLE, IT WASN'T TO WIN PRIZES...
IT WAS TO PROVE I WASN'T AN EVIL MEANIE.
I'VE NEVER WANTED A THING SO MUCH.
BUT I CAN'T KEEP THIS.
THERE'S SOMEBODY HERE WHO NEEDS IT MORE THAN I DO.

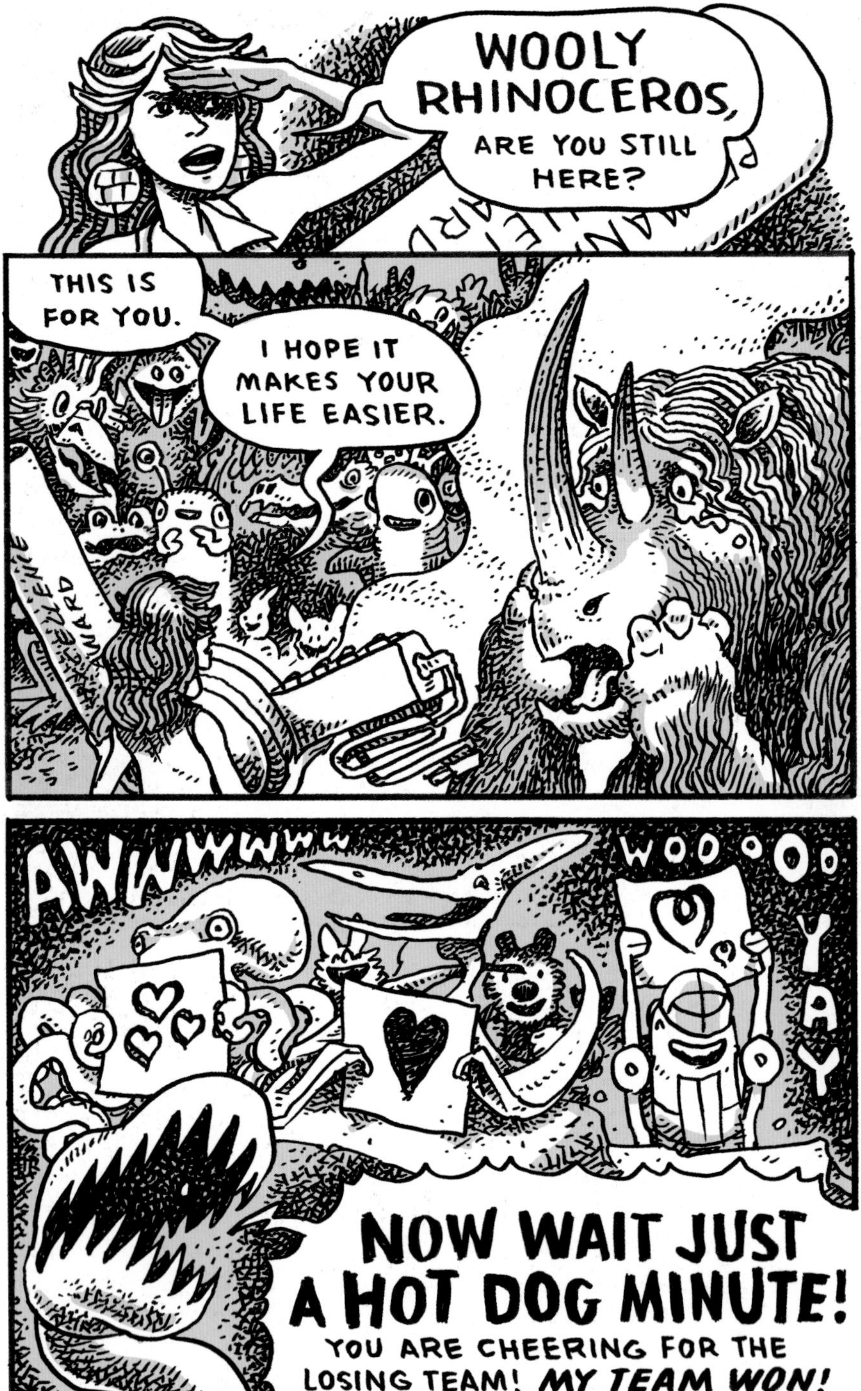
WOOLY RHINOCEROS, ARE YOU STILL HERE?
THIS IS FOR YOU.
I HOPE IT MAKES YOUR LIFE EASIER.
AWWWWWWW
WOOOOOO
YAY
NOW WAIT JUST A HOT DOG MINUTE!
YOU ARE CHEERING FOR THE LOSING TEAM! *MY TEAM WON!*

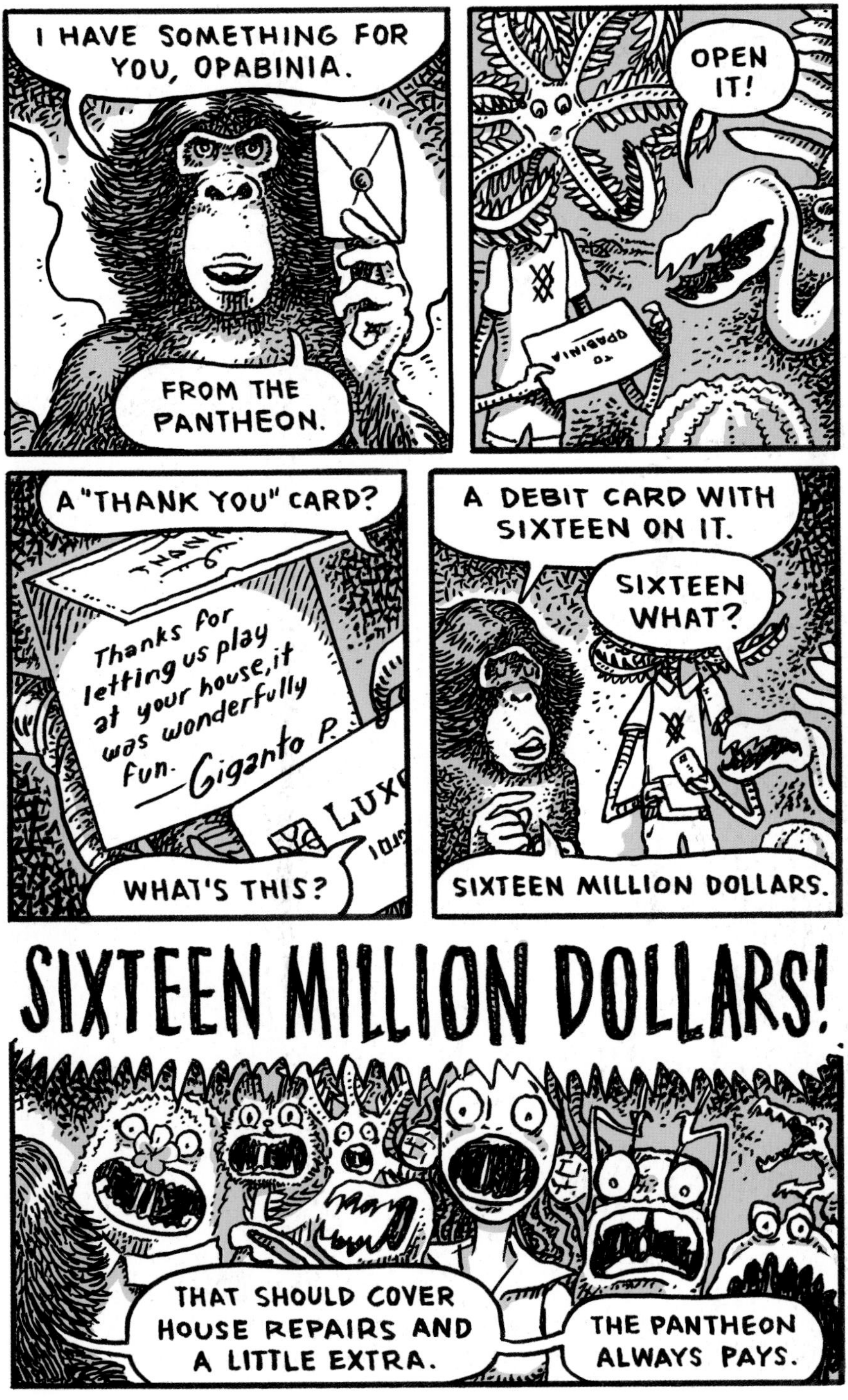
I HAVE SOMETHING FOR YOU, OPABINIA.
FROM THE PANTHEON.
OPEN IT!
TO OPABINIA
A "THANK YOU" CARD?
Thanks for letting us play at your house, it was wonderfully fun. —Giganto P.
WHAT'S THIS?
A DEBIT CARD WITH SIXTEEN ON IT.
SIXTEEN WHAT?
SIXTEEN MILLION DOLLARS.
SIXTEEN MILLION DOLLARS!
THAT SHOULD COVER HOUSE REPAIRS AND A LITTLE EXTRA.
THE PANTHEON ALWAYS PAYS.

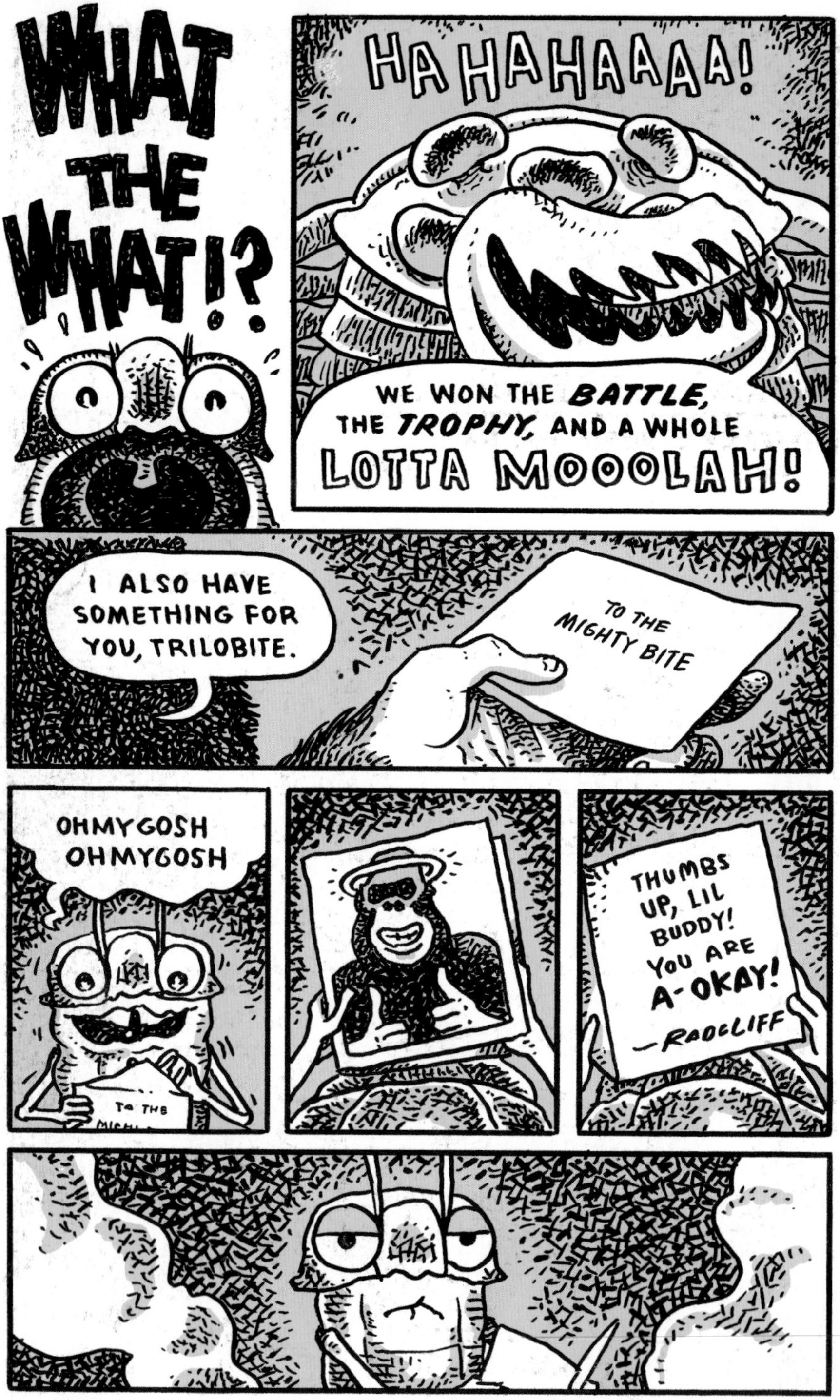
WHAT THE WHAT!?
HA HAHAHAAAA!
WE WON THE BATTLE, THE TROPHY, AND A WHOLE LOTTA MOOOLAH!
I ALSO HAVE SOMETHING FOR YOU, TRILOBITE.
TO THE MIGHTY BITE
OHMYGOSH OHMYGOSH
TO THE
THUMBS UP, LIL BUDDY! YOU ARE A-OKAY! —RADCLIFF

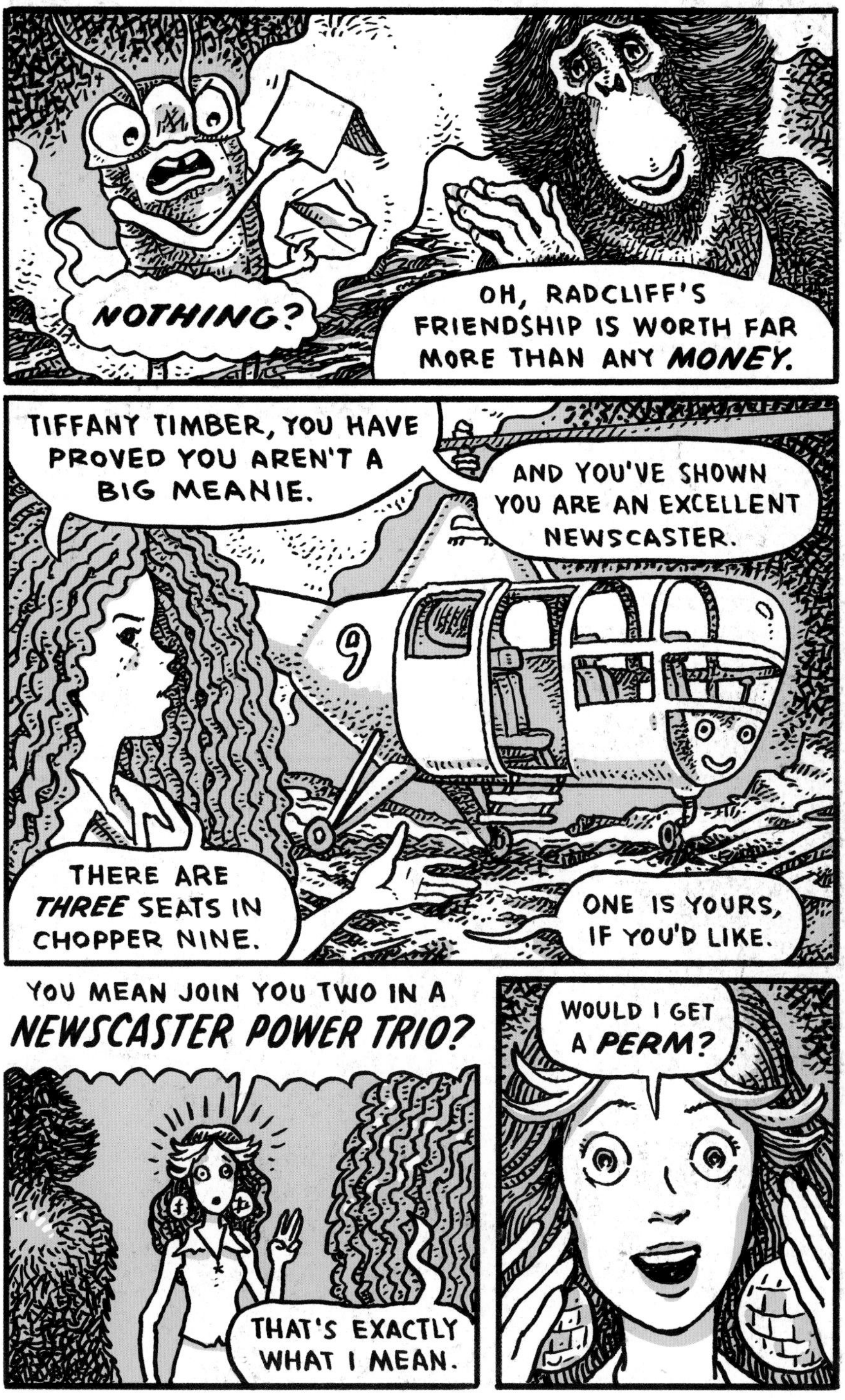

NOTHING?
OH, RADCLIFF'S FRIENDSHIP IS WORTH FAR MORE THAN ANY MONEY.
TIFFANY TIMBER, YOU HAVE PROVED YOU AREN'T A BIG MEANIE.
AND YOU'VE SHOWN YOU ARE AN EXCELLENT NEWSCASTER.
9
THERE ARE THREE SEATS IN CHOPPER NINE.
ONE IS YOURS, IF YOU'D LIKE.
YOU MEAN JOIN YOU TWO IN A NEWSCASTER POWER TRIO?
THAT'S EXACTLY WHAT I MEAN.
WOULD I GET A PERM?

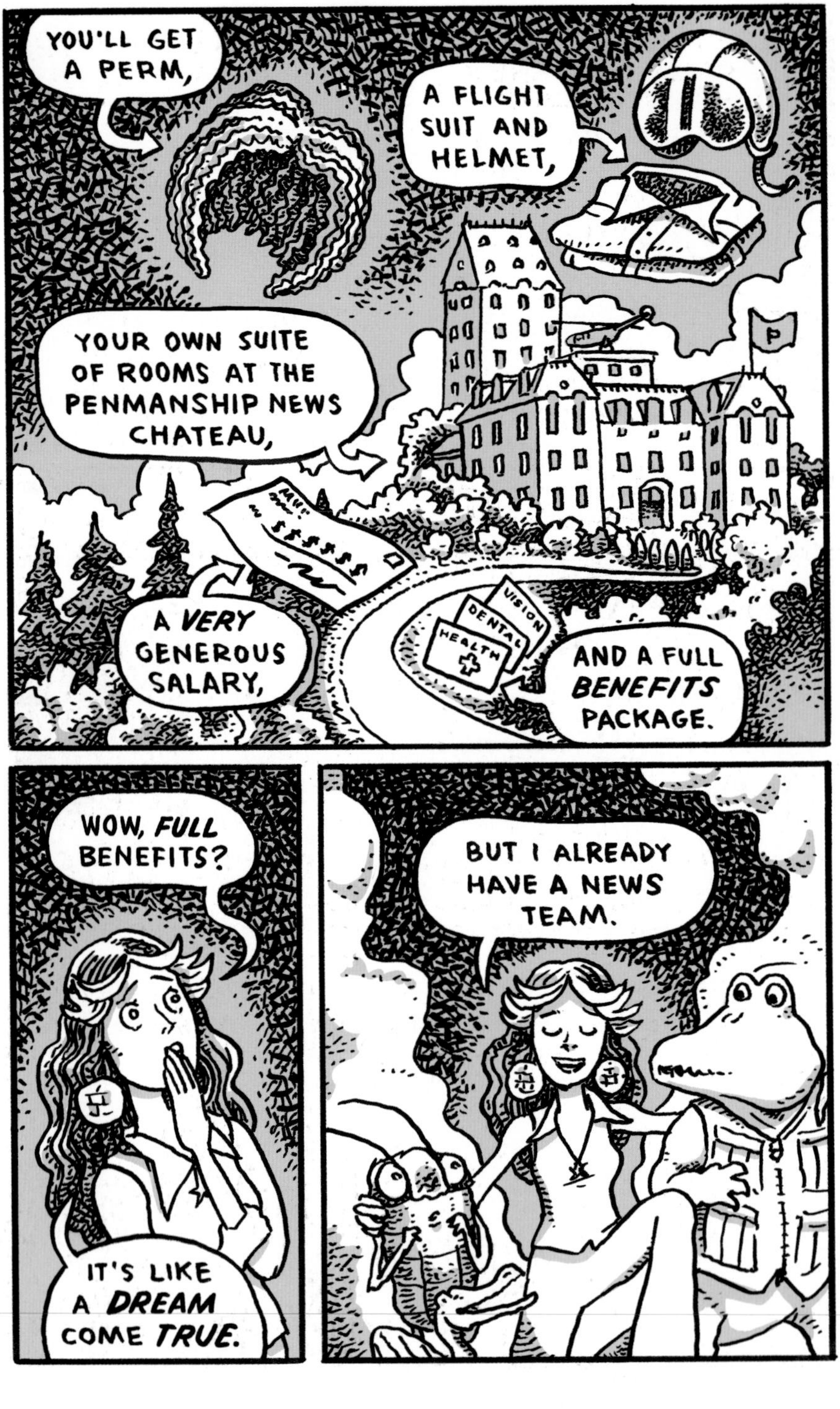
YOU'LL GET A PERM,
A FLIGHT SUIT AND HELMET,
YOUR OWN SUITE OF ROOMS AT THE PENMANSHIP NEWS CHATEAU,
A *VERY* GENEROUS SALARY,
AND A FULL *BENEFITS* PACKAGE.
VISION
DENTAL
HEALTH
WOW, *FULL* BENEFITS?
IT'S LIKE A *DREAM* COME *TRUE*.
BUT I ALREADY HAVE A NEWS TEAM.

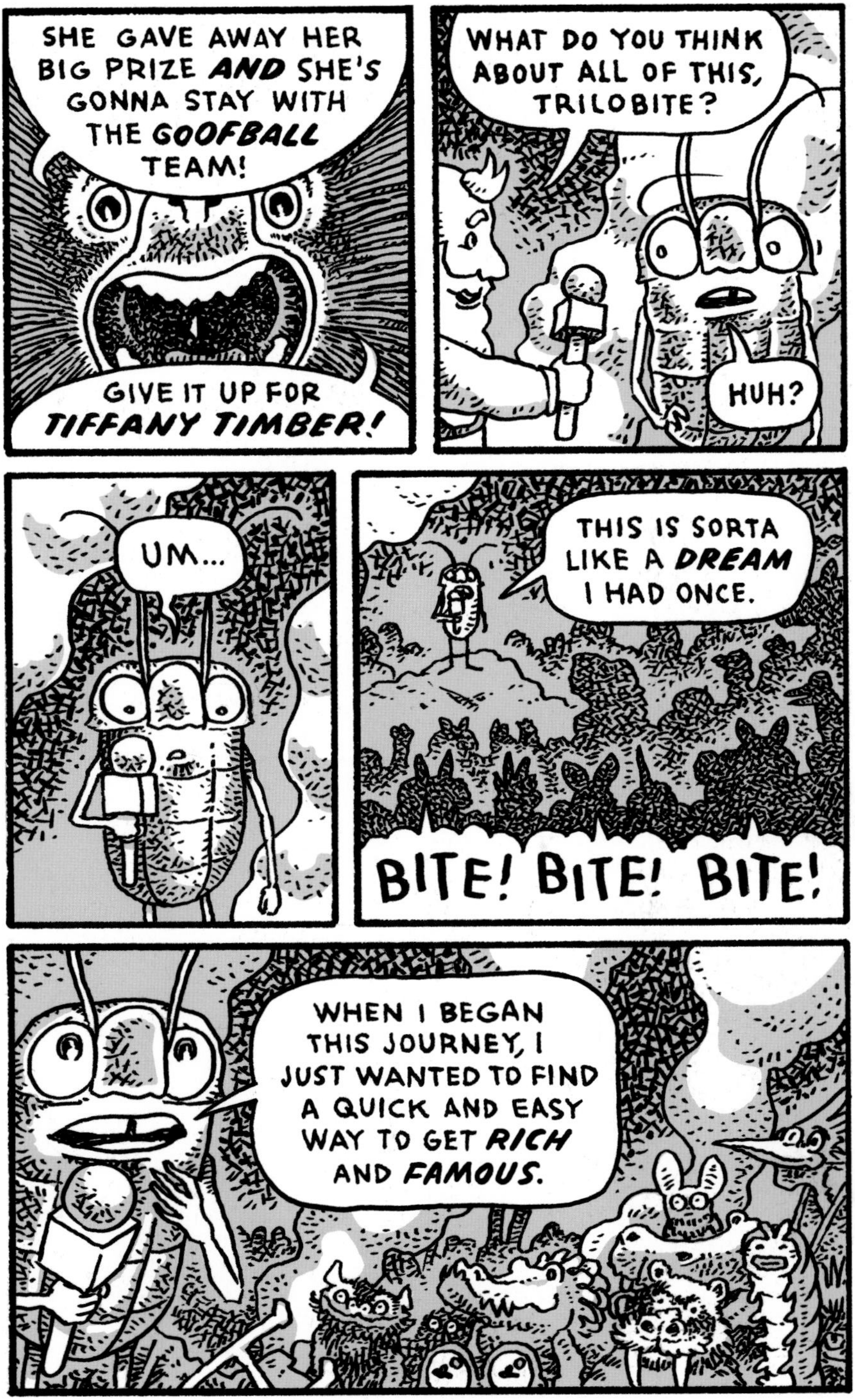
SHE GAVE AWAY HER BIG PRIZE AND SHE'S GONNA STAY WITH THE GOOFBALL TEAM!
GIVE IT UP FOR TIFFANY TIMBER!
WHAT DO YOU THINK ABOUT ALL OF THIS, TRILOBITE?
HUH?
UM...
THIS IS SORTA LIKE A DREAM I HAD ONCE.
BITE! BITE! BITE!
WHEN I BEGAN THIS JOURNEY, I JUST WANTED TO FIND A QUICK AND EASY WAY TO GET RICH AND FAMOUS.

BUT I'VE LEARNED THAT THE *TRUE* RICHES ARE THE *FRIENDS* I'VE MA--

HEY!

AMBER!

I'M GIVING MY BIG SPEECH!

GIVE IT!

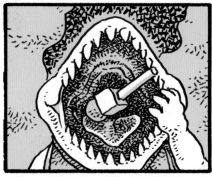

CHOMP

YAYYY

BITE! BITE! BITE!

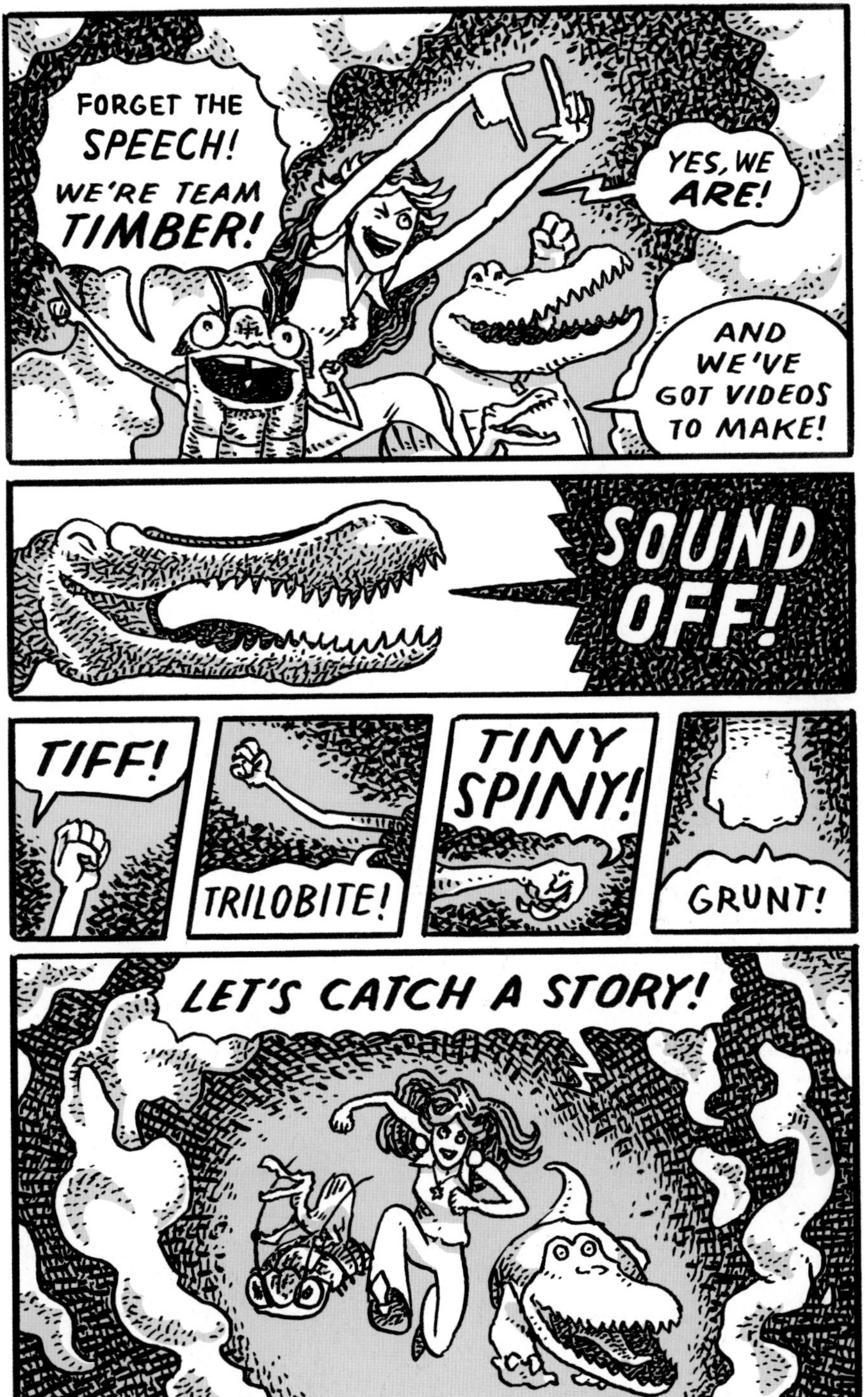
FORGET THE SPEECH! WE'RE TEAM TIMBER!
YES, WE ARE!
AND WE'VE GOT VIDEOS TO MAKE!
SOUND OFF!
TIFF!
TRILOBITE!
TINY SPINY!
GRUNT!
LET'S CATCH A STORY!

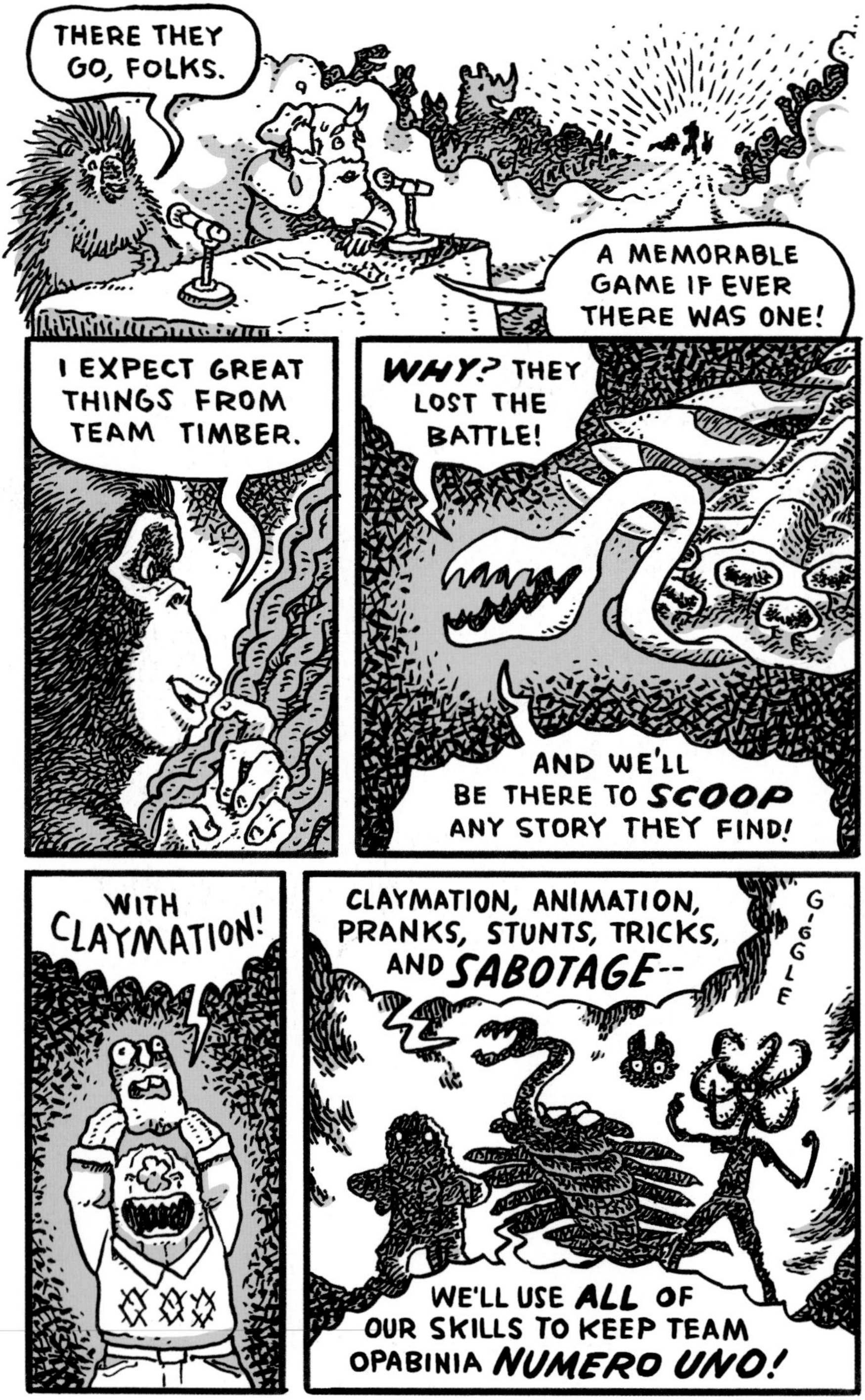

THERE THEY GO, FOLKS.
A MEMORABLE GAME IF EVER THERE WAS ONE!
I EXPECT GREAT THINGS FROM TEAM TIMBER.
WHY? THEY LOST THE BATTLE!
AND WE'LL BE THERE TO SCOOP ANY STORY THEY FIND!
WITH CLAYMATION!
CLAYMATION, ANIMATION, PRANKS, STUNTS, TRICKS, AND SABOTAGE--
GIGGLE
WE'LL USE ALL OF OUR SKILLS TO KEEP TEAM OPABINIA NUMERO UNO!

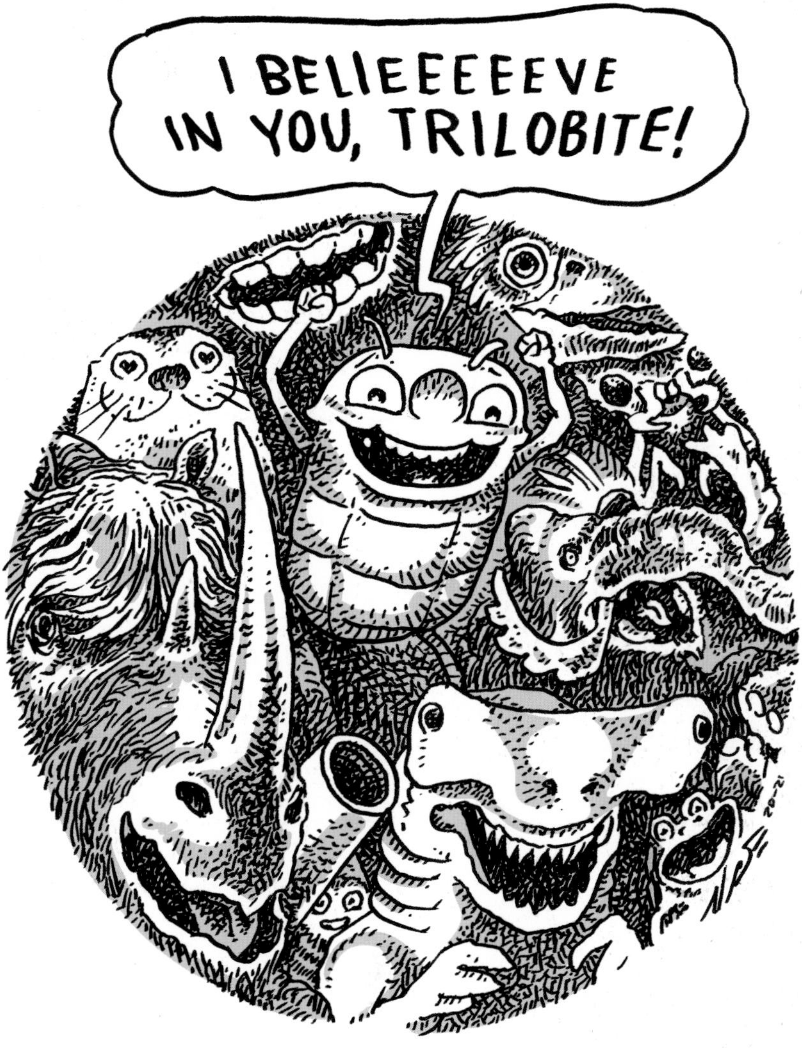
I BELIEEEEEVE IN YOU, TRILOBITE!

THE END

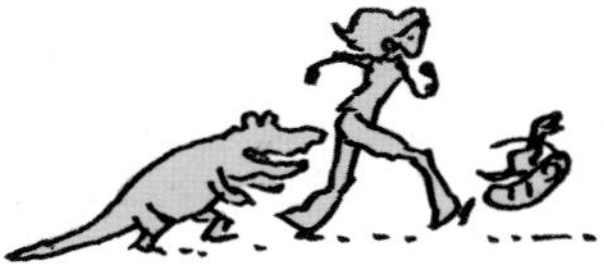

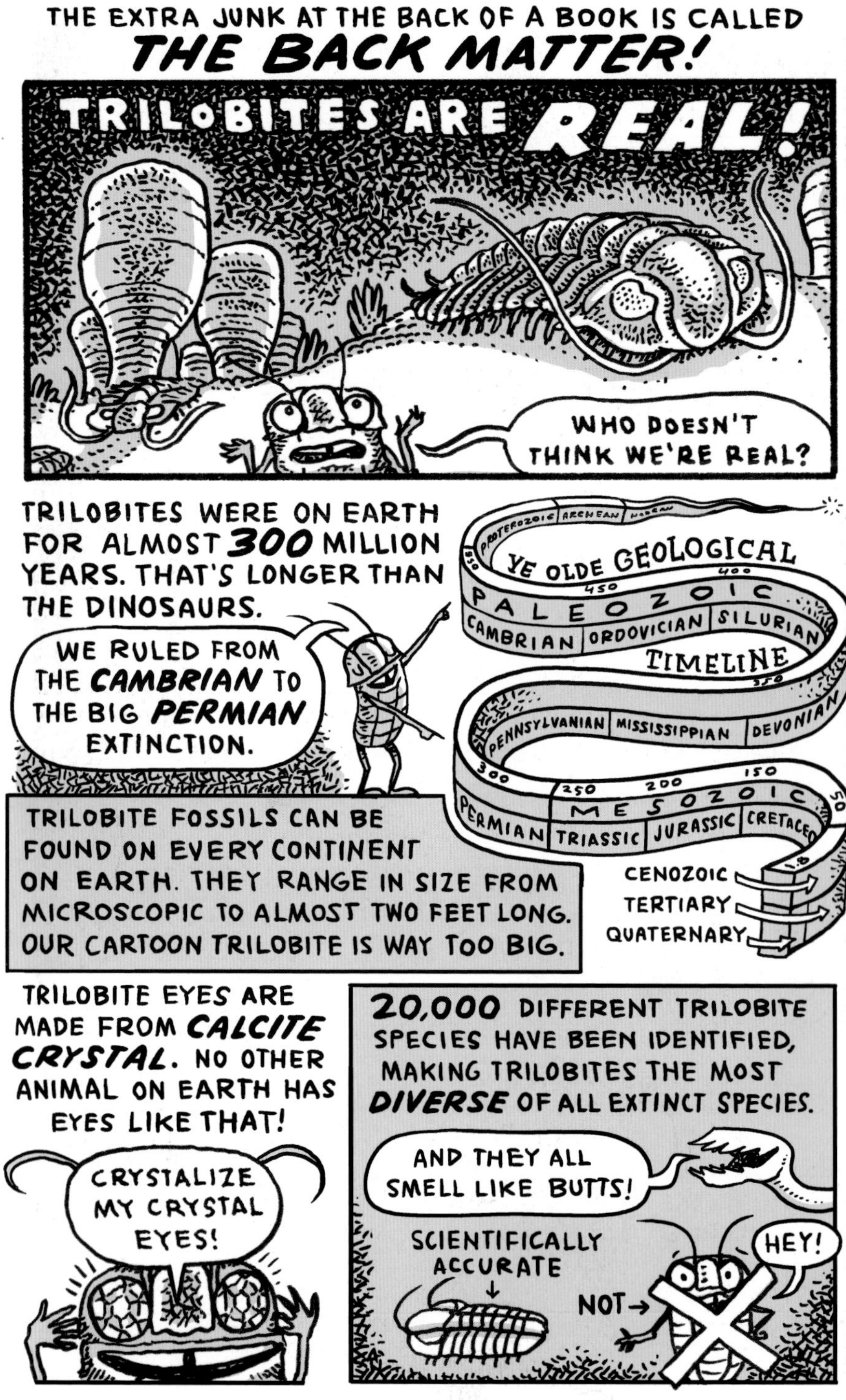
THE EXTRA JUNK AT THE BACK OF A BOOK IS CALLED
THE BACK MATTER!
TRILOBITES ARE REAL!
WHO DOESN'T THINK WE'RE REAL?
TRILOBITES WERE ON EARTH FOR ALMOST 300 MILLION YEARS. THAT'S LONGER THAN THE DINOSAURS.
WE RULED FROM THE CAMBRIAN TO THE BIG PERMIAN EXTINCTION.
YE OLDE GEOLOGICAL TIMELINE
PROTEROZOIC
ARCHEAN
HADEAN
550
450
400
350
300
250
200
150
50
1.8
PALEOZOIC
CAMBRIAN
ORDOVICIAN
SILURIAN
DEVONIAN
MISSISSIPPIAN
PENNSYLVANIAN
PERMIAN
MESOZOIC
TRIASSIC
JURASSIC
CRETACEO
CENOZOIC
TERTIARY
QUATERNARY
TRILOBITE FOSSILS CAN BE FOUND ON EVERY CONTINENT ON EARTH. THEY RANGE IN SIZE FROM MICROSCOPIC TO ALMOST TWO FEET LONG. OUR CARTOON TRILOBITE IS WAY TOO BIG.
TRILOBITE EYES ARE MADE FROM CALCITE CRYSTAL. NO OTHER ANIMAL ON EARTH HAS EYES LIKE THAT!
CRYSTALIZE MY CRYSTAL EYES!
20,000 DIFFERENT TRILOBITE SPECIES HAVE BEEN IDENTIFIED, MAKING TRILOBITES THE MOST DIVERSE OF ALL EXTINCT SPECIES.
AND THEY ALL SMELL LIKE BUTTS!
SCIENTIFICALLY ACCURATE
NOT
HEY!

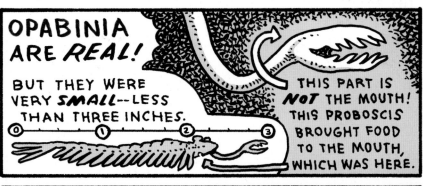

OPABINIA ARE *REAL!*

BUT THEY WERE VERY *SMALL*--LESS THAN THREE INCHES.

THIS PART IS *NOT* THE MOUTH! THIS PROBOSCIS BROUGHT FOOD TO THE MOUTH, WHICH WAS HERE.

AMBULOCETUS ARE *REAL!*

YEAH, BABY.

CRINOIDS ARE *REAL!*

AND THEY ARE VERY *BORING.*

WOOLY RHINOS ARE *REAL!*

BOO HOO!

NEWSCASTERS ARE *REAL!*

BUT UNLIKE EVERYONE ELSE ON THIS PAGE, WE ARE NOT *EXTINCT.*

GNOMES ARE *NOT REAL!*

WELL BUST MY BUTTONS!

WHAT DID I JUST READ?

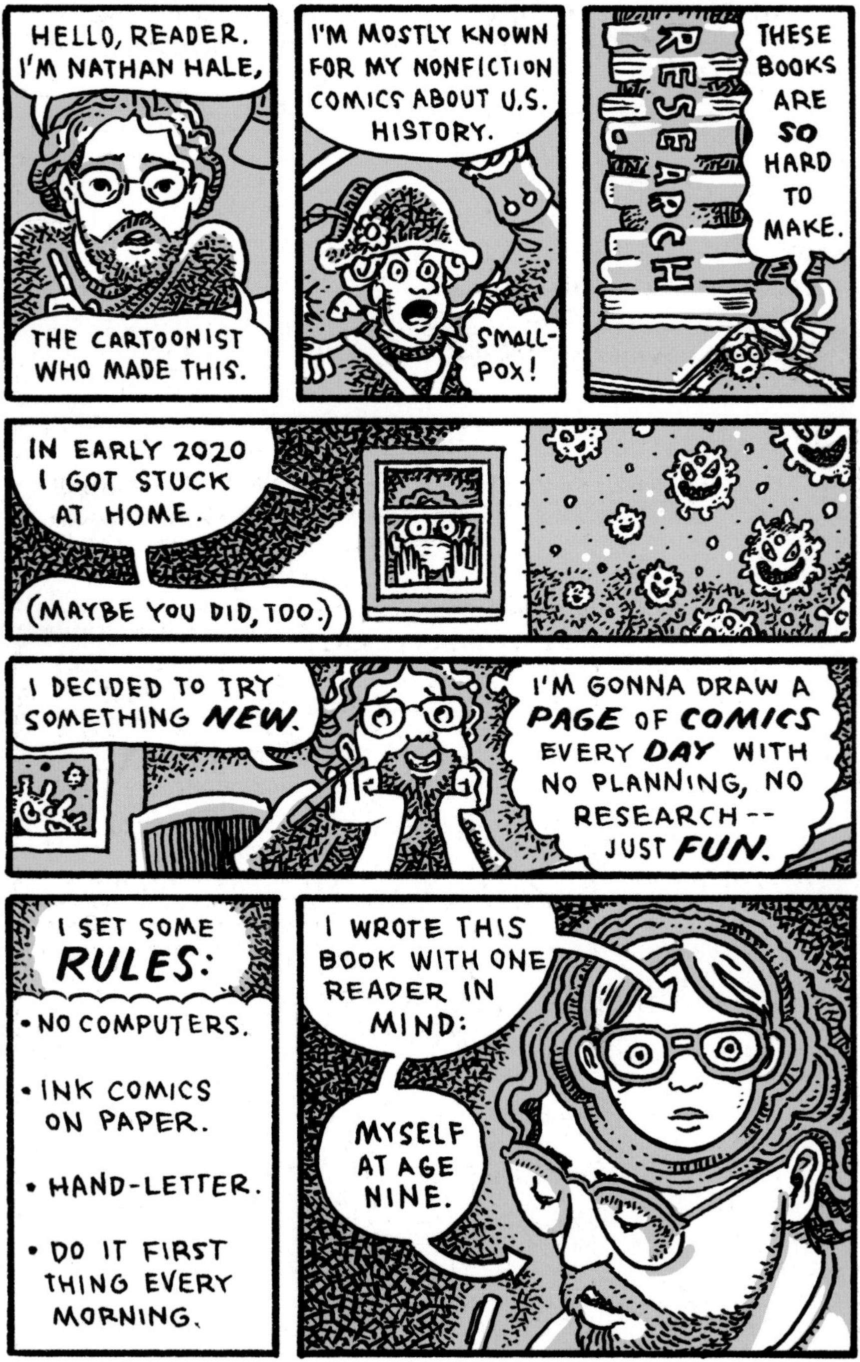
HELLO, READER. I'M NATHAN HALE,
THE CARTOONIST WHO MADE THIS.
I'M MOSTLY KNOWN FOR MY NONFICTION COMICS ABOUT U.S. HISTORY.
SMALL-POX!
RESEARCH
THESE BOOKS ARE SO HARD TO MAKE.
IN EARLY 2020 I GOT STUCK AT HOME.
(MAYBE YOU DID, TOO.)
I DECIDED TO TRY SOMETHING NEW.
I'M GONNA DRAW A PAGE OF COMICS EVERY DAY WITH NO PLANNING, NO RESEARCH -- JUST FUN.
I SET SOME RULES:
• NO COMPUTERS.
• INK COMICS ON PAPER.
• HAND-LETTER.
• DO IT FIRST THING EVERY MORNING.
I WROTE THIS BOOK WITH ONE READER IN MIND:
MYSELF AT AGE NINE.

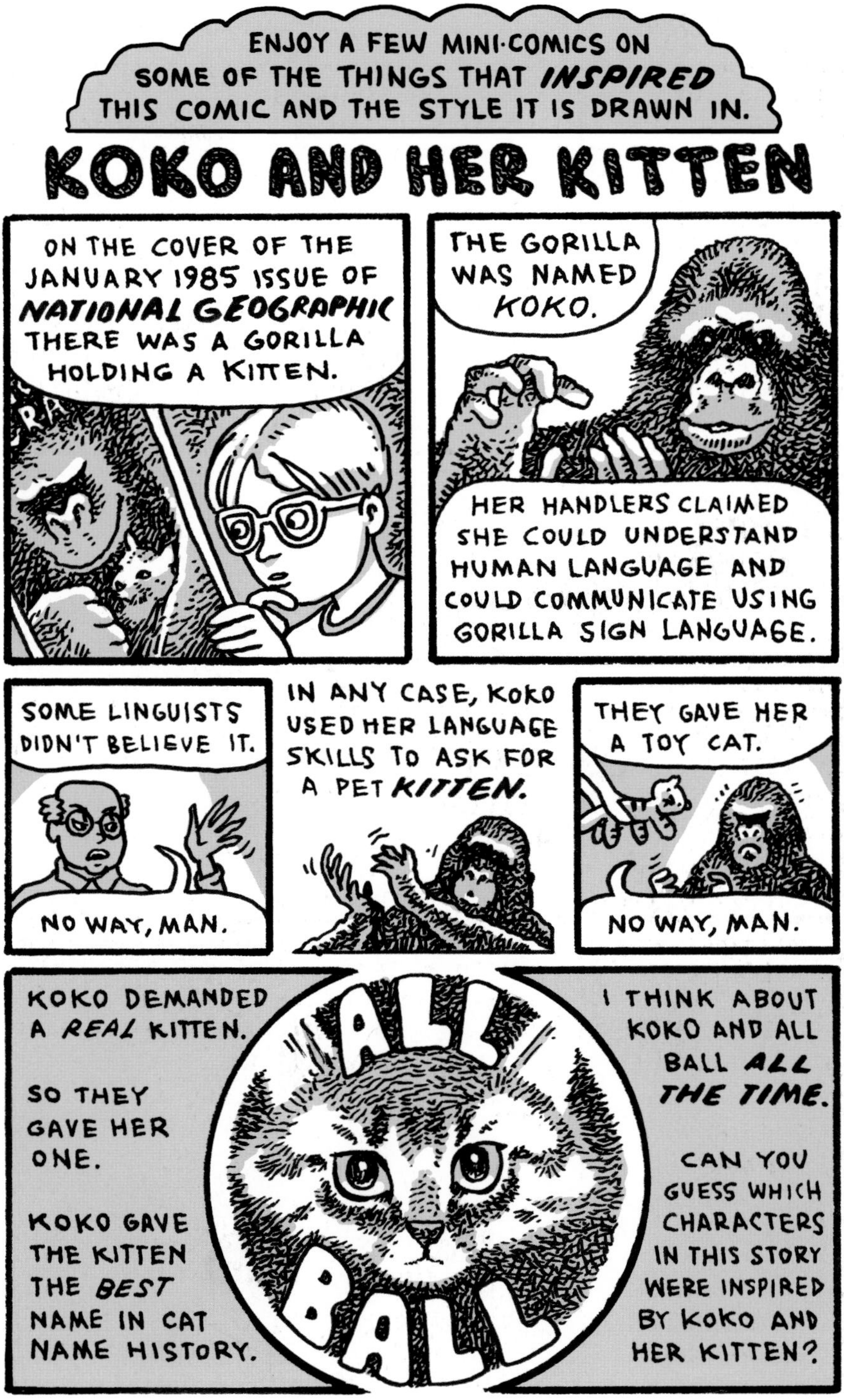
ENJOY A FEW MINI-COMICS ON SOME OF THE THINGS THAT *INSPIRED* THIS COMIC AND THE STYLE IT IS DRAWN IN.
KOKO AND HER KITTEN
ON THE COVER OF THE JANUARY 1985 ISSUE OF *NATIONAL GEOGRAPHIC* THERE WAS A GORILLA HOLDING A KITTEN.
THE GORILLA WAS NAMED *KOKO*.
HER HANDLERS CLAIMED SHE COULD UNDERSTAND HUMAN LANGUAGE AND COULD COMMUNICATE USING GORILLA SIGN LANGUAGE.
SOME LINGUISTS DIDN'T BELIEVE IT.
NO WAY, MAN.
IN ANY CASE, KOKO USED HER LANGUAGE SKILLS TO ASK FOR A PET *KITTEN*.
THEY GAVE HER A TOY CAT.
NO WAY, MAN.
KOKO DEMANDED A *REAL* KITTEN.
SO THEY GAVE HER ONE.
KOKO GAVE THE KITTEN THE *BEST* NAME IN CAT NAME HISTORY.
ALL BALL
I THINK ABOUT KOKO AND ALL BALL *ALL THE TIME*.
CAN YOU GUESS WHICH CHARACTERS IN THIS STORY WERE INSPIRED BY KOKO AND HER KITTEN?

MY UNCLE WAS A GEOLOGY STUDENT. ONCE, WHEN HE VISITED, HE BROUGHT ME A BAG OF GEOLOGY STUFF.

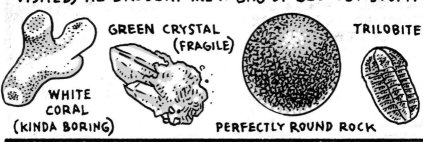

WHITE CORAL (KINDA BORING)

GREEN CRYSTAL (FRAGILE)

PERFECTLY ROUND ROCK

TRILOBITE

THE TRILOBITE GOT PLAYED WITH THE MOST.

PEW   PEW

I THOUGHT THE SPHERICAL BLACK ROCK MIGHT BE A **GEODE**...

WITH A CENTER FULL OF CRYSTALS.

CURIOSITY GOT THE BEST OF ME.

I WENT AND GOT A HAMMER.

THERE WERE NO CRYSTALS,

ONLY WHITE SAND.

ONCE, I TOOK THE TRILOBITE OUTSIDE AND BURIED IT.

THEN I DUG IT UP IN FRONT OF MY COUSIN.

OH MY GOSH! I JUST DISCOVERED A FOSSIL!

WHAT!?

A RELIGIOUS EXPERIENCE

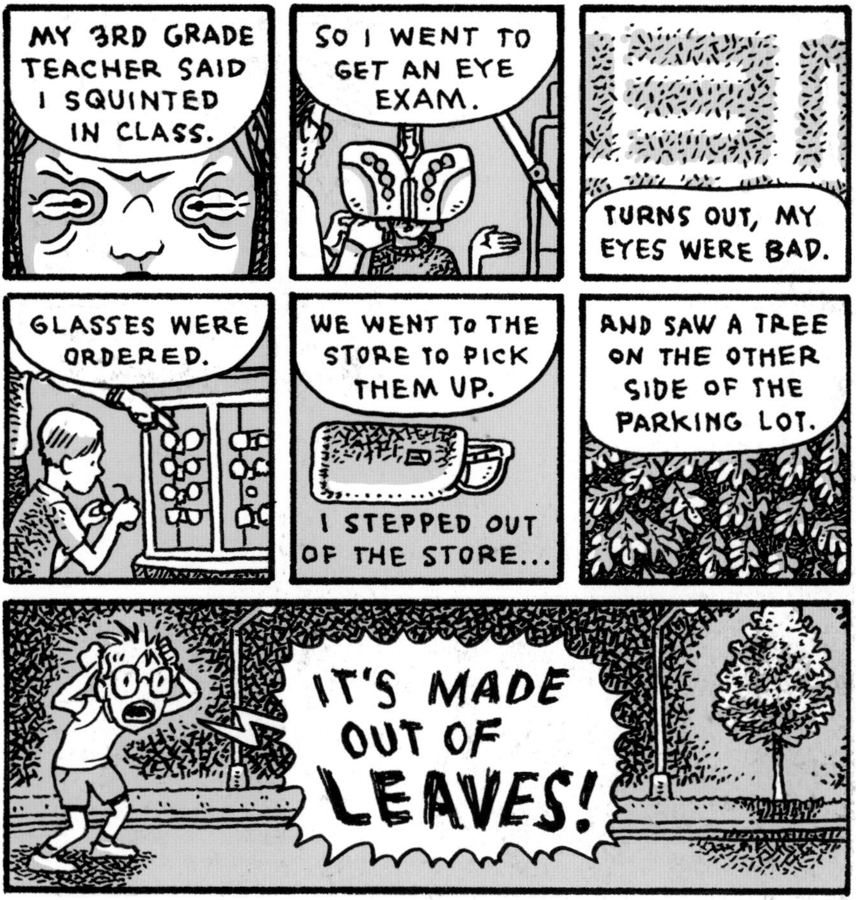
MY 3RD GRADE TEACHER SAID I SQUINTED IN CLASS.
SO I WENT TO GET AN EYE EXAM.
TURNS OUT, MY EYES WERE BAD.
GLASSES WERE ORDERED.
WE WENT TO THE STORE TO PICK THEM UP.
I STEPPED OUT OF THE STORE...
AND SAW A TREE ON THE OTHER SIDE OF THE PARKING LOT.
IT'S MADE OUT OF LEAVES!

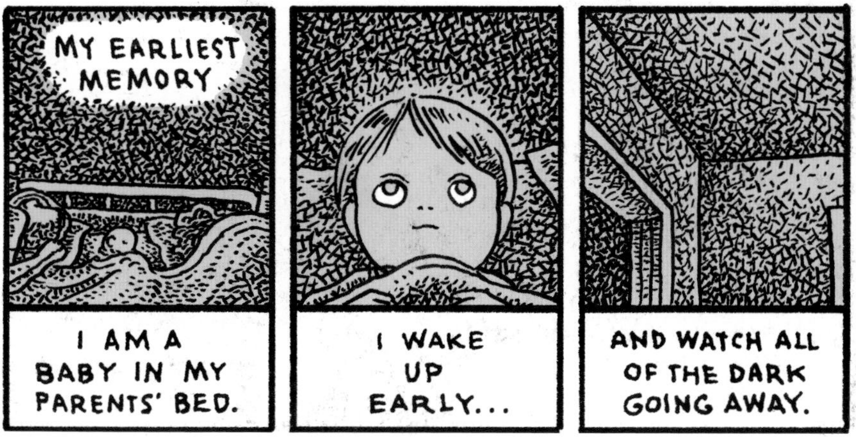
MY EARLIEST MEMORY
I AM A BABY IN MY PARENTS' BED.
I WAKE UP EARLY...
AND WATCH ALL OF THE DARK GOING AWAY.

THE BOOK BUTLER

IF YOU'VE READ THIS FAR, YOU MUST BE A *TRUE COMICS CONNOISSEUR!*

YOU *MUST* READ ALL THE OTHER NATHAN HALE BOOKS!

ONE DEAD SPY

THE HAZARDOUS TALES-- TRUE STORIES FEATURING ACTS OF *VIOLENT HISTOROCITY!*

ONE TRICK PONY

APOCALYPSE TACO

GET UNDER THE COVERS WITH THESE *SCI-FI HORROR THRILL-FESTS!* THEY'RE ABSOLUTELY PACKED WITH *CREEPY CREEPING CRAWLIES!*

DO YOU ENJOY *COW-GIRLS?*

RAPUNZEL'S REVENGE

CALAMITY JACK

* WRITTEN BY SHANNON AND DEAN HALE.

IF YOU KEEP READING THEM, HE'LL KEEP MAKING THEM! HE'S NOT GOING *ANYWHERE!*

HAZ TALES·13
MIGHTY BITE·2
????

MWAHAMWAHAHAHA

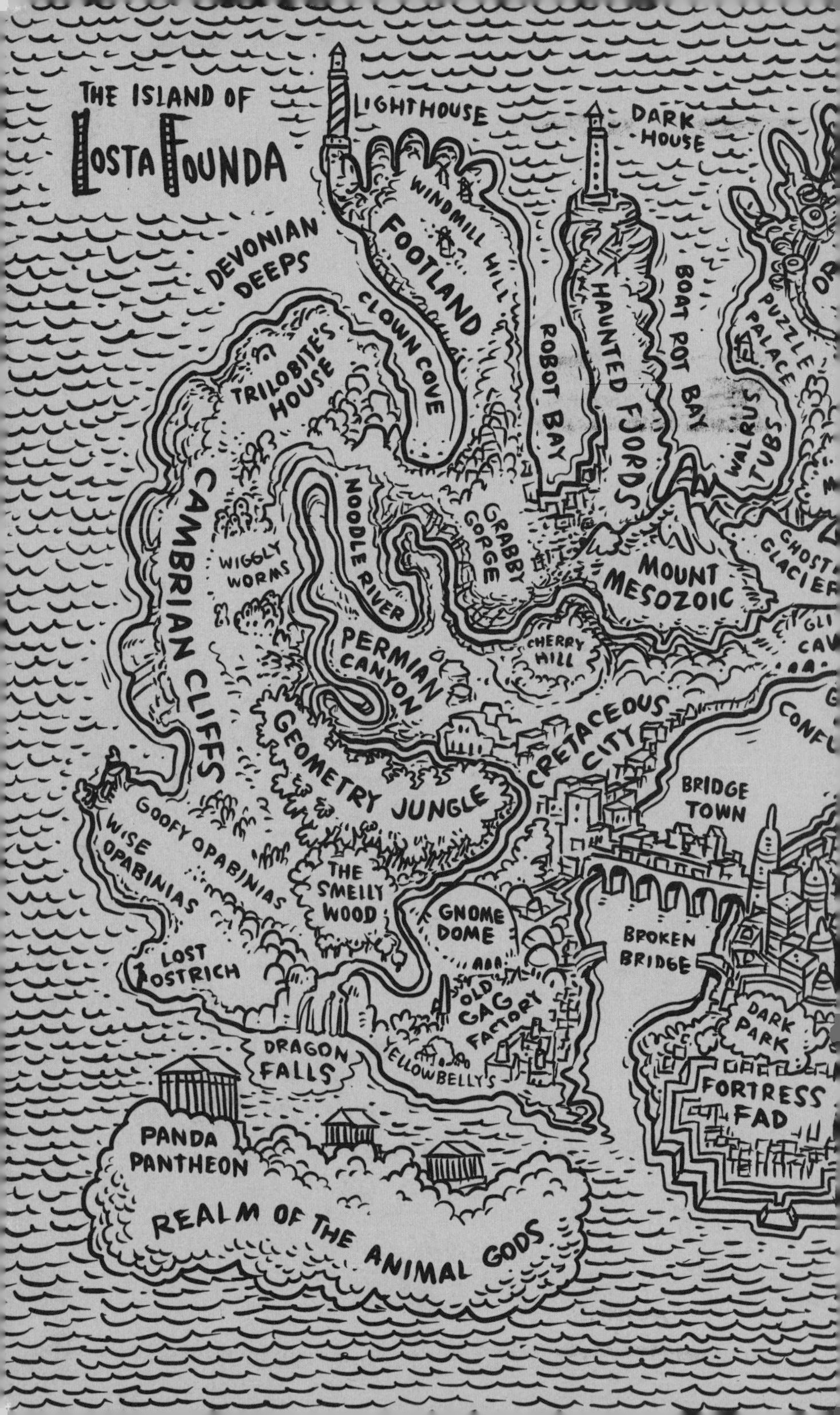
THE ISLAND OF
LOSTA FOUNDA
LIGHTHOUSE
DARK HOUSE
WINDMILL HILL
FOOTLAND
DEVONIAN DEEPS
CLOWN COVE
TRILOBITE'S HOUSE
ROBOT BAY
HAUNTED FJORDS
BOAT ROT BAY
PUZZLE PALACE
WALRUS TUBS
GHOST
CAMBRIAN CLIFFS
WIGGLY WORMS
NOODLE RIVER
GRABBY GORGE
MOUNT MESOZOIC
PERMIAN CANYON
CHERRY HILL
GEOMETRY JUNGLE
CRETACEOUS CITY
BRIDGE TOWN
WISE OPABINIAS
GOOFY OPABINIAS
THE SMELLY WOOD
GNOME DOME
BROKEN BRIDGE
LOST OSTRICH
OLD GAG FACTORY
DARK PARK
DRAGON FALLS
YELLOWBELLY'S
FORTRESS FAD
PANDA PANTHEON
REALM OF THE ANIMAL GODS